WHITCHURCH STOUFFVILLE PUBLIC LIBRARY

WS504606

WITHDRAWN

P9-DEH-522

JAN 2 8 2010

ARMS-COMMANDER

TOR BOOKS BY L. E. MODESITT, JR.

L. E. Modesitt, Jr.

ARMS-COMMANDER

TOR®

A Tom Doherty Associates Book / New York

WHITCHURCH-STOUFFVILLE PUBLIC LIBRARY

This is a work of fiction. All of the characters, organizations, and events portrayed in this novel are either products of the author's imagination or are used fictitiously.

ARMS-COMMANDER

Copyright © 2009 by L. E. Modesitt, Jr.

All rights reserved.

Map by Ellisa Mitchell

A Tor Book
Published by Tom Doherty Associates, LLC
175 Fifth Avenue
New York, NY 10010

www.tor-forge.com

Tor® is a registered trademark of Tom Doherty Associates, LLC.

Library of Congress Cataloging-in-Publication Data

Modesitt, L. E.
    Arms-commander / L. E. Modesitt, Jr.—1st ed.
        p.   cm.
    "A Tom Doherty Associates book."
    ISBN 978-0-7653-2381-1
    1. Recluce (Imaginary place)—Fiction.   I. Title.
    PS3563.O264A89 2010
    813'.54—dc22

                                    2009036273

First Edition: January 2010

Printed in the United States of America

0 9 8 7 6 5 4 3 2 1

For all the women cursed as tyrants in getting the job done when their male counterparts are only considered tough

LORD-HOLDERS OF LORNTH

Southern Lords:

Lord	Holding
Henstrenn	Duevek
Keistyn	Hasel
Kelthyn	Veryna
Orsynn	Cardara
Mortryd	Tryenda
Rherhn	Khalasn
Jharyk	Nuelda
Jaffrayt	Fhasta
[None]	Rohrn

Northern Lords:

Lord	Holding
Barcauyn	Cauyna
Deolyn	Lyntara
Chaspal	Lohke
Maeldyn	Quaryn
Spalkyn	Palteara
Gethen	The Groves
Shartyr	Masengyl
Whethryn	Tharnya

The angels came with blades of gray,
and shining bright with silver slew
all those who fought in sun or dew,
then brought a bladed peace to stay.

Oh, do not fear the angels' wrath,
Nor run with man's heroic herds.
More fear those golden sweetened words
Of lords who've strayed from order's path.

NORTHERN

CANDAR

Gulf of Candar

Gulf of Murr

RECLUCE

EASTERN OCEAN

The WORLD

E.Mitchell 1995

OCEAN

AUSTRA

GULF OF AUSTRA

Brysta

Valmurl

NORDLA

WESTERN OCEAN

Swartheld

Luba

Cigoerne

AFRIT

Atla

Swarth River

MEROWEY

HAMOR

Westwind

I

In the late afternoon on the Roof of the World, the guards stood silent on the practice ground, their eyes fixed on the blackness rising just above the western horizon as Istril stepped out of the main door of Tower Black and crossed the causeway. Saryn, arms-commander and former command pilot, stood beside Ryba of the swift ships of Heaven and Marshal of Westwind. The tip of the Marshal's wooden practice wand touched the ground, and she gestured toward the silver-haired guard and healer to approach.

Istril continued her measured pace toward the Marshal and the arms-commander. The other guards waited, their eyes moving from the Marshal to Istril and back again, while Saryn of the flashing blades studied the darkness rising in the western sky.

The silver-haired healer halted three paces from Ryba and inclined her head. "Marshal?"

"What do you think of that?" Ryba glanced from the pregnant and silver-haired healer to the west, beyond the imposing ice needle that was Freyja. "That has to be the engineer."

Darkness swirled into the sky, slowly turning the entire western horizon into a curtain of blackness that inexorably enfolded the sun, bringing an even earlier twilight to the Roof of the World. For a moment, Freyja shimmered white, then faded into the maroon darkness that covered the high meadows and Tower Black.

"I could already feel the shivering between the black and white," Istril said slowly. "So did Siret."

"And you didn't tell me immediately?" asked the Marshal.

"What could we have done? Besides, it's more than him. More than the healer, too. Something bigger, a lot bigger."

Ryba shook her head before asking, "Do you still think it was right to send Weryl?"

"He's all right. I can feel that." Istril paused. "That means Nylan is, too . . . but there's a lot of pain there." Her eyes glistened, even in the dimness.

"When the engineer gets into something . . . there usually is." Ryba's voice was dry.

Saryn said nothing, wondering still how Ryba could be so chill.

"He doesn't do anything unless it's important." Istril continued to look past Ryba toward the horizon.

"That just makes it worse, doesn't it?" Ryba's voice was rough.

"Yes, ser."

It's worse because you forced him out, you and your visions. But Saryn did not speak the words, nor look in at the Marshal. *Visions have high prices, and deeper costs.*

After another period of silence, Istril nodded, then turned and walked swiftly back across the practice ground and the causeway into the tower.

For a time, Ryba continued to study the growing darkness of a too-early night as the faces of the guards shone bloodred in the fading light. Then, Saryn gestured, silently, and the guards slipped away, filing quietly back into the tower for the duties that never ended.

The faintest of shivers ran through the ground beneath the Marshal's and the arms-commander's feet, and the meadow grasses swayed in the windless still of unnatural twilight.

Another ground shudder passed, then another, as the gloom deepened. The Marshal waited . . . and watched. Then, abruptly, she turned and walked back across the practice ground and the causeway into Tower Black.

Long after the Marshal had returned to Tower Black, Saryn remained on the stone causeway just outside the door to the tower, her eyes still gazing toward the west and the darkness that glowed, framing the ice peak of Freyja, as if to suggest that even the mightiest peak on the Roof of the World was bounded by forces beyond mere nature.

Between darkness and darkness. Again, she did not voice her thoughts. That, she had leaned from the engineer and the singer . . . that was unwise.

II

And the guards of Westwind hardened their hearts, hearts as cold and as terrible as the ice that never leaves Freyja, against the power of any man in any land under the sun. For Ryba had declared that Westwind would hold the Roof of the World for ages, and that Tower Black would stand unvanquished so long as any guard of Westwind remained.

Saryn of the black blades of death said nothing, although she demurred within her heart, for she knew that Westwind had been built of the darkness of Nylan and would stand unvanquished only until an heir of the darkness that had toppled great Cyador returned to Tower Black and cloaked the walls of Westwind in ice as cold and hard as that which covered Freyja, ages though it could be before such might come to pass.

Yet Westwind prospered, for to Ryba came women who had long since tired of bondage and of bearing children who, if male, too often died in warfare and mayhem or under the yoke of great labor and, if female, bore children until they died as well. For such women, the cold of the Roof of the World was the least of tribulations, and in their freedom, they took up the twin blades first forged by Nylan, then by Huldran, then others, who had learned well from the master of darkness.

And Saryn trained each and every one of them so that the least able of any who carried the twin blades was more than a match for twice her number, and with the bows formed of order itself by Nylan, even a man-at-arms in full armor was but as a fat boar ready for slaughter.

With those blades and shafts, they dispatched the brigands of the Westhorns so that traders and others could travel the heights unmolested, and for that safety, all were content to pay tariff to Ryba. Still, those who would cross the heights traveled but in late spring, summer, and early fall; for once the snows fell and the ice winds blew, none traveled the Roof of the World, save the angels of Westwind.

All was well in Westwind in the days that followed the fall of Cyador, for though the winters were long and chill, Tower Black was warm and well-provisioned . . .

> *Book of Ayrlyn*
> Section I
> [Restricted Text]

III

With the coming of spring on the Roof of the World, most of the snow around Tower Black and its outbuildings had finally melted, rushing down the stone-lined channels to the reservoir and the waterfall. The one exception was on a shaded section of the north side, where more than a yard of snow and ice yet remained. Once the reservoir was full, the water that came over the spillway followed the old channel to the cliff, where it poured downward into the small lake below, created by another stone-and-earth dam that Nylan had designed to provide power for the mill and ceramic works beyond the dam, although Saryn had been the one to oversee the actual construction.

Saryn walked swiftly along the south side of the stone road from the tower up toward the smithy. So early in the season, the ground around the tower was swampy, and her boots would have sunk up to the calf everywhere except the arms practice field, which had been laid over stone and was well drained, and the stone-paved roads and causeways. The starflowers had begun to bud, covering the stone cairns to the south and east with green, but the delicate blooms bent to a gentle though still-chill breeze out of the north. The south-facing sloping meadow to the north and east of the tower was a pale green haze. Saryn could remember all too well when it had been seared gray. Now, even the small stone cupola from where Nylan had wielded the last laser in all of Candar, and perhaps the first and

last in the world, had been removed, its stones incorporated in the foundation of the larger complex of towers and quarters that Ryba had ordered
begun the previous year. Just to the south of the foundation and the courses
of stones that reached head height in some places was a low building—the
so-called guest cottage—where messengers or travelers could stay, not
that the interior was all that elaborate.

A squad of junior guards was running through warm-up exercises as
Saryn left the practice field behind. They were the newest of more than
two companies of guards—nearly two hundred armed women—and another hundred who had some weapons training. Saryn shook her head.
Who—except Ryba and Nylan—would have believed Westwind could have
mounted an effective armed force of so many women? And who among the
marines and ship's officers who had landed more than ten years earlier
would have realized that those ten years would have been filled with
fighting off attack after attack—largely because Westwind was controlled
by and for women?

She kept striding up the stone-paved road, and, shortly, she stepped
through the half-open door into the far warmer air of the smithy. Both
anvils were in use. Cessya and Huldran worked a short-sword blade on the
larger, and Daryn and Ydrall used the smaller to forge arrowheads, with
Zyendra standing by. Nunca and Gresla—two junior guards—alternated
working the forge bellows. Neither Huldran nor Cessya looked up until
Cessya took the partly worked blade from the anvil with the tongs and returned it to the forge for reheating.

Daryn gave Saryn a quick glance and a nod, but did not miss a beat
with his hammer. The year after Nylan and Arylyn had departed Westwind, Daryn had asked to be allowed to help at the forge, pointing out
that his artificial foot made him a poor field worker and an even poorer
hunter, but that it mattered little in the smithy. Because he'd been willing
to undertake the dirtier work and pump the bellows whenever asked,
Huldran had agreed . . . and Ryba had said nothing. Although Ydrall had
begun almost a year before Daryn, after nine years she and the one-footed
man were about equal in smithing skills, and both were adequate smiths.

Daryn had also become a father twice, and both his son and daughter
were with Hryessa, the brunette local who'd shown such fire and such a
zest for arms that she'd become the guard captain of the second company.
Saryn had no doubts that Hryessa was actually a better leader than Llyselle,

the captain of first company, but Llyselle had been one of the original angels from the *Winterlance,* and her experience—as well as her silver hair—
had resulted in her becoming the first guard captain, after Istril had refused
to take the position, noting that her healing skills made it ever more difficult to kill.

Saryn stopped well back of the anvils, then asked Huldran, "How long
before you can provide the last twenty blades?"

"Arms-commander," Huldran replied, "with everything else, it's going
to be midsummer."

The master smith might have asked why Saryn had pressed over the
past year for another two hundred blades—enough to equip another full
company with the twin blades—when there was only a handful of guards
even available to begin forming a third company. But such decisions were
made by the Marshal of Westwind, and none questioned Ryba.

"Arrowheads?" Saryn asked, her words directed at Daryn.

"We're still way ahead of the fletchers, ser," replied Daryn.

"As for the bows, Commander," Huldran said, "we've tried everything, but if we start with the composite strips, we burn what little of the
composite is left. If we try to forge even the thinnest iron around it, we get
something that separates when there's any tension on the bow."

"So how can we get bows with power and compact enough to use from
the saddle?"

"Falynna comes from Analeria. She was a bowyer's apprentice because her father didn't have any sons. They use horn bows there. They can
pierce armor. She's been working on several since last summer, and I've
got some ideas about strengthening the central core . . ."

Saryn listened as Huldran explained before asking, "How soon will
you know whether this will work?"

"Two weeks at most, ser."

Saryn hoped the idea would work because wooden bows with pene-
tration power were too long and only a score or so of Nylan's smaller composite bows remained.

Once she finished with the smiths, Saryn headed back down toward the
practice field. Above her on the road, two squads of the newest recruits were
walking toward the stables, doubtless for their tour at mucking out the stalls
and using the wheelbarrows to cart the manure down to the fields, largely
for root crops that would last through the long and cold winters.

Three other guards walked up from the practice field. Flanking Hryessa were the two more experienced guards acting as squad leaders for the newest recruits.

". . . keep them working on the exercises to build their arms and shoulders."

Saryn smiled.

"Ser!" offered Hryessa, catching sight of Saryn.

"Guard Captain," returned Saryn. "A moment, if you will."

"Yes, ser." Hryessa gestured uphill toward the stables. "I'll be with you two shortly."

Saryn waited until the two guards were several yards away. "How are the recruits in your newer squads doing?"

"About the same as any others after their first winter on the Roof of the World. Vianyai looks to be the most promising." Hryessa had picked up Temple well enough to be conversant in both Old Rat and Temple, one of the reasons why Saryn had made the spitfire a guard captain.

"She's the one that brought in the snow cat after the blizzard?"

Hryessa nodded. "She's not the strongest, but she wants to be the best."

"That sounds like someone else . . ."

The faintest touch of a smile appeared at the corners of Hryessa's mouth, then vanished. "We'll see. Jieni works hard, too. They all do, I'd have to say."

Saryn nodded. The remoteness of Westwind and the reputation of the angels weeded out women who were not serious about changing their lives long before they reached Westwind.

"Of the latest to come before the snows last autumn, there are twenty-six from Gallos, and nine from Analeria," the arms-commander said, not quite conversationally.

"Relyn, you think?" Hryessa pursed her lips. "It could be. The only one to mention the one-handed man in black was Saachala. She claims she never heard him, but her cousin did. Vianyai said that Saachala had only brothers, and that was why she fled Passera."

"Passera? She crossed all of Gallos, then the Westhorns?"

"It cost her dearly. Her child will come due by summer. The healer says it will be a girl."

Ryba might appreciate another future guard, but every local woman who had arrived in Westwind had paid dearly in some way. That might also be why few declined to be trained to bear arms. "I need to report to the Marshal."

"Yes, ser." Hryessa nodded, then hurried up the stone road toward the stables.

As she walked swiftly down toward the causeway, Saryn caught sight of three slender figures in gray at the eastern end of the practice field, practicing bladework with wooden wands. Kyalynn and Aemra were pressing the third—Dyliess, the daughter of the Marshal, who, at almost eleven, already could handle the twin blades better than most of the Westwind guards. But then, she'd been trained from birth, not so much by Ryba as by Saryn and Istril. The three silver-hairs—that was the name the locally born guards called the trio of Dyliess, Kyalynn, and Aemra, the daughter of Istril and a year younger than the other two, so alike that they might have been full sisters rather than the half sisters that they in fact were.

"Technique!" called Saryn. "All three of you are relying on speed and not your technique! If you're going to practice by yourselves, do it correctly."

All three lowered their wands.

Aemra smothered a grin. Dyliess and Kyalynn inclined their heads solemnly.

"Do you three want to join the recruits up at the stables?"

"No, ser."

"I didn't think so. But why don't you go up there and offer to walk the horses while they're cleaning the stables? Keep them on the road. Otherwise, you'll end up having to clean them as well. The ground's too swampy. You can tell the guard captain that I sent you."

"Yes, ser."

The three hurried toward the tower to put away their wands. Saryn followed, closing the heavy door behind her and starting across the gloomy lower foyer when she saw a junior guard coming down the steps with a basket heaped with linens and other cloth.

"Why aren't you with the others?" asked Saryn.

"I'm the one assigned to the healer today, ser," replied Calysa. "I was taking these over to the bathhouse to wash."

"Go ahead, then." With a faint smile, Saryn stepped to one side.

The young woman looked around before asking, "Guard Commander?"

Saryn had almost started up the steps but halted at the hesitant words of the girl, a thin figure who had walked the roads and trails all the way from Fenard in the waning days of the previous fall, literally clawing her way through the last snowdrifts to a guard post three kays below the ridge overlooking Tower Black. "Yes, Calysa?"

"Is it true . . . that . . . ?" The brunette looked away.

"Is what true, girl?" Despite her irritation at being waylaid on her way to see the Marshal, Saryn refrained from snapping because Calysa never complained, never whined, and gave her all to anything she was asked to do.

"The stones, ser. They say that they were cut from the heart of the world by . . ."

Saryn wanted to shake her head. Nylan had been gone little more than ten years, and already the engineer was a legend. The mighty Nylan . . . the mage who had humbled two rulers, then toppled the white empire, if with Arylyn, the singer of life and death. And the man who had fled the wrath of the terrible Ryba, she reminded herself. "Yes, every stone in Tower Black was shaped in fire by Nylan. Is that what you wanted to know?"

Calysa nodded, but a question remained in her eyes.

"And you also want to know why someone so mighty would leave Westwind?" Saryn smiled wryly. "He and Ryba did not view matters in quite the same fashion, and she can see not only what is but what will be. Not even Nylan wished to cross her knowledge of what was, is, and will be." That was an oversimplification, but after years of having to explain, Saryn knew what satisfied the young women who had sought Westwind as a refuge.

"Thank you, ser."

"You best get on with the wash," Saryn said, gently but firmly.

"Yes, ser." Calysa continued on with the basket.

Saryn made her way up the solid stone steps that formed the center of the tower, all the way to the topmost level—and the Marshal's study.

At the sound of Saryn's boots, Ryba lifted her eyes from the maps spread across the simple circular table and rose from the straight-backed chair. "How is Huldran coming?"

"By midsummer we should have enough blades for another full company. She can't duplicate the bows, not the way Nylan did them—"

"If you please." Ryba's voice was cool. "Just the status."

"One of the Analerian herder girls has been working on ways to make a better horn bow, and Huldran has some ideas for coring it that might work."

"What about firearms?"

"With all those white wizards?" Saryn shook her head. "Using black powder for explosives and roadwork is one thing, but making firearms by hand would take far longer than the blades. We haven't found any sulfur anywhere in our territory, or even nearby. And the white mages could explode the powder in battle. We've barely managed to trade for enough sulfur for explosives for the roadwork."

"Save it. No more roadwork this year, not that requires blasting. Press the smiths for all the blades and arrowheads they can deliver. How much of the second company can you mount?"

"About two-thirds without any spares. All of them if we had to," Saryn conceded. "We were hard-pressed for fodder for the mounts we had this winter."

"We'll have to find a way to do better next year. Much better." Ryba's words were calm, as if finding another fifty mounts and five months of fodder for them was the easiest of tasks upon the Roof of the World.

Saryn merely nodded, then asked, "Why are you so concerned about weapons for a company we won't likely fill for another few years?"

"We'll fill it sooner than that. We have to."

"Who's likely to cause trouble? It can't be from Lady Zeldyan in Lornth or Lord Gethen, not after . . . all that happened there."

"Lornth isn't the problem. Lady Zeldyan has her hands full with the Jeranyi and Ildyrom's son. It took five years for the Jeranyi to sort out which of Ildyrom's sons would be Lord of Jerans. That's why they didn't resume hostilities against Lornth, but that could all change soon, now that Zeldyan's son is getting old enough to rule. It's one thing to remove a woman, but the lord-holders there tend to think twice about going after male rulers."

"Nesslek's what . . . eleven?"

"The years are longer here. He's twelve in terms of Sybran years, and at fifteen local years he can rule, even if he really leans on his mother and his grandfather."

"Karthanos . . . ?"

Ryba nodded. "Gallos. Not Karthanos himself. I've received word that

Lord Karthanos is ill. He may recover. He may not, but he will not rule Gallos for much longer, and his son hardly has any love for Westwind."

"Oh?" asked Saryn.

"Do you recall how Balyea came here?"

"Yes. She's the beautiful one who brought her mother and the wagon and the looms. Without her . . . we'd be far less well clad."

"She brought a small chest of golds to allow her sons to remain with her."

The two boys had barely been more than babes in arms. Even now, they were only six and seven. "She said that she was fleeing an abusive husband and that Westwind was the only place she could be sure she would not be reclaimed."

"I'm more than certain that Arthanos was abusive, but he wasn't her husband."

"Arthanos? She's never mentioned his name. Not that I know." Saryn paused. "Oh . . . he's *that* Arthanos? She was his mistress, then?"

"Exactly. He's a very nasty piece of work. His oldest brother was part of the small Gallosian contingent in the attack on Westwind, and did not survive. Not all that surprisingly, his next-older brother died last fall in a riding accident. Now his father is ill . . ."

"Does he know that Balyea is here?"

"He tortured enough people to discover that." Ryba might have been discussing what road needed to be paved next.

"When will he attack?"

"Late spring or sometime in summer, well before the harvest in Gallos. We'll need all the explosive devices you can manage."

"Arthanos will have white wizards."

"They aren't that good at detonating explosives buried in rock and soil, especially those that aren't all that close."

Saryn understood that Ryba saw—and foresaw—more than anyone logically could, but she'd yet to have been wrong when she said something was going to happen, and that meant another war—or series of battles. And more deaths. Given the position of the angels of Westwind and Ryba's determination, Saryn's only choice was to work to make certain the deaths were overwhelmingly those of the Gallosians.

IV

In the late evening, Saryn and Istril sat in the darkness of the long room that doubled as the dining hall and common room of Tower Black, across from each other at the corner of the long table nearest the iron stove in the hearth. Neither needed light, not with their nightsight. Unlike Istril, who was full Sybran and bred to the cold, Saryn fully appreciated the residual heat from the stove. The bark tea remaining in her mug had cooled to lukewarm, but she enjoyed the warmth of the mug in her hands.

"We need more men," Istril said, her voice low.

Saryn's eyes darted upward, in the direction of the topmost levels of Tower Black.

"I know how Ryba feels," the silver-haired healer continued. "Because many of the locals arrived pregnant or with children, it doesn't look like that big a problem yet. But it will be."

"There have been a few children born here from others," Saryn offered. "Certainly, your three silver-tops—"

"Only one of them is mine, and half the time I'm not sure about that," Istril said dryly. "They belong to each other more than to their mothers. Still . . . the three and Hryessa's daughters are the only ones conceived and born here."

Saryn could sense the hint of pain behind Istril's words. Unlike any of the others, Istril had given up her son, Weryl, to his father when Nylan had left Westwind. Both Saryn and Istril knew that had been for the best. Neither spoke of it often, and then only fleetingly.

"We can't keep counting on refugees," Istril went on. "Each year they have to go through more to reach Westwind. It's harder for those coming from the east. We have to find a way to get men who will fit with Ryba's visions and views."

"You want to turn men into what women are in the rest of this world? The men of this world would rather die, those worth having, anyway." Saryn's thoughts went back. Thousands of men had died trying to destroy

Westwind. For what? To try to deny a few hundred women the right to live the way they chose?

"No," replied Istril. "Why couldn't we establish a better model? We could use crafters. What if we told the women who have come here to let their relatives know we welcome crafters, and that they would never have to bear arms or pay taxes—they call them tariffs here—but the price for that life was to pledge absolute obedience to the Marshal?"

Saryn shook her head. "Even if some would come, she's not ready for that."

"After ten years? How can there be a future for Dyliess if there are no men? Ask her that. How will her heritage go on? How will ours . . ." Istril's voice died away. "I'm sorry."

"It's all right. Nylan wasn't my type, and Mertin never lived long enough . . ." Saryn took a sip of the cool tea, more to give herself time to think. "It might be . . . it just might . . ."

"What?"

"If we plant the idea that it will happen, if only after her death . . . and then ask if she would rather establish something that she can control, with rules and traditions . . ."

"You're the only one she talks to about such."

"And very seldom," Saryn replied dryly. "I'll have to be careful about when I bring it up and exactly how I approach it. She gets less approachable every year."

Istril's smile was faint and sad.

"How are those concentrate pills from the willow bark working?" asked Saryn quickly.

"I don't know that they're any more effective than the liquid, but they're a lot easier to give, especially for the younger children. I can slip them inside a morsel of cheese or softened bread, and they don't taste the bitterness. They only hold down the fever. It doesn't help with the infection chaos, except that the body is more able to fight when the fever's not really high."

"I wish we had more . . ."

"Soap and water are the biggest help. That's one place where the military discipline helps. They just have to wash up frequently."

"I've told Llyselle and Hryessa that those who are lax should be assigned to cleaning the stone drainage channels and the millraces, and especially the sheep pens and the stables. It seems to help." Saryn laughed softly.

"Do you know what Ryba has in mind for dealing with the Gallosians?"

"Not yet." Although Ryba had said little, whatever strategy the Marshal adopted would be efficient and deadly.

"Maybe we could capture a few of the younger men, ones who are little more than boys."

"They'd probably have to be wounded or disabled."

Istril nodded. "With no future back in Gallos."

"We thought that might hold Narliat and Relyn," Saryn said. "Ryba will remember. She doesn't ever forget." *Or forgive.*

"It's worked with Daryn, and Relyn hasn't caused us any harm. His words might even have brought us some of the guards we now have."

Neither mentioned that Narliat had died for his treachery.

Saryn yawned, then set her mug on the table. "It's been a long day." They all were, but spring and summer seemed short, even with the long days, because so much was necessary to prepare for the long winters.

Istril slipped from the bench and stood. "Good night." She turned and headed for the stone staircase.

"Good night, Istril." Saryn stood, then walked the length of the hall and into the kitchen, where she set the mug on the wash rack. She would have washed it, but she'd have wasted more water doing it than leaving it to be washed with the morning dishes. Then she walked slowly back through the empty dining hall—crowded to overflowing when in use, even with four shifts for meals—and up the stone steps toward the fourth-level cubby she rated as arms-commander.

Somewhere, she heard a child's murmur, and the quiet "hush" of the mother.

There should be more, she reflected, realizing again that Istril was right. But . . . talking to Ryba about men or children was always chancy. *It has to be done, and you're the only one who can.*

That thought brought little comfort as she settled onto her narrow pallet.

V

As they passed Tower Black and headed along the stone road leading up the slope to the northeast, Saryn and Siret rode near the front of the column, with but three guards before them, a full squad behind them, and three carts following them. Two of the carts were empty. The third held goods captured from the occasional brigands who had disregarded the borders of Westwind.

"What do you want most from the traders?" asked Siret, her eyes on the ridgeline above, where two mounted guards waited, surveying both the north and south slopes.

"The usual—flour, dried meat, and some of the herbs, like that brinn. Any cloth that's not too expensive, and whatever sulfur we can lay our hands on."

"No tools?"

"No. Huldran and Ydrall forge better tools than anything that Kiadryn will have. The problem we're going to have before long is iron stock. We're close to running through all those iron crowbar blades that we've accumulated over the years. So we'll need iron—unless we can find our own mine. That doesn't look likely from what little I know about geology."

As the two neared the top of the ridge, Saryn checked the twin blades at her belt and the extra one in the saddle sheath. She didn't carry one of the rare composite bows. She wasn't that good an archer, and she was far better using an extra blade or two as a throwing weapon.

One of the two guards stationed on the ridge rode forward when Saryn reached the crest of the road. "Commander," offered Dyasta, "we haven't seen any outliers, and third squad swept through the trees below us, all the way out to the flat."

"Thank you. Carry on."

Once Saryn was halfway down the northern side of the ridge, she concentrated her senses on the stand of evergreens below the road leading down to the ceramic works and the mill. She'd never had the degree of order-sensing that she'd seen in Nylan or Ayrlyn, but she got a feeling of reddish white unease whenever there were many people with weapons in an area, and she could sense "flows" when there were people around. Her senses were dependable only for about a kay and a half. Unlike Nylan and Istril, her senses didn't flatten her if she killed someone.

Once she was convinced that there were no hostiles flanking them, she turned her attention to the traders who were, at least in Candar, really a cross between traders and armed opportunistic pillagers. They had planted their banner on the flat to the west of the evergreens that sloped unbroken and gradually downward toward the northeast—before another set of rocky peaks rose some ten-odd kays to the north. Between was the road that wound to the northwest, then back to the north, snaking its way across the northern section of the Roof of the World for long kays before it began to descend into the hills of southwestern Gallos.

There were five carts lined up behind the traders. None of the carts, save the first, which was filled with kegs and barrels, looked to be as full of goods as in previous years. Standing beside the trading banner was Kiadryn, a sandy-haired man with a broadsword in a shoulder harness, similar enough to the one his father, Skiodra, had worn that it might have been the same—except Saryn couldn't imagine Skiodra giving up anything, even to his son.

Kiadryn was as broad-shouldered as his father, but not nearly so tall. He'd taken over the trips to Westwind while his father—at least according to Kiadryn—had concentrated on the trade with Lydiar and Hydlen, and other areas farther east, generally beyond the Easthorns.

The three guards reined up, some five yards from the banner. Siret and Saryn halted their mounts even with those of the guards but on the side away from the traders. Siret dismounted, handing the reins of the mare to one of the guards, and stepped forward to meet the trader.

"Greetings," offered Kiadryn.

"Greetings, honored trader," returned Siret.

"I have not seen the most honored Marshal in some time," said the trader.

"She has seen you. She sees across the Westhorns and how you have attempted to keep far from the arms of the Gallosians." Siret smiled politely. "But that is another matter. You have come to trade."

"Indeed we have, honored lady, but matters that have come to pass will make our trading less pleasurable and more costly."

"Ah, yes." Siret nodded politely. "You are going to tell me that harvests were slender last fall, and that the rainfall so far this spring has not been promising, and that there is less water in the rivers and streams of the lands to the east of the Westhorns." She raised her eyebrows.

"All those are true, indeed, but . . ." Kiadryn paused. "Karthanos's presumed heir has also declared that any who trade with you will have their goods and golds confiscated."

"That should not be a problem for you," suggested Siret. "You have already decided not to remain in Gallos. Your father has moved his base to Hydelar, and you are negotiating with the traders of Suthya and the Lady Regent of Lornth."

Saryn was as surprised as Kiadryn by Siret's statement, but she kept an impassive face.

Kiadryn did not speak for a moment. Then he inclined his head politely. "As always, honored lady, your knowledge encompasses more than most would realize. Yet the harvests in Lornth were not what they could have been. I have not seen the harvests so poor as since . . . for many years, since I was a youth."

"Since the year in which Lord Karthanos sent his armies against the Roof of the World, perhaps?" asked Saryn.

"That might be, honored Commander." Kiadryn smiled just slightly.

"That is all true enough," countered Siret, "but the harvests in Lornth were far better than in Gallos. You would rather arrive in Lornth with golds and hard goods than with those which might perish on the trip, especially if you were to be caught in the heavy spring rains that may come to the western slopes of the Roof of the World in the days ahead . . ."

As the pretrading sparring eased into the negotiations on goods themselves, Saryn watched, her eyes and senses mainly on the others in the trading party, and upon the evergreens farther to the north. Kiadryn would not break the truce of the trading banner, but for enough golds, the trader—as his father once had—could certainly be induced to conduct trading while others attempted to move into a position where they could attack the Westwind contingent.

She also scanned the men with Kiadryn, keeping in mind her discussion with Istril about recruiting suitable men. Out of all those with the trader, there was only one who looked to be less than fifteen, and he was continually playing with the hilt of the blade at his waist.

Saryn did not stop her surveillance until she and Siret were at the ridgetop on their return and heading down the paved road to Tower Black.

"You were studying the trader's men," observed Siret. "Istril said she'd talked to you."

"I didn't see any that might fit in at Westwind, did you?"

"I'm not that desperate . . . I'm not desperate at all."

Saryn looked sideways at the healer-guard. "There aren't many like the engineer."

"It's better that he's not here," Siret said. "Better for him and Ayrlyn and Weryl, and better for Westwind. There's a time and a place for each of us. We have to choose where we belong and when. The engineer knew when to leave. Sometimes, it's best to stay. Istril and I know that we belong here." Siret shrugged, as if embarrassed.

Saryn had to wonder whether the healer was seeing what she thought was best for Saryn or what she sensed. "Do you have . . . visions, like Ryba?"

"Occasionally, an image comes to me, but none of them make sense. I've seen a city with a glistening white tower and watched that tower melt like wax under a blinding light like a nova. There's no city like that, and not even the engineer wielded that kind of power. I've seen black-iron ships, but they say that this world has only ships with sails." Siret shrugged. "Those kinds of visions don't seem very useful. Who knows if they're even true . . . or if they will be? What about you, Commander?"

"No visions. I can sense what the weapons will do, and where people with weapons lurk, if they're not too far away. That's about it." *Except for the feel of things swirling around me.*

"Those skills are useful for an arms-commander."

"So are your healing skills," Saryn pointed out.

"There's pain with those. When I can't help someone enough, it hurts," Siret said. "I'd just as soon we didn't have to fight anyone."

"On this friggin' world?" Saryn laughed harshly.

"I know. There's not much choice."

Neither spoke for a time, but when they neared Tower Black, Saryn turned to Siret once more. "If you would lead my mount back to the stables . . . Ryba will be waiting."

"Better you than me, Commander."

Saryn reined up and dismounted where the road and causeway to the tower joined, then handed her mount's reins to the healer before hurrying into the tower and up to the topmost level.

Ryba was standing before the narrow open window, looking in the direction of Freyja. She did not turn. "Come in, Saryn." After a moment, she asked, "How did the trading go?"

"The flour was far more costly, over a silver a barrel," Saryn said. "Kiadryn didn't have as much as we would have liked. That was all he could get because the harvests in Gallos were especially poor. We took all ten barrels. He had a keg of sulfur . . ."

Once Saryn finished her report, Ryba asked, still looking out the window, "What did you learn? Besides the fact that Gallos had poor harvests last fall?"

"The harvests were poor everywhere. Scanty as we know those in Lornth were, elsewhere they were worse. They won't be any better this coming year. The snowpack was lighter, and we haven't had much in the way of spring snows or rains."

"We'll need to do more work on the expansion, then. I'd thought we'd have a few years."

Saryn couldn't help the puzzled look that crossed her face.

The Marshal actually sighed before she replied. "Saryn . . . I see things. Everyone thinks I see a map of the future. I don't. I see images, sometimes groups of them, and sometimes not for months at a time. All that I've seen about our times since landing has come to pass. The images haven't necessarily meant what I thought they did. Nor did they always occur when I thought they would happen. Wild as I thought some of them were, what led to them often I could not have guessed even with an imagination far wilder than mine. Some of the images I see are of only partial success. Some are of failure. Some of those I tried hard to prevent. I did not succeed. Because I wondered about how true they might be, I've always written them down. No, I won't share them. But I have to try to piece where each one fits. There's an image of the new section of Westwind, with guards struggling to complete a section against fall snows, with women so jammed into Tower Black that there's hardly room to move." Ryba stopped, turned from the window, and looked at Saryn. "Now . . . tell me what I should do. If I turn more guards to cultivating and gathering in a time when harvests are lean, will that be enough to sustain us when Arthanos sends his army against us? And will this lone tower suffice for protection against an army when we don't have the engineer or his magic laser?"

"We have you, ser," Saryn pointed out.

"For better or worse." Ryba's face remained expressionless. "You'll have to work in more arms training. They'll be tired, but then they'll be tired when they have to fight."

"More stonework?"

"More of everything, and we can only hope that it will suffice." Ryba turned back to the window. "That's all."

Saryn slipped out of the small chamber. When Ryba was so distant, she'd had another vision. Saryn just hoped it wasn't that terrible.

VI

Just past midafternoon on sixday, as Saryn walked down from the stables, she saw Ryba and a guard wearing the green sash of a courier ride up to Tower Black, followed by two other guards. The Marshal vaulted out of the saddle, then handed the reins of her mount to the courier, and hurried inside, as the other three rode past the causeway. Did the courier mean an urgent message? Why had Ryba gone out to meet the courier, or had she been riding with a road patrol? Saryn didn't bother asking Zandya as the courier rode past, nodding to Saryn. She knew that Ryba wouldn't have told Zandya. Besides, Saryn would find out soon enough.

Still . . . she wondered as she continued down toward Tower Black. Couriers early in spring usually were not the bearers of good tidings—not for Westwind, at least. She studied the ground flanking the road, now far firmer than it had been, and that had allowed the guards to return to full training with mounts.

The stones on the tower causeway were dry, but there was far too much loose sand and grit there. She'd have to mention that to Hryessa.

Saryn had barely taken three steps across the entry foyer when Dyliess bounded down the stone steps. "Mother . . . I mean, the Marshal. She'd like to see you if you're free, Commander."

"Thank you, Dyliess." Saryn smiled, knowing full well that Ryba never would have used the phrase "if you're free."

"You're welcome, Commander."

Saryn headed up the steps, slipping past two guards cleaning the wall on the third level, and making her way to the topmost level of the tower.

Ryba was in her working grays, with the usual black belt and boots, but there were splatters of mud on her trousers, and her riding jacket was draped across the back of one of the straight-backed chairs at the round table. She turned from the window. "You saw the courier?"

"I did. You two looked to be in a hurry."

"We were." Ryba held up a scroll. "I've thought something like this might be coming. I'd thought it might have happened last fall, but I didn't expect it while I was riding with third squad. So I rode back here with the courier. A Suthyan envoy should be here on eightday . . . with some traders."

"An envoy? What might he want?"

"From Suthya? Think, Saryn."

"He'll suggest we don't trade with Lornth and offer a cloaked bribe and a threat?"

"That's by far the most likely possibility, but it will be very veiled in generalities and the like. Or he might suggest that an alliance or trade with Suthya might be to our benefit, given what is likely to happen in Gallos."

"Or both," offered Saryn. "Do you want a demonstration of what the best archers and Hryessa's top squad can do?"

"That might be useful. I'd also like you . . ." Ryba smiled, but did not finish the sentence.

"My little act?"

"It can't hurt, if only to make their envoy wary."

Saryn nodded. Whether one dealt with lands where rulers used cavalry or worlds using neuronets and mirror towers, shows of prowess were necessary. *And that need is almost endless.*

"I don't like it, either," Ryba added, "but these people have been conditioned so that, without a show of power, even repeated displays of it, they can't respect others. They respect tyrants, not coordinators. That's where the engineer went wrong. He's out there looking for a way to make things work without force."

"For someone who didn't like force, he mustered a frigging load of it. The whole world shivered. Cyador's pretty much collapsed, and what was left of their fleet sailed off to Hamor. That was what the traders said some years back."

"Something like that. A good chunk of the eastern section of Cyador is reverting to that strange forestland, and most of the rest of the country is in chaos. It will be for years, if not centuries, until someone musters enough force to put things back together."

Saryn just nodded, although she had the feeling that Ryba was seeing what she wanted to. "Have you actually . . . visualized . . . that?"

Ryba shook her head. "I never get any insights there. I think it's because there are too many possibilities for now."

"Do you know when on eightday the Suthyan will arrive?"

"Plan for a demonstration in late afternoon, before the evening meal. And have the juniors clean up the guest cottage."

"I checked it the other day, but it won't hold all that many armsmen."

"Duessya will have to clean out the end section of the stable, then. That's more than adequate for Suthyan armsmen. I'll see you at supper."

"Until then." Saryn smiled, then turned and left the study, walking down all the flights of stairs to the tower's lowest level.

A Suthyan envoy? And Ryba had been expecting him for half a year?

VII

The wind whipping around Tower Black on sevenday night when Saryn finally dropped off to sleep told her that the weather was about to change. When she woke in the early chill the next morning, a thin layer of wet snow lay across the fields and meadows around Westwind, but the roads and causeways were only wet. By the time the white sun first cleared the peaks to the east, the blue-green sky was empty of clouds, and the snow had nearly all melted away, but the air was chill. Even in midafternoon, when she had received word from the scouts that the Suthyan party was less than a glass away, and she walked back downhill after checking the stables, the air was cold enough that her breath steamed as she entered Tower Black.

Ryba was standing inside the foyer, talking to Dyliess.

Saryn stopped well short of mother and daughter, out of courtesy, although she could hear their words as clearly as though she had been standing between them.

". . . don't see why we couldn't. We shoot better than any of the guards."

"Because that would be too great an insult. It would only make them more intransigent," the Marshal said.

"They're already intransigent, Mother."

"No." The single word was low, but carried enough ice and force that Dyliess stiffened.

"You will not. Now . . ." Ryba continued more softly. "You will keep the other two out of sight, but you three may observe from the second level of the tower. I want you to watch closely enough that you can describe Envoy Suhartyn perfectly and tell me exactly what sort of man he is and what he is thinking at each moment. I also would like you to be able to pick out any member of their party who appears dangerous."

"Yes, ser."

"Good. Round up the other two and take your positions. Not a word . . . and you cannot let them see you."

Dyliess turned and hurried up the steps.

Saryn waited several moments before crossing the black-stone foyer. "Everything is in readiness, Marshal."

"Except for my daughter and her accomplices."

"She wanted the trio to be part of the demonstrations?"

Ryba nodded. "It would do no good, as we both know."

"It might frighten them into building an alliance with everyone against us, you think?"

"That's possible. Right now, the rulers of those lands bordering the Westhorns all have the idea that disaffected women from their lands and elsewhere comprise the majority of Westwind. They can accept that, if reluctantly. If they see that we're able to actively train and develop another generation in addition to those who flee, that will intensify their opposition. Right now, that's outside their belief structure. They just don't think that way, and I'd like to leave it like that as long as possible." There was the briefest pause before the Marshal added, "And please don't tell me that we can't keep training youngsters if they aren't born here. You're right about men, but I don't have to like it."

Saryn understood those words were the greatest concession she'd get from Ryba on that.

A single horn triplet echoed down from the upper levels of the tower.

"It won't be long now before the Suthyans are here," Saryn said.

Ryba and Saryn walked from the base of the stairs across the foyer, halting just short of the closed ironbound door that afforded access to the causeway where the Suthyan envoy and his escorts would rein up. Only when the Suthyans were in position would the two women step out to greet the functionary and his entourage.

"He has two squads of troopers." Ryba wore a silver-gray tunic, belted in black, above black trousers and boots.

"That's enough to protect him and not enough to be considered a challenge."

"It's also an expression of their beliefs. They're traders who'd rather not spend any unnecessary golds. In the end, they'll be easier to handle than Arthanos."

"Because they'll weigh the cost of losing men against the dubious value of controlling inhospitable territory, while Arthanos will fight to maintain the myth of masculine superiority?"

Ryba nodded. "But traders are more likely to deal in treachery because it costs fewer golds."

The tower door opened, and Llyselle stepped into the foyer. "The envoy is here, Marshal."

The Marshal stepped forward, and Saryn followed, a pace back. Once outside the tower, Ryba halted on the wide single stone step above the stone-paved causeway. Saryn stood by her left shoulder and Llyselle by her right.

Suhartyn and a half score of Suthyans were reined up on the causeway, with guards on each side. The remainder of the Suthyan force was reined up on the road leading to the stables. Saryn had also taken the precaution of stationing several archers inside the tower windows overlooking the causeway.

For a moment, Ryba said nothing. She just stood there, radiating authority. Then she spoke. "Welcome to Westwind, Suhartyn, as envoy and honored guest. While we can provide but austere hospitality, that we do offer."

"I am pleased to be here, Marshal. All have heard of Westwind. All know that the only entry is as a guest, and we look forward to learning more about the Roof of the World."

"We will be pleased to let you see Westwind." Ryba smiled. "Once you have had time to settle in the guest cottage and your men in the auxiliary barracks, we will be offering you some demonstrations on the arms field that I am most certain you will find entertaining."

"Entertaining, Marshal? Or of great interest?" Suhartyn offered a smile that was half-pleasant and half-ironic.

"We would hope that you would find it both interesting and entertaining. After that, your men will be fed, and after that you and your closest advisors will join me and mine."

"You are most gracious, Marshal . . ."

Saryn sensed that Suhartyn had expected Westwind to be far more elaborate than he had found it and that he had expected a far grander welcome, perhaps because of all the rumors that had filtered across Candar in the past years.

"Grace we can provide, most honored Suhartyn, but expansive and elaborate banquets are limited here on the Roof of the World. But then, when we arrived . . . there was nothing here. In another ten years you will not recognize it." Ryba gestured. "My guards will escort you, and, in a glass or so, we will meet on the arms field for some diversion."

Suhartyn bowed from the saddle. "We look forward to that, and to learning more about Westwind, for there must be far more here than meets the eye."

"You will learn what you need to, and very little will escape your eyes. Of that, we are most certain." Ryba inclined her head.

Saryn said nothing until the Suthyans and the two guard companies were well out of earshot, riding slowly up the stone road west of Tower Black. "I'd like to see how that pampered trader and his men would fare up here in winter."

"About as well as I'd fare in Armat in midsummer," Ryba replied dryly. "Is everything in place?"

"All the targets are set, and Hryessa's first squad will mount up once everyone is gathered on the field. The other companies will be deployed in and around the tower and the stables, just to make sure that our guests behave."

"I'll leave you, and I'll join you when the envoy heads down to the arms field."

Saryn nodded and took her leave.

The sun was approaching the western horizon, seemingly barely a hand above the highest peaks, turning the glistening ice needle that was Freyja into shimmering golden white, when Suhartyn, flanked by four armsmen, walked onto the arms field. Ryba and Saryn stood waiting with ten guards from Llyselle's second squad. Behind the envoy and his guards followed four other better-dressed men, also with guards. All wore heavy winter leather jackets, unlike the riding jackets of the Westwind contingent. Two of the four Suthyans following the envoy wore uniforms, and two wore more ornate riding garments.

"We are here at your pleasure, Marshal." Standing before Ryba, Suhartyn was slightly shorter and considerably more rotund. His ginger beard was well trimmed and shot with gray, and his wary eyes were guarded by dark pouches beneath. His voice was high, not quite unpleasant. "What are we about to behold?"

Saryn felt Suhartyn's company would prove wearying over time.

The Marshal gestured to the south end of the arms practice field, a good half kay from Tower Black and the stone road up to the stables. Ten woven brush-and-wood targets, each roughly the size and shape of a mounted armsman, stood solidly anchored in the stony ground. The section of each target that resembled a rider had a tunic and a breastplate and a battered helmet. "In a few moments, you will see. We should walk a bit closer."

Suhartyn nodded, then inclined his head northward. "I see that you are building a larger hold uphill from the black tower."

"After a time, any successful community finds it must grow," replied Ryba, moving toward the targets. "Growth on the Roof of the World requires solid stone and careful planning."

"I can see that you have, what, several full companies of your guards?"

"We do, and we will have even more before long. Guards are not our only defense, as you may recall. Our abilities do not lie in just the numbers and skills of the guards, as Lord Sillek and his sire discovered."

"Ah, yes. How could anyone forget that? Still . . . that was some time ago."

"You should watch the demonstration, Envoy Suhartyn. It might answer some of your questions. If not, afterwards, I will be more than pleased to do so." Ryba's voice was calm and cool, like a polished short sword.

Saryn had stepped back, matching steps with the four men behind Suhartyn, the closer two of whom wore officers' cold-weather jackets of a dark green wool.

One inclined his head. "You're the arms-commander?"

"I am. Saryn. And you?"

"Lygyrt, Captain of Horse. This is Undercaptain Whulyn."

Lygyrt was young, barely twenty local years, while the grizzled Whulyn looked to be a good ten years older than Saryn . . . and probably wasn't. Saryn marked him as the equivalent of a noncom who'd come up through the ranks, even more rare in Candar than in the UFA.

"Then you both should find the demonstrations of interest."

"I'm certain we will," Lygyrt replied.

Whulyn nodded brusquely.

Ryba stopped in the middle of the field. Almost as she did, the twenty riders of Hryessa's first squad, two abreast, started down the stone road at a quick trot. Lygyrt and Whulyn immediately began to watch the guards. The other two Suthyans, more richly dressed in golden brown leather coats with black brocade-trimmed sleeve cuffs, did not survey the riders but kept their eyes on Ryba and Suhartyn.

Saryn glanced to Catya, the nearest guard, then inclined her head toward the two civilians, both with short-trimmed beards, doubtless the equivalent of Suthyan gentry—or dressed to convey that impression. Catya nodded and dropped back slightly, easing gradually westward so that she took position behind the two. Another guard—Trecya—joined her.

Whulyn's eyes flickered toward the two guards as they shifted position, then back to Saryn, before returning to scrutinize the mounted squad as the riders turned onto the packed gravel on the west end of the arms field.

Just before the southwest end of the field, the column turned, and the riders urged their mounts into a canter, then a gallop, with the guards on the north side holding their mounts back just enough that each file was staggered, but with each rider maintaining the same interval between mounts.

Each target received two flung blades, released from ten yards away. Every one struck the torso area of the designated target.

"Rather impressive," offered Suhartyn, "if not terribly practical in large battles."

"They're not finished," said Ryba.

At the end of the field, the squad turned right and headed back westward along the south end. They continued due west up the long slope that served as the archery range.

"Bows?" asked Whulyn, looking at Saryn.

She nodded. "At two hundred yards."

Near the top of the slope, short of the cliffs that formed a natural backdrop, the squad turned and re-formed. Barely had they done so than their bows were out. Each guard loosed three shafts.

In instants, every single target had sprouted shafts.

"You will notice that every shaft penetrated a vital area," Ryba said conversationally.

"Picked squads can do that," noted Suhartyn.

"Have you ever seen one that could do what that squad did?" Ryba looked hard at the Suthyan.

"I'm certain it is possible," Suhartyn said pleasantly.

"Indeed it is. We just proved that. But have you seen any other squad do that?" She paused. "Still, we have another demonstration."

Two guards ran across the field carrying a leather-covered sphere slightly less than a yard across. They set it on the ground twenty yards in front of the Marshal, then ran back to their positions with a squad to the east of the Marshal.

"Do you see the ten archers on the road above the smithy?"

Suhartyn turned. "Yes."

"They are a different group, and the distance is about three hundred yards." Ryba raised her arm, then dropped it.

In instants, the wicker globe became a hedgehog of feathered shafts.

"One hundred shafts in a target a yard across at three hundred yards in little more than a score of heartbeats."

Saryn could sense the concern and the tension in the two Suthyan officers, but none from Suhartyn. Didn't the envoy have any idea just how accurate the archers were?

"That is most impressive marksmanship," acknowledged Suhartyn.

"In the field, of course, they would all target different armsmen, all across the front lines, so that any charge would slow, if not halt. Then they would pick off those trapped behind."

Whulyn nodded, if almost imperceptibly. Lygyrt glanced at his under-captain, but Whulyn did not look at his superior.

"We have one last demonstration for you, Envoy Suhartyn. Would you indicate an officer to accompany my arms-commander?"

Suhartyn turned. "Undercaptain? If you would?"

One of the junior guards led two horses out onto the field. Saryn mounted her gelding, where the heavy black hood was draped over the front of the saddle. Whulyn was almost as quick with the other mount, and he rode beside her as they headed uphill on the road.

Less than a hundred yards above the northwest corner of the field, Saryn turned her mount and reined up. Then she extended the heavy black hood to Whulyn. "Look it over, then put it over my head."

Whulyn edged his mount closer with an ease of long experience, then bent forward.

Saryn leaned toward him, waiting until the hood was in place. "Is there any way I can see?"

"No." Whulyn's voice contained veiled amusement. "There wouldn't be, would there?"

Saryn managed to keep from smiling, not that the undercaptain could have seen her expression under the hood. "No. There's no trickery involved. You can follow me to watch and see what you think."

"Thank you, Commander." The amusement had vanished from Whulyn's voice.

Using her senses, Saryn guided the gelding back down the road toward the arms practice field. Her free hand checked the blades in the shoulder harness and the one in the sheath at her knee. At the west end of the field, she turned south, then, once she was past a point even with Ryba and Suhartyn, she urged the gelding eastward and into an easy canter.

When she was still a good twenty yards from the wicker target, she released the first blade, smoothing the flows and sending it toward the breastplate once worn by a Lornian lancer. The second blade was away at about fifteen yards. Then she turned the gelding, and with her back to the target, flung the last blade.

She slowed the gelding gradually, wishing she hadn't had to ride on the field, then turned and rode back to where Ryba, Suhartyn, and the Suthyan captain stood. After reining up, she removed the heavy black hood and gently tossed it to the captain. Ten yards away, all three blades were buried to their hilts in the iron breastplate, each spaced two fingers from the one beside it.

She dismounted, and a guard hurried up and handed Saryn another blade, which she slipped into the left shoulder scabbard one-handed. The guard took the gelding's reins and led him away. Saryn walked forward to Suhartyn, inclining her head politely. "I trust that these small demonstrations provide some idea of what our guards can do."

Suhartyn, a good half head taller than Saryn, smiled politely. "You are all most impressive. But there are not that many of you."

"There were less than forty of us when we destroyed the thousands of Lornth," Ryba replied calmly. "We would prefer not to fight, because fighting wastes golds and resources. That is why we destroy all those who try our patience. It keeps us from wasting resources too often."

"Ah . . . yes."

Saryn slowly drew the short sword, then looked to Lygyrt. "Would you like to see if you could put this blade, or your own, through the breastplate of the target?"

"I'd prefer not to dull my own."

Saryn reversed the short sword and extended it, hilt first, to the captain.

She and Lygyrt walked to the target.

The captain jabbed, and the short sword skittered off the iron. "This is a useless, blunted weapon."

"Please return it to me, then." Saryn extended her hand.

The officer reversed the weapon and offered it.

Saryn took the short sword, stepped back some three paces, summoned the blackness around her, and released the blade. It turned exactly once before the tip sliced through the iron, directly below the middle blade of the three she had thrown from horseback. Like the others, it buried itself up to the hilt.

Lygyrt swallowed.

Saryn smiled. "It doesn't seem that blunt to me. All the short swords are balanced to be used as both blade and weapon."

". . . demon-woman . . . all of them . . ."

". . . wouldn't have one chained and stripped bare . . ."

Saryn ignored the mutters her senses picked up and walked back across the field to where Suhartyn stood beside Ryba.

The Marshal turned to Suhartyn. "Do you still think it was a trick?"

"Perhaps . . . I should have said that it was a form of magic."

"And all of the archers were using magic?" Ryba paused. "I suppose skill with weapons is a form of sorcery."

Whulyn had dismounted and returned the mount to a guard. He said nothing when he rejoined Lygyrt and the two nobles.

Ryba half turned so that she could speak to both Suhartyn and the others. "That concludes our little demonstration. We have tried your patience, and it is time for your men to be fed in the main hall at Tower Black. The rest of us will meet there in two glasses for the banquet. Perhaps we should call it a dinner. There will be places for you and up to a half score others."

"We will be there, and we look forward to conversing and enjoying your hospitality." Suhartyn inclined his head.

Saryn could sense something, particularly from one of the two well-dressed men who had said nothing, not while she had been in earshot, anyway. But she said nothing until the Suthyans had left the field, and she and Hryessa walked toward the tower, following Ryba.

"They're planning something," Saryn told the guard captain. "Have two squads watching their armsmen at all times. If they try anything, kill anyone who lifts a weapon."

"Yes, ser."

Once she entered the tower, Saryn went to the armory. There, she drew another short sword before heading up to her small corner of the tower, where she slipped out of the riding jacket and battle harness and donned a formal sword belt, slipping the blade into the scabbard. Then she walked down to the main hall, to wait and watch while the Suthyan armsmen were fed, followed by the Westwind guards.

Almost two glasses later, Suhartyn appeared, accompanied by seven others, including Lygyrt, Whulyn, and the two bearded nobles who had watched the demonstrations. As the Suthyans entered the tower foyer, Saryn noted that all wore blades, if single, and all weapons were sheathed in highly ornamental scabbards.

Once inside, the envoy inclined his head to the Marshal, then nodded toward the blond-bearded man. "This is Lord Calasyr of Devalona, the most distinguished of our party."

"Not lord," protested Calasyr, who wore a blue-and-green tunic trimmed in silver. "My father is lord. I might be such if I live long enough."

"And High Trader Baorl, of the House of Aramal."

The older dark-haired and bearded man smiled and bowed to Ryba. "Marshal. Word of your abilities has spread far, but not of your impressive personage."

"Thank you, Trader." Ryba gestured toward the main hall. "I believe a modest dinner awaits us."

Saryn flanked Ryba as the Marshal led the way.

Those from Westwind at the table were Ryba, Saryn, Istril, Llyselle, Siret, Hryessa, Huldran, Ydrall, and Duessya. Suhartyn was seated to Ryba's right, with Calasyr to her left. Saryn sat to Calasyr's left, with Istril across from her. Trader Baorl sat down the table from Istril, while Lygyrt was on Saryn's left and Whulyn to Istril's left.

At each place was a crystal goblet and a large porcelain plate bearing the crest of Westwind that Ryba had designed. The formal dining accessories were seldom used, and only for comparatively small dinners, since there were settings sufficient for just twenty-five.

Once everyone was seated, and the goblets filled, Ryba raised hers. "A welcome to our guests, for you have traveled far through rugged terrain."

What was served in the ceramic pitchers was not properly wine, but more like an ice-wine from the bitter wild grapes that Istril had managed to use her senses to, as she put it, "tame." The resulting liquid was half table vintage and half brandy, odd but smooth and drinkable. Far too drinkable in larger quantities, Saryn knew.

"And our thanks for your hospitality," replied Suhartyn, lifting his goblet.

Saryn but sipped from her goblet, as did Undercaptain Whulyn, she noted, while the captain drank less sparingly.

"How did you come to be a captain in the Suthyan horse?" she asked.

"A younger son in a trading house has few honorable options. That is most true if one's talents do not run to trading and counting." Lygyrt lifted his goblet slightly. "And you, Commander, how did you come to command the arms of the Roof of the World?"

"The Marshal commands, Captain," Saryn replied evenly, almost softly. "I do what is necessary to carry out those commands."

"But . . . you are most talented with arms."

"The Marshal is also most talented with arms, and she has had many more years experience in fighting and leading."

"It is said that you who are true angels were born on another world."

"That is true, and we have fought in the darkness and cold between worlds. But all at Westwind are angels."

"Yet you remain here?"

"We had no choice. The vessel that carried us between worlds failed, and we made landfall here."

The servers appeared with large serving platters, holding sliced wild boar that had been cold-marinated for several days, then slow-roasted. Another set of platters held fried lace potatoes, and another a heap of mashed local turnips, in a white sauce. Two baskets of fresh-baked bread also appeared.

"Excellent," exclaimed Suhartyn, after a bite of the boar.

"Simple as this is, our usual fare here is even simpler," Ryba said. "We can only maintain a small herd of cows through the winter, and the chickens are not grown this early in the year."

"Early in the year?" asked Baorl. "This is late spring."

"It is late spring for you in Suthya," replied Istril, "but the last of the snow and ice around Westwind melted away but two weeks ago. Some snow in the shaded areas above us may last all summer."

"It is chill indeed here," observed Calasyr, "and yet some of you wear but summer garments." The young noble lifted his right hand, and a reddish whiteness swirled around it—except the chaos wasn't from his hand, Saryn realized, but from his large and elaborate gold ring.

"That is why they need trade, Lord Calasyr," said Suhartyn. "The season is too short here to be certain for them to grow the wheat corn."

"Ah, yes," added Baorl, "trade. But trade can also be uncertain, even in the best of times. And it is said that Lord Karthanos is loath to let traders travel from his lands to Westwinds."

"It is no secret that the lands of Gallos are not as amicably disposed toward us as are . . . others," replied Ryba. "Still, many do trade with us."

"Mainly through Lornth, I believe," suggested Suhartyn. "If any ill should befall Lornth, as might have happened had Cyador not collapsed in ruins, even the most doughty of traders might find it difficult to reach the Westhorns . . . except, of course, from Suthya."

"What ill might befall Lornth?" asked Ryba. "Its regents have offended no one, so far as we have heard."

"One never knows," said Calasyr, gesturing extravagantly. "It is said that some of the older holders in Lornth fear that the regent's rule may not lapse even when Lord Nesslek reaches his majority."

"We, in Suthya, of course," added Suhartyn, "would like to remain on good terms with all, especially with Westwind, whatever might occur in Lornth."

"Unlikely as that might seem at the moment," continued Calasyr.

Even though she followed Calasyr's gestures closely, Saryn couldn't determine how he managed it, only that the chaos—poison presumably—was suddenly in Ryba's goblet. Before Ryba could lift the goblet again, Saryn half stood, turned, and grasped it with her left hand.

"What . . . ?" The Marshal half smiled, but immediately released her grip and let Saryn take the vessel.

Saryn set the goblet before Calasyr, the short sword in her right hand. "You, Lord Calasyr, have a simple choice. You can swallow what you put in the Marshal's goblet, or you can swallow cold iron—"

The blond man bolted to his feet, a poignard coming up and aimed toward the Marshal.

Two blades went through him, one from in front and one from behind. He stood there . . . wavering, then started to topple forward. Hryessa stepped forward and grabbed the back of his tunic, pulling him away from the table. Saryn eased her blade from between his ribs.

Llyselle's blade tip was at the back of Suhartyn's neck, and Huldran had cold iron on Baorl. Ydrall and Duessya had moved behind the two officers.

The envoy paled, and the high trader slowly put his hands on the table, palms up.

"Suhartyn . . ." Ryba said coldly. "I expected better of you."

"I didn't know. I didn't!"

"Siret?"

"He's telling the truth about that. I'd guess he suspected treachery but not by Calasyr. I don't think he was told."

"Of course. They feared that we'd detect any lies on his part."

Ryba's smile was cold as she stood. "Does your council fear a collection of distant women so much that they would try such treachery?" She shook her head. "I doubt it. Like all thieving merchants, they merely looked for the cheapest way to their ends. And like all dishonest traders, you and they will end up paying far, far more as a result of your dishonesty. As for you, and your men, you have one glass to depart Westwind. You may leave the tower now."

Suhartyn inclined his head.

"And take that carrion with you." Ryba glanced toward Calasyr's corpse.

As the Suthyans filed out, with two Suthyans Saryn had not met carrying Calasyr's body, Whulyn lagged behind the others, slightly. Saryn moved toward him as he neared the archway between the hall and the foyer. "A moment, Undercaptain."

The grizzled officer turned. "Yes?"

"Neither you nor the captain was party to Calasyr's plot, were you?"

"No. Why do you say that?" An ironic smile flickered at the corners of his thin lips.

"Because of who each of you happens to be. What will your superiors say?"

"We'll likely be cashiered if we return to Armat."

"You might consider serving Lady Zeldyan of Lornth, in that case."

"That might only postpone the inevitable, Commander."

"It might . . . but what is inevitable to one land is not necessarily so to another."

Whulyn nodded. "I appreciate your concern, Commander, but I must ready my men. I assume they are well."

"Unless they lifted arms, you will find them well."

"I told them not to, and they obey. Good night." The undercaptain turned and hurried to follow the other Suthyans.

"What was that about?" asked Ryba.

"I was trying to recruit a good officer for Lady Zeldyan. She, and we, could use such."

"That she could. I'll need to talk to you in the morning, but I want you personally to make sure every last Suthyan is off the Roof of the World before the next glass is turned."

"Yes, ser." Saryn nodded and hurried toward the tower door.

Out on the causeway her gelding was waiting, held by Aemra.

"I can hold horses while others bear arms, Commander. The horses will not disobey me." Even in the dim light cast by the pair of lanterns framing the tower door, the calm behind the silver-haired girl's smile was obvious.

"Thank you." Saryn took the reins and mounted, then urged the gelding across the causeway to the road and uphill.

She could sense that Llyselle's entire company was mounted and stationed in squads along the road. With the guards in place, and with the Suthyans effectively under Lygyrt's—and Whulyn's—command, Saryn had few doubts that all the Suthyans would be well away from Westwind within Ryba's time limits.

Still, she'd have scouts follow them and hold a squad on standby for the night.

VIII

Oneday morning, after grabbing some bread and cheese from the kitchen, Saryn was out of the tower well before sunrise. She didn't feel as tired as she might have, even though she'd been up late the night before checking with the scouts and patrols to make certain that the Suthyans were gone—and that they stayed on the road home to Armat.

Her first concern was with the horses. Dealing with the Suthyans had meant more riding and less rest for the mounts, and it was still early in the year, when the horses were not as well conditioned as they would be later. That was one reason why she wanted to check with Duessya.

The head ostler was inspecting the front hoofs of a mare when Saryn reached the stables. Saryn stepped away and started to walk through the stables. While she didn't have the sensitivity of either Istril or Siret, if she concentrated, more like opening her senses wider, she could feel pain, but it was more like a needle jab than the overwhelming agony that she'd seen flatten Nylan and Istril.

She walked the entire length of the stables and back, but didn't sense that any horse was in great pain or agony.

Duessya waited, looking like she'd gotten less sleep than Saryn. "Yes, Commander?"

"How are the horses?"

"A handful will need to be rested, but most are in good shape. The Suthyans and their mounts aren't used to the heights or the cold. We didn't have to work ours nearly that hard."

"There are lots of things they're not used to." Saryn's words came out more tartly than she had intended.

"They do not like women with cold iron."

"And minds of their own," added Saryn. "How many more foals are we expecting?"

"Just two. We have ten in all, and they're all healthy . . ."

By the time Saryn had finished with Duessya and was walking back down the road, the junior guards were lined up on the field for exercises and arms practice.

Ryba had crossed the causeway and walked across the corner of the field to join Saryn.

"Good morning, ser," offered the arms-commander.

"Good morning, Saryn. Have you heard anything more about the Suthyans?"

"They were all headed northwest, but I have scouts following them. We can't be sure for several days where they're going . . . except that it's away from Westwind."

"The envoy did not seem overly impressed with the skill of the guards," said Ryba.

"I don't think he knows much about arms," replied Saryn. "The undercaptain understood, but I doubt that any of the senior officers will listen to him."

"In a society where position is granted by birth and gender, junior officers who come up through the ranks are ignored almost as much as women." Ryba's laugh was both low and harsh. "In all of Candar, Westwind is the only land where women and ability are recognized."

But you feel almost the same way about men as the Suthyans, Lornians, and

Gallosians do about women. Is that really any better? Saryn knew better than to voice that thought.

"What do you think about the timing of the envoy's visit?" pressed Ryba.

"It was early in the year."

"Exactly. That suggests that someone has planned something."

"There's no sign of the Suthyans bringing up more armsmen."

"They won't. They prefer to have others fight for them, whenever possible."

"That does suggest that they're working with the Gallosians." Saryn paused but for a moment. "I thought that it might be a good idea if I took a squad farther east to look into matters."

"If you hadn't suggested it, I would have," replied Ryba. "Arthanos has no love of Westwind, and he might even have been the one to put the Suthyans up to their treachery."

"In hopes of weakening Westwind before he musters forces for an attack on us?"

"That's a foregone conclusion. When were you planning on leaving?"

"I'd thought we'd leave on threeday."

"You might be better making it tomorrow."

That alone told Saryn that Ryba was more than casually concerned. "Yes, ser."

"After we warm up, I need to spar. So do you."

That was also true, Saryn knew.

IX

For early spring on the Roof of the World, the day was warm enough for Saryn to shed her riding jacket as she accompanied first company's second squad down through the pass to the north and east of the high valley through which the traders had come. Despite the clear sky and the direct whitish sunlight beating down through the greenish blue sky, snow was still drifted into piles in the shade under the massive evergreens on each side of the road. Saryn still found herself amused at what she now considered a "road." The only proper roads in the Westhorns were those around Westwind, stone-paved and generally level, although the guards had, over the past several years, paved certain sections of the packed-dirt ways around the Roof of the World, just to keep them from washing out, as well as building several short stone-and-earth bridges.

Rocky steep cliffs rose away from the stream and the narrow road, barely wide enough for two mounts abreast, or one cart or small wagon. In places, Saryn saw glints of ice. Even so, an alpine muskrat scurried from the near-freezing water into a concealed burrow.

"Do you think the scouts actually saw brigands?" asked Murkassa, the squad leader.

"They saw armed men," replied Saryn. "Either brigands or armsmen from Gallos. There were just two riders, and there weren't any tracks that suggested a larger group."

"I'd lay a wager on scouts for armsmen. Brigands would know that few men, even those with coins and weapons, travel the Westhorns in spring."

"And not women and weapons?" asked Saryn with a laugh.

"We're still the only women with weapons. We'll be the only ones for a long, long time."

"Even with Westwind as an example?"

"People don't change. Even my mother couldn't believe I'd leave," said Murkassa. "My father beat her every time he didn't like what she fixed for dinner, but she wouldn't leave."

"You left," Saryn pointed out.

"I was frightened." Murkassa laughed. "When I realized that I was frightened all the time, I decided to leave and make my way to the Westhorns." She paused. "Most women have never heard of Westwind, except when men talk about us as worse than the white demons."

"I can see why you left your family, but why did you come to Westwind?"

"There was nowhere else to go." Murkassa shrugged. "Anywhere else would have been like where I grew up, and worse, because no one at all would have cared."

"You don't miss men?"

"I don't miss men like my father and my brothers. I would that there had been more like the engineer, or Relyn, or Daryn, but having no men is better than having those that I knew." Murkassa smiled. "Besides, you angels will provide. You always have."

Saryn wasn't so certain about that, especially in finding suitable men, those who were not either hopeless or hopelessly arrogant.

At that moment, ahead of the squad, Saryn saw one of the outriders rein up, while the other turned and began to trot back up the road toward the rest of the squad.

"Commander! Bodies on the road!"

"Arms ready!" ordered Murkassa.

"Ride down to the edge of the pass. Hold up there until I can see what we might face." Saryn couldn't sense any living brigands or weapons, but there might be some beyond the outriders, farther east than her sensing skills could reach.

"Yes, ser."

Saryn urged her mount forward at a quick trot. There wasn't any point to moving faster on the uneven downhill section of the road, with its winter-twisted humps and ruts. She rode almost two hundred yards before the road began to flatten, and the rocky edges of the pass walls began to widen out into the small and largely wooded semivalley that lay beyond the pass.

The outrider, a freckled young redhead, waited for Saryn, her mount turned so that she could watch both the squad and the other outrider who had reined up ahead.

"There are two on the road." The young guard pointed. "You can see the cart poles, but the cart horse or donkey is gone. Like as not anything of value went, too."

Saryn still could not sense anything . . . except the faint reddish white residue of death that lay over the small grassy area to the south of the road. With the light wind out of the south, all she could smell were road dust, trees, and the soggy vegetation that bordered the stream to the north of the road. "You ride with me. We'll take our time."

Alert as she was, all Saryn could see or sense as she neared the second outrider and the cleared area by the overturned cart were the two West-wind guards. Still . . . there was something in the woods, but too small to be a brigand, hiding under a spreading evergreen bush.

The two guards, their blades out, flanked Saryn as they rode slowly forward. Saryn reined up short of the oiled and weathered wooden cart, overturned in all likelihood to see if anything of value had been hidden beneath it. Her eyes ran across the carnage. Two men, both graying slightly, had been cut down within yards of the cart, but they'd died fighting, from the slashes and the blood. One had his temple smashed in. Their garments had been disarrayed, and a belt wallet lay half-open on the road between the bodies and the cart.

Easing her mount around the cart and onto the softer grassy ground to the south, Saryn reined up again. There had been three women, one much older and white-haired. She'd tried to flee and been run down by a rider and struck from behind. The other two, one of whom looked barely out of girlhood, had been stripped from the waist down, and used by the brigands before their throats had been cut.

Saryn swallowed as she saw the figure of a small child in the grass. Beyond the dead child was another body, that of a pregnant woman, also half-naked. Saryn could sense that both the mother and the child within her womb were dead.

Abruptly, she stood in the stirrups and gestured to the waiting squad. "Join up!"

As she waited for the squad to reach her, she looked back at the bodies. She frowned, realizing that all the dead, except the white-haired woman, were redheads. How likely was that?

"Brigands, it looks like to me," offered Murkassa, when she finally reined up beside Saryn. "Bloody bastards."

Saryn studied the bodies for a time, looking back toward those of the men as well. There was something about them. Then she shook her head. "Armsmen. The weapons used on them . . . they're too good for common ruffians."

"Why would they attack travelers? With the men, they weren't headed for Westwind."

Saryn stiffened. There was something, and now that she was closer, she could tell that what she sensed just inside the edge of the woods was no animal. "Someone's still alive." She turned in the saddle, then nodded. "Detail a few of the guards to make a cairn over by the trees. I'm going to see . . ."

"Do you need an escort?"

"No . . . I'm pretty sure it's a child." Even so, Saryn rode slowly around the cart and the bodies toward the darkness of the tall evergreens, letting her senses take in what lay before her, one of the short swords in her hand, ready to throw or use as necessary. The closer she got to the yard-wide trunks of the tall pines, the more certain she was that a girl hid there.

Saryn rode forward, slowly, then halted her mount at the edge of the trees. "We won't hurt you. We're all women. We're from Westwind. You'll be safe now." She eased the short sword back into its scabbard.

The figure huddled under a scrub evergreen did not move.

After a time, the commander eased her mount forward and into the tall evergreens, stopping well short of the girl. Saryn wanted to tell the girl that she'd be safe, that everything would be all right. She didn't. Instead, she waited, letting her senses take in the trees and the life deeper in the shadows. After a time, she spoke again. "Those who attacked you are gone."

A small face continued to peer through the evergreen bush, as if afraid to move.

"You'll be all right, now." Saryn continued to wait, not wanting to press the girl, but afraid that if she dismounted or made any other moves toward the child, the girl would run deeper into the trees, where it would be even harder to find her. Besides, someone chasing her was the last thing the girl needed.

As she sat in the saddle, waiting, Saryn glanced back, but Murkassa had matters well in hand, and half the guards were already gathering stones for a cairn. That was better. The girl didn't need to see what had happened to the others.

"You . . . you don't have the silver hair. Are you an angel?" The girl spoke slowly into the silence. "Ma said we'd be safe if we got to the angels." She stood up, almost as if she were offering herself as some form of sacrifice.

Saryn swallowed. She wanted to vault from the saddle and take the child in her arms. Instead, she blinked back the burning in her eyes and smiled as warmly as she could. "We are the angels of Westwind, and you will be safe with us. Can you walk over here so that you can ride with me?"

"My feet hurt . . . the rocks . . ." As she spoke, the girl slowly stepped around the bush and moved toward Saryn. Her hair was red, like that of all those slain, and she already had traces of freckles on her face, especially on her cheeks. She wore calf-length gray trousers and a faded gray tunic over some sort of undertunic. Streaks of blood ran across her feet and ankles. When she reached the shoulder of Saryn's mount, she lifted her arms. Her brown eyes held both trust and fear—or those were the feelings Saryn sensed.

Saryn leaned down and lifted her, amazed at how thin and light the child was. *She must be close to starving.* Then she set the girl before her and turned the mount. "We're going to join the others." After a moment, she asked, "What's your name?"

"Adiara, Angel."

"Where are you from?"

"Neltos."

Saryn had never heard of it, but then, there were all too many places in the world whose names remained unfamiliar. She wondered if she'd ever learn them all. "Where is Neltos?"

"The market town is Meltosia. We didn't go through Kyphrien. We went around it at night. Ma didn't say why. She made me promise to be quiet."

"Where were you going?"

"Ma and Da said we were going to Suthya."

"Did they tell you why?" Saryn reined up on the road. She was careful to keep her mount pointed away from the overturned cart although the guards had already moved the bodies to the edge of the clearing, where they were piling stones over them.

Murkassa eased her mount closer to the commander's.

"Lord Karthanos . . . he was doing bad things to folks like us. That was what Da said."

"Folks like you?"

"You know, Angel. Redheads. We turn red in the sun, too." Adiara stopped speaking, and she looked at the squad leader. "You don't have silver hair. Are you an angel?"

"I am from Westwind . . . now," Murkassa replied. "The commander is truly one of the angels. She came from the stars. So did the Marshal, and she has black hair."

"Not all of the guards of Westwind have silver hair," Saryn said gently. "Some do, and some of their daughters do, also."

"You have children?"

"We are women," Saryn said, somewhat dryly. "Some of us have children."

"Will you take me with you?"

"Yes." From what the girl had said, Saryn doubted she had any relatives who would want her, and Saryn had no intention of riding down through the eastern Westhorns and through Gallos on the off chance of finding any who might want Adiara. "You must understand that Westwind is cold much of the year."

"You won't let anyone hurt me, will you?"

"No." Saryn paused, then asked, "Will you tell me when all this . . . happened?"

"This morning, Angel. We stopped for the night down at the other end of the vale. There's a pool in the stream. There was a hole in the rocks where we could shelter. We had only set out . . ." Tears seeped from the girl's eyes. "Ma told me to run . . . and not look back." She shuddered, and her hands clutched the base of the horse's mane.

"How many of them were there?" Saryn asked quickly. There was little point in allowing Adiara to dwell on the actual events.

The girl looked around, taking in the twenty guards, mostly around the cairn, except for the outriders posted as guards. "As many as you . . . I think."

"No one ran after you?"

"A man rode after me, but he didn't go into the trees."

Saryn nodded. "Did he try to follow you farther? Did he say anything?"

"He said I was too young to bother with. Someone else said I'd die in the woods."

"Miserable brigands," murmured the single guard beside Murkassa.

Adiara raised her head. "They were not bandits . . ." She shivered. "They wore armor under their rags. Uncle Rastyn said so. Then, they took out their swords . . ." Her words stopped.

"That's enough," Saryn said gently, wrapping one arm around the girl, who had started to shiver again. "You've told us enough."

For a time, the only sound in the clearing was that of rocks dropping on rocks as the guards finished the cairn.

"What do you plan?" Murkassa finally asked.

"To go hunting," replied Saryn. "They'll expect it. So we'll have to be careful. Very careful." *Careful enough that we can remove all of them.* "The girl will have to come with us."

"It might be good for her."

Would it? Saryn had her doubts.

"Will you catch them, Angel?"

"We'll see what we can do." Saryn wasn't Ryba. She couldn't see whether she and the squad would be able to deal with the false bandits, but they did need to know more, and only by tracking the armsmen could they learn what was behind the attack on the travelers.

X

The false bandits had left tracks easy enough to follow as they had headed eastward, in the general direction of Gallos and the next valley, where the roads split into those to Lornth, Gallos, and northern Lornth or Suthya. The hoofprints had all been similar, with an imprint of "G" within a square, indicating that the mounts had been shod by the same smith or farrier, most likely in the service of the Prefect of Gallos.

Even though the brigand armsmen had close to half a day's head start, as second squad continued through the afternoon at a moderate walk, Saryn could sense that the Westwind contingent was gaining ground. In late afternoon, when the white sun had dropped below the tops of the western peaks, and the road was covered in shadow, the squad neared another stream.

"Ser!" called Chyanci, one of the outriders, who had reined up at the edge of the water on the south side of the road. "Over here!"

With Adiara still seated before her, Saryn eased the big chestnut gelding toward the outrider and the stream.

Not only were there hoofprints trampled into the mud, but Chyanci leaned down and pulled a grayish cloth or rag with blood on it out of one of the scrub oaks growing on the uphill bank of the stream. "Looks like one of them was wounded, maybe pretty badly. Some of the blood hasn't hardened."

"They can't be all that far ahead," offered Murkassa. "How close do you think we are?"

"I'm no tracker," Saryn admitted, "but the imprints in the mud are still crisp. That discarded wound dressing hasn't hardened. I can't sense anyone that close to us. They're more than a kay away, but I'd guess less than ten kays. They're probably going to stop near where the three roads branch in different directions."

"What do you have in mind, ser?"

"We've pushed the mounts some," replied Saryn. "I'd rather not press that hard. They're not going back to Gallos, and we'll take them on our terms."

Murkassa nodded.

"I'll go ahead with the outriders to make sure that they're still headed east. I don't want us surprised, either." Saryn eased the gelding closer to Murkassa, then said to Adiara, "You'll have to stay with the other guards."

"I can do that, Angel."

"Good." Saryn lifted the girl and passed her across to the squad leader. She was still surprised at how light the girl was for her age, which had to be around eight or nine. "Find a good bivouac site somewhere along the stream here."

"We'll take care of it, ser."

Saryn turned the gelding. "Chyanci, Abylea!"

"Yes, ser." The two outriders rode to join Saryn.

"We're going to scout out the road to the east." The commander turned her mount and headed through the dip in the road where a spring rivulet ran to join the larger stream. Then she urged the mount into a fast walk along the flatter section of road on the other side. The two outriders followed her.

For the next kay, Saryn sensed only small creatures, except for a mother bear hidden away with cubs and a red deer doe. After that, as the road began to rise once more, and the snowdrifts under the tall pines got deeper, she sensed less large life. The hoofprints continued up the gradual incline, but she could see that the slow pace of the riders was slackening even more.

Still, after almost three kays, she felt that she and the other two were only slightly closer to the Gallosians. The light was fading, and she knew the road would climb for another kay before leveling out, then descending into the valley to the northeast. While she had nightsight, the others didn't. But she felt better knowing that the Gallosians weren't that close . . . and that their mounts were tired. She'd also have wagered that the guard mounts were in better shape. She had no doubts that her guards were.

"Hold up. We'll head back now."

"Do you think they'll make the valley tonight?" asked Abylea.

"If they do, they'll have tired mounts. They probably plan to stay there and rest for a day. That's unless they come across more helpless travelers." Saryn turned the gelding.

"Will we attack tomorrow?"

"That depends on what the day brings. We'll attack when we can be certain of the outcome." Saryn's voice hardened with the last words. She didn't want a single Gallosian returning to Fenard and Arthanos.

In the twilight, the two outriders exchanged glances.

"Let's go." Saryn urged the gelding forward, back down the road toward second squad. At least the grade was gradual enough that it wouldn't be that hard on the horses.

Even so, by the time Saryn returned to the bivouac area, twilight had given way to night across the Westhorns, and a small cookfire was burning. Saryn noted that Murkassa had found dry deadwood so that there was little smoke. Now wrapped in a blanket, Adiara hunched close to the fire.

Saryn rode over to the first tie-line where the mounts were tethered and two guards stood watch. She dismounted, unsaddled, and rubbed down the gelding before walking slowly toward the small fire.

"Any signs of them, ser?" asked Murkassa, standing as the commander approached.

"Not within about four kays."

"There's no easy approach to us. I've posted sentries where we'll get plenty of warning."

"We may need warning, but not from them." Saryn took a long swallow from her water bottle. "They're trying to make the crossing valley. They'll wait there for a day or two. I don't think they even know we're following them."

"No. Women don't track down armsmen. You'd think they'd know better after ten years," said Murkassa.

"Why would they? We've protected travelers and routed anyone who came at us, but we haven't actually tracked and attacked anyone."

"Wouldn't they think we might when they started to send squads to terrify travelers?"

"No," Saryn replied. "Women in Gallos wouldn't even consider that. They have the idea that we're like the females of most species—females will protect their own and their cubs, but they won't go that far from their territory to chase a marauder." She smiled. "We're about to change their ideas."

At that moment, Adiara turned and looked up from the fire, her eyes wide.

Saryn could sense the mixture of feelings within the girl—sadness, anger at the death of her mother, exhaustion, but most of all, something like awe, as if she had seen a glimpse of something she had never seen before.

XI

Fiveday dawned bright, with frost across everything, and a rime of ice on the still waters at the edge of the stream. The thin layer of slushy snow in the shade had a crunchy crust of ice on it that would soften by mid-morning. All that was usual for spring on the Roof of the World, and morning duties were quickly completed, so that Saryn and second squad were riding eastward long before the sun cleared the taller peaks.

As they started up the gradual incline in the road that Saryn had scouted the night before, she turned in the saddle toward Murkassa, riding to her right. "You've got five bows. How many are good with them?"

"All, ser. I've trained everyone, but the five who carry them are as good as anyone in the guards. All of them can put the shafts through plate, sometimes at a full gallop. Zanlya can hit a moving target the size of a pearapple at fifty yards, sometimes close to a hundred."

Westwind shafts, thought Saryn, *with arrowheads forged by Nylan before he left*. Those arrowheads were the ones that the guards spent glasses searching for after they'd used them against brigands . . . or poachers. That was something on which both Ryba and Saryn agreed. The replacement arrowheads forged by Daryn, Huldran, and Ydrall were good . . . but not so good as those done by Nylan. Everyone knew it, and no one ever said so.

Sometimes, the guards sang the song Ayrlyn had written about Nylan, but never when Ryba was around. Saryn smiled briefly as she recalled the engineer's embarrassment at the opening lines: *Oh, Nylan was a smith, and a mighty mage was he* . . . She also wondered if the former comm officer had composed the song just to assure Nylan's legacy.

"How long will we be riding, Angel?" asked Adiara.

"All day," replied Saryn. "You'll have to ride with some of the others soon."

The girl nodded solemnly.

A glass or so later, Saryn turned the girl over to Raena, one of the junior guards, and joined the outriders. That way, she could sense any dangers as soon as possible.

For a time, Saryn and the two outriders rode silently along the high stretch of road between the evergreens and shaded snowdrifts. The air was chill enough that the only scent was the faintest hint of pine and spruce.

"Do you think they'll have attacked more travelers?" Abylea finally asked.

"I hope not. It's early in the year for travelers, except for traders, and I don't think they'd want to attack traders." Saryn shrugged. "They might not be that smart, though. If the traders start avoiding Fenard especially, that won't make the Prefect happy."

"But he's the one who had to have ordered the armsmen—"

"We don't know that, not yet. Besides, rulers don't always understand what happens as a result of what they order. They just think they do." Saryn couldn't help but think about the UFA marshals who had ordered the *Winterlance* into a battle that ended up throwing the ship into another universe. There were always unintended consequences . . . even for those like Ryba, who could glimpse a corner of the future. Unlike the senior UFA officers, or the traders of Suthya, Ryba understood that.

By midmorning, Saryn and the outriders were leading second squad down the long and winding slope into the crossroads valley.

"There's a thin plume of smoke," reported Chyanci. "Over there, back by the knoll on the southwest side. That's the high ground."

"The only tracks on the road are theirs," said Abylea.

"The only recent ones," corrected Chyanci.

"Hold up here. They can't see us," said Saryn. Just as important was the fact that she couldn't sense any of the Gallosians. "I need to talk to the squad leader."

Saryn turned the big chestnut back uphill. As the commander neared the squad, Murkassa ordered a halt and rode to meet Saryn. "You've found them? How far ahead are they?"

"Another two or three kays. It looks like they're in the crossroads valley, on that knoll to the south of the roads, by the stream where most travelers camp. There aren't any other recent tracks on the road. We can ride down the road for another kay or so, but then we'll have to move into the trees and move southwest to the base of the knoll. First, we'll see where the sentries are. I'd like to take them out with the bows, without alerting the others. Then, half the squad will proceed up alongside the trail from the road to the knoll but hold short of where they're camped, far enough back so that the others aren't alerted.

"The bow-guards need to move in through the trees to the south. I'll lead them in to take out the sentries and position them. If we don't alert the main force, I'll take them to the north side of the knoll, and once we're there, they'll start loosing shafts, as silently as possible. The moment that the Gallosians recognize they're under attack, I'll sound the horn, and you sweep up the trail. As soon as you cross into the encampment, we'll come in from the trees."

"What if they spot us first?" asked Murkassa.

"They probably won't. If they do, we'll move back to give the bow-guards chances at picking them off. Then we'll withdraw and do it again . . . until they either catch up, and we take them on, or they retreat, and we just keep loosing shafts and picking them off until they turn to fight. Or until they're all dead." Saryn added, "Oh . . . just before you start the attack, you'll have to find a hidden spot to put Adiara. Tell her not to move. We might need every guard."

"Yes, ser." The squad leader nodded. "That should work."

From what she'd seen, Saryn knew it *should,* but more often than not, "shoulds" never happened. "Call up the bow-guards. I'll take them and Chyanci. You and Abylea lead the rest of the squad after us. I'll send Chyanci back to give you the word when to split off."

Murkassa nodded. "Bow-guards forward!"

A quarter glass later, Saryn was leading the line of guards through the evergreen woods, mostly pine with some spruce and a handful of junipers. She concentrated on sensing a clear pathway to the wooded slopes of the knoll on which the Gallosians were encamped. The going was slow as she avoided two gullies and several low and bushy pines that blocked a direct route. When she could truly sense the first armsman, she nodded. She let a half smile of relief cross her lips when she sensed the second clearly, as well as vaguely feeling the larger numbers up the knoll to the west. The first sentry was stationed under a small pine growing from between the boulders at the top of a hillock that offered a view of the crossroads. The second sentry was on the other side of the trail, slightly farther downhill, and positioned to watch the western road to Lornth. Although the two were about a hundred yards apart, and within earshot of each other, neither could see the other.

"Quiet riding," ordered Saryn.

After easing the chestnut through half a kay of pines, sometimes through snow close to half a yard deep, she reined up, then motioned for Zanlya, the lead bow-guard, to join her.

"The sentry is about a hundred yards ahead, at the same level on the slope as we are, but he'll be to your right once we come up on him, under a pine looking down on the valley." Saryn pointed through the pines in the direction of the northernmost Gallosian sentry. "I want him taken out without a sound. Let the others know, then have Chyanci pass the word to the squad leader to have her hold up until we head back this way."

Zanlya nodded.

Once Zanlya had passed the word, Saryn eased her mount forward, slowly. Covering the last fifty yards or so seemed to take longer than had the previous half kay through the pines.

Finally, she reined up and gestured to Zanlya for the bow-guards to move into positions where all could loose shafts at once. The wind was light, but it was blowing from the northeast, and that wasn't good. Not when there was the faintest snuffle or muted whinny from the sentry's mount, tied to a smaller pine lower on the slope to his south, and between him and the short trail leading from the road to the encampment.

The Gallosian stood and eased forward from where he had been sitting on a boulder. From there he scanned the area to the northeast, where the three rough roads met. He was still looking when the first shaft took him in the back of the shoulder. Another took him lower in the back, and he staggered.

"Oh . . ."

Two more shafts struck him, one in the neck, and he slumped forward.

Saryn *thought* his muted cry had not carried, but she concentrated on sensing the second sentry, across the trail to the south. When the other sentry did not show any alarm, she urged the gelding forward, along the lower north side of the knoll, then through the trees just below the first sentry's position until she and the bow-guards were almost at the edge of the trees bordering the trail, just a few yards higher than the second sentry.

He was pacing back and forth along a narrow space above the lower bushes and trees that grew out of a charred area, possibly a campfire that had gotten out of hand years earlier.

Zanlya glanced to Saryn, raising her eyebrows, and gesturing.

Saryn understood. The sentry was some fifty yards away. Still, there was no way to get closer without breaking cover. "Go ahead."

Zanlya waited until the sentry was pacing back in their direction before saying, "Fire." Her words were just loud enough for the other four to hear, and the hiss of five shafts being released at once was softer than the rustle of wind through the needles of the pines.

Only one struck the sentry directly, but it slammed through him just below the breastbone. A second lodged in his arm. In the moments when he looked around, his mouth opening to call a warning, three more shafts struck. He staggered, then slowly sank from sight.

Saryn could sense his pain. While he was dying, and would not be able to warn the others, he would not die quickly. She pushed that thought aside. The women who had been abused had not died quickly, either.

"This way," she ordered quietly.

The five bow-guards followed her back the way they had come, then westward along the side of the knoll. Murkassa rode out from between two massive pine trunks, then halted.

Saryn reined up for a moment just yards from the squad leader. "The sentries are down. We need to hurry. Take up a position on the trail. When you hear the horn, ride up and sweep through. We'll stop firing before you enter the encampment."

"Yes, ser."

As Saryn flicked the reins to urge the gelding forward, she could feel her head throbbing from all the concentration on sensing where people and weapons were. After the long winter, she was definitely out of practice. Tracking game wasn't the same thing, even through frigid snows. As almost an afterthought, she leaned back and slipped the small trumpet-like horn from the saddlebag and tucked it inside her riding jacket.

After riding another hundred yards, she could sense clearly the Gallosians scattered around the encampment ahead and to her right. Most were gathered to the south side, roughly in the middle, but they were not in any sort of formation.

She turned in the saddle again. "Zanlya . . . we're getting close. When I stop, take positions in a line abreast right at the edge of the trees. The clearing will be on our right. Silent signal. Once I drop my arm, loose shafts. Make every shaft count, but use every one."

The lead bow-guard nodded.

Saryn slowed the gelding to a slow walk through the thin layer of slushy snow, easing him closer and closer to the edge of the pines, but at an angle so that the six of them would not be close to being able to be seen until they were in position to loose shafts. She was also counting on the thickness of the overhead canopy to keep them in deep shadow.

The trees ended less than twenty yards from the northern edge of the encampment. Most of the armsmen were gathered near one of the fires, listening to a taller man. All the Gallosians were looking in his direction and away from the trees on the north side.

A few words drifted out to Saryn, words that only she could hear, and only because of the heightened senses that had come when she had found herself on the Roof of the World. Nylan had claimed that all the officers had gained various strange abilities because they had used the *Winter-lance*'s neuralnet. Saryn didn't know the reasons, but at times like these she was glad enough for them.

". . . take the northwest road in the morning . . . halfway to Middle-vale . . ."

Saryn eased the gelding partly behind the trunk of one of the giant pines and positioned him so that she could ride directly into the camp when the time came. Then she waited.

Zanlya raised her arm.

Saryn raised hers, then dropped it.

Shafts hissed from out of the woods.

For several moments, nothing happened, even after shafts cut into and through several of the armsmen.

"The bitch-demons!"

"To arms! Every man to arms!"

"Mount up!"

Saryn lifted the trumpet and bugled out an off-key call. The only thing useful about it was that the sound was loud, loud enough to carry to the trail to the west of the encampment.

An armsman jumped from the fire and turned, then grabbed his blade and charged toward the trees and the bow-guards. A shaft took him right in the chest.

The bow-guards kept loosing shaft after shaft, enough that the Gallosians sprinted toward the southwestern edge of the encampment, where the horses were picketed on a tie-line. The clustering of men provided an even better target for the archers.

The rumbling of hoofs signaled the arrival of the rest of second squad.

"Cease fire!" snapped Saryn. "Stow bows. Blades out. With me."

She urged the chestnut forward, one of her three short swords in her right hand.

One Gallosian had managed to mount and had his big blade out as he charged her.

Saryn flung her blade, sense-guiding it into his chest, then pulled her second blade into play, running down a lagging Gallosian and slicing down across the side of his neck.

For the next few moments, all she could do was hack and parry, before she wheeled clear of the handful of armsmen remaining on their feet.

From the corner of her eye, Saryn caught sight of a Gallosian riding along the south side of the clearing, spurring his mount in the direction of the northwestern trail. "Murkassa! Spare one for questioning!" Then she turned the gelding and gave him his head. She didn't want anyone to escape. If Arthanos's men vanished, he wouldn't be able to say much in public, especially if Ryba sent him and the other local rulers a message noting that brigands who had murdered innocent travelers had been hunted down and killed.

After a few moments, the fleeing armsman glanced back over his shoulder. Saryn could sense the man's apprehension, even before he jabbed his heels into his mount's flanks, trying to force more speed from the flagging mount. That did not help him, because Saryn's gelding was closing the gap with every stride.

Suddenly, the armsman urged his mount into a gap between the trees on the north side of the trail, well below where the bow-guards had attacked the sentry. Saryn followed, not without some trepidation, ducking immediately so that a low-hanging branch didn't remove her head—or her—from the saddle.

After less than fifty yards the Gallosian turned, short of a wall of evergreens, and pulled out a half-and-a-half blade from his shoulder harness. He grinned.

Saryn didn't even give him time to bring the heavy blade into position before throwing her second short sword, using her senses to smooth its flight while drawing the third blade from the saddle sheath before her. The last blade wasn't necessary. The thrown blade sliced into the Gallosian's chest so quickly and cleanly that he didn't have time to look surprised before he slumped forward in the saddle. After a moment, the heavy iron weapon dropped from his lifeless fingers. A slight *clank* followed as the metal hit a patch of rocky ground.

It took Saryn far more time to recover the weapon and corner the skittish mount than it had to chase and kill the false bandit, but before all that long she was leading the captured mount with the body of the armsman across it back toward the valley at a fast trot. She hadn't dared take any more time to strip him, not until she was back with second squad.

She needn't have worried. By the time she reached the top of the knoll where the Gallosians had been, the only figures on horseback were the Westwind guards, although two were having wounds dressed, and a third—the young Gerlya—lay unmoving on the sparse grass beside the trail leading down to the road.

"The squad leader's over there, ser," called Chyanci, pointing in the direction of the eastern end of the clearing. "Abylea's got the girl."

"Thank you." Saryn kept riding through the encampment, where gear and bodies lay strewn in every direction.

More than half had died from the shafts loosed by the bow-guards. Several had clearly been struck down before they had been able to raise a defense. A grim smile crossed Saryn's lips. She had no doubts that her attack would have been called something uncharitable by the Gallosians, except that Westwind would write the history.

At the end of the clearing, Murkassa and three guards half circled a large pine, under which was a man. Saryn could see that the man—little more than a youth, really, with but the barest hint of a blondish beard—had neither a blade nor a scabbard at his waist, nor a harness for a broadsword. Despite a leg that was clearly broken, he had propped himself up with his back against a pine trunk, and he held a dagger in his left hand.

Saryn could sense the agony as he glanced from one guard to the next. "Hold off!"

"Ser?" questioned Murkassa.

"I'd like some answers, squad leader, and there's no one else able to give them, from what I can see."

Murkassa glanced around, then lowered the blade she could easily have thrown. "Vynna! Keep that bow ready. If he so much as twitches that knife, pin him to the tree . . . but in the shoulder so that he can still answer the commander's questions."

"Yes, ser."

"Put down that sticker if you don't want a shaft through you," Murkassa ordered the young man.

Slowly, he slipped it into the belt sheath. The faintest wince crossed his face.

Saryn could sense some of the pain, and she was thankful, once again, that she did not possess the sensitivity that Istril and Siret did. She rode closer, but halted her mount a good five yards away. "What's your name?"

"Dealdron, Commander."

"Where in Gallos are you from, Dealdron?"

"Fenard. Outside the walls."

"Why were you and the other armsmen pretending to be brigands?"

"That was what the undercaptain ordered, ser."

"Who ordered him?"

"He didn't say, ser. He wouldn't have done it if the majer hadn't told him . . . or someone higher up."

"Who might that have been?"

"I don't know, ser."

"How many people have you killed, Dealdron?"

"Not a one, ser. I was here to take care of the mounts."

While Saryn sensed the truth of his words, she had to press him. "Do you expect me to believe that?"

"I didn't kill anyone. I didn't. I didn't hurt anyone, either."

"Why did you let them kill innocent travelers?"

"I didn't know . . . that was what they were going to do." He swayed slightly on his good leg.

"And I suppose you had nothing to do with the women?"

"No, ser." The young man's eyes glistened, but Saryn wasn't sure how much was from the pain of memory or the pain of his broken leg. "I didn't do anything except unharness the cart horse. I didn't."

Saryn could sense the truth of those words, as well as the faintness coming over the young man, but before she could say anything, he staggered, then pitched forward.

"Murkassa . . . we need to get his leg splinted. He's coming back with us."

"Yes, ser." The squad leader's voice was neutral.

Saryn could sense the displeasure beneath the calm words. She gestured for Murkassa to ride closer before asking, "No one else escaped, did they?"

"No, ser. You got the only one who tried to ride away." The squad leader's eyes dropped to the unconscious man. "He's still one of *them*."

"He was telling the truth. He didn't kill anyone. They didn't even trust him with a blade. I want the Marshal to hear what he told us." Saryn paused. "Don't you think she should?"

Some of Murkassa's displeasure faded. "Then what?"

"That's up to the Marshal . . . as always."

After a moment, Murkassa nodded. "She should hear what he has to say."

"Get his leg splinted. He has to survive the ride back."

"Yes, ser."

Saryn could feel that Murkassa was satisfied with Saryn's reasons, but the instinctive desire to kill any man associated with the murders and rapes, even indirectly, told Saryn, again, how hard it was going to be to work any more men into Westwind. The attempt by the Suthyans to poison Ryba hadn't helped that attitude, either.

Yet . . . it had to be done, she told herself. About that, Istril was right.

XII

Even though it was well after dark when Saryn and second squad rode down the causeway past Tower Black and up to the stables, and later than that before mounts and gear and guards were settled, and even later before second squad was fed, Ryba was waiting by the stone staircase when Saryn left the common dining hall. Ryba wore her usual grays, if with a black-and-silver leather belt and black boots. Her black hair was short, almost ship style, as always.

"If you'd join me, Saryn? I do have some brandy up in the study."

"Thank you. I could use that."

There was no beer at Westwind, and what wine there was came from the wild grapes and other fruits less than suitable for eating. The vintage, if it could be called that, was tolerable, but the quantity was definitely limited. While they could have traded for wine or beer, other goods were far more necessary, and only occasionally did a trader throw in some beverage as a sweetener. That was doubtless how Ryba had gotten the brandy.

"I thought you might."

As Ryba turned away and started up the stone steps, Saryn was again struck by the darkness behind those green eyes, much more than by the circles under them. So often had she heard Ryba moving around in the night that she no longer wondered whether the Marshal slept—only how she survived on so little sleep.

As they passed the levels of the tower, Saryn caught murmurs of conversations, all low.

". . . there they go again . . ."

". . . commander's not been back much more 'n a glass . . ."

". . . hush there, little one . . ."

". . . sore all over . . . guard captain likes seeing me black-and-blue . . ."

Saryn smiled briefly at the last. In her first year at the institute, even with all the martial arts she'd studied as a youngster—and the first year on the Roof of the World—she'd felt that way all the time.

As Saryn stepped through the narrow doorway at the top of the tower stairs, Ryba said, "Please close the door, if you would."

Saryn did so, then turned.

The small study held but a circular table, four chairs, and a wall chest. A narrow door—closed—led to a sleeping chamber. The single window was covered by a heavy gray woolen hanging. The only light was provided by a small oil lamp in a brass wall sconce, a reminder to Saryn that for all of her other talents, Ryba did not possess nightsight, or chose not to let anyone know if she did. With Ryba, Saryn was never sure, but cultivating a certain uncertain mystery was just one of the ways the Marshal exercised power—that and absolute ability with weapons.

Ryba lifted a small cylindrical bottle and poured a brownish amber liquid into two small crystal goblets, then took one of the four straight-backed chairs around the small round table. "The goblets are from an officer's saddlebags that survived the Lornian attack. I seldom use them."

Ryba's use of both brandy and goblets worried Saryn as she took the chair across from the Marshal. Ryba lifted her small goblet, waiting for Saryn to do the same.

Saryn raised hers to meet Ryba's, then waited just slightly to take a sip of the brandy. Even the slightest swallow warmed its way down her throat, and she placed the goblet on the plain polished and dark-oiled pine surface of the table.

Ryba set her goblet down, and asked, "Why did you bring that arms-man back? You should have killed him with the others."

"I thought it was the thing to do."

"You go on feelings more than you admit, don't you?"

"Sometimes that's all you have to go on," replied Saryn.

Since none of second squad had talked directly to Ryba, the Marshal had either overheard the others when they ate, or she'd seen Dealdron in one of her glimpses of what would be. There was little point in asking how Ryba had learned. "Let me tell you what happened."

"Go ahead." Ryba fingered her goblet but did not lift it.

"We ran across a family—two families—that had been slaughtered by brigands—except for one daughter who had escaped into the woods. . . ."

Saryn proceeded with a factual detailing of all that had happened, ending with, ". . . and we brought back the girl, and we did end up with fourteen additional mounts, as well as supplies, weapons, and coins."

"What were your casualties?" Ryba took the smallest sip of her brandy.

"We lost Gerlya to a wild cast of a battle-ax. Suansa's arm was shattered, but Istril thinks it can be healed. It will take a good year before she can use it well, though. Three other guards took minor slashes."

"One in twenty, Commander. You know that's not good. Even for twenty-one of theirs. The working standard is one to fifty. It is early in the year, but . . ."

Saryn had heard those words often enough, and she understood the mathematics as well as Ryba. They were literally the margin for survival. The bows helped, in small engagements, because of their range and power, so long as the guards could use the trees and the terrain, but that would change if Arthanos sent an army, because it would include companies of archers who would just turn the sky black with shafts. Archery accuracy mattered more in small engagements, but mattered far less against an enemy who could launch enough shafts that arrows fell like rain.

"What about the one Gallosian you brought back? You still haven't addressed why he was worth saving . . . except saying your feelings told you to. With you, I'm sure it wasn't because of his looks. Or did you even have another reason?"

Inside, Saryn couldn't help bridling at Ryba's words, but she replied evenly, "First, I wanted to see if we could find out more from him, especially if you questioned him personally. Second, he didn't take part in the actual killings or the assaults on the women. He didn't have anything to do with any of it, except holding the horses. His back is scarred from whipping."

"It doesn't matter. He'll end up just like all the others on this world. We don't need men like that."

"What sort do we need?" asked Saryn quietly.

"That's my decision, not yours."

"I can't carry out your decisions, Ryba, if I don't know what standards you have in mind. You've as much as admitted that we do need more men here. With that leg of his, he can't do much harm right now. Istril and Siret and you should be able to tell whether he meets your standards before he's well enough to cause trouble—assuming he's that type. I don't think he is, but I'll leave that judgment up to others."

"You're so accommodating, Saryn."

And where men are concerned, you're impossible. "I do my best for you and for Westwind. You should know that by now."

"I know that you do what *you* think is best. That is not necessarily what *is* best."

"Not having at least a number of men who are acceptable here at Westwind is not good. We all know that. So do you."

"That is not so critical now. Arthanos is."

"You're right," Saryn said carefully. "The problem is that, if we wait until the problem of men is critical, it will be too late to do anything about it." She did not take another sip of the brandy.

"Then . . . Dealdron is your responsibility."

"You still should question him," Saryn replied. "You'll doubtless discover more than I did, and he needs to know just how intimidating you can be."

"I think I can manage that," Ryba said, her tone so dry it was cutting.

Saryn inclined her head politely, then lifted the brandy goblet and sipped. "This is good."

"It is. Did you know that, while you were gone, Dyliess managed to hit the center of the swinging targets from seventy yards?"

"She takes after you . . ."

"She has some of my better traits, and some of his, but she's far more practical than her father . . ."

Saryn smiled, but did not relax, as Ryba continued.

XIII

After breakfast and the morning muster on the causeway outside Tower Black, where duties were handed out for the day, Saryn headed back into the tower to meet with Istril but found Istril coming up the steps from the lower level.

The healer smiled. "Suansa's doing well, and the other three are fine."

"Is the girl all right?"

"Adiara's healthy. She needs to eat more, and she's scared of her own shadow. The trio have taken her under their collective wings for now."

"That's good." *Good for her, and for Westwind.* "How is the Gallosian's leg?"

"It wasn't badly mangled, not for that kind of injury. The bone end didn't break through. The splint repositioned it, and he'll heal. A couple of the whip wounds had chaos in them. Not bad, and I took care of that." Istril paused. "You scared him worse than the broken leg."

"Me? All I did was tell Murkassa not to kill him."

"Oh? He saw you kill three men, then ride down another and bring him back dead. I did tell him that was what you did—and that you were the one who taught all the others to fight. He seemed to need that."

"Why?" Saryn snorted. "So his fragile male ego wasn't shattered by seeing his comrades slaughtered? Besides, Ryba designed the training, and you have as much to do with it as I do."

"Maybe at first. Not now. You know I'm limited to teaching blade skills for defense."

"Those are the most important," Saryn pointed out.

"You're kind to say that."

"Did the Gallosian say anything about Karthanos or his son? Or anything else?"

"No, ser. He did ask why we bothered to save him. I told him that was because he hadn't taken part directly in the massacres. He asked how I knew. I just told him the truth—that you knew when someone lied."

"So do you."

"He was more interested in what you thought."

Saryn shook her head. "I need to talk to him more before Ryba does."

"You got her to agree not to kill him?"

"So long as he behaves himself. If he doesn't, it's my responsibility."

"Will you tell him that?"

"Only that his life depends on his good behavior." Saryn nodded and headed down the stone steps.

She found Dealdron propped up on a narrow bed in the lower level of the tower—in what Saryn called sickbay, a term meaningless for all the local-born guards—who comprised most of those at Westwind. While his face was pale, and she could sense the chaos around the broken bones, she could also recognize that he was what she might have called passably handsome. That might cause problems, especially after her promise to Ryba.

"How are you feeling?" Saryn shifted from Temple into Old Rationalist.

"Better than if I were not feeling." Dealdron's words bore a different cadence than did those of the Lornians or those who lived west of the Roof of the World. The Gallosians and the Lornians didn't speak different languages so much as differing dialects, suggesting that their common origin wasn't that far back, not as languages went. "What will you do with me?"

"That depends on you. If you're well-mannered and prove yourself useful, you might have a long, healthy life here. If you don't, then you won't have much time to worry about it."

The young man nodded slowly. "The healer said that you are the arms-commander for all of Westwind. You rode out on patrol with but twenty . . . blades."

"Even the Marshal rides with patrols." *Not that often in recent years, but she still does.* "Shouldn't someone who commands others be willing to do all that she orders them to do?"

"Rulers . . . most rulers . . . do not ride . . . not in the fore . . ."

"We aren't most people." Saryn decided to change the subject. "You know horses. What else do you know?"

"Some things."

"What things?"

"My father was a plasterer. I can do that."

"Can you make the plaster?"

"Of course." Dealdron's tone suggested that making plaster was elementary. "If you have a kiln."

"We fire pottery."

"That is too hot."

That meant that they could build a plaster kiln. "Could you make plaster here on the Roof of the World?"

"Is there limestone here?"

"We haven't looked," Saryn admitted.

"There is limestone in many places."

"Could you find it?"

Dealdron glanced down at his splinted leg.

"It will heal, and you will walk as you did," Saryn replied to his unspoken question.

"Then if limestone is here, I will find it."

"What else can you do?"

"A man can only do so much."

"Whereas women can do many things," replied Saryn ironically, "and do them well without having to talk about it."

Dealdron merely looked bewildered, as if Saryn had replied in Temple or another language foreign to him.

"Who was your undercaptain?"

"Flassyn. He came from Subas."

"What did he say the squad was supposed to do?"

Dealdron's eyes moved ever so slightly so that he was not quite looking at Saryn, but not obviously avoiding her, before he spoke. "He said nothing until we had ridden out two days from Fenard. Then he said that they had to kill as many travelers as they could to prove the angels could not keep the Westhorns safe."

"Did he give orders to violate the women?"

Dealdron moistened his lips. Finally, he looked straight at Saryn. "No, ser. It was not like that. He said . . . he didn't much care what happened to them so long as they ended up dead."

"What did you think about that?"

"I did not like it."

"Why didn't you say anything?"

Dealdron looked directly at Saryn. "The eightday before we left Fenard, I said that they were riding the horses too hard. I got whipped for speaking out. Some armsmen agreed, but the undercaptain said I wasn't ever to question him. So he whipped me . . . and put salt on my back."

Saryn sensed the truth in the words. "You won't get whipped here."

"You will just kill me if I do not obey. Is that not so?"

"Not quite. If . . . if you have a good reason, then we'll listen. If you're being willful or stubborn . . . that's another question."

"Another inquiry?" The puzzled look appeared once more on Dealdron's face.

Saryn almost smiled. Some idioms didn't translate into Old Rat. "Another matter. How many armsmen is Lord Arthanos mustering to bring against us?"

"I cannot say, ser. He has raised ten new companies since the fall . . ."

Ten *new* companies? A thousand more armsmen?

When Saryn finally finished interrogating Dealdron, she left and crossed the lower level to the base of the stone steps, where she paused, dissatisfied in a vague way that she could not identify. Finally, she made her way up to the main level.

Hryessa was waiting for her in the entry foyer of Tower Black. "Commander? The day before yesterday, while you and second squad were gone, Murgos . . . he's the sometime trader from Rohrn . . . he brought these missives for the Marshal." Hryessa handed the three to Saryn.

Saryn recognized the script on two. One was addressed to "Ryba, Marshal of Westwind," and the second was addressed to "Dyliess, in care of the Marshal of Westwind." The third bore only the words "The Marshal."

"They arrived two days ago?"

"Yes, ser."

"You didn't want to take them up to her?" Saryn smiled wryly.

"No, ser. I know better when those two arrive. I knew you would be back before long."

Knowing the chill that Ryba could project—and her anger—Saryn could understand the guard captain's reluctance either to deliver the missives or merely to leave them for Ryba. "Wait here for me."

With the three heavy sealed missives in her hand, Saryn walked up the stone steps past the now-empty spaces on the upper levels and the area that had once been an arms practice area during the winter until too many bodies had filled the tower. As she neared the top level, she called, "Marshal . . . I have some missives for you."

"The door is open." Ryba's words were cool.

Saryn climbed the last three steps, aware that she was breathing a little heavily. She wasn't in the condition she should have been, or would be later in the spring. Then she stepped through the open doorway and set all three sealed missives on the table, directly before Ryba, who sat with her back to the window.

"These didn't come today."

"They came while I was gone. They were waiting for me to give to you."

"They all fear to hand me anything from him."

"Do you blame them?"

"No." Ryba's green eyes fixed on Saryn. "If you would wait below until I read these."

"Yes, ser."

"While you're waiting, I'd also like you to consider another problem. Too much of the guards' business is being handled in the local tongue. We need to keep Temple the language of the guards. I've asked Istril to think on this as well. The young ones must speak Temple first." Ryba held up a hand. "Don't say a word. You've insisted that the guard captains give commands in Temple, and the guards all know those. That's not enough. We need to work in schooling for the children and the new guards. Schooling in Temple."

Saryn inclined her head, turned, and made her way out back down to the main level.

"That was quick," said Hryessa.

Her words were in the degraded form of Old Rationalist that the locals used, Saryn noted. "She asked me to wait until she read the messages."

"So fortunate you should be."

"She also wants us to use Temple for everything and teach it to the young ones."

Hryessa frowned. "Only you angels know it well."

"You speak it, and it might give us an advantage in battle and in trading, especially in years to come when all the young ones know it."

The guard captain shrugged. "As the Marshal wills."

Always as Ryba wills. Nylan understood that early. Yet what could those like Llyselle, Istril, and Siret do? They were full-blooded Sybrans, and trying to live in the hot lowlands would have been a slow death sentence. And the women who had fled to Westwind would suffer the same fate as those slaughtered by the false brigands. Even as a half-Sybran, Saryn had found the lowlands oppressive the few times she'd visited Lornth.

After a moment, Saryn smiled at Hryessa. "You might as well get on with your duties."

"Yes, ser." Hryessa offered a smile that contained both understanding and sympathy.

"Commander!" Ryba's voice carried down the five levels of the stone stairs with ease.

Saryn retraced her steps back up the tower. No sooner had she stepped into the small study than Ryba gestured for her to take the seat across the circular table from her. Saryn did, but did not speak, waiting to hear what Ryba had to say.

"You know that Nylan has sent Dyliess a letter every year on her birthday?" Ryba's words were not quite a question.

"I had wondered when the first messages always came in the spring, and there was always one from the west, sometimes through Lornth, for you."

"They have to come from there. Nylan and Ayrlyn are living like hermits in some forest to the southwest, but there's always a letter for Dyliess . . . and another one for me. One with information he thinks I'll find useful."

Saryn did not comment.

"It usually is," Ryba continued. "The engineer has always known what is useful."

"Has Dyliess read the letters?" Saryn asked.

"Yes. I've read them to her since before she could read. I make copies for her now. I've kept the originals in a book for her." Ryba frowned. "The engineer is generally kind and thoughtful in his writing. He also is careful not to write anything he thinks will offend me."

"Dyliess doesn't speak of him."

"I've told her not to, except to me, or to you, if she chooses. It's better if everyone thinks of him as both mighty and departed for good, and not as a father who is human enough to write letters." Ryba laughed, softly and bitterly. "If only once a year, long as those missives may be."

"She must know that he hasn't forgotten her."

"That's true." Ryba glanced over her shoulder toward the window, still closed, but with the gray hangings pulled back to allow the morning sunlight to pour into the small chamber, illuminating the dust motes that hung in the air.

"Is there anything I should know, then?" asked Saryn. Ryba would not have mentioned the letters without a reason.

"He wrote that our troubles to the west are not over, and that, without aid, Lady Zeldyan may have difficulty holding Lornth."

"She does provide a buffer," Saryn temporized. "Do her difficulties lie with Lord Ildyrom's son? The Jeranyi have always been a problem."

"That's but one aspect of it. The Suthyans have reclaimed Rulyarth as well, and have imposed close-to-punitive tariffs on goods bound to Lornth."

"She's being squeezed on both sides then. Do we have to do anything?"

"Both young Deryll and the Suthyans would be far less to our liking as neighbors than is Lady Zeldyan. Still . . . we will have to see, after we deal with Arthanos and the Gallosians."

Saryn had the chilling sense that Ryba had already seen. "The Gallosians . . . and not the Suthyans?"

"The Suthyans fight with golds . . . or use them, or the promise of golds, to get others to fight. We will have to face the Gallosians first. After we deal with Arthanos, you'll be the one who goes to Lornth," Ryba went on. "Whatever happens, I won't send you to your death. That much, I do know."

Ryba was quite capable of lying—except that Saryn would have detected it, and Ryba knew that. Still, from what Saryn had seen in the underspace battles with the demon towers, what she'd felt on the neuronet, and what she'd experienced and observed in the ten years since the angels had come to the Roof of the World, some forms of living might well be worse than death, not that she wished to experience either. *But why would she mention that she would not send me to my death?*

"Would you like to question the Gallosian now?" Saryn asked quietly.

"I'll do it this afternoon in the common room before the evening meal, with at least a squad of guards present . . . and you, of course, and either Istril or Siret, whoever happens to be more available."

"Yes, ser."

"That will be all."

Saryn nodded, then turned and made her way back down the cold stone steps of Tower Black, wondering, as always, just what Ryba had foreseen and exactly why she intended to send Saryn to Lornth.

XIV

Just past midafternoon, Saryn sat at the end of the trestle table nearest the hearth in the main-floor great room. To her right was Llyselle, and to her left sat Murkassa.

". . . the scouts reported that half the Suthyan party took the road to Lornth and that the trader was with that group," Llyselle said. "The others took the northern road, the one to Middlevale, which avoids most of the Lornian lands on the way to Rulyarth and Armat."

"The trader is traveling through Lornth . . . or part of it. Have you told the Marshal?"

"No, ser. We just got word."

"I'll tell her, then, after we finish. What else did they discover?"

"Nothing else about the Suthyans. We'll need to send a team to repair some of the bridges . . ."

After Llyselle finished her report, Saryn walked up the stone steps to Ryba's study.

Ryba turned from where she stood at the window. "What else is it, Saryn? More about the Gallosian?"

"No, ser. We may have another problem. Half the Suthyans, and the high trader, but not Suhartyn, took the road to Lornth."

The Marshal nodded, almost as if she already knew. "That's not surprising. Trader Baorl will try to discover any weaknesses, while ostensibly trading, and will be able to give the Suthyan Council a more current report on Lornth's strengths and weaknesses. Doubtless, he will also spread untruths about Westwind."

"That won't make matters any easier for me . . . if you're still planning on sending me."

"I am, especially after what you just encountered. We'll talk about that later."

Saryn could sense that Ryba didn't want to say more, and wouldn't. She also knew that pressing the Marshal would only make matters worse. "Yes, ser."

"Don't worry about it, Saryn." With those words, Ryba turned back to look out the window.

Saryn made her way down the steps, then to the smithy to see how much progress had been made on blades.

Later, just about a glass before the evening meal, Huldran and Ydrall brought Dealdron up from the lower level, the same way all guards with injured legs were carried, in a basket seat suspended from a wooden yoke, each end of the yoke borne by one of the two smiths. They set him on a bench facing the cold hearth . . . and Ryba. Saryn stood on the right side of the wooden chair where Ryba sat, with Siret on the left.

Dealdron's eyes took in the trio one after the other—the arms-commander with her reddish golden brown hair, the black-haired and stern-featured Marshal, in silver-gray and black, and the silver-haired healer. The Marshal surveyed the wounded man without speaking.

After a momentary hesitation, the Gallosian bent forward, held the position for a moment, then straightened, looking to Ryba, then to Siret, and finally to Saryn. "Sers . . . most honored Angel and Marshal, I would offer more respect, but I cannot rise or bow without falling."

"That is obvious." Ryba's voice was cool. " 'Marshal' or 'ser' will do."

Dealdron inclined his head. "Yes, Marshal."

"What did you do before you became an armsman in Gallos?"

"Ser . . . I was not an armsman. I was an assistant ostler to the Prefect's Cavalry."

"Before that?"

"My father is a plasterer. I was working as his apprentice, but . . . times were hard, and my older brother, he was needed more, and I had helped at the local stable."

"Why were you with the armsmen who were pretending to be brigands?"

"The majer sent me because they needed someone to take care of the horses. He did not want to use armsmen as ostlers."

"Did anyone say that they might have to fight the guards of Westwind?"

"Ah . . ."

Again, Ryba waited.

"The undercaptain said that, if they came across any, they would take great pleasure in killing them. He also said that was not the main task. He said we were to rob and frighten away all the travelers and to kill those who would not be frightened."

"Why did you allow the women travelers from Neltos to be ravaged and killed?"

"I had no way to stop it, ser, only a belt dagger."

"Did you know that was what the undercaptain had in mind?"

"No, ser. Not until he said . . . that he didn't care what happened to them."

Saryn caught sight of several nods among the guards, nods not of approval, but acknowledgment of the attitude of the late undercaptain.

"You had no idea that he felt that way?"

Ryba looked at the Gallosian impassively, waiting.

Finally, Dealdron spoke, slowly. "I had heard that he was . . . hard . . . on women, but I never heard that he had injured one."

"Beyond a slap or a bruise or two, you mean?" Faint irony tinged Ryba's words.

"I did not know he would kill or order women to be . . . abused."

"Did you think he might?"

"I did not know, ser. I had only taken care of the mounts before the majer sent me with the undercaptain."

"I asked what you thought."

"I did not think about it, ser. Not until I saw what was happening."

Saryn could sense that Dealdron truly believed that, and that the young man truly had not understood the situation with the travelers until he believed he could do nothing. Her eyes took in Istril, who slipped into the chamber and along the wall until she was some five yards back from the Marshal.

Although Ryba had to have seen Istril, her expression did not change as she asked Dealdron, "You expect me to believe that you encountered no other travelers until you came across that group?"

"We saw tracks, but they hid in the woods or in other places before we could see where they had gone. The undercaptain was not going to split up the squad chasing peasants through the trees. He thought someone might ambush us."

"You were whipped. How did that happen?"

"We had ridden hard the first days out from Fenard. I told the undercaptain that he was being hard on the horses and that they would not carry us well if he kept pressing them. He laughed. He had his men tie me to a tree, and he whipped me."

"You stood up for horses . . . and not for women?"

"Ser . . . the first time I crossed the undercaptain, I was whipped. I did not think I would have lasted so long as the travelers if I had said anything."

"So very courageous of you."

"Courage is useless when you are dead, ser. I could not have helped them."

True as that was, Saryn had doubts as to whether Ryba would see it that way.

Ryba looked to Siret. The healer nodded.

"How did your leg get broken?"

"I was trying to calm the horses after the attack. I was in the wrong place. Everyone was dying, and I crawled to a tree. I thought I might climb it, but the branches were too high."

"How do you think other Gallosians would fare against the guards?"

"Most would not, I think. The Prefect's Company would do best. They would lose, but they would kill many of your guards."

"Is there any other company that good?"

"Lord Arthanos is training two special companies. That is what I have heard some say."

"What do you know about Lord Arthanos?"

"I have only seen him. I have not tended his mounts. He has never spoken to me. I have never handled the mounts of those companies he has commanded."

"A cautious reply. What have you heard about him?"

"He is brave and capable with both blade and bow. His voice can be heard above men and horses. He does not accept failure. He does not like excuses. He is said to be fair . . . mostly."

"When is he not fair?" pressed Ryba.

"I have only heard—"

"When?" The single word was like a shaft of ice.

Dealdron swallowed. "He is fond of wine, ser."

"And he is less than fair when he has had too much?"

"That is what is said. I do not know that from what I have seen."

"There seems to be a great deal you have not seen," observed Ryba.

"I have heard that angels can tell when a man does not speak the truth. I would not wish to say what I do not know."

Ryba glanced to Siret, who nodded once more.

"How many men does he have in arms?"

"It is said that he will have ninety companies . . ."

"Who are the best captains in the Prefect's forces . . .

"How many companies are ready to fight . . .

"How many archers . . ."

Ryba's questions seemed endless, but the Marshal took less than a full glass before she stopped and looked squarely at Dealdron. "You may remain here in Westwind for now. Once you are healed, then we will talk again, and we will see what sort of man you are." Ryba turned to Saryn. "Have him eat with the junior guards but at the lower end of the table."

"Yes, ser."

Ryba lowered her voice, and Saryn bent forward to catch the words. "Have Duessya talk to him about horses. And have Siret talk to him about building. See what they think." Ryba turned from Saryn, stood, then said to the assembled guards, "I thought you should hear what Dealdron had to say. Please share what you learned with those who were not here." In the silence that followed, her eyes ran across the group. For the briefest moment, her gaze stopped at Istril, who stood at the side of the chamber behind the guards. Istril met Ryba's eyes without turning away. Neither spoke.

Then Ryba smiled pleasantly and strode between the tables to the back of the chamber and out into the foyer, to return to her study until the last seating for the evening meal.

Saryn waited until the Marshal was well clear of the chamber before she spoke. "You're dismissed to your regular duties if you have any at the moment."

As the guards rose, Huldran looked to Saryn.

"Move him to the table where he'll sit. He can wait up here for half a glass."

"Yes, ser."

Saryn watched as the two smiths picked up the Gallosian. She could sense the pain from him as they lifted him under each arm and carried him to the end of the table farthest from the hearth, not that it made any difference with no fire. Then she walked toward Istril.

The healer said nothing until Saryn stopped less than a yard away. "She knows you're trying to get around her." Istril's words were barely a murmur.

"She always knows," replied Saryn. "That's why she's the Marshal." What she didn't voice were the questions that rose in her thoughts: Was knowing always enough? And how much did Ryba's knowing restrict what she would try or accept?

XV

Right after morning muster on the causeway outside Tower Black, Saryn hurried up the stone road to the smithy. While the starflowers at the edge of the fields were almost in full bloom, before long they would be lost in the grasses, leaving only the tall and individual stalks of the bloodflowers in easy sight. Behind Saryn, the junior guards moved to the lower exercise field and took their positions for the morning arms drills. Even the handful of older women who would never be guards took part in the basic drills, both for reasons of fitness and in case of undetected marauders, or the white demons forbid, an attack on Westwind itself.

Saryn pushed aside that thought as she reached the smithy.

The forges were hot enough already that the building was more than comfortably warm when Saryn stepped under the stone lintel of the entry door. Huldran had just set down her hammer as Ydrall returned something to the forge to reheat.

"How is the bow project coming?" asked Saryn.

"We've tested the new bow against the composite ones," offered Huldran.

"And?"

"Why don't you go see? Falynna just left with the second one to try it out at the range."

Saryn could sense a certain satisfaction from the smith. Was the horn bow just somewhat better than the short yew bows, or was it equal to the composite bows Nylan had forged? Or equal to a long yew bow? Or somewhere in between? "You're pleased."

"I'm hopeful," replied Huldran. "It was more work than we thought, but Falynna figured it out."

Saryn managed not to frown. They didn't need weapons that took forever to forge or fabricate. "That sounds like a lot of effort for just one bow."

Huldran shook her head. "If it works, it won't be that hard to produce a goodly number of bows each year. Figuring out how to do it was the problem."

"Let's hope it works out." Saryn turned, walking swiftly out of the smithy and continuing up the road. A narrow gully was forming on the left side of the road, caused by snowmelt runoff. The junior guards would have to build up the outside edge of the runoff channel. Some hundred yards uphill from the smithy, Saryn followed the narrow stone path westward until she reached the archery range. A sandy-haired guard stood at the edge of the range.

"I thought you were following me," said Falynna, a stocky and muscular guard whose head barely reached to Saryn's shoulder. "So I waited."

"That's the bow?" Saryn studied the double-curved weapon.

"That it is, Commander. And a sweet weapon she is, almost as good as the mage-made weapons, and better for us, I think, because we can make more like her."

"How quickly?"

"That's the one problem. This one took over a year. We can get enough horn and sinew for fifty to a hundred every year, but the setting time should be almost a year."

Saryn winced. More bows next year wouldn't help deal with Arthanos now. Still . . . a number of good bows would make a big difference over time. "So we could equip all the guards in the next four or five years."

"I would think so." Falynna extended the already-strung bow. "Would you like to try?"

"No, thank you. You're far better with the bow."

"Then we'll see." Falynna gestured uphill toward the figure made of twisted branches in the form of a mounted armsman. The upper part was securely fitted with mail breastplate and helmet. She lifted the bow, nocked the shaft, drew, and fired in a single smooth motion.

Saryn saw and sensed the shaft slam through the middle of the breastplate.

Falynna half turned. "Through the plate at a hundred yards. Now, we'll see about two hundred." The archer walked westward, down the slight slope.

Saryn walked with her. At a marker post, Falynna stopped and turned.

Saryn looked back up the long grassy slope. The target figure seemed so small, yet Falynna thought she could not only hit the target, but possibly penetrate the iron breastplate.

The archer loosed another shaft that arced uphill, then slashed downward with enough force that the entire target shivered as the arrowhead cut through the iron of the breastplate.

"That'll do." Falynna's words were matter-of-fact.

"We won't be in many places where we'll have a clear line of fire for more than that."

"That's true. It's not like the grasslands," observed Falynna. "We will need arrows with longer shafts with these bows. I couldn't use a full draw because the shaft wasn't long enough."

Strike harder than penetrating plate at two hundred yards? "How far?"

"Farther than I can aim accurately. Close to four hundred yards."

"You've done a great job," Saryn said. "You and Huldran. Mostly you, I believe."

"Huldran did help, with the core," replied Falynna, "and with the glue. We can't get enough fish for fish glue. Huldran found a way to combine rabbit skin, hide, and resin from the dwarf blue pines into something that doesn't dissolve in water once it sets."

"We'll need as many as you two can make," said Saryn.

"I figured as much, ser."

"Thank you." The arms-commander turned from Falynna and began to walk back up the slope. In time, the bows would make a huge difference, but would they have that time?

After leaving the archery range, Saryn took the path farther uphill to the quarries beyond the stables—a squarish area cut from hard reddish rock. The red stone was not quite so hard as the black granite from which Nylan had carved out the building stones for Tower Black, carefully enough that the pillared spaces he had left still served as Westwind's stables.

As Saryn neared the quarry, the sound of hammers, those of guards working down in the quarry and the measured blows of a stonecutter nearer to Saryn, grew louder. At the northeast edge of the quarry, Saryn stood in the shadows of the cliff, watching Siret as the healer, who was also a stonecutter, worked. The blackness that had surrounded Nylan when he had worked either stone or iron gathered around Siret as well, if not quite so intensely as it had around the engineer. On the other hand, Saryn had the feeling that Siret's techniques with the hammer and chisels were more deft. But then, she'd had more time to practice than Nylan had when Saryn had last observed the engineer years ago.

Abruptly, Siret set down the hammer and looked toward the shadows.

Saryn stepped forward across the cut-stone lip of the quarry to where Saryn stood.

"Do you need something, ser?" asked Siret.

"I was just observing," said Saryn. "You're working the stone the way the engineer did, maybe even better."

"I don't think so, ser," replied Siret, not looking directly at the commander, but not actually looking away, either.

"I do. I've seen you both." Saryn let the silence hang between them for a moment. "You've never said anything about it."

"What is there to say?" Siret lifted the hammer, struck the chisel, and an improbably long wedge of stone split away from the block. She turned the stone on the flat ledge she was using as a work surface, then struck again. In what seemed moments, a dressed stone rested there.

Two guards immediately hurried over from where they were stacking rough blocks and carried the dressed stone to the wagon that waited at the end of the road up from the stables.

"Just as Nylan built Tower Black," Saryn said, "you'll build the rest of Westwind."

"I'm not looking for that. I'm looking for a safe future for Kyalynn. That means a bigger stronghold. That takes stones and healthy women." Siret waited as the two guards returned and lugged a rough oblong of stone up and set it on the ledge.

After the guards had walked down into the quarry to fetch more rough blocks, Saryn asked, "What do you think about Dealdron?"

"His leg is healing. Your guards did a good job of splinting it."

"That wasn't what I meant. You're one of the few who can sense . . . you know what I mean. Will he fit into Ryba's plans, do you think?"

"You can tell if people tell the truth, Commander."

"Feelings are harder for me."

Siret looked at the woman who had been a UFA command pilot. "Weren't they always, ser?"

"You're suggesting something." Saryn offered a grin.

"To heal or work metal or stone . . . you have to feel. If you let yourself feel too much, you lose your effectiveness as a commander and a warrior, like the engineer did."

Saryn hadn't seen that Nylan had lost much effectiveness, not until after he'd destroyed thousands, then conveniently collapsed. "That may be, but what about Dealdron?"

"He'll work out fine if you don't ignore him." Siret emphasized the "you" just slightly.

"Why me?"

"He believes in earned loyalty. You've earned it. So far, no one else has."

Saryn didn't care for the implications of Siret's words, but she had to accept what the healer sensed and knew. "Have you talked to him about building techniques?"

"He knows some things we don't. He's also afraid that he wasn't that good a plasterer and that we'll find that out."

"Since we don't know anything about it, that might be difficult." Saryn's words were dry. "But don't mention that to him."

"I didn't, but he knows enough that he'll find out."

"That can't be helped, can it?" Saryn laughed. "He'll figure it out anyway if he hasn't already. There's not any plasterwork anywhere in Westwind. He'll see that, sooner or later."

Siret replied with a half smile.

"Can you teach anyone else to cut stones the way you do?"

"None of the locals . . . Oh, they can handle the hammer and chisel, but they don't sense where to strike and at the right angles. Daerona is a decent mason and a stone setter." Siret paused. "The one who's likely to be the best is Aemra. She likes it, and she comes up here and helps me in the afternoons."

"She's barely ten."

"She's better at it than anyone else."

"Does Ryba know?"

"She may, but I haven't told her. Neither has Istril. Istril'd be just as happy to have her daughter as a stonecutter. Aemra's also artistic." Siret walked to the end of the rock shelf, where she bent down and lifted an oblong of stone.

Saryn swallowed. The front side bore a sculpted face—that of Istril, although the hair was barely roughed in place, as was the neck. Even so, Istril's grace—and something else, perhaps a trace of the pain that seemed to go with healing—was embodied in the stone.

"Aemra did that?"

"No one else. It's to be a present. Istril hasn't seen it."

"You might have her work on a bust of Ryba as well."

"She wants to finish this one first before she does. She is only ten, Saryn."

The arms-commander nodded. Why was it that everything connected with the engineer created complications, even a daughter he'd never seen?

XVI

Every time a great angel leaves the Roof of the World, those who rule in lands far and wide should tremble and prepare for times of trouble, for each who leaves is unlike any other, and each shall leave her footprint and her name upon the lands she touches for ages to come.

There will be those who bear blades that none can parry, and few who oppose them will survive, and none will prosper. There will be those whose words are more deadly than slings and arrows, and those whose very countenance will charm beasts and yet freeze warriors . . .

Yet the first and last to leave Westwind shall also be silver-haired, save that both will be men, and destruction and rebirth will be their heritage, intertwining through the ages so that none will know from whence either came, nor the reasons why their actions will so afflict the world with changes that will lead to yet other changes, ceaselessly, all along the river of time.

Of those between, those upon the Roof of the World and those who descend to mold and form the Legend will free women to be what they should and can be. They will topple lands, and rebuild them, and they will create cities and places of art and beauty that will last through the ages, and yet the men who rule elsewhere will call them tyrants and worse.

Especially will those who follow the path of the white demons fear and condemn the angels and what they have wrought, and those selfsame demon followers will rip chaos itself from the earth itself and slash their way through mountains to strike at the lands of peace and prosperity where women rule. And yet all that will come to naught, high as the cost will be to those who would defend the Legend.

For in the end will the heritage of the Legend triumph, though it may not seem as such to those who behold that heritage and the fruits that it will bear over the endless years . . .

Book of Ryba
Canto I, Section IV
[Original Text]

XVII

Over the next eightday, the Roof of the World warmed, as much as it ever did. The root crops continued to grow, and the hardy redberry bushes showed signs of blossoming. Predictably, Ryba showed irritation at the time it would take to create the horn composite bows, then ordered the bow-making to continue as quickly as possible with the limitations.

Because a thundershower was drenching Westwind in midafternoon on sixday, Saryn decided to stay inside until it passed and undertake a thorough inspection of Tower Black from the level below Ryba's quarters to the lowest level, which held the carpentry shop as well as sickbay and the armory. Everything was largely in place on the upper levels. Sickbay itself was empty, and she walked quietly to the carpentry shop, stopping well short of the entry archway when she saw Dealdron seated on an old bench, using a small plane to smooth out a headboard for one of the narrow pallet bunks that would be used by the younger guards. After a time, he set the plane down and slipped a small knife out of his belt, one so small it fit almost within his palm. He began to cut a design in the middle of the headboard. Behind him, several other guards worked on various projects, but none paid much attention to the young Gallosian.

"Why are you doing that?"

Saryn couldn't see the speaker, but sensed it had to be one of the silver-haired trio because of the swirl of blackness that surrounded the girl.

"Flowers are supposed to bring pleasant dreams," replied Dealdron. "Carved flowers last longer than real ones, and there are few flowers in winter."

"What kind of flower is that?"

"It's a ryall. There aren't many. They grow in rocky places where little else grows, and they do not bloom often."

"What color are they?" Aemra stood, stretching and holding a stave she had trimmed to fit the broken bucket on the narrow workbench before her. She slipped it into place, with just enough force that it was clear she had shaped it perfectly. Then she turned and waited for Dealdron to reply. Behind her appeared Adiara, who looked at the Gallosian, half fearfully.

"They're black, mostly, with thin lines of white that outline the petals. A ryall is bigger than the one I'm carving. Each flower is bigger than a guard's hand."

"They don't sound pretty." Aemra stepped over toward Dealdron and studied the small carving. "I like the carving, though."

"They're not pretty. They're beautiful, like an icicle or a foggy morning."

"Icicles are freezing, and foggy mornings are cold and damp," Aemra pointed out.

"Here on the Roof of the World, that might be true. They still can be beautiful."

Saryn concentrated on feeling what was happening between the two, but so far as she could sense, there were no feelings on Dealdron's part beyond exactly what she heard in his words and tone. Aemra was curious and possibly a bit pitying when she looked at the young man's splinted leg, but the pity vanished as she looked at the first cuts of the design.

"I suppose so." Aemra didn't sound that convinced.

Dealdron didn't press the issue but bent forward and continued to cut and deepen the lines of the ryall. Saryn sensed the dull throbbing in his leg, but the young man kept working, and Aemra went back to carefully measuring and cutting a second stave for the other broken bucket on the workbench. After a time of watching, Saryn stepped into the carpentry shop. Several of the guards glanced up, then resolutely looked away.

"Commander," Aemra murmured, inclined her head, then stepped away from Saryn and closer to the bench. Adiara did not move at all, her eyes fixed on Saryn.

"What are you doing here?" asked Saryn, looking squarely at Dealdron. "Did the healers say that you could leave sick bay?"

"They told me not to try to climb the steps without help. Here . . . it is not far, and there are no steps. I can at least smooth wood. I asked Vierna. She seemed to be in charge."

"You carve as well, I see," added Saryn. "Did you consider that someone might not like a flowered headboard?"

"You have many guards, ser. I thought there might be one . . ." Dealdron lowered the tiny knife, then shrugged.

"There are probably a few." Saryn smiled. "If you want to carve de-signs, I'll get you a drawing of the Westwind crest."

"Might I ask a favor, Commander?"

"You can ask." Saryn stopped, although she had been about to turn and leave the shop since she had little else to say.

"I was never trained in arms. Your guards would have spitted me like a capon if I had had to fight. Could I take the exercises that even the older women do in the morning?"

"You are barely walking."

"That is true. I could only do some of the exercises, but I could begin to learn."

"It's not really necessary, is it?"

"Commander . . . ser . . . if you would . . ."

"Yes?" Saryn had to work at not snapping. She'd never liked male puppy dogs.

"There are but three things that will happen to me. The Marshal will order me killed. You will send me away from Westwind. Or I will stay in Westwind. If I obtain a little training in arms, it will do me little good against what I have seen of you and your guards. If you send me out, I will need to fend for myself because every man in Gallos will turn against me, and those in other lands will as well because they will know me only as a stranger. Any skill in arms will help me survive. And if I am allowed to re-main here, then would it not help if I could at least defend myself should any outsiders attack?"

Saryn couldn't help smiling, if slightly. The Gallosian did have a few points, and that suggested that he might show some promise . . . and he wasn't begging, just explaining. The rigor of the exercises and the training couldn't hurt in instilling more respect in him, either.

"You may begin the exercises with the junior guards whenever the healers allow you to do so—only the basic exercises that you can do with-out hurting your leg. Once you are healed, then we will see."

Dealdron inclined his head. "Thank you, Commander."

"We'll see," Saryn repeated, not wanting to commit to more. After a moment, she turned and stepped back through the archway, all too con-scious that Dealdron's eyes were on her.

As she walked back up the steps, her boots barely whispering on the stone, the way he had phrased the last alternative struck her. *If I am allowed to remain here.* That suggested he might want to remain. Was that because returning to Gallos might be a death sentence . . . or a sentence to a life of misery because he'd been captured?

She shook her head. Men! Why did they have to think that if a woman bested a man in anything, the man was worthless? At the same time, she was impressed by way the young man had stood up to Ryba, without bluster but without begging, and by his efforts to prove he had worth. He'd made the decision to learn more, but how much of that was because he was calculating that would make a favorable impression and how much because he had an honest desire to prove himself? She'd sensed both, but more of the latter, she thought.

Time would tell which was more important to him. She hoped it was the desire to prove his worth and improve himself . . . but she wasn't counting on it. Not after ten years on the Roof of the World, fighting off all too many men who wanted women as serfs or slaves.

XVIII

A glass before the evening meal on sixday, after the thunderstorm passed, Saryn hurried up to the stables to meet with Duessya, the head ostler of the Westwind Guard. She'd asked Duessya to question Dealdron, but between Duessya's duties and Saryn's, more time than Saryn would have liked passed before she had a chance to meet with Duessya again.

The tall guard stood at the west end of the stables, peering at the runoff channel that angled southward away from the stables and joined the stone channel on the south side of the stone-paved road leading down past the smithy to Tower Black.

"What is it?" asked Saryn. "You look worried."

"We're gettin' more water in the channel. Must have something to do with the quarry."

"It's south of here."

"May be so, Commander, but nothing else has changed, and there's nothing says water can't run northward when it goes downhill."

"I'll tell Siret. Some of her assistants can handle that. Daerona should be able to do it." Saryn paused. "I wanted to ask you if you'd talked to the Gallosian about horses."

Duessya nodded. "On threeday. He knows about dealing with hoof rot, and he says he can make up a pasty solution that will help, but you can't use it too much because it will crack a mount's hoofs. Like us, he thinks the best way is to keep 'em out of the wet and mud and to clean and dry the whole hoof area every time they come back from a muddy ride. He thinks it would be better if we had more hoof picks . . ."

Something else that needs to be forged. Would there ever be an end to what they didn't have, or what they didn't have enough of?

". . . thinks we ought to add some of that coarse high grass to their feed in the winter . . . says that eating the rough grass seems to keep 'em warmer in cold weather. It also might keep their teeth from getting too sharp when they can't graze. Leastwise, might not have to float their teeth so much."

"That might be useful. The young ones could gather the grass just before the snows hit. Anything else?"

Duessya frowned for a moment, as if trying to search her memories. "Lot of little things. When he heard the stables were stone, he did say that it might be better if the mangers were set so that the hay or feed didn't touch the stone."

"Condensation," mused Saryn. "Cold stone catches the dampness, turns it into little rivulets. If there's anything left in the bottom, the water that collects on the stone could drip down and spoil the hay or anything above . . ."

"Oh . . ."

"We should give him a try here once his leg is healed more." Saryn paused. "Thank you for talking to him. Once he can walk, you'll have to decide if he'd be a help."

"Anyone who'd be interested in the horses besides riding them would help." Duessya shook her head.

As she left, Saryn studied the stone runoff channel. It definitely was running higher.

Her steps were long and quick as she headed back down to Tower Black to catch Istril after her afternoon blade session with the older guards. Between trying to work out a plan for teaching Temple and accelerating arms training for the inexperienced young and newer guards, and all the other minor and continual items brought to her attention, Saryn hadn't seen Istril except in passing in days. She was striding past the smithy.

Istril was leaving the practice field but stopped and waited at the edge of the road once she saw the arms-commander. "You've been running everywhere lately."

"No more than you," replied Saryn. "How is Suansa doing with that arm?"

"It's healing. Likely be harvest before she'll be close to having any real strength in it."

"What about the Gallosian?"

"He's as bad as some other people I know."

Istril's voice was even, but Saryn could sense a certain amusement. "Go on."

"I had to spend some time explaining what he could safely do and what he couldn't and why." Istril began to walk down the road toward the causeway and the tower beyond.

Saryn glanced at the water in the stone runoff channel beside the road, then back to Istril. "Did he tell you that he wants to learn the basic arms exercise and training?"

"He did. I told him he shouldn't try even the basic exercises for another eightday, except for the simple arm-strengthening ones that he can do sitting down. He really doesn't need those, but I gave him some of those crude weights you had Huldran forge years back. I said they'd build up his arms more. That might keep him from doing what he shouldn't."

"Duessya thinks he knows a lot about horses. She didn't say it quite that way, though. What do you think about him as a person?"

"He's very polite. I think you should talk to him regularly. He might say more to you."

"If he won't talk to you . . ."

"That's not what I meant. It could be Llyselle, or Hryessa, or Ryba, but every so often he should have direction from someone who's an authority figure. You're definitely that."

"You have something in mind, Istril."

"I do. The same thing you do, if you want him to fit in. You just can't dump a man, especially a wounded one, into Tower Black without someone occasionally reinforcing the chain of command and the fact that women run things. Healers aren't in that chain."

"I'll take care of it."

"More than every few eightdays, I'd suggest."

Saryn shook her head. "I don't even know that I like him . . . but he's young enough that he just might be able to adjust."

Istril nodded.

"All right. I'll talk to him." After Istril said nothing, Saryn added, "As soon as I can."

"Thank you, Commander."

Once Saryn reached Tower Black, she found Dealdron sitting on a bench in the carpentry shop, watching as Vierna and an apprentice turned over a broken trestle table to replace the center pedestal legs.

The young Gallosian looked up at Saryn. "Ser?"

"Istril tells me that you're trying to do too much and that you'll hurt your leg more if you do."

"I feel useless . . . ser."

"You've been working in the carpentry shop, and you've made several bunks."

"Mostly. There are things I cannot do on one leg."

"It's better to concentrate on what you can do and not what you can't. That way, some things of value actually get done."

"They aren't what I do best."

"No. They probably aren't," replied Saryn. "But they're things that need to be done, and someone needs to do them. Everyone in Westwind ends up doing some things that they don't do as well as they do other things; but if you keep at the distasteful jobs, you can get better so that you don't spend as much time at them." She added, "If you want to prepare yourself for arms training, you could also exercise with the weights."

"I can lift them."

Saryn realized that the idea of weight-training repetitions wasn't one with which Dealdron was familiar. "Of course you can. But how many times in a row can you lift them?"

The Gallosian frowned.

Saryn walked over to the nearest wood bin and rummaged through it until she came up with a length of oak close to the size of a short sword.

She carried it back to Dealdron, then thrust it at him. "Hold it as you would a blade—one-handed."

"It is but wood." His face wrinkled in puzzlement as he took the billet.

"Just hold it." Saryn watched. Before long, she could see his arm begin to tremble. Unlike pine or spruce, oak was heavy. "Keep holding it."

Tiny beads of sweat began to appear on Dealdron's face, then the wood billet began to droop.

"Keep holding it," Saryn said calmly.

Finally, Dealdron had to lower the oak. Frustration warred with puzzlement on his face although he did not speak.

"Iron is heavier than oak," Saryn pointed out. "You could only hold that perhaps a tenth part of a glass. Do you think battles are over that quickly? What would happen to you if your arm got tired when someone was charging at you?"

The young man did not reply.

"What would happen?" Saryn asked again.

"I'd get wounded, or I'd have to get out of the way."

"And what would happen to the guard behind you? Or her mount? Or the formation and the other guards?"

Dealdron just looked stoically at Saryn.

"You've seen Westwind. We can't afford unnecessary casualties because someone doesn't want to train hard enough. That's why there were twenty-one dead Gallosians down in the vale and only one dead guard. Working with the weights will strengthen your arms so that you'll be better able to handle a blade when your leg heals. The healer will show you how to use them. Listen to her." Saryn managed to keep her voice level, but she could sense the unseen darkness swirling around her. That wasn't good. She needed to keep the flow of forces even.

"I am sorry, Commander. There is much that is new to me."

"There's much that is new to everyone who comes here. Those who learn are those who remain and who survive." What else could she say to him?

Abruptly, he lowered his eyes, if but for a moment. Then he said, "I will do as you say."

She understood that his words were not so much a capitulation as a statement that he would try what she said . . . and hold her responsible for the results, if only in his own mind.

"And as the healer tells you. You will not improve if you do not learn the proper way to lift the weights, just as a rider cannot improve when she rides improperly." She offered a polite smile. "I will talk to you later, and I will check with the healer as well."

Then she turned and headed toward the stone staircase. Again, she could sense Dealdron's eyes on her back as she left the carpentry shop.

XIX

When Saryn walked toward the arms practice field on oneday, she saw Dealdron standing at the back of the least experienced guards, his crutches laid on the hard ground beside him. Saryn frowned, wondering how he could do even the upper-body exercises without losing his balance. Then she saw a tripodal frame that the Gallosian had strapped to his leg at midthigh. He couldn't move much that way, and if he did, the movement was bound to be painful. Still, the frame did allow him to work on some of the exercises without losing his balance.

Saryn couldn't help but admire the young man's determination. Once she reached the field, she slipped into the exercise formation on the side closest to the road. She'd run through three exercises when Ryba appeared and joined in, effortlessly matching Saryn, movement for movement. Saryn found it hard to believe, again, that Ryba was ten years older than she was.

Once the group warm-up was over, Ryba turned to Saryn. "I need to spar."

"I could use a round or two," admitted Saryn.

"How about left-handed?" asked Ryba, producing a pair of weighted wands.

That was fine with Saryn. For years, when she sparred with anyone besides Ryba, she used her left hand and worked mainly on technique and how to anticipate moves from the slightest indications. Even so, she never sparred against the Marshal with real blades, even blunted ones. The killer instinct of an ancient Sybran warrior-queen was all too strong in Ryba.

Saryn took one of the wands, then stepped back.

A number of the older guards stopped to watch. The juniors weren't allowed that choice, and Siret broke them into instructional groups where—also with wands—they were drilled in basic skills.

Ryba took her position, then waited. So did Saryn, knowing that Ryba was willing to wait to see what her opponent would do first. After several moments, Saryn flicked the wand just a touch, and Ryba moved to the right. Saryn slipped the thrust that followed, but had to dart sideways to avoid the counter. She moved in quickly, so that Ryba had to circle away.

As always in sparring between the two, there were few even grazing blows, no matter what either attempted, because both had seen and survived so much and because each reacted so quickly. In the end, after both were sweating and breathing heavily, Ryba stepped back.

As Saryn did the same and blotted her forehead with her forearm, she saw Dealdron standing to one side, from where he had clearly been watching. Beside him Aemra had just finished telling Dealdron something.

Saryn looked directly at Dealdron, but the young man quickly looked away.

"You've been practicing. Left-handed, I mean," observed Ryba. "Walk with me." Ryba turned toward the road, heading up toward the smithy.

Saryn gestured to Llyselle, indicating she was leaving. The senior guard captain nodded. Saryn hurried to catch up to the longer-legged Marshal.

Ryba said nothing until the two were well out of earshot of the other guards. "It's time for you to leave for Lornth. Immediately."

"Why now?" Saryn recalled her sole other visit to Lornth, the large town that was effectively the capital of what amounted to a city-state, not even truly a nation. While its borders were not surveyed down to the nearest kay, the area controlled by Lady Zeldyan as regent ranged some seven hundred kays north to south and six hundred east to west. "Control" was a relative term because allegiance was often token in places distant from Lornth. Then, with the loss of the port of Rulyarth and the surrounding area several years before, control of lands some two hundred kays by three hundred had shifted back to Suthyan rule.

"We're going to need more saltpeter and sulfur, and there's nowhere else to get them. I don't like it any better than you will," replied the Marshal.

"We can't forge enough firearms, even if we could keep the white wizards from exploding the powder."

"Leave the weapons development to me. You're the only one with enough seniority and experience who can also survive the spring and summer heat down there."

"That may be, but what do I have to offer them in return?" Saryn asked.

"The Suthyans gave us that. They don't want us to trade with Lornth. You point out that we'd prefer to be on good terms with our immediate neighbors and that we're not exactly enamored of the Suthyan approach to dealing with women in power—"

"I can only mention that to Zeldyan personally. Her father won't take that well, nor her cousin Kelthyn."

"Especially Kelthyn. Young as he is for a regent, he holds the old attitudes."

"He's a tool of the older lords."

"Tools can be used by others than those who created them," Ryba pointed out.

That may be, but discovering how can be costly. Saryn only said, "That's sometimes possible."

"You'll find a way."

Whatever the cost, but we never speak of that.

"Just remember this. Everyone is a captive of the social structures of their past. They believe that men and women have different places in society, as do foreigners. Call it 'place-ism,' if you will. All the locals in Candar, at least all those we've encountered, believe that a woman's place is childbearing and at the hearth. Only if her husband or consort is dead or notoriously weak can she be accepted in a position of power and authority, and only as an exception for a short period of time. That's until her male offspring is old enough to take his place as the one in control. Zeldyan's facing a loss of power within years. She knows that will be a catastrophe because all the pressures on her son, Nesslek, will force him to repudiate her and her policies, and he'll end up repeating the follies of his sire and grandsire."

"Because to continue the wiser course of his mother would brand him as weak and as Zeldyan's tool?"

"Exactly."

"And I'm supposed to use that to get her to support us?"

"It's one tool. If you can find others, be my guest." Ryba stopped, gestured toward Tower Black, then toward the low but growing walls of the far larger new keep and barracks. "Westwind will endure. We just have to assure that future is as strong as possible."

Ryba's tone left no doubt that she intended to let nothing stand in her way to that goal, and Saryn merely nodded.

"How many guards will you need?"

"A squad should be sufficient if I can take Hryessa as well."

"Llyselle can handle things here, and Murkassa can act as captain of second company while you're gone. She'll be taking over the new third company anyway, and that will give her more experience." Ryba paused. "All of Hryessa's first squad are proficient with the bows. You'd best take enough to arm them all."

"When do you expect me to leave?"

"As soon as possible. You'll be gone at least two eightdays, and that's if the weather and the Lornians cooperate."

That was hardly likely, given the ever-changing weather around and over the Westhorns, especially in spring and early summer.

"I'll need several days to set things up."

"Whatever it takes. You're not one to procrastinate." Ryba stopped. "That's all I had for now. Just let me know when you have everything arranged."

"I will."

"I know." The Marshal nodded, then began to run uphill, as she did most mornings.

Saryn turned and headed back toward Tower Black. Once she was abreast of the practice field, she spent almost a quarter glass observing and making mental notes. Then she walked to the causeway and across it into the tower, where she made her way down to the lower level.

There she waited until Istril finished replacing a dressing on a young guard, and the woman left.

"What happened there?"

"Carelessness with the grindstone in sharpening a blade," replied the healer. "She isn't the first, and she won't be the last."

"Some of them only learn when they get hurt."

"More than some, but less than if they were men." Istril offered a crooked smile.

"Speaking of men, I saw that tripod device that Dealdron was using."

Istril nodded. "He brought it to me, and we ran through which exercises he could do and which he shouldn't. It can't hurt, so long as he's careful, and it's bound to improve how he feels. Also, he can use it in the carpentry shop, and Vierna says that he's been quite a help there, especially with simple pieces—the ones like bunks and straight wardrobes and bunk chests."

"Why is he pressing so hard?"

Istril laughed. "He may not be educated, but he's far from stupid. He watched a squad of guards destroy his outfit with only one fatality, while you dispatched three of them, and you've told him that his life depends on how well he acts. He's clearly a survivor, and to survive means obtaining your approval and the Marshal's. For him, that means doing things of value. I think your approval means more to him, though."

"Mine?"

"He asks more about you and whether you'd approve."

"But Ryba makes the final decisions."

"For this culture, she seems too high for him to impress her. He also sees that you make the day-to-day decisions."

"What about Adiara?"

"She's not a problem."

"Are you suggesting that Dealdron could be?"

Istril shrugged. "I don't know. On the positive side, Aemra likes him, and she's got a good feel for people."

"He's too old for her."

"Not that way. He's more like an older brother who needs a little direction. Sometimes, Dyliess and Kyalynn help him, too. They've decided he needs lessons in Temple."

"Why?"

"They have this idea that, if they can teach him Temple, that will shame some of the newer guards into learning it."

"I doubt that will work."

Istril shook her head. "It just might. The trio can be very persuasive, in their own manner of doing things. Dyliess has her mother's steel and her father's stubbornness and charm."

Saryn hadn't recalled Nylan as being charming although he certainly hadn't been obnoxious.

"You never looked, Commander," Istril said quietly. "He could be quite charming if anyone showed the least interest. He cared more than most saw. That was another reason why he had to leave."

"You're right. I never saw that."

"It was there. It's rare in men, but there are some who have it. Not many."

"Would you . . . if he'd stayed?"

Istril shook her head. "He's the kind who invests in one woman, and that woman is everything. Women say that they want that in a man. Most don't, not really. They want to be worshipped that way, but the cost of that is too high. It doesn't work over time if they don't love in return. I couldn't have. The Marshal never did."

"Ayrlyn did?"

"She did. That was why I could let Weryl leave. I could see that."

"Do you ever see . . . the way Ryba does?"

"I get glimpses. He's happy."

Saryn could see the brightness in the healer's eyes. "I'm sorry. I didn't mean . . ."

"That's all right. You'll understand."

It wasn't until Saryn had left the lower level and was riding down to check on the sawmill and the kilns that the oddity of Istril's last words struck her. The healer hadn't said that Saryn did understand, but that she would.

Just what else had Istril foreseen? Could Saryn persuade her to reveal more?

XX

Over the next two days, Saryn felt as though she ran from organizing one thing to another, but late on threeday afternoon, she finally headed up the stone staircase of Tower Black to check a last time with Ryba.

Just before she reached the open door, the Marshal said, "Come in, Saryn."

When the arms-commander entered, Ryba was standing by the open window. She half turned. "I'm assuming that you've briefed Llyselle and Murkassa. You're leaving early?"

"I did. We'll leave before sunrise. I'm taking four spare mounts. They're from the Gallosians, and we'll use them as pack animals as well."

Ryba pursed her lips. "I've thought it over. You'd better take half of Hryessa's second squad as well. You can work that out, can't you?"

"We'll figure it out."

Ryba stepped forward and extended a leather wallet. "There are twenty golds' worth of coins there. About half is in silvers. I'd like to send more, but that's all we can spare right now. Lady Zeldyan and the regents should be hospitable enough that you'll only need the coins while you're traveling."

Saryn took the leather wallet, slipping it into the inside pocket of her jacket. "Besides a commitment for saltpeter and sulfur, and the other useful goods, what else do we need?"

"You know the goods. See what you can discover about Kelthyn . . . and Ser Gethen's health. Find out what you can about Deryll. It could prove useful to you in some fashion."

"Ildyrom's son? Do we know anything about him except his parentage?"

"He was successful in eliminating or besting all his brothers."

"He's ruthless, or clever, or lucky. Beyond that?"

"He wants the western part of Lornth back as part of Jerans, and he's doubtless building the forces to take it. That's all we know."

"What about white wizards?"

"Zeldyan doesn't have any. Not unless one has appeared in the past year or so, and that's most unlikely. The engineer took care of all of those who served Lord Sillek. The Suthyans probably have some, but who knows where any who survived the fall of Cyador might be?"

"Is there anything else you want me to convey to Lady Zeldyan and her coregents?"

"Not directly. The information about Suhartyn's veiled proposals, and your presence should be enough. Try not to stay too long." Ryba's faint and ironic smile conveyed the sense that she knew Saryn's reply before the arms-commander spoke.

"I have no desire to stay a moment longer than necessary. It's already going to be hot and sticky down there, and most of the towns will stink." *And I'll miss the cleanliness and showers here at Tower Black, not to mention the clean mountain air.*

Ryba nodded. "It will do you good to see the men of Lornth as well."

Saryn flinched inside, but she only said, "They'll likely be just as overbearing as the Gallosians, except not quite so overtly."

"If you're fortunate."

This time, Saryn nodded. "Is that all?"

"That's all. If I think of anything else, I'll tell you at supper or in the morning when I see you off." Ryba turned back to the window, her eyes veiled.

As Saryn walked slowly down the stone steps, she thought over Ryba's words and expressions. The Marshal had seemed distracted, and yet focused and removed, all at the same time. And she looked more drawn. But was she, or had it happened over time, and Saryn hadn't noticed the gradual change?

When she reached the lowest level of the tower, Saryn found both Siret and Istril in sickbay, and both were silent, as if they had heard her boots on the stone steps and were waiting. "My ears are burning," the commander said lightly. "Exactly what were you discussing? Or should I ask what you were saying about me?"

"We were talking about the Gallosian," replied Siret. "Aemra has taken an interest in his carving. He's actually done several good copies of the Westwind crest on new bunks. That created a problem."

"Oh?"

"Everyone wanted one. So we switched them for your bunk and mine and Siret's," said Istril. "No one could complain about the angels getting them."

Saryn hadn't exactly approved carving the crest on bunks all over the tower. Was Dealdron going to be like so many men and push every limit?

"You did say crests were acceptable," Istril said.

"What about the one he did of the ryall?" Saryn sensed something was going on.

"He did three of those," said Siret blandly.

"Three?"

"Aemra persuaded him to."

"So the trio each have flowers? Flowers?" asked Saryn.

"They are wildflowers." Istril grinned.

Saryn shook her head. "I don't believe it. You . . ."

"They're only girls," said Siret.

"They're guards."

"They're still girls who will be guards . . . when they're older. Let them have a carved flower or two." Istril's voice was firm, and she looked directly at Saryn.

"Anyone can have anything carved on their bunk," Saryn said dryly. After a moment, she added, "Anything suitable, and no larger than the Westwind crest. Flowers, crests, animals, designs." She wasn't about to fight that battle. "And the design and the carver have to be approved by Vierna. That's just so things don't get scratched into the wood."

Siret and Istril exchanged glances.

Siret nodded. "Yes, scr."

"We'll tell Vierna," added Istril.

After a moment of silence, Saryn said, "I need a moment with Istril."

"I'll be in the carpentry shop." Siret stepped through the doorway and out of sickbay.

"What is it, Commander?" asked the older healer.

"The other day . . . you said that I would understand about sensing things. What exactly did you see?"

Istril offered a shrug. "I couldn't explain it, Commander. Sometimes, what I see is as much feeling as foresight. There's something all tied up with you and this trip and . . . people. I can't say what. I had a good feeling about it, though. Or not a bad one, anyway."

Saryn could sense the truth of that, but she also knew that Istril had seen more than she was willing to say. "That's all you can say?" She tried to keep the irritation out of her words.

"That's all I'd best say. I might make it worse if I said more. You know why."

Saryn did. Trying to avoid or change what Ryba or the healers foresaw usually just made matters worse, often far worse.

"Except," added Istril, "be kind to Lady Zeldyan."

"That doesn't sound good."

"How could it, in her situation? Besides, being kind to her will only help you and us."

While that was obvious, Saryn knew Istril was right and only trying to help. "One last question. The Marshal seemed drawn and tired. How is she? Physically, I mean? She doesn't have some lingering illness or anything, does she?"

"There's nothing physical wrong with her. She just sees too much. She's trying to sort out what's useful and what isn't. Then she has to decide what she—and we—can do."

"She's always had to do that," Saryn replied.

"She's getting better at it. She's written out an entire book of things. It's for Dyliess and whoever becomes Marshal after her." Istril paused. "How would you like to know chunks of future history and have to act on that knowledge? I wouldn't want to. You'd never know if you could change things or if you should have done something different."

Saryn nodded slowly. "Did she tell you that?"

"No. Not in words. I just . . . know."

"Because you can do a little of it?"

"A little is too much. I wouldn't want to know more."

Saryn understood that. That kind of knowledge could be a set of chains. Was the tiredness she'd seen in Ryba the result of struggling with and against those chains? She shook her head. Was there any doubt about that?

Finally, she said, "Thank you."

XXI

Saryn's eyes studied the narrow road that wound downward through a slope strewn with boulders, the smallest of which dwarfed her gelding. From the infrequent pockets of soil gathered on the sheltered side of the giant stones grew occasional junipers, few overtopping the rocks themselves. Another three kays below and to the west, the road reached the flat and grassy floor of the narrow river valley that stretched a good ten kays before entering another gorge, one that neither the road nor the guards could follow. Instead, they would have to climb, riding over another pass through the still-rugged lower range that was the last before the hills of eastern Lornth. With the white sun pounding down on the rock, Saryn had already removed her riding jacket and folded it into her saddlebags.

Her undertunic stuck to her back in places. One-handed, she lifted the water bottle from its holder and took a long swallow.

As Saryn's eyes and senses scanned the rocky waste ahead, for some reason, one of Ryba's parting instructions came to mind, in particular, the way in which Ryba had worded it. She had stated that finding out about Lord Ildyrom's son Deryll might prove useful to Saryn. Not to Westwind or Ryba, but to Saryn. Exactly what had Ryba meant? At the time, with her greater concern about what the high trader and the Suthyans were doing, Saryn had taken it as a guideline for her negotiations. Now she wasn't so certain, especially since both Istril and Ryba had made similar statements. Just what had they foreseen? She knew why neither would tell her, but that didn't make her any happier.

After another swallow, Saryn slipped the water bottle back into its holder and shifted her weight in the saddle, then turned to survey the riders who followed. No one was straggling. Her eyes flicked forward, toward the outriders, a good half kay ahead. They hadn't seen anyone in at least a day, nor had she sensed anyone, but that would likely change before long.

"This makes Westwind look like a garden, ser," observed Hryessa, riding for the moment beside Saryn.

"Compared to much of the Westhorns, Westwind is, and it's much more comfortable than Lornth is going to be when we reach it."

"For you, ser," Hryessa replied with a grin. "Some of the guards still have their riding jackets fastened all the way up."

"Ryba and Istril would be in undertunics by now, covered in sweat," Saryn bantered back. "Maybe not that damp, because it's dry here, but they'd be hot. Once we get where the air is damp . . ." She shook her head, although it would be another day before they emerged into the high hills southeast of Lornth.

"Do you think we'll run into any brigands?"

"Not if they're smart, but with those types, you never know. I'm more concerned about some of the local holders in Lornth. Trader Baorl likely stirred up trouble of some sort."

"With men like that, you can count on it. We can handle it." Hryessa's tone was dismissive. "Men . . ."

"You seemed to have worked out things well enough with Daryn."

"He's different. He also knows what I'd do to him if he ever did anything wrong."

Saryn laughed. "I think all Westwind knows that."

"He likes Dealdron," offered the guard captain.

"Did he say why?"

"He said that Dealdron works hard and doesn't feel sorry for himself, and that he's a crafter at heart."

"But he's trying to learn arms as well," Saryn pointed out.

"It doesn't get in his way of working in the carpentry shop, and Vierna says he's better than anyone there but her and Dyosta."

"He was an apprentice plasterer . . ."

"They have to work with wood a lot, not just stone. People want plaster everywhere, and they have to carve it into decorative shapes, too."

"If he happened to be so good at it, why did he join the Gallosian armsmen?"

"Daryn says that was because his older brother was lame and couldn't do anything else but help their father, and times were hard. There wasn't work for two apprentices."

Dealdron had told Saryn there had only been work for one apprentice, but not that his brother was disabled. She had to wonder what else she didn't know about him.

"He works hard," Hryessa repeated.

Saryn turned in the saddle to look squarely at the captain. "You've said that."

Hryessa shrugged. "He seems to be a good man. He's decent-looking, and he's kind to the children. We don't have many."

"I argued with the Marshal to keep him alive and allow him to stay at Westwind."

"That was good of you, Commander. It was wise, too. Some guard will be most fortunate to have him as a consort."

"It's too early for that. Less than a season isn't enough to determine how Westwind suits a man, especially not until his leg is fully healed. Then we'll see."

Hryessa offered an embarrassed smile. "Ser . . . we already said something like that."

"In my name, I'd wager? Don't tell me that some of the guards were already making a play for him?"

"Ser . . . Daryn, the two woodcutters, and old Covyn are the only men left in Westwind."

"And the Lornians who were crippled by the engineer."

"I said 'men,' ser."

"The healers and I have been working to get the Marshal to allow more men."

"That'd be a good idea, and before too long."

"I said that, too, Captain."

"Yes, ser." Hryessa's voice was even and polite.

Saryn could sense a certain veiled amusement behind the words. "Would you mind telling me why you're suddenly so concerned about Dealdron?"

"The trio have taken an interest in him, ser, but it's like . . . sister-brother. The girls just a bit younger aren't likely to be so wise."

"And it might not stay sister-brother for the trio, either. Is that what you're telling me?"

"No, ser. The trio are real clear about their feelings. You can see it in the way they act with him and the way he acts with them. But that won't last with the others."

Saryn could sense that Hryessa was absolutely certain about the trio and Dealdron, but there was something else there. "What else?"

"Nothing that I could say, ser."

Saryn wasn't going to get any more out of Hryessa. When the captain didn't want to say more, she didn't, and nothing changed that.

"Do any of the younger ones make plays for Daryn?" she asked, more to indicate she wasn't about to press than to seek information Hryessa wasn't about to provide.

"Not more than once," replied the captain with a laugh.

If so many of the guards hadn't been so badly beaten and abused, or disliked men in general, the problem would have come up even sooner. In a way, Saryn was surprised, in hindsight, that it hadn't surfaced before, but then some of the emotional scars were fading, and some of the junior guards had come to Westwind as young girls with their mothers. They'd been young enough that they didn't have quite the same level of negativity as the older guards.

All that just reinforced Istril's concerns about the need to change matters with regard to men, and that was likely to result in more tension between Saryn and Ryba. Yet Istril was right, and Hryessa's comments just reinforced that concern.

Still, there wasn't anything Saryn could do at the moment, either about Dealdron or men in general. She had to admit, for all of her initial skepticism, that Dealdron seemed to be a good person . . . but there was something about the way he looked at her when he didn't think she was watching, not that she felt anything wrong or negative . . . but . . . still . . .

She shook her head, then scanned the road ahead, but she sensed no others besides those from Westwind.

XXII

By midafternoon on twoday, Saryn and first squad were out of the hills, past the smaller hamlets, and riding down a gentle grade between meadows and recently planted fields. Just before Saryn and Hryessa rode Xanda, one of the junior guards. She carried a standard bearing a parley flag since Saryn didn't want anyone thinking the squad was the forerunner of an invasion force, especially with the possibility that the Suthyans might have spread that sort of false rumor. She just hoped that the locals recognized the white banner with the blue circle for what it was.

Ahead was a kaystone rising out of the green early grass that would brown under the summer heat. Saryn had to squint to make out the words once engraved in the stone and almost weathered away. HENSPA—3 K.

"Ayrlyn said something about this place."

"Good or bad?"

"Good."

"Let's hope it's still that way."

Just beyond where the road flattened out ahead was a low hill on the right side of the road. On the mostly level ground between the road and the slope rose a holding of some sort, with a large barn and several outbuildings, and three small houses. Beyond the holding, the road curved to the northwest around the hill. Two men and a boy were working on a stone wall of a corral beside one of the smaller outbuildings. The boy pointed, and the men turned. Then one said something, and the three watched, stone-faced, as Saryn and the guards rode past.

Once they were halfway around the curve, Saryn could see where the brown clay road straightened and led into the town. A scattering of huts or cots, set almost haphazardly on small plots of land, flanked the road for about a kay. Beyond them were more regularly placed stucco dwellings. Once most likely white, the houses were tinged a brownish tan, with gray-tile roofs.

"More of the black sheep." Hryessa pointed to a small flock to the right of the road, tended by a small barefoot girl and two scruffy dogs.

Closer to the town proper, under a porch of slanted planks on a rough timber frame, a graying woman struggled with laundry in a wooden tub held together with woven bark strips. Several chickens pecked in the dirt beside the hut. The light breeze carried various smells to Saryn, and she wouldn't have wanted to look into the source of any of them.

No one actually closed shutters, and that did happen, Saryn had heard, although she hadn't seen it on her one previous trip to Lornth. Two bent and graying men, standing outside a smithy, stared. From inside came the sound of a hammer on metal, and the faint odor of hot iron and charcoal drifted around Saryn.

The square in the center of Henspa was anything but impressive, with a modest pedestal and a weathered statue in the center, surrounded by a low brick wall that needed so much repointing that it appeared likely to collapse in a strong wind. Of the buildings around the square, the only two that had received much care were the chandlery, where the two crossed candles had been recently repainted yellow, and the inn, the next building west of the chandlery. The inn boasted a signboard with the glossy black image of a well-endowed bull. By comparison, the cooperage across the square from the inn and the chandlery was so dingy that Saryn couldn't even tell what sort of finish might once have graced the plank siding and the drooping shutters. Even the pair of display barrels flanking the door were stained from rust oozing from their hoops.

"Angels!" boomed a loud voice. The man who stepped out from under the shade of the inn's porch was a giant, but his mahogany hair and well-trimmed beard were tinged with streaks of gray. He looked directly at Saryn, who signaled for the squad to halt.

"You'd be one of the angels, I take it?"

"Yes. We're traveling to Lornth to meet with the regents."

"I'm Essin. I run the Black Bull here. My ma, it's half hers, she said any-time any angels came to town, she wanted to talk to 'em. Been that way ever since . . . well . . . a good ten years. Be a good thing, especially now. We don't have enough rooms for all of you, but you can have the stable, and you and the other angel there, you can have the big room."

"We couldn't pay for all that," Saryn said with a smile.

"Oh . . . there'd be no charge for the rooms, just for any meals."

Saryn sensed the man's honesty, but she didn't understand why he'd make such an offer.

"Not my idea. It's Ma's, and she pretty much still runs Henspa." He shrugged. "I do as she wants. Anyway, you spend time talking to her, and you get the stable and the rooms."

Saryn offered a smile. "That's the best offer we've had on the whole journey."

"You really headed to see the regents?" His eyes moved to the parley flag.

"Yes. They need to know some things."

"As if that'd be anything new." Essin shook his head. "If you'd have the stable, it's behind the inn. Take the lane there." He pointed. "Once you've got your . . . folk . . . settled, if you'd not mind, Ma would enjoy talking with you here on the porch."

Saryn turned to Hryessa. "If you and the squad would check out the stable . . ."

"Yes, ser."

For a time, neither Saryn nor the innkeeper spoke.

"You don't see many of the local lord-holder's armsmen here, do you?" she finally asked.

"Haven't seen any of Lord Jaffrayt's men in years, except for the ones that come every harvest with the tariff collector. Pretty much leave us alone, and we like it that way."

"What about traders?"

"Not many. We get some factors around harvesttime, looking for spare grain or cattle, or black ewes. Not interested in much else that we have here. Except there were some Suthyans here an eightday or two back. Only one trader and a bunch of armsmen. Talked to a few folks, and Ma, then left."

"What did they say?"

"Ma would have to tell you. I wasn't there." Essin shook his big head. "Don't much care for traders in fancy clothes. Means they cheated someone."

"So what pays for the inn?"

"Didn't say we didn't get travelers. Mixed bunch. Enough. Sometimes not enough, but Ma put enough aside for the rough times, what with the rents from her other lands."

"How do people make a living here?"

"Like folks everywhere. Some farm. The bottomland west of the river fetches up good maize, and the higher land does oats and wheat-corn pretty good. Wool from the black sheep brings a fair price, and we got a tin mine a bit south. Slow going there, but it helps."

At that moment, Hryessa rode back from the lane and reined up. "Looks good, ser."

Saryn nodded to Essin. "You've got a deal, innkeeper. How much for supper?"

"Two coppers each, with one lager. Another two coppers for the second lager."

"And fodder?"

"A silver for oats, and that's a cup for each mount, and all the hay they can eat."

Almost a gold. Saryn couldn't have afforded that every night, but with only two more days, three at the most, to Lornth, they had enough, and the mounts could use the fodder. "Agreed." She nodded to Hryessa, then dismounted and handed the gelding's reins to the captain. "I'll be with you in a while."

Saryn climbed the three wooden steps to the porch, keeping a bit of distance from the overlarge innkeeper, out of habit.

"Ma! Got your favorite guests." A rolling chuckle followed Essin's words.

Favorite guests? Saryn couldn't sense any menace in the man, but his words bothered her because they suggested a certain familiarity.

A woman a good head taller than Saryn opened the front door of the inn. Holding to her arm was a white-haired woman.

The older woman moved slowly, if steadily, but her brown eyes were bright and centered immediately on Saryn. "I'm Jennyleu. You're one of the real angels, aren't you? Could tell it right away. Something about all of you." She settled into the straight-backed wooden chair, then released her grip on the strong forearm of her young escort. "Sit down over on the bench, Lessa."

The woman smiled, her eyes turning to Saryn before she settled onto the backless bench.

The commander sensed that Lessa had seen angels before.

Essin picked up the other bench and set it down in an easy movement right in front of the chair. "You might as well be comfortable."

Although she seated herself, Saryn wondered how long she could take the hard wood after all the riding.

Jennyleu continued to study Saryn for several moments before speaking. "It was ten years ago, almost to the day, as I recall. Two angels rode in. One of them was carrying a child in a pack. No-good cousins, Gustor and Buil, went after 'em with blades. The one angel fellow, he wasn't all that big, tried to warn 'em. Buil tried to stab him in the back. Next thing I knew, both of them were laid out in the road—right out there—dead as a pair of slaughtered oxen. He took care of them with those little swords, threw one of them right through Buil."

Saryn nodded. She'd never heard the story, but it had to have been Nylan and Ayrlyn.

"You know about that?" asked Jennyleu.

"I never heard the story, but I know who they were."

"What ever happened to him?"

"He was the one who destroyed the Cyadoran army when they attacked Lornth. After that, he headed to the Great Forest." That was what Nylan had called it.

"*He* was the mage that turned the skies black and toppled all the cities in Cyador and drowned two or three of them?"

Those were details Ryba hadn't passed on. Finally, Saryn said, "That was Nylan. Ayrlyn helped him."

"Seemed like nice folks," said Jennyleu.

"They were," murmured Lessa. "I saw how good he was with the boy."

"Grandchildren are worse than children," snorted Jennyleu. "They know everything." Her eyes returned to Saryn. "You know any more about them?"

"He sends messages occasionally. Cyador, he says, pretty much fell apart."

"That's what we heard here." Jennyleu shook her head. "I told Wister and his boys not to mess with him. Coulda told the Cyadorans the same thing. They were always a nasty bunch, anyways. Never satisfied with what they had. Always trying to grab more. The Suthyans are sorta like that, too, except they want to buy everything cheap." Her eyes twinkled.

"Your son said some Suthyans came through here a few eightdays ago."

"Fancy-dressed fellow spouted nonsense about you angels killing a fellow at supper."

"We did. That was after he tried to poison the Marshal, then went for her with a blade. The Marshal turned the rest of them out in the darkness."

"Figured it might be something like that." Jennyleu nodded. "Sneaky bastards, those Suthyans. Told 'em to go on their way. Not before I got Essin to tariff 'em double for the feed and fodder." She laughed softly.

Essin laughed. "They don't count that well, either. Overcharged them, and they never caught it."

"Some people in Lornth might believe the trader," suggested Saryn.

"Not real folk, they wouldn't. Even the lord-holders wouldn't believe 'em."

"What do you think about the regents?" asked Saryn.

"What is there to think? Anytime Lady Zeldyan wants to do something that makes sense, the lord-holders start making noises like they'd make her boy overlord now and be his regents rather than her. Mostly, it's the menfolk causing problems, 'less they listen to a good woman."

Saryn laughed. "You and the Marshal agree on that."

"We haven't seen many raiders since she started patrolling the Roof of the World, not for long, anyway. That's more than the lords and regents in Lornth ever been able to do." She paused. "You didn't say why you were going to Lornth."

"We wanted to talk to her about the Suthyans. They tried to buy off the Marshal—before they tried to kill her. We thought Lady Zeldyan should know."

"Like as not, she knows how treacherous the Suthyans are. Making that young idiot Kelthyn understand is another thing. He likes being regent more than doing what he ought."

"Was Lord Sillek like that?"

"No. One reason why he's dead. He kept trying to keep the old lord-holders from warring with Westwind. His mama, Lady Ellindyja, wanted revenge 'cause you angels killed her consort. A course, even if he was over-lord, Lord Nessil wasn't any better than his lord-holders. He was just meaner. She kept stirring up trouble . . . you all know what happened."

"How do you know all this?" asked Saryn.

Jennyleu laughed. "Haelora. She's my niece. Vernt's, really. She and her consort, they've got an inn off the square in Lornth. The Square Platter. Vernt staked 'em, years back. She writes good letters. Not all that often, but the gossip's good."

As she listened to Jennyleu, Saryn couldn't help but find herself liking the straightforward old woman and wishing that dealing with the regents would be that direct.

XXIII

Despite Jennyleu's comments about the Suthyans and Saryn's worries, travel for the next two days was uneventful, past hillsides filled with in-hospitable ironwoods and hamlets populated by Lornians who were nei-ther friendly nor unfriendly—just wary. On fiveday morning, under a clear green-blue sky and less than a glass after setting out from their camp on the hillside lands of a halfway-friendly herder, Saryn caught sight of a rider in brown, stationed on a rise nearly a kay ahead. Abruptly, he turned his mount, but before he disappeared, she caught the glint of sunlight on metal—armor of some sort, she thought.

"You think that was a scout, ser?" asked Hryessa, easing her mount along beside Saryn.

"He was a scout. He wasn't wearing purple or blue. Those are the Lorn-ian colors."

"Local lord-holder, then."

"That's the best option." Saryn certainly didn't want to run into Jeranyi or Suthyan forces, since that would have proved the regents had no control away from the capital city.

Almost half a glass passed before Saryn caught sight of a kaystone ahead on the right, one newer and considerably more elaborate than any they had passed earlier. The oblong stone sat on its own pedestal and bore the name DUEVEK in elaborate Anglorat lettering. The name was framed by a sculpted frieze depicting sheaves of grain.

Saryn blotted her forehead, already damp in the still air. "Of course, the road's down here where it doesn't catch the wind," she murmured, more to herself than anyone.

Past the kaystone, the road turned more due west, toward the town proper, but to the northeast of the town was a flattened hilltop on which stood a walled villa, and a wide road leading down from it to the main road. While there were scattered cots on the left, with small plots and outbuildings, the lands on the right were empty of habitations, with just wide meadows and tended fields. Farther away were orchards.

"These have to belong to the local holder." Saryn gestured to the left. As she did, she caught side of the dust on the road down from the villa— and she began to sense . . . something.

She turned to Hryessa. "That scout told the local lordling we were coming. Have everyone ready arms and string their bows, all of them. We're about to be stopped. We couldn't outride them. Their mounts are fresher. I'd like to talk them out of anything foolish, but I'm not counting on it."

"No, ser." Hryessa eased her mount to the side. "Guards, to arms! String all bows!" Then she rejoined Saryn.

The two—and Xanda, still bearing the parley flag—continued to ride toward the town ahead, followed by the thirty Westwind guards. As they approached the point where the road from the villa met the main way, Saryn concentrated on the armsmen. The local armed riders were uniformed in brown, and had taken a position across the road. There was also another group of riders hidden behind a small orchard to the right of the road.

"We'll play stupid," Saryn said quietly. "We'll stop, but with enough distance to use the bows, if necessary. We probably will, because there's another group behind that orchard there."

"We could just ride the ones here down and kill them," suggested Hryessa.

"We have to let them see the parley flag and give them an opportunity to do the right thing. We just won't give them much of a chance to do anything else." Even with the local lord-holder's forces more than half a kay away, Saryn could sense the hostility. "We'll halt a good thirty yards out. Have the archers ready to take out the leader and the first rank at my command."

"Yes, sir." Hryessa let her mount drop back, then turned and began to convey Saryn's orders. Before all that long, she rejoined the commander. "They understand. They'll take care of the first rank and as many others as they can if they attack."

"They probably will," said Saryn sourly. "We'll just have to see, though."

The locals, in brown leathers, with brass-trimmed breastplates, were reined up across the main road a good hundred yards before a junction in the road. The left road—the main road—headed into Duevek. The well-maintained but narrower way led uphill to the elaborate walled stone villa and outbuildings, all with shimmering red-tile roofs. The middle track skirted the base of the hill and doubtless rejoined the main road northwest of the town.

As the guards reached a point about forty yards from the armsmen, Saryn called out, "Guards, halt! Staggered formation!" Then she eased the gelding to the shoulder of the road to allow the guards, already staggered, a clear field of fire.

In a lower voice, Hryessa turned in the saddle, and ordered, "Ready arms."

"You're blocking the road," Saryn called.

The squad leader stationed at the west end of the formation glanced at the parley flag, then at the armed squad. "Parley or not, you're not welcome."

"We're on our way to Lornth to meet with the regents."

"Anyone can offer a parley flag. That doesn't mean you're friendly. Those weapons, small as they are, don't suggest friendship."

Saryn refrained from pointing out that, if the Westwind force had not been friendly, they certainly wouldn't have ridden up without attacking. "We didn't go to arms until you blocked the road. We're not fighting each other. That was ten years ago. Westwind and the regents have a treaty," Saryn said politely. "Now . . . if you block our way, that breaks the treaty."

"The regents don't say how we run our lands. The only place you're headed is back to the Westhorns, if you can make it."

"Are you telling me you—or your lord—refuses to honor the treaty and a parley flag?"

"You aren't coming any farther into Lornth."

"We are," Saryn said. "We have the duty and the right to talk to the regents."

"You only honor conditions when it suits you."

Saryn had a good idea where that had come from. "We honor those who hold to them, not those who use them to attempt poisoning and murder." Her words made no impression, not that Saryn would have expected it.

"I have my orders. Nothing you say will change that."

"That may be. But I don't think your successor would like to explain how you lost an entire squad in a few moments. Undercaptain, or squad leader," Saryn said. "You have two choices. You can let us pass peacefully, or you can let us pass over your dead body."

"You're women. There's nothing special about you." He shouted, "To arms!"

"Fire!" snapped Saryn.

Before he could spur his mount forward, the squad leader slumped forward in the saddle. So did the six riders in the front rank.

"Charge!" ordered someone from the rear of the body of armsmen.

"Fire!" Saryn ordered again, the black currents around her amplifying her voice, even as she drew the first of her three short swords.

Another rank of armsmen went down, with the exception of two men partly shielded by the squad leader's mount, which had half reared. In moments, the arrows sleeting across the space between the two forces had reduced those in brown to a mere handful. Even so, that handful charged the guards.

"Charge!" ordered Hryessa.

In moments, the guards had swept though the remaining brown-tunics, and had reversed their mounts. Saryn had held her ground, concentrating on the second group of Lornians, now breaking clear of the orchard and less than a hundred yards away. "Captain! Attack from the south!"

"Archers!" snapped Hryessa. "Line abreast on me!" The captain gestured.

Not all of the Westwind archers caught the command, but twelve managed to get into formation.

"Fire!"

The roughly three volleys that the guard archers loosed were enough to halve the number of able-bodied attackers even before they were within fifty yards.

Saryn found two Lornians aiming their mounts directly at her. She forced herself to wait until they seemed almost upon her before throwing her first blade, smoothing the flow and using her order-skills to guide the weapon, even as she drew the second and parried the wild swing of the on-coming Lornian, then back-cut across his neck before he could recover.

The melee that followed lasted less than a tenth of a glass, and by the end, every one of the brown-clad Lornians was either dead or wounded se-verely enough to be unable to fight.

Saryn reined up and studied the road. Close to forty dead and wounded. For what? She scanned the road up to the villa, but it remained empty. The locals had clearly received orders to attack, or to keep the angels from reaching Lornth, if not both. She could see the hand of the Suthyans in that, but why would a local lordling throw in with Baorl? Or were matters that unsettled in Lornth?

Hryessa rode over and reined up. "We've secured the area, ser."

"What are our casualties?"

"Three slashes. None that serious. For all the fancy uniforms, these boys weren't that good. The blades aren't bad."

"Pack them up."

"We've recovered most of the shafts and arrowheads, but some will need to be reworked."

"What about our mounts?"

"Two won't make it."

"Take the ten best of their mounts. Use two for replacements, and load the rest with the blades and anything else of value. Let's find one of the survivors who looks to be able to take a message back to his lord or who-ever. Then we need to be moving out."

"Still to Lornth?"

"It's looking more important than even the Marshal thought."

"I don't care for that, ser."

Neither did Saryn. "We need one of the riding wounded."

"There are only two. They're over by the banner."

Saryn turned and rode the twenty or so yards to the left side of the road, almost opposite the west end of the orchard that had shielded the second group of attackers.

The two men in brown leathers were the only Lornians still horsed. Both were weaponless. One was black-haired, and both hair and beard were shot with white. Blood oozed from a crude dressing around his lower right arm, and a thin slash ran across his forehead. The other looked young enough to be his son, but with pale red hair and a strong nose, he in no way resembled the older Lornian. Pain contorted his face as he held a crooked lower right arm in place with his left.

Saryn reined up several yards from the pair, flanked by Westwind guards with blades in hand. She looked at the older armsman. "You are free to return to your lord and to tell him the price he has paid for dishonoring the parley flag—and for consorting with the enemies of both Westwind and Lornth. You can take your friend here with you." She inclined her head toward the fresh-faced Lornian.

"The Lord of Duevek will not be pleased, Angels." The dark eyes flicked from Saryn to Hryessa and back to Saryn.

"That is possible. We're not pleased with your lord. Nor will the regents be pleased with him. That makes us even. Now . . . ride back to your lord and tell him to send retainers to remove these carrion and clear the road. You can also tell him he should be glad the regents have a treaty with Westwind, because, otherwise, he'd have suffered far worse. We've only taken the mounts necessary to replace those injured by his attacks—and the weapons used against us."

"There are far more armsmen in Lornth than angels in Westwind."

"That is very true," Saryn replied. "You lost forty men. We lost none. You attacked first. The last time that happened, when Lornth attacked Westwind, we lost thirty, and you lost thousands. Think about it. In fact, you and your lord should think very hard about it." Saryn felt the conflict boiling within her. Given the Lornian male arrogance, she wanted to slit the man's throat on the spot as much as she needed him to convey the message. Given what might lie behind the walls of the villa on the hill, she had no intention of delivering it personally. Yet she could sense the swirling of both order and chaos around her. At least, that was the way it felt.

Abruptly, the man's eyes widened, and he swallowed once, then twice. "Yes . . . Angel . . . I will tell him." He swallowed again. "Might I go . . . ?"

The younger man turned white and swayed in the saddle, then stiffened in greater pain, clearly because he'd moved the broken forearm.

"Go." While firm, Saryn's voice contained as much resignation as anger, and she watched as the pair started up the narrow road toward the villa. "What was all that about?" Then she turned to Hryessa. "One moment, he was all bluster, and the next, you'd have thought I was like the engineer when he was using the laser."

The captain's lips quirked into an ironic smile. "You looked much like the engineer, and a bright blackness gathered around you. It's fading now."

"You don't seem all that worried."

"You are an angel, Commander. All of you true angels have such moments. That is a mark of the angels."

Saryn wondered about that, but introspection could wait. "We need everyone to mount up and get moving." She pointed to the narrow middle road. "We'll take the narrow track around the town, not the main road. I don't imagine we'll be exactly welcome right now."

"They were stupid," Hryessa said.

"That's because it's been years since we really exerted any force over Lornth," Saryn pointed out tiredly. "People who are raised to think women are worthless have a tendency to forget what conflicts with their beliefs."

"This lord will not forget."

But how many others are there who already have?

As Saryn urged the gelding forward, she turned back for a moment to see if anyone followed, but the road was empty, except for the dead and wounded. For a moment, she looked back at hillside and the villa occupying it. If one had to live in Lornth, there were worse places. Set on the hilltop and open to the Westhorns, there would be cool breezes most of the year, and the river wasn't that far. Duevek itself wasn't a bad town . . .

She shook her head. She doubted she'd ever see either Duevek or the villa again, because she certainly wasn't going to return the way they'd come. That would be asking for even more troubles she didn't need.

XXIV

Lornth stood in the middle of a valley entered through a gentle pass in the rolling hills and on the higher ground west of the river. As Saryn rode closer to Lornth in late midafternoon, the already-small holdings grew even smaller, with the space near the cots filled with gardens or crowded pens for livestock. A cat watched from under a scraggly bush, and a nondescript brown dog tied to the post of a rickety porch kept barking as the squad passed, but no one left the cot to investigate. Then the packed-clay road changed into a stone-paved highway—about two kays out from where the randomly crowded cots with their tiny plots were replaced by dwellings whose stucco was a pink so pale it looked white, especially under the bright spring sunlight. The larger dwellings had courtyards with walls finished with the same pinkish white stucco.

As Saryn neared the first of the more-permanent-looking stucco dwellings, a dark-haired and pregnant woman froze in place and almost dropped a shirt she was hanging on a line when she caught sight of the guards riding toward Lornth. Ahead and rising above and to the west of the modest dwellings and structures of the town was a taller red-stone tower that Saryn recognized as part of the palace complex. As the guards approached the town proper, they were assaulted by a series of odors, most of them unpleasant, if not revolting, all emphasized by the warm stillness of the air. The side of the road to Saryn's right held a stone-lined sewage channel, with pools of filth along the bottom, a stark contrast to the cleanliness of Westwind.

Once they were into the town, Saryn saw that the side streets were narrower and darker than she recalled, if paved irregularly, and all had sewage channels on both sides. Some of the larger buildings lining the wider main avenue were of the same reddish granite as the tower and the palace walls. The scattered handfuls of people along the streets reacted in different ways, some gaping, some retreating into the shops, and some remaining apparently oblivious as the guards rode past.

Beyond the small square in the center of the buildings, marked by a pedestal and a statue of Lord Nessil, the avenue narrowed for the three-hundred-odd cubits it continued, flanked by taller, more ornate dwellings, before ending at what passed for a green. On the far side of the green, two hundred cubits away, rose the wall and the palace complex beyond it, all constructed of a pale pink granite.

Saryn gestured for Xanda to take the road that circled to the right around the patchy grass of the green. As she and the guards followed the standard-bearer, once again it struck Saryn that Lornth was still little more than a big town and a keep with a low wall, hardly that defensible. Was that because Lornth was far from the borders with other lands? Or because it was that poor? Were the regents powerless to exact enough in taxes for a more impressive capital? *Tariffs* was the local term, Saryn reminded herself.

A set of wooden but ironbound gates in the ten-cubit-high wall around the palace and its outbuildings stood open, if guarded by four armsmen, two on each side. As Saryn raised her arm to order the Westwind contingent to a halt before the open gates, a young armsman—an undercaptain from his uniform—burst out of the guardhouse just inside the gates and came to a halt in the space between the gates. His eyes took in Xanda and the parley flag. Then he looked to Saryn.

"I'm Saryn, the arms-commander of Westwind. I came to see the regents."

"Ah . . . yes, Commander." The undercaptain paused. "Were they expecting you?"

"No. I would doubt it. When we discovered what the regents should know, it wouldn't have made much sense to have sent a messenger when we would be here almost as quickly." *And we're not about to have sent a single messenger through Lornth, anyway.*

"I don't . . ."

"We'll wait here," said Saryn with a smile. "You can go request instructions."

The young officer glanced at the thirty armed women, then back at Saryn. "It might be best if you entered the courtyard and waited inside while I check on where you'll be billeted."

Saryn could sense no scheming and no malice in the young officer, only apprehension and worry. In that, in a vague way, he reminded her of Dealdron, although she suspected that Dealdron might well be more perceptive than the Lornian, officer or not. "We can do that." She turned to Hryessa. "Have them ride through and form up inside and to the right."

"Yes, ser."

The undercaptain watched as the guards rode through and re-formed on the stone pavement that stretched across the front of the palace. Then he walked swiftly across the uneven paving stones toward a smaller side door, avoiding the main steps—only six, Saryn noted—that rose to a modest receiving archway. Beyond the archway was a set of brass-bound double doors. The undercaptain walked to the lower door to the right of the steps and disappeared within. With the main body of the palace rising some three stories, the building stretched perhaps two hundred cubits from end to end, with the red-stone tower centered in the middle, but at the rear.

"You took him off guard, Commander," observed Hryessa.

"He recovered. I don't think he's ever seen so many armed women before." Light as Saryn's voice was, she was concerned. They had arrived without being observed, or if they had been, word had not been passed to the regents or the palace staff.

"You'd think someone would have reported our nearing the city," said Hryessa. "We'd have known if thirty armsmen approached Westwind."

"You would think so," replied Saryn. "If they did, no one told the guards."

While they waited, Saryn studied the front courtyard of the palace, an expanse of unevenly laid cobblestones a good seven hundred cubits across the front and with perhaps a hundred cubits between the wall and the mounting blocks at the base of the wide stone steps leading to the main entry. The area behind the palace proper was also paved, with a series of two-story outbuildings set before the rear wall of the complex, presumably stables, barracks, and workshops of various sorts. Scraggly grass had sprung up between the cobblestones, imparting a ragged look to the courtyard, and the lowest line of stone on that part of the north side of the outer walls of the palace bore the greenish sheen of moss or lichens. Outside of the gate guards, Saryn saw only two other individuals—armed doormen standing at the top of the main steps, one on each side of the entry archway.

After a time, the small door beside the base of the main entry staircase opened, and the undercaptain hurried back toward Saryn and the guards. With him was another armsman.

The undercaptain halted well short of Saryn. "The Lady Regent bids you welcome to Lornth. There is ample room on the main floor of the second barracks for your . . . troopers. The adjoining stables offer enough vacant stalls for your mounts, and there are quarters on the second level for your officers, Commander. Lady Zeldyan would like to offer you quarters in the palace. Once you have refreshed yourself, she would like to greet you personally."

"Thank you, Undercaptain." Saryn inclined her head. "If you could direct us . . ."

"Squad leader Cardaryn and I would be most happy to do so."

The undercaptain understood a commander's concerns because he walked beside Saryn as the armsman led the way around the north side of the palace. The second barracks were those in the rear at the far west end, and while they appeared well tended from outside, it was clear that no one had used them recently. Once Hryessa was satisfied, and Saryn and the guards had stabled and groomed their mounts, the undercaptain and Saryn walked across the rear courtyard to the nearest door. She carried her own saddlebags.

"This is the south wing of the palace, where guests are housed," offered the undercaptain, opening the brass-bound door. He led the way up a flight of steps and turned to the right. The wooden floors creaked under his boots. "Your chamber is at the end on the left."

A young woman scurried out of the end door, then stepped to the side, almost against the ancient dark, wood-paneled wall, and bowed her head. "Your chamber is ready, Angel." Her eyes lingered on the battle harness and the pair of blades it held.

"Thank you." Saryn smiled.

The undercaptain stopped at the door and turned to Saryn. "One of Lady Zeldyan's ladies-in-waiting will escort you to her quarters once you are ready, Commander. She should be here shortly, but Lady Zeldyan suggested that you not rush."

"Thank you." Saryn smiled politely.

He stepped back, then turned and walked swiftly back down the hallway, wide for a dwelling but narrow for a ruler's palace, only a fraction over two yards in width.

Saryn stepped out of the dim corridor and into the corner chamber, large enough that it might well have been a third the size of the great hall of Tower Black—but the ceiling was far lower, barely above the fingertips of Saryn's fully extended arm. Centered on the north wall was a large bed with a high headboard, carved with ornate images of armed men and cornered animals. Pale green hangings framed the headboard. Three long but narrow windows, recently opened, Saryn suspected, looked out on the front courtyard, while two on the south wall overlooked the side courtyard.

Between the two south windows was a narrow fireplace, and against the west wall was a large armoire, its carvings matching those of the headboard, with a dressing table to the left, and a washstand in the corner, with two large bowls of water, one warm, and towels on the side rungs. To the right of the armoire was an ancient weapons rack. A writing desk was set back slightly from the middle window of those opening to the front of the palace. The dark wooden floor was largely covered with a green carpet, bordered in purple.

After closing the door behind her and slipping the bolt into place, Saryn eased the weapons harness off and draped it over the arms rack beside the armoire that she scarcely needed. While she did not dawdle, it was close to half a glass later by the time she had washed up and changed to one of the cleaner uniforms she had remaining. While no one had knocked on the door, she had sensed someone outside and assumed that the woman waiting was her escort.

When she finally did open the door, a very young woman, scarcely older than any of the Westwind silver-haired trio, stepped forward and offered what seemed to be a cross between a bow and a curtsy.

"Honored Angel . . . I am here to escort you. Tomorrow, you will meet the regents in the tower council room, but Lady Zeldyan thought it would be more suitable for you two to talk in her private chambers."

Not only suitable but doubtless far more discreet. "I look forward to seeing the lady."

The route to Zeldyan's chambers was simple. They walked almost the length of the palace and past the top of a large formal staircase to the north end of the palace, up one flight of stairs, then back to the left perhaps ten yards to an unmarked door.

A single armsman stood outside. He did not look at Saryn as the young Lornian woman opened the door, but Saryn could sense his curiosity.

"The angel, Lady." The escort stepped back to allow Saryn to enter.

Saryn nodded to the young woman. "Thank you." Then she entered the chamber.

The door closed behind her, and she stood in a sitting room that featured three windows looking out on the front courtyard, but with an archway leading into a chamber to the left.

A slender blond woman, with piercing green eyes, wearing black trousers and a tunic trimmed in purple, stood from a small square table with a chair on each side and on which were set several covered dishes, two bottles, and a pair of goblets. "Welcome to Lornth. Undercaptain Maerkyn indicated that you are an arms-commander?"

"Saryn, Lady Zeldyan. I am the arms-commander of Westwind." Saryn inclined her head politely. She could see strands of white intermingled with the blond ones, and there was a slight darkness under Zeldyan's eyes.

"Seldom do angels leave the Roof of the World," offered Zeldyan. "Never have any done so without cause. I would doubt that the Marshal has sent her arms-commander and more than thirty guards were there not great cause."

"There is certainly cause for concern, Lady."

"I imagine you could use some refreshment, and I thought we might talk while you refreshed yourself. I've arranged for your guards to be fed in the barracks mess and for your officers to join ours this evening."

"Thank you."

"Please sit down." Zeldyan gestured to the chair across from her, then reseated herself.

Saryn took the chair, thankful that it had a thick cushion.

"I can only offer red or white wine, Commander . . ."

"Saryn, Lady."

"Then you must call me Zeldyan when we are in private. Red . . . or white?"

"I like both. Whichever you think the best." Saryn sensed a welter of emotions behind the regent's collected facade, most clearly anxiety and curiosity, and a touch of fear.

"The red, then." Zeldyan filled both goblets half-full, then lifted her goblet. "To your safe arrival here."

Saryn raised the goblet before her in return. "And to your grace and hospitality." She took a small sip of the deep red vintage, appreciating the natural fullness and the hints of flowers.

Zeldyan set down her goblet and removed the tops of the three porcelain dishes. "This one has small lamb pies. These are currant-and-meat-stuffed potato skins, and these are cheese pastries. I prefer the cheese, but the currant stuffing is also good."

"And the lamb?" asked Saryn with a smile.

"Good, but very filling."

Saryn took one of the cheese pastries, just large enough for a single mouthful, and found it moist and surprisingly light. "It's very good."

"It was one of my mother's favorites."

Saryn sensed the momentary sadness . . . and realized that Zeldyan's mother was dead. She'd known that one of the other regents—Ser Gethen— was her father, but no one had ever mentioned Zeldyan's mother. "I can see why."

After a time, Zeldyan took a sip of her wine. "You have come far."

"And with reason. Earlier in the spring, we found a large body of Gallosian cavalry in the lower reaches of the Roof of the World. They were posing as bandits and attacking travelers and traders who were attempting to cross the Westhorns."

"Knowing how your Marshal pledged to keep the Westhorns free of brigands, I imagine you took some action."

"We did. All the armsmen are dead. We have their ostler at Westwind." Saryn took another sip of wine, and one of the currant-stuffed skins. "We also discovered from the ostler that Lord Karthanos's son— Arthanos—has not only removed all of his brothers, but that he has also recruited some ten additional companies, and it appears likely that they will attack."

"From what you have said already, that would appear likely . . . and perhaps unfortunate." Zeldyan sipped her wine. "Yet . . . you are here, rather than in Fenard."

"We had thought, as a result of that occurrence, and another, that Lornth and Westwind might have similar interests. We also have seen few traders, apparently for reasons linked to what we have learned, and the Marshal was interested in obtaining some sulfur and saltpeter and thought you might be of assistance."

Zeldyan frowned, but behind the frown was more curiosity than anything . . . and worry. "I fear I have yet to understand why our interests might coincide."

"The Suthyan Council sent an envoy to Westwind, accompanied by a high trader named Baorl and the son of a Lord Calasyr. That is how they were represented. The envoy and the lord's son were seated beside the Marshal." Saryn paused, waiting for a reaction.

"That sounds as it should be."

"The Suthyan envoy talked generally about the difficulties Westwind faced in finding traders to supply its needs given the problems that might arise among our neighbors."

"Was that how he phrased it?"

"I believe the exact words were something to the effect that 'If any ill should befall Lornth, even the most doughty of traders might find it difficult to reach the Westhorns . . . except, of course, from Suthya.' He also made an observation that the older lord-holders in Lornth feared that you and the other regents would not turn over power to your son when he reached his majority." Saryn knew she was conflating two statements, but the truth behind them remained. "The Marshal seemed unimpressed, and the young lord attempted to poison the Marshal's wine. When he was given the choice of drinking the wine or swallowing iron, he attempted to attack the Marshal. Needless to say, he did not succeed, and the Marshal expelled all the Suthyans from Westwind within the glass, bearing his body, despite the darkness and the chill of the evening."

"That seems unduly generous." Zeldyan's voice dripped with sarcasm.

"Had we slaughtered them all, who would have believed us?" Saryn smiled politely. "What happened after that is even more interesting. . . ." She went on to explain how the Suthyan party had split and how Ryba had dispatched her to Lornth. ". . . and now I find myself reporting to you that, because of the Suthyans, we were forced to defend ourselves against an unprovoked attack when we were riding here to warn you about the Suthyan intentions toward Lornth."

"An unprovoked attack? By whom?"

"The armsmen of Duevek." Saryn went on to explain.

Zeldyan nodded slowly. "What does the Marshal think the Suthyan intentions might be?"

Saryn sensed that, while the events were a surprise to her, the general situation was not entirely unexpected. "She does not yet know of the attack by the Lord of Duevek, but even before that her feeling was that the Suthyans were planning for some sort of attack against Lornth, possibly shortly after the likely attack by Arthanos against Westwind." Again, Saryn was guessing in her representation of Ryba.

"She must be greatly gifted with foresight to have seen all that, even before it happened." This time the irony was gentle. Behind the words was a mixture of worry and skepticism.

"She has seen much that has come to pass, often long before it has, Lady Zeldyan."

"That may be, from what I have seen with the black mage and the flame mage. Though they helped us, they cost us most dearly."

Black mage and flame mage? Saryn realized she had to be talking about Nylan and Ayrlyn. "They cost the Cyadorans far more dearly."

"Yes. Cyador is no more, not as it was. But Lornth is not as it was, either. The lands they scoured with fire south of Rohrn all the way to Clynya have only begun to recover . . . even now."

". . . and you have so few armsmen that the Suthyans have retaken Rulyarth and threaten Lornth itself," finished Saryn.

"You do not ask for much," Zeldyan said, "not for such a long journey, but why do you need such comparatively useless items as saltpeter and sulfur?"

"To create things that are more useful against the Gallosians."

"And not against Lornth?"

"We are few in number, compared to either Lornth or Gallos. We wish to be left in peace. Lornth has done so. Gallos has not. Why would we wish to anger and trouble a land with whom we are at peace? Especially when we face the attacks and enmity of two others?"

Zeldyan laughed, with a bitterness not revealed in the sound but only the feelings behind it. "I thought as much, but one must ask."

Saryn said nothing but took a sip of the wine. Her goblet was still almost half-full.

"You have given information, and you have weakened one who might yet be a traitor," Zeldyan went on. "Yet you do not offer us much hope."

"What would you have of us . . . of me?" replied Saryn.

"Whatever you can offer . . . after you deal with the Gallosians." A tight and wry smile crossed Zeldyan's lips, then vanished. "Unlike my sire and

Kelthyn, I know one cannot demand of angels. One can trust their word, and I would like your word that you will provide what assistance you can so long as it does not require you to lose Westwind to Arthanos."

"I cannot commit Westwind, Lady."

"Can you commit yourself, Angel?"

Saryn did not speak for a moment. Zeldyan knew Saryn could read her feelings, and the regent was hiding nothing—not her fears, nor her wish to preserve what she could for her son, and for those who would follow. *We have to have the sulfur and saltpeter . . . or Westwind will not survive . . . and how many women and their children will die then? What hope will remain to the others who look to Westwind and the legend that Ryba is forging?*

"I will give what I can of myself and what I can raise, Lady, if you ask it of me. That is all I can promise."

"You will have all the saltpeter and sulfur I can summon." Zeldyan smiled, and there was relief, hope . . . and anxiety behind the expression. "You might try the lamb . . . or more of the stuffed skins . . ."

Saryn understood that what lay before her was her supper, and she almost smiled at Zeldyan's finesse in keeping Saryn away from the others in the palace before they met more formally. As she picked up one of the small pastry pies, Saryn wondered how much she would rue her promise.

Yet . . . what else could she have done? *What other real choice did you have?*

XXV

The next morning, Saryn was awake early, but within moments after her feet hit the thick carpet over the wooden floor, there was a knock on her door.

"Yes?" She walked to the wardrobe and pulled out the dressing gown left for her—the first such that she'd seen in the more than ten years since she'd found herself in Candar.

"Would you like your breakfast, Commander?" asked a feminine voice.

Saryn pulled on the gown and tied it shut. "Now would be fine." She walked to the door, pausing to let her senses range beyond it, but there were only two women in the hall. Neither radiated hostility, only worry and apprehension. She slid the bolt back and opened the door.

Without looking at Saryn, the serving girl hurried into the chamber, where she quickly laid out a place on the small writing table, then set out all the items on the breakfast tray. She straightened and bowed. "Will there be anything else, Commander?"

Saryn glanced over the breakfast—a small loaf of fresh-baked bread, with a dish of dark conserve or jelly; several strips of ham; a mound that looked like egg and cheese; a sliced pearapple; and two pitchers, gray and green, with two mugs. "That will be fine, thank you."

Another bow, and the serving girl was gone, but another young woman entered, and she quickly replaced the washbasin and the two pitchers of water. She, too, vanished as quickly as she had come, and Saryn found herself alone as she seated herself at the side of the table, looking out through the window to her left. The table was set just far enough back that she could see the early-morning shadows on the courtyard below.

A note was set on one side of the tray, folded and sealed, the imprint presumably that of the Lady Zeldyan. Before starting to eat, Saryn broke the seal and read:

> Commander:
> The regents would be pleased to meet with you at the tenth glass of the morning to discuss matters of mutual import and concern. In the meantime, the palace and grounds are open to you.

Below the precise Anglorat script was a single letter—Z.

The breakfast offered far more than she normally ate. Because the greenjuice was bitter, she only drank the cider, although it bore a trace of fermentation. After eating, Saryn washed and dressed, only to hear another knock.

"Yes?"

"Commander . . . I'm here to take whatever you need washed . . ."

That was welcome news. "Please come in."

Saryn gave the young laundress almost everything she had brought, except the uniform she wore and another that passed for a dress uniform.

She'd thought about wearing that but decided against it, because she was meeting the regents officially, but not formally.

Then she followed the laundress out of the chamber, almost past a startled-looking young woman.

"Commander—"

"I need to see to my guards." She had probably slept far too late and spent too much time on breakfast, and she needed to see how they had fared.

"The regents will be expecting you in a glass and a half."

"I will be ready. You can accompany me . . . or wait here. I'll be checking the barracks." Saryn hurried down the corridor and down the south steps she had taken the night before, out the door, and across the uneven pavement of the rear courtyard.

Even before Saryn reached the second barracks, Hryessa stepped out into the courtyard, looking more rested than she had on too many of the previous mornings.

"How are they?" asked Saryn.

"Everyone's fine. The food is decent, better than what we've had, and there was plenty. I figured we wouldn't be traveling today. So I've got everyone cleaning their gear and equipment and washing uniforms."

"And Kalasta and the other wounded guards?"

"They're healing well."

"Good. I'm meeting with the regents shortly. I met with Lady Zeldyan last night."

Hryessa raised her eyebrows.

"She's worried, but she's promised the saltpeter and sulfur. She didn't say how long we'd have to wait for it." *Or if the other regents will agree with her decision.* That was something Saryn didn't see any need to mention. Not yet.

"How long will we have here?"

Saryn shrugged, offering a wry smile. "I couldn't say, but I wouldn't plan on leaving before tomorrow at the earliest." She paused. "Until I know more, they'd best stay within the palace walls. I don't think Lornth will be that friendly to Westwind guards. They can certainly take care of themselves, but doing so might create some injured males and their pride—if not worse. We don't need that."

"I'm afraid you're right." The captain shook her head.

Saryn wondered how many years—or generations—it might be before that changed . . . or if it ever would. "What about grain for the horses?"

"There's enough. I had to run down the ostler in the other stable for fodder. This one hasn't been used in years. Even that one is only half-full." Hryessa looked to Saryn.

"It doesn't look good, but any help we can get is better than none." Saryn hated the triteness of her words, true as they were. "I'd like to walk through the stables."

The stables were clean but dusty, as if they were unused and had been cleaned quickly and perfunctorily. Still, reflected Saryn, after she left Hryessa and crossed the courtyard back toward the palace proper, they offered better quarters and shelter than anywhere so far.

The young woman was waiting in the second-level hallway. She'd clearly been pacing back and forth. "Commander . . ."

"We still have a little time, don't we?"

"Yes, Commander."

Saryn nodded. "I'm Saryn, and you are . . . ?"

"Lyentha." Her eyes did not meet Saryn's.

"What are your duties, Lyentha?"

"I serve the Lady Zeldyan, Commander."

"What do you do in serving her?"

"I assist her in dressing, and in overseeing her wardrobe and that of young lord Nesslek. I help her in planning the food for the palace. When we have receptions or the year-end ball . . ."

Saryn listened for a time, interspersing occasional questions, before asking, "The staff appears smaller than when I was last here. Is this something recent?"

"I couldn't say. I've been here but a year and a season."

"I've met Lord Gethen once before, but Lord Kelthyn was not a regent. What can you tell me about him?" Saryn offered a winning smile and tried to project warmth.

"He is the eldest son of Lord Weald. His sire perished . . . with Lord Sillek."

"When Lord Sillek was forced by the older lords to attack Westwind, you mean?"

Lyentha nodded.

"He is less than favorably disposed toward us, I would judge, and I can understand that, but why is he so cool toward Lady Zeldyan?" That was a guess on Saryn's part, but from what Nylan had written and Zeldyan's actions in seeing Saryn first, it certainly wasn't unreasonable.

"I'd not be the one to say."

"What might others say, then? You must have heard. After all, Lady Zeldyan has done her best in a most difficult situation."

Lyentha glanced down the corridor, one way, then the other. "He is a cousin of Lord Sillek. It is a distant relation, but he is the only lord-holder with a blood tie."

"Has he pressed for Lady Zeldyan's hand . . . and she refused?"

Lyentha looked down. "I could not say, Commander."

Saryn could sense the answer. "So he will go out of his way to put pressure on her, either to force her to accept his offer or to discredit her in the eyes of the other older holders."

"I could not say that."

"You have said nothing, and I appreciate your discretion." Saryn nodded. "Perhaps we should make our way toward wherever I am to meet the regents. If you would lead the way . . . ?"

Lyentha headed down the steps to the main floor and northward until they passed through an older stone archway that opened onto a foyer, part of the original tower. To the left was a polished door of old and dark wood. Beside it stood a guard with a decorative brass breastplate and a sheathed short sword. He looked at Saryn, then at the table beside him.

Saryn smiled, then unfastened the formal sword belt and laid the belt with the attached and sheathed Westwind blade on the table. In close quarters, she could always use hand-to-hand, not that she expected that kind of trouble. Trouble, but not that kind.

Lyentha opened the door, and announced, "The commander is here."

"Have her enter," replied a pleasant male voice.

Saryn stepped through the door.

The chamber held no table, but three chairs in a semicircle, and two others—empty—facing the three. The heavy but worn dark green carpet had a purple border decorated with intertwined gold vines and leaves. The walls were dark-paneled, and the only natural light came from the pair of high windows in the back wall, and from the four brass lamps in wall sconces.

Lady Zeldyan sat in the middle chair, with her father, Lord Gethen, to her left, and Lord Kelthyn to her right. Kelthyn was not at all what Saryn had expected. Although seated, he looked to be of moderate height, with short-cut but wavy brown hair and a neatly trimmed squarish beard, slightly redder in shade than his hair. His blue eyes appeared guileless. His tunic was a deep blue that brought out his eyes and was trimmed in a darker blue.

Saryn bowed to the three. "Regents."

"If you would be seated, Saryn," offered Kelthyn, his voice pleasant.

Saryn bristled inside at the instant familiarity, but she smiled politely and replied, "Thank you." She omitted any honorific as her sole response to the youngest regent's inherent arrogance, then settled into the chair closer to him. She could feel his intense and instant dislike of her.

"Zeldyan has offered a summary of why you are here," Kelthyn continued, "but it would seem that your journey to confirm a hostility of which we are already aware affords Lornth little knowledge that we do not already possess."

"That was always a possibility," Saryn replied, "but given the nature of the treachery and the possible cost to Lornth, it seemed unneighborly not to make certain you were aware of how deep and far-reaching the enmity held against you by the Suthyan Council happened to be."

"That was most thoughtful of you, but of little consequence—"

"Commander," interrupted Zeldyan, her voice like cold steel cutting through Kelthyn's honeyed words, "I understand you ran into some difficulty on the way. Could you explain this?"

"Lady Zeldyan, as you suggested, we did indeed encounter some small difficulty on our way here. That difficulty, I fear, emphasizes the danger facing Lornth."

"Oh . . . and what might that be?" Zeldyan's politeness concealed amusement.

"Our difficulty concerned the actions of the Lord of Duevek. His men attempted to block the road and dissuade us from riding to see you. Although we were riding under a parley flag and stayed to the road, he sent two squads against us, first to block the road, then to attack us from behind." Saryn shrugged. "When they charged us, we were forced to use . . . persuasion. The kind with long shafts."

Even Gethen stiffened.

"That is an outrage!" snapped Kelthyn.

"We were under a parley flag, and their undercaptain called them to arms. He seemed unable to understand the parley flag, and he claimed that the regents did not rule in Duevek."

"He said that?" asked Gethen. "In those words?"

"Exactly, and most clearly."

"And then?" pressed Zeldyan.

"He ordered his men to attack. After we removed him and his front line, his assistant ordered the survivors to charge us, and another group attempted to attack us from behind."

"You do not seem that much the worse off," observed Kelthyn, his voice gently sardonic.

"We are not. Three guards suffered minor wounds. They will recover. There were perhaps five survivors out of forty from those who attacked us. We sent them back to Lord Duevek with the message that he should not presume for his regents." Before any of the regents could say more, Saryn pushed on. "What is most interesting is that the Suthyan trader who had been part of the delegation that came to Westwind under the guise of trading talks had not returned to Suthya directly but had proceeded to Lornth and to Lord Duevek. One of the delegation to Westwind attempted to poison the Marshal. When he was given the choice of drinking his own poison, he declined and attempted to use his blade to kill the Marshal. He failed and died. The Marshal was most considerate, given the situation. She merely expelled all the remaining Suthyans . . ." She went on to explain the Suthyan effort to isolate Lornth, ending with, ". . . and under those circumstances, the Marshal felt that it was not only wise, but neighborly, to send someone of stature to inform you."

"Someone of stature," repeated Kelthyn politely. "I suppose it is a most kind gesture. Yet it would seem that where you angels go, death always follows."

"We came in peace," Saryn said. "We came to warn you. Death came to those armsmen because they did not wish us to reach you. Why, that I could not say. I might surmise that Lord Duevek sought a personal advantage with the Suthyans, but I could not say. I also might surmise that the Suthyans seek to increase divisiveness between Westwind and Lornth and between Lornth's regents and its holders . . . but I could not say that."

"It would appear you managed to convey that quite clearly without saying it," replied Kelthyn.

"Lord Kelthyn," said Gethen, stressing the word *lord* ever so slightly and ironically, "I might point out that, whatever you may think of Westwind and its Marshal, in this matter, it is rather clear that they and we have little to gain in squabbling between us. The Suthyans gain much by such squabbling."

"I yield to your great wisdom and experience in this matter, Lord Gethen." Kelthyn's smooth and well-modulated voice contained no hint of the contempt Saryn sensed. He turned to Saryn. "I believe you have requested some odd trade goods in measure for your information and support of Lornth. Is this not true?"

"It is."

"And can you promise that such will not be used against Lornth?"

"I can promise that they will not be used against Lornth, assuming that Lornth does not attack Westwind. Certainly, Lord Kelthyn, you would not expect me to foreclose self-defense."

"No, I would not expect that, but do you honestly expect the Suthyans to ally themselves with the Gallosians?"

"No," replied Saryn. "I expect the Suthyans to use the Gallosians and anyone else to their advantage, whether it be the Gallosians, Lord Deryll, or holders here who might seek to profit."

"As they always have," added Gethen dryly.

"Could they not be using Westwind?" questioned Kelthyn.

"They tried. When that failed, they sent High Trader Baorl to visit Lord Duevek."

"Could it not have been that the Lord of Duevek was merely concerned to protect his lands? To see the vaunted guards of Westwind advancing . . ."

"Thirty-one women on the highway, who avoided both his town and his fortified villa? Why would we ride six days into Lornth if we were merely raiding? And then ride here and tell you about it?"

"You make a most convincing point, persuasive as it is meant to be." Kelthyn leaned back slightly in his chair, as if to signify that he had said what he would say.

"It may take several days to gather those items which you require," said Zeldyan.

Saryn understood the unspoken question that followed. "We understand and appreciate your helpfulness. Given the chance of misunderstandings, we have ordered our guards to remain within the palace walls for the time being."

"Most prudent," said Gethen.

"It is best to be prudent when that suits the situation," added Kelthyn.

"You have made that point yourself, often by example, Lord Kelthyn," added Zeldyan sweetly. She turned her head to Saryn. "We may wish to make inquiries of you again, Commander, before you leave. For now, you are free to leave while we discuss other matters."

Saryn rose and bowed. "Thank you. I will be most happy to address any other matters you may wish."

None of the regents spoke while she departed.

Once she was outside the tower chamber, she reclaimed her sword belt, not that she feared a direct attack, at least not in Lornth. She did need to make her own inquiries about a route that would return them to the Roof of the World without going through Duevek. There was little point in tempting fate unnecessarily.

XXVI

After she had left the regents, Saryn took her time touring the palace, then began what amounted to an inspection tour of the outbuildings. The few armed guards she saw observed her closely, but no one hindered or questioned her. While everything was reasonably clean and ordered, she couldn't help but notice water stains around windows on the north end of the palace and in several places, along the top edges on the interior of outside walls. Many of the chambers on the third level on the south end of the palace were empty even of furniture. The fireplaces in several guest chambers had been bricked up. The large kitchen had massive hearths, but not even the simple stoves of Westwind, and some of the hearths had not been used in some time. Drains in the stables had been dug up and crudely replaced and reset.

As much to take her mind off what she had seen as anything, she spent the later part of the afternoon working in the rear courtyard with various guards on their blade skills. Several of the palace armsmen watched, if covertly.

She was about to begin sparring with Hryessa when the middle rear door to the tower section of the palace opened and Lady Zeldyan emerged, walking across the courtyard with a boy who had to be her son, followed by two armed guards. Rather than beginning to spar, then interrupting the exercise, she waited for the pair to reach them.

"Commander, this is my son, Nesslek. Nesslek, this is Arms-Commander Saryn."

Although only eleven, Nesslek was but a hand shorter than Saryn. His face was oval, with fine but strong features, topped with thick blond hair. He smiled politely and warmly, then bowed. "Commander Saryn, my mother has spoken much about you . . . and well."

Saryn could see that he was already the kind who charmed women. "And she has spoken with pride about you."

Before Nesslek could say more, Zeldyan spoke. "I had heard you were practicing. Would you mind if we watched?"

"Not at all. We are using weighted wands, not blades."

A look of puzzlement crossed Nesslek's face.

"We train to kill," Saryn said to him. "And there are not that many guards in Westwind that we can afford to kill or wound each other."

"Your blades are short, like an inside sword," observed the young heir.

"They're more effective on horseback. We also throw them when necessary."

"Does that not leave you vulnerable?"

"The arms-commander carries three into battle," Hryessa interjected. "She never misses."

"Have you killed many men?" pressed Nesslek.

Saryn managed a smile. "As many as necessary and far more than I would have liked to. That is the nature of using weapons successfully."

That brought another expression, not quite a frown, yet not exactly thoughtful.

"So long as men do not wish any land to be ruled by women, such deaths will be necessary, but I can wish they were not." Saryn stepped away from the lady and her son and nodded to Hryessa.

Both Zeldyan and Nesslek watched for close to half a glass as Saryn worked with Hryessa, first right-handed, then with her left, and at last with wands in both hands.

Finally, Saryn stepped back, breathing hard and soaked with sweat. She was glad that the laundress was washing all her soiled uniforms—except for the one remaining clean one—not that she had that many.

"Would you like to try?" asked Saryn, reversing the weighted wand and extending it.

Nesslek took it . . . and then grasped it more firmly.

"It's heavier than it looks." Saryn smiled.

"It is indeed," replied Nesslek, reversing the weapon and handing it back.

"Is that one reason why many have underestimated your guards?" asked Zeldyan. "Because your weapons do not seem too impressive?"

"It may be, Lady. Also, the guards are very skilled with their bows."

"The longbows . . . how can you ride with them?" inquired Nesslek. "Besides, they are best used for hunting, not fighting."

"We use a double-curved shorter bow. They're powerful enough to put shafts through armor at two hundred yards, and the guards are trained to pick up different individual targets and lead them. We don't fire blindly."

"How do they fare against armored cavalry?"

"A squad of guards wiped out an entire Gallosian squad and incurred one fatality and three minor wounds," Saryn replied. "This detachment wiped out two squads that attacked on the way here—that was after a day of travel against fresh mounts. We lost no one."

Nesslek glanced to his mother.

"It's true," Zeldyan said. "Those who attack the angels seldom live to regret their folly."

Saryn sensed the old pain and bitterness behind the pleasantly spoken words. "I would that it were otherwise, Lady, but when a land is few in numbers, and its people have nowhere to go, one has no other choices."

"No, you do not." She looked at Nesslek. "You may go now. I will rejoin you shortly."

Nesslek inclined his head politely to his mother, then to Saryn. "Good day, Commander."

Both Saryn and Zeldyan watched as the youth turned and headed back toward the palace proper. The boy was handsome enough, Saryn thought, but she had the feeling that he was likely to be the type easily swayed by promises of glory and heroism. There had also been something about the bows . . . as if using a bow was looked down upon, or even cowardly.

"I had another reason for coming out here, Commander." Zeldyan smiled. "I had thought you might like to have supper with my father and me. It will be simple, just the three of us, but we would enjoy your company."

"I'd be pleased and honored."

"Thank you. So would we." Zeldyan inclined her head. "I'd best see to my wayward son."

Only when Zeldyan had returned to the palace did Hryessa speak. "They want something from you, I'd wager. More than your company, ser."

"I'm certain that they do, but it will be interesting to see what it might be . . . since we have very little to offer."

"Except ourselves. Be careful that you do not commit to what we cannot do."

"According to the Marshal, we can do anything." Saryn didn't bother to keep the edge out of her voice.

"You can do anything, ser. The rest of us are less able."

The tone in Hryessa's voice caught Saryn, not because it was sardonic or ironic, but because both the words and the feeling behind them embodied complete confidence in the arms-commander. "I can do a few things others can't. That's true of all of you. You've seen what a lousy archer I am." That was accurate enough, because arrows flew farther than Saryn could reach with her senses, unlike the blades she relied upon.

"Yes, ser." Hryessa's voice was pleasantly agreeable.

Saryn could sense the disagreement behind the words, and she wanted to shake her head. Instead, she said, "Could you talk to the armsmen here in the palace about the best way to avoid Duevek, especially if we have any carts or wagons?"

"I've already asked about maps, ser, and they've promised some by tomorrow. They would like to see us gone. I think the maps will arrive."

"Good . . ." Saryn shook her head. "You don't need me."

In return, Hryessa grinned. "It's not about maps, ser. We need an angel."

Less than a glass later, Saryn headed back to her chambers to wash up and change into what served as her dress uniform, although it lacked the adornments she'd seen on other officers the few times she'd left the Roof of the World.

Just before twilight, the same young lady-in-waiting who had escorted Saryn to meet with the regents reappeared and escorted her to a small dining room on the main floor at the north end of the palace.

Two figures stood talking inside the chamber, but Gethen and Zeldyan immediately turned.

"There you are," offered Zeldyan warmly. "I'm glad you're joining us." She moved toward a table that was roughly eight cubits long, but was set with three places, one at the east end, and one on each side. She took the end place and gestured to the one at her left.

Saryn waited until Zeldyan had started to take her seat before slipping into the chair she had been offered.

Gethen seated himself last and with a smile. "It's not often a old man gets to eat with two beautiful women."

"Two younger women, at least, and only one of them beautiful," replied Zeldyan, inclining her head to Saryn.

Saryn concealed her surprise because she could sense that Zeldyan believed every word. "I fear you are far too modest, Lady."

"Always has been," added Gethen.

"The red pitcher has red wine, from Father's vineyards, no less, and the gray has a gentle white, but not from any of our lands." Zeldyan smiled. "I prefer the red, but the white is good."

Saryn poured the red into Zeldyan's goblet, then into her own, before handing the pitcher across the table to Gethen. The serving girl brought just two items to the table—a pastry-covered casserole dish and a large basket of bread.

"It's just a fowl-and-vegetable pie." Zeldyan handed a large silver serving spoon to Saryn.

"Thank you." Saryn served herself an ample helping, then handed the spoon back. She did not eat—or drink—until Zeldyan did, although she sensed nothing amiss in either the pie or the wine. She took several bites and sipped the wine. Both the fowl pie and the wine were good, but certainly not outstanding.

"Thank you for allowing Nesslek and me to watch you spar."

"And me," added Gethen. "I was watching through a glass from the tower."

"What did you see?" asked Saryn, allowing a grin to cross her lips.

"I saw that Kelthyn could have used the observation," replied Gethen. "I've seen him work out, and he wouldn't have lasted three strokes against you or the other one."

"Hryessa is a guard captain. She is most accomplished with both blade and bow." Saryn turned to Zeldyan. "Did Nesslek say anything about the sparring?"

"He seldom does, but he was most reflective."

That could mean anything, thought Saryn.

"He should have noticed." Gethen shook his head. "Your choice of officers guards your back well, Commander."

"Those who accompanied us are almost as good."

"Could you train others to be that effective?" asked Zeldyan.

"In time . . . if they wanted to work that hard. I don't think most arms-men do."

"Why do yours, then?" asked Zeldyan, with little inquiry in her tone, as if she knew the answer but wanted Saryn to offer it.

"Our guards know that they have no choice. There is no one to rely upon but themselves. They see that great skill is the best way to assure their future. And, of course, the Marshal does not accept slackers or sloppiness."

"Nor do you, I'd wager." Gethen's voice was dry.

"We all do what we must." Saryn shrugged. "I did not see Lord Kelthyn depart. He must have left after our meeting. If I might ask . . . how did he seem?"

Zeldyan laughed, humorlessly. "Kelthyn was not pleased, although he was most polite and circumspect. I'm certain you could tell that."

"He did seem less than pleased," observed Saryn. "I got the impression that he didn't like being put in a position where he couldn't disagree without seeming totally unreasonable."

"Ah . . . yes . . . young Kelthyn always likes to seem reasonable," said Gethen. "That is so even when he is least reasonable."

Saryn could sense the age and fatigue in Gethen, but the older man's eyes were intent and clear, giving the impression that he was trying to draw out something. "There are always those who cultivate the impression of warmth and reason."

"Are you one of those, Commander?"

"I think not. Although women are supposed to be more devious than men, I have great difficulty in looking for the least obvious path to an objective. No one has ever accused me of great warmth, either." Saryn smiled at Zeldyan. "Unlike you, who combine warmth and shrewdness."

"Shrewdness without power avails one little." Zeldyan paused, then asked, her tone casual, "Do you think the Suthyans will attack you first . . . or us?"

"I do not think they will attack Westwind at all. Not at present, at least. They have seen how costly it would be, and they measure everything by cost. I am not certain that they will attack you, either. Not directly, in any case."

Gethen frowned, but Zeldyan nodded.

"What else can they do that is not direct?" asked Gethen. "They've already taken Rulyarth and exact high tariffs on goods coming upriver to us. It also appears they have persuaded the Gallosians to keep traders from the east from traveling to us overland. They are trying to enlist Deryll to their cause as well. What is left?"

With Gethen's last words, Zeldyan focused on Saryn.

"More of what happened to us with the Lord of Duevek, except directed at you and Lady Zeldyan as regents. The old holders are not pleased with matters as they are . . . are they?" Saryn took a sip of the wine, then another mouthful of the fowl pie.

"Are they that foolish?" Gethen snorted, then, after a moment, went on. "Of course they are. They think that if they overturn the regency they can reestablish the old ways, with one of them as overlord. Each believes that he will be the one the others will accept."

"When all the squabbling and fighting is over, and no one can still agree, and swords remain bloody," added Zeldyan, "the Suthyan Council will offer to make Lornth part of Suthya. Most of the lesser holders will finally agree after they find they have no golds left, and the Suthyans will then pay them to overturn the handful of larger ones. Those who remain will beg to be part of Suthya just to end the bloodshed."

"You paint a dismal picture, daughter."

"What other picture is there? Already, half the holders offer excuses rather than their tariffs, so much so that we have half the armsmen that we had five years ago, and that number was but a third of what Sillek took against Westwind and lost." Zeldyan looked to Saryn. "You see to what state we are reduced when the only one in whom we can trust is the arms-commander of the land that destroyed us."

"We did not destroy you, Lady. Your holders did. We did not invade Lornth. We only asked to be left in peace."

Zeldyan's lips tightened, and Saryn wished she had not had to say what she had.

"That is so, much as it pains me to admit it. Lady Ellindyja, may the demons rend her spirit forever, set all this in motion. I feared it then, and I begged Sillek to stand against his lord-holders. But he did not, and we cannot change that. You had to do what you did to survive, and I cannot change that." Abruptly, Zeldyan straightened. "We cannot change what will be, and nothing more we say here tonight will alter that." She lifted her goblet. "Best we enjoy each other's company. Do tell us what you found of interest on your journey here. Are the ironwoods as desolate as ever?"

After sensing the pain and frustration within Zeldyan, Saryn offered a smile as warm as she could make it. "I would not call them desolate, but rather severe and forbidding. Majestic in their own fashion. The size of the streams and rivers is also a wonder, because in the heights, they are so small, and yet in Lornth they have grown so large . . . there are valleys in the lower mountains with little but boulders in them, many standing alone, and some nearly the size of the palace here . . ." Saryn went on to offer the best travelogue she could, trying to keep her tone light.

At some point, the serving girl removed the platters and set before each of the three a small pielike dessert consisting of thin leaves of pastry with a mixture of honey and berry jam between. Saryn did enjoy that, as well as the stories Zeldyan told of being a young girl in The Groves.

In time, some three glasses after she'd entered the small dining room, Saryn made her way back along the empty corridor to her quarters. She had to admit that, despite the earlier part of the dinner, the latter part had been pleasant and that having supper with just three people had been far more enjoyable than eating alone, or than eating amid a score or so in the hall in Tower Black.

Just how many years had it been since she'd had a small and intimate dinner?

Later, after undressing, as she lay on the wide bed in the guest chamber, all too awake, she couldn't help but believe that Lornth looked to be on the verge of collapse or rebellion, if not both. What had she done in promising to help Zeldyan? Even after dealing with Gallos, assuming Ryba's plans were successful, what could Saryn possibly do?

What should she do?

XXVII

Eightday at the palace was quiet, and although Saryn ate supper again with Zeldyan, but not with Gethen, who had departed for his estates, the lady regent was most careful to keep the talk to matters other than the relations between Lornth and Westwind, the Suthyan threat, and the problems posed by the old holders. Zeldyan did not mention Saryn's pledge, either, but it hung over the commander like an unseen burnished blade, and she fretted about why she had given her pledge so easily. Ryba certainly would not have. Yet for all her worry . . . it had felt right, and that nagged at her even more.

She was both relieved and glad when, late on oneday, the first creaky wagon arrived, bearing barrels of saltpeter and smaller kegs of sulfur. Two more wagons arrived on twoday. Saryn wondered about returning the wagons and the swaybacked horses that pulled them, but Zeldyan insisted that both could be sent back later, whenever practicable.

Saryn didn't protest, and on threeday, she and the guards set out, at first retracing the route they had taken previously. The following day, they took a ferry across the river at the narrows to follow a road that, had they gone its full length, would have taken them to Rohrn. After another two days, they turned eastward and eventually recrossed a stone ford north of Henspa. Twilight was turning to evening as they entered the town, but Saryn was still sweating, and she kept having to blot her forehead, while her undertunic was plastered to her body.

The big innkeeper Essin stood out on the porch of the Black Bull. "I thought you might be back," he called as he left the porch and walked toward Saryn, still mounted on her gelding. "Same terms as before?"

"That would be acceptable," Saryn replied.

"Ma's doing poorly, but she told me she wants to talk to you. She said you'd be back. Just come in here when you're set. I'll tell the girls to heave to . . . be a simple supper."

"Simple is fine." Any decent supper they didn't have to prepare would be welcome, and Essin's charges were moderate enough that they might actually return to Westwind without using all the golds that Ryba had provided.

"I'll tell Ma." Essin paused. "I was hoping . . . she's pretty sick."

"I'll be there," Saryn promised, "but I'm not like the other angel. I'm not a healer." What was she, really, besides a pilot who'd discovered a talent for weapons and killing in a strange and magical world she still wasn't certain she truly understood?

"Be good for Ma to see you."

Saryn could sense the disappointment in the big man, and his concern and love for his mother, but all she could say was, "I'll be there." Then she rode around to the stables.

After making certain that guard details were posted for the wagons and that horses and guards were settled in, as well as after grooming her own gelding, Saryn finally made her way across the rear courtyard and back into the inn where Essin was waiting.

"Be another half glass or so before supper's ready," he announced.

"That's fine," Saryn replied. "Where is your mother?"

Essin gestured toward the narrow staircase, then started up. Every step creaked under his boots, and the wooden panels on each side of the staircase vibrated as well. Saryn followed several steps behind. By the time she reached the top, Essin was standing by the open door at the end of the hallway to Saryn's right. She walked toward him, grateful that the floorboards didn't shake under her boots as they had under his, and followed him into the chamber, some three yards by four.

The white-haired woman was propped up with pillows in a narrow bed. Her face was drawn, and the circles under her eyes were black. Her eyes remained as intent as Saryn recalled, but her voice was hoarse. "Told Essin you'd be back afore long." She smothered a cough.

"Word is that the Lord of Duevek had some difficulty when you passed through his lands." Essin looked to Saryn expectantly.

"He blocked the road and said we had no business going to the regents. His undercaptain sent half a company of cavalry against us. They ended up wounded or dead, mostly dead."

Jennyleu laughed, a dry, cackling sound. "Coulda told the lord that. Wouldn't have done any good. None of the men who rule understand." A racking cough punctuated her words.

Saryn studied the old woman with her senses, picking up hints of the reddish white chaos she knew was some kind of illness.

"Essin said you got wagons . . ."

"Trading goods from the regents," Saryn admitted.

"You going to help them if it comes to that?"

"Lady Zeldyan seems to be the only one who doesn't want Westwind destroyed." That wasn't quite true, Saryn realized, even as she spoke. Zeldyan might not mind the destruction of Westwind; she just didn't want Lornth to pay any more for Westwind's annihilation. "Or to go to the trouble of doing it, anyway."

". . . don't like not telling the truth, do you, Angel . . . ?" Another series of coughs racked Jennyleu, so much so that her pale face turned red, then almost gray.

Saryn found herself stepping forward and grasping the old woman's forearms. While she was no healer, she had to try to do something. Using the darkness, much as she might have with her blades, she cut away the reddish white that she knew was wound chaos, or infection, but only that, and nothing that felt "physical." After that, she smoothed and ordered with the blackness.

A wave of dizziness passed over her, but she straightened, released the older woman's arms, and stepped back, putting her hand on the footboard of the bed to steady herself.

Essin looked at her strangely but did not speak.

"What did you do?" asked the old woman, after a long silence.

"Something . . . I can't describe, but . . . I think it will help you get better." Saryn studied Jennyleu with her senses again. Most of the chaos had vanished, and she had the feeling that the rest was fading.

"That's better." Jennyleu smiled. "I'll be able to rest now."

"You shouldn't talk anymore," Saryn said. "Not for a while."

"I feel better already."

"Ma . . . you heard the angel. It's time to rest."

"All right . . . suppose you've listened to me more 'n few times about things like that." Jennyleu paused, then said, "Feed her good, you hear."

"Yes, Ma." Essin stepped back to the door, then out into the hallway.

After a last look and a smile at Jennyleu, Saryn followed the innkeeper.

Once they were down in the front foyer of the inn, Essin turned and looked hard at Saryn. "You said you weren't a healer."

"I'm not. I just know a few things. I helped her a little. She's a strong lady."

"You helped her more than a little."

"I hope so, but I can't promise anything."

"She said she wanted to see you when you come again."

"I don't know if that will be soon," Saryn pointed out. "The last time was years ago."

"You didn't stop here then."

"I didn't know enough to stop in Henspa." Saryn grinned in the dimness of the foyer, lit by but one oil lamp in a wall sconce. She still felt slightly light-headed.

"You will next time." Essin gestured to the dimly lit public room. "You need to eat."

She wasn't about to argue, not as tired as she suddenly felt. Was that because of what she'd done for Jennyleu? Ayrlyn, Istril, and Siret had always said that healing left them exhausted, but Saryn had never thought of herself as a healer. "Lead on, innkeeper."

XXVIII

Late on fiveday, a full eightday after they had reached Henspa, she and the guards—and the wagons—finally pulled up outside the stables at Westwind. Along the way, they'd had to replace one wheel, brace an axle and hope it held, and use the spare mounts to help the drays up the steeper grades. They'd also seen no other travelers, traders or otherwise.

Saryn groomed the gelding, then slung her gear over her shoulder and walked through the darkness down the road past the smithy, whose forge had been banked glasses earlier, and into Tower Black. She closed the heavy wooden door behind her and took just two steps when young Dyliess sprang up from where she had been sitting on the bottom step of the stone staircase.

"Commander . . ."

"I assume the Marshal wants to see me, Dyliess?"

"Yes, ser. At your earliest convenience."

"Tell her that I'll be there as soon as I drop my gear."

"Yes, ser." The silver-haired girl inclined her head, then turned and hurried up the steps.

Saryn followed, stopping momentarily to leave her gear in her own small cubby before resuming the climb to the top level of Tower Black. There, Ryba was waiting, seated at the small table, on which were set an amber bottle and two goblets. The single wall lamp offered more than enough light, given Saryn's nightsight.

"Brandy again?" asked Saryn.

"You look like you could use it."

Saryn took the empty chair and watched as Ryba half filled the small goblets, not really brandy snifters. Then she took a small sip, letting the liquid warm her mouth before swallowing.

"What took you so long?" Ryba finally asked.

"Success," replied Saryn dryly. "We've got the sulfur and saltpeter. The Lady Zeldyan agreed to help immediately, but it took a bit to persuade the other regents—and several days to gather everything . . ." She gave a brief summary of the journey, ending with, ". . . I hadn't realized how much the wagons would slow us down coming back up to the Roof of the World."

"How much were you able to obtain?"

"Three small wagonsful," Saryn replied. "And the loan of the wagons and the dray horses. We lost a wheel, and one of the wagons will need to be rebuilt before it goes anywhere."

"Do you think we need to return them?"

"No one will complain, but it still would be a good idea."

Ryba looked hard at Saryn. "Exactly what did you have to promise for all that?"

"My personal help to the lady, but only after we deal with the Gallosians."

"Your personal help?"

"I could not commit Westwind."

"Saryn . . . I would not . . ."

"What else did I have to offer? I'm no trader. I'm a former space pilot with skills in weapons and some ability to lead people. After this last trek, I'd never want to be a trader."

Abruptly, the Marshal nodded. "Each of us is slave to what must be."

"Must be . . . or might be?" asked Saryn.

Ryba smiled sadly. "Don't you think that I've tried to change things from what I've seen? So far my attempts to change things have led to what has occurred, and so have my attempts to avoid changing things."

"Predestination? No free will? Do you really believe that?"

"No. But I do believe that our exercise of free will leads to what will be and that there's only one future. No matter what the talk may be about multiple universes branching off from any decision, we each only have the one future that we choose with each decision."

Only one future, and that dictated by the exercise of free will? At that thought, Saryn took another, larger, sip of the brandy.

After a time, she asked, "When will the Gallosians attack? Sooner than you thought?"

Ryba nodded. "There are more scouts from the east, more refugee women, and no other travelers or traders." She paused. "You've had a long trip. The kitchen should have a late supper ready for all of you in a bit. Go and eat. We'll talk more later."

"Until later." Saryn rose and turned toward the open door.

Behind her, Ryba remained at the table, looking nowhere.

Saryn slowly made her way back down the steps to the main level.

There, Istril stood in the front foyer of Tower Black, as if she had been waiting for Saryn to descend from the Marshal's chambers. "Welcome back."

"Is anything the matter?" asked Saryn.

"You've changed."

"Changed? What do you mean?"

"You're more ordered. More black than chaos. Except that's not right . . . they almost flow around you in ordered patterns."

"What does that mean?"

"You already know that the more black you are, the harder it will be for you in battle, among other things. You've tried to avoid changing, and you have been successful, more than any other. But you've finally changed, and you look . . . you feel . . . different."

Saryn smiled wryly. "You wouldn't be telling me that if you didn't have something in mind. What's happened here that Ryba isn't likely to tell me?"

"Besides the score or so of Gallosian scouts that have vanished? Or her trips up into the ice fields? Or the forty-odd Analerian women and their daughters who appeared last eightday?"

"Forty? Is Arthanos conducting some sort of purge in Analeria?"

"According to several of the women, he discovered that women actually serve as village elders and several village chiefs are women. One of them was killed because she had the temerity to be overheard by a Gallosian officer saying that she didn't understand what all the fuss was about Westwind. The other villages nearby petitioned Karthanos to recompense the village, and Arthanos responded by burning them all to the ground."

"Did they bring anything but the clothes on their backs?"

"You sound like Ryba."

"I don't mean to, but . . ."

Istril sighed. "Ten of them had burns that had gotten infected. One died. We saved the others. Seven or eight might make good guards with training, and most of the girls look healthy. There are fifteen girls and five boys, but none of the boys are over five. Arthanos had something to do with that. He captured the youths and men and killed any who wouldn't join his army."

"He sounds as bad as the Rationalists. Worse, actually."

Istril just smiled sadly.

"You don't think so?"

"We have a lot of time, especially at night, to think, Commander. I've thought a lot. Most rulers believe what they do is for the best. It might be best for themselves, or it might be best for what they believe in. Or for the people. Or for whatever god there is. Not many people do anything just to do it badly."

"You don't think there's a difference between rulers?"

"Of course there is. Some are effective, and some are not. Ryba's effective. Lord Sillek was not. Arthanos appears to be quite effective in raising an army. Ryba will be effective in destroying it. The Suthyans will be effective in profiting off everyone's misery."

"You're saying that Lord Sillek didn't believe enough in attacking us?"

"What do you think, Commander? You've been to Lornth. I haven't."

"His widow seemed to think he had doubts. Is that what it's all about? To be effective, you have to believe in what you're doing? To the point that it costs everyone around you?"

"I don't know. I've just thought about it a lot."

"Maybe that's why tyrants are effective," Saryn said. "Because their beliefs are so important that they let nothing stand in their way. But is that the way things should be?"

Istril said nothing.

"Or is it just the way matters have to be?" Saryn didn't want to think about that, not as tired as she was. "How are all the injured and wounded?"

"No one's been hurt seriously since you left, except for the refugee women. Dealdron's healing well. His leg is in a walking splint. You probably ought to talk to him tomorrow, after you talk to Siret."

"Now what?"

"Siret can explain better than I can. It's not that kind of problem. He works hard, and he works long. He doesn't argue, and he always wants to do better."

"Then . . . what?"

"It's late, Commander. Could the three of us talk tomorrow?"

"That might be better," Saryn conceded, even as she wondered what the problem could possibly be. Still, the fact that she couldn't even guess suggested she wasn't thinking clearly and that Istril was right about waiting to talk it over until the next day.

XXIX

Saryn rose early on sixday and sought out Llyselle because she wanted a full briefing on what had happened in her absence. The guard captain was leaving the kitchen, where she'd obviously grabbed something to eat before starting her day.

"I thought I'd see you early, ser," mumbled Llyselle, after swallowing the last of a biscuit.

"It might be a good idea if you briefed me." Saryn gestured toward the archway that led into the carpentry shop since she could tell that the shop was empty at the moment, although she had the feeling someone had been there not too long before.

Llyselle followed her, and once they were out of easy earshot, stopped and began to report. "The Gallosians have been sending scouts toward the three approaches to Westwind. I won't say that we've gotten all of them, but we've added almost another thirty of those crowbar blades to the trading/iron stockpile. I sent Siret and a squad down lower. The Gallosians are gathering wagons and setting up a staging base not that far below the entrance to the north pass. All the refugees have been avoiding the usual passes and coming up over the southern hills, the way that leads from Analeria, even those that aren't from there . . ."

Saryn listened for a time before asking, "How long do you think before they'll set out?"

"They're planning a major campaign. At least two eightdays, maybe three or four."

Saryn thought about sending a squad to harass the staging camp with arrows, but that was likely just to waste shafts. Better to save those for when they could make every one count. "How is the training coming for the new guards?"

"Slow. Too many of them are here because they have no place else to go, not because they want to be here."

"They can't be encouraged to head to Lornth?"

"They're mostly Analerians. They think Lornth's as bad as Gallos."

Saryn sighed. She should have realized that after what Istril had said the night before. "That's going to be a problem."

"We're overcrowded. Most of them are in the stables for now, and that's fine for the moment, but when the weather turns in the fall . . ."

"Can we turn them to doing something on the new barracks and keep?"

"Siret has a bunch of them hauling stones . . . and there's one who actually knows something about masonry. But the rest . . ." Llyselle shook her head. "They're farmers, and half of what they know won't work on the Roof of the World."

Saryn wondered if what Dealdron knew about masonry was enough to be helpful. She'd have to ask him. "They'll have to learn or freeze." Then she shook her head. "No one has the time to teach them more than the minimum now, not until we deal with the Gallosians. Have your guards continue to keep a close eye on the Gallosians. For the moment, that's all we can do. I should know more in a day or so." Saryn hoped that was so.

"Yes, ser."

Saryn followed Llyselle's example of grabbing several biscuits from the kitchen before checking the armory, as well as running a quick inspection of the tower. Before all that long, she was out on the arms field limbering up with all the other guards. After Istril's comments of the night before, Saryn positioned herself so that she could watch Dealdron. No sooner was she in place than Ryba joined her.

The Marshal said nothing, and Saryn could still watch Dealdron. The young Gallosian now wore a bulky brace and splint on his leg and was able to do a much wider range of exercises. He did each precisely, yet with a certain awkwardness that suggested that they were not yet habit.

The sparring sessions followed, and Saryn squared off against the Marshal. She was on the defensive, possibly because she kept trying to watch Dealdron. She was startled, but not exactly surprised to find that the trio of silver-haired girls had taken on the duty of instructing Dealdron. As she continued to catch glimpses, one after another of the three worked with Dealdron, and not a one showed him favors or mercy. If anything, they pressed him more than would have been usual for an inexperienced guard. The only mercy they showed was not striking his injured leg.

At the end of the sparring, Ryba inclined her head to Saryn. "You could concentrate more, Saryn."

"I have a few things on my mind."

"The trio can take care of themselves. I'll see you this afternoon." With that, Ryba turned and strode uphill toward the stables.

Once the rest of the guards broke from their sparring sessions and split up for their daily duties, Saryn motioned to Istril and Siret. Under a sky that held scattered clouds, the three gathered at the west end of the causeway, where it joined the road to the smithy and the stables.

"Now . . ." began Saryn, looking at Istril, "last night you said you had something to say about Dealdron, except that it wasn't that he was a problem. Just how is he doing?"

"You saw him during the exercises and the sessions . . ." began Siret.

"Did you see him working with the trio this morning?" asked Istril.

"I saw them working him over pretty unmercifully. If they've been doing that very long, he's got to have bruises over most of his body."

"He asked for someone to press him as hard as possible. We thought they'd be ideal, because, even with the leg, he's strong, and they need to learn to deal with strength and discover that technique has its limits. He needs to learn technique, and besides . . ." Istril broke off.

"No one else besides you two and Llyselle will press them?" asked Saryn.

"They are looked on as the heirs to the Marshal."

"Only one is," Saryn pointed out.

"She doesn't treat them that way," replied Siret. "It's as if they're all hers, at least when it suits her."

"They are sisters, and it would be worse if she openly favored any one of them," Saryn pointed out. "What else can she do? It seems to me that she and you are all doing the best you can." She paused. "But what does this have to do with Dealdron?"

"He's still looking for your approval," Istril said.

"I haven't even been here."

"That doesn't matter."

Saryn would just have to deal with it. "I'm going to talk to Dealdron. I'll also see what he knows about stonework. If he knows something, can you use his help?" Saryn looked to Siret.

"We can use any help we can get. While the weather's good, he'll be more use there than in the carpentry shop. We need to finish the walls on the new barracks."

"If he could be a help, when should he start . . . I mean, with his leg?"

"I'd give him another eightday at carpentry," suggested Istril. "That way, he'll be stronger, and he can finish those foot chests that Vierna never had time to do."

"Why not?"

"Because things like bunks and replacement shutters and trying to teach new guards some basics so that she doesn't have to do everything take up most of her time."

Saryn nodded tiredly. *It's always been like that. For ten years, never enough of anything.*

"You're right," said Siret, looking from Saryn to Istril. "There's something there . . ."

"Something what?" asked Saryn.

"About you, ser."

"Could you two just say what you mean?"

"We can't, ser," replied Istril. "Not the way you mean."

"Tell me what you can, then."

The two exchanged glances. Finally, Istril said, "We see or feel, but it's like half feeling, half seeing mixed together, a blackness or a reddish white when people like the engineer—"

"I know that. The blackness is more like order, and you can move things and build and heal with it, and the reddish white is chaos, and it tears things apart. Those mages that were with Lord Sillek used the whitish red chaos to throw their thunderbolts or whatever they were."

"You, ser . . . you sort of had them all mixed together, except now there's more of both the black and the white, and they're all separate."

"Why would that be?" asked Saryn. "I haven't done that much that's different. Maybe not anything."

"With us," added Siret, "it was healing. The more we did, the blacker things got. Have you tried anything like that?"

"Just once . . . just a little bit."

"That could do it."

"Just once?"

"Sometimes, it only takes once," Istril said dryly.

Saryn found herself both flushing and trying to stop the urge to laugh. "You two can be impossible."

"Yes, ser," agreed Istril. "You will talk to Dealdron?"

"Later. Is there anything else I should know?"

"No, ser. Not right now."

"Good." Saryn turned and began to walk up the road toward the smithy, thinking over what the two healers had said. Why would her trying to heal Jennyleu incline her more toward separating order and chaos? Would that hurt her ability in battle? How much?

Huldran was checking the forge fire when Saryn entered the smithy, but immediately turned and walked to meet the arms-commander. "Ser?"

"How are the bows coming?"

"Good as we can do, ser," replied Huldran. "We'll have near-on thirty frames laid down by the middle of summer. That's all we've got enough horn and glue for right now."

"Arrowheads?"

"Daryn and Ydrall have been working on them steadily . . ."

Saryn listened as Huldran provided a rundown on everything in the smithy.

". . . and the Marshal ordered seven of these, ser." Huldran pointed to a series of objects on the workbench against the smithy wall. Each resembled a funnel a half yard across at the larger end, but the end of the funnel was capped with a heavy wedge. Beside each was a circular iron plate, designed to plug the larger end. "She didn't say why, but she gave me a drawing with the specs."

Saryn nodded. The design suggested clearly what Ryba had in mind for the Gallosians. "They're designed to . . ." She paused. "They'll have a special use against the Gallosians."

"Be helpful to know what that is," replied Huldran.

"They're designed to focus a blast," Saryn hedged. "Where, I don't know."

"Fill them with old-time powder?"

"Something like that, but I'd have to ask her."

"Wicked-looking devices."

With that and suspecting their use, if not in exact detail, Saryn could agree.

From the smithy, Saryn walked up the road to the stables, where she found Duessya instructing a group of young guards on which stalls to clean. She stayed in the shadows until the head ostler finished, and the guards fanned out to their assigned chores.

"Commander. The mounts you brought back were fine, and the spares you picked up along the way are all in good shape. A couple of really good mares, and the one stallion has promise. The drays . . . though . . . they're a sorry bunch. Old and overworked."

"Can you get them in better shape?"

"One for sure. Another one . . . maybe. The third . . ." Duessya shook her head.

"Do what you can." Saryn sensed no one near. "Do you know where the Marshal went?"

"I'd not be the one to ask her, ser, but she was headed toward the ice fields to the northwest. She's ridden there several times this season."

Ice fields? Why does she need to go there? "I wonder why."

"She brings back ice, but I'd guess that's not why she goes. She doesn't say, and she always goes alone."

"Is there anything else I should know?"

"Well . . . ser . . . not about the horses . . ."

"Is that a polite way of suggesting that we'll lose horses to the weather, come fall, if you don't get the stable space back from all the newcomers?"

"Winters are real chill up here, ser."

"I know. The Marshal and I are working on it."

"Thank you, ser."

After she left the stables and headed back down to Tower Black, Saryn couldn't help but wonder how long they could juggle the problems of too many people and too little space, not to mention those of food and fodder for the next winter. And those problems didn't even include the difficulties with Lornth, Suthya, and Gallos. Once she reached Tower Black, she hurried down to the carpentry shop.

There, Dealdron was working on planing sections for foot chests for the newer guards. At the other end of the shop, Vierna was instructing two new guards on what looked to be the proper way to sharpen a saw.

Dealdron stopped and set the plane on the workbench. "Commander, ser."
He looked Saryn directly in the eyes.

Since she'd been gone, he'd had his hair trimmed short and shaved off
the short beard. Without it, he looked older, surprisingly, and passingly
good-looking. She pushed that thought away, even as she sensed that the
directness of his gaze was anything but a challenge. She realized that he
was making a determined effort only to look into her eyes. "You seem to
be doing better with the exercises and the sparring."

"I could not have done worse than when I started." A faint smile followed his words. "I wake up sore every morning from the bruises that the
girls have given me the day before."

"How did you end up sparring with them?"

Dealdron shrugged apologetically. "There was no one else. The older
guards are beyond me. The newer guards are not so strong as me and
could not teach me what I need to know."

"What do you need to know?" pressed Saryn.

"Enough to defend myself when attacked. More would be better."

"You think we will be attacked here?"

"You will be attacked. That is certain. I thought Lord Arthanos would
have no trouble reaching Westwind. Now . . . I am less sure."

"Why?"

"Your Marshal, she is . . ." Dealdron paused. "She is the spirit of the
mountains. There is no other way to say it. She is like the winter storms.
No one ever defeats winter."

Saryn hadn't thought of Ryba that way, but the image fit. She didn't
see how Dealdron could have formed such an impression, so seldom did
the young man even see Ryba, except from a distance. "How did you decide that?"

"I can see what I see, Commander."

That was all he was going to say, Saryn realized. "Where are you sleeping now?"

"I have a corner here in the shop. That seemed better."

"It probably is." After the briefest pause, she asked, "Dealdron . . .
what do you know about masonry . . . stonework?"

"A little, ser. Sometimes, my da . . . my father, he had to redo some of
the stonework when he was replastering older places. He spent a little time
as a stonemason's apprentice. He didn't like it. So he became a plasterer's

apprentice. He taught me some stoneworking because my brother had trouble handling the heavier stones. Getting the stones cut right is hard, and when they're not finished proper-like, over time they can settle and crack any plaster laid over them . . ."

As she listened, it appeared to Saryn that plastering in Candar included what she would have called outside stucco as well as interior wall finishing. "It sounds like you know more than a little about stonework."

"I know some things."

"In another eightday, or so, once you finish more of the foot chests, and your leg is stronger, you'll start working with Siret on stonecutting."

Dealdron frowned, and Saryn could sense his concern.

"No . . . you haven't done anything wrong," she replied to his unspoken question. "We need to finish at least part of the barracks before winter. If we don't, we'll lose horses to the cold because we're using parts of the stables to shelter refugees—"

"Refugees?"

Saryn realized that the Rationalist word for "refugee" wasn't in the local vocabulary. "The women and children who fled Analeria because Arthanos tried to kill them."

"What is the word the angels use?"

Saryn told him the word in Temple, then asked, "Are you trying to learn Temple?"

"As I can, Angel," he replied in Temple.

"Keep at it. Istril or Siret will tell you when you're to start at stonecutting."

"Yes, ser. Whatever you think best, ser."

As she turned and headed out through the archway from the carpentry shop, Saryn was struck by what lay behind his words—or what did not. There was no feeling of resentment or anger, just a calm acceptance of her decision. She also realized how wasteful traditional low-tech cultures could be. Dealdron was intelligent and talented—and he'd accomplish far more in Westwind than he ever would have been allowed to do in Gallos . . . even with Ryba's concerns.

And Istril was right. For all his background, Dealdron was a good man.

XXX

Ryba did not return from the heights until late afternoon, and then she sent Aemra to fetch Saryn from the armory. Saryn set aside the blade she was sharpening and hurried up the stone steps that seemed to get longer as the day progressed.

Ryba was seated, waiting. The table was bare. She gestured to the chair across from her.

Saryn seated herself, and since Ryba did not speak, asked, "How are you finding the ice fields?"

"That suggests you want to know why I've been riding to the heights. Do you really think that knowing that would be useful to you as arms-commander, Saryn?"

"I couldn't say without knowing what you're accomplishing up there . . . besides returning with ice to preserve various foods."

Ryba smiled, a distant expression. "Do you know why I need to ride up there?"

Wasn't that what I just asked, if more politely? "I'd appreciate it if you'd tell me, ser."

"Don't humor me, Saryn."

"I already asked, politely . . . Ryba."

The iron in Ryba's voice began to soften as she spoke. "The more bodies that are crammed into Westwind, the harder it is for me to sort out what I truly see from what I worry about. I find that in the quiet and the cold amid the ice, matters become clearer."

Are matters ever really that clear? Or are they just clear for you?

"You will find, in your own time, Saryn, that clarity of vision and purpose are everything. You cannot be distracted by what might be, or what might have been. There is only what was, is, and will be. All the rest are either wistful thoughts or useless nightmares." Ryba smiled, an expression filled with a mix of emotions that Saryn wasn't certain she wanted to know. "That doesn't mean you won't have both, in great measure. You just have to learn to know what they are and set them aside. One of the great weaknesses of most men is that they fail to recognize early enough which dreams are possible and will become real, and which are vain hopes."

"Was the engineer that way?" Saryn kept her voice low.

Ryba looked hard at Saryn before her expression changed to one more amused and enigmatic. "The engineer was the kind of man who is the most dangerous. Upon occasion, he could turn unreality of the most impossible kind into hard accomplished fact, but he never understood the longer-term implications of each of those transformations."

"The longer-term implications?" prodded Saryn gently. "Doesn't every action have a consequence? Why would there be greater implications from a set of acts that appear at first sight to be less probable to result in success?"

Ryba laughed. "You've seen it, and you don't understand? How likely was it that a single engineer who barely understood the natural laws that enable magery on this world and a singer could destroy the mightiest power on the continent of Candar?"

"Rather unlikely, but they did," Saryn pointed out.

"Precisely. And what has happened as a result?"

"Lornth is weaker, but it remains independent."

Ryba smiled coldly. "Had Cyador taken even the southern half of Lornth and held it, Lornth would have been forced to accept a position as a vassal state to Cyador, and Suthya would not even be attempting designs on Lornth. In turn, Arthanos would not even be considering moving a force into the Westhorns. By accomplishing the improbable and what was considered impossible, the engineer created a set of circumstances that actually weakened Westwind."

"Weakened us? We would have had Cyador as a neighbor."

"Had Cyador taken Lornth, that would have returned the empire to its largest historical territorial borders. Cyador could not have afforded to expand any more, certainly not in the next century. Westwind would not have been seen as a danger, but as a buffer, a small land that neither Gallos nor Cyador would have wished the other to have, but which neither really would have wanted. In turn, that stability would have blocked the Suthyan expansion into Rulyarth and kept the Suthyans at bay, and we would have been free to trade with all three. Cyador would not have cared if women fled to us because it would have made Lornth more stable. Karthanos and his son would not have been able to complain if discontented women left their land for Westwind."

"So you're saying, by destroying Cyador, Nylan threatened the survival of Westwind?"

"He increased the level of that threat. That much is certain." After a pause, Ryba added, "That is why I struggle to see what will be, because the ripples in reality created by his acts distort what will now occur."

Saryn certainly hadn't thought in those terms, but she'd seen enough of what Ryba had foreseen to know that the Marshal was no mystic and, in some way Saryn did not pretend to understand, could see pieces of a future that was unknowable to anyone else, at least so far as Saryn could determine. "What do we do now, then?"

"What we must, you and I together, and you and I separately." Ryba cleared her throat. "We have at most four eightdays . . ."

Saryn listened intently, trying not to be distracted by all the implications of what Ryba had said earlier.

XXXI

Saryn completed all the tasks and planning Ryba had requested, from assigning duties to various detachments to planning the logistics of transporting the various devices and explosives. Before dawn on fiveday, she and Ryba and second company's third squad were riding eastward along one of the approach routes to Westwind.

Ryba seemed disinclined to talk, and Saryn wasn't about to initiate either questions or conversation when the Marshal was so self-absorbed. While Ryba had been somewhat distant as a ship commander, over the years at Westwind she'd become even more self-contained. Not exactly withdrawn, because she trained with the guards and ate with everyone else, but there was definitely a space between her and others, even when she was in the middle of a group.

Midmorning came—and went—before Ryba spoke. "This is still the way they'll come."

Saryn had her own idea as to why the Gallosians would take the road that Ryba and Saryn followed, the most northerly route out of Gallos toward Lornth. There were no truly narrow passes all the way to Westwind, although there was one valley surrounded by rocky cliffs, but the cliffs were a good half kay from the road. "Even though it's the most obvious, ser?"

"Obvious or not, after all we've done to harass them, they won't take a road where easy ambushes are possible. That's one reason why I ordered the attacks."

"So that they'd take the most open road?" On the face of it, that made no sense.

"The road that *seems* the most open. Appearances aren't always what they look to be."

Saryn could understand that, even if she didn't recall why that would be so on the route they were traveling.

Not until late afternoon did they reach the west end of a comparatively shallow valley running generally east to west, whose northern side was comprised of rocky hills that footed taller and snowcapped peaks and whose southern side largely comprised a long mesa with sheer cliffs overlooking the valley. As Saryn recalled, the valley extended almost eight kays, and at the eastern end, which she could not see, was a slightly deeper bowl-like depression, to the east of which was a moderately good-sized stream.

Ryba reined up at the top of the pass, just before the road began a straight and gentle descent. She studied the entire valley, then she nodded to the squad leader. "Forward."

Halfway down the incline, nearly a kay farther along, the Marshal again halted and surveyed the valley, particularly the cliffs to her right, the ones buttressing the rocky mesa. To Saryn, it was obvious that the Marshal was comparing something she had seen—or foreseen—to what she was now seeing, measuring everything with her eyes. The Marshal gestured for Saryn to ease her mount closer.

Saryn did so, reining up when she was almost stirrup to stirrup with Ryba.

"The middle section of the road, down there." Ryba pointed. "Right in the middle of the valley. You can see that there aren't any trees to the south of the road, just mountain meadows sloping up to the base of the cliffs. It looks like a gradual incline, but it's steeper than that. There's a mass of rock ready to break loose on the side of the mesa. When it does, it will reach the road and still be a good ten yards high."

How can she be so certain? "That much rock will make the road impassable."

"Yes, it will." Ryba could have been acknowledging that the sun would set every day.

Saryn understood. In addition to hopefully burying part or all of Arthanos's army, such an avalanche would reduce the number of routes through the Roof of the World to two, both of which had narrow passes that were far more easily defended and controlled.

"You see that overhang?" asked the Marshal. "Where the reddish stone bulges out?"

"Yes, ser. Is that where you want the explosive penetrators, or whatever you call the iron funnels that you had Huldran forge?"

"Precisely. How long will it take you to get them in place?"

"Two or three days, but it could take an eightday. It's hard to tell from here. We can cut across from the pass back there to reach the mesa, and there's a saddle that looks clear enough. But we'll probably have to use ropes to place them. The rock on top looks rugged and not too stable, and we don't want to trigger anything before Arthanos's army is down below."

Ryba nodded. "You'd best get started as soon as we return. I'm counting on you to determine the optimum placement so that the entire overhang comes down."

"How will we know when to set off the charges?"

"It will be sunny enough. We'll use mirrors. Smoke if it's not sunny. I'd prefer mirrors. I want the bastards to see what's coming."

They're not all bastards. A lot of them are poor armsmen just following orders.

As if she had read Saryn's thoughts, Ryba replied, "We've been here ten years. We've never attacked their lands. We've never invaded. We've never threatened. But they keep trying to stop those who would join us. They've cut off trade and supplies. Even after we destroy this army, the winter will be long and hard. Destroying ten thousand armsmen will keep Gallos off our back for a good twenty years, if not longer, and we'll need every year." She paused, then continued in a softer tone. "In your own time, Saryn, you'll see. You'll come to understand that there are times when any sign of fairness or decency is only perceived as weakness, that there are times when only being a tyrant will suffice for the greater good. You will wonder, time and again, if you're rationalizing when you do what must be done. Remember that when a male ruler does what is necessary, he is a strong and forceful leader of his people. When a woman does exactly the same, she's a cruel bitch who is extreme and unfair." Ryba laughed, harshly. "Already, the world has begun to forget what Nylan did to Cyador and how many tens of thousands perished. You saw that with the Suthyans. Yet two lands and the holders of a third want to attack and destroy a single settlement of perhaps five hundred women and children. Why? Because Westwind is ruled by a woman for women." After another brief silence, she finished. "It's better to be a just tyrant who provides freedom than a dead ruler who tried to be fair in an unfair world."

Strangely, Saryn heard no bitterness in Ryba's tone. Her words had been delivered with a pleasant yet chilling calmness.

Abruptly, the Marshal turned her mount. "We've seen what we came to see."

Saryn eased the gelding around and beside the Marshal. They had a long ride back.

XXXII

Ryba and Saryn returned to Westwind late on sixday, and Saryn started working on her own expedition sevenday morning. She assigned Hryessa's fourth squad, two carts, plus the two decent wagons of those that she had brought back from Lornth. Standing just downhill from the smithy, Saryn watched while Huldran, Ydrall, Cessya, and Nunca loaded empty penetrators into the two wagons. Huldran had added a metal loop on each funnel so that the penetrators could be lowered on a rope, as necessary. The two carts were at the powder house beyond the quarry, where the kegs of finished powder were being loaded.

Except for fourth squad, whose guards were getting their gear together, the remainder of the guards were on the arms practice field, sparring.

Saryn's eyes drifted across the groups, then stopped on Dealdron and the trio, who were on the section of the field immediately below the smithy. There was something happening there, involving order, but Saryn couldn't sense what it might be. She waited until Huldran and Cessya had lowered another iron funnel and plug plate into the first wagon, then said, "I need to check something. I shouldn't be too long."

"Yes, ser."

With that, Saryn eased down the slope, at enough of an angle, she hoped, that it wasn't obvious that she was more interested in the trio and Dealdron than in the newer guards toward whom her steps appeared to be directed. Although Dealdron still wore the heavy splint, he was moving more easily than he had an eightday earlier, and his blocks and parries were much surer. Dyliess was attacking him with her weighted wand, and, as sure as some of the young man's moves were, Dyliess still wove her wand through and around his efforts enough that she struck him on his good thigh once and got a solid crack on his ribs another time.

The use of order wasn't coming from Dyliess, Saryn realized, but from Aemra, who was somehow using it to help Dealdron anticipate Dyliess's attacks. She continued to try to sense what the youngest of the trio was doing, but from what she could tell, somehow Aemra was not so much guiding Dealdron's moves as making him more aware of what Dyliess was doing.

Saryn had never seen order-skills used quite that way, let alone by girls who weren't even properly women yet, but it was clear from the way Aemra was helping the Gallosian that she, and doubtless the other two, had been doing something like that for a time. If they had used that skill among themselves, that did explain why they performed so much better than would have been normal for even skilled junior guards.

Abruptly, Aemra glanced from Dealdron to Saryn, then back to Dealdron, but Dealdron did not falter, even when Aemra stopped helping him. He did get hit again, if by a glancing blow.

Saryn could only obtain the sense that Aemra was measuring something . . . and that it involved Saryn. Whatever heritage they had received from their parents, especially from their father, made it difficult, if not impossible, for Saryn to sense much of what Aemra was feeling, but then she had been able to do so less and less as the three had grown older.

"Aemra . . . a moment." Saryn's words were not a question.

"Yes, ser." The youngest of the trio walked away from the two who continued to spar.

"You were using a touch of order to help Dealdron learn moves."

"Yes, ser. We had to." Aemra kept her voice low, so low that Saryn could barely hear her. "He's strong enough, ser, but he doesn't have any sense of where the blades go, where they can strike. We're using a lot less. He's almost got it, now."

"Why?" asked Saryn.

"It's not like that, ser. He's . . ."

"Like a clumsy big brother," added Kyalynn, who had followed Aemra. Her voice was also low and intense, as if she didn't want Dealdron or anyone else but Saryn to hear. "He was going to get himself hurt bad if we didn't help." She shot a glance at Aemra.

Saryn caught that the look was a warning, but couldn't sense about what Kyalynn was cautioning the younger girl. "Does the Marshal know this?"

"No, ser," interjected Kyalynn. "Please don't tell her. We're almost done, and you wouldn't want him killed."

"We helped him enough so he can defend himself against lowlanders," added Aemra.

Saryn hadn't thought that Ryba would have Dealdron killed, but when order and her daughter were concerned . . . Still, while Saryn couldn't sense all that much from the trio, two things were clear. There was no love, lust, or romantic attachment involved, and the three really were just trying to give the young man what amounted to a chance at obtaining the skill to be able to defend himself.

"Why?" she repeated.

"Mother says . . . we need him, and so do you," replied Aemra. "We were just trying to help, because no one else was."

"He . . . he's like a puppy dog," added Kyalynn.

Saryn wanted to laugh at the efforts the two were making to conceal something, and she probably would have—if she'd been able to determine what they really had in mind. But she could only sense what they didn't have in mind. "What are you two hiding?" The question was worth asking, if only to see their reaction.

"We're not hiding anything," protested Aemra indignantly. "We're just trying to help you."

"If we get him so he can defend himself," added Kyalynn, "then he can do whatever you need him to do."

Both statements were true, and both girls believed them . . . but there was more, and Saryn knew she wasn't going to get to whatever else was there. She finally did laugh. "All right. Don't hurt him too badly, and listen to your mothers."

"Yes, ser."

Saryn turned away and started back toward the smithy.

"Saryn!"

At the sound of the Marshal's voice, the arms-commander turned again and headed toward Ryba, who was walking over from the east side of the practice field.

"What was all that about?" asked Ryba.

"I wanted to know how they felt Dealdron was coming and if he'd had enough training so that he could spend more time with Siret doing stonework."

A brief look of amusement crossed the Marshal's face. "He probably does know enough to defend himself. The girls can be quite thorough. How soon before you leave?"

"Another glass or so. We're loading out now."

"Good. I got another report. Arthanos is still getting supplies, and the scouts think he returned to Fenard. If that's so, we have several days, possibly more, but I'll keep you posted."

"I'd appreciate that," Saryn replied politely.

"It would still be good if you placed everything as soon as possible. Then take a position there and wait for us. Take care. I'll see you in about an eightday." With a nod, Ryba headed back toward Tower Black.

Saryn hurried toward the smithy and the carts, still pondering her exchange with the girls and Ryba's reaction. The Marshal could be most protective of the trio, and yet, for all of Ryba's former doubts and concerns about Dealdron, she hadn't seemed in the slightest worried about the three sparring with the young Gallosian. She'd been amused . . . but about what? It couldn't just have been about the bruises Dealdron was taking, could it?

Comforting as that might have been, Saryn didn't think so.

XXXIII

Eightday afternoon found Saryn stretched out on rough red rock, peering over the edge of a precipice, a rope fastened tightly around her chest. Some ten yards behind her, toward the center of the mesa, two guards from fourth squad held the other end of the rope. A chill wind whipped her short hair around her face as she tried to see down into a split in the rock a yard and a half in width. On the other side of the split was a stretch of rock some fifty yards in width, and a good two hundred yards from east to west.

Another gust of wind slammed into her, half-inflating the back of her riding jacket. She could feel the pressure of the wind lightening her body, as if trying to pull her away from the rock, but after a moment, the pressure lessened. She understood all too well why the top of the mesa was barren, except for a handful of stunted trees. Wind or no wind, she needed to find where to place the explosive penetrators, not only where they would dislodge the most rock but where she could make sure that the fuses could be lit with the right timing. She edged forward until her head was well out over the opening between the mesa and the spurlike section of rock, trying to see and sense whether the narrow crevice was wide enough to lower the penetrator into it as far as necessary and whether a targeted explosion would break the section loose.

She couldn't see any light farther down in the crevice, but there was a thin line of light halfway down on the north end that suggested that section might be easier to break away. She needed the bulk of the overhang to break loose, but that was the part opposite from where she was stretched out. If that section didn't break away, there wouldn't be enough rock cascading down into the valley below to reach the road with the volume necessary to be effective.

After easing back just a bit, Saryn tried to relax enough to let her senses probe the depths below. At first, she could sense nothing except small creatures she thought might be some form of bat. After a time, she began to sense faint lines, some of them more like dark gray, and others more a pinkish white gray. Below her, and to her right, near where she "felt" the crevice ended and the two sections of rock joined—or split, depending on which way she looked at it—there was a "knot" of both blackness and the faintest whitish red. Was that a vulnerable spot where she could place one of the penetrators? Or was it a stronger area that the chaos could not weaken?

Could she find a smaller area—a much smaller one—somewhere else on the mesa with the same sort of knot where she could experiment to see what the knot was? That would have to wait. She glanced at the sky to the west, which was darkening rapidly as a line of thunderheads began to build, as they often did in the afternoons over the Roof of the World. Finally, she rose to her feet and edged some fifteen yards to the north, until she felt she was standing above the knot. She slipped the charcoal-grease stick from its bag, then knelt and scrawled a large arrowhead, its tip pointing toward the juncture of order and chaos.

As she stood, another gust of wind buffeted her, and she crouched and moved back away from the edge of the cliff, moving carefully over the patches of crumbling rock. She glanced westward again. She had about a glass before the storm reached the mesa, and they needed to be off the exposed surface and back down in the rough rocky shelter they'd put up in the middle of some ancient twisted mountain pines in the saddle between the rise from the lower hills to the west and the mesa. The mounts and the wagons and carts were almost a kay farther down, because that was as far as anything with wheels could go and because there was no shelter at all for the horses any farther up the rocky saddle.

She hurried westward, back along the edge of the crevice another fifty yards or so, followed by the two guards holding the other end of the rope. Then she knelt, close to the middle of the long crevice, and again tried to sense the order below on the sides of the crevice. The dark gray and pinkish gray lines were almost random, and there were no junctures or knots.

She stood and moved back, then walked farther west, where she tried again. This time, she sensed another juncture, slightly less obvious than the first one. She took out the grease stick and marked the stone, then glanced northward. Dark sheets of water engulfed the peaks north of the hills on the other side of the valley. The grease ought to hold the marker in place, but, if not, she could always locate the junctures again, now that she had a fair idea where they were.

Her last attempt was near the end of the crevice, where it was barely a yard in width, but, as she suspected even before she tried to sense any weakness in the rock below, the patterns of darker gray were more defined—stronger, she thought—than those of the pinker gray. She stepped back and motioned to the two guards. "We're heading back down to the shelter."

"Yes, ser."

As she walked back toward the west end of the mesa, and the sloping, rocky, ridgelike saddle back down to the upper camp, she stopped. Had she sensed something like another juncture?

"Just a moment," she called to the two guards, even as she was moving toward the edge of the cliff. Since what she sensed was several yards, if not farther, below the lip of the cliff, she flattened herself and edged forward until she could look partway down. What she had found was an outcropping of rock projecting from the cliff some twenty yards below her. Over the years, the stone around the outcrop had peeled away, leaving a ledgelike formation a few yards long that projected out perhaps a yard and a half.

Saryn's problem was simple enough. She had no way to exert force on that outcropping to see whether the juncture she sensed represented strength or weakness. Although she was personally convinced it was weakness, she couldn't very well go on feelings alone when so much was at stake.

At that moment, several long rolls of thunder echoed across the valley toward the three guards. Saryn glanced northward. The storm was definitely moving quickly toward them.

"Frig . . ." How could she test her idea?

If the darker gray represented a form of order . . . could she somehow move it out of the juncture, divert it, smooth its flow into the cliff . . . and let the pinkish gray dominate?

Another roll of thunder washed over her, and she could sense the concern of the two guards at the other end of the rope. Saryn forced herself to concentrate on the order-chaos knot at the base of the isolated small ledge below her. While it *might* be easier to work on the pink, somehow, that didn't feel right. She took a slow breath, then used her senses to try almost to stroke the grayish order away from the juncture.

Another gust of wind whipped across her, stronger than any of those that had swept the top of the mesa earlier. She kept trying to ease the gray away from the pink, and several smaller strands retreated into the cliff proper . . . and re-formed, as if completing a circuit.

Crack. . . .

Saryn could feel the stone shudder beneath her, and reflexively, she grasped a stone protrusion in her right hand. The ledge slowly leaned out away from the cliff, then, after a second *crack*, dropped away and plummeted toward the scree nearly a thousand yards below. Saryn looked down to follow it . . . and wished she hadn't. The red chunks of rock at the bottom of the sheer drop looked incredibly distant. She quickly concentrated on easing back from the edge while keeping a firm handhold on the solid outcropping her right hand clutched.

At the same time, she couldn't help but wonder. In both atmospheric and space piloting, she'd had no problem in looking down; but on top of rocks on a planet that had no aircraft, she found being at the top of a cliff incredibly disconcerting.

She pushed those thoughts away as she stood and walked back toward the two guards. They needed to get off the mesa before the thunderstorm finishing crossing the valley and swept down on them.

"Any luck, ser?" asked Hoilya, the taller of the two guards and the one closer to Saryn.

"More than I'd hoped for, but we'll have to come back early tomorrow and start positioning the devices." That would be even more difficult than finding where to place them had been, Saryn suspected.

"We need to hurry," she added, as another roll of thunder announced the oncoming thunderstorm.

Heading down off the mesa, she couldn't help but wonder if order and chaos could be used like power flows, with variations on current and voltage. *But . . . order and chaos?*

XXXIV

Each of the penetrators had to be filled with powder, with the fuse placed and sealed with wax, even before any could be lowered into place. Saryn had had each one filled and fused, but not lowered, because the afternoon thunderstorms turned the crevice into a waterfall, and she couldn't be certain that the fuses would stay dry under such a deluge. Instead, they remained on a rocky rise on the mesa, covered with the personal tarpaulins of individual guards, which were waterproof enough to keep the devices dry. That meant, unfortunately, that Saryn and fourth squad would have to place each one essentially at the last moment, once they had word that the Gallosian forces were about to enter the valley. It also resulted in Saryn and those at the upper camp ending up wetter than they would have liked.

Slightly after noon on fourday, Saryn finished inspecting the penetrators and began to walk back westward on the mesa. Unlike many afternoons in the Westhorns, the sky remained clear, without any sign that an afternoon thunderstorm might be building. With luck, Saryn thought, there wouldn't be any more storms until the time came to place the weapons.

"Commander! The Marshal's headed up here." Thalya, one of the younger guards in fourth squad, ran from her observation post. "You can see her standard."

That meant Arthanos was on the march, but how far he was from the valley was another matter. Saryn picked up her pace, but Ryba and three guards had reined up short of the twisted pines and waited for Saryn. As Saryn neared, Ryba eased her mount forward.

"Marshal, welcome to one of the more lovely and fertile spots on the Roof of the World," offered Saryn sardonically.

"I can see that. How are you coming with the weapons?"

"We can't lower them into place until the day the Gallosians enter the valley. The thunderstorms drench where they need to be. But they're filled and sealed and in their harnesses near where they'll be placed. We've used most of our personal waterproofs to keep them dry."

Ryba merely nodded. "Arthanos and his army are moving westward along the route we anticipated. He could make the valley in two more days, but it might be three."

Saryn forbore to point out that Ryba, not Saryn, had been the one to foresee which of the three approaches the Gallosians would take. Instead, she said, "I thought I'd leave Klarisa here to light off the penetrators. That way—"

"You need to be here," Ryba interrupted. "Everything depends on the penetrators, and no one else has your skills."

"But as your arms-commander, I'm totally out of touch up here."

"I can rely on you, and none of the other guards really understand explosives."

All of what Ryba said was true, but it wasn't the whole story, Saryn knew. "What else?"

"I can't be certain matters will work out unless you're here. Besides, I'll have both the captains you trained."

"What exactly do you have in mind?" asked Saryn.

"A barricade across the road that will appear after we've cut off their advance company. It will look like a picket of pikes."

"Placed so as to slow them down and put them in a battle formation, where the easiest ground to flank us is south of the road on the sloping meadows where no one can hide?"

"Approximately . . . yes."

"How many men does he have?"

"He couldn't fill all the companies, it appears. There were still around eight thousand. There are a few less now. I'm having the best archers pick off as many officers and squad leaders as they can from a distance. That should give them the impression that we don't have the troops to fight a massed battle. It will also keep outliers close to the main formation."

Saryn turned and glanced back at the valley below and to her right. Not surprisingly, what Ryba planned wasn't all that different from what she'd had in mind.

"We had an interesting morning," Ryba said.

Saryn didn't like the way Ryba said "interesting," but she just looked back at the Marshal. The circles under the Marshal's eyes were dark, and a tracery of fine lines radiated from the corners of those eyes. Fine silver hairs were interspersed with the short jet-black. With a jolt, Saryn realized that Ryba was no longer young, something she had known, but not really felt. *Not until now.*

"We captured two Gallosian scouts. The older one was the obnoxious, dominating-male type. The younger one was just worried. Scared, even. The obnoxious one decided to tell me that Arthanos would torture me within a digit of my life for all that I'd done, and that I ought to let him go. Before he started talking, I'd thought about it, because releasing him would have confused them and showed a certain arrogance. But then . . . he spat at me."

Saryn winced.

"I changed my mind," Ryba continued. "Instead, I took off the battle harness and the dagger, and had them remove his scabbard and check him for hidden weapons. Then I told him that he could go free if he bested me, but that I'd kill him with my hands and feet if he couldn't. He couldn't wait to charge me. I smashed his knee, broke one arm, then the other. I could have broken his neck, but that wouldn't have done what was necessary. So I crushed his throat and let him suffocate. It didn't take very long."

"And you sent the other one back?" asked Saryn.

"I told him that was what an unarmed woman could do to the most experienced armsmen. Then I had Murkassa take him—and the broken body of the arrogant one—down to where he could ride and report to Arthanos. I told her, while he listened, to kill him if he didn't ride straight to the Gallosian lines."

"You're trying to infuriate them even more, aren't you?" asked Saryn.

"Fury weakens. It impairs judgment, and it burns out strength too soon. Besides, I'm tired of men who seem to think that might makes right but only when they have the might."

"They may kill the younger scout because he didn't fight," Saryn pointed out.

"They may. That's his problem and theirs."

Saryn saw no point in commenting on that. "You still haven't said when I'll know to light off the fuses on the weapons."

"We'll flash you with the mirrors. Just long flashes. From there." Ryba pointed to a low hillock on the south side of the road not far from the southern end of the mountain meadows.

"Won't the signaler have to get clear?"

"That hill is higher than it looks from here."

"What if there's no sun?"

"There should be," replied Ryba. "But if there's not, we'll torch a fire with a column of smoke—heavy smoke. I brought some oil mixtures that do that. Just make sure that they explode at close to the same time."

"I've timed the fuse burn rates, but it's still a guess. Some of the fuses have to be longer than I'd like."

"I'm sure you'll work it out. Remember, Saryn, the future of the Legend lies in your hands."

The future of the Legend?

"The Legend of Westwind and the hope of women on this forsaken world," Ryba added.

"It rests more on you," Saryn replied. "You're the one who created Westwind."

"And you'll help save it. You'll see." Ryba smiled, a trace sadly, then turned her mount. "We need to get back down. You understand why I came, I trust?"

"Yes." *To make sure I'll detonate the explosions that will destroy more than eight thousand men and who knows how many mounts.*

"Sometimes, there are no good choices, no matter what those who might follow will say."

As she watched the Marshal ride slowly downhill, Saryn shook her head. She had never envied Ryba, and she certainly didn't now.

XXXV

Even by midmorning on fiveday, Saryn was getting a bad feeling about the line of thunderstorms to the northeast. They looked darker than most, and she could hear the distant rumbling of thunder. Also, thunderstorms that formed earlier in the day were more severe. So far she'd had no word from the Marshal as to the progress of the Gallosian forces, but no news meant that Arthanos wasn't all that close. Not yet, anyway.

By just before noon, the line of thunderstorms had reached the other side of the valley opposite the mesa, and rain was beginning to fall there.

Saryn had been careful to place the penetrators on rock high enough not to be flooded but low enough that they weren't anywhere near the highest points on that part of the mesa. But still . . . she looked toward the oncoming ominous clouds and the sheets of rain that looked black in the gloom cast by the thick and towering clouds blocking the sun. The penetrator casings were iron, and there were far more lightning flashes than she'd yet seen in a mountain thunderstorm.

There certainly wasn't time to move the penetrators off the mesa, not when it had taken most of a day to get them up there, and with the intensity of the oncoming storm, Saryn wasn't certain that anywhere would have been safe. Probably she should have waited to cart them onto the mesa, but she'd always hated to be forced into doing anything at the last moment.

Now . . . by being too prepared, she might lose everything.

Could she use her skills with the "flow" of order to draw or keep the lightning bolts away from the penetrators? How? Was it even possible?

What was a lightning bolt? She didn't see how it could be order. Was it some form of chaos-bolt, like those flung by the white mages?

She walked hurriedly eastward toward the mesa, angling her path so that she reached a point just a few yards down from where the rock surface flattened into the mesa top and a handful of yards back from the cliff overlooking the valley. The gusting chill winds whipped at her, and she had to refasten her riding jacket. Then she sat down on one of the tumbled rocky chunks and concentrated on the nearest edge of the thunderstorm, no more than a kay away.

At first, all she could sense was a swirl of chaos. Rather than probe, she just let her senses absorb the swirling winds and water droplets. Before long, she began to grasp that, for all the chaos, there was a pattern there, and an interplay between order and chaos.

Cracckkk! A blast of energy slammed somewhere down into the valley, but it was close enough that for several moments Saryn heard nothing. Then tiny high-pitched bells rang in her ears before her hearing began to return.

Scattered rain droplets began to pelt her, and she tried again to absorb the pattern or patterns within the approaching thunderstorm. Somehow the water droplets collected or embodied order. That order was tossed up by chaos high into the storm, then dropped, only to be hurled upward once more. With each cycle, more order was gathered . . . and so was more chaos, except the chaos, she realized, was being drawn from the ground or rocks beneath the storm.

That's it! Lightning is chaos cloaked in order . . . and it actually flows in both directions at once. Somehow . . . somehow, she had to create enough of an order-barrier around the weapons so that the order strength of the storm wouldn't draw chaos from the mesa and through the iron casings of the penetrators, but from a point at least a few yards away from them.

She began to scramble over the rocky ground and bare rocks in the direction of the weapons. She didn't want to get too close, but she just couldn't handle order flows from a distance. Nylan might have been able to, but she didn't have his skills.

She stopped well over fifty yards from the weapons, dropping behind a block of red rock that offered protection from flying iron or lightning—she hoped. The rain droplets were falling faster and harder, and another roll of thunder shook the air. Saryn forced herself to concentrate.

First, she tried to sense any order-pathways around where the weapons were. There were only three, and they were faint. There didn't seem to be much chaos, either. But she could sense a distant rush of it moving from the north end of the mesa, as if it accompanied the wall of rain that had begun to sweep toward her and the weapons. All Saryn could think of was to try to braid the three faint order-pathways into a loose pattern around the penetrators. That might divert the buildup of chaos to another higher area of the mesa. If she could make it work . . .

She kept trying to reinforce those order-barriers while, all around her, a sort of pressure built, not order, but not exactly chaos, either. She felt as though she were being pressed into the rock, even while water poured down on her.

Crack! Crack! Crack! . . .

Scores of miniature lightning flashes—or slender reedlike stalks of order and chaos—flared across the higher rocky hump to the south of the waterproof-covered penetrators. The bitter smell of ozone—something she hadn't expected to smell again after she'd left the *Winterlance*—filled the air around her. At the same time, her ears reverberated. When the reverberations finally died away, and the rain subsided to something more like a shower, there was a deep silence—except that in the distance, she could hear the faintest roll of thunder. She glanced up and to the southwest. Another lightning bolt flared against a ridgeline of a peak perhaps three kays away, but the sound she heard was so faint that the lightning strike should have been more like ten kays away.

Soaked as she was, she needed to check the penetrators, especially the fuses, to make sure that the wind hadn't ripped them out of their oiled leather. So she extended her senses again—or tried to—except an unseen hammer slammed into her skull so hard that she staggered . . . and almost fell. For a moment, she just stood on the wet rock, water dripping off her, trying to gather herself together.

She'd seen Nylan collapse after using his skill with order too much, but that had been to destroy thousands. All she'd done was to divert a lightning bolt some twenty or thirty yards.

All? And just how much power is in one of those? She winced. She hadn't thought of it in quite that way.

After a moment, she edged toward the waterproof-covered weapons. They looked untouched, and there were no signs that the lightning had struck close. She certainly hadn't seen or felt it, but she could have missed a strike amid that last set of blasts. She paused. If any had been struck, shouldn't it have exploded? Or could the powder be slow-cooking?

She wished she could use her senses to check the penetrators, but even the thought of using them at the moment brought on a throbbing in her skull. Finally, she hurried toward the still-mostly-covered weapons. They were cool to the touch, and no water, or anything else, had gotten to the oilskin-covered and rolled fuse cables. After repositioning the water-proofs, she stepped back and glanced up. The northern sky was almost clear—a crystalline greenish blue, and the storms were already well to the southwest.

As she turned and walked carefully back over dampened, red sandy soil and rain-slicked red rock, she couldn't help but think about Ryba. After ten years of being Ryba's arms-commander, Saryn had come to assume, if tacitly, that Ryba's visions were true. What if they were not? And even if they were—this time—would what she saw always come to pass? Was that why Ryba kept most of them to herself? Somehow, Saryn doubted that Ryba had foreseen everything that had happened with Nylan.

She kept walking through the scattered droplets that were tapering off to nothing, making her way off the top of the mesa and down toward the upper camp. As she neared the twisted trees, she could see that a Westwind guard waited, her mount breathing heavily from the ride up the hills and over the shoulder.

Saryn waved and hurried toward the woman.

As Saryn drew closer, the guard said something, but Saryn couldn't hear the words. She stopped and looked closely at the guard. "I'm sorry. I didn't hear that."

"A message from the Marshal, ser."

Saryn only heard some of the words, but by watching, she got the meaning—or close enough, since the guard then extended a folded sheet of paper.

"Thank you." Saryn took the small square of paper and read Ryba's precise script.

> Commander—
> Arthanos will reach the pass at the end of the valley no later
> than noon tomorrow. So far, he has lost almost two compa-
> nies of cavalry.

Under the words was Ryba's seal.

Saryn could only hope that she didn't have to deal with another thunderstorm, especially at the time when the Gallosians finally reached the valley.

XXXVI

Saryn woke just after first light, cold, stiff, and sore. Her head still throbbed, if faintly, and her uniform was damp. The sky was as much gray as green-blue. Thankfully, Klarisa had detailed one of the guards to bring up the coals into a small fire. As she stood close to the flames, Saryn silently thanked the squad leader for the warmth. Three others from fourth squad stood around the fire, none close to the arms-commander.

Although it had not frosted, Saryn suspected that it had been almost that cold. The brisk wind out of the west made the air seem even more chill, though summer was almost upon the Roof of the World. But then, full summer wasn't all that warm on a mesa top in the heights of the West-horns. With a west wind, Saryn reflected, they were less likely to get a thunderstorm, but the valley below would be warm by afternoon, possi-bly almost hot—at least by angel standards, cold as it was before sunrise.

"Ser," Hoilya ventured, "how long will it be before the Gallosians reach us?"

"I'd guess today. It might be as late as tomorrow."

"Just as soon they get here," murmured one of the others. "Colder up here than doing picket duty at the stables . . ."

Not as cold as it will be if we don't get more quarters built and get people out of the stables. With that thought, Saryn turned from the fire to look down-slope at a rider she had just sensed, a guard pushing her mount as much as possible. That urgency suggested the guard bore news of Arthanos. Saryn waited, since the rider could cover the remaining distance far faster than could Saryn.

". . . wager she's going to tell us the Gallosian bastards are on the way . . ."

Saryn wouldn't have bet against the guard's aside.

When the rider finally neared, Saryn stepped away from the fire and walked several yards to meet her. "Greetings."

"Ser, the Marshal sent me. The Gallosians were less than ten kays from the east end of the valley when they made camp last night. They should reach the valley by late morning or midday. The Marshal requests that you be ready to act on her command by midmorning."

"Thank you. Once you've rested a moment, you can leave your mount and take one of our spares. You can tell the Marshal we will be ready for her command."

Saryn turned to call for Klarisa, but the squad leader was already hur-rying toward Saryn.

"We're to expect the Gallosians by midmorning. If you'd show the messenger which spare mount she can take to return to the Marshal, and then muster your squad up at the weapons. We need to lower the penetra-tors and set the fuses."

"Yes, ser."

Saryn turned and ran, if carefully, up toward the top of the mesa, then toward the northern edge, stopping when she could see the east end of the valley. The sun was beginning to clear the peaks to the east, and she had to squint to scan the thin line of brown that was the road, but there were no riders in sight, and she didn't see dust farther to the east. The thunderstorm of the afternoon before hadn't lasted that long, only enough to dampen the top of the ground, and the Gallosian army would raise some dust.

She doubted that the Gallosians were that close, since most commanders wouldn't begin a day's march through mountains in total darkness, and Arthanos would have had to start in darkness to reach the valley by sunrise. Even so, she and fourth squad couldn't waste time.

Why can't anything be easy? She shook her head. If they'd already placed the weapons the day before, the storm would have soaked them and the fuses. By avoiding that problem, they faced the difficulty of having to lower and position the penetrators on short notice. That didn't take into account the various ailments she had from having to protect the weapons from lightning. At least all the ropes and harnesses were ready to go. She took a last look at the eastern end of the valley, still in shadow, then hurried to the weapons cache. The last members of the squad slipped into the formation before the still-covered penetrators as she neared.

"Ser, fourth squad stands ready," Klarisa reported.

"Good. First, have them move the weapons to the marked staging points on the edges near the crevice. We'll move them all before we lower any into place."

"Yes, ser." Klarisa turned. "Uncover the weapons. Stack the waterproofs. Divona, Hoilya, Shenda, you take the first weapon. Agala, Yulia, and Rheala, you get the second one . . ."

Saryn walked swiftly toward the third marked location. That was a critical point. She had decided that two of the weapons were necessary there, one on each side of a slight bulge in the crevice wall. Lowering the second one into position on the west side of the bulge would be difficult because some two yards above where Saryn wanted to position the penetrator, the crevice narrowed to a point where it was only a few handspans broader than the weapon. She eased herself to the edge of the crevice and looked down, but it was hard to see in the early light. From what she sensed, no rocks or debris had fallen to block lowering the weapons. She straightened and headed back to the cache. She could carry ropes and harnesses.

By the time Saryn had the ropes and harness for the first two weapons in place, the rest of fourth squad had the weapons in the positions she'd marked with rocks and charcoal grease, and the guards were carrying the remaining ropes and harnesses into position. Saryn took several moments to check the valley. Still no sign of the Gallosians, for which she was grateful.

Once the harnesses were fastened around the weapons, the ropes tied to the harnesses, and all ready to be lowered into place, Saryn had Klarisa gather fourth squad. When everyone was there, she made her speech brief.

"We're going to lower the two weapons for the third position first, then those on the second, then the fourth, the first, and the fifth and sixth last. I'll be near the edge, and the squad leader will relay my instructions. Make sure you let the weapons down slowly . . . very slowly. One guard will have to hold and feed the fuse, and once the weapon is positioned, the ropes will have to be secured to the heavy stakes." She nodded to Klarisa. "That's all."

"You heard the commander. Let's go."

Saryn flattened herself on the uneven and rocky surface slightly east of where the guards would lower the weapon. Two guards eased the first of the two heavy penetrators out over the edge of the crevice drop-out, then positioned themselves to feed the thick rope and keep it from being cut by the stone as four guards behind them bore most of the weight of the weapon.

"A little more toward me!" Saryn watched the penetrator creep downward. "Good . . . a little slower now . . . hold it! Move it away from me, just a bit . . . That's it. Now, ease it down . . ."

Even though she wasn't the one lowering the weight and struggling with the ropes, and despite the cool breeze, Saryn was sweating by the time the first penetrator was lowered and secured. The second one took longer, with all the maneuvering around the narrow spaces above where she wanted it placed, but it, too, was in place before that long. The next four weapons were lowered into place and secured relatively quickly, all with the fuses set in place and held by stones until they were ready to be lit off.

With one to go and midmorning approaching, Saryn could definitely see a pall of dust rising from the road leading down into the east end of the valley. "Last one!" she called.

Because the sixth position, the one farthest to the west, was also the narrowest section of the crevice, it took much longer to lower and position the weapon, so much so that Saryn felt it had taken almost as long for that single penetrator as for all the others. So she was surprised, once it was secured with its fuse in position, to discover that, while the dust cloud had almost reached the valley, the Gallosians were not actually in the valley. From the east end of the valley to the section where Ryba had planned for the avalanche to strike was close to three kays, and that meant at least another glass, if not two, before Saryn had to light off the penetrators.

She turned to the squad leader. "We've got a glass or so. Have the squad pack up and have everything ready to go. We'll likely have to leave quickly once we're done."

"Yes, ser." Klarisa hurried off.

Saryn checked the small leather bag that held the striker and tinder and tied it shut. She fingered the smooth splinters of fatwood in her riding jacket, now open to the breeze, just to reassure herself that they were there. Then she blotted her forehead and turned from where she stood on the eastern end of the mesa to see if she could see the Westwind forces, but the road through the middle of the valley still looked clear. For a time, she watched, first checking the western end of the valley, then the eastern one. The western end seemed empty, but all that meant was that Ryba had her forces concealed, most likely in the forest north of the road. When exactly would Ryba bring the guards out of hiding and spring her defense to halt the Gallosian advance and force the Gallosians into a more concentrated formation?

"Everything's set for us to ride out, ser," said Klarisa from behind Saryn. "Do you see any of ours?"

"Not yet." Saryn squinted, then nodded. "Wait a moment. I can see their advance squad. It's about half a kay into the valley."

"You think the Marshal will try to pick them all off? So that no one gets back?"

"I'd guess so, but she didn't tell me what she plans." Saryn tried to moisten her lips, but her mouth was dry. "I'd better get some water. We could be waiting here for a while."

"I'll send one of the guards to get your water bottle."

"That might be best. Thank you."

For the next while, Saryn continued to watch the road, but the lead Gallosian squad rode onward, without opposition. Behind them, the first companies of the vanguard began to emerge from the wide pass. They did not stop, but continued along the road after the advance squad. Saryn checked the sky, but it remained a clear green-blue, with no sign of clouds and a steady brisk wind out of the southwest.

"Ser . . . your water bottle."

Saryn turned and took the bottle from the guard. "Thank you, Rheala."

"My pleasure, ser." After a moment, the guard asked, "How long will it be?"

Saryn shrugged. "It could be a glass, but it's more likely to be two or three."

"It doesn't take that long. You can see their lead squad is almost in the middle."

"No . . . but the Marshal will want all of the Gallosians, or as many of them as possible, in the middle of the valley before we strike. That will take longer. Once they discover we have guards there, and intend to make a stand, they might even stand down to rest their men. They might even wait an entire day."

"Would they wait to attack at dark?"

"That's unlikely. We're better in the dark, and Arthanos knows that. He could wait until tomorrow, though. We'll just have to see."

From her vantage point on the mesa, Saryn could make out several squads of Westwind guards emerging from the forest to the north of the road and swinging in behind the Gallosian advance squad. Then another squad rode out from the woods about half a kay in front of the Gallosians. While Saryn was too far away to see the details, several Gallosians toppled from their mounts. That had to be a result of Westwind archers. Several more Gallosians fell while the advance squad seemed to mill around. Then the remaining Gallosians turned back toward the main force—only to encounter more arrows and a charge from the force behind them.

Before all that long, the section of the road between the main Gallosian force and the hill that Ryba had pointed out to Saryn again appeared empty, with the dead and wounded dragged out of sight and the captured mounts led off. The Westwind forces were mustering on the west side of a rise in the road that was just high enough, Saryn judged, to keep them concealed from the oncoming Gallosian vanguard.

Saryn took several swallows from her water bottle and kept watching, with most of fourth squad circled loosely around her.

Almost a glass passed. All of the main Gallosian force was now in the valley, and the two full vanguard companies were within half a kay of the concealed Westwind force.

Whether the vanguard had scouts out, or sharp eyes, someone had clearly noticed something, because the Gallosians moved into an attack formation and simply kept riding toward the Westwind forces. Saryn didn't understand that strategy, unless Arthanos had calculated just how many Westwind women there were, and unless he felt that without the great male mage Nylan, Ryba was simply posturing. Whatever the reasoning, it was clear that the overall strategy was simply to keep attacking, beginning with the vanguard, until the force of numbers destroyed Westwind.

For the vanguard, that strategy was largely suicidal. After weathering a hail of targeted arrows, less than half the vanguard even closed with the Westwind companies, and many of those armsmen might have been wounded. In little more than half a glass, scattered handfuls of Gallosians were fleeing eastward, and the rest were dead or otherwise out of combat.

Within moments, a set of wagons appeared, moving forward of the Westwind positions, where guards began placing frameworks across the road and in a semicircle around the crest of the valley road. Saryn continued to watch as the Westwind guards stood down, remaining in a loose formation visible for at least a kay to the east. All the time, the main body of the Gallosian forces continued westward, with cavalry leading the way, followed by marching armsmen, with another set of cavalry troopers behind. In the rear came close to twoscore supply wagons.

As noon came . . . and went . . . the Gallosians kept moving toward the Westwind defenses. Once they were within clear sight, they halted, then re-formed, with the foot moving to the front and taking the road and some distance on each side of it, and the cavalry flanking the foot, if with the larger portion on the open south side.

Ryba had either judged Arthanos correctly—or her visions had been accurate in regard to the Gallosian strategy. Arthanos was not even attempting finesse. He knew how few the Westwind guards were and intended to overwhelm them by sheer force of numbers.

Then . . . a flash of chaos flared across the Westwind pike line, and flames and ashes rose. When the flames died away, and the smoke and ashes had been blown clear, a large gap appeared in the framework of pikes. The Gallosian forces continued to advance, and a second chaos-bolt transformed another section of the wooden piles into flame, ashes, and charcoal.

"They've got mages, ser," offered Klarisa, her voice worried.

Saryn nodded. "Let's hope they don't have too many." Arthanos had at least one white mage. That was why he was so confident. The mage—or mages—had to have determined that there were no mages among the Westwind fighters. And there were not, because, while Istril and Siret were in the valley, they were being held back for healing afterward. There was no point in wasting either in battle, because at most they could kill a single Gallosian, and then they'd be useless as healers for some time. While Saryn had some abilities along those lines, she'd certainly never faced a chaos-wielder, and she was kays away from the battle.

"How long now, ser?" asked the squad leader.

"I'd guess another quarter to half glass, but it depends on how fast the Gallosians move." *And when Ryba signals.* Saryn glanced toward the hillock that Ryba had pointed out. While she could make out riders and mounts there, no one was signaling, not that Saryn expected a signal yet. The rear of the Gallosian forces was not yet far enough into the valley, and the cavalry and the footmen at the front had not yet even reached the smoldering and useless wooden pikes.

Ryba couldn't have foreseen the mages. She wouldn't have wasted the effort to build the pike frameworks, ruses or not. Saryn frowned. *Or would she?*

Ryba did not order a charge, and the mounted guards remained shielded by the crest of the hill—for the moment.

Saryn could see that Ryba had ordered the archers to fire again, because some of the cavalry fell, and there were places in the Gallosian lines where the advance slowed. Then, still shielded by the hill, the Westwind guards wheeled and began to ride to the southwest, directly toward the hillock from which the signal was supposed to come. The Gallosians continued to advance along the wide front, as if no one had noticed anything at all.

The cavalry on the meadows to the south of the road began to move more rapidly. That made sense, because they were higher and were the first to see the Westwind withdrawal. The lines of the Gallosian mounted forces became even more ragged, while the Westwind guards rode up the hillock and re-dressed their lines—in the staggered fashion that would allow them to fire shafts downhill at the attackers.

How long before Ryba signaled? Saryn glanced to the east end of the valley. Most of the armsmen in the main body of the Gallosian forces were well within where the avalanche would sweep—if Ryba's visions were right . . . if Saryn's judgments on where to place the weapons happened to be accurate . . . if she had calculated the fuse burn times correctly . . .

So many ifs . . .

The Gallosian cavalry hadn't reached the foot of the hill that held the Westwind contingent . . . not yet. Ryba hadn't signaled. How long should she wait? Saryn asked herself.

Her eyes focused on the Gallosian forces. Some were clearly being taken down by Westwind shafts, but the losses scarcely slowed the mass of men and mounts pressing toward the base of the hill.

A flash of something flitted past Saryn, and she immediately looked directly to the top of the hillock, concentrating intently. For a time she could see nothing. Then the light flashed past her again, and she realized that Ryba, or whoever was using the mirror, was sweeping the mesa, as if she could not see where Saryn and fourth squad were.

Saryn immediately moved to the fuse on the first penetrator, opened the leather bag, and removed the striker and the tinder. It took several strikes before the tinder caught, but once it did, she immediately slipped one of the fatwood splinters from her jacket and held it over the tinder, waiting until it was burning brightly. Then she lit the first fuse.

"Fourth squad! Back!" she ordered as she stood.

She walked swiftly to the second fuse and lit it, then the third and fourth, close together, and after them, the remaining three. Following her own advice, she moved back from the edge of the mesa and knelt, waiting, hoping that the weapons would work . . . and work as planned. If not, almost all of the Westwind guards would be overrun and slaughtered—unless they fled . . . and that would only prolong the eventual outcome . . . all that if Saryn could not trigger the avalanche necessary to wipe out most of the Gallosians.

She could sense the running reddish chaos of the fuses, and all felt as though they were burning at almost the same rate, and that they would trigger the penetrators at close to the same moment. Just before the fuses burned down to the penetrator casings, Saryn found herself holding her breath.

Whummmp! Whump! Whump! . . .

The entire mesa seemed to rock with the force of the explosions, but that was only the sound, Saryn realized, and all she felt was the slightest tremor from the stone beneath her feet. Small fragments of rock pelted down on and around her, and reddish dust puffed up from the north side of the mesa. A faint rumbling growled away from her, then subsided.

Saryn could sense that most of the overhang remained in place, although some of the stone had fragmented away.

Now what?

She had no more explosives, not to speak of, and no more penetrators in which to place them, and certainly not enough time to do either. But she *had* to do something. She had to.

She didn't even look into the valley. There was no time for that. She walked quickly to the edge of the crevice, just opposite the largest bulge in the overhang, stopping just a yard or so back from the break in the stone. She tried to feel the junctures of order and chaos. Four of them were gone—the ones targeted by the first, fourth, fifth, and sixth penetrators. The second juncture was there, but so weak that it was more like a tangle of strands of order and chaos.

Saryn had no idea how to break the bonds holding the mass of rock to the mesa, but she had to find a way . . . and quickly. She'd changed the flow of the order-lines around the penetrators to protect them from the lightning. Could she change the flows around the junctures so that the order and chaos didn't intertwine?

She immediately reached out with her senses to the weaker juncture and began to ease the dark gray strands away from the pinkish gray ones. The effort was more like trying to move water with a rake or fan air with a small leafless branch . . . or part hair with a toothless comb.

Still, after a moment, the weaker tangle separated, but the strands immediately re-formed—flowing around the single remaining juncture, which began to vibrate. Saryn turned her efforts to the remaining juncture, pressing harder, smoothing, parting the currents, or the strands, edging the flows away from each other, and yet, as she did, she realized that the separate flows became stronger, as if parallel flows of order and of chaos were stronger. As each dark strand separated from what seemed to be its complementary pinkish gray one, Saryn could sense a growing reddish white ball of chaos growing around the disintegrating juncture, yet somehow contained—if barely—by a ball of grayish order.

As the last strand flowed away, Saryn could feel the chaos flaring toward an intense whitish red . . . and she instinctively flattened herself on the stone, yelling, "Down! Everyone! Get down!"

The explosion that followed shook the entire mesa, and was so massive and loud that Saryn heard nothing at all. Just silence, and pressure.

Then a second blow hammered her into the rock, and her skull felt like it was being split in half. At the same time, rock fragments pelted down and kept pelting down. Although her eyes were closed, Saryn felt as though scores of invisible needles were jabbing through them and into her brain.

Then . . . she felt nothing.

Dampness on her face brought her back.

"Ser . . . ser . . ."

Someone was pressing a damp cloth across her forehead, and she was lying on her back.

"I'm . . . all right." She wasn't. Not exactly. Her head was splitting, far worse than when she had tried to manipulate where the lightning struck, and her eyes were tearing so badly that she could see almost nothing but blurred colors and figures.

Slowly, she sat up. "It broke loose, didn't it?" She looked at the guard she thought was Klarisa.

"Yes, ser."

Saryn struggled to her feet. Even without her numbed senses, she could feel the fear in the squad leader. She blotted her eyes. After several moments, she could see, if intermittently, since her vision blanked out with each unseen hammerblow on her skull, but she could tell the large section of the mesa was gone. Where the crevice had been was the mesa's edge.

Klarisa looked at Saryn, then down at the valley.

Saryn turned. The entire middle section was shrouded in brown-and-gray dust.

Shrouded . . . a good word.

"Ser . . . what did you do?" the squad leader finally asked.

"What had to be done." Saryn looked down into the slowly clearing dust, watching as the higher ground of the hillock finally emerged. While it was surrounded by tumbled rock, stone, and earth, fighting continued on the slopes, where at least a company of the Gallosian cavalry had managed to ride high enough to avoid being swept away by the tide of rock and stone.

Saryn felt helpless, but there was nothing else she could do, only watch. Even if she had been down in the valley, her head throbbed so much that she knew she wouldn't have been any good in a battle, or not much. Had Ryba guessed that? Saryn frowned. That couldn't be, because if Saryn hadn't had to use her skills to help the penetrators, she wouldn't have had the headache . . . but then most of Arthanos's army would have escaped.

The end of the fighting did not last that long, endless as it seemed to Saryn, and, finally, Saryn could see a few Gallosians—both mounted and on foot—scrambling onto the rocks below the hillock, trying to escape the remaining guards. She turned her head away, not really wanting to think about the casualties—on either side.

"Ser? It looks like the Marshal won . . . didn't she?" asked Klarisa.

"We survived . . . and they didn't." *For now.*

Would it always be like that? Winning by destroying massive forces and taking huge losses in the process? Why, when everyone would have been better off without such battles?

Abruptly, she looked back toward the easternmost part of the valley—and saw nothing. As her vision returned, she made out a company of Westwind guards emerging from the forest on the northern side of the road and bearing down on the ten or so supply wagons that had not been engulfed in earth and rock. The remaining Gallosians were scattering.

"Klarisa, we need to mount up and head down there. We can't do any more here, and they'll need us." Saryn walked back down to the upper camp and her mount, without an answer to her questions.

XXXVII

By the time Saryn and fourth squad had descended from the mesa and ridden down the next set of slopes, then made their way along the road until they had nearly reached the western end of the mass of churned rock and earth and sand—a half kay west of the hillock—the sun had dropped behind the western peaks and ridges, and the entire valley lay in shadow. Because her vision continued to vanish unpredictably, Saryn was forced to rely on Klarisa.

Ryba rode up to meet Saryn, easing her mount to a halt, almost stirrup to stirrup with the younger woman. "I knew I could count on you. You had trouble, didn't you?"

"Yes." After the ride, and the events of the past two days, every part of her body ached, her head and eyes most of all. "We managed. How about you?"

"All told, we lost thirty-one guards." Ryba's voice was hoarse.

"How many of the Gallosians survived?"

"We don't know for certain, but no more than a few hundred. A handful rode north and managed to get onto a few higher places, and the last two companies—his rear guard—managed to escape. I didn't have second company chase them. The wagons were more valuable." Ryba frowned. "It's going to be the demon's own time getting them over or around that mess you created. It might take days."

"What about our wounded?" Saryn lost her vision again, with another thunderclap inside her skull.

"There are another forty or so, but the healers tell me that most of them will make it." Ryba's voice was hoarse. "The ones who died—they were more than a tenth of all those at Westwind, and that doesn't count the wounded. Gallos has to lose nine or ten thousand men before it's a serious loss. Every loss is still serious to us."

"They won't try again, not soon."

"Thanks to you, no. Not for another few years, or a generation at most, before some other younger son or hothead decides that having a land ruled by women is insufferable to the mighty male ego." Ryba's voice dripped with acid bitterness.

At that moment, Saryn's vision flickered back, and she saw the heavy dressing on Ryba's upper left arm. "You were in the front lines, weren't you?"

"Second line, but one company of theirs was good. Not as good as us, but much better than anything we've seen."

"One of those special companies," suggested Saryn.

"In the end, it didn't matter. They all died, too."

"All of them?"

"They couldn't face the fact that they weren't that special. Not one would surrender. There seems to be a certain disgrace to being bested by a woman at arms." Ryba snorted.

"So . . . you didn't spare anyone?"

"I'm not that cruel, no matter what Arthanos told his men. There are close to a hundred wounded and fifty who did yield. We took their weapons, and let them have two of their wagons and sent them back to Karthanos. I also sent a message with them, suggesting that peace would be far less costly than war. I also said we had no intentions on his lands, but that we would suffer none on ours, nor on traders or others who wished to travel the Westhorns."

"Will he get it?"

"I had Istril with me. I gave it to a wounded undercaptain. She said he was honest and would deliver it." Ryba's smile was twisted. "We will see."

"What about their mages? How many did they have?"

"Two, I think. Chaos-fire isn't that effective against an avalanche." Ryba paused. "I'm going to take two squads, along with the wounded, and head back to Westwind first thing in the morning with Siret. I'm leaving you in charge here to manage getting the Gallosian wagons to the road and acting as our rear guard."

"I can do that," Saryn said dryly. *But I'll need someone who can see all the time.*

"I know. I need to think about the Suthyans." Ryba laughed, sardonically and hoarsely. "We can't block every road in the Westhorns, or we won't have either travelers or trade."

Saryn looked pointedly at Ryba's bound arm, only to find that, again, she saw nothing except a sparkling blackness punctuated with what felt like blows to her skull and eyes. "Are you sure you're all right?"

"It's only a slash. Istril says that it will heal but not to use it for a while."

"Please don't." From the pallor Saryn had seen briefly in Ryba's face and the tiredness in her eyes and posture, Saryn had the impression that the Marshal's wound wasn't just a slash. She couldn't use her own senses to tell, not at the moment, and she wondered how long it would be before she regained her own abilities.

"I doubt that I could. If you'd look things over and take charge, I'd appreciate it." Ryba paused. "Hryessa and first company are east about a hundred yards."

As the Marshal turned her mount, Saryn tried to extend her senses, since her sight had not returned, and before dizziness and pain washed away her perceptions, felt another locus of chaos, and a splint of sorts, on Ryba's lower right leg. *Second line?* As she forced herself to try to relax, Saryn had her doubts about that.

She had to wait for a time before her sight returned, and she could urge the gelding forward, riding toward several wagons and what looked to be a camp ahead on the right side of the narrow road.

Hryessa was mounted, and when she caught sight of Saryn, rode to meet the arms-commander, easing her mount around the end of one of the wagons. As the captain neared, Saryn reined up. She could see several guards stretched out in the wagon, one with a dressing that covered her entire upper face.

"Arms-commander, you are back. When the top of the mountain exploded, we feared that none would survive and return."

"It wasn't as bad as it looked," Saryn replied. "How bad was it here?"

Hryessa reined up close to the arms-commander. "It was terrible, but our guards, they were magnificent. The Gallosians were beasts. Some had sabres smeared with poison, and others . . ." She shook her head. "I worried that the Marshal waited too long, but she did not. If she had called for you to bring down the rocks any earlier, there would have been many more Gallosians who escaped their fate."

"Where did you come up with that last company to take the wagons?"

Hryessa grinned. "We used barely trained junior guards, but they were led by first squad. The Gallosians in the rear were not thinking after they saw their army disappear under the rocks."

"Was that your idea?"

"I offered it to the Marshal. She agreed. It was a long wager, but we need the supplies."

"I'm certain we do. The Marshal will be taking two squads and the wounded back tomorrow. We have the task of salvaging everything we can and getting those supply wagons from the other end of the valley here."

"I already have guards searching for the best path through the woods."

Saryn smiled. "You're ahead of me."

"Is that not what a captain is for, ser?"

"A good one, and you are," Saryn said with a laugh she did not feel, as her vision vanished again, and she swayed in the saddle.

XXXVIII

All in all, it took nearly two full days for Saryn and the remaining healthy Westwind guards to reorganize and to move the ten supply wagons less than three kays through the woods, as well as collect anything useful that could be reclaimed from the avalanche and from what the surviving Gallosians had discarded in their flight. Personally, Saryn suspected that the fifty-odd Gallosian mounts they had captured might well prove to be of the greatest value, those and the supply wagons themselves, since they would allow Westwind to send its own traders out with enough cartage capacity to bring back meaningful quantities of goods.

Finally, at first light on oneday morning, they set out on the return journey to Westwind. Saryn rode just behind Hryessa's first squad, which provided the outriders and scouts and served as vanguard. Beside her rode Istril, since Hryessa was leading the vanguard.

Saryn said little for the first several glasses after they left the valley, lost as she was in her thoughts about the battle. She really hadn't had time to think about it since she'd rejoined the main force, not with all that she had been required to organize and supervise, not to mention that she had worried that some of the Gallosians might turn into marauders, whom she wouldn't have been able to discover. Her ability to sense anything without blinding herself or risking unconsciousness had only begun to return late on eightday, and she hadn't pressed herself. She still had spells during which she could not see.

On one level, she understood why Arthanos had tried to destroy Westwind, but she had trouble understanding emotionally. Even if he had succeeded, he would have lost hundreds of men, if not thousands . . . and for what? To destroy only a few hundred women in the middle of mountains that no one really wanted? Was it an attempt at revenge for the fact that Balyea—his former mistress—had left him for Westwind? Saryn almost couldn't believe he had mounted such a massive campaign because he opposed a tiny land where women ruled . . . and yet she could.

"You're deep in thought, ser," Istril finally said.

"I'm still having trouble with the idea that a ruler's son would sacrifice thousands because he couldn't stand a few women who didn't have to bow and bend to men."

"There are men like that everywhere. Some places have more, some less, but all have some. It's not just men, either. Some women would like it the other way."

"It's a sad comment on people."

"Everyone wants to be in charge."

Saryn wondered about that. Did everyone want to be in charge, or did most people just want control over their own lives?

When she did not say anything, and the silence dragged out, punctuated only by the sound of hoofs on the road, Istril spoke again. "It's a good thing you were the one on the mesa to loose the rocks. You had to use order and chaos in addition to the explosives, didn't you?"

Saryn glanced around. No one else was riding that close to them. She nodded. "Some."

"More than some. I could sense it down in the valley. So could Siret."

"I'm not like the engineer," Saryn protested. "It was nothing compared to what he did."

"No, you're not. What you did was different. But it wasn't nothing. The entire side of the mesa exploded. It was loud enough to stop everyone for several moments."

And then the killing resumed. Saryn's smile was bitter. Who was she to talk about other people's killing? "I couldn't hear for a while."

"I can imagine. It was worse than that, wasn't it? You're still pale . . . order-frayed, and it's almost three days later. You lose your sight at times, don't you?"

"I can't complain. I survived in one piece, and thousands didn't."

"That's true, but you paid in a different way. People who use a lot of order or chaos do. But you're not quite like either the engineer or Siret or me, or even the white mages. You're not black, and you're not white. There's a grayness around you, and it's getting stronger, and your eyes, they're sort of silvery instead of straight gray. What does it feel like?"

Grayness? "I hadn't even noticed it," Saryn admitted.

"I'd suggest you do." Istril's words were gentle. "How do you see order and chaos?"

"Order . . . chaos—they're more like flows . . . like winds through the air or water through the ground . . . or even unseen electrical fields or currents . . ."

Istril frowned. "I don't sense it that way. Siret doesn't, either, and neither did Nylan or Ayrlyn. Flows?"

Saryn nodded. "The order or chaos in or around things . . . they just look like they're stationary, but they're really not. Everything is moving, all the time. That's the way it seems, anyway. That could just be me, though."

"How could everything be moving? There's order and chaos: But cold iron, it has order in it, and it doesn't move."

Saryn shrugged. "I can't explain it. That's just the way it seems to me." She wasn't about to try to explain how to integrate magic and higher-level physics on a world that half the time she wasn't sure even ought to exist— except that she'd seen and felt . . . and caused . . . enough death to know that it was a *very* real world.

"I don't think anyone's going to argue with what you did, ser. Or how you did it. They're just glad you did."

"No. The Marshal just wants results." *And she's never much cared how she gets them.*

"That's true of most people who run things," Istril pointed out.

Am I like that? Saryn smiled sardonically. She hadn't cared all that much about all the deaths she'd caused with her use of order and chaos flows—just that she wiped out Arthanos's army. But still . . . She shook her head. She had more than a little thinking left to do, but that could wait . . . for a while.

"Do you think most of the wounded will recover?" she asked.

"Most, but some won't ever use an arm or a leg right again, and some probably won't think very well . . ."

XXXIX

By fiveday morning, three days after Saryn had returned to Westwind, matters seemed to have settled back close to the normal routine. Saryn stood on the northern side of the arms practice field, her back to the smithy uphill behind her, looking out across the guards as they gathered for the morning exercises and drills. The first thing that struck her, as it had every morning since her return, was the smaller numbers of guards on the field, almost a third fewer, as a result of deaths and casualties. The second was that Dealdron, who now wore a lighter splint on his leg, was lined up behind all the junior guards, looking directly at her.

She ignored his scrutiny and began her own exercises. Only after the exercises and after she'd sparred two rounds with Hryessa did she look again in Dealdron's direction.

The younger man was being pressed by two of the trio simultaneously, and for a moment Saryn wondered why, since he certainly wasn't as skilled as any of the three. But as she watched, she realized they were putting him through a defensive drill, where he was only to block all attacks. He did not block all of them, but he had definitely improved. At the same time, while his movements were precise and even smooth, there remained an awkwardness about them.

From Istril's reminders, and her own nagging conscience, she knew she had to talk with Dealdron, and before long, but that conversation was something she had put off. She knew she could do that no longer.

"The Gallosian won't make an armsman," said Ryba from behind Saryn's shoulder. "Not if he practices for years." The Marshal wore a light splint on her leg and a dressing on her arm.

"No," replied Saryn, "but he's better than some of the Gallosians and Lornians, and he wouldn't get slaughtered out of hand now. His defense is better than his attacks."

"He's strong enough that he gives the girls an understanding of why technique is important. They'll need that. For such, the Gallosian is useful."

That was about as much acceptance as Saryn was going to get from Ryba about letting Dealdron remain at Westwind. "He's been helping both Siret and Vierna."

"He's trying to earn his keep, unlike some men."

"Like Gerlich and Narliat?" While Saryn thought the veiled reference was to the two who had deserted Westwind, only to recruit locals to try to overthrow Ryba, she wanted the Marshal to make it clear that she wasn't referring to Nylan.

"Exactly. The engineer worked hard. I'm not that petty, Saryn."

"I'm sorry." *How am I ever to know? Sometimes you are, and sometimes you're not.*

"I have to be hard, Saryn, but I try not to be petty or small. You will see, in your time. When a woman leads, even other women, anything less than firmness is weakness. Westwind cannot afford any impression of weakness. Arthanos thought we were weak because we had not shown great power in close to ten years. Power must be exercised to be believed, especially in dealing with men." Ryba's voice softened. "That will be hard for you, because you try to be fair, and fairness can also be viewed as weakness, especially in this world."

"I've seen that."

"You have, but you will come to feel it as well. It can make you bitter and force you to question the worth of what you do. Do not let the questions overwhelm you." Abruptly, the Marshal smiled, and her tone lightened as she spoke. "I sound like a Rationalist preacher. I didn't mean to. I'll see you later."

"Yes, ser." Saryn nodded as Ryba turned and began to walk, limping, uphill toward the road and the stables.

After keeping the guards exercising at arms for a bit longer, Saryn dismissed them to their duties, then headed down the road and across the causeway. When she strode into Tower Black, she nearly ran into Istril, who was carrying a basket of dried herbs, possibly brinn.

"You look like you're headed to battle or an execution . . . but don't worry," offered the healer, "Ryba's already left for the ice fields."

"I know. I hadn't planned to talk to her."

"Well . . ." said Istril with a smile, "if you're looking for Dealdron, he's already up at the quarry. He always walks straight up there after arms practice."

"Is he still sleeping in the carpentry shop?"

"You haven't looked?"

"I've been occupied."

"What do you have against him?" asked Istril gently. "You're the one who saved him."

"He looks at me as if . . . I don't know."

"As if he's grateful? As if he's trying to prove to you that he was worth saving?"

"Something like that," Saryn admitted.

"Little Adiara accepts him, without reservations, and she lost her family to the Gallosians he was ostler for. Why can't you?"

Saryn didn't have an answer. Finally, she shrugged. "I don't know. There's . . . something there."

"Well . . . he is handsome in his own way," Istril pointed out with a mischievous smile.

"I know, but it isn't that."

The healer nodded. "He'll be able to do without that splint in another few eightdays."

"And?"

"That's all." Istril smiled again.

Saryn couldn't read what lay behind the smile, not with the shields that the healer had raised, and that bothered her. "Thank you."

When she left the tower, Saryn walked directly up the road past the smithy. She glanced to her right as she did, seeing a good half score of guards working on setting and mortaring stones on the barracks wall, under Daerona's direction. She paused. From where had the mortar come? Dealdron? At that thought, her vision vanished.

She took several deep breaths, then walked more carefully. After perhaps ten yards, she could see again. Once she reached the quarry, she found Siret busy dressing stones, but the stonecutter and healer stopped and motioned Saryn toward her.

"How is Aemra coming with her sculpture of her mother?" asked Saryn.

"She's polishing it. It should be finished by full summer." Siret paused. "He's over at the other end, setting wedges."

"He's helpful, I take it?"

"Good enough that I can spare Daerona to do the stone-setting and mortar on the barracks walls. Aemra helps up here with the stone dressing."

"Where did the mortar come from?"

"Where do you think it came from?"

Saryn shook her head, ruefully. "How is the stonecutting coming? Will you have enough to finish the new barracks before winter?"

"If we don't run into trouble. We've got almost enough for the rear wall now. Daerona claims she'll have three courses set all the way around by the end of the eightday. After that, things will slow because we'll be out of mortar."

"He'll have to go down to the canyon and make more. That will slow the quarrying."

"For now. He's working with a couple of the Analerian women who are strong enough to handle the quarrying. By midsummer, they might be some real help." Siret nodded.

Saryn understood. She was just slowing Siret's work. "Thank you." She turned and walked to the west end of the quarry.

When Dealdron saw Saryn standing there, he set down the heavy sledge and walked to meet her. "Arms-commander."

"Were you the one who made the mortar while most of the guards were gone?"

"It was not that hard." Dealdron shrugged. "No one was using the kilns, and there is a thin layer of limestone in the lower cliffs. It is almost buried under the other rock. Many stones were cut and waiting to be placed in the barracks walls. Without mortar, the walls could not be built. The girls helped me cut the wood. It would have been better to make charcoal first, but it can be done with green wood. I showed them how."

Saryn tried to sense what he was feeling . . . and discovered that trying to do so was like trying to peer through mist. *Why?* He wasn't a mage, and he didn't have unseen darkness clinging to him the way Istril and Siret, or even Ryba, did, although the Marshal's talents did not seem to run to manipulating order or chaos. Was it just that he was what he claimed to be, a simple ordered man? And that simplicity and order made it hard for Saryn to sense his feelings? Or was there just a hint of order-darkness?

"Ser?" prompted Dealdron. "Have I offended you? Or failed in some way?"

Saryn realized that she'd just been looking at him, saying nothing, and she forced a pleasant smile. "No. You have worked very hard. Even the Marshal has said that you have made yourself very useful, and from her, that's high praise."

"I have tried to follow what you told me."

"You've done well," Saryn admitted. "I should have told you that sooner, but I . . . my thoughts have been elsewhere."

"You were worried about Arthanos." His words were but a statement of fact. He smiled. "I did not think he would prevail."

"Why not?" asked Saryn, genuinely curious.

"No one in Candar, perhaps in all the world, can stand against you and the Marshal. That I have seen."

Even through the sense-mist that was not quite an order shield, Saryn could make out the conviction and belief behind the words. "We're not that powerful."

"The guards said you tore down the side of a mountain and flung it at Arthanos's men."

"It wasn't exactly like that," Saryn tried to explain. "There was already a crevice in the rock, and we used explosives . . . and other skills . . . to weaken it so that it fell and rolled down the mountainside and over the Gallosians."

Dealdron frowned. "Could anyone else have loosened part of a mountain and let it fall on an army?"

Saryn forced a laugh. "I wouldn't know, and I don't think I'd like to find out." After the briefest pause, she asked, "How is your leg?"

"The healers say that I will not need the brace before long."

"You'll still have to be careful."

"I will take care. I haven't done anything the healers told me not to do."

"Good." Again, she paused. "That's all I wanted to talk to you about. Just keep up the good work."

"I can do no less, Arms-Commander." He inclined his head politely.

Saryn sensed there were words not spoken, but she did not press. Instead, she turned, but she could feel his eyes on her back as she began the walk back to the smithy, where she needed to check with Huldran on the progress in forging replacement arrowheads for all those lost in fighting the Gallosians.

XL

Over the next eightday, matters remained quiet on the Roof of the World. The air warmed into summer, and Dealdron headed down into the lower canyon with the trio and other guards to make more lime for mortar. The less-severely-wounded guards resumed their duties, and progress on the new barracks, which would be, in time, the lower level of a much larger complex, continued. Saryn had very few losses of vision, and only for a few instants. Just after midday, she was standing outside Tower Black, enjoying the sunshine and taking a break from what she had been doing—sharpening blades.

"Saachala had a little girl this morning," said Istril as she joined Saryn.

"How are they?"

"Both are fine."

"Ryba will be happy with that."

"So is Saachala. She still wishes she could have ridden against the Gallosians."

Saryn could understand Saachala's hatred, considering the reason the young woman had come to Westwind pregnant. "She'll have years of dealing with them."

"How long do you think they'll behave?" asked Istril.

"Another ten years, fifteen if we're fortunate."

"You're as cynical as the Marshal."

"Realistic," countered Saryn. Even in the UFA, she'd seen the subtle discrimination against women. Had a man accomplished what Ryba had done as commander of the *Winterlance*, he would have been a flotilla marshal at the least, and the UFA was almost chauvinism-free compared to

Candar. But then, Candar hadn't had to deal with Sybran warrior-women, and the UFA had. "Cultures don't change easily, sometimes never, unless great force is applied, and Ryba can't do that yet, except once in a while."

"You mean you can't. She couldn't have done it without you."

"Let her take the credit."

"Or the blame?"

"Either way."

Abruptly, Istril gestured. "The road patrol is bringing someone in under a parley flag."

"Gallosians, you think? Who else would need a parley flag?"

"We'll see."

Almost a quarter glass passed before the riders reined up on the causeway outside Tower Black. There were but four men, three armsmen and an older man in a more formal uniform.

Klarissa was the squad leader at the head of the detachment, and she inclined her head. "This is Arms-Commander Saryn, second only to the Marshal in Westwind."

Saryn straightened.

The officer, whose brown beard bore traces of white, bowed his head to Saryn. "Commander, I have a message from the Lord-Prefect of Gallos for the Marshal of Westwind."

"I'd be happy to present it to her," said Saryn.

"I have been ordered to wait for her response, Commander."

Saryn looked squarely up at the officer and smiled politely. "I will tell her that, as well."

His eyes widened as he met her gaze, and he quickly extended a sealed parchment envelope, lowering his eyes ever so slightly when she took it.

Saryn crossed the yard or so to the tower entry and stepped inside. She took her time climbing the stone steps to the uppermost level of the tower, thankful she didn't have to ride into the heights of the ice fields to find Ryba.

The Marshal was seated at her table, with the door open to her study, writing in some sort of ledger, which she closed as she saw Saryn. "Yes?"

"You have a message from the Prefect of Gallos." Saryn stepped forward and handed the envelope to the Marshal.

Ryba took it. "From the Gallosians? I saw the parley flag."

"The officer wore a Gallosian uniform. He said he'd been commanded to deliver the message and wait for your response. He was nervous and telling the truth."

"We could make him wait, but that wouldn't inconvenience Karthanos at all and would just alienate the poor officer, who was probably sent because he'd upset his mightiness or whoever is running Gallos for the Prefect." Ryba slipped out her belt knife and slit the envelope, then extracted the single sheet of parchment within.

She read it and handed it to Saryn without comment. Saryn scanned the short document.

> Marshal:
> Continued conflict between our lands is less than practical or advisable.
>
> Therefore, in the spirit of conciliation and friendship, the land of Gallos accepts your offer and reaffirms its commitment to respecting the previously established boundaries between Gallos and Westwind. Gallos will continue to respect the rights of travelers and traders to cross freely those boundaries, subject to whatever tariffs each jurisdiction may impose.

Under the bottom line was simply the seal of Karthanos, Prefect of Gallos.

Saryn looked to Ryba. "That's as much of a concession as you're going to get, unless you invade Gallos and sack Fenard."

"That will do." Ryba shook her head. "It has to."

"It isn't signed, only sealed. Do you think that's because Karthanos is too sick to reply, but someone fears we'll do worse if they don't reply?"

"Does it matter? The seal offers the commitment. Besides, what would we do if they try again? Drag out this communiqué?"

"You'll reply in similar terms?"

"Slightly more graciously, and with polite words suggesting that it would be a shame if similar devastation had to be wreaked on either land in the future."

Saryn nodded, although she shared Ryba's judgment that Gallosian forbearance would lapse with time . . . or with a new ruler.

"How are you feeling?" asked Ryba.

"Fine. What about you?" Saryn couldn't help but glance down, although she couldn't see the leg brace that had replaced the splint on Ryba's leg.

"It's still uncomfortable, but it wasn't a break, more like a hairline fracture. I worry more about you. You were looking fairly washed-out after the battle . . . for more than an eightday."

Saryn started to say that what she had done had taken a great deal of effort. Instead, she just nodded. "I think everyone was tired afterward." *Those who weren't dead.*

"What do you intend to do about your pledge to the Lady Zeldyan?"

"Nothing now," Saryn replied. "I said I would offer my personal help, if requested, after we dealt with Gallos. That doesn't require me to volunteer to run down to Lornth immediately."

"You were rather generous with your offer, as I may have noted before, Saryn. What if you are needed here?"

"I thought it necessary, Ryba. If we did not obtain the saltpeter and sulfur, I felt we could not defeat the Gallosians. If we could not, I would not be . . . available to help the Lady Zeldyan. I had nothing else to offer."

"What else did you offer?"

Saryn shrugged. "Only as many guards as you would spare and who would choose to go." Again, that wasn't precisely what she had said, but it was close enough. "The only absolute was my personal assistance." That was perfectly true.

"If she requests you, that will weaken us more, even if you take only two squads."

"That's possible, but anything that leaves the regents in control of Lornth will strengthen Westwind."

Ryba nodded. "She will ask . . . sooner or later. Let us hope it is later."

From what she had seen in Lornth, Saryn feared it would be sooner.

The Marshal nodded. "Go offer the Gallosians modest refreshments and water for their horses, and tell them that I will have a reply shortly. You may return for it after they are fed."

"Yes, ser." Saryn turned and headed down the stairs.

Had Ryba already seen that Saryn would have to go to Lornth with two squads? How much else had she seen? Saryn certainly wasn't about to ask.

XLI

More than two eightdays passed, and Saryn regained control of her vision and all of her abilities to sense order and chaos flows. The road patrols reported travelers returning to the Westhorns; a trader in leathers even came to Westwind. Dealdron returned from the lower canyon with kegs filled with lime, and Aemra told Istril that Dealdron had showed her everything necessary to create the lime and the mortar. The last of the horn bows were set in their frames for their long curing. More Analerian women appeared, asking for refuge, and some even brought goods and tools and small wagons, and a horse or two. The walls of the new barracks continued to rise, and the foundations of the larger keep planned by Ryba took shape.

And Saryn kept worrying, wondering when she would hear from Lady Zeldyan.

On the fourth threeday of summer, in late afternoon, as Saryn made her way back down from the smithy to Tower Black and the armory, where she anticipated more work in sharpening newly forged short swords, she saw three guards riding down the road from the ridge to the north of Westwind, accompanying two unfamiliar riders. Although neither rider bore a banner, the purple-and-green uniforms announced their purpose clearly enough.

Saryn reached the causeway well before the riders did and stood there waiting as they neared, then reined up.

"Commander," offered Haesta, "the Lornians have a message for you."

The younger courier eased his mount forward and extended his gloved hand . . . and an envelope on which was written in ornate script: Saryn, Arms-Commander of Westwind.

Saryn looked at the envelope again, then up at the courier. "Thank you." She turned to the guards. "See that they are fed and their mounts taken care of."

, JR.

"We'll take care of your mounts. Then you can eat," said Haesta. "This way . . ."

Once the guards escorted the riders back across the causeway and onto the road up toward the stable, Saryn slit the envelope with her belt knife and extracted the single sheet of parchment.

> Dear Arms-Commander—
> On behalf of the Regents of Lornth, I would like to invite you to meet with us, at your earliest practicable convenience, to discuss in what manner your assistance might be most valuable.

Below Zeldyan's clear and flowing signature was her seal.

After a moment, Saryn walked toward the entry to Tower Black. She did not replace the parchment in its envelope, but opened the heavy door one-handed and stepped into the tower.

Ryba was standing in the foyer, alone. "The Lady Regent has requested you go to Lornth."

Saryn crossed the distance between them and handed the Marshal the single sheet.

Ryba read it, then looked up. "Politely worded."

"But a definite reminder of my pledge."

"Do you intend to keep it?" asked Ryba. "You are not strictly obligated to do so. It was made under duress."

"That doesn't matter, does it? If I do not go, no one will trust the word of Westwind except when backed by force of arms, and that will require that every pledge be so backed."

"That is true. Did you think of that when you pledged your assistance?"

"I did. That was why I pledged only my personal aid."

Ryba shook her head. "Zeldyan knew you would not come alone. No matter how we try, we end up enmeshed in the affairs of the others. That's the way of the world—on all worlds."

"I'm not asking for great support. A squad would be enough, and there must be that many guards who would be willing . . ."

"You will need two," affirmed Ryba, "and Hryessa. A good second-in-command will be vital for you."

"Are you sure you can spare two . . . and a good captain?"

"We can't afford to have you fail, and you'll need two squads for you to have a chance at succeeding."

"Why two?" Saryn knew that Ryba had foreseen something, and Saryn wanted to see if she could get Ryba to reveal more of what might be.

"Two squads aren't threatening enough for any of those holders opposing Zeldyan to claim that Westwind is invading Lornth, but our two squads are worth a company or more of the lord-holders' armsmen, especially under you and Hryessa. You also may be able to recruit and train some Lornian women . . . that is, if you're there a while, perhaps two more squads, and that would give you a full company. You may be there that long, unfortunately, because internal unrest is not something that is quickly or easily resolved, as you will discover."

"We might need some spare mounts," suggested Saryn.

"You can take ten of the captured Gallosian mounts. We might have trouble enough with fodder this fall and winter."

"What else do you suggest?" asked Saryn.

"Additional blades. We can't spare many, but we can spare an extra for each guard."

"You're saying that I'm likely to be there a long time," Saryn replied with a wry smile. "How long, do you think?"

Ryba shrugged. "What I foresee doesn't come with dates attached. You've seen that already. Nor do I understand exactly the context of the images. I've seen you in snow and cold rain, though. That suggests you won't be done with what you need to do by the end of harvest. I can spare but twenty golds, and half that because you were so careful on your last trip. You will have to make certain that the regents support your guards with food and fodder. At that, you will be far cheaper than any other armsmen." Ryba's smile was cold, yet wry. "You can take two of the wagons for supplies and spare equipment, and two of the drays. Since one wagon fell apart, and we had to rebuild it, and since you are coming to the aid of the regents, that is only fair. Also, the Suthyans will only supply or bribe a few Lornian lord-holders. That is because they wish the revolt to be long and bloody, so that Lornth will fall easily into their hands. Do whatever you must do, wherever that may lead. I would that it were otherwise." Ryba shook her head. "When will you leave?"

"We can leave by eightday, if that is agreeable to you."

"That's likely for the best. From what you have said, the Lady Zeldyan would not request your assistance unless matters were truly urgent. You are her last hope, and possibly our best chance for keeping hostilities from our western borders."

The Marshal's words carried resignation and sadness, Saryn could tell, both from the feelings she could sense and from the tone of the Marshal's voice. "Then it will be on eightday."

Ryba nodded.

Saryn offered a wry smile, then turned and headed out to find Hryessa.

From Ryba's comments and suggestions, and the fact that Ryba had allowed Saryn to take Hryessa and the two squads of her own choice, Saryn was well aware that not only would she have a long and hard struggle in trying to preserve the regency from the greed and the chauvinism of the lord-holders of Lornth, but that even Ryba was uncertain as to where matters would lead or exactly how long Saryn would be away from Westwind.

Lornth

XLII

Saryn had started down the steps to the main hall before dawn on eight-day, when she heard Ryba's voice from above her on the stone staircase. "Saryn . . . I'd like a word with you . . ."

Saryn headed up to the top level of Tower Black, where Ryba waited, fully dressed.

"Come in and close the door."

Saryn did so. Ryba stood by the circular table and looked at Saryn. "I have not said too much to you about what you must do in Lornth. That is because I do not know so much as I would like. I cannot tell you how vital it is that you do not hazard yourself unnecessarily. You can sacrifice guards if you must, but without you, Westwind will have nothing." Ryba's lips quirked into an ironic grin. "Needless to say, such an unnecessary sacrifice would not benefit you, either. One way or another, Lornth will not survive in its present form. The old lord-holders who will not abandon their male-only traditions will have to be crushed, or they will destroy the regency. The regency may not last in any case, but whoever or whatever rules Lornth must not include the tradition-bound holders, or we will be at war within a handful of years."

"Even with the devastation there, and what is likely to come?"

"If they survive, they will seek to blame us and plunder Westwind for what crumbs they can find. We do not need another war."

"So . . . you're sending me as much for Westwind as because I pledged."

"More for Westwind. I respect your honor, but my goal has always been to change Candar so that there are places where women have at least equal rights and power compared to men. Without Westwind and what you must do, that cannot happen."

Ryba's words scarcely surprised Saryn. "I think I always knew that."

There was a moment of silence before Ryba spoke again. "Saryn . . . no matter what you think, I do wish the best for you."

Those words and, even more, the clear feeling of truth behind them did surprise Saryn. "Thank you."

"You'd best get something to eat. You have a long journey ahead of you." Ryba paused. "One last thing, and it is advice you will not like. To succeed you will need to be more ruthless than any man, for only then will they respect you."

"I hope it does not come to that."

"It will. It always does." Ryba stepped forward and opened the door.

Saryn nodded, then departed, heading down to the main hall to eat.

Less than a glass later, she was mounted and at the head of her small force, reined up on the road outside Tower Black where it met the causeway.

"Is everything set?" Saryn looked to Hryessa.

While Saryn would have liked to have checked every guard's gear personally, she knew that doing so would have undermined her subordinate—unnecessarily, since Hryessa was every bit as meticulous as Saryn herself. The arms-commander glanced back at the wagons waiting behind fourth squad. Both were in far better condition than when she had brought them back to Westwind, as were the two drays pulling them.

"Yes, ser. We're ready to head out. We made the transfers you approved for the two with small children, and that took care of anyone who shouldn't really be going to Lornth."

Saryn nodded. She'd told the guard captain that they might end up stuck in Lornth over the winter if things did not go well. "How does Daryn feel about your going to Lornth?"

"He hasn't said. He doesn't have to. He doesn't like it. I can tell." Hryessa shrugged. "I told him you needed me, and the Marshal said so. That means he has to stay and take care of Elaya and Ryntyr. He's good with them. That's not a problem. He's tended some of the other young ones, too, when it was necessary. He's a good man."

Saryn looked across the causeway. Standing just outside the door to Tower Black was a small group of people, among them Daryn and Hryessa's son and daughter, and four other familiar figures—the three silver-haired girls and Dealdron. Ryba was not among those seeing the detachment off, but Saryn would not have expected that of the Marshal.

Elaya and Ryntyr waved to their mother, and Hryessa blew them each a kiss, then flicked the reins of her mount. "Company! Forward!"

Saryn took a last glance at Tower Black and the handful of people standing before it on the causeway.

Dealdron looked at Saryn, his gaze steady, but she could not sense what lay behind his eyes, only that it was not hatred or anything like it. *Wistfulness? Why would he be wistful?* She offered a pleasant smile, then eased the chestnut gelding forward, wondering how long it might be before she saw the tower again.

XLIII

Unlike her last travels, when she returned from the battle with the Gallosians, Saryn found the descent from the Roof of the World to the hills of eastern Lornth both quick and uneventful. Less than five days later, she and her detachment rode into Henspa just before sunset. Essin the innkeeper was waiting on the porch of the Black Bull.

"I thought we'd not be seeing you again so soon, Angel."

"I didn't think so, either. How is your mother?" Saryn asked Essin.

"Much better, and I thank you for that. She would like to talk to you, I'm certain, once you've seen to your guards."

"I'd be happy to."

"And she'd be pleased. There are not that many who come to Henspa these days."

"Have you seen any more Suthyans?" asked Saryn.

"Not a one, and only a sole Jeranyi trader, taking the long way back, telling tales of how the Great Forest grows vaster day and night, swallowing up whole towns, but leaving a village here and a village there."

"Why was he there?"

"Like all Jeranyi, he was a thief. Like as not, he hoped to glean riches from the ruins, and two fine wagons he had. Jersen said that he had a pair of cupridium blades."

"Cupridium?" Saryn had never heard that word.

"Silvery metal harder than cold iron and more flexible than copper. That's what the old Mirror Lancers used, back in the time of Lorn the Mighty and his son, Kerial."

"Lorn the Mighty? Was Lornth named after him?"

"So they say. Anyway, Marleu wouldn't let her father even think of purchasing the blades. Said cupridium belonged to the past and wouldn't stand up to the black iron of the angels. Smart woman she is." Essin shook his head.

"I'd best tend to my mount," Saryn said. "Then I'll be back to talk to your mother."

She flicked the reins and rode slowly past the inn and up the narrow lane into the rear courtyard and the stables. More than half a glass passed before she'd finished grooming the gelding and going over matters with Hryessa and could make her way back through the inn to put her gear in the room she'd share with the guard captain.

When she came down the steps, Essin was waiting in the foyer. "Ma's on the front porch. She says it's cooler there."

The white-haired Jennyleu turned her head as Saryn stepped out onto the covered porch. "You've changed, Angel."

"Not that much," demurred Saryn.

"Your eyes are silver, like they'd reflect what's inside folk, and there's a seriousness there. Why did you come back?" A smile lingered on the old woman's face as she shifted her weight on the chair beside the bench in the twilight.

"The regents requested that I return," Saryn said, settling onto the bench, facing Jennyleu.

"The Lady Zeldyan needs you, as does her sire, but all the other lord-holders will fear you. Especially the Lord of Duevek."

"We will take the longer route to Lornth and avoid Duevek. I do not wish to create more problems for the regents."

"Ah . . . but you will. Even an old woman such as I can see that."

Saryn laughed gently. "You see it because you are a woman of much experience."

The white-haired woman snorted. "Doesn't take much experience to see that the old lord-holders'd be looking for a ruler who'd let them line their own purses. Young Nesslek like as not would be following his mother and his grandsire once he becomes overlord, or he'd be questioning the lord-holders as to why he shouldn't. Neither would they like."

Saryn nodded, although she wasn't that certain about young Nesslek's integrity, particularly if he were flattered and promised great glory. "How did it come to that?"

"Generations back, Lornth was a province of Cyador. You knew that, did you not? Then, the Mirror Lancers withdrew to the west and south, but the Protector of the Steps to Paradise still demanded his tariffs, and they were not light, and many that were levied were not paid. Before long, one of the officers of the Mirror Lancers and his company returned. He took over the town of Lornth, then others, until all acknowledged his superiority. Then he proposed a treaty with Cyador where but a quarter portion of the tariffs went to the emperor in Cyad, and half went to him. The other quarter he returned to the holders. Any holder who complained was killed and his family thrown off their lands, and those lands were awarded to a follower of the Lord of Lornth." Jennyleu smiled enigmatically.

"And that was how the house of Lornth was founded?"

"That has also been how it has maintained its position, by power alone. When the black and flame angel destroyed Cyador, they destroyed any fear the holders had of the great and ancient kingdom. They also weakened the house of Lornth so that the regents had not the golds nor the armsmen to put down the stronger holders who did not pay their tariffs."

"Such as the Lord of Duevek?"

"He is one of those, but only one, Angel."

"You know all of this because of your daughter in Lornth?"

"My niece, Haelora."

"The one who has the inn there? I never had a chance to meet her."

"It's right off the square . . . the Square Platter. She says you can't miss it. I couldn't say. We never got so far as to Lornth. You know, Vernt staked her and her consort."

"I remember. You told me, and she writes good letters."

"Ah, yes. Letters." For a moment, Jennyleu's eyes twinkled. "Tell me about Westwind, Angel."

"What would you like to know?"

"Whatever you care to tell me."

Saryn nodded. "Westwind sits in a small valley on the Roof of the World . . . where the Marshal and the guards live is in Tower Black . . . and every stone in it was cut from the rock in a single year by Nylan, the black mage you met . . ."

XLIV

Two glasses after sunrise on sixday, Saryn's detachment was headed due west, ten kays out of Henspa, under a high haze that turned the morning sky a silvery greenish blue. Early in the morning as it was, the day promised to be the hottest that Saryn had yet experienced in Candar . . . or anywhere else, for that matter, and it wasn't even near the height of summer. She hadn't even bothered with her riding jacket and certainly wasn't looking forward to the heat of the days to come, not at all.

Inside her tunic was a letter introducing Saryn to Jennyleu's niece Haelora, which Essin had handed her just before she had mounted to leave the inn. That introduction Saryn intended to pursue. An innkeeper in Lornth had to know things that the regents would not, and even from what little Saryn had heard about the land of Lornth, it was clear she'd need every bit of information she could find or dig up.

She shifted her weight in the saddle and looked along the road before the column of guards, riding two abreast. The lands to the west of Henspa—and the river—consisted of low, rolling hills that looked to get flatter the farther they were from the river. While some of the land was pasture, and there were a few orchards and woodlots, most was cultivated. For whatever reason, the road on the west of the river did not follow the watercourse at all but headed away from it for almost fifteen kays, then turned north at the town of Ornath and continued onward for another twenty kays before rejoining the river some fifteen kays to the northwest of Duevek.

Saryn squinted to make out what was causing the dust in the road a good two kays west of the outriders. As she watched, she could see, headed toward the Westwind riders, a large high-sided and roofed wagon, the kind merchants and traders often used, its wheels churning up dust. Less than half a kay from the outriders, the driver turned his team and wagon onto a side road southward and whipped the pair of drays into something like a fast trot.

"Poor fool," observed Hryessa from where she rode beside Saryn. "He's only hurting his drays. If we wanted to catch him, there'd be nothing he could do."

"Are we that fearsome? Forty-odd women, two wagons, and ten spare mounts?"

"Forty-odd armed women, ser, from a place that has slaughtered thousands of their men."

"We may have to trade on that fear," prophesied Saryn.

"What does the Lady Zeldyan want from us? Beyond your counsel?" An amused and knowing smile crossed the captain's lips.

"You know as well as I. She wants us to preserve Lornth for her son to rule, though she has not said that in so many words." *In any words, in fact, but what else could she desire?*

Hryessa turned her head toward Saryn. "Is that possible?"

"We'll find out, and before too long."

"What if it is not possible?"

"Then we will do what we can to protect Westwind." What exactly that might be, Saryn had no idea, except that, given the holders of Lornth, it would be neither easy nor bloodless.

Saryn and her detachment passed few carts and wagons on the ride through Ornath and back to the river, making camp on sixday night at what passed for a way station near the ruins of what might once have been a town. After an early start on sevenday, two glasses' ride brought them to a flat stretch between two hills and a kaystone proclaiming that Haselbridge lay but three kays ahead.

Saryn could sense riders nearby and was not surprised to see a group appear on the low rise perhaps half a kay ahead, just off the left shoulder of the packed-clay road where it crested the next hill. She could sense no others, but all that meant was that there were none within a kay. "Riders ahead," she said quietly but firmly to Hryessa.

"Ready arms," said Hryessa, turning in the saddle. "Pass it back on the quiet."

"Ready arms . . . Ready arms . . ." the murmured command whispered back through the guards.

As the Westwind detachment neared the crest of the road, Saryn could see that the waiting riders were drawn up almost in formation. On the right side of the road was a scrubby section of pasture that sloped steeply down to the river, still running almost to the top of its banks with the late runoff from the Westhorns.

"Hail, Angels!" The call was loud, cheerful, and sardonic, and came from an angular man attired in a rich maroon waistcoat over a thin but fine linen shirt. He was mounted on a gray stallion, slightly forward of the other eight riders.

"Hail!" returned Saryn, studying the caller. He looked to be a young lord or heir, whose wavy brown hair was longer than that of most arms-men, crafters, or tradesmen, and his entire being radiated arrogance.

"Where might you be headed?"

"To Lornth." Saryn reined up short of a position that would have brought her opposite the lord-holder or lordling. Behind her, Hryessa brought the guards to a halt. "And you?"

"We were out for a ride." He bowed in the saddle. "Keistyn, of Hasel. Welcome to my lands." The cheerful words still carried a sardonic and de-meaning overtone.

Saryn inclined her head, if but slightly. "I have not had the honor of meeting you before, but please understand that we are only passing through with no ill intended to anyone in Lornth."

"That is most reassuring," replied the lead rider, "for many have feared the blades of the angels of the heights." He paused. "I do not believe you introduced yourself, Angel."

"Saryn, Arms-Commander of Westwind." Saryn studied the eight armsmen behind Keistyn. All carried in shoulder harnesses the long and massive blades favored by most men-at-arms in Lornth, and all wore red tunics trimmed in black. Three looked young and fresh-faced, and two were clearly hardened veterans of some sort. The remaining three were ex-cessively beefy, with a certain cruelty behind round faces, the kind of cru-elty that seemed to come from self-indulgent and overweight males, Saryn reflected.

"And what might a fearsome arms-commander be doing here in the lowlands? I had heard that the angels had asked a favor, and when the re-gent had granted it, you had returned to your heights, never to trouble Lornth again."

"We have not come to trouble Lornth," Saryn replied pleasantly, "but to respond to a request of the regents. Because the regents, unlike the Gallosians, who paid most dearly for their faithlessness, have kept their word and faith, when the regents asked us to return to meet with them, we were pleased to accede to their request."

"I had not heard of the faithlessness of the Gallosians, but being people of little honor, could you have expected otherwise of them?" A short bark of laughter followed.

"Until someone proves otherwise, we accept their word," Saryn said. "They proved otherwise, and the Prefect's son, Arthanos, and his army of nine thousand are no more." She smiled politely at Keistyn.

"Nine thousand . . . I beg your pardon, Angel, but that seems . . . unlikely." A skeptical smile followed Keistyn's words.

Saryn shrugged. "Unlikely as it may seem to you, that is what happened. Sooner or later, you will hear, and there will doubtless be those who will not believe." She paused. "But that is what happened. You should recall that, twice, Lords of Lornth attacked the Roof of the World, and both perished. The second time armsmen from all across Lornth perished as well. You might also recall that a single mage who left Westwind brought down the great empire of Cyador. Doubting is all well and good, Lord Keistyn, but it is also dangerous to doubt what has already occurred, especially when thousands have already died because they, in turn, doubted."

"Oh . . . I do doubt. I doubt anything that I have not been able to verify myself, or through those I trust to be most truthful."

Saryn smiled coolly. "I think you will find that angels do not stoop to lies or duplicity, but that is a matter in which you will find your own way."

For just a moment, Saryn could sense that her words had chilled the young lord, but that chill was followed immediately by anger so strong that Saryn cast out her senses again to see if other armsmen lurked nearby. To her relief, she could sense none.

"I will indeed find what is true. I always do, Angel." Keistyn smiled warmly. "Unlike many, I do not hamper myself with outmoded strictures, for a lord must do what he must to preserve his heritage."

"You are most forthright, Lord Keistyn. I appreciate your directness, and I will convey that to the regents, as well as your courtesy in greeting us."

"There is always a time for courtesy, but we will not delay you longer, for you have many kays to ride before you reach Lornth."

Saryn could easily feel the anger and the hostility behind the warmly spoken and cheerful-sounding words, an anger so raw that it burned like chaos within Keistyn. She also saw no purpose in revealing what she sensed. "That we do, Lord Keistyn, and the regents await us."

"I am most certain that they do and that they will tell you much. The Lady Zeldyan, especially, is a warm and most charming lady." Keistyn smiled once more. "But I am most certain that you know that, and I digress." He bowed from the saddle a last time, then turned his mount and rode down the back side of the rise, followed by his armsmen, toward a narrow road that stretched westward to where it passed between two wooded hills, flanked by a smaller stream that meandered out from the hills generally eastward toward a small stone bridge perhaps two kays farther along the road and just outside of Haselbridge.

Saryn nodded to Hryessa.

"Company, forward!"

Saryn urged the gelding onward, her senses still focused on the departing Keistyn and his armsmen, even while she waited to hear what Hryessa might say. They rode down the other side of the rise and past the road that Saryn supposed led to Keistyn's holding or country lodge.

"Lord Keistyn sounds pleasant and cheerful," observed Hryessa. "I do not think he is either."

"Why not?" asked Saryn.

"He smiles, and even his eyes and his voice are warm, but they lie. He is evil behind all his pleasant words and smiles. So were those with him. Did you not see that?"

"I saw we should not trust Lord Keistyn the length of a short sword, perhaps even less."

"Much less. He is the kind that men so often trust because he seems warm and friendly, until he places knives in their backs."

"And twists them," added Saryn.

Hryessa nodded, her eyes straying to the west and the nine riders.

Another thought struck Saryn. There were only two even halfway-direct routes from Westwind to Lornth, and one led through the Lord of Duevek's domains and the other through Lord Keistyn's lands. She had chosen their route to avoid Duevek . . . and had been met and greeted by Keistyn, as if the young lord had been expecting the Westwind contingent. That suggested a number of possibilities, none of them exactly to

Saryn's liking, and that Keistyn and Duevek might well be allied in more than their dislike of the regency.

If even a fraction of the holders in Lornth were like Kelthyn and Keistyn, Saryn could see why Lady Zeldyan and Lord Gethen had their troubles. Still . . . short of wiping them all out, which hardly seemed possible, she had to wonder exactly what she could do to help Zeldyan.

XLV

As on her previous journey to Lornth, when Saryn and her detachment rode the last kays toward the town in the late afternoon of eightday, they saw no scouts who might have conveyed information on the presence of Westwind guards to the regents. When they entered the town proper, the only reaction was a sullen sort of fear, where women eased away from laundry tubs and into their summer-sweltering stucco houses, dragging children after them, until the guards had ridden well past.

Even more pungent smells rose from the stone-lined sewage channels into the still, hot air, mixing with the odor of hot, and at least some burned, cooking oils. The unpleasantness of the odors intensified as the guards rode into the center of Lornth, with its narrow and roughly paved streets. Those out on the streets glanced toward the riders, then generally looked away.

When Saryn saw the small square ahead, with its statue of Lord Nessil, she began to search intently in all directions for a signboard or something that might indicate the presence of the Square Platter. Not until she was past the statue did she finally catch a glimpse of a signboard with a cream-colored square platter set against a green backdrop, down perhaps half a block on the right side of the second narrow side street on the south.

Then she rode through the narrower section of the avenue, with its taller and more ornate dwellings, and out onto the road around the green before the palace, whose pale pink walls looked even more washed-out in the late-afternoon summer sun.

"To the right!" ordered Saryn, gesturing for the scouts riding ahead to follow the right section of the road circling the now-browning patchy grass of the green.

The ironbound gates stood open, and Saryn had to wonder if they had ever been closed. Probably not, because the ten-cubit wall around the palace complex was hardly enough to stop a determined enemy of any great numbers, although it might suffice against a mob. But then, Saryn wondered, could the lord-holders or anyone else raise a large force?

As Saryn raised her arm to order the Westwind contingent to a halt before the open gates, an older armsman half hurried, half waddled out of the guardhouse just inside the gates and stopped dead, not even reaching the space between the gates.

"I'm Saryn, the Arms-Commander of Westwind. I came to see the regents. At their request."

"Ah . . . yes, ser. I had not heard," stammered the guard, looking past Saryn at the ranks of mounts and guards, his eyes wide.

"We will take the same rear stables and quarters we did on our last visit," Saryn announced. "I would suggest that someone inform the Lady Zeldyan that we have arrived."

The guard gulped, looked at the armed women, and finally replied, "Yes . . . ser."

"Thank you." Saryn nodded to Hryessa.

"Company! Forward!"

The hoofs of the Westwind horses clattered on the unevenly laid cobblestones, seemingly the only sound in the large courtyard, as Saryn and Hryessa led the detachment toward the paved area behind the palace proper, then to the two-story outbuildings set before the rear wall at the far west end of the complex. The scraggly grass between the cobblestones had turned brown, as had some of the moss on the lowest stones of the palace walls.

"You were not so polite this time," murmured Hryessa.

"Now is not the time for deference to mere armsmen," replied Saryn. "They need to understand that we stand for the Lady Zeldyan." Saryn was far more concerned than she had been on her previous visit. Surely, after a request from the Lady Zeldyan, word should have been passed to the armsmen. Or did Zeldyan fear that, if Saryn did not arrive, her authority as regent would be even further weakened?

"This is worse than before," murmured Hryessa. "How can they let half a company of armsmen approach the main hold of Lornth and not know?"

"That is why we are here, I fear," replied Saryn.

An ostler rushed out of the first stable, his eyes wide, then ducked back inside.

"Company! Halt!" ordered Hryessa, as she and Saryn reined up in front of the second stable.

Saryn eased her gelding aside while Hryessa turned her mount to face the detachment, then said, "Most of you know the drill. Mounts to the stables, then guards to the barracks and make sure everything is as it should be. Dismissed to duties!"

Saryn had barely dismounted when she saw an armsman hurrying across the courtyard from the rear of the palace. As he neared, she could make out the features of the same junior officer who had greeted them earlier. Unfortunately, she could not remember his name.

"Commander!" called the undercaptain.

Saryn waited until he stopped a yard from her. She'd once thought that he resembled Dealdron; but it was clear, now that she looked, that he did not. She could sense the mixture of consternation and even fear stirred up within him. "Yes, Undercaptain?"

"The Lady Zeldyan conveys her apologies for your not being recognized. She had not anticipated that you would respond to her invitation so speedily."

With a smile, Saryn replied, "Her invitation did say that she wished to meet at our earliest convenience. We have obliged her."

"Yes, ser. As soon as you have your guards settled, she would very much appreciate a brief meeting with you personally."

"I would be happy to do so. It should not be that long."

Less than a quarter glass later, Saryn and the undercaptain walked across the rough stone pavement of the rear courtyard to the door on the south wing of the palace and up the single flight of steps. Saryn carried her saddlebags and a second bag with other uniforms and items she had thought she might find of use.

"The same chamber as before?" she asked.

"Yes, ser."

Saryn turned to the right, noting that the air in the corridor was warm and stale.

A young chambermaid—the same one as before, Saryn thought—hurried from the end door, then stepped to the side, her eyes wide before she dropped them, and said, "Your chamber is ready, Commander."

"Thank you." Saryn smiled.

The girl glanced up, fleetingly, her eyes taking in Saryn's battle harness, before they dropped again.

Saryn did not doff the harness and blades after she set her gear on the writing table, but she did take a moment to locate a clothesbrush and used it to remove the dust from her boots and uniform before she turned. "I'm ready."

"Yes, ser."

As she walked down the corridor beside the undercaptain, she could sense the chambermaid following, if at a discreet distance. She also managed to drag up the name of the undercaptain from her memory by the time they passed the top of a large formal staircase in the middle of the palace and reached the north staircase, where they climbed another flight of stairs, then walked to the same unmarked doorway where Saryn had been before and a single armsman stood.

Saryn nodded. "Thank you, Undercaptain Maerkyn. I trust I will see you later."

"Yes, ser." Maerkyn stepped back.

Saryn could sense the chambermaid peering out from the stairwell and watching the three figures outside the private chambers of Lady Zeldyan.

The guard outside the study looked at Saryn and her weapons.

Saryn looked through him, her eyes cold, projecting a flow of total command.

The man stepped aside.

Saryn nodded and opened the door.

". . . never seen that . . ." came the faintest murmur before Saryn closed the door behind her and smiled. There would be more than a few things happening that Lornth had not seen before if she had anything to do with it.

Lady Zeldyan had already stepped away from the small square table set before the middle window of the sitting room. On the table were two bottles and a pair of goblets. Zeldyan wore a purple tunic and trousers trimmed in black, and her silver-and-blond hair was drawn back away from her face. The darkness under Zeldyan's eyes was more pronounced than it had been earlier.

"If you would sit down . . ." The regent waited to seat herself until Saryn began to take the other seat. "I can only offer white or amber wine . . . Commander . . ."

"Saryn, if you would."

"Only if you call me Zeldyan . . . which you have not done . . ." Zeldyan's smile was impish, and the amusement behind it startled Saryn so that she did not reply immediately.

"White or amber?" asked the regent.

"Whichever is lighter, I think."

"The white, then." Zeldyan filled both goblets, then lifted hers. "To your courtesy in heeding my request."

Saryn returned the gesture. "And to your grace." She took a sip of the clear white vintage, pleased at its light, slightly fruity flavor . . . and its coolness.

"You came armed." Zeldyan's smile slipped away.

"I came prepared, Lady."

"I did not expect an even-larger party than when you came earlier in the year. I do not know whether to be complimented or worried."

"Westwind wishes you to remain regent. The Marshal allowed me half a company . . . and some spare mounts and equipment. We also returned two of the wagons and drays. The other cart . . . barely survived the trip to Westwind, and the dray would not have survived the return."

"All will be surprised that you returned two," replied Zeldyan sardonically.

"The palace seems . . . rather empty, and I did not see Nesslek . . ." offered Saryn.

"In the summer, few wish to remain in Lornth who do not have to. Nesslek is at The Groves with his grandsire."

"Is that for the summer . . . or because matters are less than desirable here in Lornth?"

"He is spending the summer with his grandsire, as he has often done, and as I did as a child."

"Of course." Saryn nodded, understanding fully that Nesslek was where Zeldyan thought he would be the safest. "The holdings near there are most friendly to your sire?"

"All those near The Groves are most faithful to my sire . . . and to the rightful heir." Zeldyan sipped her wine.

"The regents did not request my presence, did they? You did. The others don't even know we're here. Or they didn't until we arrived."

"They will not know for a time. Those loyal to Kelthyn have already left Lornth for the season. Little occurs here in high summer."

"What would you have of me, Lady?" Saryn took another sip of the cool wine.

"Whatever you can do to assure that my son lives to his maturity . . . and to succeed his father."

"That suggests that there are those who wish otherwise . . . besides Kelthyn," Saryn observed quietly.

"There are those."

"I do not think that you would wish more killing and violence."

"No ruler or regent *wishes* that," replied Zeldyan.

"You will pardon me, Lady, but I know little of the holders of Lornth. Besides those of the regents, I know only of the Lord of Duevek, who was both rash and impolite, and who is doubtless under the influence of the Suthyans, and Lord Keistyn, who met us briefly on the road through his lands."

"What did you think of young Keistyn?" Zeldyan's voice was even, but in the thoughts behind the perfectly modulated tone, Saryn could sense the lady's dislike.

"He was most polite, and his voice and eyes were warm and cheerful. No holder in Lornth can be that warm to a party of Westwind guards without dissembling."

"His father perished when the Cyadorans attacked." Zeldyan laughed. "Lord Chentyr of Hasel had taken care to position himself most carefully, well out on the flank, claiming he was there to support my brother, Fornal. When Fornal charged, Chentyr did not, but a stray chaos-bolt from the Cyadoran mages was deflected from the mage Nylan and struck Chentyr. Not even cinders remained. Yet Chentyr was a paragon of virtue compared to his son."

"That would suggest the son has little love for either you or Westwind."

"On the few occasions he has been here in the palace, he has always been volubly pleasant and most courteous."

"And the same is true of Lord Duevek?"

"Actually, he is Lord Henstrenn of Duevek, or Henstrenn, Lord of Duevek, just as Keistyn is Lord Keistyn of Hasel, or Keistyn, Lord of Hasel, although the common folk often just call whoever holds the lands Lord Duevek or Lord Hasel or, in my father's case, Lord Groves."

That made a sort of sense to Saryn. "How am I to know who might be truly a friend of the regency, who might not, and who has yet to decide?"

"I have already considered that . . . Saryn." Zeldyan drew a folded sheet of parchment from somewhere below the table and extended it.

Saryn opened and studied it. There were three columns of names, but nothing else. After a moment, she smiled. The first column was headed by Gethen, Lord of The Groves, the second by Henstrenn, Lord of Duevek, and the third by Maeldyn, Lord of Quaryn, a name that Saryn did not recognize. "Where is Quaryn?"

Zeldyan extended another parchment, one clearly older, and colored. "This is a map of the holdings of Lornth, as they were when Sillek's father became Lord of Lornth. Some boundaries have changed, and, for now, there is no Lord of Rohrn, since almost no one there survived the Cyadoran chaos-fires. But that should help you know what holdings there are. I would request you return the map to me when you no longer need it."

"Thank you. I will." Saryn smiled but let the expression drop as she asked, "What plan do you have in mind in which I might be helpful?"

"I had thought that together we might visit some holdings."

"Beginning with those in the second column? The first name first?" Saryn raised her eyebrows.

"That was my thought, once your guards and their mounts have had some time to recover from their trip." Zeldyan smiled. "The holders are required to host the retainers of the Lord of Lornth, and the regency, once a year, for up to an eightday. That will provide some relief to our treasury and allow you to meet them and them to meet you . . . and your guards."

"Do you think it wise to take both squads on these visits?"

"What would you suggest?"

"I have not seen many armsmen here in the palace," ventured Saryn.

"At present, there is less than a company. There is a full company at The Groves."

"You aren't leaving yourself much protection."

"I need little. All know that in less than four years, Nesslek will be overlord. Besides, were I to die in some unfortunate fashion, my father has the right to name another regent. Only one is named by a vote of the lord-holders. If anything happens to Nesslek, however . . ."

Saryn understood. Still . . . there were other matters to work out. "We do represent Westwind, and it is possible that women who are displeased with their situation may come to us, for we are far closer here than on the Roof of the World."

"I had not thought of that." Zeldyan frowned. "It would not do to have consorts deserting their men. Nor would it be seemly for your guards to entice women of Lornth."

"What about young women, or single women without consorts or children?"

"What will you tell the others?"

"That we are a fighting unit, and that while we will accept those who can be trained to fight, we cannot not break up households or act in a way that might orphan children, not when we are here as your guests."

"I do not know . . ." mused Zeldyan.

"Would any man truly want a girl who wants to be a Westwind guard?"

"I could point that out. It would work with most."

"Those who would not accept that will find other reasons to dislike us," Saryn said.

"You may not seek out those girls."

"I'll make sure that the guards all know that and obey."

Zeldyan sighed. "Nothing is as simple as one would like it."

"No. What else do we need to discuss?"

The regent glanced out the window. "There is much you need to know about Lornth. We should begin over supper. Do not worry about your guards. I've told the kitchen to take care of them."

"You're most kind," replied Saryn.

"No . . . I'm being practical, and I dislike eating alone." Zeldyan rose from the table. "We will eat in the breakfast room, though. It's far less austere."

Saryn rose and followed the regent from the sitting room.

Over the course of supper, a simple meal of cutlets and rice in a cheese-cream sauce with early peaches from the south, she heard far more about the various lord-holders of Lornth than she had ever imagined she would need to know . . . and yet, the fact that Zeldyan knew such a range of facts and trivia suggested that it was far from trivial. Even so, Saryn's brain was reeling under the impact of names and deeds and the grievances and slights claimed by holders she had not even known existed two glasses before.

Early evening passed, and it was full night when Saryn made her way to the upper level of the barracks and the single occupied officer's room, where Hryessa was poring over an ancient folder of maps.

"Ser?" Hryessa rose from the ancient straight-spoked oak chair.

"What have you learned?"

"There's no army here at all, less than a company."

"There's only one other company, from what the regent told me, and that's at The Groves, guarding Lord Nesslek."

"Are we here just to guard the regent, then?" asked Hryessa.

"No. We're here to see that Nesslek lives to become lord." Saryn shook her head. "The Lady Zeldyan has requested that I accompany her, with one squad, to visit various holders over the remaining course of the summer, and possibly through harvest. I'd thought I'd take fourth squad for the first visits and alternate squads after that, but you'll have to take charge of whichever one is here."

Hryessa nodded. "I thought it might be something like that."

"I got the regent to agree that you could accept recruits, provided that they're not married . . ." Saryn explained the rest of what she had covered with Zeldyan. ". . . if any who have been beaten or abused persist, all you can tell them is that, if they reach Westwind, it is unlikely the Marshal will turn them away, but you cannot hazard the guards here or Westwind itself."

Hryessa nodded. "I hate telling 'em that."

"You made the trip. So did every woman there."

"More tried and didn't reach Westwind."

"I know, but we can only do so much."

"Another thing, I'd suggest, ser," said Hryessa. "We shouldn't restrict the guards to the palace, not if we're going to be here two seasons."

"Yes?" Saryn waited, although she had her own ideas.

"I'd recommend we let them go into Lornth, but only in groups of three."

"Three?"

"It's a mite harder to persuade two others to do something stupid than just one, and one or two guards might not be enough in some situations."

"Three it is," agreed Saryn, "but no more than three groups at any one time, unless both squads are here, and then it can be six, and not tonight. I need to tell the regent."

"That's fair."

Dealing with the guards and their relations with the people of Lornth was likely to be far easier than dealing with the lord-holders, reflected Saryn. Far easier.

XLVI

Although Saryn rose early on oneday, soon after she started to wash up, her breakfast arrived, as if the chambermaid who delivered it had been waiting in the corridor and hurried down to the kitchen to fetch the tray. Saryn gulped the not-quite-warm fare down and finished dressing. She was in the courtyard before the barracks in time for the morning exercises that she and Hryessa had agreed to continue while they remained in the lowlands. She had just finished sparring with Hryessa—left-handed and using the weighted wands—when one of the palace armsmen hurried across the courtyard. Saryn stood back and waited.

"The Lady Zeldyan wished to inform you that Lord Henstrenn of Duevek will be paying her grace a visit at noon. The lady thought that you might wish to join her before he arrives."

"You may tell Lady Zeldyan that I will be most pleased to join her."

"Yes, Commander." The armsman bowed, then turned and hurried off, clearly pleased to be away from Saryn and the Westwind contingent.

"The Lord of Duevek? The same bastard whose men attacked us the last time?" asked Hryessa, blotting her damp forehead.

"The very same." Saryn frowned. Zeldyan had suggested that Saryn and the guards make Duevek their first visit, and they had planned to leave Lornth on fourday. Now . . . Henstrenn was already approaching Lornth. "If you'll excuse me, I need to find Undercaptain Maerkyn."

Finding the undercaptain wasn't all that difficult since he was in the duty room of the first barracks, sitting in a straight-backed chair, his boots on a bench. He bolted to his feet so quickly that his fine black hair, short as it was, sprayed out from his scalp for an instant, and Saryn wondered how she ever could have thought he resembled the blond-haired and diligent Dealdron. "Yes, Commander?" His eyes took in Saryn's sweat-damp working uniform for just a moment before he looked back directly into Saryn's eyes . . . then away.

"Undercaptain, I am not all that certain as to how messages are carried from the regents. I thought you would be able to enlighten me." Saryn not only watched the young officer but concentrated her senses on him. All she could feel was concern and puzzlement.

"The regents have a squad of couriers here at the palace."

"A courier carried Lady Zeldyan's message to me to Westwind. Was that courier one of the armsmen from the palace?"

"Yes, ser."

"To whom do they report?"

"They all report directly to Overcaptain Gadsyn."

"And you're in charge of the other company of armsmen here now?"

"Yes, ser."

"Who commands the company at The Groves?"

"That's Captain Tuulyr, ser."

"So Overcaptain Gadsyn is in charge of all the armsmen and couriers?"

"Yes, ser."

"Were you the one who gave the message to the courier?"

"Yes, ser . . . but it was sealed, ser."

Saryn could sense the truth . . . and a certain growing anger within the undercaptain. "And it arrived sealed, as it should have. Who was the courier? Is he here in Lornth?"

"Klaemyn, ser, and he's on the roster for today."

"We need to talk to armsman Klaemyn."

"Courier Klaemyn, ser."

"If you would lead the way . . ."

Saryn didn't have far to walk, because the chamber that Saryn would have called the couriers' ready room was in the same barracks, except at the far east end, nearest the gates.

There were three couriers in the room. Two were polishing their brass,

and the third was doing something with his scabbard. All three straightened. "Ser!"

"Maesyn, Zubael . . . you two can take a walk for a while," said
Maerkyn.

The remaining courier, one of the two who had been working on his
brass, stiffened. He looked older than the other two and vaguely familiar
to Saryn, but she couldn't have sworn that he was the one who had delivered Zeldyan's message. Like Maerkyn had been, he was worried but puzzled, and Saryn could sense his questioning as to what he might have done
wrong.

"You were the one selected to ride to Westwind, weren't you?"

The courier/armsman looked to Maerkyn. The undercaptain nodded.
"You're to answer the commander's questions."

"Yes, ser."

"Where did you stop on the way to Westwind?"

"Just at the way stations, ser. We were told to make haste."

"I'm curious, Klaemyn. Who were your escorts when you rode to Westwind this last time?"

"Daelyst, Reagor, and Salastyn, ser. They're with the undercaptain's
company." The courier went on quickly. "We always have armsmen for the
longer runs, where it might be difficult to deliver a message without armsmen."

"I can see that."

"You were the one I gave the message to, ser. You remember that, don't
you?"

Saryn could sense the truth there. "I do, and there's no question that
you delivered the missive directly to me. Did you stop only at way stations
on the return?"

"Except once, ser. Daelyst said that we could stop at Lord Henstrenn's
on the way back, that he knew the undercaptain of the armsmen there.
The timing was right, and we needed a place to sleep, and we're allowed
to stop at holders' keeps. Lord Henstrenn's armsmen welcomed us right
well. We had a good supper, and a good breakfast." Klaemyn shook his
head. "Last really good meal for Daelyst, poor fellow."

"Poor fellow?" asked Saryn.

"He started feeling poorly the next day, and he fell out of the saddle
dead the day after, just as we were getting near Lornth, almost back. It

must have been a flux or something. That's what the local healer said in the nearest hamlet."

"I'm very sorry to hear that," replied Saryn, and she was, but not because she cared greatly for the dead courier. "Do you recall the name of the undercaptain at Duevek?"

"Branslyd. That was what Daelyst said."

"Undercaptain Branslyd," mused Saryn, trying to fix the name in her mind, before she asked, "You never let anyone else see or touch the message I gave you?"

"No, ser! We're not allowed to do that. I even slept with it, ser."

"Did you sleep well at Duevek?"

The slightest frown crossed Maerkyn's face, but the undercaptain said nothing.

"Yes, ser. Good bunks, good food . . . the best night's rest on the whole run."

Saryn nodded. "Thank you. You've been a great help."

Once they were well away from the courier's standby room and back in the duty chamber, Maerkyn looked at Saryn. "Ser, might I ask . . . ?"

"You might, but I'm not at liberty to say. Not yet. Not until I talk to Lady Zeldyan."

"You don't think—"

"So far, Undercaptain," began Saryn, trying to speak formally and indirectly, rather than bluntly, "I have no reason to believe that you or any of those currently under your command did anything improper or disloyal. I doubt that anything I discover will change that. That does not mean that others have not done so, unfortunately."

As Maerkyn took in her words, Saryn could sense his remaining anger being replaced by a mixture of concern and curiosity. Finally, he asked, "Might I ask why Westwind is so concerned about the regency?"

"It's very simple, Undercaptain. We like neighbors who are friendly. We get concerned when those rulers who are friendly find themselves in difficulty, particularly when those who are creating the difficulty appear to be far less friendly to Westwind. In short, we'd prefer to help our friends rather than having to fight those who might supplant them."

"You think the regency is in straits that dire?"

Saryn looked straight at the taller officer. "Don't you?" She kept her eyes fixed on him.

"I'm . . . not the one to say . . . Commander."

"You're loyal to the Lady Zeldyan and Lord Nesslek, Maerkyn. I appreciate that. So do they, I'm certain, but loyalty does not require blinders." Saryn smiled. "Sometimes, it does require tact, and that is a quality that I've often found difficult to master when dealing with those who use polite words to conceal less-than-honorable intent."

Maerkyn looked even more puzzled.

"Let's just say that honor is as honor does, Undercaptain, not as it speaks. Now . . . I need to meet with the Lady Zeldyan. Thank you for your help, and I'm sorry if I'm not totally forthcoming."

"Commander . . . you need not explain." Maerkyn's words were cool.

"I don't have to, and I would like to, but that has to be the regent's decision, because it bears on Lord Nesslek's safety." Saryn *thought* she sensed a thawing in the undercaptain's coolness. "Until later, Undercaptain."

"Commander." Maerkyn inclined his head more than was merely perfunctory but less than he probably would have to a male superior.

After she left the duty room, Saryn made her way back to her quarters, stopping only momentarily to check with Hryessa. Then, once she had washed up and changed into a clean uniform—and left the battle harness in her chambers, changing to a formal sword belt with a single short sword—Saryn made her way to Zeldyan's private chambers, only to be informed by Lyentha that Zeldyan was in the lower tower council chamber. A few moments later, Saryn walked into the lower chamber, where Zeldyan was seated in one of the chairs—now around a circular table that had not been present when Saryn had last been in the chamber. Even in midday, with the brass lamps lit, the dark-paneled chamber was gloomy enough that Saryn wondered how Zeldyan could read the ledger before her.

"I saw you crossing the courtyard with young Maerkyn, and he did not look particularly happy," offered Zeldyan, without rising from her chair.

"He was not, but I trust I left him in a better humor than then. I talked with your courier, and, although I cannot prove it, I know that my message to you was intercepted and read by Lord Henstrenn and returned to the courier without his knowledge of its absence. That might well explain why Keistyn was waiting to see me when we returned. Had I returned with less of a force, I doubt I would have made it safely to Lornth."

"You are certain of this?"

"Keistyn was waiting, and I wouldn't be surprised if Henstrenn was prepared as well in case I went that way. The armsman who arranged for the courier and his escorts to spend the night at Duevek was familiar with an undercaptain there. That armsman woke up ill the next morning and died two days later, supposedly of a flux, just before he was to reach Lornth. The courier admits he had a filling supper at Duevek and slept extraordinarily well that night." Saryn shrugged.

"You are most suspicious, Saryn." Zeldyan's laugh was light and bitter. "That does sound like Henstrenn, leaving no way for anyone to prove anything."

"Proof may be necessary for public action, but suspicion is sufficient for private precautions."

"What precautions do you suggest?"

"Those will depend on what Lord Henstrenn has to say."

"True." Zeldyan closed the ledger and gestured to the chair at her right. "Join me. It should not be long before his lordship arrives. Henstrenn may be many things, but he is always punctual and attentive to the details, particularly those that do not inconvenience him greatly."

A few moments after the tower bell rang announcing the turning of the glass at noon, the study door opened, and Lyentha announced, "Lord Henstrenn."

Henstrenn, Lord of Duevek, was almost what Saryn expected, an older and more handsome version of Keistyn, his black hair shot with streaks of iron gray, and a warm smile on his face as he advanced toward Lady Zeldyan, his boots so light on the stone, then the worn dark green carpet, that his movements seemed almost feline. He stopped and bowed, then said, "My Lady Regent." Then he turned to Saryn, and added, "Arms-Commander."

Like Keistyn, Henstrenn had a deep, warm, and powerful voice, one whose friendliness could not have been more at odds with the coldness behind it, Saryn sensed, but she merely replied pleasantly, "Lord Henstrenn."

"When I heard that the Arms-Commander of Westwind was visiting the regents," Henstrenn went on, "I thought I would pay my respects to all the regents and the arms-commander." He paused. "But apparently, I was mistaken about all the regents being present."

"Your courtesy in wishing to see the arms-commander is much appreciated," replied Zeldyan. "Please be seated."

Henstrenn slipped into the seat directly across the table from Zeldyan with feral grace. "Will we be seeing the other regents?"

"My sire has indicated he is involved in training Lord Nesslek, and since I have not heard where Lord Kelthyn is located, it was not possible to contact him in a timely manner," replied Zeldyan. "We frankly did not expect that the arms-commander would respond so quickly."

Henstrenn smiled warmly, as did his deep brown eyes. "I have heard that the Marshal of Westwind is not one to tarry. Once she discovered Lord Arthanos marching an army toward the Roof of the World, she destroyed it." He looked to Saryn. "Or are those reports incorrect or overstated?"

"Lord Arthanos had about nine thousand men, mounted and foot," replied Saryn. "All but about two hundred perished."

"I had not heard the details. Perhaps you could enlighten me as to how this amazing destruction was accomplished."

"I am not privy to all the weapons that the Marshal has at her disposal." *Most, but not all.* "I do know that her archers alone slew hundreds, and that we could find no trace, even of the bodies, of most of those who perished."

"Mighty sorcery, it would appear, must have destroyed the remainder. Would you know just what type of sorcery, Arms-commander?"

"I could not possibly describe the means by which it happened, Lord Henstrenn. I can only say that when the smoke and dust cleared, there was no sign of Lord Arthanos and his army, save a company or so of rear guards and ten supply wagons." All that was perfectly true, if misleading. For a moment, Saryn could sense that, in some way, her words had discomfited the man, if but for a moment.

"It must be of some concern to those in Westwind that their safety rests so entirely on one person, mighty as the Marshal must be."

"That is no different from the ruler of any other land, is it?" replied Saryn. "The responsibility lies upon the ruler to find the people and tools by which he or she can best protect the land and those upon it."

"Lord-holders share that responsibility, if on a lesser scale," offered Henstrenn. "We must balance what has been with what is best for the future, commensurate with the resources at hand."

"You state that concisely and well," said Zeldyan.

"Thank you, your grace. Now that the arms-commander is indeed here in Lornth, might I ask what your plans are?"

"You may indeed, Lord Henstrenn. We will be visiting a number of holdings so that the holders may meet Commander Saryn and come to understand better why it is good to have an ally such as Westwind between us and Gallos . . . as well as flanking Suthya."

"You realize, Lady Zeldyan, that we would not have difficulties with Suthya had Lornth in an earlier time not taken action to seize certain lands and the port of Rulyarth?"

"That is an interesting way of putting it, since Rulyarth and the lands along the river had belonged to Lornth for centuries until they were seized a generation ago. Reclaiming what was historically ours should not have been unexpected by the Suthyans."

"No, Lady, but taking it without the means to hold it for long exposed us to greater danger than not taking it at all. Still . . . I would not dwell on Suthya, for what is past is past."

There was a silence, although Saryn could sense Zeldyan's concealed anger. After a moment, Saryn said, "As you may have heard, Lord Henstrenn, because traders do tend to cross the Roof of the World, we do occasionally hear intriguing bits of news. One that the Marshal found of great interest was that a Suthyan trader apparently visited several holdings in Lornth. What seemed strange was that he took no goods with him, just armsmen bound to the Suthyan Council. Because your holding is closer to the roads that the traders follow, I was wondering what else you might be able to add to what the Marshal conveyed to the regents."

Henstrenn was not surprised by Saryn's words, either in expression or within, which confirmed for her that he already knew that she knew of his dealings with Baorl. "I could not possibly add to anything that the most powerful Marshal of Westwind has determined to have occurred. I would say that any holder who would protect his people will listen to all sources of information, but listening does not mean that loyalties change in the slightest, only that one listens, just as you, Lady Zeldyan, and the regents listen to me and to the arms-commander."

"You're most persuasive, Lord Henstrenn." Zeldyan smiled. "You are also most astute. Of all the holders you know, who might be among the best for the arms-commander and me to visit—besides yourself, since you have been so kind as to make yourself available here?"

"Ah . . . there are so many who have doubts about the efficacy of allying Lornth to a power about which they know so little . . ." Henstrenn paused, as if he were thinking, before continuing. "But I might suggest Lord Maeldyn, or perhaps Lord Spalkyn."

Saryn could sense a calculation behind Henstrenn's suggestion, one, she suspected, designed to push Zeldyan away from the very names he had suggested.

"Do any others come to mind?" Zeldyan's inquiry was sweetly voiced.

"If one wanted to find out how those near Lord Deryll feel about Westwind, you might consider visiting Lord Barcauyn."

"That is a most interesting possibility," admitted Zeldyan. "We will give your thoughts careful consideration, Lord Henstrenn. And how is your most lovely and obedient consort?"

"Myleanda is well. She is visiting her cousin at the moment."

"Oh . . . I had not heard that. She and Keistyn are so different . . ."

"Different as we may all be, we do share a great concern about assuring that Lornth remain strong . . . as I know you do, Lady Zeldyan."

"I am so glad to hear you say that," replied Zeldyan. "You, above all, are known for keeping your word and commitments."

"You are most kind," demurred Henstrenn.

Saryn managed to keep a pleasant smile on her face for another quarter glass or so while Zeldyan and Henstrenn traded apparent pleasantries.

Finally, Zeldyan rose from her seat, and, after a moment, as Henstrenn did, so did Saryn.

"I am so glad that you came to see me and to meet Commander Saryn," Zeldyan said warmly. "I'm sure that you'll be telling your acquaintances about her, and how much better it would be to have Westwind as an ally in these . . . difficult times."

"They could, indeed, be difficult times, and we all must take care to choose wisely for Lornth, Lady Regent . . . as I know you will." Henstrenn bowed to Zeldyan, then turned slightly to Saryn. "I'm pleased to meet you, Commander Saryn, here, rather than in a less . . . hospitable situation, and I trust you feel as I do."

"Indeed I do," replied Saryn with yet another smile she did not feel. "It's well to learn about someone in person so that you don't judge that person on what others say."

"Do not let us keep you," said Zeldyan. "Do convey my best to your consort."

Zeldyan did not reseat herself until several moments after the study door closed behind the departing Henstrenn. When she sat back down, so did Saryn.

"I didn't realize that Keistyn and Henstrenn were related by consortship," Saryn said.

"Saryn," said Zeldyan gently, "in some way or another all of the seventeen major holders in Lornth are related to each other. With whom else could they consort?"

Saryn concealed a wince. No wonder Lornth was in trouble.

"Now . . . we should discuss whom we should visit, and in what order. I'm inclined to follow Henstrenn's suggestions."

"So that you can point out to Kelthyn that you did . . . and because those names were on the list anyway?"

"At times, doing what someone says they want is the best way to disarm them." Zeldyan smiled. "Besides, he did not wish me to visit Maeldyn. That was why he suggested him."

Saryn smiled back at the regent. Zeldyan was no one's fool.

XLVII

Given the way inns operated, Saryn decided that she would visit the Square Platter after midmorning on twoday. Again, as she and the three guards rode from the palace to the square and down the side street, men and women alike glanced at them, then quickly looked away.

When she dismounted outside the Square Platter, she handed the gelding's reins to Yulia. "Just wait here for now." She studied the inn, a narrow brown-and-yellow brick building some fifteen yards across the front, with three windows on the right side and one on the left side of a large single door. Both the door and the shutters were painted a deep burgundy. A covered porch only two yards deep extended the width of the front, and a narrow brick-paved lane on the left side of the building presumably led to stables and a rear courtyard. She turned and stepped up onto the narrow porch.

The tall and broad man who stood beside the door looked at Saryn, then at the three Westwind guards, still mounted, before he said, "I don't think you're welcome here."

Saryn smiled politely. "I'm welcome. I'm here to see Haelora. I have a letter from her aunt in Henspa introducing me to her."

"I said—" The man stopped, realizing that the short sword was at his throat.

"What's all this about?" Another man, older and paunchier, stepped out of the inn. His eyes flicked from Saryn to the armed guards and back to Saryn.

"I'm here to see Haelora. I have a letter of introduction from Jennyleu. Your man wants to keep me from her." Saryn lowered the short sword only slightly.

Abruptly, the second man shook his head, almost ruefully. "You're an angel, aren't you?"

"Saryn. I'm the Arms-Commander of Westwind. I was asked to meet with the regents, but I've stopped at the Black Bull three times now . . ."

"Jennyleu couldn't resist sending you to see her niece." He shook his head, then looked at the tall man. "Rhytter . . . don't ever cross one of the angels. I don't want to tell your family how you ended up dead."

Rhytter's eyes narrowed. "You going to let them in here?"

"You want to die over it?"

"I think I'll be finding another job." Rhytter turned and walked off the porch.

Saryn just waited, looking at the prematurely balding blond man who was probably younger than she was.

"Don't worry about it. He never has liked women all that much. I'm Vanadyl, Haelora's consort and half owner of this establishment."

"Saryn." She displayed the envelope. "From Jennyleu."

"Come on in."

Saryn followed Vanadyl inside and into a narrow foyer.

"Haelora! Got a surprise for you!"

The woman who hurried through the archway from the public room to the right wore a burgundy skirt and blouse, and a cream-colored apron. She looked at Saryn, as if not quite certain what to say.

"The angel here's got a letter from your aunt. Oh, she did what we couldn't. Rhytter said he wouldn't be working here anymore."

"Fancy that." Haelora was as blond as her husband, but unlike many of the women of Lornth, whose hair was long and either braided or bound back, hers was cut not that much longer than Saryn's. Also, unlike her husband, she was slender and muscular.

"This is from your aunt." Saryn extended the envelope.

Haelora opened the envelope. When she finished the letter, she shook her head ruefully. "Only Aunt Jennyleu'd have the nerve. Says she owes her life to you."

"I helped a little when she was ill earlier this summer."

"More than a little if she put it in ink," suggested Vanadyl.

"She writes that I'm to help you." Haelora paused. "Begging your pardon, Angel, but what sort of help could a poor innkeeper provide?"

"Information." Saryn looked at the younger woman. "We're here to help Lady Zeldyan. There seem to be a number of lords who feel like Rhytter did."

"Glad he's gone," replied Haelora with a laugh. "Wouldn't have been working here if he hadn't a been Ma's youngest cousin. Since he left on his own, I'm not obligated anymore. What sort of information?"

"What you hear. What people are worried about. How people feel about the regency."

Haelora gestured to the public room. "Best we take one of the front tables. Folks know not to bother me there if I'm talking to someone. That's where I haggle with everyone."

"And she haggles well," added Vanadyl. "Otherwise, we'd not be in business." He turned back toward the narrow desk against the wall, where a ledger lay open.

"But he keeps the accounts," replied Haelora, leading the way into the public room and toward a table in the corner farthest from the archway, where she settled into a chair from which she could watch both the archway to the main foyer and the smaller archway to the kitchen.

"Do you have any children?" asked Saryn.

"Just Maryla. She's but eleven and one of the best cooks in Lornth. Runs the kitchen right well, she does. You wanted to know what worries folks? They worry that their wallets are too thin, and they don't see 'em getting any fatter. They don't see the regents doing much to help them. Leastwise, the Lady Zeldyan doesn't spray coins like Lord Nessil's consort did—a new dress every eightday. He wasn't much better, with all his gold-and-purple tunics."

"What do people think about Lady Zeldyan?"

"I don't know as they think much, excepting she's trying to do her best. Most folk just want to have enough for small comforts and be left alone."

"What about Lord Kelthyn?"

"Oh . . . Lord Snotnose . . . he near-on rode down old Bethamie last winter, then yelled at her for not getting out of his way, then talks real cultured to the fellow he's riding with. Can't say as many folks even pay much attention to him. I wouldn't know that much, save that Bethamie's daughter is Maryla's friend. Now . . . Lord Gethen, he's gentlefolk. Some of his armsmen come in here. Never heard a one speak ill of him, and more than a few tales of how he helped a widow or an orphan on his holding. Wouldn't be surprised if some wouldn't take a blade for him."

"Did you ever hear anything about a Lord Keistyn?"

"Can't say as I have."

"Henstrenn?"

"He's the Lord of Duevek, isn't he? Only thing I ever heard here is that he's been hiring armsmen, anywhere he can get them. Been doing it for nigh on three–four years. Have to wonder where he gets the golds, when most of the lords haven't been adding any armsmen at all."

"What bothers you most these days?"

"Not having enough paying customers coming through the doors." Haelora laughed.

Saryn laughed as well.

"You wouldn't know what's going on at the palace, would you?" asked the innkeeper. "Seems like we don't get near as many palace armsmen anymore."

"I know one company went north to Lord Gethen's holding with the overlord-heir," replied Saryn. "There are only half as many armsmen here now. But . . ." Saryn grinned. "You wouldn't mind if some of the Westwind guards came here when they're off duty?"

"Their coppers are as good as anyone's, aren't they?" Haelora smiled. "Besides, these days, it's not like we're turning away folks. We'll give 'em more for their coppers than most, and we don't water the beer or the wine."

"That's good to know." Saryn rose. "Thank you. You won't mind if I stop when I can?"

"That I wouldn't." Haelora stood. "You'd be welcome anytime."

As she left, Saryn just hoped that would always be the case.

XLVIII

In the end, Zeldyan decided that the first regency visit should be to Lord Barcauyn.

"That way," she had explained to Saryn, "you will see for yourself how little the eastern border means to the holders of the west. Then we can make our way farther north to see Lord Maeldyn and possibly Spalkyn, then visit Lord Deolyn before heading back and stopping at The Groves on the way."

"You think Deolyn will tell us something of the Suthyans?"

"Either in words or actions," Zeldyan replied.

And that was how, after a ride of four days that took them slightly south and all too far west for Saryn's comfort, even with all of fourth squad and a squad of Maerkyn's armsmen, they entered the holding of Cauyna. In time, she found herself sitting on the expansive second-story terrace of Lord Barcauyn's villa, looking at the hills to the east beyond a meandering and placid stream, on the far side of which was the town of Arkyn. On that sevenday evening, the setting sun bathed the hills and the town in a reddish light, while the villa shaded the terrace, and a breeze from the east made the air almost pleasant for Saryn.

The comfortable cushioned wooden armchairs were set in a semicircle, facing outward, with Lady Zeldyan in the center chair, the gray-haired Barcauyn to her right, and Barcauyn's eldest son, Joncaryl, to her left. Saryn was seated beside Barcauyn, while another son, Belconyn, sat beside his older brother. Barcauyn's consort was nowhere to be seen.

". . . a great surprise to see you, Lady Regent," rumbled Barcauyn. "A most pleasant one, I must say. I had thought all your attention was devoted

to the difficulties to the east." He glanced toward Saryn. "The presence of
the arms-commander gives me hope that now the regents might pay
greater attention to our difficulties here."

"There are difficulties everywhere these days," replied Zeldyan. "How
do you view the problems . . . to the north?"

"What problems? We had not the forces to hold Rulyarth, and we did
not. The Suthyans wanted the port in a way that would have been far too
costly for us to hold. Yet they will trade with any who care to trade. They
care little for expanding, now they have reclaimed what they believe is
theirs. On the other hand, that demon Deryll will bleed those of us in the
west dry."

"We will talk of Deryll in a moment," Zeldyan said smoothly. "I have
heard words that suggest the Suthyans have been in rather close contact
with the Prefect of Gallos."

Barcauyn laughed, a deep, rolling sound. "Most likely with his departed son." He turned to Saryn. "I understand that Arthanos squandered
an army of close to ten thousand men trying to retake the Roof of the
World."

"Nine thousand, Lord Barcauyn," replied Saryn. "A few hundred
escaped." She paused, if briefly. "He may have thought of it as 'retaking,'
but as I understand matters, when the Marshal created Westwind, the
lands in question were thought to belong to Lornth. Perhaps I should
leave sleeping snakes cold, but I have great doubts that, had he been successful, Arthanos would have returned the lands on the Roof of the World
to Lornth."

"Ha! Right you may be, but it's not worth talking about, because your
Marshal assured it didn't happen, and I've never seen much gain in jaw-
ing about how things might have been."

"Nor I," answered Saryn. "I only raised the point as an indication that
Gallos and Suthya are not to be dismissed when considering what may
happen."

"In the future, when Karthanos dies, and he well may have already,
from what I hear, there will be a contest over who will be the next prefect.
That prefect will have to consolidate his power. Only then, and that will be
years from now, will anyone need to fear Gallos, and I dare say that your
Marshal will put a stop to any designs that prefect has on the west. The
Suthyans always want someone else to fight for them, so that they can sell

weapons and goods to both sides. So long as we do not fight, they cannot profit from selling weapons and food. But the west, that is where the threat to Lornth lies. If I look to the hills that mark the west of our holding, I see all that separates us from the Jeranyi. Beyond those hills are grassy plains stretching all the way to Bornt. Those are the demon-cursed grasslands that spawned the Jeranyi." Barcauyn's voice was level but not free of the bitterness behind it. "You may not remember it, Lady Regent, for I was barely more than a boy when they last swept out of the hills into the western hamlets of the holding. They made off with hundreds of cattle and sheep and a score of women. I even knew one of the girls they took. Lovely thing."

"You didn't go after her?" asked Saryn.

"It's a day's ride from there to here. My father did send me out to see what they had done and to offer some coins to those who lost livestock. The Jeranyi were long gone when we arrived, and trying to track them into the hills and out into the grasslands beyond . . . that would have been senseless." Barcauyn shook his head. "After that, Ildyrom and his bitch consort turned to raiding the south, and little around Rohrn was spared. The one good thing that came out of the battles between the angel mages and the Cyadorans was the devastation that fell on Jerans. We've had ten years without a single raid, but the Jeranyi are riding again, and closer and closer to us." He turned to Zeldyan. "That is why I fear the Jeranyi far more than those on any other border."

"The Jeranyi are far greater devils than all others on our borders," murmured Joncaryl.

Belconyn nodded, not quite enthusiastically.

"You make a strong argument, lord, and I hear your concerns." Zeldyan smiled sadly. "Yet, as a child, I saw our armsmen at The Groves fending off Gallosian and Suthyan raiders, and those in Clynya were beset by the Cyadorans. Lord Deolyn has told me about Suthyans who were not so interested in trading as taking. On all sides are enemies." She glanced to Saryn. "In the past ten years, the only land that has done much against our old enemies has been Westwind, sad as that may sound, and you know of my own grievous losses in regard to Westwind."

"What does Westwind say, then, Arms-Commander?" asked Barcauyn.

"You know what we have faced with Gallos, and for the moment, they are less of a threat. After that, we tracked Suthyan armsmen up to the lands of Lornth. What they were doing there, we do not know, for we would not intrude in following them. The Suthyans have attempted both bribery and treachery to attempt to persuade Westwind to ally with them against Lornth. We have not. That is one reason why I am here."

"Would you have us fight your battles, then?" Barcauyn's voice turned chill.

Saryn turned her eyes . . . and the flow of dark power . . . on the lord. "We ask no one to fight our battles. We came to the regents because Lornth has treated with us fairly, and we thought they should know what we had learned about Suthya and the traders' intent. We have no need and no desire for lands beyond what we hold."

Barcauyn sat back in his chair, silent for a long moment.

Joncaryl frowned, as did his brother.

"Ah . . ." Barcauyn finally said. "I see now why you are arms-commander. Yet you seem more like a mage, for all the arms you bore when you rode in."

"All the arms?" asked Joncaryl, adding quickly, before Saryn could respond, his voice light, not quite mocking, "I saw your guards—and you, Commander. Tell me . . . are those daggers the only weapons you have?"

"They're short swords, not daggers, and we also use bows."

"The blades are really only long daggers, it looks like to me."

"They can be very effective, especially in close combat," replied Saryn.

"I don't see how, not against a proper blade," pressed Joncaryl. "You give away far too much space."

"They've proved that against anyone who's tried." Saryn smiled politely.

"Then they couldn't have been very good with their blades . . . begging your pardon, Commander. And bows . . . well . . . they don't prove much about their wielder."

Saryn could sense the inflexible arrogance of youth, yet felt as well that she could not afford to concede the point, not when the reputations of the Westwind Guard and Westwind itself were at stake. "So far, over ten years, Lord Joncaryl, every force that has attacked Westwind or her guards has failed, most killed to the last man."

"That was because of magery, not skill at arms, at least from what I've heard."

"Magery played a part in destroying whole armies. That I will concede, but in smaller conflicts settled only by arms, even when faced with larger forces, the guards triumphed overwhelmingly."

"You'll pardon me—"

"Words seldom settle such matters of opinion," interjected Barcauyn smoothly. "If I were younger, I'd give it a try in a thorough sparring, perhaps against you, Commander." He shrugged. "I am too old to spar, but I would like to see how you might fare against a truly skilled man-at-arms, such as my son. Perhaps tomorrow?"

"I'd be most happy to demonstrate in sparring," Saryn said, even as she knew that the contest had been a setup.

"Excellent!" Barcauyn beamed. "Now . . . if we might talk of other matters . . . ones more pleasant before we repair to the dining chamber to eat . . ."

Saryn understood. From that moment on, nothing of substance would be discussed, and tomorrow, she would have to prove what she and the guards could do with weapons—again.

XLIX

Saryn joined Zeldyan for breakfast in a small room off the main hall of the villa. Zeldyan was quiet, perhaps because Saryn was preoccupied and did not eat all that much of the heavy and hearty fare, which included heavy ham strips, a cheese, egg, and noodle concoction, and hot, fresh, dark bread. Saryn appreciated the bread most. After eating, she excused herself and went to ready herself for sparring with Joncaryl, limbering up and exercising just enough so that she didn't feel mentally cloudy.

There was no question as to where the sparring would take place. The west courtyard contained a well-maintained and swept paved area in the center of which was a large circle marked by inlaid black stones. The courtyard was also where the armory was located, its ironbound and heavy oak door distinguished by the round shield affixed thereto. In the center of the black-rimmed yellow shield was a crest featuring a mailed fist crossed with a deep blue flower that Saryn did not recognize.

Saryn brought her fighting blades, a pair of blunted blades, and a set of wooden wands down to the section of the western courtyard below the terrace—what amounted to a private arena, since people could sit on the terrace and watch sparring over the low balcony wall. She laid the weapons out on one of the benches set against the villa wall—right below the west terrace, still partly shaded by the morning sun.

Above her on the terrace a group was gathering, one that included Zeldyan, an older graying woman who was likely Barcauyn's consort, and two young women. Behind her, she sensed several other figures approaching. She half turned from the bench.

"What are those?" asked Joncaryl, gesturing to the wands.

"Sparring wands," replied Saryn, already sensing the young man's contempt.

"I can't say as I've ever seen such," added Barcauyn from several paces behind his son.

"We use them because it reduces injuries when guards are learning."

"That may be fine for your guards, but not for armsmen," said Joncaryl. "Blunted blades are one thing, but I will not stoop to wooden planks."

Saryn smiled politely, looking up slightly at the well-muscled young man. "I would not think of having you stoop to anything, Lord Joncaryl." She stepped to one side, then toward his father. "Lord Barcauyn, we use wands because our short swords are, despite their size, rather deadly, even when blunted. I will endeavor not to cause any permanent harm to your son, but I ask your understanding that, even with a blunted blade, injury is possible."

"It is also possible to you, Commander," Barcauyn pointed out. "Far more possible, I would judge."

"We will see," replied Saryn. "I will use a pair of blunted short swords." She stepped forward and picked up the blades, one in each hand.

Joncaryl accepted a long and wide blade from his brother Belconyn.

"You have seen the circle," said Barcauyn. "I had it swept just a while ago so that your footing should be firm."

"What are your limits for sparring?" Saryn asked.

"We try not to kill the other person," said Joncaryl, "but it is up to each fighter to protect himself . . . or herself."

Saryn nodded. Given the culture of Lornth, that was about what she expected, but it was better to ask and know than to risk health or life on false assumptions. Blades in hand, she walked to the center of the circle and waited for Joncaryl to follow and face her.

The heir to Cauyna raised the massive blade that looked to be far more than a hand and a half and began moving it through a series of moves, meant to be intimidating.

Saryn just watched, letting her senses take in the flow and the rhythm of Joncaryl's moves and blade, holding her own blades at the ready.

She could sense the growing anger in the tall and muscular young lordling, as if he expected her to move first. Instead, she smiled, waiting.

Joncaryl finally moved, a restricted and controlled circle of steel that was almost a defensive thrust.

Saryn slipped to the side, circling to his left, merely avoiding his blade.

Joncaryl widened his circling thrust, and Saryn kept moving, sideways, but not retreating.

From a circling probe, Joncaryl unleashed a slash, and Saryn used the right blade to deflect his heavier weapon downward, coming across with the left and letting the flat strike the back of his arm before she danced back.

Joncaryl didn't seem to notice and launched a series of attacks.

Again, Saryn used the short swords to deflect his heavier weapon, thwacking him moderately on his right thigh.

"You can't even stand against a heavy blade," he said with a laugh.

"That's not the point," she replied.

Another flurry of slashes followed, none of which came close to her body, despite the greater length of his blade.

After the last one, before he had fully recovered, Saryn moved closer, and on the next series, easily slid or parried his attacks.

"You're not so good," he muttered, lowering his voice to add, "another loudmouth with little daggers."

Saryn smiled and parried again, and again, until, within moments, she had the opening she wanted, and with the blade in her right hand, she caught the heavy weapon on the trailing edge and jammed it down toward the stone pavement, moving even more inside the arc of the big blade and bringing up the short sword in her left hand.

At the very last moment, Saryn turned the edge of the blade so that the flat slammed into the right side of Joncaryl's jaw. She could hear the *crack* of breaking bone, but, knowing the young man's rage, in his moment of pain she stepped forward and brought the flat of the other blade down across his forearms with enough force that his hand-and-a-half blade slipped from his fingers and clattered on the courtyard stones.

Then she swept his feet from under him and stood with one blunted blade at his throat, the other ready to strike were he unwise enough to try anything else.

"Do you still think my little daggers are toys, Joncaryl?" She stepped back, still watching him with one foot on his big blade.

The young man struggled to his feet. "Magery . . . it was magery."

"Joncaryl!" snapped Barcauyn. "Cease! The commander could have slain you three times over. She tapped you twice when she could have struck. Her only magery is what she can do with those short blades. If you are too stupid to understand that, then you are too stupid ever to inherit a holding."

Those words froze Joncaryl. His eyes flicked from his sire to Saryn and back to his sire.

Saryn could sense Barcauyn's twin anger—both at her and at his son—and she turned to him, if keeping an eye on the angry heir. "Lord Barcauyn . . . I apologize if I have caused difficulty. What you have just seen is one reason why I am here."

Anger warred with puzzlement on the face of the older lord.

"We have been forced to kill far more good men than we ever wished," explained Saryn, "all because none wished to believe that we could and would defend ourselves. We will continue to defend ourselves, if we must, but we would rather not slaughter those who know not what they face." She sheathed one of the short swords.

"Might I ask how long you trained with those blades?" asked Barcauyn.

"From when I was about five." She didn't mention that it had been for a competitive sport on Sybra, not blood.

"On the far side of the Rational Stars?"

Saryn nodded. "It was a point of honor." That was certainly true.

"Only . . . women?"

"No. Both men and women. Our ship just carried more women than men, but the warrior tradition is stronger in women."

"I would find that strange, had I not seen you fight."

Joncaryl's eyes flicked back and forth between the arms-commander and his father.

"Now . . . there is one more thing you should see." Saryn smiled sadly. She was coming to hate what she was about to do.

"You wish to spar with someone else . . . with what you have already shown?"

"No, that would be unfair." Saryn pointed to the round shield beside the armory door. "Would you mind if I used the shield as a target? Even if I damage it?"

"No," said Barcauyn, his voice puzzled. "It's just an old shield."

"Thank you."

Saryn turned, lifted the blade, then hurled it at the shield, smoothing the flows and imparting that sense of black strength to it.

Thunnk!

Barcauyn's mouth dropped open when he saw the blade, buried to a third of its length through both the iron-plated shield and the wood behind it.

Belconyn's face paled, and he looked at his wounded brother, then back to Saryn.

Up on the terrace, Zeldyan's hand went to her mouth for just an instant.

And Saryn had the feeling—from all of them—that they thought she had suddenly become something like a mountain snow leopard that had just dispatched a handful of armsmen. She inclined her head to Joncaryl. "I am truly sorry, Joncaryl, but I have learned that few ever believe that a woman smaller than many men could excel at arms."

Belconyn walked over to the shield and tried to pry the blade out. He could not budge it.

Saryn followed him. "If you would excuse me . . ." She had to use order flows to smooth away the restraints. Even then, it took all of her strength to reclaim the blade. She looked at it. Blunt as it had been, it would still need a great deal of work even to return it to that state. She sheathed it and walked back across the dusty paving stones toward Barcauyn.

She had gained the understanding of the lord and father and made an enemy of the son and heir. Yet anything that would have been to the satisfaction of the son would not have convinced the father.

She stopped short of the holder. "I must also apologize to you, Lord Barcauyn . . . but I have found that I lack great persuasive powers, except through my blades. I truly wish it were otherwise. If you would excuse me . . ."

"Of course." While the lord's voice was steady, there was a certain relief behind the words.

Only then did Saryn glance upward at the terrace, extending her senses as well. The muted murmurs were so low that she could not make out what was said, but what she did notice was that neither of the two girls—or young women—looked all that distraught, but Lady Barcauyn's face was filled with worry. Out of the welter of feelings, she could feel most strongly concern and a certain sense of horror. Amid those various feelings was one thread of satisfaction, and that had to be from Zeldyan, although Saryn was not absolutely certain.

She gathered all her blades and the practice wands and walked back into the villa and up to the guest quarters on the second level. Once in the large chamber, she washed up again, then sat down before the writing table in the quarters she had been given.

There was a knock on the door. Saryn could sense Zeldyan. "Yes?"

"Might I come in?"

"Please."

Zeldyan slipped into the chamber, closing the door behind her. She looked at Saryn. "I saw you spar in Lornth, and I was impressed . . . but you could have killed young Joncaryl within instants, couldn't you?"

"Yes," Saryn admitted. "I struck him gently, and he did not understand. Then he started insulting me under his breath."

"I thought so. When he considered it, so did Lord Barcauyn. You have left him sorely troubled."

"I trust I have not upset matters too greatly."

Zeldyan shook her head. "You have not. But I must confess that when I saw you fight, I saw death held in restraint. Each time I meet an angel, I fear more. You have already changed all of Candar, and yet there are but a handful of you. For all the power I saw in the black one, I fear you more."

Saryn laughed softly. "I'm just like you, Zeldyan. I'm trying to make my way in a world I didn't create in a place I never expected to be, dealing with men who don't like women who have any sort of power and ability."

"We share that," admitted the regent. "Yet I must dissemble and smile, and play one against another, and lean upon the reputation of my sire, the position of my late lord, and the tradition of the land. You . . . you can strike fear into their hearts."

"I wish that it were merely respect. Men hate women they fear. They will often respect, if grudgingly, men whom they fear."

"We will do what we must." Zeldyan paused. "I have told Lord Barcauyn that we have many to visit and will be departing on the morrow."

"I'm certain he was agreeable."

"He was. He did suggest that, if I could manage it, I should set you and your guards against Deryll."

"Doubtless he'd prefer mutual annihilation." Saryn's tone was bitter and dry.

"He well might, but even he thinks Deryll would be the loser. I have no doubts." Zeldyan inclined her head. "I will soothe Barcauyn, as I can."

Saryn merely nodded.

She remained in her quarters for a glass, if not somewhat longer. When she finally emerged, she followed the corridor toward the western terrace, but before she reached the terrace, Joncaryl stepped out from a side hallway.

"Do you wrestle?" asked Joncaryl, a crooked yet sly smile on an injured face, already turning black-and-blue. Pain mingled with anger behind the words.

"After a fashion," replied Saryn politely. "Except we call it unarmed combat, and it's designed to kill people as quickly as possible without using weapons."

The smile vanished. "Are all your people like that?"

"Not all the guards are trained in that. Just those who were trained from birth to be warriors." That wasn't exactly true in the Sybran sense, but it was accurate enough for Candar, and the young man wouldn't have understood the distinctions no matter how hard Saryn tried to explain.

Even so, she could sense Joncaryl's puzzlement, and she continued, "Angels are trained to do whatever they do in any way necessary and possible. We were fighting an enemy across the stars. Weapons could be destroyed in an instant. We were trained to be able to kill with anything at hand . . . or with nothing. You don't train armsmen that way. We do."

"You're not . . . armsmen. You're killers."

"No," said Saryn. "We're only killers when people try to kill us or take our land. I offered to use wooden wands against you. I struck you lightly to warn you. You paid no heed. Westwind never attacked Lornth and never attacked Gallos. Both paid no heed and attacked us."

"But it was a matter of honor."

"For us, it was a matter of survival. We had nowhere else to go. Survival trumps honor any moment of the eightday."

"Without honor . . . there is nothing." Behind Joncaryl's words was a sense of exasperation . . . and anticipation.

Saryn sensed someone moving from behind her, and whirled, using Belconyn's momentum to throw the younger brother into the wall. A second movement broke the dagger from his hand. While his hand was limp, Saryn was fairly certain she hadn't broken his wrist, but he wouldn't have much use of the hand for days.

At that moment, Zeldyan and Barcauyn appeared, walking through the archway from the terrace. The lord's eyes went from Belconyn, who was supporting his injured wrist with his good hand, to the dagger on the polished tile floor, then to Joncaryl, whose face bore an expression of anger mixed with shock.

"Both of you. To your quarters. You will remain there until I determine what to do with you. Be grateful that you are still alive."

Saryn said nothing, but watched both young men as they hurried away. The dagger remained on the polished floor tiles.

"What happened, Commander?" asked Zeldyan, clearly preempting the lord.

"Joncaryl attempted to find out what I knew of wrestling while his brother approached from behind me." Saryn shrugged. "I tried not to injure Belconyn too much, but his head will ache from where he hit the wall. His wrist should heal. It's not broken."

"You can tell that?" asked Zeldyan.

"Yes, Lady. If I'm near someone."

Barcauyn's countenance was ashen. "I must offer my deepest apologies for the unforgivable behavior of my sons."

Saryn paused a moment. "Lord Barcauyn, I accept your apology, and appreciate your grace in this matter. Also, because Lornth has no experience with women warriors, I understand your sons' failure to understand my abilities at first. What I find . . . distressing . . . is not their failure to understand, but their inability or unwillingness to understand once I showed those abilities, and their subsequent anger. I attempted to show Joncaryl what I could do without hurting him. His response was to taunt and belittle me under his breath when we sparred, then to have his brother attack me from behind while he distracted me. Were I a man, they would have accepted my abilities without question, and I hope you will understand that I find that distressing as well."

"You must admit that it is not common to see a woman of your skills," ventured Barcauyn.

Saryn could sense a certain irritation, even anger, in the lord and bit back the statements she might have made and nodded politely. "It has not been common in the past, but it will be far more common in the future, and I would hate to see your sons injured or even killed because they did not recognize that women can also be fearsome warriors. I would hope, with all my heart, that Westwind will never have to fight with Lornth again. That is one reason why I am here, so that you and other lords can see the value of Westwind as an ally rather than as an enemy." She paused and softened her voice. "I am sorry for the injuries to your sons, and for any distress I may have caused you in this matter."

"Commander." Barcauyn smiled faintly. "You have my admiration. My distress is as much at myself for failing to understand truly what you represent. You must understand that you are changing the world. That change is hard on those of us who have worked so hard to preserve our heritage."

"I understand that, Lord Barcauyn, for I have lost my heritage and must make my way in a world as strange to me as the one you fear Westwind may be creating is strange to you."

"You are a woman, and you talk of making your way." The lord shook his head. "Women in Lornth, in all of Candar, do not speak so."

"They have not spoken that way in the past, but they will in the future. Even if I had not come to Lornth, matters would still be changing, because women have seen what other women can do."

"That may well be, but times of change are not easy for anyone."

"No, they are not." Saryn paused, then added, "But they are always far harder on those who stand against what must be."

"If you will excuse us, Commander," said Zeldyan gently, "I need a few words with Lord Barcauyn."

Saryn nodded politely. After they passed, she walked out to the west terrace. It was empty . . . and unlikely to see anyone but her while she remained there.

L

Supper on sevenday was quiet and private, with only Lord Barcauyn, his consort, Lady Zeldyan, and Saryn. The atmosphere was also formal and chill. During the entire meal, Lady Barcauyn said fewer than twenty words, even in response to Zeldyan's questions. Not a single word was directed to Saryn, who sensed a smoldering anger from the lady, clearly directed at her.

After all the events of sevenday, Saryn was glad to be up early on eightday, and even happier once they had ridden out of the villa and through the still-quiet town of Arkyn, headed eastward. By midmorning, they were headed north on another clay road, slightly wider, but no more traveled, under a slightly hazy sky, with a warm breeze at their backs. Saryn turned in the saddle, slightly, and asked, "What did Lord Barcauyn say to you, if anything, after his sons' actions and yesterday's . . . events. He was very polite at supper. Excessively."

"We talked about what the other holders might do in regard to the regency and with regard to the Suthyan meddling. He is still greatly concerned about Deryll and the threat he sees in the Jeranyi. And, among other things, he apologized several times for offending my champion." Zeldyan smiled wryly. "It appears as though that might be your role. He said that never had he seen someone so small who was so deadly."

"He should see the Marshal, then," Saryn said.

"He understands that you could have killed Joncaryl, or crippled him for life."

"The problem is that Joncaryl doesn't understand that. Nor does Belconyn. I don't think they ever will." Saryn glanced at the road ahead, but there the only riders were those of their party, and not a wagon was in sight anywhere. "Were the girls on the terrace his daughters?"

"They were. There is an older daughter who is consorted to the younger son of Lord Mortryd, who holds Tryenda."

"I was never actually introduced to his consort," Saryn pointed out. "Was that because she would have refused such an introduction?"

"I'm certain she would have," replied Zeldyan. "She is . . . overly devoted . . . to her sons."

"So her presence at supper was by command of her consort?" *His way of declaring that he is the one who is lord of the holding.*

"That can often happen in Lornth. More than once I did not speak at a meal when Sillek became overlord."

"Women must obey, but they don't have to pretend to like it?"

"I fear that is only true of those who are lord-holder born."

With what Zeldyan had said earlier about the relations between lord-holders, that made sense. A consort could afford to express her dislike passively because the lord might still need the support of her father or brother or cousin . . . or not wish to alienate them unnecessarily.

"Joncaryl would have chopped me up if he could have," Saryn pointed out, "and he and his brother would have knifed me in the back hall. And Lady Barcauyn is angry at me?"

"She worries that he may have to fight for the remainder of his life, and will die young because he was bested by a woman, one far smaller than he. Even Barcauyn worried about that. His hope is that your prowess will become known widely enough that Joncaryl will profit from surviving your blades. Lady Barcauyn is less certain that such will happen."

For a moment, Saryn almost felt sorry for Barcauyn. The lord was caught between a chauvinistic tradition, an arrogant and spoiled son, and an excessively partisan consort and overly devoted mother. Still . . . "Lord Barcauyn was the one who pressed for the sparring match, and Joncaryl was totally insufferable. If I had demurred, Westwind would have no credibility, and I'd be of no support to you," Saryn pointed out.

"But you would not be bested by any man. You would die before allowing that. Is that not true?"

Am I that stiff-necked? Or is it just because this frigging place treats women so badly?

"Is it not true?" asked Zeldyan again, gently.

"I'd like to think I'd have enough sense to recognize anyone who was superior, man or woman. The Marshal is a better warrior than I, and I'd be foolish not to acknowledge that."

"But you will not be demeaned by those who are lesser in ability."

"I'd rather not be," Saryn admitted.

"Rather not?" Zeldyan offered a smile that was enigmatic, but behind it, Saryn sensed more—that Zeldyan believed Saryn inflexible and unwilling to submit to any man in anything.

Saryn just shrugged. After they had ridden another hundred yards or so, she asked, "What do you think Barcauyn will do?"

"Angry as his consort may be, he will not move against me. Not so long as you remain in Lornth."

That's just frigging fine. To keep these chauvinist idiots from undermining the regency, I have to stay in Lornth sparring against idiots with crowbars and sweating my way through summer and harvest . . . and who knows how much longer.

"Tell me about Lord Maeldyn," suggested Saryn, "and his holding."

"I have not talked with him often, and not in some time. He always seemed a man who kept his counsel to himself. I would judge him as one not to make hasty decisions."

"That doesn't sound too bad."

"No . . . but sometimes those who do not wish to make hasty decisions make no decisions at all, or make decisions by not making them."

Saryn had seen enough of that in her life. "What about his heirs?"

"I know little of them, save that he has at least one son and two daughters."

"And the holding?"

"Unlike many, there is more than one town, but all three that might be called such are smaller than most holding seats. The largest is but half the size of Carpa—"

"That's your father's holding?"

"It would have been Fornal's, but it will go to Nesslek, now."

Zeldyan's words confirmed that her brother had had no children—or no sons, at least.

"I'm sorry. What else about Quaryn?"

"The largest town is Ryntal, and Maeldyn's keep overlooks the town. There are large woods in the hills to the north, and swamps beyond them . . ."

Saryn listened intently.

LI

Several glasses before they reached Ryntal on threeday, Zeldyan dispatched one of the couriers traveling with them to alert Lord Maeldyn to their arrival. To Saryn's eyes, as they rode into the town in late afternoon, Ryntal didn't look all that much smaller than Lornth itself. Like most of the towns she had seen in Candar, it was located on a small river, although that description of the watercourse was charitable. Most of the dwellings incorporated more of a mixture of brick and timber, suggesting that good building stone was harder to come by—or that brick and timber were more readily available. The buildings were mostly neat and well maintained, and there were small barge piers on the river.

"Does the river flow into the one at Rulyarth?" asked Saryn.

"I don't know the name of this river, but it does flow into the Yarth. That's how Maeldyn gets his wool and hides to the traders there. Carpa is also served by the Yarth, and Father sends his wines down it. He used to, anyway. With the way the Suthyans have been refusing to pay what the vintage is worth, he's been aging it more, hoping that prices will increase."

"Has that worked?"

"Not so far. He took to drying the lower-quality grapes and sending the kegs of raisins to Gallos by the northern route. He didn't get as much, but it kept him from having to take whatever the Suthyans offered for the wine."

Saryn could see the square ahead, and while there looked to be a raised brick-and-stone platform in the middle, no statue graced the square. "Do they use the square as a marketplace at times, or . . . ?" She wasn't quite sure how to finish the question.

"Some towns do. I don't know about Ryntal."

Saryn could see that more than a few people along the streets were beginning to look at the riders, especially when they saw Saryn and Zeldyan, and the Westwind guards directly behind them. She could catch some of the murmurs and words.

". . . that's the Lady Regent . . ."

". . . who's with her . . . woman wearing blades . . . don't see that . . ."

". . . whole bunch of armed women . . ."

As they rode into the center square, Saryn scanned the buildings, seeing a chandlery, a cooperage, even a fuller's, and, on the west side, a gracious-looking inn with wide porches supported by yellow-brick pillars. The roof over the third story was made of pale yellow tiles, and the shutters and trim were also painted yellow. Not surprisingly, the signboard showed a yellow house, and the words beneath read *Yellow Inn*.

The main street continued northward beyond the outskirts of the town. Less than a kay farther, a paved road angled up a low rise to a mansion surrounded by a low wall, a three-story dwelling that faced generally west, with covered porches on all sides, except the colonnaded front, and on all three levels. When they reached the crest of the road, Saryn could see that the rise was the south end of a long ridge. Stables and outbuildings flanked a stretch of yellow-brick pavement extending along the ridge for half a kay. Beyond the last of the structures began a forest that not only covered the ridge but spilled down both sides and continued northward into the higher hills. A gray-haired woman stood behind the railing of the lowest porch on the north side, and a man dressed in brown livery stood on the pavement below the porch railing.

"Welcome to Quaryn, Lady Regent!" called the woman in a loud and cheerful voice. "If you and the commander would care to dismount there, Feiltyr will see to your mounts and conduct your officers and armsmen to the guest barracks."

In less than a quarter glass, Saryn found herself standing in a second-level corner room with a cool—at least for Lornth—breeze blowing though the open windows. She could see the rear courtyard, with a fountain that fed watering troughs, where both Zeldyan's armsmen and the Westwind guards had almost finished stalling their mounts and were being directed toward the barracks flanking the stables. She turned from the window and toward the curtained nook of her room, which contained an actual tub, half-filled with warm water, and a table piled with soft towels.

She did not resist that temptation, even washing her hair, although she was thankful that she had kept it barely longer than the shipboard military style she'd grown accustomed to years before. She took her time in washing and dressing in a clean uniform, but when she did descend to the main level of the mansion, she was met by a black-haired and black-eyed young woman.

"Commander, I'm Ilys. Mother asked me to escort you to the porch. It's much more comfortable out there."

Saryn followed the lithe Ilys along the wide central hallway, past a formal dining chamber on one side and a very formal sitting room on the other, then out through a set of double doors onto the porch. Lady Maeldyn rose from where she had been sitting.

"Arms-commander . . ."

"Lady Maeldyn, your graciousness—"

"Anyna . . . please call me Anyna. The thought of the Arms-Commander of Westwind calling me 'Lady' is absolutely preposterous."

Saryn couldn't help smiling, not so much at Anyna's words but at the directness and truthfulness behind them. Anyna meant exactly what she said. "Then . . . Anyna, thank you, and I am Saryn. I cannot tell you how much I appreciated the thoughtfulness of the bath awaiting me."

"Nonsense. After a long dusty ride in the summer, that's a courtesy for anyone. We even have showers in the barracks . . . I hope that . . . we did put your guards in a different barracks . . ."

"Showers are all that we have in Westwind," Saryn said. "They'll be as grateful as I am."

"Good. That's settled." Anyna gestured to the cushioned chair across a low table from her. "You don't mind if Ilys joins us?"

"I'd be pleased."

Anyna smiled, and so did her daughter, as Ilys took the more straight-backed chair to the right of Saryn.

"Zeldyan will be here shortly, but I would like to ask you a few questions if I might."

"Certainly."

"Is it true that you gave Barcauyn's loutish son a thorough drubbing?"

"Ah . . ." Had Zeldyan already told Anyna that, or had word reached the lady some other way? "I tried to be gentle with him, but . . . in the end I had to break his jaw and dump him on the stone before he understood."

Both mother and daughter laughed, almost unrestrainedly.

Saryn wasn't quite certain how to respond.

"We're a bit different here," Anyna said after she stopped laughing. "We have mountain cats and giant boars here. I insisted that Maeldyn train the girls, as well as Chaeldyn, with arms. Ilys is almost as good as her brother, and Abaya will be at least that good if she stays with it."

"Could you work with me?" asked Ilys.

"If you're willing to use wooden wands."

"Please don't say you want to use real blades," interjected Zeldyan from the door to the porch. "That was Joncaryl's first mistake . . . of many." She crossed the porch and settled into the cushioned chair on Anyna's left.

"Do all guards train with the wooden blades?" asked Ilys.

"Until they're very good, and sometimes beyond," replied Saryn. "The Marshal and I only spar against each other with wands."

"Is that because you are good?"

"Well . . . we would prefer not to kill or injure each other."

"Wooden wands," said Anyna. "Definitely." She turned slightly to face Zeldyan. "When I received your message, Lady Zeldyan, I sent a rider to summon Maeldyn, but he could not possibly return before tomorrow afternoon. That is perfectly acceptable to me because I never have had the opportunity to meet you, and never would I have a chance to meet someone like the arms-commander. Maeldyn would worry that you would corrupt me, Commander, but I'm too old for that kind of corruption . . ." A warm but light laugh followed those words. "When the Westwind . . . issue came up years ago, I told Maeldyn that any bunch of women who were desperate enough to fight were to be avoided at all costs. He did not believe me, totally, but he was wise enough to follow my advice. He also refused to treat with Trader Baorl when that snake slithered through here late in spring."

"I understand that Lord Henstrenn received the trader," Saryn said.

"That does not surprise me. Henstrenn thinks he should hold Lornth . . . begging your pardon, Lady Zeldyan, and he would treat with the white demons if he thought it would help him become overlord. The Suthyans are almost that bad."

"Kelthyn seems little better, from what little I've seen," suggested Saryn.

"With the notable exception of your consort," began Zeldyan dryly, "I would suspect that ambition of at least half the holders in Lornth."

"Ambition often grows most unrestrainedly in those with the least ability to manage it," replied Anyna.

At that moment, another figure stepped out from the doorway onto the porch—a much younger girl bearing a tray. She carried the tray out to the small table before her mother and set it down there. On the tray were three crystal carafes and five fluted crystal glasses.

"Thank you, Abaya."

Abaya nodded politely and took the chair beside her sister.

"I can offer you white, amber, or red wine. The amber and red come from our vineyards, and the white from those at Hendyn. All are good, but I personally prefer the red."

"The red," replied Zeldyan.

"Red, please," said Saryn.

"And I know what you two want," said Anyna with a smile, looking at her daughters. As she lifted the carafe of red wine, she looked to Saryn. "I hope you won't mind, but I would so like it if you would tell us about Westwind, what it's like on the Roof of the World, and what the Marshal is like."

"I'll do my best," replied Saryn. "Westwind itself sits in a valley sheltered on the north by a ridge. The most important building is Tower Black. . . ."

LII

After a good night's sleep and a leisurely breakfast with Zeldyan and the women of Quaryn, Saryn retrieved the weighted wands from her gear and brought them to the courtyard directly behind the rear porch. Both Ilys and Abaya were waiting, dressed in exercise tunics and trousers and riding boots.

"Why do you use the shorter blades?" asked Abaya.

"Because they're more useful in a wider range of circumstances. Also, they're better suited as a weapon for women, especially on horseback."

"But the blades Father uses are much longer . . ." Ilys didn't finish the sentence.

"I can throw my blades farther than his reach." Saryn kept her voice even.

"I saw what you did at Cauyna," said Zeldyan from the porch, where she sat with Anyna. "If it's not too . . . intrusive, might I ask how many men you've killed by throwing a blade?"

Saryn glanced up at the regent. "I've never kept track, but it's well over a score, perhaps two or three times that."

For just a moment, Anyna's face froze, and Saryn could sense the shock.

"You should understand that Westwind has been under attack in some way every year. Just this year, I've been in three battles or skirmishes. In every one, we've been outnumbered. The only way you can survive those odds is to kill them without suffering many casualties."

Zeldyan nodded. The surprise slowly faded from Anyna's face, but not from within her.

"Can't you just drive them away?" asked Abaya.

"That doesn't work. They'd just come back, and that means twice as much risk for us. They have thousands of armsmen. We only have hundreds of women . . . and their children."

"Do you have children?"

"No. The Marshal does, but I don't. Her daughter is about your age." Saryn picked up one of the wands and handed it to the younger daughter. "We'll start with one." Then she stepped back. "Take your position."

Abaya immediately took a stance.

"Put your feet a little closer together. They don't have to be quite so far apart with a shorter and less weighty blade . . ."

A glass or so later, Saryn stepped back. "I think that's enough for today."

"Oh . . ." came from Abaya. "I was just getting better."

"Thank you," said Ilys, smiling and inclining her head.

"Thank you," added the younger sister quickly before turning and looking up at her mother on the porch. "She's very good."

"I know. I watched her. Now . . . go get cleaned up so that you'll look presentable for your father. I hope it won't be that long before he arrives."

"Yes, Mother." Abaya nodded, then looked to Saryn. "Father lets us exercise and ride and spar, but only if we look like ladies the rest of the time."

Once Abaya and Ilys had left, Saryn said, "Lord Maeldyn sounds un-like other lords with respect to his daughters."

"Maeldyn is quite aware of both the proprieties and the realities." Anyna laughed. "He's also cognizant that they tend to conflict. Thank you for taking the time with them."

"How could I not, when so few girls are given the chances that you've given yours?"

"Do you train all the girls at Westwind?" asked Zeldyan.

"When they're old enough." There was a moment of silence before Saryn spoke. "If you'd excuse me, I'd like to check with the guards."

"Oh . . . don't let us keep you. We're not exactly going anywhere. I do hope it won't be that long before Maeldyn returns."

Saryn wasn't certain whether she should be eager for the lord's return or not as she made her way farther along the courtyard until she found Klarisa. The squad leader had just finished sparring drills and turned. "Commander."

"Squad leader. How are matters?"

"The quarters are good. They have showers. The stables are clean, and there was plenty of food for breakfast, and even some fowl eggs with porridge and bread."

"And your guards and mounts?"

"Garlya's mount is lame, but we brought two spares. How long will we be here?"

"Until tomorrow, at least, possibly a day longer, but I wouldn't count on that."

"Then we will wash everything we can now."

Saryn nodded. "How are things going with the Lornian armsmen?"

"They are very respectful." Klarisa grinned. "They have been even more respectful since you sparred with Lord Barcauyn's son."

Saryn's smile was as much sad as wry. Again, respect came only at the edge of a blade.

Later, after Saryn had washed up and after a light midday meal, Saryn, Zeldyan, and Anyna were talking on the northern porch when Lady Maeldyn pointed to the northeast.

"I do believe I see Maeldyn and Chaeldyn on the ridge trail. It won't be all that long before they're in the courtyard."

Saryn followed the gesture and was slightly surprised to see that there were only six riders and two packhorses, certainly a small party for hunting, from what she had heard about the massive hunts with scores of men and staff. As she watched, no more riders emerged from the woods, and the six finally entered the north end of the long courtyard through the open gates.

"They're not bringing back that much game," observed Zeldyan.

"Maeldyn brings what we need," replied Anyna. "We don't maintain that large an establishment here. There are only about thirty armsmen here and just five staff. Of course, Maeldyn also pays the twenty armsmen who are patrollers in Ryntal, Hendyn, and Corsaera, and he can call them up as necessary."

So Lord Maeldyn was supplying the patrollers who kept peace in the towns?

"Do other lords follow that practice?" asked Saryn.

"My father does," replied Zeldyan, "and Lord Deolyn might. I think it used to be more common, especially here in the north."

Before that long, the riders had reined up outside the stables and dismounted. One, presumably Lord Maeldyn, spent some time talking to a youth before turning and walking quickly past the courtyard fountain and toward the mansion.

As the lord strode up to the porch, Saryn studied him with both her eyes and her senses. Maeldyn was of medium height, less than a span taller than Saryn, and thin-faced, with a long chin and narrow lips that imparted the impression of dour grimness. His thinning hair was black but without a trace of gray. His tunic and trousers were a light brown, close to tan, and his riding boots were polished dark brown.

Once he climbed the five steps to the rear porch, his first gesture was to step forward and wrap his arms around Anyna. "I'm home, dearest. Chaeldyn is settling the mounts and gear." After that brief but warm gesture, he turned to Zeldyan. "Lady Regent." Then he faced Saryn. "You must be the arms-commander." Maeldyn's voice was cool and clipped, and his brown eyes seemed almost flat.

"I'm Saryn, Lord Maeldyn."

"Maeldyn will do here at Quaryn. More than do." The warmth of his fleeting smile was totally at odds with his voice and severe demeanor. "If you ladies will excuse me, it has been a long ride, and I'd prefer to be somewhat more presentable."

"Of course, dear," replied Anyna. "I'll have the girls ready wine for when you join us. Supper will be ready at the usual glass."

"Thank you." Maeldyn nodded to the three women. "I will return shortly, but I doubt you will miss me." A quick grin creased his thin face before he turned and headed inside.

Saryn had to admit to herself that he was anything but what she had expected, especially after her previous experiences with Lornian lords.

"I thought he would be back soon," said Anyna.

Before long, Ilys and Abaya appeared with carafes of wine and a tray with small pastries. Not that long after the girls set the two trays in place, Chaeldyn appeared, a youth not quite fully mature with his father's thin face, but with green eyes and just enough roundness in his cheeks that he looked merely serious rather than dour. He took a chair between his sisters, offering a "Good afternoon, your graces," with a nod to the regent, Saryn, and his mother, in that order.

"It won't be long, now," said Anyna.

As she finished her words, Maledyn stepped out onto the porch. "Ah . . . lovely afternoon."

Saryn wouldn't have called it lovely, but bearable, on the shaded porch with a light breeze out of the north, but she nodded polite agreement.

Only after Anyna had filled all the wineglasses did she turn to her consort and ask, "How was the hunting, dear?"

"We took care of what was needed. We tracked and killed the two boars who were rooting into the gardens and fields near Hendyn, and we let the locals kill some of the excess deer north and east of town here. They've been encroaching on the orchards, and that's not good for the harvests. They like the pearapples, especially . . ."

As Maeldyn summarized the hunting trip, Saryn noted that, while the three children were included, their chairs were set back just slightly, so that they did not break the line of sight between adults, and that they remained quiet, unless addressed directly. She also could sense that, even beyond his words, Maeldyn didn't like hunting but regarded it as a necessary duty.

". . . and I was happy to get your message, dear, and to learn that the regent and the arms-commander were visiting." Maeldyn lifted his goblet and took a small swallow. "Good, especially after a long ride." Then he looked to Saryn. "I imagine the hunting is something on the Roof of the World."

"We have red deer and some mountain boars. The snow leopards can be a real problem in winter. Hunting when the snow's over your head, even on skis, gets to be a chore quickly."

Maeldyn glanced at Abaya. "You had a question?"

"Yes, Father." The youngest child looked at Saryn. "How deep does the snow get? Is it like that all winter?"

"The snow starts to fall in late harvest, but except on the ice fields, it doesn't stick until midfall. By the time winter starts, it's thigh deep in many places. By midwinter, it's higher than I am. We do use horses to pull scrapers and plows to keep some of the roads mostly open, but just the ones around Westwind."

"How do you keep the water from freezing?" asked Anyna.

"We have fired-clay pipes from one spring, and they're deeply buried. They go into a cistern in Tower Black." Saryn shook her head. "The showers in the winter can be very cold."

"Water piped into the tower," commented Maeldyn. "Most ingenious."

"Most necessary when it would freeze solid otherwise."

"What other ingenious devices do you have?"

"We do what we can." Saryn shrugged. She wasn't about to get into stoves and overshot waterwheels.

"I don't think the commander is going to share too many secrets," observed Maeldyn. "I can't say that I blame her."

Saryn sensed no anger behind the lord's words, merely quiet amusement, as if he had expected her response.

Maeldyn nodded to his son.

"Commander, ser, I heard that when Lord Sillek attacked Westwind, the angels hurled fires so great that all but a handful of men were burned to ashes. Ah . . . sometimes . . . stories . . ." Chaeldyn did not finish the question.

"What you heard was true," Saryn said. "We still wish it had not been necessary. That is one reason why I am in Lornth. We would like those who rule Lornth to remain friendly to Westwind, as the regents have been."

"The regents would certainly prefer that," said Zeldyan lightly.

"So would most thinking lords," added Maledyn.

Less than half a glass passed before a thin, redheaded woman appeared at the doorway to the porch.

"I do believe that supper is ready," announced Anyna.

Maeldyn rose and stepped to one side. "After you, Lady Regent." His eyes fixed on Saryn, and he said in a low voice, "If I might have a quick word with you, Commander Saryn?"

Saryn nodded and waited until the others were on their way into the mansion.

"You're not the type to like hunting, either, are you, Commander?"

"Only when necessary for food or to prevent damage to crops or orchards."

"As many people as you've killed, you don't care much for that, either, do you?"

"No . . . but I will do what's necessary."

Maeldyn nodded. "As will most women, and that is why it would be foolish for the holders of Lornth to change the regency. Come . . . we should enjoy supper." He gestured toward the door.

Saryn crossed the porch and followed the others into the dining chamber. There, Maeldyn sat at the head of the table, with Saryn to his left and Zeldyan to his right, while Chaeldyn sat beside Zeldyan, and Ilys beside Saryn. Anyna sat at the end opposite her consort, with Abaya between her mother and Ilys.

"Ah . . . stewed traitor birds with sand-stuffed cactus, seasoned with slime-moss." So deadpan was Maeldyn's announcement that, for an instant, Saryn almost believed it.

Abaya giggled. "Father!"

"Was I mistaken? Perhaps we're having fermented turtle with snake-skin stuffing and . . ."

"Father . . ." Ilys's single appellation carried fond exasperation.

As dinner continued, Saryn realized that the dour-looking lord was anything but dour and the first lord, besides Zeldyan's father, that she could say she respected and possibly even liked.

LIII

The next oneday found Saryn, Zeldyan, and their armsmen and guards riding northeast through woods on a hilly and winding muddy clay road that was little more than a lane. Three days of solid riding through light and drizzling warm rains had left Saryn feeling thoroughly wet everywhere although the rain had stopped for the moment. The damp heat hadn't seemed to bother Zeldyan nearly so much, unsurprisingly. When Saryn had ridden out of Quaryn on sixday, she had been genuinely sad to leave the one place she had visited thus far in Lornth where she had felt welcome . . . and even valued.

Saryn looked to the Lady Regent riding beside her. "Tell me again that Palteara isn't that far out of the way."

"It isn't," replied Zeldyan. "If we were riding directly to Lyntara and Lord Deolyn . . . now that would be a ride. But we only add two days this way, and Lord Spalkyn can meet you. Besides, it is a pleasant ride."

Pleasant had different meanings for different people, Saryn reflected, brushing away another of the voracious biting flies that the forest harbored—and which seemed to prefer Saryn to all the other riders. She glanced up at the gray clouds above the trees. Were they thinning? She wasn't certain how much of a blessing a clear sky would be, not with all the moisture in the air and on the ground and vegetation. "I'd just get steamed faster," she murmured under her breath.

"You should try it in the winter . . ." Zeldyan broke off her words, laughing. "I tend to forget. You know far more of cold and winters than any of us."

After they rode up another wooded hill, only to see more of the same ahead, Saryn turned to Zeldyan. "Is it wooded all the way to Lord Spalkyn's?"

"No. I'd judge we'll be out of the woods and hills by a bit after midday."

Saryn could sense people in huts down side lanes in the woods, and there were cart and wagon tracks on the road, and hoofprints as well, yet they never saw anyone on the roads. Was it habit for the locals to avoid large parties of riders? What did that say about Lornth?

Just as Zeldyan had predicted, less than a half glass after midday, they rode up a long slope and at the top of the ridge, the mix of deciduous and coniferous trees grave way to a plateau of slightly rolling fields and pastures, with an occasional lines of trees that had to be orchards.

"If I recall correctly," the regent announced, "Spalkyn's holding is another glass ahead on a low rise to the north of the road. He holds most of the highlands here."

"We're not all that far from Suthya, then?"

"We're not that far from the lands Suthya stole from Lornth," replied Zeldyan. "They don't really even control them. Spalkyn and Deolyn have both had difficulties with raiders. The Suthyans just burned out our lord-holders, and now they collect tariffs from the people, and buy what they can as cheaply as possible and sell what people need as dearly as they can."

Feudalistic mercantilism, thought Saryn. "I can see why Lord Sillek wanted to retake Rulyarth."

"His aims were superior to his means, and Lady Elindyja was less than helpful. Had she supported his efforts in dealing with Rulyarth and not insisted on revenge against Westwind, we would be in a far better situation."

"What happened to her?"

"She died a bitter woman the year before last. It would have been better had her death occurred far sooner."

Even Saryn was surprised at the hatred and anger that lay behind the mild words, but she managed to reply. "Revenge for the mere sake of revenge seldom accomplishes anything."

"Too many in Lornth are so obsessed with honor and revenge that little gets accomplished."

"Too many men, you mean?" asked Saryn.

"Since women seldom count, who else?"

There wasn't much Saryn could say to that. She just continued to ride beside the regent as they continued across the rolling lands of the plateau that Zeldyan had called highlands, a term Saryn wouldn't even have considered attaching to the lands. Another half glass passed before they caught the first glimpse of Palteara.

Even from a kay away, Saryn could see how the location of Spalkyn's lands had affected the holding proper, which was truly a hold. A wall a good fifteen cubits high circled the ground below the knoll, and two low towers framed the single gate. All the stones were a dull gray and brown. The lowest level of the mansion set on the flattened top of the knoll had no windows and only a single door. Although there were terraces on the upper levels, they were bordered by stone walls that looked to be chest high, and the second-level windows were narrow. Not until the third level were there wide and spacious windows. Although the complex wasn't laid out to withstand a prolonged siege, it was clearly strong enough to withstand and hold off raiders or marauders and anything short of an army.

The heavy wooden gates swung open as Zeldyan and Saryn rode closer, presumably in response to the regent's banner, but Saryn saw only a pair of guards, both of them very young, as they rode in.

"Lady Spalkyn awaits you at the house, Lady Regent," called one.

Once the entire column was inside the wall, the gates swung closed with a heavy *thunk*. The paved lane did not run directly up the center of the knoll but along the right side and climbed more gradually past the mansion to another gate in the wall of the courtyard to the rear of the structure. The courtyard gate was open.

A dark-haired woman stood behind the wall on the second-level balcony. When Zeldyan reined up, she called out, "Lady Regent! I was so glad to get your message and to see you here."

Saryn sensed both distress and hopefulness behind Lady Spalkyn's words.

"Maerila, what is it?"

"Marauders . . . more than a score of them. They started burning houses and barns near Tearan last night. Spalkyn rode out with every man he could raise early this morning, right after he found out." For the first time, Maerila's eyes took in Saryn and the Westwind guards. "They're . . . women. I'd hoped . . ."

"Maerila," said Zeldyan firmly, "they're Westwind guards—the ones from the Roof of the World. They came to help me. They can certainly help Spalkyn."

"They're the ones . . . oh . . . oh . . ."

"How far is Tearan?" asked Saryn. *There's no point in fluttering around if Spalkyn truly needs help.*

"Ten kays or so to the northeast," answered Maerila.

Saryn looked at Zeldyan. "We'd better head there now. You and your armsmen can guard the holding. There's no one else to do it. The raid could be a feint to draw defenders from here."

"Spalkyn said that was possible," offered Maerila, "but he said he couldn't leave the crofters to face them alone. He needed every man."

"How many did he take?" asked Saryn.

"He had a score, maybe a few more."

That was all he could raise?

"You should take a few of my armsmen and my banner," Zeldyan insisted. "Otherwise, both sides might end up attacking you."

"Just a few." Saryn looked up to Lady Spalkyn. "Do you have someone you could spare to be a guide? That way we can be certain of getting there sooner. We will need to give the horses a breather before we set out, though."

"Wualaf knows the lands as well as anyone. He can't help much in a fight, but he can ride with the best."

"We need a guide. We'll take care of the fighting." Saryn just hoped that there weren't hundreds of marauders rather than scores. "Where can we water the horses?"

"The fountain and water troughs are straight back, beside the stables. Do you need food or grain?"

"Some of each, if you can spare it and find it quickly," replied Saryn, wondering exactly what she'd let herself and the guards in for . . . and hoping that the results would be worth it—and not too costly.

LIV

Wualaf and Saryn rode near the front of the column, just behind the outriders, along a back road that wound back and forth in a sinuous path, generally leading to the northeast and presumably toward Tearan. The white-haired man had only one arm, but his dark eyes were bright, and his words were clear. They were also endless.

". . . over the next hill are the apple orchards belonging to Mazias . . . best apples in the highlands, not that there are apples anywhere else in

Lornth because where it's lower the brown rot gets to the trees . . . Mazias'll
let you know about every tree in his orchards if you'll give him but one
word, because after that you won't get in any more . . ."

Finally, when Wualaf paused to take a drink from his water bottle,
Saryn asked, "Could you tell me about Tearan? Where we'll be fighting
and what the ground is like?"

"Ah . . . yes . . . Tearan . . . there's been more fighting there than anywhere in Lord Spalkyn's lands, and that'd be because once there was a
swamp there, and someone—perchance the Pantarans"—at that, the old
man laughed before continuing—"they filled in the swamp, and it's better
and more fertile than bottomland. You can still see the ancient stone courses
in places, you know. Then, too, it might be as because it's off the old, old
road through the hills to Rulyarth . . . and raiders can take that way without anyone seeing 'em . . ."

In time, the old forester got around to describing the terrain in detail.
". . . really not even a hamlet anymore, maybe six or seven cots on the rise,
if you can call it that with the barns in the dell below 'em. That way, they're
sheltered from the northwest winds. They can blow bitter-like, sometimes
for an eightday or more . . ."

"Just seven cots? How many able-bodied men and women are there?"

"You figure maybe three–four to a cot, but they're farmers, not a one
really knows one end of a blade from another. Any who didn't hole up or
run got killed right quick. That doesn't count the folks got cots farther out
in the fields or in the east orchards . . ."

"Do these marauders come in large bands?"

"Large enough to deal with folks who don't traffic much in arms."

"Large enough?" *Why is it that all of Zeldyan's allies have so few armsmen
and resources?*

"Maybe a score, two sometimes."

"How good are they with arms?"

"Good? Not all that good. They're not really armsmen, but if you can
use a blade, and the other fellow can't, you don't have to be that good."

Wualaf had a point, Saryn thought, but she hoped he was right about
the level of ability of the marauders. She'd prefer not to have any casualties or losses, but that wasn't likely. Even the worst blades occasionally got
fortunate, especially in a melee.

The afternoon got warmer, and Saryn's undertunic was soaked through well before midafternoon, but she kept plying the old forester with questions and taking in the answers.

The sun still hung a good hand above the hills to the west when Wualaf said, "Tearan lies around the next bend in the road past this one. Once you get to the top of the rise up ahead, anyone there can see you."

Given how low the rises were, that was understandable, but Saryn would have preferred a bit more warning. "Company halt!" She turned to Wualaf. "Is there any way to get closer without being seen?"

"Well . . . you might be able to go around the rise to the left, then through the maize fields there. Don't know as how they've got the rows running. Folks might not like their maize being trampled, but it's close to high enough . . ."

"Squad leader! Ready the guards. Hold until I return. If I don't, use your judgment to save Lord Spalkyn and his men." Saryn eased the gelding off the road and alongside the hedgerow, if a tangle of plants and weeds barely neck high on the gelding could be called a hedgerow. She kept on until she could slip into the maize, riding along one of the wider rows between the plants, trying to keep her sleeves from getting held and ripped by the tough green leaves. She had to keep her head down, but she managed to rein up near the end of the field, where she could see some of Tearan. On top of the rise, two outlying cots were smoldering ruins, and the doors of the five others either hung open or had been ripped off their hinges.

From what Saryn could sense, Spalkyn and his retainers were barricaded in the largest barn, the one on the west end. Ranged in a circle around the structure were at least forty figures in motley garments and with weapons ranging from a cut-down pike to broadswords, hand-and-a-half blades, and even old cavalry sabres. Yet only four or five were mounted.

Where were all the mounts that Spalkyn had to have brought? And how had all those raiders gathered without horses? She tried to sense or see more. Several horses were in the barn, and she thought there might be others. She could also sense bodies everywhere, and more than a few of those were large enough that they could only have been horses.

She also sensed one figure, around whom was gathered a reddish white mist of chaos. She frowned. If the man were a chaos-mage, even a weak one, why hadn't he used his fire-bolts?

Then she sensed the sheep in the barn, along with the horses. *Of course . . . if they fire the barn, they destroy all the livestock.* They'd already looted the cots, but the livestock and mounts were far more valuable than most of the goods of the crofters. The situation was a standoff . . . for the moment. She forced herself to study all the buildings and where everything was located before she turned her mount back through the maize.

The detachment was waiting when she returned, although Saryn could sense the squad leader's unease . . . and Klarisa's relief when she caught sight of Saryn.

Saryn reined up. "Squad leader? You have ten archers?"

"Yes, ser."

"We'll walk the mounts until we're almost in view of the marauders. They don't have any sentries posted. When I give the order, you and the archers move to a solid canter and stay on the road until you can circle and take the higher ground to the west. Don't worry about archers. I didn't see any bows, and if they have one or two, they won't have time to use them. As soon as you're in position, start firing. Once they break, stow the bows and block that end. If they don't break toward you, charge them, but we don't want any to escape if we can help it. The half of the squad with me will be riding more slowly, but directly toward them. We won't charge until they break or charge us. I'd like you to put as many shafts into them as you can." Saryn looked to the young armsman with the regent's banner. "Once we begin the attack, you're to swing up to the high point on our flank, in a position where Lord Spalkyn and his men can see you clearly. The marauders will, also, and that might spook them more. Your task is to display the banner and defend it, and it's more important than it sounds, because, if anyone escapes, we need them to know that the regent's forces were here. We also need Lord Spalkyn to know that."

"Yes, ser." The young armsman's voice was even, but Saryn could sense both worry and relief.

In the momentary silence Wualaf's low murmur was clearly audible. "She hasn't even looked past the maize field."

"The commander doesn't need to. She can see with more than her eyes," said a guard in a low voice.

Saryn ignored both comments and looked to Klarisa. "Fourth-squad archers, lead off. Armsmen, you follow the archers, but take your time. We'll split when we reach the lane up toward the hamlet. Wualaf . . . best you stay behind the armsmen and the banner."

"I can do that."

For the next several hundred yards, Saryn could sense nothing, not that she expected to, but she was relieved when her force swung around the last bend and headed up the gentle slope. The marauders had moved closer to the end barn, and the chaos-mage was with them.

"Archers! Forward!" Saryn ordered. "Fourth squad, on me!" As she rode forward, slowly and deliberately, she drew one of her three blades. At the same time, she spent a moment concentrating on tracking Klarisa and her half of fourth squad.

So intent were the raiders on the barn and Spalkyn's men that Saryn had led the squad a good thirty yards toward the flattened area before the three barns before a single member of the motley crew turned. While Saryn and her guards rode another ten yards, the raiders just looked.

Saryn could sense that Klarisa and her archers were not yet in position. So she raised her hand and reined up.

"They're just boys with little blades!" called out someone.

". . . can't do a thing . . ."

". . . not real men . . ."

". . . what you going to do, boys?"

Abruptly, the shafts from the archers began to strike.

Four or five of the raiders went down before anyone began to react. Then a short man mounted on a gray with a pair of sabres waved one in the air. "Get the pretty boys!" He turned his horse and started toward Saryn and the guards.

Saryn waited until the sabre-wielder was closer, hardly ten yards away, before she threw the blade, smoothing the flows and drawing a second blade. The short sword slammed through the man's chest, and he staggered, gaping at the blade, before he lurched forward in the saddle, then sideways, half off his mount, his leg caught in a stirrup and his body dragging the gray to a halt.

"Archers! Hold your fire!" Saryn ordered, letting the order flow amplify her command. "Company! Forward!"

For the next few moments, everything seemed a blur to Saryn as she tried to keep her eyes and senses on the mounted raiders, and those on the ground, who could unhorse a guard by striking at the legs of the mounts.

She parried and cut, slashed and parried, working her way toward the barn.

Hssst!

Fire flared by her, so close that she felt her short hair had nearly crisped from the chaos-flame—and that only her residual hold on the order and chaos flows and her continuing movement had saved her from being charred. Glancing around, she realized that the chaos-mage had escaped the fray in the barnyard and was standing on the edge of a loading dock on the east end of the barn, gathering and concentrating more chaos.

At the same moment, another marauder charged at her.

Saryn angled the gelding toward the other rider, parried his wild swing, then slipped the blade and back-cut. She could sense the pain of her cut, perhaps because she was so close, and it disoriented her for a moment, but she turned the gelding just in time to see and sense a chaos-fire-bolt flaring toward her.

Somehow, she managed to smooth and shift the chaos flows so that the small fire-bolt sputtered into a section of bare ground. Immediately, the chaos-mage concentrated, and a second fire-bolt arched toward Saryn and those members of fourth squad behind her. With the speed of the fire-bolt, Saryn was pressed even to divert it slightly, and it slammed into the ground before her, close enough that she could feel the heat for a moment.

How could she strike back? She had no idea of how to throw order or chaos. But . . . iron . . . cold iron, didn't that work against the white mages? Yet . . . she was a good forty yards from the mage, and she was tired.

She tried to hold to her sense of the order and chaos flows around her, then urged the gelding directly toward the white mage. For a moment, the man just looked at her. Then an even smaller firebolt wobbled toward Saryn, but she managed to "angle" the flows so that the chaos slid to the ground on her left side. The mage jumped from the loading dock and started to run.

Whether he was running or not, Saryn didn't care. As soon as she was within ten yards, she released her second blade. Tired as she was, the blade only took him in the shoulder, but fire flared from around where it had penetrated. In moments, all that remained was a charred corpse.

Saryn scrambled to unsheathe her last blade, but when she turned the gelding, she discovered that there was no immediate need.

Several raiders had scattered, and one was riding up the slope to the northeast, spurring his mount for all he was worth. The rest were either dead or wounded, from what Saryn could see. Klarisa was crossing the barnyard, and Saryn didn't even recall seeing the squad leader bring the other half of the squad into the melee.

The squad leader reined up. "We've got a good half score wounded here, ser. The raiders, that is. We've some slashes and cuts, but nothing too serious—except for Larya. She took a pike. Must have ripped open something. She bled to death before the fighting was over."

Saryn winced. Even dealing with marauders who didn't know that much about blades, there were casualties. She hadn't considered that a ragged marauder would know how to use a pike against a rider, and she'd have to watch for that in the future—and go over it with the guards and squad leaders. "Bind up the captives' wounds quickly, those you can. We'll leave what's done after that up to Lord Spalkyn. We can't care for them beyond now, and they're on his lands. I'll tell him."

Klarisa glanced past Saryn toward the barn, where a man of moderate size wearing a breastplate over a dark tunic stepped away from the armsmen there, who had followed him out into the yard filled with bodies.

Saryn counted eleven men. *Eleven left out of a score.*

The heavyset lord walked tiredly toward Saryn, the broadsword not completely into the shoulder scabbard. As he neared her, he pulled off the antique helm, revealing a short and full brown beard. "Our thanks, Captain . . ." He broke off as he took in Saryn's face and the twin-bladed shoulder harness. "Who . . . you . . . with the banner, I expected . . ."

"The Lady Zeldyan sent us with her banner, Lord Spalkyn. There wasn't time to explain. I'm Saryn, the Arms-Commander of Westwind. We've been accompanying the Lady Regent on visits to holdings . . . We did leave most of a Lornian squad at your holding with the regent and your consort, just in case the attack here was a feint." Saryn paused for just a moment. "Is it better to hold here or return?"

"I'd say return . . . but it's getting dark . . ."

"We can scout in the darkness, if that worries you . . ."

"You really are the Arms-Commander of Westwind? Why are you here?"

"We were sent to help the Regency. I'm one of the few angels who can survive the summers here," Saryn said. "The guards I brought are mainly women from Gallos, although a few are from Lornth. We trained and equipped them."

"They're all women? Just from Candar? With all the raiders they killed? You must have taken down forty. There were more than threescore . . ."

"We did have five Lornian armsmen." Saryn didn't point out that she'd worried more about those five because her guards had far more experience than the Lornians.

"I won't say that I understand," Spalkyn replied. "I don't. I am truly grateful that you arrived when you did." He paused. "I would like to return tonight if that is possible."

"We need to take care of our wounded—and yours—and collect horses, weapons, and recover what shafts we can. We will also need some rest for the horses before we set out, and we will have to travel at a moderate walk. And we'll need to be your guests for an extra day or so."

"For what you've done, I think I can manage that." Spalkyn's eyes drifted back across the slope, where the guards were already stripping the dead.

"There are ten or so captives. We'll have to leave them for your people. We're not equipped to handle prisoners."

"Those that can walk will come with us. Those that can't . . . the crofters can handle."

Saryn could sense that leaving the badly wounded marauders didn't set well with the lord, but she could also sense his deeper anger at the attack.

"I'll see how the crofters are doing. I think most of them made it into the fields and into cover. I hope so . . ." He turned and began to walk back toward the barn.

Saryn watched him for just a moment, then looked across the barnyard in the twilight.

Sixty-odd marauders coming after a small hamlet? It doesn't make sense. Not unless someone paid them . . .

Unfortunately, she had a good idea that was the case . . . and from where the coins had come . . . as well as the feeling that they well might run into more raiders before they ever reached The Groves and young Lord Nesslek.

LV

Late as they had finally ridden into Palteara hold on oneday night, Saryn did not sleep all that well, and she woke with the first strong light of the morning, with scores of thoughts and concerns circling through her mind. She couldn't help but think over what had happened when Klarisa had reported the evening before that most of the raiders had wallets and coins in them . . . coins that Saryn had ordered to be pooled, then split among the guards, with a quarter of the total reserved for her to defer any expenses she might have to bear.

"Some even had silvers," Klarisa had said. "Why would they be attacking a farm hamlet?"

"Why do you think, squad leader?"

"They had to be paid . . . ser."

"That's my thought. Most likely by the Suthyans."

Klarisa had nodded, but Saryn had sensed the woman's anger at the thought that someone had paid out-of-work armsmen and ruffians to raid and kill poor crofters. Then, too, Saryn couldn't understand why Spalkyn didn't have at least some armsmen as retainers, near as he was to the border with Suthya. Beyond that, she also had to think more about how to counter chaos. Before, she'd never had to deal with it—and she hadn't known she'd even had that much ability. And there was the question of archers . . . or the lack of them. Joncaryl had sneered at the composite bows.

She snorted softly. She'd find out about the bows in time. Lack of a weapon by enemies wasn't nearly so big a problem as a weapon she didn't know how to counter effectively. If she'd faced a really strong white mage, she'd have been the one turned to charred ashes.

Still . . . order and chaos were everywhere, except they were part of or embedded in some materials so deeply there seemed no way to remove them or even to move such materials. In other places or other materials, order and chaos seemed to move with only a thought. Some aspects were obvious. Iron was endothermic, essentially an ordered energy sink . . .

L. E. MODESITT, JR.

For a time, she just thought.

Then she rose and washed up, dressing quietly. After that, she moved silently from third-floor guest quarters down to the second level. As she neared the breakfast room, she could hear voices, those of Spalkyn and his consort. She stopped to listen, wondering if she should intrude.

". . . thought she was a young captain at first . . . should have known . . . the way she slaughtered that hedge mage . . . but you see what you expect . . ."

"You wanted her to spare him?" There was a certain scorn in the woman's voice.

"No . . . his fire-bolts killed most of the ones we lost. It was just . . . she didn't hesitate, even while he was fleeing, and she *threw* that blade through him . . . woman looks so pleasant . . . almost harmless . . . unless you look behind her eyes."

"I thought you never looked at other women's eyes, dear . . ."

A loud snort followed, after which Spalkyn went on, "Those women . . . almost felt sorry for the marauders . . . They didn't stand a chance . . . frightening in the field."

"I don't feel a bit sorry. I'm just glad they came in time. So should you be."

"I'm glad enough for that . . . I just wonder . . . did the old Cyadorans know something?"

Saryn wanted to know just what that had meant, but neither of the two spoke. So she scuffed her boots on the worn wooden floor, then coughed, before making her way to the arched entry to the breakfast room. "Good morning."

"Commander." Spalkyn immediately stood from his place at the end of the small table. "I hadn't thought you'd be up this close to dawn. Not even the children are awake."

"I'm sorry. I didn't sleep all that long."

Gesturing to the place at his left, Spalkyn reseated himself. "Would you like hot cider?"

"I would, thank you," replied Saryn, easing into the ladder-backed chair.

"We were talking about yesterday," offered Maerila, who was dressed in maroon trousers and a white shirt, with a sleeveless pale green vest. While her garments were clean and pressed, Saryn could see that they were anything but new. "Your guards are quite accomplished with their weapons, Spalkyn was telling me."

"Unhappily, that is a necessity. We're always outnumbered." Saryn took the liberty of filling the mug before her from the porcelain pot with the slightly chipped handle, then taking a small sip of the warm liquid. The cider was spiced, if sweet, and helped soothe a throat she hadn't even realized was sore.

"Outnumbered or not, your presence was the only thing that saved us." Spalkyn shook his head. "You must think me terribly improvident not to have at least a squad of armsmen."

"I know too little of Lornth and of you, Lord Spalkyn, to make a judgment. With your lands so close to Suthya, I must admit that I wondered about that."

"I was deeply indebted to Lord Nessil, as well as to Lord Sillek, Commander. But when Sillek attacked Westwind, Maerila was close to death after the birth of the twins. I chose not to leave her, but the only way to discharge my obligations was to finance and send an entire company, including the two squads I had raised and trained here. At that time, Sillek had reclaimed Rulyarth, and . . ." The brown-eyed lord shrugged.

"You've been paying off all that for years? Death golds, as well?"

"A lord must honor his obligations. The harvests went well last fall, and I paid the last and began to raise a full squad of my own armsmen. Now . . ."

Saryn had a sudden thought. "I do not wish to seem unduly . . . inquisitive, but the way in which you said that you had paid the last suggests that you had to borrow against harvests or the holding. I was wondering who outside Lornth might know of your situation."

Spalkyn laughed, softly and ruefully. "Doubtless every merchant house in Armat or Rulyarth. There was no merchant house left in Lornth who could provide the golds, not after the black angel visited devastation on the south and the Cyadorans."

"I wish that I could make some recompense," said Saryn, "but what—"

"Say no more," interrupted Maerila. "You saved his life and half of his squad, as well as most of the crofters' dwellings and stock. No one could ask for more."

"You had something in mind, I think," said Spalkyn.

"We stripped the corpses of the marauders . . ." began Saryn.

"As you had every right to," pointed out Maerila quickly, almost as if she were afraid her consort would contradict her.

"Every marauder had coins. Some had silvers," Saryn finished quietly. "There were threescore, and even had they taken every head of stock . . ."

"You're saying that they were paid to attack my lands."

"There's no way to prove it, but let me tell you why if you would not mind."

"Please." The words were calm, but Saryn sensed a cold anger behind them, one not directed at her, although she was not certain how she knew that.

"This spring, the Suthyan Council sent an envoy to Westwind . . ." Saryn went on to tell the entire story, including the side journey of Trader Baorl to Duevek and the ensuing attack on Saryn's squad on her first trip to Lornth. ". . . so you can see why I have some thoughts about who might have paid the marauders to attack your lands."

Spalkyn nodded, slowly.

"But why?" asked Maerila. "We are among the poorer holdings, as you have discovered."

"That may be why," suggested Saryn. "It costs less to create trouble and dissension and to undermine the regency and foment a civil war so bloody that eventually the stronger lords will beg for the Suthyans to take over. The weaker lord-holders, of course, will have no say."

"No," replied Maerila. "They'll be dead."

Saryn could sense someone else moving toward the breakfast room—Zeldyan, she thought—but whoever it was stopped, possibly to eavesdrop, as Saryn herself had earlier.

"Hmmm . . . and why are you here, then, Commander?" asked Spalkyn.

"Because for the past ten years, Lornth has been a good neighbor, and neither Suthya nor Gallos has been. Westwind would not wish to see Deryll and the Jeranyi take Lornth, and especially not the Suthyans. We do not have golds to help, and we have few armswomen, but the Marshal sent what we could spare. Possibly more than she could spare," Saryn added.

"Help? How?"

"To support the regency."

"How do I know you are not fomenting the very trouble you claim to be trying to prevent?"

"Because she's telling the truth, Spalkyn," said Zeldyan, stepping into the breakfast room. "Also, not saving you and having everyone squabble over your lands and which child will be consorted where would certainly cause more dissension than saving you did. Especially given that you have but one son and the twins."

Saryn sensed something more behind those words, something about the son, and she also had a good idea that Maerila could have no more children.

Zeldyan took the chair across from Saryn and poured herself a mug of cider.

"It's no secret that both Zalana and Zerlina will need matches with strong men, and that one will need to run Palteara," added Maerila.

Saryn would have liked to point out that much of the trouble in Lornth might have been lessened, both for Zeldyan and apparently for Lord Spalkyn, if strong women were allowed to hold and rule. She said nothing.

Spalkyn cocked his head.

Saryn could hear footsteps on the steps, then youthful voices.

"Father! You're back!" Two lithe redheaded girls rushed into the breakfast room and threw their arms around their father, one on each side.

"He is indeed," added Maerila. "Girls, please say 'Good morning' to Commander Saryn. She is the reason why your father is back hale and healthy. And to the Lady Regent."

"Good morning, Commander. Good morning, Lady Regent." The words were nearly simultaneous, and both inclined their heads politely, first to Saryn, then to Zeldyan.

The girl closest to Saryn asked, "Do you really live on the Roof of the World?"

Saryn laughed. "Not that way. We have a holding there, like your father does here. It's called Westwind, and I'm the arms-commander for the Marshal. Her name is Ryba, and she has a daughter about your age."

"Where's Paultyr?" asked Maerila.

"He's still sleeping. You know how he is."

"Indeed I do. Please take your chairs, girls."

Saryn took another sip of the cider, enjoying the moment.

LVI

Neither Zeldyan nor Saryn wished to impose unduly on Lord Spalkyn, but it was still fiveday morning before Saryn felt the guards—and their mounts—were ready to ride. Part of her caution lay in her concern that they had not seen the last of raiders or other difficulties that might require arms, and she wanted the horses well rested. Although they mustered the guards and armsmen at a glass past dawn, Spalkyn, Maerila, and the twins were all on the terrace, watching to see them off. Both twins waved, enthusiastically, while the lord and lady watched quietly.

As they rode down to the main gate, Zeldyan turned in the saddle, and said to Saryn, "You've won over Spalkyn . . . and Maerila, and that's not easy. I should take you everywhere."

"So I can terrify the bullies and reason with those who think?" retorted Saryn with a laugh.

"Over the years, I've heard of worse approaches," replied Zeldyan with a smile.

"It doesn't seem to work with people like Keistyn and Henstrenn . . . or Kelthyn."

"Even past experience with force doesn't work with some. Did Arthanos learn anything from Gallos's past dealings with Westwind?"

"He didn't seem to." Much as she knew that Zeldyan's words were true, that truth still depressed Saryn. Why were there those who would not stop until they were destroyed? Was it just that they could not believe that they were mistaken . . . or mortal? Even Ryba worried about that, although, Saryn had to admit to herself, much of Ryba's worry in recent years had been hedged by her tendency to put others in the front lines . . . or dispatch them to Lornth.

"Do you think there are not lord-holders like him here in Lornth?" Zeldyan's voice was dry and cutting.

"I had hoped to find that most were not, but I have the feeling that all too many are."

"As it is and will be all across Candar," replied Zeldyan.

The mild air turned warmer and heavier with the sun, until, again, Saryn felt hot and damp all over, early as it was in the day. She tried not to think about what it would be like by midafternoon and concentrated on watching the road ahead and trying to sense whether anyone was lurking nearby and out of sight.

They had ridden for a good glass before Saryn turned to Zeldyan, and asked, "What's Lord Deolyn like?"

Zeldyan laughed. "Different and not predictable. That's all I can say. Beyond that, you'll have to make up your own mind."

"What are his lands like?"

"They have more hills than here, and his tenants and crofters have more livestock and orchards, rather than field crops. Because it takes more land, his estates are somewhat more extensive. He has a master beekeeper and is known for his clover honey."

Sweets . . . Saryn had almost forgotten what they tasted like, except for the molasses candies sometimes carried by traders, and she'd found those unsatisfying and somewhat sicky-bitter in their sweetness.

"Sillek said that half Deolyn's golds came from the honey, and that he had to send a squad of armsmen to accompany any shipment to the river-barge piers."

"Whose lands lie between Spalkyn's and Deolyn's? Will they be discomfited if you do not stop to visit them?"

"Whethryn and Chaspal. They'll hardly be upset. Relieved, rather, I would think, because feeding and entertaining us is not uncostly . . . and neither has the extent of estates as do Spalkyn and Deolyn."

"But Spalkyn . . . he could not afford a single squad—"

"He could have sold land, but it would have beggared his future."

Land-poor. "How many lords face similar situations?"

"They do not tell a widow regent, Saryn, but I would judge one in three face some problems. Spalkyn's was the worst, but Rherhn of Khalasn is not far behind."

"That is why tariffs to the regency are not what they should be?"

"Part of the reason. It does no good to beggar a lord, especially a loyal one, and force him to sell lands to a rich lord who is less loyal."

There was little that Saryn could say to that, although she thought that it might be better to sell lands to those who were not lords—like

Jennyleu. Obviously, that wasn't done, either for practical or legal reasons.

As she rode on, Saryn's thoughts still drifted back to her encounter with the white mage. Although he might only have been a hedge mage, his fire-bolts had come uncomfortably close to turning Saryn and some of the guards into charred flesh and ashes. While she'd seen Nylan and even Ayrlyn create order shields, she'd tried that approach over the past few days, and it didn't seem to work for her, possibly because neither order nor chaos seemed static to her, and it took far too much effort to try to erect any sort of barrier.

Abruptly, she tried to squash one of the biting yellow-and-black flies that seemed to pester her more than anyone else, but the fly buzzed off, circling around her head for yet another attack. She'd been able to change the junctures in rock. Were there similar junctures or nodes in the air? Ones that she could shift to create a barrier against things like pesky flies? Or at least create a bit of a targeted breeze to blow it away from her face and neck?

She glanced at the fast-moving cumulus clouds, puffy with shades of gray, moving slowly across the eastern sky, then tried to sense the flow or interplay of order and chaos within them, but they were beyond the range of her senses. *What about the air around you?*

She concentrated, just on feeling, sensing the air, all too quiet at the moment. There were eddies that were not exactly junctures or nodes but mixed the tiniest bits of order and chaos.

After several moments, she tried to smooth one of the eddies somewhere above her left shoulder. The eddy dissolved, and a slight puff of warm air ruffled her too-damp hair, hardly enough to push away a pesky fly, and too hot to be exactly cooling. Still . . . it was a beginning.

Oh well . . . you'll have a few more days on the road to practice . . . Even with that thought, Saryn wondered if she'd ever gain a fraction of the control that she'd seen in Nylan or even in the hedge mage.

LVII

Late on eightday afternoon, Saryn and Zeldyan had just seated themselves on the north porch of Lord Deolyn's hilltop mansion, looking at a meadow that sloped down to a small pond created by an ancient rock-and-mortar dam. Beyond the pond was another hill, covered in straight rows of apple trees whose fruit was showing signs of crimson, reminding Saryn that summer was fleeing, and that she seemed to have accomplished comparatively little.

Deolyn was unlike any other Lornian lord. His short blond hair, interspersed with silver, lay in tight ringlets close to his scalp. His bright green eyes almost seemed to bulge over a narrow nose and a small, silver, brush mustache. His face was deeply tanned and lightly wrinkled, and he was barely Saryn's height. He wore a green tunic with yellow trim, the colors of his holding.

The three sat in a semicircle around a low table that held two carafes and three blue-tinted crystal goblets. Saryn was using her slowly increasing order-chaos flow skills to arrange the faintest breeze to waft over her and keep various tiny flying creatures from her.

"The white comes from Spidlar," said Deolyn. "I wouldn't have it except it was a gift. The red's from my high vineyards. It's dry, but holds a good taste."

"The red, please," replied Zeldyan.

"For me as well, thank you," said Saryn.

Zeldyan smiled, lifting the goblet she had taken from Deolyn. "To worthy lords."

"To worthy lords," seconded Saryn.

"To worthiness, wherever it may be found," responded Deolyn in a high tenor voice before sipping from the goblet, then lowering it and looking at Saryn intently. "So you're the fearsome arms-commander!"

Behind the cheerful voice was what Saryn would have termed good-natured coolness.

"I'm the arms-commander"—Saryn smiled—"but I'd never claim to be fearsome."

"No point in that at all. If you are, you don't need to trumpet it, and if you're not, you're lying, and that's to no one's benefit." Deolyn looked intently at Saryn, then glanced at Zeldyan. "I can hold my own in battle, but you're better off having the commander on your side."

"I know that, Lord Deolyn, but I'd be interested to know why you think that."

"She has to hold your interests more dearly than any one lord-holder possibly could. She would not be here were this not so. She also would not be here if she were not more than a match for any commander in Lornth. The Marshal of Westwind could send no less. Westwind cannot risk any impression of weakness."

Deolyn's understanding impressed Saryn, but she waited to see Zeldyan's response.

"Do you think the Marshal's interests are those of the regency?"

"I would not say that," replied Deolyn. "Her interests are in a peaceful Lornth that will not attack Westwind. At present, those interests are in supporting the regency, for so long as it remains in power."

"And if it does not?"

"Then I would not wish to be a lord-holder in Lornth, even as I am." Deolyn's smile was warm enough, but behind it lay worry. "Those who would replace the regency would find themselves bound to attack Westwind—or be attacked by those who would. That would be so, even were the Suthyans not distributing coins and mercenaries to some who oppose Westwind and the regency."

"To whom are those coins and mercenaries going? Do you know?"

"I do not know all their destinations, but it is no secret that in Duevek lies your greatest foe. I would guess that Keistyn of Hasel is also receiving coins, and Kelthyn of Veryna, if only to keep young Kelthyn from snapping at your legs. Other than that . . ." Deolyn shrugged.

"Oh?" Zeldyan raised her eyebrows, then her goblet, and sipped.

"It's simple enough, Lady Zeldyan. Your strongest supporters are in the north, and some of those are wavering, despite your sire. Your bringing the arms-commander—and her slaughter of the Suthyan marauders—solidifies that support. That's well and good, but what do you intend to do about Henstrenn and Keistyn . . . and that puppet of theirs, Kelthyn?"

"What do you suggest?" Zeldyan smiled pleasantly.

Saryn could sense the regent's worries behind the smile.

"Crush them quickly, and one by one, before they unite against you and your sire."

"With what do you suggest I crush them? My two companies?" asked Zeldyan. "And how will I explain to all the other lords who will flock to them for fear I will turn on them next?"

"You have at least three companies with the commander's forces, I would judge."

"We brought but half a company." Saryn tried to focus a breeze on herself as she spoke.

"They are worth twice their numbers. I saw them ride in, and I saw how much deference the armsmen gave them. The Lady Regent's squad leader conveyed to my captain that the single squad from Westwind took on and destroyed more than threescore Suthyan marauders."

"They were not armsmen, but a motley gathering of marauders," replied Saryn.

"Half or more were former armsmen, and you lost but one woman." Deolyn smiled. "Henstrenn and Keistyn may delude themselves, but I will not. All of our armsmen have other tasks and duties. Yours may as well, Commander, but it is certain that they are trained first to kill. Even your weapons speak to that. Men prefer long blades because they believe such proclaim their masculinity. Your blades are far better for mounted combat. I have heard that you alone have killed many by throwing blades through your enemies." The blond lord shrugged. "It may be that I have heard in error, but I do not believe so." He glanced at Zeldyan. "Have I?"

Zeldyan shook her head. "She sparred with Lord Barcauyn's son and could have killed him three times over in moments. He failed to understand, then insulted her, and me. She broke his jaw with the flat of her blade and threw him to the stone. Then she flung a blade through a shield and half through an oak door behind it. None could remove it, save her."

Deolyn nodded, then looked to Saryn. "You could kill without weapons, could you not?"

"I am no mage, but I was trained to kill with arms, hands, elbows, knees, whatever opportunity might be offered."

"It is there for those who would see," pointed out Deolyn. "I may not see all, but I see enough, and I will stand behind you both."

Saryn understood what lay beneath his words—that Deolyn's support rested in part, if not in whole, upon Westwind's backing of the regency . . . as Ryba had obviously foreseen.

LVIII

The wind blew through the doors at the north end of the room, beyond which was the verandah with a fountain whose splashing was just loud enough to drown out the sounds from elsewhere in the structure, which was, Saryn realized, neither a castle, a palace, a keep, a villa, nor a mansion, but a dwelling that incorporated some features of each. The verandah beyond the fountain, where Zeldyan sat in the shade talking to her son, might have been more suited to a villa, but the study, where Saryn had just seated herself in a captain's chair across from the gray-haired Gethen, might better have belonged in a castle or a mansion, especially with the dark wooden bookcases filled with leather-bound volumes.

After another four hot days on the road, Saryn was grateful for the breeze cooled by the spray of the fountain and for the chilled white wine that Gethen had provided. She was also happy that she was not expected to prove as much, as least not directly, although she was still concerned as to exactly how Gethen regarded her—and Westwind.

"You've met a number of the lords of the north," said Gethen. "What do you think of them?"

"They impress me far more than those of the south I've met." Saryn paused and took another small swallow of the cool wine. "Rather, I'd say that I liked and appreciated them better. I fear that Keistyn, Henstrenn, and Kelthyn might be more impressive in battle, except perhaps for Deolyn. Lord Barcauyn speaks more loudly than he fights, I fear, and might lack caution in some situations. Lord Maeldyn . . . I don't know."

"Maeldyn is more formidable than he appears," said Gethen. "Between them, he and Deolyn could raise close to three companies of decently trained and mounted armsmen. They would not compare to your guards, but they would be a match for Henstrenn and Keistyn."

"I would hope so since we did remove almost half a company of Henstrenn's armsmen in the spring."

"By now he will have replaced them, doubtless with the help of Suthyan golds."

Saryn had few doubts about that possibility. "If I might ask, why did Rulyarth fall so easily back to the Suthyans?"

"After the losses we sustained against the Cyadorans, no lord would offer armsmen to help me hold the city and the lands surrounding the river. I was selfish enough not to wish to lose everything I had for lords who would offer nothing. Those who were willing to help me, such as Spalkyn and Maeldyn, had too few armsmen remaining to make a difference. Only Deolyn had more than a company, and I saw no point in both of us losing everything."

"Especially since you had already lost a son."

"I lost two. Relyn never returned after he was wounded on the Roof of the World."

"He lost a hand," Saryn said. "Nylan crafted him a false one, with which he could hold a dagger, but he vowed he would never return to Lornth. He was strong and healthy, and better than ever with a blade when he did leave Westwind for the east."

"He was bitter, I suspect, about how Lady Ellindyja manipulated Sillek into offering lands for any who would destroy Westwind and concealing just how powerful you angels were. Like Fornal, he was proud and wanted to earn lands, not be given a pittance, which would have been all I could have bequeathed him. If he returned to Lornth, he would have had to fight lord after lord, and he would not have beggared me and Fornal to obtain arms and men. He was too honorable for that." Gethen shrugged sadly. "I cannot say that events and you angels have treated those of The Groves easily."

"We never attacked anyone," Saryn pointed out. "Nor did we raid any lord."

"No . . . you did not." Gethen sipped from his goblet. "But it mattered not. The lord-holders of Lornth have always been most sensitive to any incursion upon what they see as their rights and privileges. They have also been unwilling to support any overlord who does not appear to have the ability to compel them to submit. Without the support of The Groves and Lord Deolyn, my daughter and grandson would have perished soon after Sillek. That was another reason why I could not hazard my forces in Rulyarth and why we struggle to maintain two full companies of arms-men here."

Saryn nodded. The more she traveled Lornth and the more she heard, the more she felt like the majority of the holders were spoiled brats who could only be held in check by absolute force. "How did it come to this? Are all the lands in Candar so?"

Gethen's smile was both sad and bitter. "I can only guess. Cyador was always feeling out those lands on its borders, especially in the south of Lornth, but the emperors tended to leave alone those whose reaction cost them golds and trained troops. Whether those lord-holders actually won against Cyadoran forces mattered less than the costs to Cyador. In time, only those lord-holders who were most foolhardy and willing to fight could manage to hold their lands . . ."

"And that is why the southern lords are so touchy about honor and lands and privileges?"

"I do not *know*. I can only surmise, and that surmise is based on legend and what I have seen in the lord-holders I have known." He took another sip of the wine.

"Do you know why all the lords in Candar are so fearful of women having power in their own right?"

"Again, I can but guess. Power and lands have survived only in the hands of those who have been able to fight for them. Until you angels arrived, no woman existed who could hold her own against a man . . ."

Because no one would train them, no doubt, but Saryn did not voice that thought, continuing to listen, although she thought that there was more that Gethen was not saying.

". . . it was felt wrong to grant power to a woman, except in the name of an underage heir, because she could not defend herself, save by the sufferance of the other lord-holders."

"And now?" asked Saryn.

"Now, Commander, you have come and proved that you are a woman who can best other lord-holders, and that has many greatly concerned that you will raise up other women to do the same, and few lords would wish yet another challenge to their lands and their privileges." Gethen smiled, sadly, once more. "You will either make my grandson's heritage or destroy it, but Zeldyan has no one left to turn to, save me, and a few lord-holders of the north, and we cannot prevail alone against such as Hen-strenn, not when he is being bribed by the Suthyans to cause difficulty." Gethen glanced up. "Here come my daughter and grandson." He stood.

So did Saryn.

As Nesslek entered the study, the youth studied Saryn.

She could sense his puzzlement, but not exactly the reasons behind it although she guessed that Zeldyan had told her son what Saryn and the guards had done, and the youth was trying to understand how it was pos-sible, as if he could still not understand how a woman could have done what his mother had told him. Saryn had the unhappy feeling that little that she or Zeldyan had said or might say would make that much of an impression on Nesslek, much as she hoped she was wrong.

"We should go eat," suggested Gethen, breaking the silence. "And you both can tell us of all that occurred on your travels, for little has hap-pened here, most thankfully."

LIX

Zeldyan, Saryn, Gethen, and Nesslek stood in Gethen's study on sixday afternoon, just having left the dining chamber after a long and filling midday dinner.

"We will not be long," Zeldyan said, turning to Nesslek, "but we need to discuss some matters with your grandsire. You can wait on the veran-dah if you like. Then you can take us on a tour of the vineyards. I have not had such a chance in years."

Nesslek looked at the map spread out on the study desk. "Maps are not lands or holdings, and you already know all the roads to Lornth."

"Commander Saryn does not, and there are other matters she needs to know."

"Maps won't tell her those." Nesslek's voice was not quite dismissive.

"No," replied Saryn pleasantly. "Maps do not show the lord-holders or the people, or their ability or their will. But they do show the lay of the land, and what lies where, and often, if the map is good, the best ways to get from place to place. No one knows everything that a map shows. A good leader needs to know both people and maps, and many other skills as well."

"And you need to go," said Zeldyan firmly.

Nesslek looked as though he were about to object.

Saryn turned her eyes on him directly and let a sense of order flow from her to the impertinent youth. *Go . . . and obey your mother.*

Abruptly, Nesslek swallowed. Then he inclined his head. "Yes, Mother. I'll be on the verandah." He did not look at Saryn nor nod as he hurried off.

Zeldyan said nothing until Nesslek had left. Then she asked quietly, "What did you do?"

"I just looked at him," replied Saryn.

Zeldyan glanced to her sire.

Gethen nodded, then chuckled. "That she did. It was a look I'd not disobey, even at my age. It would have frozen Lady Ellindyja in her tower in midsummer, and none ever did that."

For a moment, Zeldyan said nothing.

After a long pause, Saryn spoke. "It would not have been right for me to speak, but I was angry. A child, especially one whose mother is a ruler, should never question her, and certainly not in public. I fear he saw my anger, and if that was so, I do apologize."

Zeldyan smiled faintly. "That he would fear you . . ."

"My anger would matter little," Saryn said, "if he did not know that I support you."

"And that you are as fearsome a warrior as any he has known," added Gethen. "The boy, whether we like it or not, is much like your brother."

"And pride and rashness were his undoing." Zeldyan's voice was bitter.

"We do what we can, daughter. In the end, children become men and women and make their own choices."

Saryn felt uncomfortable, as if she were in the middle of a private conversation. "I am sorry. It was not my place . . ."

"Nonsense," said Gethen. "He may become Overlord of Lornth, but it will only lead to his ruin if he does not understand that the world has changed and that there are fearsome women as well as men." He laughed gently. "There have always been fearsome women, but many times no one would admit it."

"You did not say a single word," said Zeldyan to Saryn.

Even so, Saryn could feel the sadness behind the Lady Regent's words.

"He must also learn about what is not said, daughter," added Gethen.

"I would that Nesslek could accompany us back to Lornth, especially with Saryn," said Zeldyan. ". . . but . . ."

Personally, Saryn suspected that a few eightdays in the company of the silver-haired trio of Westwind would have done Nesslek more good than being with Saryn herself, but that certainly wasn't feasible. Then, Westwind's regimen had clearly benefited Dealdron, and the time spent recovering in Westwind had helped Zeldyan's brother Relyn as well.

"He would be safe on the journey," Gethen pointed out, "especially with your armsmen and the commander."

"But then what? There are others we must visit, and they are not so friendly as those in the north. If he comes with us, that brings one set of risks, and if he remains in Lornth . . ."

"Then you are weakened in what you do," said Gethen.

"You do not mind?"

"Hardly. Since your mother . . . it's good to have him here—he can be a pleasure at times—and he can work with Tielmyn on his skills with weapons. He might be a bit more diligent now."

The wry humor in Gethen's voice brought a touch of a smile to Zeldyan's face, but it faded quickly.

Gethen moved to the map spread on the desk. "Do you intend to take the west river road, or the old road to the east?"

"The west road is far swifter," Zeldyan replied. "The only hold close to the road itself is Masengyl. Lord Shartyr will be pleasant enough, and it will not hurt to drain some of his golds, seeing as he is too inclined to follow Jaffrayt."

"Lord Jaffrayt does have a well-trained pen," conceded Gethen, "if not one so temperate as it might be."

"Is he the kind who can complain in writing in a way that almost seems like praise unless you read the words closely?" asked Saryn.

"That would be a fair description of Jaffrayt. Occasionally, he is less circumspect, although he is always most courtly in person—as is Lord Shartyr. Shartyr can be exceedingly charming." Zeldyan smiled wryly. "When he was younger, he was much admired by women who should have known better, and he still believes himself that exceedingly handsome young lord."

"You do not want to tarry on the road," cautioned Gethen.

"No. But a stop of a day or so at Masengyl will leave the horses far more rested when we return to Lornth."

"What will you do when you return?"

"After resting the horses and letting all in Lornth know we have returned, we will visit some of the weaker holdings, such as those of our dear friend, Lord Jaffrayt, to suggest indirectly that his tacit alliance with Keistyn and Henstrenn is less than advisable. Hopefully, we can keep everyone quiet until winter. That will purchase another year, and, if the harvests are good, also help in building up the armsmen at Lornth."

"When would you like me to return to Lornth with Nesslek . . . and Overcaptain Gadsyn and your first company?"

"If I had my way, he would remain here through the winter, but that would create another set of difficulties. I would judge the best time would be at the height of harvest, when our southern lords are worrying about their yields and golds," replied Zeldyan. "If matters change, or you think otherwise, then I yield to your judgment."

Gethen nodded. "Perhaps your visits will quiet some of those who have raised rumors."

"They will reassure those who need it least, quiet those who are undecided or wavering, and irritate those who have no sense and never will. The last, unhappily, also have the greatest number of armsmen."

Saryn understood all too clearly that Zeldyan had used the Westwind guards to solidify her support among the northern lords so that she would be in a better position to take on the recalcitrant lords of the south . . . or at least delay any immediate acts on their part.

"You will set out in the morning?" asked Gethen.

"At dawn. That will allow us to make Masengyl in two days, and arrive late enough that Shartyr will delay in sending messengers to those who might be interested until the next day."

"Because it would be all too obvious?" asked Saryn.

"Shartyr prides himself on not being too obvious," replied Zeldyan.

"If he sent a messenger in the darkness, even if we did not discover the act, that would proclaim his concerns to whoever received the message, and that would not serve him well, either."

Saryn accepted Zeldyan's reasoning, but she also understood the unspoken words behind the situation—that the regent's power rested on little more than a frayed thread, and one that might well have already snapped had Saryn not appeared.

Had Ryba seen that, as well? Saryn wondered if she would ever know.

LX

The late-summer sun's white heat blistered its way through the clear green-blue of the sky the entire two days of the ride from Carpa to Masengyl, and the closeness of the road to the River Yarth assured that the air was not only hot but damp—as were Saryn's uniforms. The first night found them in the small town of Zadrya, where Zeldyan exercised the regent's prerogative and commandeered the only two inns for night.

An early start on eightday morning, and a long day's ride, brought them to the town of Gaylyn, and Masengyl, the hold of Lord Shartyr, just at sunset. As they rode across the causeway over an ancient dry moat, Saryn could see immediately that Masengyl was a hold that dated back centuries, with moss and darkened stones on the lower walls, while the upper ends of the crenelated parapets were bleached a light gray that was almost white. The recessed gates in the main walls suggested that the causeway might once have held a drawbridge lowered from the twin towers.

A single player trumpeted their arrival from the southern tower. As she rode past the open gates, Saryn noted another thing. While the wrought-iron straps and braces binding the heavy wooden gates were black with age, the massive hinges had been recently oiled and cleaned, and the blades presented by the squad of armsmen clad in green-and-cream uniforms and arrayed in formation on the steps to the inner keep were polished . . . and sharp.

At the top of the stone steps stood a tall man arrayed in green and silver who waited until Zeldyan and the entire group had halted. Then he waited longer until the courtyard was totally silent. Finally, he spoke.

"My Lady Regent, we are so glad that you have chosen to grace us with your presence and that you've taken the time to visit Masengyl. If we had known sooner, we could have offered you a truly grand reception." The silver-haired and angular lord turned his flashing smile, and his slightly yellow teeth, toward Saryn. "Arms-Commander! Such a great honor. Seldom have any holders had two such powerful and noted women in residence at the same time, however brief that residence may be. We will endeavor to make your stay as refreshing and as restful as possible, but not without offering you the best repast possible on such very short notice . . ."

"We deeply appreciate your hospitality, Lord Shartyr," replied Zeldyan, "and particularly your support of the traditions of Lornth that the regency has continued to maintain."

"And in the name of the Marshal of Westwind," added Saryn brightly, "I also thank you for your kindness, especially toward those with whom you have far less acquaintance."

"Both of you are most charming to a lord who so seldom sees power and beauty combined. I bid you welcome and look forward to dining with you." Shartyr bowed and stepped back.

Another trumpet flourish sounded, and Shartyr stepped back into the keep.

"Shartyr does like appearances," murmured Zeldyan, before she rode forward to the keep staff who awaited her at the foot of the main steps.

Saryn rode beside Klarisa around the side of the main keep, following a functionary in dark green-and-gray livery.

"Squad leader," Saryn said in a low voice, "find out everything you can about the arms and armsmen of the holding, and who may have visited. Do it casually, and don't mention a word to anyone else until you report to me . . . after we leave tomorrow."

"Yes, ser." Klarisa nodded.

"Keep your eyes open and post a watch."

Once Saryn was satisfied with the arrangements for the guards, she walked back across the courtyard to the side door of the keep. She carried her own saddlebags.

There, at the door, the nearly silent functionary bowed. Beside him was a young woman. "Mistress Eralya will see you to your quarters, Commander."

"Thank you."

Eralya bowed in turn. "If you would follow me . . ."

Not until they reached the third level and Eralya had closed the chamber door did the young woman speak again. "Commander, if you need anything . . . anything at all . . . I've poured warm water for you, and fresh towels." The girl's eyes flicked to the battle harness and blades.

"Yes," said Saryn gently, "I carry them all the time. All Westwind guards do."

"Yes . . . Commander . . ."

Saryn could sense that the girl wanted to ask something but dared not. So she went on, trying to determine what that might be from Eralya's reactions. "We train all the women and girls in Westwind to handle blades and bow, but we're not the demons some think we are. That's one reason why we're with the regent. We'd prefer to be on friendly terms with her, and see the regency continue peacefully until Lord Nesslek reaches his majority. The Gallosians weren't so friendly, and now they're without an army . . ."

"Is it true . . . you're really an angel?" Eralya finally whispered. "And you come from beyond the Rational Stars?"

Saryn nodded. "Our ship was damaged in battle, and we could not return. We had to land on the Roof of the World."

Abruptly, the girl bowed again. "If you need anything . . . just ring the bellpull there . . . doesn't matter how late it be, Commander . . . or how early."

"I trust I won't have to bother you, Eralya, but thank you."

"Being my pleasure, Commander." The girl backed out through the doorway, closing the door behind her.

Why did she want to know about our coming from beyond the Rational Stars? And why the Rational Stars? Saryn wondered, not for the first time, what superstitions lay buried in Lornian culture. She turned and surveyed the chamber. While it was on the third level, it was at the rear, if on the side away from the kitchen, but overlooking the barracks and stables. The rear walls of both barracks and stables were either part of or directly against the walls of the hold itself. She counted four barracks, each of two levels, and what looked to be four stable buildings. Her chamber was large enough, and furnished with a dark wooden bed, whose headboard was carved with military emblems and crests, but the old weapons rack, the plain wash table, and the location of the room at the end of hallway seldom used was an indication of the lower level of mere arms-commanders, at least in the eyes of Lord Shartyr.

After washing up, she donned the dressiest uniform she had, not that it was terribly so, but she had the feeling that Shartyr would be splendidly attired. When she descended to the main level and the salon adjacent to the dining area, she was not disappointed.

Shartyr wore a shimmersilk tunic of brilliant green, trimmed in silver, over black trousers and boots polished to such a state that they reflected the oil lamps in the polished-brass wall sconces. With him was a younger woman, if somewhat older than Zeldyan or Saryn, also dressed in a green gown, but of a darker shade. Zeldyan was attired more plainly, in a simple but elegant high-necked, deep blue gown. All three stood before an open set of double doors through which flowed a slight breeze, if one barely cooling.

Shartyr inclined his head to Saryn. "This is my distant cousin, Amelyna, who has been keeping me company this summer. Amelyna, this is Saryn, the Arms-Commander of Westwind. You know, the fearsome warrior-women of the Roof of the World."

Amelyna inclined her head and bowed, murmuring, "Commander."

Saryn sensed subdued but clear fear in the attractive black-haired woman and merely returned the greeting. "Amelyna."

"As I was telling my Lady Regent," continued Shartyr, "there will just be the four of us tonight, but the splendor of the company will surely compensate for the lack of others. Might I offer you some wine? I do recommend the golden amber."

Saryn glanced to the goblet in Zeldyan's fingers, which held an amber vintage. "How can I refuse the recommendation of a lord of such noted taste?"

"I can see that my Lady Regent has been telling tales again." Shartyr laughed warmly.

Zeldyan sensed little real warmth behind the words. "Only about your tastes and your grace and wit, and surely that is no secret among the lord-holders of Lornth."

"Certainly not to my Lady Regent," replied Shartyr.

Even without her ability to sense people's feelings and order-chaos flows, Saryn would have been able to pick up on how the use of "my Lady Regent" grated on Zeldyan, even though she gave no outward response to the words.

Shartyr glided to the high circular table on which rested several carafes. After setting his own goblet down, he half filled the remaining empty one—of pale green crystal—and returned, holding his own goblet in the other hand, and tendered the goblet to Saryn.

"Thank you." Saryn offered a polite smile.

"I trust you will find it at least as flavorful as anything found in the heights."

"Far more flavorful, I am certain," returned Saryn. "The Roof of the World is not kind to subtlety or subtle flavors, and I doubt that it will ever be."

"You see, Shartyr," Zeldyan said, "she understands you are a master of subtlety."

"My dear Regent, you do me too much honor."

Saryn took the smallest sip of the wine. It was good. "This is one of the best wines I've had since I've been in Lornth."

"That is because it is one of the best wines in Lornth," replied Shartyr.

"You must be able to sell it to the Suthyans for a goodly price," suggested Saryn. "Pardon me, but my inquiry does show my lack of subtlety."

"One can be too subtle about some matters," commented Zeldyan.

"Alas, I part with some of it for practical purposes, and for not so much as it is truly worth, yet one must do what one must in these troubled times."

"Have you hosted many others this summer?" asked Saryn. "You have such a distinctive keep here."

"Distinctive?" Shartyr laughed. "It is one of the oldest in Lornth, and its greatest distinction is that I have been forced to spend many golds in rebuilding it. My father, alas, was not the best in managing the lands, and so I have had to spend much time almost as a factor and trader in order to make things prosper once more."

"You have done well," added Zeldyan. "Your armsmen look most accomplished, and you have, what, six companies?"

"Hardly that, my dear Lady Regent. I have barracks that will hold eight, and adequate stables, but no lord-holder of Masengyl has maintained any number close to that in generations. I count myself fortunate to have two companies. Of course, having the space does mean that I can accommodate your men." Shartyr turned to Saryn. "And your guards, without any crowding."

"For which the guards and armsmen are both grateful," replied Saryn, "as am I, and, I suspect, so is Lady Zeldyan. Tell me, since I am new to Lornth . . . you must come from a long tradition of success with arms. A hold this strong and this established would not seem likely to have endured without such."

"Such a perceptive inquiry," mused Shartyr, beaming at Amelyna, "don't you think so, dearest?"

"She recognizes your stature and worth," replied the black-haired woman, her voice barely short of simpering.

"As do all in Lornth," added Zeldyan.

"I cannot claim much prowess in arms," admitted the lord-holder. "Without such, I am most careful in selecting those who are, for are we all not judged not just by what we are and what we do ourselves, but by what those with whom we surround ourselves are and do?"

"Most certainly," replied Saryn. "It is clear that you have thought this matter through with great foresight, as you must have many things."

While Saryn had no doubts that she and Zeldyan would survive dinner and the evening, it was clear that it would be exceedingly and politely cutting and arduous, and that she would learn little except just how courteously slithery Shartyr could be.

LXI

Saryn was more than happy to leave her chamber—and more than ready to depart Masengyl—early the next morning. Dinner had been as long as she had feared, and as tiring, given that she had to watch every word and weigh every phrase uttered by Shartyr. As she fastened her gear behind her saddle, while the other guards were doing the same, Klarisa hurried over to her.

"Commander?"

"What did you find out?"

"There are four barracks buildings," said Klarisa. "Each can hold two companies. One is filled with armsmen. The second is half-filled. Lady Zeldyan's armsmen were in the third, and no one else, and we were in the fourth."

"Had the third and fourth barracks been used recently?" asked Saryn.

"They were clean. The storage areas were empty, and there was some dust. They have been used, but only for short periods. I did ask one of the old women who clean the buildings. She said that armsmen in brown and yellow had stayed here in early spring, and in early summer a company in blue and gray also stayed for several days. A company of armsmen in orange and black left little more than an eightday ago. She does not know what lord they belonged to because no lord accompanied them. They did not speak much, except among themselves. They were headed north." Klarisa paused. "Blue and white are the colors of Lord Orsynn, but I do not know whose are blue and gray, orange and black . . . or brown and yellow."

Klarisa's recollection of Orsynn's colors reminded Saryn that the squad leader was from Lornth. "Brown and yellow are the colors of Duevek." Saryn was hardly surprised that Henstrenn had visited Masengyl, but she had no idea whose men sported orange and black. "What else?"

"Lord Shartyr has always bred horses, but he has been selling more of them in the last seasons, yet there are more in the stables, and more grain has been laid up." Klarisa paused. "I would not claim to know everything, but I would venture these lords are readying for war."

Saryn nodded. "At the very least, they're preparing for some sort of fighting. Let me know if you find out anything else . . . or if any of your squad does."

"Yes, ser."

Once Saryn was mounted and had made certain the guards were ready, she rode across the courtyard to the front entry of the keep, where Zeldyan was saying her farewell to Shartyr.

As Saryn reined up, Shartyr turned and smiled. "You do look fearsome in battle garb, Commander. Remind me not to cross you."

"I doubt that you need any reminders about anything, Lord Shartyr," replied Saryn. "A lord who can offer such hospitality to a former enemy on such short notice is extraordinarily formidable himself. I do thank you for your charm and grace, and for your skill in enlightening me about so many facets of Lornth that I had not considered."

"It was more than my pleasure." Shartyr bowed.

Saryn inclined her head politely, then turned her mount back toward the section of the courtyard where fourth squad had formed up. She could sense a certain play of chaos around Shartyr, as well as a clear dislike of Saryn. That hardly surprised her.

Within moments, Zeldyan rode to join Saryn. The two women followed the Lornian outriders and scouts out through the massive gates and across the causeway onto the road to Gaylyn. Not until they were a good kay east of the small town and almost on the river road south to Lornth did Saryn ease her gelding directly beside that of Zeldyan and close enough that those riding ahead of them would not catch her words.

"What lord-holders have colors of blue and gray and of orange and black?" asked Saryn.

"A brilliant blue and dark gray? Those are Lord Jaffrayt's. The orange and black are those of Veryna. No other lord has those particular colors."

"That's Lord Kelthyn." Saryn paused. "A company of his armsmen were here, without him, an eightday ago, and they were headed north."

"North? A company?" Zeldyan's face clouded. "We didn't see any trace of them. They must have taken the old east road. I'll need to send a courier to The Groves."

"With escorts," suggested Saryn.

Zeldyan nodded. "If Father is warned, he should have more than enough armsmen to handle a company—if it even comes to that."

"Could they be headed anywhere else?"

"To any northern holding," Zeldyan pointed out. "That's the problem."

"But wouldn't that . . ."

"Yes. It would mean a war among the holders. But unless they do something that offends those who support the regency, I cannot afford to attack any of them."

And once you find out, it may be too late.

"Nor do I have enough armsmen to chase a single company across Lornth. Nor any mages, not that any have such . . . these days."

That might be, but how long before one of the rebels finds one . . . or the Gallosians or Suthyans send one? Again, Saryn found herself regretting something—this time, that she hadn't worked more on ways to deflect chaos-bolts. She also couldn't help but wonder how matters had gotten so bad . . . except that she was beginning to understand—and Ryba's words came to mind—"To succeed you will need to be more ruthless than any man, for only then will they respect you."

LXII

. . . All was well in Westwind in the days that followed the fall of Cyador, for though the winters were long and chill, Tower Black was warm and well provisioned, and the goods and plunder gained from the defeat of the Lornian forces fed the angels for a time, but only for a time.

Yet all was not well beyond the Westhorns, for to the east the Prefect of Gallos had sickened, and treachery infected his land. His youngest son removed his brothers and made himself ruler in all but name. Fearing the example of Westwind, the treacherous son first drove out all those from Analeria who believed that women and men should share equally in duties and rights, scourging them, and slaying any man who respected his consort. He declared that none could travel the Westhorns nor trade with the angels. Then he raised a mighty host to bring against the angels of Westwind. For he believed that, with the departure of Nylan, no mages of power remained upon the Roof of the World, and warriors though the remaining angels might be, they could not withstand the horde of armsmen that he led westward toward the heights of Westwind itself.

Yet Ryba marshaled all the angels, including those who had fled Gallos, upon a hill in the middle of a valley before a Gallosian force so numerous that they were locusts upon the land, ready to swarm over the small host of the angels and devour them. When they rode up that slope to smite and destroy the angels, Ryba signaled the sun, and the mountains trembled, and shuddered, and shuddered yet again, until half of a great mountain split away from its firmament and buried all but a few score of that horde, leaving no sign that any so engulfed in that wave of rock and soil had ever existed. And all Gallos mourned, and the darkness of grief hung heavy over the land, with orphans and widows weeping streams into the streets of towns and hamlets. And the Lord Prefect took to his deathbed.

Yet in the north, in the depths of Suthya, remained those who saw the calamities that befell Gallos as an opportunity for their own gain, and they spread coins across the troubled land of Lornth, suggesting to each lord who received such largesse that he, and he alone, should become the Overlord of all Lornth, because it was not fitting for Lornth to be ruled by a widow whose lord had failed to subdue the angels of Westwind.

As in all matters where knowledge is lacking, those in Suthya did not comprehend the depth and breadth of their folly, for Ryba dispatched Saryn of the black blades and her host to bolster the regency of Lornth. Yet when the lords of Lornth first beheld Saryn, they perceived but a woman of stature smaller than themselves, seeing even less than the fresh-faced undercaptain she resembled in form. And they gathered together, and said, "We will make an end of her and of the regency." While they spoke thusly to each other, each in his heart desired to make an end of all those who would contest his claim to the lordship of the land, and each armed more and more of his retainers, thinking that he, and he alone, would triumph by the might of blades and bows. And some among them even enlisted the aid of their ancient foes to the west, enticing them with the honey of plunder and golds.

In the growing darkness that surrounded Saryn, as she crossed the contending holdings of Lornth, she yearned but to staunch the flow of blood and the jealous strife that plagued so many of those who held lands . . . yet until she raised her dark blades and the forces behind them, none save the regent widow would listen to reason, only to the lure of golds and power. And so it was in the end, that their greed and their blindness turned them against the widow regent, who but wanted to save and heal the land. . . .

Book of Ayrlyn
Section I
[Restricted Text]

XLIII

Another long day's ride brought Saryn and the regent's party back into the palace courtyard just before sunset on oneday evening. As Saryn rode slowly toward the second barracks and the rear stables, she straightened in the saddle. Ahead were Westwind guards, standing in formation at attention, with Hryessa at one end.

"Present arms!"

Blades flashed into position, but something about the entire scene nagged at Saryn for a moment—until she looked more closely. There were three full squads of guards. Had Ryba sent two more squads? But as she rode closer, she could see the last squads consisted of unfamiliar faces, and some were very young. Had that many recruits come to Hryessa? Saryn just hoped that the recruiting had been voluntary—very voluntary. Even so, Saryn drew and raised a blade in response and led fourth squad past the arrayed guards to the stable. There, she had Klarisa dismiss fourth squad to unsaddling and grooming before she dismounted to meet Hryessa.

"Welcome back, Commander," said the guard captain, with a grin.

"I see you have a few recruits," Saryn said, smiling back.

"Yes, ser . . . and that is not all. There is almost another squad, but they are not well trained enough to join in a formal drill yet. We do not have enough mounts for all, either. Or blades, but Daryn has the old armorer's forge, and he is working on that."

"Captain," said Saryn, torn between laughing and being appalled, "if you would explain?"

"Within a day of when you left, some of the girls who had been pressed into being harlots came to Shalya. They asked if they could become guards. As squad leader, Shalya came to me." Hryessa shrugged. "From what I have seen, the Lornians do not care much for what happens to women without coins, and we will be able to use them. So I followed your instructions."

"And?" prompted Saryn.

"We have over forty in training. I saw we would not have blades enough. I know the Marshal would not have food enough for so many in the winter to come. So I sent four guards with a message to the Marshal asking for what blades she could spare. She sent back the four guards, and ten more who volunteered, with a wagon. There were but ten more short swords, besides those carried by the new guards, but the wagon held many worthless or broken blades, and Daryn and some of his tools. The Marshal sent me a letter saying that sending Daryn would be best . . . because he was a man and would work harder for me at forging the blades we needed."

"Daryn's here? What about your children?"

"They came, too. No one minds. Oh . . . and she sent you a letter also." From her tunic, Hryessa withdrew a sealed envelope and handed it to Saryn.

Much as she would have preferred to read the missive alone, Saryn opened it, breaking the seal and letting the wax fragments fall onto the paving stones of the courtyard. She paused as her eyes followed the wax for an instant. The scraggly grass around the courtyard was gone.

Another example of Hryessa's initiative? She shook her head and turned her attention to the letter. She needed to know what the Marshal had written before she committed herself to anything else.

> Saryn—
> The future of Westwind depends on you, yet I can only spare what I have sent. With the recent influx of even more women from Analeria, we cannot feed more than what we have here now, possibly not even those if winter descends early. That is one reason why I could spare another half squad to support you.

If you can find a way to send flour or cheese or other staples before winter sets in, we would appreciate it.

Please remember what I told you in parting.

The signature was an ornate, single "R."

Saryn lowered the missive. Just what had Ryba foreseen? She looked to Hryessa. "Exactly how did these . . . recruits know we would accept them?"

"You said the guards could go into the town. Some went to the cafes and the taverns, especially the Square Platter. They're more friendly there." Hryessa shrugged. "Word got out."

"How did the guards have the coins to frequent the taverns?"

"They did not have too many, but"—Hryessa smiled—"you must remember that there were many dead Gallosians not buried by the mountain who had no further need of rings and coins, and not all the coins found their way to the Marshal's strongboxes."

That certainly figured, Saryn realized. She'd been in so much pain after the avalanche that she hadn't been as attentive as she should have been. "It's all been as easy as that?" She tried to keep the ironic tone out of her voice.

"No, ser. We've had problems. I have two women locked in the armsmen's brig, and every day the local patrol chief comes to make sure that they are still there. One, I think, should be whipped, and set free somewhere well away from Lornth. She stole silvers from the Square Platter, but we replaced them. The other"—the captain shook her head—"she took a blade and killed a man and a woman. I talked with the regent's undercaptain. He said that any punishment that is merited by the regent's armsmen is handed down by the overcaptain and approved by the regent. I said that you and the regent would decide the punishment for the two."

Saryn withheld a sigh. She expected some problems, but not a recruit murdering a former lover or whatever the man had been. "Tell me more about the killing."

"The woman's name is Fynna. I believe she was really a harlot, but no one would say. She took a blade to a bouncer at the Green Dog, fellow named Ritta or something like that—"

"Rhytter?"

"I think that's it. Anyway, the two with her tried to grab her, but she vaulted over a railing and put the blade into another harlot. That was when the two guards got her. They weren't gentle. They carried her back here."

"We can't have that," Saryn said. "Rhytter might have deserved it, but with her killing two, like that, there's no question on what has to happen."

"No, ser."

"I'll tell the Lady Regent, but I think she'll agree with a death sentence. Don't say a word until I get her agreement, though."

"No, ser."

Saryn could sense the relief in the guard captain, as if Hryessa knew that had to be the sentence, but she wanted Saryn's agreement. "I'll need to stable the gelding first, though."

Hryessa nodded and stepped back, an enigmatic smile on her face.

Saryn turned to lead the gelding into the stable when a tall blond figure strode from the stable. For a moment, she was shocked. Then she shook her head and asked Dealdron, "What are you doing here?" Behind her, she could sense Hryessa slipping away.

"I came to make certain that someone was here to take proper care of your mounts," replied Dealdron. "I am not as good a fighter as your guards. I can fight well enough against those who are not guards that no one will need to protect me, and that will free a guard for what else must be done."

"The Marshal said you were useful," Saryn said. "I do hope so."

"I am not so useful as Daryn. He came to make sure that there was someone to repair and reforge the blades. None of the lowland smiths can do that."

"I suppose he would know that." She paused, then asked, "What about you? What can you do that the lowland ostlers and plasterers cannot?"

"Defend myself, if badly, and know that it is best not to argue with an angel."

Saryn managed not to laugh, although she suspected Dealdron had kept much of what he'd thought to himself. "How did you persuade the Marshal to let you go?"

"I did not. I just slipped into the wagon and waited. Daryn helped." Dealdron shrugged. "I think she knew that was what I would do."

"Then why . . . ?"

"She said that you needed help and that Westwind needed you to be successful. I can help, if in a small way, and I would not be able to if it had not been for you."

"And you don't totally trust the Marshal so far as men are concerned?"

"The Marshal will keep her word," replied Dealdron. "How she will keep it I cannot say. I know how you will keep yours. That is one reason why I am here."

Saryn glanced toward the palace. "I'll talk to you later about how to keep making yourself useful, not that you seem to need any advice from me. I need to talk to the regent."

"I have always listened to you." Dealdron smiled. "Have I not?"

Saryn shook her head, again, even as she admitted, "So far."

He extended his hand for the gelding's reins. "I will unsaddle and groom him, and your gear will be safe."

"Thank you."

Even after he led the gelding into the stable, and she turned and crossed the courtyard, now clean of the sparse grass that had infested it, she felt as though Dealdron's eyes were on her back. Although she appreciated his devotion, she couldn't help but worry that he was already making her into something she wasn't.

Saryn made her way to the upper-level private study, where Lyentha ushered her inside, past the guardsman, who resolutely looked away from Saryn and her weapons.

Zeldyan sat at the table, where several missives were neatly stacked. "You have that look upon your face, Commander."

"What look?" Saryn offered what she hoped was a puzzled smile.

"The pleasant one that hides news you think I will not find to my liking." Zeldyan sighed. "Little news is to my liking these days. What is yours?"

"Mine does not bear on the land of Lornth, but upon a murder and a theft committed by two of the young women who asked to become Westwind guards . . ." Saryn went on to explain, ending with, ". . . and it is my judgment that the thief should be whipped publicly, then sent as a servant or the like to another town. The one who killed Rhytter must be publicly executed, and soon, so that the people of Lornth know that Westwind will not tolerate offenses."

"If you would send the thief to Rohrn, that might be best. They need people there, and she will find work. The other . . . Will you need an executioner? An axeman?"

"No. I'll take care of it personally."

"You would execute one of your own?" asked Zeldyan.

"She's my responsibility. It would be wrong and cowardly to turn it over to anyone else."

"I appreciate the courtesy of your coming to me, but you didn't have to, you know?"

"I think I did. I will announce that the sentence is in accord with the laws of both Westwind and Lornth. While I do not wish to wait, I would think that at noon the day after tomorrow might be best. That way, there will be some notice to the townspeople."

"Even that will not please Henstrenn and Kelthyn, you know? If you did nothing, they would claim you flouted the laws of Lornth. Now, they will claim that you are a ruthless killer, even of those who flee to you."

"A ruthless, heartless, killing bitch?" offered Saryn.

"They will not use those words, but that is what they will suggest."

"So be it. The alternative is worse."

"All choices for a woman in power are unsuitable. We can only pick the one that does the least damage."

"That's true of all rulers, I would think," Saryn offered, not sure that she believed her own words.

"It is, but the people, and especially the lord-holders, are more willing to forgive men when they make the best of two bad alternatives."

Saryn silently agreed, but merely asked, "Have you had any word about any of the southern lord-holders?"

"Only a missive from Lord Jharyk of Nuelda. He is greatly concerned because his men have seen Jeranyi riders within a few kays of his lands."

Saryn frowned, trying to remember where exactly Nuelda was located.

"Nuelda is southwest from here, north of Rohrn and Cardara, and on the old borders with Jerans," explained Zeldyan. "If I had heard from Jaffrayt or Keistyn, I'd let them use their own armsmen and hope they took heavy losses. But Jharyk has been most loyal to my father . . ."

"And he supports the regency because of that loyalty?"

Zeldyan nodded.

"Do you need to send armsmen yet?"

"He did not ask . . ."

"But a loyal lord-holder should not have to ask, especially of a woman regent?"

"There is that."

"Can you send him a missive telling him that you will be sending him aid shortly?"

"I cannot strip the palace . . ."

"We have some recruits. I can take a full squad and a squad of them."

"They are not as well trained, the new ones."

"No, and some of them may die. But then, two-thirds of the original angels died on the Roof of the World in the first year."

Zeldyan's mouth opened, just slightly. "I did not know."

Saryn could sense something. If she'd had to guess, it would have been that the regent would have said something suggesting that it was no wonder the angels were so cold toward Candar. "We've never said. Now, it makes no difference."

"The more I learn about you, Saryn, the more I fear what you bring to Lornth. Yet . . ."

"Neither of us has many choices." Saryn forced a smile.

"No . . . as women, we do not."

"Is there anything else I should know?"

"Not at this moment."

"Then, if you will excuse me . . ."

"Go . . . do what you must, as will I."

Saryn inclined her head, then turned and departed.

She still needed to make her way to the Square Platter to talk to Haelora and explain what would happen, but it was already getting late, and Haelora had said, clearly, that she preferred to talk about things in the mornings.

LXIV

Saryn was up early on twoday morning. She had to admit she did enjoy being able to eat when she wished and to hand her dishes and laundry off to the chambermaid, since she'd done her own laundry at Westwind, as did everyone. Just those two conveniences made it easier to get out in the courtyard early to supervise and observe the exercises and drills.

After the initial drills, she drew Hryessa aside. "Do the palace armsmen exercise or drill?"

"They practice arms at times," replied the captain. "They don't exercise."

"Riding drills?"

"No. We haven't seen any."

"What do they do?"

Hryessa shrugged. "They watch us. They accompany messengers. They serve as gate guards. They go out at night and drink too much. Mostly at the Green Dog."

"Which is why the guards go to the Square Platter?"

"It's quieter. The wine and ale are better."

Saryn nodded politely. "Where did you get all the gray cloth for their uniforms?"

"We traded a few extra items that Daryn brought hidden in the wagon. Plunder he had the foresight to bring."

"More than a few items, I'd venture, to get cloth for forty women, and all of it yours."

"First company's," replied Hryessa. "Things the Marshal would have no use for but that could be traded."

"You had them sew their own uniforms?"

"We had to sew ours when we became guards. So should they. No one complained. I did let them work it out among themselves. That was because two of them had been trained as seamstresses."

"And scabbards?"

Hryessa grinned. "We found old leather ones here that had been piled up as useless, but since our blades are smaller . . ."

"You've done well." Better than Saryn might have done in her place. "A little later, I'll need a pair of guards to ride into town. I need to talk to the owner of the Square Platter."

"How about three? Two seasoned and one recruit."

"You're trying to get them used to all sorts of duties?"

"I want to give them the sense of being guards. We've been pushing them very hard with the exercises and the drills."

"You have a feeling about Lornth?"

"It's not a good feeling, Commander. Things are too lax here. I think the overcaptain was stricter than the undercaptain, but Overcaptain Gadsyn hasn't been here all summer."

"He's detailed to protect the overlord-heir. That's why he and the other company are in Carpa and have been all summer."

"They can't protect him here?"

"Not if all the southern lords attack Lornth. His support lies with the northern lords."

"It is stronger now that you accompanied the Lady Regent?"

"I hope so."

"It is," said Hryessa firmly.

"I'll leave you to the rest of the exercises. I have a few matters to deal with. If you could have those three ready after the exercises?"

"Yes, ser."

Saryn stepped back and glanced around the courtyard. She had no idea where the armorer's forge might be, but she just checked the chimneys and followed her nose and senses to a building in the northwest corner of the walls. Once there, she stepped through the open door.

Daryn was already hard at work. Standing over the anvil, beating metal into shape, the smith looked drawn, and there were circles under his eyes. He did not look up, although Saryn could sense he had seen her enter. While she waited, Saryn surveyed the armorer's shop. From what she could tell, only a few dusty tools—still hanging on the rear stone wall—had been left behind—besides the forge and the large and small anvils that were anchored to heavy posts extending into the ground beneath the stone slab flooring. Daryn was working with tools he had forged himself. In the far corner, a small boy and girl played with some wooden toys. Both stopped and stared at Saryn for several moments.

She smiled, and they went back to playing, but the girl kept sneaking looks at Saryn.

The one-footed smith finally replaced what looked to be a section of an older blade in the forge and looked up.

"You've been working hard," Saryn said.

"I have no choice, Commander. The new guards need blades. Hryessa will give me no peace until they all have them. These blades will not be so good as those in Westwind. I can forge better blades, but I do not have the time if all are to have enough blades . . ."

"Like the rest of us, do the best you can with the time and material you have."

A crooked smile crossed his face. "What else would I do?"

"You're doing a good job, and I appreciate it. Thank you." Saryn returned the smile, then left the armorer's shop to find Dealdron. She had mixed feelings about talking to the ostler.

Dealdron was, of course, in the stable, checking the hoof of one of the horses. He looked up. "This one can't be ridden for a time, not unless you want to risk losing a rider."

"Just tell the captain and the squad leader. They'll listen. If they have a problem, tell them to come to me."

The ostler eased his way out of the stall, closing the half door behind him and looking intently at Saryn.

"How long have you been here in Lornth?" she asked quickly.

"Two eightdays tomorrow."

"And what have you discovered?"

Dealdron shrugged. "I have no coins. So I have only walked through the town with some of the guards twice. It is a small town, much, much smaller than Fenard. It is cleaner, a little. From what I have heard, coppers go farther."

"What about the palace? What have you seen here?"

"I would show you something . . . this way. I did not want to mention it to the captain."

Saryn could sense nothing but concern. "Lead on."

The young ostler turned and walked another ten yards, finally stopping and pointing. "This is a feed barrel."

Saryn refrained from saying that she knew that much, but only nod-ded. "There's something wrong with it?"

"Not the barrel." Dealdron took the wooden scoop and slipped it into the feed mix. He brought it up, easing the feed mixture onto the half of the barrel head remaining, then setting the scoop aside and spreading out the feed on the wood. "See . . . the oats have been mixed with chaff, and there are far too many of the tiny oats and hulls. There is far too much chaff."

"You're telling me that the regent is getting shortchanged on her feed? Or are our horses the only ones getting the poor feed?"

"I have checked the feed in all the stables. It is all the same. I cannot say why. I only know that there should be more grain and less chaff and tiny oats. For now, I told the captain that we should feed the horses more, perhaps half again as much. I did not tell her why. I just said that they needed more feed."

"That won't hurt them?"

Dealdron shook his head. "There will be more to clean up in the stables and stalls. If we are here into colder weather, the horses will be warmer."

"The chaff is like the coarse grass?"

"Not as good, but it helps."

"What else have you been doing? When you aren't taking care of horses?"

"Sometimes, I watch Daryn and Hryessa's two. Sometimes, I talk to the armsmen. They fear your guards. They are right to fear them." Dealdron shook his head. "I have watched them practice their weapons. I am as good as some of them, and you know how poorly I do against the better guards. They almost do not seem to care. Can you help this regent, ser?"

"We have already. Whether it's enough and whether what else we can do will be enough, only time will tell." She paused. "It is a very good thing that Hryessa is training more guards."

"She is hard on them. Some she will not take, perhaps half who come."

That didn't surprise Saryn. "Not every woman is suited to be a guard." *And even of those she accepts, more than a few will be killed before this is over.* "I need to get my mount."

"I already saddled him. I had heard you would be riding into Lornth."

"Do you listen at the eaves?" Saryn couldn't help smiling.

"I cannot serve the guards and their commander if I do not know what is needed." Dealdron smiled sheepishly.

"You might ask me."

"You often do not have time to tell me," he replied gently.

Saryn couldn't argue with that, not the way things were going. "That's fine. But . . . if you're not certain, and can, please ask."

"I will. I would not go against what is good for you."

"Thank you." Saryn followed Dealdron to the larger stall at the end, where her horse was indeed saddled and waiting, then led the gelding out into the courtyard. No sooner was she in the saddle than three guards rode toward her and reined up. She knew two of the guards—the gray-eyed Dyala and the redheaded Kayli.

"Commander, this is Cenora," offered Kayli. "She's one of the newer guards."

"Commander . . . ser." The younger guard inclined her head. Her hair was cut short, and she wore the same gray trousers and tunics as the other guards, but the gray was slightly lighter. She also carried but a single blade in the shoulder harness.

Saryn could also sense apprehension, even a touch of fear. "Welcome to the guards, Cenora. It's going to be a very interesting year. For the moment, we're just riding into Lornth, to the Square Platter. I need to talk to the owner."

"Yes, ser." All three responded almost as one.

As Saryn rode out through the gates and around the green outside the palace walls, she couldn't help thinking that everywhere she looked and went, matters were worse than she had thought, and it didn't look as though she was seeing any improvement. Had her presence and that of the Westwind guards made matters worse?

She shook her head. The feed was the same as when they had come. Nesslek had already been at The Groves. The officers commanding the palace armsmen hadn't been changed since before she had arrived the first time. The palace had already been falling apart.

By the time Saryn had ridden past the larger houses between the green and the square, she had noticed several other things. More than half the once-fashionable dwellings had been shuttered, but whether for the summer, or for other reasons, she couldn't tell. The handfuls of people on the street barely gave her a glance, but it was an avoidance based on apprehension, not on fear, nor on familiarity. One other thing was very obvious when Saryn dismounted in front of the Square Platter. There was no bouncer on the narrow porch.

She stepped up onto the porch and went inside, but she didn't immediately see anyone. Before she could call out, though, Vanadyl hurried up.

"Commander . . ." He bowed.

"If she's here, I would like a few moments with Haelora or you and Haelora."

"She is. I think she would be more than ready to talk with you. If you wouldn't mind going to the front table, I'm sure that she will join you there soon."

"Thank you."

After Vanadyl left, heading toward the kitchen, Saryn entered the public room and walked to the table in the right front corner. She didn't bother to seat herself but looked out the window at the three guards. Dyala was explaining something to Cenora, who was nodding.

Two men hurried by, but neither even looked at the three guards. *That* was a change, Saryn thought.

Haelora walked toward Saryn. "I was thinking I should have heard from you sooner."

Saryn could sense a certain anger. "I'm very sorry. I've been in the north with Lady Zeldyan with half my guards." *Except they're no longer half.* "We just returned last night, and you'd said you'd prefer to talk in the mornings. I heard that one of our recruits took a blade to Rhytter. That's why I'm here."

"He mighta deserved it. I don't know. Fynna was no great shakes, either."

"No, I don't think she is," Saryn concurred.

"What are you going to do with her?"

Saryn could feel that some of Haelora's anger was fading. "She'll be executed in public. Her sentence will be carried out on the front palace green at noon tomorrow."

"Yet she came to you . . ."

Behind the words was a mixture of emotions, and Saryn tried to address them. "She did, and then she broke the rules and killed two people. As you said, Rhytter might have deserved it, but the other woman didn't, and we don't like our guards going off and killing people. Who would trust us for long if we allowed that to happen and didn't punish the one responsible?"

"Lord Nessil did. No one said anything." There was a challenge, and resignation, beneath the words.

"I'm not Lord Nessil. Neither is the regent."

"That'd be good." Haelora smiled, a wry yet sad expression.

"If we can make it last?"

"That'd be up to you, Commander, I fear. The Lady Regent is fair and has a good heart, but the lord-holders respect only strength and power."

"What about the people?"

"The people . . . we don't expect much. Don't tariff too high and don't rip down doors and take our daughters. Pay for most of what you take. That's what most people expect."

Saryn concealed an internal wince. "I don't think that's all. I doubt you like fighting among the lord-holders because the deaths fall on your sons and cousins."

"And now, if you fight, some will fall upon daughters."

"That is true, but they will have a chance to be more than victims."

Haelora's expression remained sad. "What will that change?"

Saryn almost said that she was in Lornth to stop the senseless fighting—except that she realized she had already been fighting in what were nearly senseless conflicts. "I can only say that I will do what I can."

"That is an honest pledge, unlike many."

Saryn looked squarely at the innkeeper. "What should I know that you know, and I don't?"

Haelora shook her head. "I cannot say . . . for I do not know what you do."

"You know I am a stranger in a strange land."

"You are, and yet you are not. You look like a young woman, except in your eyes, but you are not. Those eyes have seen what I would not wish to have seen . . ."

Saryn waited.

"Do not worry about the people of Lornth, except to save them from the worst of the lords. We can live through anything except the worst of weakness and of evil. Even that, we will survive." Haelora smiled, faintly, but not unhappily. "Thank you for coming. I will tell others, and your guards are always welcome here."

"Thank you." Saryn nodded politely. "I must go."

As she left the public room, she could sense Haelora watching her. *Why does everyone watch me leave? Because they want me to go, or because I'm something strange that they've never seen? Or both?*

She didn't have an answer to that . . . or to more than a few other questions.

LXV

Early as she had been up the day before, Saryn was up earlier on three-day and meeting with Hryessa in the small space at the west end of the barracks, assigned to the captain as a company officer.

"You've checked the platform and the scaffold?" asked Saryn.

"Yes, ser. The ropes are in place, and they'll hold her tight." Hryessa looked at Saryn. "I can't say as I like doing this in public."

"We do it anywhere else, and someone will claim we were hiding something or that we really didn't do it at all, and that they saw Fynna in Rohrn or Carpa or who knows where else. It's going to be a show, no matter what we do," Saryn said gruffly. "So we need to make it a good show— one that demonstrates that we mean what we say and that no one should mess with us, either. Besides, you have to deal with Sineada."

"That's just a whipping. She'll recover, and she might learn something from it," replied Hryessa. "You . . . that's different. You sure you want to do it, Commander?" asked Hryessa, her voice deferential. "We could use an ax."

"Do I *want* to? No. Do I have to? Yes. It sends a message that even the Commander of the Westwind Guard knows weapons . . . and needs to be treated with the same respect as any male commander."

"Men don't—"

"They don't have to. Everyone believes that they can. In Lornth, they don't believe that about women, and we have to change that." *As quickly as possible.*

At that, Hryessa nodded.

"Now . . . can we mount three squads?"

"I'd figured that, one squad on each side of the space you'll need, and one squad behind, with two guards on the platform for each of them to tie her up."

"They can handle Fynna if she gets wild?"

"Those two can. Zelha grew up tossing steers, and Marha is just as tough. If they'd been with Fynna, been a different matter."

"Good."

Once they had the details worked out, Saryn spent some time sharpening both her blades, then doing what amounted to a casual inspection of barracks and stables. Both were far neater and cleaner than when they had first come to Lornth.

At half a glass before noon, the procession from the palace began with a mournful trumpet fanfare from the gate tower. Mournful, but off-key. That was just another part of the palace staff where competence was less than marginal. *Is that true of all small kingdoms . . . or is Lornth worse?*

Saryn didn't have an answer to that question, like she didn't to so many others, and she watched as the first squad rode out and drew up in a north–south line, each rider facing east, and the first rider close enough to the stone platform that the nose of her mount was even with the west–southwest corner. The second squad rode out and took position in a line opposite the first, the distance between them the width of the platform. Then came three guards, with Rheala and Hoilya from fourth squad escorting Sineada—the girl who had been discovered stealing—with her hands tied before her. Behind them came Zelha and Marha, with Fynna between them, her hands tied behind her. Marha held the leads to Fynna's mount. Saryn and Hryessa, riding slowly, followed, accompanied by Agala, who rode slightly behind them. Behind them rode the third group of riders—the remainder of fourth squad, led by Klarisa.

Zelha and Marha led Fynna's mount directly to the stone platform in the middle of the green, from which three gallows trees rose, none of which seemed to have been used recently. They waited until Saryn and Hryessa had reined up, some ten yards short of the platform, and until fourth squad took position as an east–west line, so that the guards formed three sides of a rectangle, with the platform comprising the fourth side.

As Saryn and Hryessa waited, Rheala and Hoilya reined up at the steps on the left end of the platform, and the other two halted the three mounts at the right end. Saryn studied the crowd. From what she could see, there were more than a hundred townspeople present, possibly twice that.

Rheala and Hoilya tied the three mounts, then marched the trembling Sineada up to a space between two gallows tree supports and tied her wrists and ankles in place, then stepped back. Hryessa rode forward to the platform, with Agala riding behind her. When the guard captain dismounted, she handed the reins to the guard and climbed the five steps to the platform, carrying a whip.

"You have stolen from those you were trusted to protect," said Hryessa. "That is theft, and you will receive ten lashes from the whip. If you are ever found stealing again, you will be executed."

While Saryn wasn't totally happy about that, a second offense of serious theft was a death sentence in most of Candar, and she wasn't about to try to change it.

Hryessa did not shy away from using close to full force of the whip, until the end, when Saryn could tell that the guard captain pulled the last two lash strokes.

After the last lash, Hryessa stood back and raised the whip. "Justice is done. You are hereby banished from Lornth and will be sent to Rohrn to make your way there as you can."

Hoilya and Rheala untied Sineada and half marched, half carried her to the mount that had brought her to the platform. Then they set her on the horse and mounted beside her, moving close enough to support her, if necessary.

Hryessa returned to her mount, and she and Agala rode back to take position beside Saryn. The three—and all the other guards—waited until Marha and Zelha marched a shuddering Fynna into position and tied her there.

Then Saryn eased the gelding forward, just two yards, and spoke, using a touch of order to amplify her words across the green.

"You have killed two people you were entrusted to protect, and you used the weapon you were given to protect them. That is murder, twice over. The sentence is death by the very weapon you misused."

Saryn summoned the darkness and the flows, then stood in the stirrups, and drew and threw the short sword, smoothing and guiding its flight.

"No!!!"

The weapon sliced through Fynna's chest, burying itself to its hilt and cutting off her last scream. Her body jerked but once, then went limp.

The entire green was silent as Saryn rode forward to the execution platform.

There, the two guards moved to the body. Zelha removed the short sword and stepped to the front edge, where she tendered the bloody blade to the commander.

Saryn raised the blade and spoke, once more letting order magnify her stern words. "Justice is done, under the Code of the Guard and the laws of Lornth. Let this be a warning to any who might consider breaking either."

Saryn remained motionless, still holding the blade, while the two guards cut the body loose and carried it to the horse that Fynna had ridden, laying it facedown and sideways across the saddle before they remounted their horses. Saryn tried to use her senses to gather an impression of what the townspeople felt, but the greatest impressions she got were that, while the thrown short sword had stunned most of the onlookers, most felt that the punishments had been too quick and that both women should have suffered more.

People . . . She refrained from shaking her head and waited until the four guards dealing with Sineada and the dead figure of Fynna were in position before the platform and ready to ride. Then she looked to Hryessa.

"Guards! Return!" ordered Hryessa.

Fourth squad led the return procession to the palace courtyard.

As she and Hryessa rode slowly back, Saryn glanced to the guard captain. "They didn't want a whipping and an execution. They wanted public torture."

"Of course," replied Hryessa. "It was good that you threw the sword. That way, no one will complain in public. They will mutter, but they will not say more where we can hear it."

Once they were in the courtyard, in front of the stables, after dismounting, Saryn cleaned the blade, and her hands, before unsaddling the gelding.

When she was finished, she left the stables, heading for the palace. Dealdron was helping with the burial detail, such as it was. Not a single Lornian armsman was in sight, except for the four with gate duty.

Saryn's next duty was to report to the regent, and she made her way to

Zeldyan's study. The regent was waiting, with a carafe and two goblets of red wine. She motioned to the chair across the small table from her.

Saryn took it. "It's done."

"I saw. I watched the execution and whipping from the tower. Several hundred people were there. It looked most impressive." Zeldyan paused. "What if you had missed?"

"I would have looked very foolish. But I didn't miss. I can't afford to."

"No, you cannot. You are wise to understand that."

"Those who watched were looking for torture. I'm afraid we disappointed them." Saryn didn't bother to keep all the irony out of her voice.

"You also frightened them. They left the green quickly." Zeldyan sipped her wine, then looked up. "The courier returned from The Groves. They rode much of the night both ways."

Saryn couldn't sense grief or despair. "So far, your father's seen no sign of Kelthyn's company of armsmen?"

Zeldyan nodded. "At least he knows, and he and Gadsyn can prepare. The courier might have reached The Groves before Kelthyn's armsmen. The old east road is much longer."

"They might be headed elsewhere."

"He's sending his own messengers to the others in the north."

"You've done what you can," Saryn said.

"I have heard those words before, Saryn. When all goes wrong, they are cold comfort."

"We have to take comfort where we can." Saryn took a sip of the wine before continuing. "There's another matter . . . much smaller. One of our ostlers came with the last wagon from Westwind. He has been checking the feed for the horses, and the grain contains quite a bit of chaff and the tiny oats that are mostly hulls . . ."

"I will talk to the steward." Zeldyan smiled coolly. "I will tell him that you are concerned about the quality of the feed."

"Perhaps, at least, you could pay less or obtain more . . ." suggested Saryn.

"For a time, and then, when we are gone or occupied with greater matters, they will return to putting chaff and the poorer oats in the feed."

Saryn nodded, not in agreement, but in understanding.

"Do you know what is the saddest of all of this?"

Saryn was afraid she knew, but she merely shook her head.

"Those who have helped me more in the past season and watched my back are those who killed my consort, while those who claim to be my lords and people scheme to bring me and my son down."

"Where would you like us to visit next?" asked Saryn.

"We might try Kelthyn. If he has a company elsewhere, he might be more welcoming." Zeldyan took another sip of wine. "Or perhaps Keistyn. Think it over, and tell me what you think in the morning."

"I will." Saryn didn't press. Zeldyan was waiting for something, and whatever it might be was unlikely to be good. "We'll be doing some mounted drills later this afternoon, mainly with the newer guards."

"They already do not look much different from the others."

"They still have much to learn." *And little time in which to learn it.* "If you will excuse me."

"Of course." Zeldyan's smile was faint, concealing some sort of worry, but not, Saryn thought, about her or the Westwind guards.

Most likely about Nesslek . . . or her father—or both.

In the meantime, Saryn and Hryessa had all too much training to do.

LXVI

Despite Zeldyan's words, it was close to midday on fiveday when Lyentha appeared in the courtyard where Saryn and Hryessa were working with the wooden wands to develop the blade skills of the recruit guards.

Saryn sensed the young woman's approach and stepped back. "Yes, Lyentha?"

"At your convenience, Commander, Lady Zeldyan would appreciate a word with you. She is in her upstairs study."

"You can tell the lady I will be there in a few moments."

"Yes, Commander." Lyentha hurried off, clearly relieved.

"What do you think it is, ser?" murmured Hryessa.

"Nothing good. There have been too many messengers, and none of them have worn purple. We're going to have to ride somewhere and fight someone. This time, if it comes to that, I'll take first squad and whichever recruit squad is farthest along."

"They're really not ready, ser."

"I know that, but from what I've seen, they're as good as the locals." Saryn glanced at the waiting recruits. "Keep working them. I don't want to keep the regent waiting, and I hate postponing bad news that can only get worse."

Hryessa nodded understandingly just before Saryn turned and walked across the courtyard toward the palace.

Lyentha was standing outside the study door and opened it as Saryn approached. "The commander is here, Lady."

Saryn had barely cleared the doorway when the door closed behind her.

Zeldyan turned from the window farthest to the right. "If you would, Saryn, I have received some messages. I would like you to read the one from Lord Jharyk first." She extended a heavy sheet of parchment that had been folded and sealed rather than placed in an envelope.

Saryn took it and read, her eyes coming back to the key phrases.

> . . . already have seen two Jeranyi attacks on small hamlets, and have lost a number of my armsmen. Those with lands bordering mine have offered sympathy, but feel that they cannot assist. They point out that since help from the regency is not forthcoming, they cannot afford to stretch their limited forces . . .

"That's effectively blackmail," Saryn said. "If you don't help him . . ."

"Exactly," replied Zeldyan. "It does not help that he has always been lax in maintaining armsmen because he claims that too many of them will drive a lord-holder to ruin. Lord Nessil almost took his holding years back in order to give it to a stronger lord-holder."

Another type who wants someone else to shed their blood because defense isn't cost-effective. "Why didn't he?"

"He always paid his tariffs on time. He still does. Now . . . if you will read this one."

Saryn took the second sheet, which had been sealed inside an envelope, and began to read the words beneath the blue-and-gray seal.

My dearest Lady Regent,

It has come to my attention that you have been visiting various lord-holders within Lornth. Your diligence in doing so is
commendable, although, had those of us with the best interests of the future of Lornth been consulted, we might have
suggested that the overlord-heir accompany you, since it is
in his name and for his future that the regency exists. More
disturbing, however, is the presence of the so-called arms-
commander of the brigand land occupying sections of the
Roof of the World on such visits, for it was those very brigands who not only usurped Lornian lands but whose acts resulted in the very need for a regency.

As a lord-holder devoted to Lornth, I find that such a lack of
concern about both the future of Lornth and the circumstances that led to the present unfortunate situation suggests
consideration by all lord-holders of the need for a more im-
partial regency and one that looks to the early rule of Lord
Nesslek under such. That is, unless the present regency will
consider taking the necessary steps to reclaim Lornth's lost
lands and remove with due haste agents of those who have
caused such losses.

I remain your most obedient and concerned lord-holder.

The seal and signature were those of Jaffrayt.

Blue and gray? Saryn looked up. "Do Jaffrayt's armsmen wear blue
and gray?"

"I would think so. Those are his colors."

"This wasn't the only one, was it? There were a number of messengers."

"Yes, there were," replied Zeldyan. "There were similar missives from
Lord Rherhn of Khalasn, Lord Orsynn of Cardara, and Lord Keistyn.
Kelthyn wrote expressing concerns that the regency was not meeting the
needs of the lord-holders. Shartyr's letter was less demanding. He just ex-
pressed a need for agreement among all the lord-holders in dealing with
Lornth's future."

"So that he could claim to the others that he'd also written you but without declaring directly his opposition to you and the regency."

"He has met you. The others who wrote have not."

"If I'm counting correctly," Saryn pointed out, "you've received six letters of complaint or threat. That doesn't count Henstrenn, who's already shown where he stands, even if he hasn't put it in writing. How many of the remaining southern lords might support the regency, besides Lord Jharyk?"

"There are eight lord-holders in the south, now that there is no lord-holder of Rohrn. The only one who has not made his feelings known is Lord Mortryd of Tryenda. Although he is not actually in the south, Lord Mortryd tends to follow the southern lord-holders."

"I can take two squads, one of regulars and one of recruits." Saryn paused. "We'll need a guide, and I think we should leave under the cover of darkness. Outside of the palace, few know how many guards we have here now, anyway."

"You would do this?"

Do I have any choice? "If Jharyk and Lord Mortryd back the regency, with the holders of the north, most of the lord-holders will be behind you. If you don't send some help to Jharyk . . ."

"Then much may be lost." Zeldyan paused. "I should send a squad of armsmen with you."

"One squad . . . those who rode with us before, I think. We will leave tonight after dark."

"Let me send for Undercaptain Maerkyn to meet me in a glass. Then, before he arrives, I will tell you what you should know about Lord Jharyk." Zeldyan shrugged. "I would tell you of the Jeranyi, but there is little I can say except that they ride and strike quickly, then vanish into the plains or hills."

Wonderful. Trying to combat guerrilla warfare on horseback while helping a lord whose support is lukewarm at best.

Zeldyan lifted the bell on the table and rang it once.

The door opened, and Lyentha stood there. "Yes, Lady?"

"Please summon Undercaptain Maerkyn to meet me here in about a glass."

Lyentha nodded and closed the door.

Zeldyan gestured to the chairs and the table. "We might as well sit down while I tell you what I know."

Saryn took the seat across from the regent.

"Jharyk does not merely venerate golds. He worships them more obsessively than the ancient Cyadorans did their long-lost chaos-towers. He also obsesses over women, in a differing fashion, since he is now on his fourth consort, for various calamities befell all the others . . ."

Saryn listened, even while thinking, *And we have to help this excuse of a lord so that all Lornth doesn't fall into revolt and into the Suthyan Council's hands . . . or purses? There has to be a better way . . .* Except that she couldn't think of one, not with the limited resources she had.

Almost exactly a glass later, at least by the sand-glass on the top of the bookcase, Zeldyan finished by saying, "I don't know how much of that will prove useful, but that is what I know."

"I think all of it will be useful in one way or another. It's always what you don't know that causes trouble." Saryn rose. "I'd best start getting the guards ready."

As she stepped out of the study and started down the steps, she found Undercaptain Maerkyn headed up. The undercaptain stopped and stepped to the side of the staircase.

"Undercaptain," said Saryn in greeting, "a word with you, if you please."

"I'd be most happy, if I can be of assistance, Commander."

"What do you know about Lord Jaffrayt?"

"Besides the fact that he's said to be a direct descendant of the Pantarans, not much." Maerkyn shook his head.

"The Pantarans?"

"Oh . . . you wouldn't know that, Commander. There aren't any Pantarans. They don't exist. Whenever the old-timers wanted to blame someone, they blamed it on the Pantarans . . ."

"You're saying that he's a nobody? Or that his family came from nowhere?"

Maerkyn nodded. "That's what they say when they talk about people who claim to be more than they are."

Saryn wondered how many more expressions she'd either missed or had to learn. "Is there anything else?"

"They say he doesn't pay his armsmen very well."

That figures. "And?"

"Other than that . . . I don't know. I'm from the north, near Carpa."

"Thank you." Saryn nodded and continued down the steps, then out across the courtyard.

Hryessa had to have been watching, because she said something to Shalya, who stepped forward to take over the drills as Hryessa moved away from the guards and met Saryn.

"Were you right, ser?"

"Close enough. We're going to a place called Nuelda, and we need to leave after dark tonight, as quietly as possible. Deryll—he's the Jeranyi lord or chief or whatever—he's sending raiders there. Lord Jharyk is one of the few southern lords supporting the regency, and he's not equipped to deal with them."

"The weakest henhouse is the one that always wants guard dogs. They usually don't want to feed them, either."

"Something like that. Nuelda is a hundred kays southwest of here. It might be more. I don't trust anyone's distance estimates. Lady Zeldyan is sending one squad of her armsmen, under my command, and I'll take first squad and whichever recruit squad . . ."

"Second squad. I've moved Yulia from fourth squad to be squad leader, and put two of the recruits in fourth squad as replacements."

"Can you handle any more recruits?" Saryn asked.

"We're still getting a few. Not so many as before. That might change if word gets around to the other towns. You think we'll need them?"

"We'll need every blade we can train. And every one Daryn can forge."

"I've told him that. He grumbles, but he works hard. Dealdron has been talking to the other ostlers. He might be able to get ahold of a few more horses . . . ones that he can work with."

"Ones that are trouble but that he can train? We can't afford many others."

"Just capture as many as you can, ser." Hryessa grinned. "We've done pretty well that way."

Saryn shook her head. "We need to go inside and go over the supplies."

The two walked toward the barracks and the small space that served as Hryessa's study.

LXVII

By oneday morning, Saryn and her detachment had ridden for two days over low, gently rolling rises that held more meadows than tilled fields, and more than a few cattle and sheep. They passed orchards, but the trees were generally low, either olives or apricots, according to Saensyr, the older armsman who was acting as their guide.

"They look to be even poorer than those in the flats of Gallos," observed Shalya, the first squad leader, riding for the moment beside Saryn. "They're overgrazing the meadows."

"You're from Analeria, aren't you? Did you have raiders like the Jeranyi?"

Shalya laughed. "Our ancestors were the raiders. They settled down to become herders."

"So how do you deal with raiders?"

Shalya shrugged. "You can only kill them. They won't stay bought or bribed."

"Do you think the Jeranyi are like that?"

"Worse, from what we've heard. Even Lorn the Mighty couldn't do anything but slaughter them. That was almost a thousand years ago, and they haven't changed much."

A bit past noon, she rode back to talk with Caeris, the squad leader of the palace armsmen.

"Have you ever fought the Jeranyi, squad leader?"

"Not since I was first in service, ser. We didn't so much fight them as guard Lord Sillek's mages while they picked off the Jeranyi one at a time. Except once when they charged, and they didn't fare so well."

"We should be able to hit them with arrows from a distance . . ." mused Saryn.

"The way you hit the Suthyan raiders up north?" asked the squad leader. "You'd have to be out of sight. They don't even come close to formations. One of their tricks was to string out a company, then swarm in from all sides. Leastwise, that was what the locals told us."

"I'll have to keep that in mind. Do they use spears or bows?"

"They had short bows, but they didn't carry as far as yours."

While she talked with Caeris for a time, she didn't learn all that much more.

Then she joined up with Yulia.

"What do you think about the squad?"

"They want to be guards. They work hard. Hryessa weeded out those who didn't." Yulia laughed.

"You meant that, didn't you? She had them dig or pull out all the grass in the courtyard?"

"The captain wouldn't let anyone eat until they finished a section each day. She didn't eat, either. She told them that what she was making them do was but a fraction of what the guards on the Roof of the World endured. Only four or five quit."

That just confirmed what Saryn thought about how women—or many women—were treated in Lornth and how desperate some were to escape.

"How are they with blades on horseback?"

"They'll be all right in making or taking a charge. I wouldn't like to have them in an all-out melee, though, not yet. We've practiced breaking in unison on command. They should be able to execute it well enough not to get spitted, if the locals have pikes."

Should is one of those words commanders hate, and this just reminds me why. But Saryn just nodded and kept questioning Yulia . . . and making a suggestion or two.

Clouds began to appear in the sky to the south by midmorning. By noon, a mass of darkness loomed across the southern sky. The land the three squads were traveling was less cultivated, with more open pastures, if with scattered stands of trees, although she didn't think that the woods were anything close to original growth. They just didn't feel that old.

She turned in the saddle toward Saensyr. "I take it that there's no town nearby?"

The older armsman shook his head. "Just herders for another ten kays, as I recall."

Saryn gestured to Shalya. "Squad leader . . . send out a pair of scouts to see if there's anywhere ahead that might offer shelter."

"Yes, ser." Shalya glanced toward the darkening sky. "Looks like we've got a solid storm moving in."

In moments, on Shalya's orders, two guards urged their mounts away from the main body, then, after another half kay, past the outriders. A half glass later, a misty drizzle began to fall, but there was nowhere in sight that would have offered any real respite from the heavier rain to follow— just open fields with grain and maize looking close to harvest, and pasture, although Saryn could see woods to the west, ahead along the right side of the road.

If there's nothing ahead, we could see about the woods up there. Except, in the end, all that trees did was delay the rainfall.

Another quarter glass passed before the scouts returned. Their report was simple.

"Another two kays along, past the beginning of the woods up ahead, there's a herder who's got an empty barn and an old house with a sound roof that's only got some timbers in it."

"Nothing else?" asked Saryn.

"No, ser. He says that he's the only one for another three kays."

The mist drizzling down around Saryn wasn't that bothersome, but the sky was continuing to darken, and she had the feeling it wouldn't be that long before a hard rain fell. "If that's what there is, that's what there is." She hoped that the herder's shelter wasn't too filthy.

The misty drizzle had definitely shifted to rain by the time Saryn reined up outside the dilapidated barn that squatted before a stand of old oaks—the first truly old trees Saryn had seen since they had left Lornth.

The herder, wearing oiled leathers, gestured toward the trees. "The old place is back there, to the left and behind the barn."

"Lead the way." Saryn turned to Shalya. "I'll be back shortly and let you know if the old house is suitable."

Saryn let the chestnut gelding follow the herder along a path through knee-high weeds past the left side of the barn and through a gap in a thicket of wild berries—redberries, Saryn thought—and out into a clearing covered with sparse grass and thick moss. At the back of the clearing was a single-story dwelling that looked smaller than it was, overarched as it was by two towering oaks whose branches intertwined well above the roof whose green tiles almost matched the moss covering most of them. The dark blue glazed bricks forming the walls still retained their sheen, except for those where the finish had been crazed by time or impact. Even so, Saryn felt that, from the outside, the ancient dwelling, were it cleaned and repaired, might well provide more livable shelter than the herder's crooked timber house. A freestanding wall some six cubits wide and more than head high faced with green and blue tiles blocked direct access to the door. Faded yellow tiles formed an intertwining pattern of squares and triangles on the front of the wall.

Saryn rode up to the low wall, where she discovered an ancient hitching ring made of a bright metal she did not recognize, its shimmer seemingly totally at odds with the age of the structure. After dismounting, Saryn quickly tied the reins to the ring.

She stepped toward the herder, gesturing toward the wall in inquiry.

"All the old Cyadoran houses had them. That was so no one could look inside at the womenfolk. That's what my grandma said, anyways."

Saryn followed the herder around the wall. He had to lift the door slightly as he opened it in order to get it over the slightly buckled masonry. Saryn noted a narrow shining metal shutter in the center of the door, set approximately at eye height, and apparently made of the same metal as the hitching ring. Behind the door, inside the dwelling, was another privacy wall, but the floor between the door and the inside wall and to each end of the privacy wall comprised a mosaic. Although a handful of tiles were missing, and dust covered the remaining tiles, Saryn had no trouble making out the image of a mounted figure with a shining lance squaring off against an enormous lizard.

"Stun lizard. From the Accursed Forest," said the herder laconically, before he stepped into a room that stretched the width of the dwelling. The third of the room to the left was filled with stacks of short timbers. "Good place to dry the oak."

On the right end in the far corner was what looked like a ceramic stove. That side of the chamber was otherwise vacant, except for a solid ring of the shimmering metal set into the wall. "What's that for?" Saryn pointed to the metal ring.

"Link-ring. What Ma said, anyway. Cyadoran women who misbehaved or tried to run away had their chains linked there."

Had their chains linked there? They wore chains all the time? Saryn forced herself not to retort. Finally, she nodded and turned. Two sets of two narrow windows graced the front of dwelling, and three windows were set into the walls at each end of the room. All the windows had sagging internal shutters that were closed and did not look as though they had been moved in years. The entire floor was of dark gray tiles, many of which were cracked, but still firmly in place. After a moment, she looked to the archway leading toward the rear of the dwelling.

"Most of the back rooms are empty. Don't do as much wood as my da did. Herding brings more coins."

"Didn't anyone want to repair this?" Saryn asked. "It's not in bad shape."

"Grandma, Ma . . . they said it was no place for women, that it still held demons. Neither one'd ever set foot inside."

With that evil ring, I can see why. "How long has it been here?"

The herder shrugged. "Hard to say. Was here before my great-grandda bought the place. He didn't even know it was here, what with all the brush grown up around it."

Saryn nodded. "This will do. Thank you."

The herder glanced around the chamber, seemingly holding in a shudder, then said, "I need to get back to milking, ser."

"That's fine. We'll manage."

After he left, Saryn spent a moment studying the dwelling. For all the herder's talk of demons, she could sense no concentrations of either order or chaos. If the link-ring were removed . . . it wouldn't be that bad, but she could understand why any sane woman would be repulsed by that metallic ring. Still . . . even in its present state of disrepair, the ancient house was far more solid than most of what she'd seen in Lornth. With a modicum of work, it could be made into a comfortable dwelling with cross ventilation and a good stove for heat in the winter. And no one had ever wanted to use it for more than storage? And what was that shining silvery gold metal that age had not dimmed?

She shook her head. At least her squads would have space out of the drizzle and rain for the night. But she did have to hold in a shudder when her eyes took in the shining ring.

LXVIII

On midafternoon of twoday, Saryn's force rode into Nuelda, a small town on the west side of a nameless—at least to Saryn and Saensyr—narrow river confined between broad earthen berms that suggested the water was not always so narrow and shallow. Saryn had the Lornian squad lead the way, flying the regent's banner, and she rode at the front with squad leader Caeris. The dwellings were all of dull red brick, but the roofs were of a reddish gray clay tile rather than the turf they had seen earlier.

As in all Lornian towns, there was a central square with a raised platform in the middle, but the platform was low and of simple brick, with no statue or other adornment, and the inn to the south of it looked old, small, and mean. The passage of armed riders, particularly of armed Westwind guards, seemed to freeze those on the streets. Most just gaped, but several women dragged children inside shops.

Before all that long, the riders were following a packed-clay-and-gravel road to Jharyk's holding, located on a rise along the river, on the southwest side of the town. Unlike other holdings Saryn had seen, there were no walls around the long and low villa, with extensive outbuildings set along the crest of the rise some hundred cubits above the river. The villa, even to the square columns framing the entry, was of red brick.

Not knowing what else to do, Saryn directed the Lornian squad to form up opposite the main entry steps rising from a paved area with mounting blocks, with the Westwind squads flanking the Lornians.

They had barely completed forming up when a small man wearing a dark gray tunic and trousers, with a silvery shimmersilk vest over the tunic, stepped from the villa and walked halfway down the steps. He stopped and looked to Caeris, ignoring Saryn. "Captain . . . it's about time you arrived here."

Caeris glanced to Saryn, then said quietly, "Begging your pardon, Lord, but I'm just a squad leader. Commander Saryn here is in charge."

"A woman? That's—" Jharyk's eyes narrowed as he took in Saryn, then widened as he saw the battle harness with the twin blades.

"Lord Jharyk, I'm Arms-Commander of Westwind. I believe you have heard of Westwind. Since we did sign an agreement with Lornth some years ago, we are at peace, and in the interests of helping a cooperative neighbor, the Marshal sent me and close to a company of guards to offer some assistance to the regency." Saryn paused before adding, "Since it would take almost an eightday to obtain a complete Lornian company and ride here, and since you had expressed urgency, we agreed to take on the mission on behalf of the regency."

"How can you . . . and women help?"

"Earlier this summer we destroyed an army of nine thousand Gallosians with four companies. A number of years ago we did the same to a Lornian force, and over the past few years we've wiped out several hundred brigands and others. We have more experience at killing unwanted intruders than anyone else around. Isn't that what you wanted?"

Jharyk was silent, and Saryn could sense that he was getting angry. She turned to Caeris. "You might tell Lord Jharyk about the Suthyans, since he seems unwilling to accept my words."

Caeris swallowed, then spoke. "One squad of her women destroyed almost fourscore armed Suthyans who were attacking Lord Maeldyn's crofters. She lost one guard. They did it all with weapons and not magery."

"Why are you here?" Jharyk finally asked, as if nothing had been said before, but his eyes finally acknowledged Saryn.

"It's very simple, Lord Jharyk. You have been a supporter of the regency. Had you not been, in all likelihood you would still be waiting for assistance. Westwind prefers friendly neighbors. The regency has been friendly. Those who oppose the regency would likely not be so friendly. We help the friends of our friends."

"Why would it take so long for a Lornian company?" Jharyk demanded, almost petulantly.

"I imagine that's because they're in Carpa at The Groves, and it would take time for a courier to ride there and even more time for them to prepare, then ride here."

"There is that. Well, now that you're here, I imagine you can make yourselves useful by doing what you can to deal with those Jeranyi pests."

"We will need some information from you, or your people, Lord

Jharyk, as to where the Jeranyi have been attacking. We'll also need supplies, food, and lodging while we're here . . ."

"I'm but the poorest of lord-holders . . ."

Saryn smiled. "So you have said, but feeding and lodging the better part of a company for an eightday or however long it takes us to deal with the Jeranyi is far less costly than maintaining a full company yourself, and you can console yourself with that thought."

Saryn could sense that Jharyk was so shocked by her reply that anger didn't even occur to him. "You . . . you would talk so?"

"We've ridden all the way from Lornth because you asked for assistance, Lord Jharyk. We're here at your request of the Lady Regent. It's certainly not unreasonable to expect food, lodging, and fodder, now, is it?" Saryn smiled politely.

"For a woman so beautiful, you are not exactly accommodating . . . Commander."

"I am being very accommodating to your need to deal with the Jeranyi." *For any other accommodation, you'd better look to your present consort.*

Jharyk forced a smile. "Ah . . . I will go and summon my steward. He will settle your guards and armsmen. Then, after you have worked out matters with him, perhaps you would join me in my study . . . Commander, so that we may discuss the best way to approach matters."

"Most certainly." Saryn returned the smile with one as equally charming and false.

Saryn shifted her weight in the saddle and watched as Lord Jharyk made his way back into the villa, then glanced to Caeris.

"I'm sorry, Commander, if—"

"There's nothing to be sorry about, especially here." Saryn followed her words with a humorous smile. She could sense the squad leader's relief.

The man who hurried down the steps after a good tenth of a glass was of moderate height, and balding. He walked quickly toward Saryn and bowed deeply. "Arms-commander . . . I am most sorry that we did not know of your arrival so that we might be better prepared—"

"We understand," Saryn replied. "I am certain that Lord Jharyk did not expect us quite so soon, but we came almost as quickly as any messenger could have."

"We do not have much in the way of accommodations for as many armsmen as you have brought . . . but there is a new barn, and the stables are mostly empty at present."

"Let's see what you have, and we'll work from there. Where do we go?"

"Ah . . . around the villa . . . that way and past the staff quarters—that's the first building."

"We will meet you there." Saryn paused. "You are?"

"Boudyn, Commander."

"I'm sure we can work things out, Boudyn. We're not likely to be here at Nuelda long, unless there are Jeranyi near."

"Oh, no, Commander. The closest they have come is at Westera, and that is a good fifteen kays from here."

Saryn raised her arm.

"On the commander!" called out Caeris.

Saryn urged the gelding forward and to the left, following the packed-clay-and-gravel drive around the villa.

All in all, it took less than half a glass to work out the quartering and feeding arrangements with Boudyn, and then Saryn walked from the stables to the rear entrance to the villa, where a young woman stood waiting.

"Commander?" Her voice was unsteady, just short of trembling.

"Yes," replied Saryn pleasantly.

"Lord Jharyk awaits you in his study. If you would come this way . . ."

Saryn followed the woman along a short, covered walk, supported by square brick columns, then through a set of double doors into a wide hallway. She could see immediately that the villa was laid out so that, if doors and windows were opened, cross ventilation would occur regardless of wind direction, although the wind from the south might well bring not only coolness but a certain odor from the stables.

The study was on the northeast corner of the villa and paneled in a dark wood Saryn didn't recognize. As she stepped into the chamber, with its wide windows that offered a view of the river and the town, Jharyk rose from behind a wide desk on which were spread several maps.

"I do apologize for my . . . abruptness, Commander," said the small lord smoothly. "You must understand I never expected a force of Westwind guards coming to deal with the Jeranyi."

"I can understand your surprise, Lord Jharyk, and from what your steward said, it's unlikely that we'll be spending more than tonight here."

"You, at least, must join us for the evening meal. Ioncosa has never met . . . well . . . none of us have ever met a Westwind guard, much less the Arms-Commander of Westwind."

"I would be honored." *Not particularly pleased, but honored.*

"Good. Very good." He turned to the desk and gestured. "Here is a map of the holding . . . the hamlets here to the southwest are those where the Jeranyi struck. Westera was the closest . . . right here. I would judge that they will move either east or north from there . . ."

Saryn said little as she listened and followed the swift and jerky gestures of the lord. Chauvinistic and arrogant Jharyk might be, but he was neither stupid nor slow, and he was clearly trying to make up for being taken aback by Saryn's arrival. She was also certain that he had decided Saryn's appearance at Nuelda was to his benefit, although she couldn't sense why.

Once Jharyk finished describing what had happened where and when, Saryn asked, "Have the hamlets or cots of other holders been attacked?"

"They don't seem to have been. My lands are closest to the West Pass, though, and that's the easiest way through the hills from Jerans."

"Are the hills that hard to cross?"

"Compared to the Westhorns? Hardly. But the Jeranyi are always looking for the easy way. Steal rather than raise their own. Take a woman rather than arrange a consorting. Be a boon to all Candar if they were just wiped out."

Saryn didn't like what she was hearing. If the Jeranyi were so opportunistic, why were there no attacks on other holders at all? Was that because the Jeranyi knew Nuelda was the weakest . . . or for other reasons, such as a message from the other lords?

After another half glass, the same young woman escorted Saryn to her guest chamber. There, Saryn discovered that someone had brought her gear and laid it out—still packed—on the long table under the high windows.

"The wash chamber is through the door there, Commander."

Saryn almost felt guilty getting cleaned up and changing. Almost. When she left the room, her escort was waiting, and brought her to a set of open double doors, then slipped away.

"I hope you do not mind that it will be just the three of us," offered Jharyk, standing at the door to the dining chamber.

"No, not at all. You're very kind."

Jharyk laughed. "I'm seldom called such. You must already know that. But for all my vanities and foibles, I try not to be stupid. I'm certain you know much that I do not, and I hope to learn from you. But . . . first, may I present my consort, Ioncosa?"

Ioncosa was petite, dark-haired, and probably not much older than the youngest of the Westwind guard recruits. She was also pregnant and smiled shyly. "Commander . . . it is such an honor to have you here at Nuelda. I have always heard of the Westwind guards, but they seemed so . . . unreal. Yet . . . you are so solid, even though you're . . ."

"No . . . I'm not a giant," said Saryn with a slight laugh. "The Marshal is imposing in stature as well, but most of us are not."

Jharyk gestured toward the far end of a table that could have held twenty but was set for three. "We should be seated."

As soon as the three had taken their places, Jharyk filled the three goblets almost precisely two-thirds of the way. "Enjoy." He raised his goblet, then took a sip. "Some of the other lords in the west here make their own vintages." He shook his head. "Waste of golds and time. The soils aren't right. They're best for sheep and wool, and for dairying and cheese. So I buy good wine when times are hard and store it in the cellar. We also store the cheeses if we can't get the proper prices." He smiled at Saryn. "I've never figured out how you could support so many folk—or any folk—on the Roof of the World. Would you mind telling us what life is like up there?"

Saryn took a sip of the deep red wine. Jharyk was right about one thing. The wine was good, and she wondered where he had gotten it. "It was very hard for the first years. We do have mountain sheep . . ."

Jharyk nodded as she spoke, but Saryn could sense he would remember every word she said through the entire meal.

LXIX

In the deep darkness before the sun would rise over the hills west of Suedara on sevenday, Saryn had a far better idea why no one really wanted to deal with the Jeranyi. Four days of following tracks, sleeping in dusty barns and sheds, and sensing the riders who could only be Jeranyi scattering away through the bush-covered hills had left her feeling more than a little frustrated and very much more understanding of why Lord Sillek had just had his mages drop fire-bolts on whatever Jeranyi he'd been able to find.

Saensyr had just said, "One wastes shafts trying to use bows, and horses chasing them."

Was that another reason why the Lornians didn't use archers in battle? *It couldn't be the only reason, could it?*

At the same time, she'd also come to realize that her ability to use the flow of order and chaos in the areas around her had extended. She could now reliably sense riders and large animals at close to two kays. Part of that had to have been because of the more open terrain, but some also had come from having to use her senses so much—because there didn't seen to be any other way to discover the raiders.

She'd also discovered that the Jeranyi liked to move into position well before dawn, then strike when there was just enough light to see. That was how two more small hamlets had suffered. It was also why she was leading the three squads through the darkness along a trail well away from and west of the main narrow road. If they'd used the main road, the Jeranyi certainly would have noticed all the hoofprints. Suedara wasn't a hamlet, but a small town, with not only cots and crofters, but even a few houses of more than one room—and it was the only town with easy access from the trails leading from the West Pass that had not suffered from the raiders, and that was doubtless also why many had fled there from devastated hamlets.

While it looked to Saryn as though the Jeranyi were trying to scare everyone into Suedara for more concentrated pickings, she certainly couldn't prove that, nor could she explain why she thought the Jeranyi would make their raid into Suedara on sevenday. She'd just told the squad leaders that attempts to find the Jeranyi later in the day had failed and that Suedara offered the raiders better pickings.

"How much farther, ser?" asked Shalya through the darkness.

"About a kay before Caeris takes position. About a half kay after that, you'll take first squad up onto the rise on the right and set up with the archers out of sight from the main road . . . the way we talked about last night. Once you're in position, I'll move back with the Lornians."

Based on their early ride through the town on the way to Westara, Saryn had picked a spot more than a kay southwest of the town itself . . . for several reasons. First, she didn't want a pitched fight in the town. Second, she wanted to surprise the Jeranyi away from the town, and third, there wasn't any terrain she liked better anywhere else along the route that she thought the Jeranyi would take.

A low rise topped out some hundred and fifty yards west of the road leading out of Suedara to Westara, a road that eventually swung due west until it reached the West Pass. On the east side, opposite the ridge, lay soft and marshy ground, but that did not begin until close to a hundred yards off the road. The marshy sections bordered a small swamp that fed, if intermittently, the stream that supplied Suedara. The area Saryn had picked did not appear as confined as it was in fact.

"Do you think the Jeranyi know we're after them?" asked Shalya.

"They must know someone is after them, but I'd be very surprised if they knew there were Westwind guards among their pursuers."

They rode in silence for more than a quarter glass before Saryn eased the gelding back along the shoulder of the narrow trail until she reached the Lornian squad. "Squad leader?"

"Yes, Commander?" replied Caeris through the darkness that might have been lightening ever so slightly. Saensyr rode beside him.

"Just ahead is where I want you to take your position, in the low area behind the last slope down to the main road. You're not to move to where you can be seen . . . unless, of course, you come under attack, but I doubt that will happen. Remember . . . you're not to close off the road until the Jeranyi are under attack from first squad."

"Yes, ser."

"You understand your task?"

"Yes, ser."

Saryn rode with Caeris for another hundred yards and made certain that the Lornians were in position before riding back up the slope to the trail and joining Yulia and second squad.

"Commander," offered the squad leader.

"Squad leader. Your task is simple, but it won't be easy. You're just to block the road so that the Jeranyi can't reach the town and hold as long as you can. First squad will be attacking from the Jeranyi rear. Keep the squad together as much as possible. The Jeranyi like to pick off riders who get separated."

"Yes, ser."

Saryn did not accompany second squad all the way to their position, concealed behind the north end of the same ridge behind which Shalya and first squad were readying themselves, if almost half a kay farther from the town. But Saryn did not rejoin first squad until she could sense that Yulia had her recruits in place.

Then, while the sky slowly lightened, and the night sounds of various insects began to be replaced by another set of sounds, and the night breezes died away into an uneasy stillness, it was a matter of waiting. Before all that long, Saryn began to sense riders—far more than she had expected, more than her three squads, and possibly close to a group the size of an entire company. She checked the position of first squad again—just below the top of the ridge where they could not be seen from the road.

"Bows ready," she ordered.

"Bows ready," echoed Shalya, quietly. "Pass it on."

Saryn waited until the Jeranyi were less than two hundred yards south of the point on the road just opposite the guards. "Forward and into position."

"Forward . . ."

The twenty guards rode forward, not quite to the top of the ridge, but far enough that they could see the road before and below them.

Saryn could not only sense, but see, the oncoming Jeranyi, riding three abreast on the main road. None of the raiders were talking, and they rode quietly. She also sensed the Lornian squad beginning to move—too soon—despite her orders not to reveal themselves and not to take the road until first squad actually opened fire on the Jeranyi raiders.

So far the Jeranyi had not seen the Lornians.

"Squad leader . . . have your archers aim at the rear of the Jeranyi for the first volley, then at the leading riders for the second." Saryn hoped that might confuse the raiders . . . if they even saw the Lornian squad.

"Archers . . . first shafts at the rear ranks. Second shafts at the head of the column. Pass it on."

At the moment when Saryn could actually see the first Lornian armsmen coming down the slope to hold the road behind the Jeranyi, she said, "Loose shafts. Now!"

"First shafts away!"

After a moment, Shalya added, "Second shafts!"

Saryn watched with eyes and senses. For several moments after the first shafts ripped into the rear of the raiders, nothing happened.

Then there was a faint cry of "Archers!"

Almost immediately after the second shafts struck down some of the leading riders, one of the Jeranyi was pointing in the direction of first squad.

"Rake the lead riders again!" Shalya ordered.

Two more volleys followed, then a third, before the Jeranyi started toward the ridge.

"Bows away! Forward!" snapped Saryn. The guards needed to get up the ten yards in front of them to take the higher ground.

Shalya echoed Saryn's command, and, in moments, first squad was formed up on the ridgecrest, two deep.

Saryn judged that more than three squads' worth of Jeranyi were urging their mounts up the gentle slope toward her and the guards, and that was with at least ten or more raiders cut down on the road. All had blades out, what looked to be sabres, rather than the longer and more cumbersome blades used by the Lornians.

"Forward!" ordered Shalya.

Against the first rush, the guards had the advantages of coming downhill and the surprise when the Jeranyi realized that they were facing women.

A single rider made toward Saryn, singling her out, possibly because she was on the flank of first squad and slightly back. Saryn turned the gelding into him at the last moment, using her momentum to beat down his blade and cut upward into his neck. She swung away and back uphill, stopping to survey the situation.

ARMS-COMMANDER • • • 361

After the first flurry of blades, most of the raiders circled away, not without leaving another handful of dead. Saryn saw that the Jeranyi could have taken to the ridge and escaped down the trail, but not a single raider had taken that option.

Four of those who had flanked the guards swung back toward the main body, then saw her and charged. She urged the gelding toward the on-coming riders, releasing her first blade at the lead Jeranyi. Her senses and aim were true, and the raider went down, but the others kept coming. A second blade followed, and another raider fell.

Saryn swung the gelding to the leftmost of the riders, angling so that the other would collide if he followed, then ducked and back-cut as she passed the outermost rider. She could sense the wound, enough to inca-pacitate the man, but, once clear, she turned back, looking for the fourth rider, but he had ridden back to where the remaining, but still large, group of Jeranyi were forming up again—south of first squad on the ridge slope but at almost the same height.

As she watched, the Jeranyi formed into a tighter formation, a mounted wedge, just far enough down the hill that the Westwind force would have trouble seeing them against the rising sun.

Saryn glanced back. If first squad held, they might prevail, but the Jer-anyi also had short blades for infighting, and the casualties on both sides would be high . . . and she had but a single blade left in her hand. What could she do?

The Jeranyi began to ride toward first squad, picking up speed.

Saryn turned the gelding toward them, and less than fifteen yards from the onrushing force, flung her remaining blade at the center rider— using her skills to accelerate and smooth the flow around the weapon . . . and to create a wedge of black-edged darkness that trailed from both sides of the blade, a wedge that linked invisible junctures in the air into an un-seen black-framed whitish knife blade.

The Jeranyi's savage grin turned to a rictus of terror in the instant be-fore the heavy blade slammed through the hardened leather mail and into his chest. The two riders flanking him screamed, and all three mounts went down. So did those beyond them, and the entire center of the wedge was flattened into a pile of dead men and mounts.

Saryn found herself gaping . . .

Then a black void hammered her with emptiness and chill, shaking every sense and sinew in her frame. When that passed, she could barely see through the shimmering knives of light that flashed before her, then turned and stabbed through her eyes. While they left no wounds, the pain felt as intense as if they had, and it took every fragment of strength she had to hold herself in the saddle as she slowed the gelding.

The remaining riders turned their mounts and scattered downhill and both south and north along the road, except for a few who tried the marsh and found their mounts chest high in mud and water. Some rode right into the remaining Lornians. The others fled toward Sudara . . . and second squad.

As she stopped her mount, barely before running into the carnage she had created, Saryn shuddered in the saddle. After a moment, she turned and rode toward one of the nearest guards. "One of your blades, please?" Her voice cracked, and she hated that.

"Yes, ser." The guard's voice was filled with fear, but she immediately extended a blade, hilt first.

"After them!" Saryn forced strength into her voice, and she urged her mount forward and down toward the road into Suedara. The recruits of second squad would need all the help they could get.

"First squad! Forward!" ordered Shalya.

Saryn let the other guards pull slightly ahead of her over the quarter kay or so that it took to come up on the rear of the remaining Jeranyi, by then in a melee with second squad. She needed to be there, but she doubted that she could have lifted the borrowed blade for more than a single parry, if that.

She didn't need to use it. Caught between the two Westwind squads and demoralized, the remaining Jeranyi had little chance for escape, and in less than another half glass, the only mounted riders remaining were those in the now-bloody gray of Westwind.

Saryn sheathed the blade and fumbled out her water bottle, mostly by feel, because she could only see intermittently through the lightknives that penetrated her vision. She drank slowly.

The water helped . . . if only slightly, enough that she realized she was flanked by Dyala and Kayli, both still holding drawn short swords.

"Are you all right, ser?"

"I will be." *I hope.*

Saryn just forced herself to wait until she was certain there were no Jeranyi left in or around Suedara. Then she rode back south and out to where Shalya was supervising the recovery of weapons and mounts.

Once there, Saryn reined up short of the squad leader. "After you've taken care of the wounded, make sure that your squad recovers every single shaft and blade possible, including the damaged or broken ones. We're going to need each one."

"And the spoils, ser?"

"The standard," replied Saryn. That meant half of all coins and jewelry to the Marshal—or Saryn, in this case—for supplies and the like and the other half split among the squad, with a double share to the squad leader. She'd varied the spoils occasionally, to compensate for the lack of coins among the guards, but from now on, she needed the standard . . . if not more. All weapons were for Westwind, to be used as Saryn deemed necessary.

With a nod to Shalya, Saryn eased the gelding toward Caeris and what remained of the Lornian squad, also recovering weapons and spoils. Dyala and Kayli flanked her as she rode.

From what Saryn had been able to sense during the fight, after she had used her white-darkness-expanded blade, less than a handful of riders had managed to ride over the ridge and take the back trail. Their tracks indicated—since Saryn could sense little —that they were not headed westward, though, but almost due south, toward Cardara and the lands of Lord Orsynn. Perhaps thirty or so had escaped her dark blade and fled toward Suedara and attacked third squad. None of those had escaped, although Saryn wasn't exactly happy about the casualties.

"Commander." Behind Caeris's voice was something, not quite fear and not quite respect.

"Most of the Jeranyi are dead. Once you've completed matters here, please join up with us for the return to Nuelda."

"We're returning?"

"Less than a double handful of Jeranyi escaped. For the moment, I doubt that they will be any threat to Lord Jharyk's folk."

"Less than a . . . out of fivescore?"

"The rest are dead."

"Yes, ser."

Saryn wasn't sure, not with her uncertain eyesight, but she thought the squad leader looked a trace pale. She smiled politely and turned the gelding back in the direction of Suedara.

More than two glasses later, Saryn's combined force was back in formation and ready to ride. Given the size of the Jeranyi force and their reputation, the casualty numbers for her detachment wouldn't have seemed that bad to the Lornians—nine dead, five of them Lornians, four of the junior recruit guards, and six wounded, none seriously enough not to ride, of which three were Lornians. The regency force had also ended up with nearly forty captured mounts and, according to the count of the squad leaders, some eighty-three dead Jeranyi. Unhappily, somewhere between ten and fifteen of the dead Jeranyi had merely been wounded in fighting second squad—until the locals got to them near the end of the skirmish.

Saryn's head was still splitting. Closing her eyes didn't seem to provide much relief from the shimmering arrows of light that flashed across her field of vision and stabbed through her eyes and into her skull. She also didn't want to think about what she had done . . . or how.

After receiving final reports from the three squad leaders, Saryn ordered the Lornians to lead. Then she eased her mount into position beside Caeris, who did not look in her direction for the first kay, not until they were well north of Suedara and riding northeast toward Nuelda.

"Do you think they have more raiders around here, ser?"

"Not all that close, but I'd be surprised if this is the last that we hear of them. But it won't be for a while, and we can't stay here and wait."

The squad leader nodded slowly.

"They probably won't attack Lord Jharyk's lands soon. They've already plundered most of the towns here." As she finished, Saryn realized that many of the coppers and silvers taken as plunder had probably come from those hamlets and towns, but she wasn't about to try to figure out how to return them, not when there were no coins coming from either the regency or Westwind to support her force. But . . . she still couldn't help but feel a trace guilty.

Another half kay passed before the Lornian squad leader spoke again. "Ser . . . how did you know that they'd attack Suedara and take this road?"

"They've tried to plunder every other hamlet and town close to the end of the West Pass. This is the one with the most goods and women. They were trying to drive everyone here, then hit here and return to Jerans."

"But why this road?"

"What other road would they take?" replied Saryn with a smile.

"They could have come in from the north almost as easy, or come across the bridge into Suedara from the east. You just seemed to know."

"Sometimes, you just have to trust your judgment and act." Even as she replied, Saryn couldn't help but wonder. How had she known? It had felt obvious to her, but it had been more than that. She'd *known*. Saryn swallowed. *Does it come from sensing order and chaos flows? A feel for what must be? Or was it just a lucky guess?*

Saryn almost would have preferred the last . . . but she'd felt something beyond certainty.

LXX

Saryn did not press on the ride returning to Nuelda, and her force did not arrive until well after dark on sevenday. Even so, by the time she was riding past the nearly dark front entry to Jharyk's redbrick villa, the lord-holder, accompanied by two servants bearing brass lanterns, had hurried out to meet her. As she reined up, she could see lanterns being hurriedly lit in the villa, and presumably in the rear courtyards as well.

Jharyk stood there fully dressed, and as dapper as before. "Commander, you sent no word, and we did not expect you, especially not so soon."

"Good evening, Lord Jharyk." Saryn had no trouble discerning the irritation in the lord-holder's voice and posture. She forced the hoarseness from her voice and ignored the lightknives attacking her eyes and the throbbing in her skull.

"Might I ask what occurred?" His eyes flicked to the guards, then back to Saryn.

"You were right to be concerned." Saryn smiled politely. "There was a good company or so of Jeranyi raiders who were attacking your lands and hamlets. They had sacked all of them except Suedara, mostly before we arrived, before we could bring them to bay."

"And?"

"Ten of them escaped. The other eighty-three or so are dead."

"I presume you have recovered some mounts and goods for us . . . to compensate us for the devastation we have suffered."

"They're Jeranyi horses, and they will be used to mount more West-wind guards to serve the regency." Saryn kept her tone polite. "They were paid for in blood. Mostly Jeranyi blood, but also Lornian regency forces' blood and Westwind guards' blood."

"My people have suffered greatly. Should they have no recompense?" asked Jharyk smoothly.

"If they need recompense, Lord Jharyk, perhaps they should turn to you. You did not have to raise and train armsmen to drive off the raiders, and that surely should leave some coins. We've removed the Jeranyi for now, and, after we get a good night's rest and food and fodder, we'll be heading back to Lornth in the morning."

"You're leaving that soon? What if they return?"

"They may return, but I doubt it will be soon. Not with nine-tenths of their force destroyed."

"I see. Did you not capture any?"

"There were perhaps twenty wounded, but"—Saryn shrugged—"the townspeople of Suedara took out their vengeance on them while we were running down the stragglers." That wasn't quite true. It had happened as much because Saryn had been barely functioning, and the guards had been more concerned about weapons and stray mounts, as well as possible armed stragglers. "Whatever simple fare your kitchens could prepare would be appreciated," she added.

"After such a battle, we will manage."

"Thank you."

The evening meal was late and simple—cheese over noodles with fried cakes. That was fine with Saryn, who ate with the guards. She did sleep in the villa, if with the chamber bolted shut and a chair wedged under the door, hoping that a softer bed might let her sleep more soundly and re-cover from her use of the order and chaos flows.

Even so, she woke early the next morning, and while the lightknives had not totally disappeared, they appeared infrequently, and the throbbing in her skull had subsided to a dull ache. She washed and dressed quickly, and one of the serving girls brought her breakfast.

She was in the courtyard, ready to mount up, when Jharyk appeared again.

He appeared very subdued, and Saryn had to wonder if he'd talked to the Lornian squad leader or Saensyr. "Commander . . . I must apologize for any abruptness I may have conveyed last night. I was astounded that you returned so quickly and with such a staggering victory."

"As we both know, Lord Jharyk, it is a temporary victory. That is why it needed to be absolute. We of Westwind are most familiar with the need to destroy enemies so that it will take time for them to regroup. We always hope that will suggest a certain wisdom in not provoking another attack. At times, as with the regency, it has. At other times, as with Gallos, it has not. I would like to think that the Jeranyi would be wise. I doubt they will be. Some lords are far too interested in amassing power at any cost. In the end, they lose everything. So it has been with the Jeranyi, and so it will probably be again." Saryn inclined her head politely. "We do appreciate your food and fodder, and your continued support of the regency. We have left five mounts as some recompense. They are slightly strained, but they are basically sound, and in a few eightdays will be worth far more."

Jharyk looked at her but did not speak.

"I would that I could offer more, Lord Jharyk, but because several lords, unlike you, have been remiss in remitting their tariffs, the treasury of the regency is not what it could be." *Or what it will be, if I have anything to do about it.*

"I understand, Commander. It may be that will not be an issue in the future."

Saryn could almost hear the words "one way or another," although the lord-holder only smiled politely. "It may not be. We need to be on our way."

"Of course."

Saryn mounted quickly, checking the saddle sheath before her knee. On the ride back, she'd made certain that she again had three blades, two in her harness and one in the sheath.

Then she rode across the courtyard to where the Lornian squad was forming up.

Caeris rode to meet her. "Commander."

"Squad leader, I'm sending you and Saensyr back to Lornth with your squad and with the three wounded guards—and with all but five spare mounts."

"Ser?"

"The regent's orders were for you to defend Lord Jharyk's lands against the Jeranyi. You and your men did that admirably. We wouldn't have been able to do what we did without you." Saryn paused. "I'm very concerned that the remaining Jeranyi may cause trouble with Lord Orsynn, and we're going to follow them for a bit, just to make sure there's not more trouble. I'd be exceeding our agreement with the regency if you were to accompany us. We will take the regency banner, just so that there's no confusion."

"Yes, ser."

Even with her pain-diminished senses, Saryn sensed both worry and relief. "Also, you'll be able to tell the Lady Regent that we destroyed the Jeranyi force threatening Lord Jharyk's lands and people. She needs to hear that as soon as possible. I'll be sending a dispatch with one of my guards to confirm your report."

"Yes, ser." That thought clearly cheered Caeris.

"Oh . . . by the way, did Lord Jharyk ask you about what happened in Suedara?"

Caeris frowned. "Yes, ser. This morning he talked to both Saensyr and me. We didn't say much. Was that . . . ?"

"No . . . that was fine. He just seemed to know more than I'd told him last night. I took him offguard, and I'm sure he had more questions this morning."

"He had some. He was surprised at how few we lost for how many Jeranyi we killed. Then he thanked us and said he needed to talk to you, ser."

"He did. I think he understands more and is even more inclined to support the regency." Saryn smiled. "We'll leave together. Once we're beyond the town, you'll head to Lornth."

"Yes, ser."

Saryn rode back to first squad.

"First and second squads ready to ride, ser," offered Shalya.

"Have someone pick up the regency banner from the Lornians," said Saryn. "Then we'll head out."

"Yes, ser." Shalya turned in the saddle. "Fryada, we'll be taking the regency banner. Get it from the Lornian squad. They're expecting you."

With a nod, the guard turned her mount out from the column and headed back toward Caeris and the Lornians.

Shalya turned back to Saryn. "I'd wager that Caeris was pleased to know he could head back to Lornth."

"Relieved, I think."

"They did all right for a bunch that hasn't fought much."

"They did, but I'd wager that Caeris will have a hard time explaining losing three men of every ten to the undercaptain."

"That's because they haven't fought anyone in ten years." At times it was hard to believe that it had been only twelve years since they had left the *Winterlance* in orbit.

Saryn just nodded, her eyes going to Fryada, returning with the furled regency banner.

Once the guard was back in position, Shalya turned and checked over the squad, then ordered, "First squad . . . prepare to ride!"

Saryn rode beside the squad leader as they headed down from the holding into the town. In the early morning, the streets of Nuelda were almost deserted, and those few who were out slipped away as they saw the riders.

Saryn couldn't help but think about the casualties second squad had taken. Not all of them had been because of the shortness of the recruits' training. Some of it, Saryn feared, had occurred because of where she had positioned Yulia's squad. They'd had to face into the rising sun, not directly, but even at an angle that well might have been a problem. Saryn hadn't considered it because in the Westhorns, where all the roads and trails were beneath cliffs and mountains, early-morning sunlight was never a problem. Shadows were.

She shook her head. There was still so much she had to learn about Lornth and the lowlands . . . and she still had thoughts about the ancient Cyadoran dwelling and what it represented, although she couldn't have explained totally what it represented, beyond the clear tradition of feminine submission.

LXXI

By midmorning on fourday, Saryn and her two squads had found the road that ran as directly as possible from Lornth to Carda, the largest town in Cardara, Lord Orsynn's holding, and were riding to the south under high, hazy clouds. Thankfully, they had seen no more rain, and the last marker stone indicated that Cardara lay ten kays ahead. Saryn was again doubting the wisdom of her decision to follow the fleeing Jeranyi, but there had been more than enough hoofprints in the road dust and on the shoulder of the road that it appeared the raiders were headed toward Carda, following the road over what seemed endless rolling rises, not even hills, most of them planted in wheat corn or other crops, although a few were lightly forested.

Saryn doubted that the Jeranyi were riding to raid the town, and that suggested even worse possibilities. At least, the lightknives that had plagued her after the fight with the Jeranyi had faded away during the first day's ride from Nuelda. That had been a relief.

Ahead of the column rode a pair of outriders. As the first neared the top of the next rise, not quite half a kay away, she turned immediately and waved her partner back. Saryn immediately extended her senses to their limit, barely discerning riders in a long column headed toward them.

"Show the regency banner!" Saryn ordered. "Bring it to the fore." As one of the junior guards rode forward with the banner, Saryn glanced back at the outriders, both moving at a good canter toward her.

As the two neared the Westwind force, Saryn tried to estimate the distances. First she glanced to the last rise behind her squads, but it was almost two kays away, while the rise before them was perhaps eight hundred yards away. She sensed the position of the riders ahead, then she nodded. Her squads would reach the crest of the road while the oncoming riders were still almost a kay away and on lower ground.

The first outrider to reach Saryn pulled her mount in beside the commander. "Ser . . . there must be three companies riding this way. I don't think they saw us, and their scouts aren't but a quarter kay or so ahead of their vanguard."

"Could you tell who they are?"

"Two companies are in blue and white. The third . . . they look like Jeranyi."

"Blue and white," murmured Saryn. *Most likely Orsynn's colors.* "What's the ground like on the other side of the rise?"

"Same as here, ser. Fields of potatoes, it looks like, wheat-corn in places, close to being harvested. All of it low crops. There's nothing that would stop them from spreading out and flanking us . . . well, except in the vale way down to the west, and there are some trees there."

Except that they don't know that we're here. Not yet. Do we really want to confront them? But if we don't at least offer them the chance to be friendly . . . then what will they claim? Saryn had the definite feeling that she needed to appear with the regency banner and see how the Lornians reacted.

After a moment, she nodded. "Head back to the rise, but stay out of sight. Ride slowly enough that you don't raise dust."

"Yes, ser."

Once the outriders headed back up the road, Shalya looked to Saryn. "That doesn't sound good."

"No. It looks like the southern lord-holders are in rebellion, whether they call it that or not, and they've probably hired some of the Jeranyi mercenaries. They were probably paid to attack Lord Jharyk because he's supported the regency."

"Then they'll attack him again, won't they?"

"Not yet. He doesn't have enough armsmen to make a difference. If the southern lord-holders win, they'll deal with him later." *And if they don't, the regency will doubtless feel obligated to reward him, self-centered as he is.*

Saryn continued to study the Lornian forces as her own squads neared the crest of the road, but from what she could sense, the Lornians had yet to learn that a regency force was approaching them. *A regency force?* She shook her head, thinking about the irony of Westwind guards being the strongest forces available to Lady Zeldyan.

She still wondered about the wisdom of confronting the Lornians, but she certainly couldn't determine their intentions by fleeing from them, and she'd rather have the high ground, gentle as the southern slope seemed to be.

Less than a quarter glass passed before the Westwind squads reached the crest of the road.

"Squads halt!" Saryn ordered. "Re-form ten across, first squad on the left, second squad on the right."

"Squads halt! . . ." Both Shalya and Yulia repeated the orders, modified for their own squads.

Saryn studied the oncoming riders, who continued for almost another two hundred yards before coming to a stop.

For a time, nothing happened.

Then a single figure rode up the gentle slope toward the Westwind lines, bearing a white parley banner.

Saryn rode forward slightly and reined up, but took the precaution of unsheathing a blade and resting it across her legs.

The young man, an undercaptain, reined up. "I bring terms from Lord Orsynn."

"Terms?" replied Saryn. "Since when does a lord-holder impose terms on the regency?"

The young man scanned the ranks of Westwind guards. "How can you claim to represent the regency? You are the enemies of Lornth."

"We have a treaty," Saryn pointed out. "We are here at the request of the regency."

"The regency no longer represents the lord-holders of Lornth. Women are not fit to rule the land, and such a rule is against the natural order of life. Still . . . the lord-holders have no quarrel with Westwind, and if you choose to return to the Westhorns, none will hinder you."

"Oh?" asked Saryn mildly. "That is a most suspect assurance, given that various lord-holders have already attacked us."

"Lord Orsynn has given his assurance, and he is a most honorable lord," said the young officer.

"Honorable so long as women remain in what he regards as their rightful place," suggested Saryn, keeping her voice even. For some reason, the image of the shimmering metal link-ring in the old Cyadoran dwelling flashed into her mind.

"What other place . . ."

"Oh . . ." replied Saryn, "they might rule, or command, or otherwise infringe on the traditional prerogatives of men. And, in response to the most generous gesture of your lord, I will offer my terms in return. If he returns to his lands and swears allegiance to the regency, the regency will accept his allegiance without prejudice."

"You are outnumbered," pointed out the officer.

"We are indeed, but you may convey my terms to your lord. If he turns his forces and returns to his holding, I will know he has accepted the regency's terms."

"And if not?" The undercaptain's smile was more like a smirk.

"Then what will be will be," replied Saryn.

"He cannot accept those terms. He has pledged—"

"He broke his pledge to the regency. He can certainly break his pledge to a group of rebel lords."

"They are upholding the true traditions of Lornth."

Inherited from Cyador, no doubt. "Undercaptain . . . convey my terms. Lord Orsynn can accept or receive the consequences."

The undercaptain flushed, and Saryn could sense his anger.

"I will tell him you have refused his terms."

"Tell him my terms as well." Saryn's voice was even, but the undercaptain flinched at her eyes.

Without another word, the young officer turned his horse and rode down the slope.

"He did not even ask who you were," observed Shalya.

"We're women. In his eyes, and those of Lord Orsynn, we don't count, unless consorted to a powerful man." Saryn looked out at the more than three companies. *Can you do it again?* she asked herself. *Do you have any choice?*

For several moments, she watched the undercaptain ride down the road. Then she turned. "Squads! Re-form to five abreast, four deep."

Shalya and Yulia repeated the orders but both looked to Saryn.

"With us only two deep, they could sweep through us. Besides, I want the Lornians in a more compact formation."

For a time, the Jeranyi and Cardaran forces remained as they had halted. Then, both began to re-dress their lines, until they had three companies abreast, each with a ten-man front. After a short wait, they began to ride forward, if only at a quick walk.

"Make sure everyone holds fast," Saryn said firmly. "I can't take them on until they're close, and it's going to look like they'll run over us. We'll charge at the last moment and go through them." *Don't ask how.* "Keep the formation tight." She turned to Shalya. "Once we're through them, don't waste guards trying to capture or chase down stragglers."

"Yes, ser."

Saryn made a conscious effort to relax her grip on the short sword, her eyes and senses on the approaching Cardarans and their Jeranyi allies. With the hazy clouds, and the white sun higher in the sky, she didn't have to worry about her forces facing into a low, bright light.

As she waited, she extended her senses, beginning to link the junctures and nodes in the air into a chevron-shaped pattern, with her at the apex, and with the same knife-edge of chaos she had created before, cradled in unyielding order. She worked to extend that unseen blade far enough to both sides so that it would cover the flanks of the Cardarans.

At a hundred yards from Saryn, the attackers began a full gallop toward the regency force. Saryn waited until they were close to eighty yards away. Then she finally ordered, "Charge! Forward! On me!"

She urged the gelding into a full canter, linking the chaos-knife to her short sword and knowing that she needed as much momentum as possible to increase the force of her blade. She searched for the leading rider in the center company, her eyes sweeping the attacking force, nodding as she sensed that the attackers had fallen into a rough, if barely perceptible, wedge, with the middle of the center company at the point.

Less than twenty yards from the leading rider, Saryn finally released her blade, strengthening the links and flattening herself against the neck and mane of the gelding as the unseen black-framed whitish knife blade slashed through men and mounts, cutting them down and scattering them away from the Westwind squads.

Even before Saryn reached the shattered rear of the Cardaran force, black voids filled with cold whiteness arrowed into her, pulling and hammering at her, so much that her entire body felt as though it had been penetrated by hundreds, if not thousands, of unseen needles.

Her fingers clutched at the gelding's mane.

She started to lift her head, but she could not see through the assault of shimmering lightknives that stabbed through her eyes. She reined in the gelding, conscious of riders around her, hoping they were Westwind guards, before the needles, the lightknives, and another black void all slammed into her.

Hot darkness and chill icy white engulfed her . . . then she felt nothing.

*   *   *

As if emerging from an unseen drizzle, Saryn felt the dampness running down her forehead, water that was neither hot nor cold, and she shook her head, trying to speak, to get out of the rain.

"Commander?"

She tried to speak again, but her throat was so dry that her "yes" was more like a croak. "Water . . . please."

Someone placed a water bottle at her lips. She lifted her head, ignoring the pounding inside her skull, and drank.

Hate being weak . . . passing out in the saddle isn't a good example. She struggled into a sitting position on the shoulder of the road.

Although she could barely see between the lightknives and the pain they created, she could make out that the high, hazy clouds had been replaced by lower and darker ones. A flash of lightning flickered brightly just to the east, followed immediately by a loud crash of thunder.

Her body didn't feel bruised. Finally, she looked at Shalya. "I didn't fall . . . ?"

"We had to pry your fingers out of the horse's mane."

"What happened?"

"Your black blades scythed through the main body of both the Jeranyi and the Lornians. It looked like some thirty armsmen on the fringes escaped. We captured ten or so."

Even with her vision almost nonexistent because of the flashing lightknives, Saryn could see the gravity on Shalya's face and in her words. "How long was I out? What's the problem? What were our losses?"

"You've been out a half glass or so. We had three wounded. I don't think one will make it."

Saryn didn't see that as insurmountable, given what they'd faced.

"We found several bodies attired . . . like lords. The captives identified them as Lord Orsynn and two of his sons."

"I don't see a problem there. He, or his envoy, admitted rebelling against the regency. They attacked a force bearing the regency banner without any hesitation. They paid the price."

"Some of the captives complained that you used sorcery."

Saryn wanted to snort. "None of them thought it was unfair to attack us with six times our numbers. There is no fairness in battle. You win or lose. Did we capture many mounts?"

"A score and a half. The others . . ."

Saryn understood. Her dark scythe didn't distinguish between men and mounts. "Blades? Weapons?"

"We recovered hundreds of blades, enough that most of the captured mounts are heavily laden. More than a bit of coins as well. I haven't counted it, but I'd guess close to sixty golds. More than half came from Lord Orsynn." Shalya's face bore an expression Saryn couldn't decipher, and her light-blurred vision and pounding head kept her from sensing anything.

"What else?" asked Saryn.

"Your blade . . . it was molten when it hit, and there was a dark fire."

Saryn was vaguely amused that she wasn't surprised. "It mixes order and chaos flows." After a moment, she asked, "Did the fire upset the guards?"

"Most of them didn't see it."

"The stragglers?"

"A few were Jeranyi. I think they were breaking away even before you acted. They might have been those who were at Suedara."

That certainly made sense.

Saryn slowly rose to her feet, looking for the gelding. They needed to get back to Lornth before matters got even worse . . . if they hadn't already.

Rain began to fall out of the still-darkening sky.

LXXII

The departure of the Westwind guards from the lands of the late Lord Orsynn required a glass of riding through rain that fell in sheets, soaking through everything. There had been no help for it, since there was no shelter from the storm, a storm that Saryn was more than certain her use of order and chaos had either created or exacerbated. Once they had cleared the deluge, she occasionally looked back, but the sky remained black, suggesting that most of Cardara was being thoroughly drenched. Had she done Orsynn's people a favor or washed out their harvest?

With as much riding as they had earlier pressed on their mounts, it was late afternoon on oneday when Saryn ordered the regency banner un-furled again, and they rode back through the streets of Lornth from the southwest. While the main square and byways were not deserted, Saryn felt that there were noticeably fewer people out than she'd seen before, and that bothered her. The feeling engendered by the semideserted ap-pearance of Lornth was scarcely improved as she rode toward the palace gates . . . and found them closed.

The Lornian armsmen quickly opened the ironbound and timbered relics, and just as quickly closed them behind the returning Westwind forces.

Saryn rode directly to the rear stables and reined up. There, Hryessa was waiting.

"You brought back more mounts and plunder," said the captain. "Who else did you fight?"

Saryn swung down out of the saddle before replying. "Three compa-nies mounted by Lord Orsynn. He and the southern lords declared rebel-lion against the regency. They didn't say it that way. They claimed to be out to restore the rightful ways of Lornth. Lord Orsynn won't be restoring anything. Neither will two of his sons or his companies."

The guard captain nodded, as if such were to be expected. That chilled Saryn in a way she couldn't have described. "Undercaptain Maerkyn told me about the rebellion. Lord Kelthyn demanded that Lord Henstrenn re-place Lord Gethen as regent. When the Lady Regent refused, Lord Kelthyn vowed she would regret her failure to return Lornth to the old ways."

"Sometimes the old ways are best. Sometimes, they're not. In changing times, those who prevail are the ones who understand which ways work best for the times." Saryn paused, then asked, "Speaking of new ways, do you have any more recruits?"

"Close to two squads. Some walked days to get here. They are all will-ing and work hard, but they have so much to learn." Hryessa shook her head sadly. "Lornth needs new ways."

"The Lady Regent seems to be one of the few who thinks so." Saryn stretched, then shook her shoulders, trying to loosen tight muscles. "After I take care of the gelding, I need to talk to the Lady Regent. Once I've heard what she has to say, we need to go over things. It's going to be a long har-vest and winter."

"We will not be returning to Westwind soon."

"No. They have so many women who have fled there . . . that was why the Marshal asked if we will be able to send supplies after harvest." Saryn had already told Hryessa that, but wanted to reinforce the point. "There are hundreds of blades packed on the spare mounts. Daryn can have his pick for the best to reforge, but, before he does, would you make sure that any adornments are removed?"

"I can do that." Hryessa smiled before turning away.

Saryn started to lead the chestnut into the stables, only to find Dealdron standing there.

"Good afternoon, Commander, ser." He studied her intently.

Saryn could sense his concerns, but she only replied, "Good afternoon."

"I will unsaddle and groom your horse. You have ridden all across Lornth and fought hard battles, and there will be more to come."

"I can—"

"You can do anything, Commander. I cannot do what you can do. I can take care of your horse so that you can do what you must."

Saryn just stopped and looked at Dealdron, again sensing the concern and worry behind his open, handsome face and intent eyes. Seeing and sensing that concern for her, particularly from a man, she couldn't help smiling. "You're right. Thank you." She handed him the reins.

"And, Commander, ser . . . you need to eat, ser."

Saryn couldn't help but be touched. "I will." She turned and started across the courtyard.

She hadn't quite reached the rear door to the south wing when Lyentha stepped out and moved toward her.

"Yes, Lyentha?"

"The Lady Regent would like to see you at your earliest convenience, Commander." Lyentha paused. "Is it true that you killed an entire company of Jeranyi by yourself?"

"No. The three squads with me did that. I helped some." *More than some, but I'm not getting into that.*

Lyentha nodded, but behind the gesture was skepticism at Saryn's demurral.

"I'll be there shortly. In fact, I'll go there now."

"She is awaiting you in her private study. She said to tell you she has refreshments."

"Thank you." *Dealdron did say I needed to eat.* That thought brought another smile to her lips as she entered the palace.

The guard outside Zeldyan's third-level study resolutely looked away as Saryn approached and knocked.

"Yes?"

"Saryn, at your request."

"Please come in."

Saryn entered, closing the door behind her.

Zeldyan rose and moved from the small writing table to the conference table on which were three platters, a carafe of red wine, and two goblets. "Welcome back." She gestured toward the table.

"Thank you." Saryn took the seat across from the regent.

Zeldyan filled both goblets before she spoke, lifting hers. "To your safe return."

Saryn merely nodded, then sipped the wine and lowered the goblet.

Zeldyan set her goblet down and looked directly at Saryn. "Your message stated that you had dispatched the company of Jeranyi that had been raiding Lord Jharyk's lands. After that success, why did you not return personally with the message? Lord Henstrenn, Lord Kelthyn, and Lord Keistyn have joined with most of the lords of the south in demanding an end to my regency. They have sent a document that demands that I immediately leave Lornth and return Nesslek to their custody."

"I knew something of the sort."

"Oh? And you did not return?"

"No, Lady. I was involved in destroying Lord Orsynn's three companies. They were riding northward in the direction of Lornth. I asked Lord Orsynn to pledge his allegiance to the regency. He refused and attacked. He, two of his sons, and his forces are no more."

"They are no more?" Zeldyan raised her eyebrows. "They will re-form under some other lord."

"No." Saryn shook her head. "All but thirty died. Twenty were Jeranyi who started to flee before the battle began. We captured ten others."

"You slaughtered almost three hundred men?"

Saryn shrugged. "I could have abandoned you, or I could slaughter them. Those were the choices."

Zeldyan paled. "How terrible you angels are."

"How long do you think your son would live in the custody of Hen-strenn or Keistyn?" Saryn said quietly. "How long before your supporters were removed, one way or another?"

"I have barely a company left here to hold Lornth, and they could not stand against you alone. And so I must rely, more and more, upon you?"

"We have few choices," replied Saryn, "either of us."

"You would fight your battles on our lands."

"We would prefer to fight no battles, Lady. If we must fight, we fight where we can. What would you have us do? Leave you and the regency to fall, then destroy your enemies later at an even higher cost to both lands? We cannot allow them to destroy Westwind, and that is what they wish."

Zeldyan lifted her goblet and took a small swallow, then picked up one of the small pastries and ate it.

Saryn picked up one of them and chewed it, a miniature fowl pie, somewhat dry. She took and ate a second, somewhat warmer and juicier, then sipped the wine, waiting for the regent to speak.

"I would that you had never alighted upon the Roof of the World," Zeldyan finally said.

"Our choice was to land there or die. We did not attack anyone." Saryn paused, thinking back. The only times she had ever attacked first, she realized, was when she had dealt with the Gallosian false bandits and the Jeranyi attacking Lord Jharyk's lands, and in both cases, the enemy had attacked others first. Yet everyone seemed to believe that she was some sort of evil destroyer.

"That matters not. Your presence was an attack."

The way in which your men treat women and anyone they see as lesser is an attack on us . . . But there wasn't any use in raising that point. "What is done is done. What can we do now? Who has what forces and where are they? Do you know?"

"Lord Mortryd of Tryenda is the only other lord in the south profess-ing loyalty to the regency, but he is being threatened by Rherhn of Kha-lasn, whose forces have entered his lands. Mortryd has a small holding, and he has written that he has barely one company of armsmen, and many of those he has had to call away from the harvest . . ."

Saryn mentally called up the map she had memorized, and visualized the geographic positions. Tryenda was a narrow holding south of Lornth, sandwiched between Hasel and Khalasn, and with its north border adjoining the southern border of Nesslek's holding of Lornth. "What about Keistyn? His lands border Tryenda on the east."

"Mortryd's missive was quite clear. Lord Rherhn has always coveted the bottomlands of Tryenda and apparently sees the present unrest as an opportunity."

"How long a ride to Tryenda—the holding keep, that is?"

"It's on the north end of the holding. A day and a half easy ride."

"Do you want to get involved?" asked Saryn.

"He's promised his company to support the regency, but he won't leave his lands with Rherhn threatening him."

"So he wants the assurance," said Saryn dryly, "that you can and will support him before he'll back you and the regency."

"Exactly."

"Is it worth it for a single company?"

"If he throws in with Kelthyn and Keistyn, that's a difference of two companies. Also, some of the northern lords may question whether we will support them if they have few armsmen. Henstrenn would certainly trumpet that everywhere."

"And what if it's a trap or a ruse to get your forces out of Lornth?"

Zeldyan looked at Saryn.

"Ah . . . you want me to take care of it so that you can hold Lornth without risking what you have here."

"If it is a ruse, you can return quickly. If not, you can return with Mortryd's forces. If it is an attempt to engage your forces, there is certainly no reason for you to fight unless circumstances are favorable."

"Do you know where Keistyn's forces are?"

"One company was sighted near Veryna, joining up with Kelthyn's men. They could not return to Tryenda in less than four days."

Worse and worse.

"Most of the lands are entering harvest. They can't bring all their forces into line for several eightdays. After that . . ." Zeldyan shrugged.

"So we need to straighten out the mess between Rherhn and Mortryd before everyone jumps in?" *The guards and I have to, not you. At least, we have enough horses to switch them out and take fresh mounts.*

"I fear so."

"We will still need at least a half day to prepare." *Even if I take fourth squad this time.* "In return, I want assurances of at least ten full wagons of supplies to be sent to Westwind before the late-fall snows."

"What of friendship?" Zeldyan's voice carried irony.

"I think I've demonstrated that amply, Lady. We beat back Suthyans in the north, destroyed two squads of Lord Henstrenn's men, broke a company of Jeranyi, and eliminated three companies of Lord Orsynn's men. By warning you about the Suthyans, the Marshal lost the chance to trade for food with them. Friendship goes two ways, does it not?"

"I cannot send food to Westwind until the revolt is crushed . . ."

"I know. The roads go through Hasel, Duevek, and a corner of Fhasta. I just want your pledge." *And I will hold you to it.*

"You have it."

"Tell me more about Lord Mortryd and Tryenda," Saryn said, finally taking another pair of the miniature pastry pies.

Much later, as she left the regent's study, more questions swirled through Saryn's mind. She'd been able to prevail against the Lornians, the Jeranyi, and the Suthyans only through her use of order and chaos, and she'd been even more fortunate that years before, Nylan and Ayrlyn had destroyed all those in Lornth and Gallos who might have challenged her—except for the Gallosian mages buried in the landslide, and she had not had to get close to them. What could she do if someone used either order or chaos—or both—against her? She'd barely managed against the Suthyan hedge mage, and he was nothing compared to the white mages she recalled who had attacked Nylan.

Then there was the problem of her own guards. She had but two experienced squads, and the lack of experience was killing too many of the recruits—but there wasn't enough time to train them as well as the older guards. Yet she didn't want to turn them away because, after they'd left their homes, what they faced if they had to return there was likely to be as brutal as the fighting they would face as Westwind guards.

Even with Zeldyan's pledge, how long would it be before she could get supplies to Westwind? For that matter, given the location of Duevek and Hasel, and the fact that any pledges of passage could scarcely be trusted, how could she even have returned to Westwind without still having to fight in a civil war . . . and with even less assurance of an outcome favorable to Westwind?

LXXIII

On twoday, after more than a little thinking and planning the night before, Saryn was up early. After dressing and eating hurriedly, she sought out Hryessa a good half glass before morning muster . . . and found her leaving the officers' quarters above the barracks.

"Good morning, Hryessa. What should I know that you haven't gotten around to telling me?" asked Saryn with a cheerful smile. Bright and clear as the morning was, perfect for the second day of harvest, she didn't feel near as cheery as her smile indicated.

"The cooking for the guards is better. The Lornian armsmen have stopped watching us, and they even drill and practice at times. Our guards have no trouble in the town, but they are always in threes. They have caused no problems. Dealdron and Daryn have built two supply wagons from the unused parts and planks and timbers in the storeroom. You could take one of them to carry more rations and grain for the horses. It would not slow you."

"I didn't think there were that many spare parts around," replied Saryn. "Nor decent wood and timbers."

"Dealdron traded for some of the wood. They found some parts. Daryn forged some. They are very good wagons."

"What about blades?"

"We have enough short swords for each recruit to have one, sometimes two. Daryn is working on a second blade for each of the others."

Saryn would have liked more of the shorter blades, but that had always been a problem, even in Westwind. "Check the blades we captured. See if any are short enough to be used as a second blade."

"I did, ser. There were eleven."

Saryn nodded. "How hard are you pressing the new recruits?"

"Some of them cried at first. I had the older guards talk to them. They are better now. Before long, most will be able to hold against armsmen for a short time. Some are already better than that. Shalya said that Yulia kept the second squad doing their exercises. They look stronger."

They'll have to be. "She worked them hard, but I need you to re-form second squad," Saryn said.

"With ten of the best recruits from third squad?" asked Hryessa. "I had thought you might. And you need one replacement in first squad."

"I do, but I'm going to take fourth squad and second squad to Tryenda. First squad could use a break. It could be the last one they get for a while. Can you get fourth and second squads ready to leave by noon?"

"They will be ready the glass before midday. With a supply wagon."

"Thank you, Captain." Saryn couldn't help grinning. "Oh . . . I'll be going over to the Square Platter in a bit, after I talk to Dealdron."

"You should talk to him, Commander. I will have three guards waiting."

"I should? Why?"

"Because he is a man who would do anything for you, and there are few of them. He also can do many things."

"I'll keep that in mind." She turned and headed down the steps.

She had barely entered the stable when she saw Dealdron leading a saddled horse—not her gelding—in her direction. She waited until he neared and stopped.

"Hryessa told me that you and Daryn built some wagons."

"You will need them. You cannot travel through unfriendly holdings without more supplies, and if all the rebel lords ride on Lornth to attack the palace, you do not have the tools to defend it. So you will need wagons if we must leave." Dealdron smiled. "Also, with all the weapons you have captured, we will need to build another one."

"Daryn needs to forge more blades, not build wagons."

"He only does a little. The new guards help me, and I am training some of them to be teamsters." He paused and inclined his head toward the horse whose reins he held. "I have saddled one of the strongest mares for you. She is better than any of the other horses."

"How did you know I was riding anywhere?"

He shrugged. "It seemed that you would. The gelding should rest. So should you, but you will not. You are like the great winds that never stop."

Saryn doubted his words were a compliment. "What have you heard that I should know?"

"The Lornian armsmen are worried. Some have left."

"They've deserted?"

"Only a few. The undercaptain is pressing them to spar and drill more, but they are less than pleased. The taverns are charging half a copper more for ale, and the harvests are coming in earlier this year because the summer was hotter and drier."

Earlier harvests mean it will be sooner rather than later when the rebels can raise more troops. "Anything else?"

"We have added another sheath to your saddle, on the right side. You can carry four blades." Dealdron paused. "I heard that you were left without a blade."

"Thank you." What else could she say? The words weren't offered in the puppy-dog fashion of a boy trying to curry favor, nor were they strictly matter-of-fact. Dealdron was deeply worried that she might not have the weapons she needed.

He extended the mare's reins, and she took them. "Will it be all right to take the gelding later today?"

"The mare would be better. She is almost as strong, and the gelding should be reshod and rested."

"Then I'll take the mare." Saryn swung up into the saddle of the mare, then turned her toward the three guards riding toward her. She recognized only one of the three, the one with a dressing across her forearm. "Feyla, how is the arm?"

"Almost healed."

Saryn could sense that, as well as the fact that her arm held none of the whitish chaos suggesting infection.

"Commander, ser," Feyla said quickly, "Duena and Shayni are with third squad."

"It's good to see you. Captain Hryessa told you I'm headed to the Square Platter?"

"Yes, ser."

"It shouldn't take long." Saryn urged her mount forward.

The three others followed.

The armsmen at the gates glanced at the four riders approaching, then immediately began to slide the ancient and heavy iron bolts away before opening the gates. Two of them glanced toward the shapely Duena, then looked away quickly when they saw Saryn's eyes on them. As she rode through the gate, her senses allowed her to pick up parts of the murmured conversation

". . . that one's a tyrant . . . pin you to the wall with that short blade as soon as look at you . . . saw what she did out on the green . . . colder than . . ."

". . . bitches often the beautiful ones . . . You wonder what . . ."

"Don't even think about it . . ."

Saryn managed not to turn back and glare. *Men* . . . Except there were some who weren't that way. The engineer hadn't been. Neither, she reflected, was Daryn, although that might have been as much Hryessa's doing as anything. And Dealdron . . . had he always been that way and unable to show it? Or had he changed because she'd encouraged him? Had Istril and Siret seen that? Or even more? She pushed that thought away. There was no point in even considering such, not at the moment.

As she guided the mare around the green, then onto the avenue leading to the square, she concentrated on what she wanted to learn from Haelora. When the four turned onto the narrow street off the square and headed toward the inn, a squat, bearded man standing in front of what might have been a run-down joinery looked hard at Saryn and started to open his mouth.

She could sense the anger, and said firmly, "Not a word. The Lady Regent's better than you deserve."

The man stepped back, his face turning livid, his mouth working silently.

As soon as she had spoken, Saryn wondered whether she should have said anything at all. But then, she was tired, and getting even more weary of people, men especially, suggesting in so many ways that they didn't like women with any sort of power or authority—as if the men in Lornth had done such a wonderful job at anything except fomenting dissension.

The streets weren't any more deserted than they'd been on oneday, but they certainly weren't any more crowded, either, and the few she saw were those in common working garb. When they reached the Square Platter, the front porch was empty, but Saryn caught sight of Haelora through the front window of the public room just before she reined up. She dismounted and handed the reins to Shayni, then hurried into the inn.

Vanadyl, standing near the doorway with a pail in his hand, gestured to the public room.

"Thank you," Saryn said politely, making her way through the archway and walking to the right front table, where Haelora was seated with a ledger before her. "Greetings."

The innkeeper bowed her head but did not rise. "Honored Commander."

Saryn took the chair across from her. "Have we done something else to displease the people of Lornth?"

Haelora frowned, then spoke, quietly closing the ledger. "You've got 'em worried. Most think that the lord-holders fighting with each other and the regent . . . well . . . it wouldn't have happened ifn you hadn't come. The men, they're getting afraid that Westwind will ride down and take over. Some of the women are pleased. Most fear that, if things get worse, they'll get blamed, and their consorts will beat them. Even those who won't get beaten worry about what their menfolk think."

Why do they fret about what their consorts think? Most men here put what they want first . . . and then think about the women around them later . . . if they even bother to consider them at all. Saryn managed to nod, reminding herself that the women of Lornth didn't have the choices or opportunities that she'd had. *Or the training.* But she and Ryba and Hryessa were changing that. They had to. "Have you heard anything about the other lord-holders?"

Haelora glanced toward the archway behind Saryn, then lowered her voice. "Lord Kelthyn's agents were skulking around here last eightday, looking for armsmen with experience."

"How do people feel about that?"

"So long as the lords don't hurt them, they don't care that much. They just want to get in their harvests. Some hope that the fighting will make their crops more dear. Those are the young crofters. The older growers and sharecroppers only want to stay out of the way. Some would like to send their daughters to relatives . . . but no one knows what will happen where. They're all just waiting, biding their time. Hoping, mostly."

"And you?"

"We open the public room to anyone and hope what we make will pay for what damages follow. We serve honest lager and ale to the armsmen, but not the most costly. And we only use the chipped and cheap mugs for them."

"We all do what we have to."

Haelora nodded. "What else is there?"

I'd like there to be more to life than that, but will that ever be possible here? "When I was riding west toward Nuelda, we stayed in an old house that the herder said was Cyadoran. Was this part of Lornth once part of Cyador?"

"For a short time, in the days of Lorn and Kerial. There are a few dwellings here that old, but they are not like they were then."

"The herder said that none of the women in his family would enter the dwelling, that they believed demons still lived there."

Haelora laughed. "The only demons were the Cyadorans. Harsh as the men of Lornth can be, they are kind compared to the old ones of Cyad, that ancient capital."

That was about what Saryn suspected. She rose. "Thank you." She couldn't say that she'd learned that much, except that Kelthyn had been recruiting. That scarcely surprised her.

"You are always welcome here, Commander," replied Haelora.

Saryn could sense regret, almost sadness, as if Haelora did not think much of Saryn's prospects. "I will be back." She offered a grin. "I could not say when, though."

"I will look forward to that." Haelora stood. "Take care."

"You, also." Saryn inclined her head, then turned and departed.

She was back at the palace close to two glasses before noon, and it only took her a quarter glass to gather and pack her gear before heading out into the courtyard. Dealdron was waiting with the mare. She thought he might offer to fasten her saddlebags and gear in place, but he only held the mare while she did.

He did not speak until she finished. "I will tether her in the shade for now, while you do what you must. I will be checking the wagon harnesses." He smiled.

"Thank you."

As she turned to walk toward Hryessa, she could feel his eyes on her back and sense his feelings—a sense of wistfulness, along with clear admiration—and nothing lustful or lecherous.

Admiration . . . after what he'd seen her do to his fellow Gallosians? Yes, she'd spared him, but that was because he'd been unlike the others, and every eightday since, he'd proved her initial assessment. *But admiration?*

She doubted that would last if he'd seen what she'd been forced to do in battle after battle.

In a strange way, she almost hoped he never did see her in that light. And yet . . . that would be less than honest. She was what she was . . . and any man she might be interested in needed to see her as she was.

Enough of that. We need to get out of the palace and on the road. She walked more briskly toward Hryessa, who stood waiting by the supply wagon.

LXXIV

South of Lornth, in the late afternoon of fourday, the road was dusty but largely empty, for which Saryn was grateful. She had noted almost no one traveling northward toward Lornth, but she and her force had passed carts and small wagons heading away from the town.

Why are they going southward? Was it just because they had friends or family with whom they could stay? Certainly, heading toward the lands of the lords most likely to create trouble didn't make much sense to Saryn. *Except most of the townspeople probably don't know that. They only know that the Lady Regent is in trouble, and they're afraid to be in Lornth because they know there may be fighting there.*

Saryn glanced at the road ahead, a packed-dirt way holding generally to the crest of a low rise that ran north and south. A kay or so ahead of her it dipped slightly, before climbing to the crest of yet another gentle rise. She squared herself slightly in the saddle, knowing that she couldn't put off the task at hand, not if she and her force wanted to survive the eightdays ahead, because, sooner or later, another chaos-mage would show up to support the rebel lords, and the next one was likely to be far more accomplished than the Suthyan hedge mage she'd barely managed to handle.

How could she create a shield against the chaos-fire-bolts?

Slowly, she reached out with her senses and touched one of the nearest unseen nodes of order in the air. That was easy enough. Then she reached to another, and another . . . and another . . . Abruptly, the sunlight dimmed.

"Ser?" asked Klarisa, riding beside her, "What's happening?"

Between Klarisa's worried question and Saryn's own unsteady control of the nodes, the order-linkage collapsed, and hot sunlight flooded back over Saryn and the squad leader . . . and the first riders in fourth squad.

"Ser?" repeated the squad leader nervously.

"I'm trying to work on how to deal with white mages," Saryn said. "You might notice some strange things."

"Yes, ser. I'm sorry, ser."

"That's all right. I should have warned you."

"Do you mind if I pass it back, ser?"

"Just tell them that I'm working on a better defense against mages."

Klarisa turned in the saddle. "Don't worry if you see strange things around the arms-commander. She's practicing defenses against the white mages. Pass it back."

Saryn wasn't about to correct the idea that she knew the defenses and was merely practicing them. She just hoped that she could come up with something that worked.

Once she was sure that all the guards had had time to get the message, she concentrated on rebuilding the order-lattice that connected the tiny unseen nodes in the air around her. Once again, the light around her dimmed, but she had the feeling that the lattice she had created was more like a net than a shield. And nets didn't stop targeted energy. That she'd learned in the darkness between stars.

She released her hold on the net/lattice, and full sunlight flooded back over the squad. She took a deep breath.

What else can you do? What had she done—exactly—in dealing with the Suthyan hedge mage?

For a moment, she let her thoughts drift back to the fight with the raiders who had attacked Lord Spalkyn's crofters and how she'd dealt with the small fire-bolts. She'd *slid* them, using a combined flow of order and chaos. *Flow? Is that the key?*

After extending her senses, as she continued to ride southward, for a time she just watched/sensed the flows in the air between the order nodes and those between the chaos nodes, noting that the changes between order nodes were patterned and infrequent, while those between chaos nodes were much faster and unpredictably irregular. *Chaotic.* She smiled at that thought.

Now . . . could she meld the flows so that they would block a chaos-bolt and slide it away? Could she extend those flows so that they covered both squads?

She began by smoothing the chaos flows between two nodes that seemed to jump from place to place—as did all of the chaos nodes. Then she extended the smoothing to a third node . . . and a fourth. She could feel a certain pressure, and she tried to link in the nearest order node. A tiny star flared in the air.

That doesn't work. What about the idea of flow circuits . . . or something?

She began to connect order nodes, then tried to tie the linked chaos nodes to the linked order nodes . . . smoothing the "space" between them. Her "smoothing" tinged the white of the chaos with gray, and the black of order faded toward gray . . . but the flow seemed stronger, like a curtain of unseen gray light.

At the same time, the white sunlight falling around her out of the hot and hazy green-blue sky seemed to shift toward the red, toward a faint amber. *Cutting off the blue end of the spectrum?*

She linked in more of the order nodes to the order "circuit," but, then, the curtain seemed to stiffen, as if it might crack or buckle—if something she could not see or feel could do either. So she extended her links to more of the dancing chaos nodes, and noticed that with each added chaos node, those nodes danced around less, although it felt to Saryn as though they were oscillating, or vibrating, within themselves.

Balance . . . the flows have to balance.

The sunlight darkened into a deeper red, and she glanced around, seeing that the reddish light shadow covered all of fourth squad, but only Yulia and the first rank of second squad.

Saryn concentrated on extending the area of the parallel melded flows, weaving her order-chaos flow curtain farther behind her, trying at the same time to strengthen it, to thread in more order and chaos nodes.

The sunlight darkened yet more, giving a slight cooling to the air around her, yet sweat poured off her forehead and into her eyes, and tiny flashes of light flared across her vision. She felt herself swaying in the saddle.

Finally, she had to release her hold on the gray light-curtain. White sunlight flowed back over the squad. She inhaled deeply, then exhaled, then did so again, even though she hadn't been holding her breath.

Murmurs drifted forward from behind her.

"... scary ..."

"... most stuff she does that saves your rear is scary ... better get used to it ..."

Am I really that frightening? Saryn was afraid she knew the answer to the question, much as she pushed it away, but her answer raised a second question, one to which she had no answer. *Why does it have to be that way?*

She eased her water bottle out of its holder and took a long swallow. She'd have to rest before she tried to gain better control of the shield flows. But she couldn't stop working, not until she had them under control. She'd just have to pace herself ... for as long as it took.

She took another swallow and corked and stowed the bottle.

According to the maps, the border to Tryenda lay another fifteen kays ahead. She could rest and eat some biscuits and try again.

LXXV

The lands of northern Tryenda held the same kind of rolling rises as Cardara and the area south of Lornth, but the ground itself seemed less fertile, with occasional rocky outcrops, more meadows with sheep and scattered cattle, less cropland, and far more forested areas. The air was heavy and damp. Saryn kept blotting her forehead, face, and neck, and her undertunic was soaked through by midday on fourday.

Part of that was because of her own extra efforts in trying to find better ways to fuse the flow of order and chaos in the air into a flowing, sliding curtain that would hold against the chaos-bolts of the white mages. She could now shield both squads, but not for all that long, at least not without exhausting herself. Since she doubted that any chaos-mage she might face would conveniently go away when her flow curtain failed, she'd begun to work on her technique to put it together. At least, if she could raise it quickly, she might be able to hold it just long enough to deflect fire-bolts and then raise it again . . . if she could develop the proper technique. Or . . . she might be able to raise it just where the fire-bolt was aimed.

While she took several long swallows of water and rested, she studied the road and the fields and scattered woods through which they were riding. After a time, she realized that she had seen few tracks on the road, except those of her own outriders, for the last five kays, but she also hadn't sensed anyone around—not closer than two kays, at least. Abruptly, it hit her, and she wanted to pound her own forehead.

"Squads! Halt!" she ordered.

As soon as the guards came to a stop, she dismounted, then knelt and studied the sandy, dusty surface of a road whose spring ruts had long since been softened by a hot summer and the passage of hoofs, feet, and wagon wheels. Close inspection showed only traces of one set of cart wheels and two set of hoofs. The dust showed faint wavy lines . . . covering deeper imprints.

Saryn frowned . . . *They dragged branches. But why bother? The roads always have some horsemen . . . unless there are lots of riders . . .*

The entire situation screamed of ambush . . . but how exactly should she handle it?

Klarisa glanced down at Saryn.

"They hid their tracks. It's hard to tell, but I'd guess several companies rode this way. Not today. Yesterday or the day before. The locals must know, because there haven't been many riders or carts since then. They're keeping their heads low and hoping things blow over." *Like Zeldyan has been, but some troubles don't ever blow over. They just get worse.*

The hidden tracks suggested that a number of riders had used the road, but it couldn't have been too many because there were no obvious marks on the shoulders and no deep wagon traces. No wagons meant few supplies, and few supplies implied that whoever was riding either intended to live off the land or wasn't hostile. Given the intrigue and double-dealing that Saryn had already seen, she suspected the former . . . but suspicions were only that.

"Call in the outriders!" Saryn swung back up into the saddle.

After the three outriders had returned and gathered around Saryn, Klarisa, and Yulia, Saryn cleared her throat. "There are armsmen somewhere ahead of us. There could be several companies. Whenever you near a ridge or a higher place in the road, I want you to slow down and move up just enough to see what lies beyond. If you see any sign of anything that looks out of place or any sign of armsmen, slip back down and make your way back here. Don't raise any dust in doing it. Is that clear?"

"Yes, ser," came the chorus.

"We'll also need a place to rest, or to bivouac, where there's clean water."

Once the three had headed out again, Klarisa looked to Saryn. "How far away do you think they are?"

"More than two kays, but less than eight, because that's about how far Tryenda is from here. That's a bit of a guess, though."

"Would they not be closer? I cannot believe they would sweep the road for ten kays." Klarisa raised her eyebrows.

"They might, if they were told some women were after them . . . and they'd get a certain . . . pleasure . . . or reward, or something like that. Besides, they'd want quarters in the town."

"They would." Klarisa nodded, but there was a certain anger behind the gesture.

That was fine with Saryn.

Given what awaited them ahead, there was no point in pushing the horses, and Saryn slowed their pace to an easy walk. Even so, they covered almost two kays before the outriders returned, and Saryn halted the squads to confer with the scouts and the two squad leaders.

"What did you find out?" she asked.

"It's hard to tell for certain, ser, not without being seen," offered Chayara, the stocky older outrider—from somewhere in Gallos, as Saryn recalled. "There's a woods on a rise to the right of the road, and there are cots below it. There's no one in the cots, and it's harvesttime here. That doesn't seem right. There's no one on the road, either."

"How far do you think the town is?"

Chayara shrugged. "I couldn't say, but I'd be guessing it's less than a few kays beyond where the road turns west beyond that wooded ridge."

"Is there anywhere we can make camp out of their sight?"

"There's a tiny stream over the next rise, and it winds sort of west . . ." offered Leisi, the youngest outrider. "There's a big woods there."

Saryn turned to Klarisa and Yulia. "I'm going back with Chayara and Hanira. You take Leisi and the squads along that stream and behind or around the first rise. If there's no place suitable to make camp, just wait there. Otherwise . . . that's where we'll stay. No fires. None."

"Yes, ser."

Saryn nodded to the outriders. "Lead on."

They covered slightly less than two kays before the road angled to the left around a slightly larger rise covered in scrub and grass that looked to have been overgrazed.

"The road's too open," said Chayara. "We just went uphill here, by that path next to the stone fence there."

"Thank you. Follow me." Saryn extended her senses before she reached the top of the rise, but she reined up the mare short of the crest once she saw how open the ground was there. She closed her eyes and concentrated, building up a better picture from what she was sensing.

Chayara had been right. There were empty cots in the vale below the rise where Saryn had halted. Above those cots were armsmen and mounts—possibly two companies, although all were concealed in the trees, which comprised more of a managed woodlot than a true forest.

Could all the armsmen be there for a reason besides rebellion . . . or an ambush?

She considered what she knew. Lord Mortryd had been very clear in his missive to Zeldyan that he had barely a company of armsmen to his name. The tracks she had sensed were for far more than a single company, and that suggested several more companies' worth of armsmen waiting somewhere beyond. She very much doubted that Mortryd would send all his armsmen kays away from his hold if he were under attack.

So . . . Mortryd was under attack by those waiting in ambush, and those waiting wanted to ambush any forces sent to relieve Mortryd . . . or good Lord Mortryd was part of the rebellion, and the missive to the regents had been a ruse. Saryn would have bet on the latter. Either way, it didn't make much difference so far as those armsmen the outriders had sighted were concerned. Saryn and the guards needed to deal with them.

Saryn continued concentrating, trying to relate the exact positions of the armsmen who guarded the road. There was one squad drawn up in readiness—or semireadiness—just behind the first line of trees on the ridge overlooking the road that led into the town of Tryenda, and behind them, under cover, was at least a company.

Still, there had to be others . . . but where? Most likely, they were quartered in the town, another kay or so to the southwest . . . if her maps were correct.

She opened her eyes and looked to the outriders. "We can head back to the others."

"Yes, ser."

Saryn turned the mare, urging her back down the east side of the rise, thinking about how they could deal with the armsmen.

The woods weren't that thick, more like a woodlot, and she thought that, if she attacked before dawn through the woods, hitting the sentries with the archers, then the camp itself, that might be enough to scatter the first company. Then . . . if she moved her squads across to the other side of the ridge . . .

She nodded. *It should work.*

And if it didn't, they had the high ground and a way to retreat—even if she really didn't want to think about that possibility.

LXXVI

Saryn awoke in the darkness, jerking awake from a dream in which chaos-bolts had rained down upon her and the guards from all directions, and no matter what direction she lifted her shield, chaos flew in from another angle and turned guard after guard into flaming charcoal, then ashes.

She sat up on her thin bedroll and blotted her steaming forehead with the sleeve of her undertunic. *Let's hope that's not prophetic.* After reaching for her water bottle and uncorking it, she took a long swallow. Then she corked it and looked eastward at the starry sky. Above the hills she caught sight of a fast-moving star—except stars didn't move that fast. Had that been the *Winterlance*? Or just a slow meteor? Did she want to lie on the hard ground and try to rest for the little time left before she'd need to prepare? She shook her head. All that would do would be to make her more uncomfortable. She pulled on her boots, then her tunic, and stood, thinking.

There might be as many as three companies in different positions, poised to close in and surround whoever took the road that led into the town of Tryenda. Saryn pushed that thought away. *One objective at a time, and the first one is to crush and scatter the company guarding the road before they know they're under attack.*

During the last battle, using the chaos-knife wedge had prostrated her after a single effort. Even if all three companies were in one giant formation, there was no way she could create a chaos-knife big enough to encompass all of them . . . not and stay conscious.

Does the energy required for using order-chaos flows increase arithmetically or geometrically with the size of the application? She couldn't help but smile at the pedantry in her mental question. But still . . . could she just use a smaller chaos-order-knife at a key point? Or several of them? Without totally exhausting herself?

She'd have to see.

Saddling the mare in the darkness was little different from doing so in the day, except that Saryn relied more on senses than sight. Once all her gear was ready, and the mare tethered to a tree, she donned her battle harness and went to find Klarisa and Yulia.

They were awake, fully dressed, and talking quietly. Saryn paused and listened for a moment.

". . . don't know what she'll do . . ."

". . . whatever . . . Lornians won't like it . . ."

". . . can be ruthless . . ."

"Does she have any choice . . . how they are?"

Saryn cleared her throat and stepped forward.

"Ser," offered Klarisa.

"We'll need to get everyone up in a moment, but I want to go over what I expect from each of you. Klarisa, you and fourth squad will be with me. We'll come up the back side of the woods and get as close as we can. Then we'll ride into and through their camp. Slash and disrupt. Keep your guards mounted and moving. Tell them not to stop. Once they stop they become much easier targets. The Lornians will either scatter, or they'll regroup. If they scatter, make sure no one's left in the campsite, then form up at the front of the woods. If they regroup, we withdraw. I'll give the order. If something happens to me, it's your task to get everyone clear."

"Yes, ser."

Saryn turned to the other squad leader. "Yulia . . . you and second squad will ride along the top of the cleared area that's below the forest and above the cots. You're to wait in position beside the first barn . . . when the sky begins to lighten, move farther around the hill until you're within a hundred yards of the area just below where the Lornians were hidden in the trees. Hold there until you hear yells from the Lornians or something else that makes it clear that fourth squad has attacked. When that happens, be ready to sweep across the cleared area and cut down anyone you can. Don't chase stragglers, and keep the squad together as a unit. It's better to let some escape than to scatter the squad."

"Yes, ser. We're to sweep and re-form, then sweep back and forth across until they stop coming and you join us."

"That's right." Saryn straightened. "Get your squads ready to ride."

Less than a half glass later, both squads were mounted and formed up. Saryn rode toward the two squad leaders and reined up.

"Squad four, ready to ride," reported Klarisa.

"Squad two, ready to ride," added Yulia.

"Quiet riding," returned Saryn, easing the mare around. "Forward."

"Forward . . ."

Close to half a glass passed before the two squads split, and Saryn led fourth squad up the long, gentle slope on the back of the rise. By the time they rode into the trees, the eastern sky was beginning to lighten. After several hundred yards, Saryn could clearly discern with her senses three figures standing in the trees some yards out from the three small clearings where most of the armsmen still lay sleeping. She'd hoped to get closer than the thirty or forty yards between her and the nearest sentry, but, quietly as she was trying to ride, and as widely spaced as the trees were, almost every hoof that touched the detritus of moss, twigs, and old leaves created a crackling sound. There was just no way to approach silently.

She turned in the saddle. "Forward . . . fast walk . . . no talking . . . pass it back." Then she guided the mare directly toward where she sensed the nearest sentry to be, drawing the first of her blades. She rode to within fifteen yards of the man before he jerked into full awareness.

"Who goes there! Who is it?"

Saryn kept riding toward him and threw the blade, guiding it with order-chaos flows.

The sentry's next query ended in a gurgling sound.

At that, Saryn drew another blade and urged the mare forward into almost a trot, as fast as she dared in the gloom amid the trees. As she burst into the small clearing where close to forty armsmen were sleeping, she angled toward the fire, where a handful of troopers had gathered, her blade out and ready.

"Attackers!"

Two of the armsmen dived to the side, but a third wasn't nearly that fortunate. Saryn cut him down, then the man next to him.

"Someone's out there!"

"To the horses!"

After that, Saryn just concentrated on keeping clear of other guards and cutting down or wounding any armsman she could. Her senses definitely gave her an advantage in the gloom. In time, as the eastern sky changed from gray to deep green-blue, Saryn and fourth squad found only themselves and severely wounded or dead Lornians in or around the camp clearings in the woods.

"Re-form on the open slope!" Saryn used a touch of order to boost her voice, then turned her mount toward the open space she could make out through the trees, winding her way through scattered bodies. The only organized group she could sense was fourth squad, waiting on the slope.

As she emerged into the early-morning light, Saryn saw three guards with cuts or slashes being dressed and one empty saddle. Below her on the slope were bodies in olive green uniforms strewn everywhere. Saryn swallowed, then rode toward Yulia.

"They never really saw us, ser. Then they panicked. We just did what you ordered."

"You were very effective. Second squad casualties?"

"One dead, three wounded."

"Keep several guards in the saddle and on alert. Have the others recover weapons, but have them hurry. I'll need another blade, too, if they can find one. Then they can stand down for a bit. Oh . . . send a pair to check on the teamsters. For the moment, they can stay where they and the wagon are. And post someone at the back of the woods so that the locals can't do what we did."

"Yes, ser." Yulia nodded and turned her mount.

Saryn watched as the guards of fourth squad emerged from the trees and formed up. She waited until Klarisa had taken muster before she rode across the sparse grass and churned ground and reined up beside the squad leader.

"Fourth-squad casualties?"

"Two dead, five wounded, none seriously."

"Thank you, squad leader. Good work." *What else can you say to her? That we have to lose guards fighting in Lornth so we don't fight under worse conditions in the Westhorns?* "Send out a pair of outriders to watch the road from the town. Have the others recover what they can, then stand down. We'll likely have a glass or two before anyone decides to attack."

"If they don't . . . ?"

"We won't go looking for more trouble, but I don't want to be chased back to Lornth, either."

Klarisa nodded.

Saryn could sense a mixture of emotions within the squad leader, and added, "We can't ever be perceived as running away. That would undo everything we've accomplished, and we'd have to fight even more for years and years." *Especially after destroying a company in a predawn attack.*

"Why?"

Saryn laughed, not hiding the bitterness. "They think we're invading their land and corrupting their ruler and their ways. So they feel they have no choice but to attack us. We're here because, if the regency is overthrown, we'll have to fight Lornth again and again because their ways don't allow for women to be anything but subservient, and sometimes less than slaves. So we don't have a choice, either."

"I meant . . . why does it have to be that way?"

"I don't think it does, but so long as men in power think that way and refuse to see women as anything but lesser, we have one of two choices, and that's fight or submit."

"That's somehow sad . . . that all the ones in power want either men or women in charge."

"The Marshal thinks that it won't ever change unless women are in charge for a time."

"What do you think, ser?"

"I think she's right, but I don't have to like it." *Or the costs involved.*

The squad leader nodded.

After Klarisa had returned to her squad, Saryn couldn't help but think over the questions the squad leader had raised—not that she hadn't thought them over countless times before. The bottom line, so far as she could determine, was that many men feared women who were powerful far more than they feared other powerful men. Why? Was it as simple as the fact that they couldn't dominate powerful women sexually? Or was it that when powerful women could determine their own consorts—or at least refuse to consort with men they did not like—some male reproductive instinct was threatened?

In the end, she just shook her head. She doubted she'd ever know, and, so far as Lornth and Westwind were concerned, the reasons why mattered less than the reality that the most powerful lord-holders of Lornth still wanted to destroy Westwind and effectively enslave women . . . for whatever reason . . . even if they wanted to call that enforced subservience "a return to traditional ways."

That left the question of whether she and the guards should have ridden back to Lornth from the lands of Tryenda immediately after the morning battle. Logically, that made sense. They were outnumbered, and there was no telling whether, even with her emerging order-chaos-abilities, she could defeat the armsmen who were likely to stage a retaliatory attack. Yet . . . something within told her that wasn't the right thing to do.

So she stood and studied the slope below the woods and how the road turned coming from the town, and made her plans. Before long, one of the guards brought her a replacement blade. Saryn didn't ask if it had belonged to one of the dead guards.

Almost a glass passed before Klarisa rode over to where Saryn sat under one of the trees at the front of the woods. "They've got scouts on the rise across the way, but they didn't stay long." The squad leader looked at Saryn. "You want them to attack us?"

"It works better that way," Saryn replied. "They'll have to ride uphill, and after the way we prevailed in the woods, I think they'll want to attack in the open." She walked to the mare, untied her, and swung up into the saddle. She rode forward and to the south along the high ground just forward of the forest, with Klarisa and Yulia following her, until she had a clear view. Then she reined up and studied the attackers.

Coming around the curve in the road from the town were close to three hundred riders, with two distinct sets of uniforms among them—those in the olive green of the armsmen she had scattered and killed earlier in the morning and a smaller number in a brighter burgundy and white.

"Our tactics are very simple," Saryn said. "Fourth squad will be on my right, second squad on my left. Whoever has the regency banner will be slightly behind me. On my command, we charge downhill. If what I plan works, you two will only have stragglers to deal with. If it doesn't, break off and swing back uphill and make your way through the trees and back to Lornth. After this morning, they won't follow into the trees immediately. They'll likely think it's another trap. Is that clear?"

"Yes, ser."

While both squad leaders spoke nearly at once, because Saryn could sense the unvoiced questions from Klarisa, she added, "I'm going to try a version of order-and-chaos-blades. What version that will be depends on the way in which they attack." *And if they attack.* After another long look at the riders, still a kay away, she turned the mare and rode back to the position she had picked out.

The squad leaders followed, issuing orders.

"Fourth squad! Form up!"

"Second squad . . ."

The Westwind forces were in position in less than a tenth of a glass, but the Lornian forces had barely moved. That was fine with Saryn, because with each passing moment the sun was higher in the sky over the mostly east-facing slope.

The Lornian forces—presumably those of Lord Mortryd and Lord Rherhn—continued northeast on the road for another third of a glass until they were less than two hundred yards below the Westwind squads. Then, they formed up . . . and waited.

"They want us to attack," observed Klarisa.

"Then we should." Saryn smiled. "Have your archers start picking off men in their front ranks, but have them ready to stow their bows immediately." *Let's see how patient they can be as they lose men one at a time.*

"Archers! Ready bows!"

"Fire!"

Saryn watched as the first shafts arched down the hill and into the front ranks. Two armsmen sagged in their saddles immediately. A second volley followed, then a third, and a fourth. Gaps began to appear in the front ranks of the mounted armsmen.

Because she doubted it would be long before the Lornians lost all patience with Westwind sniping, Saryn began to create what she visualized as a much smaller chaos-order-knife than the one she had employed against Lord Orsynn's forces.

Then a single trumpet note blared forth—off-key.

The Lornians re-dressed their lines, and at the sound of repeated trumpet triplets, urged their mounts forward.

"Bows away!" ordered Saryn.

"Bows away!" echoed Klarisa.

Saryn studied the oncoming armsmen, all seemingly bearing over-large blades, but did not wait long before she drew one of her blades from her battle harness and ordered, "Westwind! Forward!"

As she rode downhill, her eyes took in the Lornians, noting that the center of the attackers was yards ahead of either flank and composed of armsmen in the olive uniforms. With slightly more than a hundred yards between the two forces, Saryn released her first blade, aimed and boosted by order-chaos flows toward the center of the attackers . . . but the linked chaos-order-knife extended less than ten yards to each side of the gray-black blade.

The moment the chaos-knife sliced through the center of the attackers, Saryn began creating a second chaos-order-blade, even smaller and more concentrated, which followed her second short sword—directed to the section of the attackers ahead and to her right.

She could see the attackers' faces, then the terror on them as a red mist sprayed through the center of those riders. Forcing that moment of horror away, knowing that she was less than twenty yards from the remaining attackers, she cobbled together a third chaos-order-blade, even as she drew the third blade from the sheath before her left knee and hurriedly and desperately flung that blade back to her left.

Lightknives stabbed into her eyes, and dark voids of white death pounded at her skull as she struggled to draw her last blade—merely for self-defense. Except she and the standard-bearer rode alone through fallen men and mounts, and the mare somehow, surefootedly, avoided falling, if occasionally moving so abruptly that Saryn barely remained in the saddle as she slowly reined up.

Through eyes that were intermittently light-blinded by the miniature knife-flares that stabbed them, Saryn could make out riders in olive and burgundy scattering downhill and southwest. Despite the unseen hammerblows to her skull and the lightknives, she turned the mare, trying to make certain that no one attacked her from behind.

That was about all she could do as the guards wheeled through the small groups of armsmen foolish enough—or stunned enough—to offer resistance.

In time, although Saryn couldn't have said exactly how long, the battle—or semislaughter—was over, and Klarisa had ridden over and reined up beside her.

"Ser? Are you all right?"

"Better than the last time, but I hope I don't have to do anything else for a bit."

"It doesn't look that way," replied Klarisa. "The ones who rode off aren't looking back."

"There are more survivors than they think," Saryn said. "We managed to defeat them without killing so many."

"You did, ser."

"If your archers hadn't goaded them into attacking, it could have been worse," Saryn pointed out.

"They don't have archers. Why not?"

That was a good question. "I don't know. Maybe because they feel that fighting should be hand-to-hand. Otherwise, it doesn't make sense. Even the Gallosians have archers. They're not that good, but they have them." *Or could it be that the Lornian lord-holders don't want to give their people a weapon that could kill lord-holders and their armsmen from a distance?* "If you can find an officer or a squad leader among the captives or the wounded, I want to talk to him."

"Yes, ser. I'll see if there's one among the captives." Klarisa turned her mount toward a small group of Lornians in the olive green who, surrounded, had lowered their heavy hand-and-a-half blades.

Saryn just sat on the mare and waited until Klarisa rode back, holding the reins of a horse bearing a young officer who cradled a crooked left arm in his right. She reined up, and the Lornian's mount slowed as well.

"The commander has some questions for you," Klarisa announced.

The undercaptain looked blankly at Saryn.

"Who ordered you to set an ambush for the regency forces?"

The young undercaptain did not speak.

"Answer the commander," snapped Klarisa.

The officer looked to the squad leader, then to Saryn. Despite her headache and her intermittent vision, Saryn "squeezed" him with order-chaos flows, and she could sense the instant fear. "I asked you a question, Undercaptain."

"Lord Rherhn . . . it was Lord Rherhn." His mouth opened wider, but no words emerged for a moment. "You attacked in the dark."

"We were supposed to ride down the road and present a nice target?"

"Attacking in the dark isn't honorable," he protested. "And the arrows—"

"Neither is rebelling against the regency, Undercaptain. Nor is attacking lands that never did you any harm. Nor, for that matter, is there any difference between setting an ambush, as you attempted to do, and attacking in the dark, as we did. If you found it honorable to use the trees for concealment, then it was certainly honorable for us to use darkness."

"It's not the same . . ."

"It's not the same, *ser!*" reminded Klarisa coldly.

The officer opened his mouth, then closed it, before adding, "Ser."

"What were you told about us and the regency forces?" asked Saryn.

After a long moment, the undercaptain replied. "Lord Rherhn said that the regency had been taken over by the Marshal of Westwind or her deputy, and that we needed to take it back, or that every man in Lornth would end up as a slave to the . . . to Westwind."

"As a slave to whom?" pressed Saryn, exerting order flows on the undercaptain.

"He said . . . the tyrants of Westwind."

Saryn suspected another word had been used, but there was little point in pushing that. "After you vanquished us, then what were you supposed to do?"

"He didn't say."

Again Saryn looked hard at the man.

"Not exactly, ser. He just said that all the lord-holders of the south were working together to reclaim Lornth for the traditional ways."

Unfortunately, Saryn sensed that the undercaptain was indeed telling what he'd been told. "When were you going to leave for Lornth?"

"He didn't say where, except that it wasn't Lornth. He said Lornth was only a symbol. He did say we'd be heading north in the next few days."

"Who were you going to join?"

"He didn't say that, either, except that we'd be fighting a real battle."

"And I suppose he'll rally the armsmen for that once we leave?"

"You killed him with that black sorcerous blade . . ."

Saryn paused. She shouldn't have been surprised, since Lornian lord-holders tended to flaunt their bravery . . . but she was.

After another quarter glass of questions, Saryn was convinced she'd learned what she could, and her head was splitting even more.

"Take him back to the other captives. Splint his arm. Then come back here."

"Yes, ser."

Saryn disliked the brusqueness in her tone, but she felt as though it had taken every bit of energy she had just to question the undercaptain. As Klarisa led the undercaptain's mount away, Saryn fumbled for one of the hard biscuits she'd set aside, then her water bottle.

She had to moisten her mouth before she could chew, but two biscuits and half a water bottle later, she felt slightly better. She also realized how fortunate she'd been not to have had to use the order-chaos-shield during any of the attacks. What could she do if she had to attack and defend all at once? She didn't have the skill or the energy to do both. The unfortunate aspect was that a good third, perhaps close to half the rebels had escaped. She supposed that, technically, she'd won, but it didn't feel that way.

What was the rebel lords' strategy? Was it simply to keep the West-wind forces occupied while they did something else? Like attack Gethen and The Groves? Or Lornth, then The Groves?

Or was it two-pronged? To wear down both the Westwind contingent and to eliminate Henstrenn's rivals at the same time? Or was that the plan that the Suthyans had given the Lord of Duevek . . . before they moved in? How could she tell?

I'm not a strategist. I'm just a fair to middling tactician . . . and an effective killer. True as it was, the last thought bothered her.

Whatever else might be happening, she and the guards needed to get back to Lornth.

Once Klarisa returned, Saryn forced a smile. "I'm sorry if I've been a little short. It takes a lot of effort to handle order and chaos."

"We all understand that, Commander."

Saryn could sense that Klarisa did understand, and that the squad leader was concerned, either about Saryn or her squad . . . if not both. "There's even more happening than I realized. Have your guards gather up all usable weapons and all the coins and any jewels as fast as possible. And as many horses as possible. Leave the captives and wounded to fend for themselves. Pass that on to Yulia as well, if you would. We need to head back to Lornth."

"Yes, ser."

"Thank you." Saryn flicked the mare's reins, letting her walk slowly down the slope to the road.

Two guards followed, their blades out.

Already, the vulcrows were circling overhead.

LXXVII

Even as late as midafternoon on sixday, Saryn's head still ached, if dully, as she rode northward along the road back to Lornth. She hadn't slept that well, unsurprisingly, not with her thoughts flitting among all the possibilities for rebellion she had envisioned, but hard biscuits and cheese had helped some in dulling the ache.

An early-morning shower had momentarily cooled the air, but that cool had turned into a steamy heat as the day wore on and as the white sun beat down through a clear green-blue sky. The road had been empty, except for the guards, and the dust kicked up by the horses was not quite so bad as on previous days, but Saryn would have traded the steamy harvest heat for dust and drier air in a moment.

In addition to the headache, she kept seeing images of the mostly young men whom she had killed, their bloody bodies strewn across the Tryendan hillside . . . and the bewildered look of the undercaptain when confronted with a woman in authority and the almost-sullen responses, as if she had no right to question him.

Why, Klarisa had asked, and Saryn had answered. The more she thought, however, the less she liked what she'd said. Oh . . . her words had been right . . . so far as they went, but what bothered her was the feeling that everything she and the guards had done so far was almost meaningless. Why were they doing what they were doing? So that a spoiled boy could become Overlord of Lornth, carrying forward the same attitudes that had created the first attacks on Westwind? So that more young men and women would fight and die in the future?

She should have thought about all that earlier, far earlier—but she truly hadn't understood, not emotionally, the depth of the misogynism embedded in the Lornian culture. Why not? What had changed her understanding? The fanatical male insistence on tradition, to the point of senseless death after senseless death? Or the inability or unwillingness to accept the superiority of a female force? The old Cyadoran dwelling, with its entire structure designed to restrain women?

And what can you do about it so all the deaths won't have been in vain?

"You look worried, Commander," offered Klarisa.

"I have to say that I am," Saryn admitted. "Every time we fight, we prove how good we are, how capable. Then we have to do it again . . . and again, and the men in this place keep looking bewildered . . . or angry . . . as if we were demons, not women."

"That's how they see us. The worst of the white demons are women. They have to be chained with gold chains to keep them from tempting men into chaos."

"They believe that here?" Saryn couldn't keep the incredulity out of her voice. "They really do?"

"Not everyone, but most folk, especially in old towns and hamlets in the south."

"But . . . women have never had any power in Candar, not even in old Cyador. That doesn't make any sense."

Klarisa shrugged. "That's the way they feel. Even my father called my sister and me his little demons. He was better than most. When he died, and we had to live with Uncle Saemat . . . that was when I left."

Why hadn't Saryn asked Klarisa or one of the guards from Lornth earlier? She shook her head. *Because you didn't know enough to ask the questions, not until after a few battles and seeing that old Cyadoran dwelling.*

Oh, in retrospect, it all made sense, if in a perfectly logical and twisted way, but it also made Saryn's last question even harder to answer.

Just what can you do to change things so history doesn't keep repeating itself?

LXXVIII

When Saryn returned to the palace in Lornth, it was early afternoon on sevenday, but as hot as any full summer day, rather than harvest day, which it was. She didn't even think about grooming the mare but handed her over to Dealdron, remembering to smile at him, before hurrying straight to find Hryessa. The guard captain was at the west end of the rear courtyard, watching as Dyali drilled a group of newer guards.

Fifth squad? Saryn wondered. Then she saw Kayli farther west in the courtyard, drilling another group. *Just how many more women have joined? From where?*

Hryessa walked quickly to Saryn. "Commander?"

"You've got more recruits."

"Another thirty or so."

"That's good . . . I think. You'll need to make ready to ride out as soon as possible—with everyone. It's not certain, but, if we do have to ride, we'll not have much time. If not, you can call it a drill. Can we mount all your recruits?"

"Yes, ser. We'll even have some spare mounts. Not many, but enough."

"Weapons?"

"We have enough. Daryn shortened many captured long sabres. They cut well enough, and the balance isn't bad. They cannot be thrown."

Saryn nodded. "I need to find the regent. We had to fight three companies of rebels in Tryenda. Our casualties weren't bad, but the rebel lords are on the march. I'll get back to you shortly."

"Yes, ser."

Saryn strode across the courtyard, into the palace, and up the stairs to the third level.

Lyentha met her outside Zeldyan's study. "She's meeting with the clerk of the treasury. She asked not to be interrupted."

"You can interrupt her, Lyentha. Or I can."

The armsman at the door put his hand on the hilt of his sword but got no farther before Saryn's blade was at his throat. "This is urgent. More urgent than either of you knows." Saryn nodded to Lyentha.

The lady-in-waiting swallowed, then rapped on the door. "The arms-commander, Lady, with most urgent news." Lyentha opened the door and stepped back.

Saryn walked swiftly in, blade still in hand.

"You may wait outside, Tregarn," Zeldyan said politely to the small, gray-bearded man who rose from the circular table, picked up a heavy ledger, and scuttled around Saryn and out of the study.

Behind Saryn, Lyentha closed the door.

Zeldyan did not rise from where she was seated at the table. Behind the regent's polite words, Saryn sensed anger. She really didn't care, not after another day on the road thinking over what she'd missed and what she should have done—and what Zeldyan had not. But she did sheathe the short sword as she stepped forward.

"You seem . . . agitated . . . Commander. Perhaps . . . we should defer this meeting."

"It could be that I am. The day before yesterday I lost more guards, and ended up killing another few hundred or so young men of Lornth because of the little power games your local lord-holders are playing. The forces of both Rherhn and Mortryd were waiting in ambush. So we ended up ambushing them. We did finally find the bodies of both lords and managed to capture an undercaptain, who didn't know very much, except that they'd been ordered to dispose of any regency forces before riding north."

"You obviously kept them from attacking Lornth. I believe that was the goal, was it not?" Zeldyan's voice remained chill. "I even believe that happened to be as much your idea as anything I expressed."

"Goal or not," Saryn said smoothly, "they were not heading to Lornth or anywhere close. Lord Rherhn said something to the effect that Lornth was an empty symbol. Now, why were you informed about Jharyk's problems . . . and then Mortryd's—all conveniently here in the south?"

"That is where most of the rebels are. And the Jeranyi."

"Indeed, they are." Saryn paused. "But one company, if not more, of Kelthyn's men was already headed north of Lornth. And another of Henstrenn's has been loitering in the north for several eightdays, and possibly even one of Lord Jaffrayt's. Unless you've heard something since we left, no one has seen Henstrenn's forces, or Keistyn's, anywhere in the south, and my guards are the only force likely to be able to stand against them."

"You forget my sire."

"Lord Gethen may well be the best commander in all Lornth, Lady, but can he stand against all the forces that have already gathered against him . . . particularly if he has no time to call together his and your supporters? His holding is not a fortress, and he cannot withstand more than a short siege."

"How would you know that?"

Saryn just looked at Zeldyan for a moment before replying. "I could take The Groves with two companies. There are far more than that already headed there." *Unless I miss my guess, and this time I don't think so.*

"You know . . . I am the regent for my son. Not you. Not anyone else. And I will decide. Not you. Not anyone else."

Saryn forced herself not to answer. She was acting more like some of the lord-holders than like Ryba, who was always cool and calculating. Another set of angry words wouldn't help, furious as she was.

"You don't contest that, now, do you, Commander?" pressed Zeldyan.

"No." Saryn shook her head, then offered a sad smile, because she felt for Nesslek, spoiled as the boy might be. "I don't. I had hoped that by helping you and Lord Nesslek, we could make this part of Candar a better place. But everything I've done has made matters worse for both of you. By supporting you, I've raised the worst fears of the southern lords and pushed them into an attack on The Groves."

At those words, Zeldyan's irritation was replaced by concern . . . and a different and deeper anger. "You *knew* this?"

"Of course not," Saryn replied. "Not until after the attempted ambush in Tryenda." *Not until after seeing the old Cyadoran house and hearing Klarisa's words about the white demons.* "That's why I pressed to get back to Lornth. That's why I used a blade to force my way in here. I wasn't raised here. It took me a while to see what was happening." *You should have seen it sooner, but maybe you didn't because you were raised in the north.*

Anger and puzzlement warred within Zeldyan.

"On the way back from Tryenda, I heard some of the old southern stories about how female demons had to be chained . . . and they see me as a demon." That was a guess on Saryn's part, but not one requiring any great leap of faith.

Zeldyan froze, if but for a moment. "They can't honestly think that . . ."

Saryn shook her head. "I doubt for a moment that the lord-holders believe that. But it makes a most convenient rationale for overthrowing you and the regency . . . and even for killing your son on the grounds that he has been fatally tempted by a woman and a female demon. Because it is a southern legend, I suspect it's not something that you or your sire, or most of the northern lord-holders, would even think about. But that's likely what they're using to motivate the lord-holders involved in this rebellion. And it's why I would strongly suggest we take all the forces we can to The Groves without any delay."

"I did not want to abandon Lornth. That would have shown weakness and encouraged more unrest."

"Without you and Nesslek, Lornth means nothing, and holding it now means a company you cannot use against the rebels. Or, if your father and Nesslek are under attack, to save either."

"You see no other choice?"

"No. Do you?"

"Then we must leave immediately." Zeldyan finally did stand.

"There's another issue we need to discuss, Lady Zeldyan."

"What else is there to discuss? We need to save Nesslek."

"So far, hundreds of men and women from Westwind and Lornth have died. Westwind attacked no one. You, so far as I can see, attacked none of the lord-holders. Let us say that we do succeed in putting down this rebellion, and your son succeeds the regency. Then what?"

"He becomes the Overlord of Lornth." Zeldyan's voice was somewhere between matter-of-fact and dismissive, behind which was irritation at Saryn, probably for stirring up things, then bringing up an irrelevant question.

"So that he can pursue the same course as his grandsire and so that we end up fighting each other for years to come? So that women who no longer want to be slaves to men flee Lornth for Westwind, and men in Lornth, especially in the south, get angrier and angrier until they force him into another war?"

"I cannot change what men feel. Neither can you," Zeldyan pointed out. "Sillek tried that. Much good it did him. Had he stood fast, he would have faced revolt as well."

Saryn could see that there was no point in pursuing that issue—for the moment. She had raised it, and that was all that she could do for the moment. "You're right . . . for now. We need to move to The Groves. I have my guard captain readying all the guards."

"I will send for Maerkyn, and we will be ready shortly."

Saryn inclined her head. "By your leave . . ."

Zeldyan raised her eyebrows, as if to ask whether her permission mattered.

"I will let you know when we are ready, Lady." Saryn stepped back, then turned and left. As she hurried down the staircase, she heard Zeldyan calling for Lyentha.

Hryessa was in the courtyard, with six others—all squad leaders, Saryn decided, as she slowed and let the captain finish her instructions to the six. Only then did she step forward.

"How long?" asked Saryn.

"Two glasses. It could be less. I wouldn't press it, though. That will give your mounts some rest."

"True enough." Saryn paused, then asked, "What about Daryn and the children?"

"He'd already worked out something with the local smith. He'll work for nothing except food and keep the children there. They'll be out of the palace and away from the fighting."

"You knew this would happen."

"Sooner or later, ser, it had to."

"We're the demons, you know?" Saryn kept her voice conversational. "The ones who are out to upset all their traditions."

Hryessa spat on the courtyard pavement. "Men like that have a reason for anything. It is never a good reason. But they have it."

How many of those reasons are just rationalizations for holding power? Is Ryba any different? Are you? "We all have reasons."

Hryessa laughed. "Always! But ours are better. Especially if we keep them to ourselves."

Saryn smiled, if momentarily. "I want to see what they're loading in the wagons." She turned and walked toward the stables. Outside the main doors, Dealdron was organizing the loading of the five wagons lined up in a row—none with horses yet in the traces.

"The spare blades and shafts at the rear. If the guards need them, they cannot wait for us to dig them out. The barrels in the middle . . ."

She couldn't help but smile as she watched him. He'd definitely been wasted as an assistant ostler in Gallos . . . or even in Westwind.

As if he had sensed her presence, Dealdron turned. "Commander, ser?"

Although she knew what he would say, Saryn couldn't help but ask, "Who will be in charge of the wagons and teamsters?"

"You are the commander, Angel," he replied.

"But you intend to be the one I give the orders to?" She managed not to smile.

"Who else will take care of the wagons and so many mounts? You would not waste good guards on the mounts, would you? I will be safer with you than staying in an empty palace in Lornth, where I could do nothing to help."

Saryn had her doubts about his safety, but she didn't want to argue . . . and he was a good teamster and the best they had with the horses. She couldn't help but smile. "How long before the wagons are ready?"

"We started readying them right after you rode into the courtyard, Commander. If all goes well, we will be loaded in less than a half glass. I did not want to put the drays in traces until we knew . . ."

She glanced at the seat of the first wagon, where two sheathed blades rested.

Dealdron followed her eyes.

Saryn looked back at him.

He shrugged. "I would prefer not to use a blade, but I would prefer to have them in case some armsmen might come upon us."

Still smiling, Saryn shook her head. "I can't imagine you'd drive a wagon after any armsmen. I won't keep you from your duties. We are leaving as soon as possible." She started to turn, then stopped. "I am glad you'll be with us." Then she walked back toward the barracks, feeling Dealdron's eyes on her back, half-surprised that she didn't mind the feeling. But then, she knew he was concerned about her and didn't think she was a white demon.

LXXIX

By noon on eightday, Saryn was wondering if there was a harvest season in Lornth, or if the people there just called the last half of an endless summer harvest. Zeldyan and the Lornian guards under Maerkyn were leading the way up the road. While Saryn had spent much of the time riding with the Lady Regent, for the last glass Saryn had ridden at the head of first squad, beside Hryessa.

"You've had a long face all day, ser," Hryessa finally said.

"A lot on my mind," replied Saryn.

"You worried about the guards, ser?"

"How couldn't I be? We're fighting in a civil war in a land where neither side is truly to our liking, just to prevent those who would be worse from taking over. To one side, we're a necessary evil. To the other, we're the horrible demons out of a near-legendary history." *It's all to preserve something that's not that good from something worse. It's not building anything, not really, and fighting to preserve the less bad . . . Does it really accomplish anything?*

Saryn glanced to her right, across the summer-dried marshes that separated the road from the River Yarth. She hadn't seen a single boat or barge on the water all day. When they had ridden south from The Groves to Lornth, there had been all manner of craft on the river, headed in both directions. Now. . . .

"Ser . . . do you see any of the new guards complaining? Even those in second squad where some got killed?"

Saryn laughed softly. "They wouldn't complain to me."

"They see us, and they see you . . . as something better. Almost all of the women with us here are from Lornth. Those from Gallos and Analeria aren't complaining, either, and they're not complaining behind my back or yours."

Saryn offered a brief smile. "Do you really think we'll change anything for the better? Here in Lornth?"

"If you save the Lady Regent, do you think she's going to cross you?"

"She might not, but every time she does something that's less traditional, or that might make things better for women, some lord-holder will complain."

"Not if we get rid of the troublemakers now."

Hryessa had a point, but it was a blade's point, deciding by force. Saryn shook her head. Had any change in any society ever been accomplished without some form of force? "I don't know. I worry about young Lord Nesslek. He still seems to think that men and size are what count."

"Men are always impressed with size. Especially if it's their own. In all manner of blades, it's how it's used, not how big it is."

Saryn laughed in spite of her worries.

"Ser?" Hryessa's smile vanished. "What will you do if the worst has already occurred?"

"We'll have to find some way to destroy whoever did it. We can't let a lord-holder who believes as the southerners do take power."

"We have but one true company. We are worth two or three of theirs, but . . ."

"If . . . if that happens, we will have to see if some of the northern lords will join the fight. Otherwise . . ." Saryn shrugged. "We will have to try something else." *And who knows what that might be.*

"You will find a way." Hryessa nodded.

What sort of a way? At what cost? Saryn feared that Hryessa was all too likely to be proved right, but to speak of that to Zeldyan would suggest that Saryn had known early enough to prevent what might already have occurred. And a grief-stricken mother was all too likely to turn on Saryn if matters turned out for the worst and if Saryn had suggested it before the fact.

She might anyway, Saryn reminded herself.

LXXX

Slightly past midmorning on a oneday that seemed even hotter than the days before, Saryn was riding with Zeldyan behind the squad of Lornian armsmen who served as the vanguard of the force. Zeldyan kept shifting her weight in the saddle, easing her mount out to the shoulder of the river road and looking ahead, then returning to the center of the road under the warm morning sun. Ahead of them, both the road and the river swung to the north, angling through a low line of hills. Before that long, the road and river would twist back to the northeast toward Carpa, some twenty kays ahead.

Sensing the tension and concern that permeated the regent, Saryn said little, not wanting to make Zeldyan worry more and also not wanting to offer false encouragement.

"Why?" asked Zeldyan abruptly, speaking for the first time in over a glass. "Why have they turned against Nesslek? Why now?"

That question Saryn could answer. "Because they think they can, Lady, because the Suthyans are paying Henstrenn and others to do so, and because your presence reminds them of how wrong they have been. By overturning the regency and removing your son, they can blame you rather than their own failings. It has often been that way in many lands on many worlds."

Zeldyan looked sharply at Saryn. "At times, I almost forget that you are an angel who has seen many worlds. Tell me, Angel, what awaits us."

Saryn ignored the slight sarcastic edge to the regent's question. "Other than lord-holders with bad judgment and a lust for power, I cannot say, Lady. I do not know when they left their holdings, how they proceeded, or how they intend to make their desires known. I do know that, whatever happens, Lornth will suffer far more than had they let the regency stand. I also know that is something that they will deny to their dying day."

"May those days be soon." Zeldyan tightened her lips and paused, before adding, "I still wish you angels had not come to the Roof of the World."

"It was not our wish, either. We harmed no one until we were attacked. We took nothing of value, and nothing that anyone was able to use before we arrived. We were attacked because Lord Nessil and Lord Karthanos were too proud and too unwilling to let us hold land that no one wanted until we came. Each attack has cost those who attacked more, and wounded their pride more, and still they lash out where they can."

"Your truths are cold comfort, Angel."

"Truth has never offered comfort, Lady," Saryn replied.

Once more, Zeldyan did not speak for a time. Then she said, "Have you ever loved?"

"Truly loved?" asked Saryn. "No . . . not really."

"Has anyone truly loved you? Truly?" Zeldyan paused. "Sillek loved me that way, you know."

"You were most fortunate in that."

"Do angels love that way?"

Saryn had to think for a moment. Certainly, Ryba didn't. But for all her feistiness, Hryessa did love Daryn. And Nylan . . . "Nylan, the one you call the black angel, and Ayrlyn love that way."

"Was that not why they had to leave the Roof of the World?"

Was it? Saryn wasn't certain that was all of it, although . . . She nodded. "Most likely."

"The Roof of the World is cold in many ways, besides its ice, I fear."

"It can be, Lady. Freedom is not always comfort." Saryn frowned. There was something . . . somewhere . . . nagging at her. After a moment, she extended her senses. Ahead along the river, in the distance, perhaps where the road ran through the hills, she felt . . . riders . . . hundreds of men.

Quickly, she scanned the land immediately around them. The mostly dried-out and low swamps filled the two hundred or so yards to the right of the road between the raised roadbed and the River Yarth. Slight hummocks bordered the road on the west, but the tallest was but a yard or two above the roadbed.

She turned in the saddle. There was a small hill less than half a kay back, barely large enough to hide their force . . . and the wagons.

"Companies halt! Outriders! Back!" Saryn ordered, boosting her voice with a touch of the order-chaos flows.

"What—?" Zeldyan looked to Saryn.

"There are at least two companies riding our way. We need to move back to the cover of that hill, where we aren't seen until they're almost upon us." Saryn gestured over her shoulder.

"We need to get to The Groves," Zeldyan said.

"I agree. But riding up to a force with greater numbers won't get us there sooner." Saryn pointed to the nearly flat field to the west. "Trying to go around them that way will only expose us, and retreating kays and kays to the last ford won't help either."

Zeldyan looked to Saryn. "It appears as though I am in your hands . . . again."

"Guard captain! Third Westwind squad leader! Forward!" Again, Saryn boosted her voice.

At that moment, Undercaptain Maerkyn rode back from the first Lornian squad and reined in beside the regent. "Why have you called a halt?" He looked to Saryn accusingly.

Saryn waited until Hryessa also rode up and reined in, then said, "Armsmen are riding this way, two kays north, just out of sight where the road comes out of those hills."

"The scouts have not reported . . ." objected Maerkyn.

"They will. Or they would have if I had not recalled them."

Maerkyn stood in the stirrups, then dropped to the saddle and looked at Saryn again. "The scouts are returning. How did you do that?"

"My voice carries," she replied politely.

Another rider joined them—Rydala, squad leader of third squad. "Ser?"

"Squad leader, there's a force headed toward us. I don't know yet whose force it is, but it's likely to be the rebels. We can't conceal all the tracks in the road, but they won't look that hard if they see armed riders ahead. I want you to take a position on the road, back toward that hill there, close enough that you can ride back on the road, not too fast, as if your mounts are tired. Before all that happens, we'll be riding back and taking position behind the hill, waiting to attack at the right moment. Your task is to be seen and let them get fairly close, then to recognize them, and appear to turn and retreat as slowly as possible without letting them catch you. They'll either pursue quickly or advance in an orderly manner. Either way, they are likely to focus on you and not be looking quite so hard for others."

"Why would that be?" asked Maerkyn.

"First, the rebel lords know that we only brought two squads from Westwind. Second, they've only seen the Westwind guards in groups of one or two squads," Saryn explained. "And those likely to be ahead haven't seen us with any Lornian armsmen."

"How many are there?" asked Maerkyn.

Saryn concentrated for a moment, then shook her head. "They're still too far away to be certain, but it feels like three companies."

Maerkyn frowned. "We have a little less than two companies."

"That may be, but the regent has decided that we need to get to The Groves, and we won't get there by pulling back." Saryn nodded politely. "If you would like to escort the regent back to the high ground behind the hill . . . ?"

Maerkyn glanced to Zeldyan, then replied, "Of course."

"I'd thought that you would take the western side of the back side of the hill, and we would take the east. That way, third squad could rejoin us easily."

"What then?" asked the undercaptain.

"We attack, and when the time is right, you leave a squad to protect the regent, and follow up and attack their weakest point . . . or any squads that are isolated and easy pickings."

"Just like that?" Maerkyn's voice verged on scornful.

"Fairly so," replied Saryn. "It seems to work. We've beaten something like four companies so far, always with two squads or less." They might have faced more than that, but Saryn wasn't about to take the time to count up the casualties. "Now . . . if we don't want to get caught in the open on the road here, I'd suggest we remove ourselves to behind that hill."

Maerkyn looked to Zeldyan. The regent nodded, then added, "She has been rather successful at this, Undercaptain. Repeatedly."

Maerkyn nodded. "Then let us withdraw to the high ground, Regent, and prepare."

Saryn looked to Rydala. "Hold your squad in place until I move the others back. Then move back closer to the hill."

"Yes, ser."

Saryn turned to Hryessa. "I'd like you to make sure that the wagons are out of sight, then lead fourth, fifth, and sixth squads. Hold back for a bit, then follow up as you see fit."

"You think they will break if we seem to be a second force?" asked the captain.

"I'm hoping so. I also want you away from me, just in case . . ."

"That will not happen, but I will be certain few escape." Hryessa's smile was hard.

As Hryessa turned and guided her mount toward the rear of the Westwind forces, Saryn had to wonder, not exactly for the first time, just what the captain had endured before coming to the Roof of the World.

The combined Westwind and Lornian forces and the supply wagons were well out of sight in less than a quarter glass, and the only riders who remained on the river road were those of third squad, all recent recruits and trainees, except for Rydala. But that was why Saryn had chosen third squad. First and fourth squads would have to spearhead the attack, and the Lornians would take casualties in dealing with stragglers and the general melee.

Saryn had gone over her battle plan with her squad leaders until they understood exactly what she wanted. In the simplest terms, the Westwind force would angle through the lead company behind a narrow chaos-blade, then swing back to head through the second company behind a second swath of chaos. After that . . . they might try a third one, or swing back and reinforce the Lornians. That assumed, as always, that Saryn could make it work.

A good half glass passed under a sun hotter than Saryn liked. The hill itself held only a few bushes and was mostly covered in browned wild grasses and weeds, although the west side backed up to grasslands that looked more hospitable.

"We cannot see the road from here. Do you expect to hear them from a greater distance than one can see?" asked Maerkyn.

Saryn waited on the gelding, behind the crest of the hill, with Maerkyn to her left and Zeldyan beyond her. From where she was, a ride of less than five yards would bring her to where she could. "I know where they are. Just a trace beyond a kay away. They've caught sight of third squad, and Rydala is acting confused, having her squad mill around for a bit . . ."

"Your guards don't mill," Maerkyn said.

"That's true, but you're one of the few Lornian officers alive who knows that." Saryn paused, then added, "They've decided to pick up their pace a bit, but they're being cautious."

She could sense the van company picking up speed and trying to catch the apparently slower and tired guards, and she began to weave together the order and chaos flows she would need before that long.

"Stand by!" she called to Maerkyn. "They're almost in position."

She could sense the undercaptain's shrug . . . and fatalism. She ignored both and raised her voice. "Westwind! Squads one and four! On me!" Then she urged the gelding up over the last part of the hillcrest and down through the knee-high browning grass that crackled with each hoof that struck it. As she came down over the rise, a quick glance confirmed that the lead riders were in blue-and-gray livery—the colors of Lord Jaffrayt—one of those who had declared rebellion. The riders on the road looked up as the guards poured over the eastern side of the dusty hill. The immediate effect of the charge was to slow the riders in the van more than those in the rear.

Saryn loosed her first short sword at close to sixty yards, but with a far narrower chaos-blade. Even so, it sliced through the heart of the entire first company. Saryn forced herself to ignore the screams and the dark voids of death that assaulted her as she drew the second blade and rode through the tunnel of death and destruction she had created and onto the wide east shoulder of the river road.

The company that followed the first one wore orange tunics trimmed in black. They did not hesitate even after seeing the carnage on the road before them, but charged toward Saryn even before she could swing her mount back to the left . . . and before she had fully gathered and smoothed all the order and chaos into a flow that she could link to the short sword.

Saryn was almost on top of the first rank—or they were nearly on top of her—before she could release the blade. While that cleared a bit of a path, she had to struggle to get her third blade out of the knee sheath, barely in time to parry the all-too-large blade of an armsman who charged in at her from the left, from just beyond the too-narrow wedge of destruction she had flung.

She managed to keep moving and deliver a back-cut, enough to get clear and begin to create a third chaos-and-order-flow knife. The riders in the third company—also in orange and black—had slowed somewhat, and that gave Saryn a few moments more as she found herself on the west side of the road. She turned the chestnut back toward the road and urged him forward toward the third company.

Since so far as she could see, there was not another company behind the third one but only some scattered riders with wagons and pack animals, she widened the chaos-blade slightly before releasing the short sword and drawing her last blade.

A wider swath of armsmen and their mounts fell before her, and were scattered by the forces she had wielded. Then, lightknives and unseen hammers pounded her eyes and her skull, but not quite fiercely enough to immobilize her, as she turned the gelding back toward the rear of the third company.

How she looked, she had no idea, but when she rode toward the disoriented rebel Lornian armsmen at the rear, they all turned their mounts and scattered away from her.

From that moment on, the resistance of the rebels seemed largely to melt away, although some individual armsmen held on, swinging their huge blades until one guard or another wore them down. Before all that long, Saryn reined up and surveyed the area, through vision intermittently blurred by lightknives.

A handful of riders in blue and gray spurred their mounts into the drying swamps, clearly trying to reach the river. Another broken squad in orange and black had managed to escape the Lornians and raced southwest, possibly toward refuge in Masengyl, or elsewhere.

Less than a quarter glass later, the road held only the Westwind and regency forces, and the wounded who could not escape . . . and all too many bodies.

Should we pursue the stragglers? She shook her head. One way or another, they needed to find out what had happened.

Saryn glanced farther north along the road . . . and saw another group of armsmen. Had she missed a whole company? No . . . they were the wounded, those who had been wounded earlier and who had followed the more able armsmen . . . and who had hung back when the regency forces had attacked.

There are not that many. Her entire abdomen tightened. That was hardly a good sign. As she watched, some of the riding wounded turned their mounts away out into the fields and grasslands to the west. The others waited, almost dumbly, as if half-stunned.

Saryn rode toward Hryessa, who had organized fifth and sixth squads to sweep through the dead and wounded, while the other four squads took up stations around the battle area.

"Ser."

"Where are their survivors?"

"Riding away from us as fast as they can. They're all heading sort of south once they get away from us. I've got most of the guards ready to attack if they try to regroup."

"What do our casualties look like?"

"Ten dead, maybe more. Four or five who might not make it. Another ten or so with wounds that should heal."

"Have them finish up the sweep of the bodies, but make it quick, for blades and for coins or jewelry, and see if there are any that look like lord-holders."

"Yes, ser."

Maerkyn rode toward the two, reining up. "Second Lornian company is re-formed, Commander. Three dead, ten wounded. We've taken station around the regent."

"Thank you, Undercaptain. I appreciate that."

"Might I ask, Commander . . . You never offered them terms," Maerkyn said. "You . . . you just attacked and slaughtered them."

"They'd already declared rebellion against the regency, and they were part of those rebel lords who had already twice attacked forces bearing the regency banner." Saryn paused, then asked, "Whose colors are orange and black?"

"Lord Kelthyn's, I believe. The blue and gray belong to Lord Jaffrayt."

Saryn frowned. She had seen no armsmen in brown and yellow or in the red trimmed in black. Had both Henstrenn and Keistyn taken the east road back toward their holdings—or toward Lornth—knowing that Saryn and Zeldyan would be on the river road, and leaving the other two lord-holders to face Saryn and the Lornians? She wouldn't have put it past either Henstrenn or Keistyn. Then she nodded. "If you would tell the regent that I need to find out some information, but that I will join you both shortly to let her know what we've discovered."

Maerkyn nodded politely. "Yes, ser." He turned his mount and headed back up toward the hillside where the Lornians had formed around the regent.

"He is much more respectful," said Hryessa.

"Yes." *I can't imagine why.* Saryn couldn't help the sarcastic tenor of her thoughts. "I need to question the rebel wounded back there." She gestured.

"You need some guards." Hryessa gestured toward the nearest guards in fifth squad.

Saryn waited until she had six guards flanking her before she rode slowly northward, finally reining up short of one of the wounded, an arms-man in gray and blue, with an arm strapped to his chest and a dressing covering what remained of his left ear. He sat almost lopsided in his saddle.

"Where did you get wounded?"

"Up north . . . the villa outside Carpa . . ."

"What happened there?" pressed Saryn.

"We fought . . . the squad leaders said we won."

"You didn't see what happened?"

"Some of them got away . . . some of 'em got us . . ." The wounded man just looked at Saryn. "That's all I know."

Sensing that he had told her all he could, she moved on to the next man, who had a crudely splinted leg that stuck out. She wondered how he'd mounted, unless his comrades had lifted him onto the horse. "What did you see?"

"Not much . . ." His eyes widened. "You're one of those . . . angels . . ."

"What did you see?" Saryn repeated.

"Lots of fighting . . . we were the first . . ."

After questioning close to fifteen armsmen—all those who seemed lucid—Saryn broke off the interrogation and rode back to the hillside to find Zeldyan, Hryessa, and Maerkyn.

They rode closer once she reined in the gelding.

Hryessa looked to Saryn. "Commander . . . your attack killed both Lord Jaffrayt and Lord Kelthyn."

"They deserved it," offered Maerkyn, if under his breath.

"That may be," replied Zeldyan, "but they are only part of the rebellion. Take their personal effects and signets and save them. Do not worry about burying them." She looked to Saryn. "You do not have good news. That I can tell. What is it?"

Saryn sensed that the regent already suspected what Saryn was about to report. "Lady . . . I have questioned some of the rebel wounded. They were the ones who were wounded in an earlier battle . . . outside Carpa."

Zeldyan's face stiffened. "What happened?"

"Those we've questioned believe that they won, but they all admit that at least some of the defenders escaped."

The regent shook her head, and Saryn could sense the despair.

"We will just have to see, Lady. Perhaps other lords came to your father's aid. It could be that they took your son to safety."

"My son . . . that is possible. My father . . ." Zeldyan's lips tightened, and her eyes brightened. "We must press on."

"We should be ready shortly, Lady." Saryn could sense the dread within the regent. Given what almost certainly awaited them at The Groves, neither of them was looking forward to what they would find.

LXXXI

Just before the harvest sun sank over the half-harvested fields to the west of the river road, Saryn and the Westwind guards led the way into the old town of Carpa. Almost every shutter was closed tight, and the only creature Saryn saw, between the slowly diminishing flashes of the lightknives stabbing into her eyes, was a brown-and-tan dog that ran down a narrow alleyway. The sound of hoofs on stone echoed in the slowly dimming light.

Saryn studied the shops and the shuttered inn off the main square, absently massaging her head with her free left hand, but she could see no signs of looting or damage. Did that mean that the rebel lords had enough sense to confine their fighting to each other? She hoped so. The land could recover if the rebel lords were destroyed—provided the shops and crops were not ravaged.

The stone bridge across the Yarth was likewise untouched . . . and empty. Saryn sensed no groups of men ahead; but she felt traces, perhaps of wounded men or men hiding, and the scouts reported nothing.

Less than a half kay east from the bridge, Saryn saw the first body, that of a man in the gray-and-yellow livery of The Groves, lying facedown in the ditch on the north side of the road. The lower section of his tunic and the upper part of his trousers were stained dark, a shade that looked black in the fading light.

She signaled for the column to halt and rode back along the shoulder of the lane until she reached the first Lornian armsmen . . . and Maerkyn and the regent.

"You might wish to stay with the undercaptain while we enter the grounds, Lady. There may be a few wounded, but no more than that, and most of those will not live."

Zeldyan shook her head. "I will join you at the van. I will be among the first to see the ruination of The Groves and Lornth."

"As you wish." Saryn inclined her head in respect. *All that lies ahead is the devastation resulting from what came before.*

The two rode back along the shoulder of the road, took position just behind the scouts, and resumed riding toward The Groves. Ahead along the gently rising road, Saryn and Zeldyan saw more figures sprawled along the road. There was no smell of fire, as Saryn thought there might have been. Several horses lay alongside the road, and ahead, the tall iron gates hung open in the low wall surrounding the structure that was half keep and half villa, if with a narrow isolated tower farther to east. As she rode closer, she could see that the only bodies wore yellow and gray, although a large soil mound a half kay to the north looked as if it had just been heaped there.

Saryn wagered that the dead of the attackers lay under that hastily piled soil.

She turned in the saddle to Hryessa. "Once we're inside the gates, have two squads flank the villa and secure it. There may be hangers-on or looters."

"Yes, ser."

Once past the gates, Saryn stiffened in the saddle. She could sense the lingering whiteness of chaos. She began to look more closely at the bodies left beside the lane. Several were charred, she realized. One charred figure still held a bow, the first one Saryn had seen in the hands of a Lornian. Was the ability of a mage to shield himself with chaos another reason why the armsmen of Lornth scorned the bow as a weapon of war? "The attackers had a white wizard with them."

"There are none . . ." Zeldyan paused. "The Suthyans, you think?"

"I don't know who else it could be. The Gallosians wouldn't send any. They may not have any remaining. The Jeranyi . . . ?" Saryn shook her head.

"Treachery . . . deceit . . . everywhere." Zeldyan's voice died away.

As they rode toward the villa, two squads moved away, one to the right and one to the left. Saryn sensed, then saw, two men running through the twilight, each with a bag in hand.

"Looters." Zeldyan's voice was flat.

Both looters staggered, then fell, shafts through their back. Saryn knew the shafts had come from fourth squad.

When they reined up at the front portico, the entire villa was dark, but one of the guards from first squad hurried forward with a striker and lit one, then the other, of the two large brass lamps flanking the archway and main doors.

Saryn sensed no one within the villa. "It's empty. There's no one in there." *Not alive, anyway.* After a moment, she dismounted, handing the reins to a guard.

"Squad two, first eight," ordered Hryessa, "escort the commander and the regent."

Flanked by guards, Saryn and Zeldyan walked through the archway and the double doors into the main foyer of the villa. Behind them strode Maerkyn.

Another guard lit the foyer lamps, revealing to sight what Saryn had already sensed. A long table had been dragged into the foyer. On it rested three bodies, one gray-haired, in a gray-and-yellow blood-soaked tunic, still wearing a sword belt, with the blade laid across his chest. The second had tightly curled blond-and-silver hair and a thin silver mustache, and wore a green-and-yellow tunic Saryn recognized. The angle of his head suggested his neck had been broken, probably from behind. His long blade had been laid out at his side The third was smaller, with thick blond hair, wearing a plain green tunic. A dagger remained in his breast, the cloth around the weapon dark with blood.

"They . . . captured him . . . and then killed him," Zeldyan said.

Her voice was cold, but the anguish behind the words was like glass knives shredding her silently from within. That was how it felt to Saryn as she looked at the youth who would never grow up to be Overlord of Lornth. After a moment, she said quietly. "He fought, Lady. He has slashes on both arms and bruises on his face."

"He was only a boy."

"He was, but the lust for power respects nothing," Saryn replied. *Especially when a woman stands in the way.*

Zeldyan said nothing for a moment, then turned to the undercaptain. "Guard them for the night."

"Yes, Lady."

Zeldyan turned back to Saryn. "I leave all arrangements to you for now. The east tower has been unused for years, since the death of Lady Ellindyja. It is a fitting place for me." Sadness and bitterness mixed in her words. Then she turned and walked back out the front of the villa, past the open doors that had not even been forced.

Saryn did not move until Zeldyan had left. Then she continued her inspection of the villa, moving toward the sitting room, then the grand salon, and the dining chamber, and the family quarters. The furniture had been largely untouched, but most small items had vanished. There were no silver candlestick holders, nothing small and metallic, no small vases, as if anything that could be quickly pocketed had been taken.

Still, as she surveyed the dwelling, she had the feeling that the looting had been quick and almost incidental, as if Henstrenn and the others had not wished to tarry, nor to take the time to search too deeply.

Saryn left Gethen's study for last, entering from the main hallway in the darkness. She could sense that the leather-bound volumes still rested in the dark cherrywood bookcases, seemingly untouched. So was the desk at one end, except for odds and ends strewn on the floor beside it, and a few scraps of paper and parchment fluttering in the light night breeze that gusted through the doors at the north end of the room. The fountain outside and beyond the doors still splashed, although Saryn thought the water's sound was muted in some fashion.

Saryn just stood in the darkened chamber, thinking.

Now what? Technically, there was no regency, although Saryn supposed that Zeldyan could claim something similar over The Groves, at least as holder for her brother Relyn, if in absentia. Henstrenn and Keistyn had obviously left with their forces by the old eastern road, sending Kelthyn and Jaffrayt down the river road for a possible battle with the regency forces. That, all too conveniently, had left the lord-holders of Duevek and Hasel in the strongest positions to claim power as Overlord of Lornth. Saryn didn't like the idea of either taking power.

Yet she had but a single company, if oversized, and more than half consisted of women who were barely beyond being raw recruits. She had a little ability with order-chaos flows. Against her were three companies from Duevek and Hasel, and at least one white wizard, and there was no telling who else might weigh in, although she'd already decimated the forces of all the southern lords except those two.

Either Henstrenn or Keistyn would be a disaster, both for Lornth and Westwind. But would the surviving northern lords support any action against them? Did Zeldyan even care any longer? Even if the other lords did not want to move against Henstrenn and Keistyn, could Saryn afford to leave them in a position to seize power?

"Commander?" came a voice from the half-open doors to the verandah, one she recognized.

"Dealdron . . . I'm here, thinking."

"There is a chamber for you on the lower level of the tower. Your guards have secured the villa and moved into the barracks."

"Thank you." Saryn did not move.

"You should eat, Commander. It has been a long day, and you used much magery."

"I'll be there shortly."

"That would be good." He said nothing more. He also did not move from his position on the verandah.

Saryn realized that he wouldn't, not short of a direct order.

With a muted sigh, she crossed the study and stepped out onto the smooth stones, then closed the doors behind her. "We might as well go."

"There is food waiting in your chamber."

"Oh?"

"Yes. You have been inspecting the villa for a time."

Saryn turned and began to walk toward the tower.

"They killed the young lord because they cannot kill you," offered Dealdron, matching her steps.

Saryn noted that he did wear a blade, a short sword.

"Now the lord-holders will claim that you have no right to be in Lornth," he added.

"I suppose there's some truth in that, but the only right they truly recognize is might. Why should I recognize any other right in dealing with them?"

"So long as you were not the first."

Saryn was curious as to why he might say that, although she certainly had her own belief. "What difference does that make?"

"If a lord seeks power over others by force when they have done him no evil, that is wrong. By using might, he has justified the right of others to use force against him."

"That may be, but . . . what about his armsmen? I've killed hundreds or more. Most of them were only following orders."

"They chose to be armsmen and to take up arms. Do you not know that every time you go into battle you might suffer the same?" Dealdron's voice was low, almost gentle in the darkness as they neared the tower, which showed but two lights, a lamp in the window of the topmost chamber and a brass lamp outside the ground-floor door.

"I do my best to avoid being killed, but . . . yes . . . it is a possibility."

Dealdron shrugged, as if to suggest that the answer was obvious. He stepped forward and opened the main door. The narrow hallway led to stone steps upward, but Dealdron gestured to the only door on the right, then pushed it open.

Saryn stepped inside. A single lamp was lit in the small square chamber with the narrow bed. A covered tray rested on the small writing desk. The floor had been swept and linens placed at the foot of the bed. Two pitchers of water and a washbasin stood on the washstand with a chamber pot in the corner. Her saddlebags were set beside the bed.

Saryn surveyed the chamber, noting the heavy bar beside the door and the inside shutters on the two windows, already closed and barred shut.

"Good night, Commander." Dealdron stepped back and closed the door.

Saryn looked at the back of the door, knowing that Dealdron had made all the arrangements for her. She sensed his pleasure at surprising her.

She wasn't certain she even wanted to consider that—not after the events of the day. And yet . . . how could she not? He was concerned about her, honestly. He found her attractive, and yet he was sensitive enough not to press her in any way. If only . . .

She shook her head, then eased the battle harness off.

LXXXII

Despite the heavy shutters, Saryn woke early on twoday and was washed up, dressed, and out of her chamber while the sky was still pale greenish blue-gray and awaiting the first glimmers of the sun creeping over the hills to the east. As she walked toward the barracks to the south of the tower, she did not see Zeldyan, but the regent's shutters were closed, not surprisingly. The lightknives had faded away . . . mostly, if with an occasional needle flaring across her field of vision, reminding her that she was certainly not back to full strength in terms of handling the order-chaos flows.

Hryessa was also up early, out checking mounts and supplies. "Good morning, Commander. You feeling better this morning?"

Saryn raised her eyebrows. She'd never said how she'd felt.

"Every time you use magery, you look like you've been run over by wild horses," Hryessa replied to the unspoken question. "That's why Dealdron went to the trouble of getting your quarters set and some food. Not the only reason, of course."

"Not the only reason?"

"Almost any woman would be pleased to have a man that handsome willing to do whatever he can to make her feel better."

Saryn shook her head. "He just wants to prove his worth."

"That he does. To you. He still takes blade practice with the better guards. Gets bruises, too."

That Dealdron saw something more, or the possibility of something more with Saryn, handsome, hardworking, and intelligent as he had proved to be . . . Was that even possible for her? "How are the guards?"

"We lost Ilysa last night. Looks like all the others will pull through."

"And the stores here?"

"Lean, but one of the head ostler's boys sneaked back last night. He said that most of the crops hadn't been brought in yet, and Lord Gethen warned the growers and crofters off almost an eightday ago. There's some stored cheeses and dried meat and enough flour in dry barrels in the deep cellars. Might have some weevils here and there. We can deal with that."

"What about making the holding more secure?"

"We've got fifth squad on patrol, with scouts out, and third and sixth are cleaning up the place and burying the dead. The horses, too. They're already beginning to smell. The Lady Regent . . ." Hryessa inclined her head toward the villa. "She'll need to decide. We can't do anything there until she does."

"I'll talk to her once she leaves the tower." Saryn wouldn't press Zeldyan, not when the regent had just lost her father and her son. A few glasses wouldn't matter, not at the moment.

"We've got the barracks kitchen open, ser."

"Thank you." Saryn smiled, then turned and headed toward the barracks. Hryessa's statement was as much a suggestion that Saryn eat as the captain was likely to make.

First and second squads were lined up to eat as Saryn neared the end of the barracks holding the kitchen. The guards inclined their heads as she passed. She did hear some murmurs.

". . . darkness around her . . ."

". . . darkness or not . . . would be a lot fewer of us without her . . ."

". . . too bad she's not the regent . . ."

Saryn almost shook her head at the last. For a woman to be Overlord of Lornth—or even regent—she'd have to kill or defeat every lord-holder in Lornth . . . and keep doing it.

After she quickly ate fried bread and some unnamed meat strips that she suspected were probably from a fallen horse, Saryn walked back into the villa, this time trying to discover where there might be hidden entrances to a strong room or the like. She'd slowly gone through the wing with the bedchambers, sensing nothing behind the stone walls, except two places where windows had been walled up and one location where there had once been a door, when a guard called from the front foyer.

"Commander, ser!"

Saryn hurried back to the front foyer, her eyes passing quickly over the bodies laid out on the long table and looking toward the young guard, who stood just inside the archway. The woman had a long smear of dried blood on her left sleeve.

"Ser . . . there's a messenger here. Right out front."

"Thank you." Saryn followed the guard out to the portico and the mounted armsman. Three other armsmen were reined up behind him.

All four wore tan tunics, with black belts and boots—Maeldyn's colors, as Saryn recalled.

"You'd be the Lady Arms-Commander of Westwind?"

"I am," replied Saryn.

"I was sent to deliver a message to Lord Gethen."

"The regent and our forces rode in last night," Saryn replied. "We arrived too late to save Lord Gethen, Lord Nesslek, and Lord Deolyn, but we did defeat Lord Kelthyn and Lord Jaffrayt and their forces on the way."

"What about the Lady Regent?"

"She is secluded in the east tower for the moment. She's just lost her father and her son. Can you convey the sense of the message?" Saryn asked.

"I don't know what was written, ser. I can tell you that Lord Maeldyn and Lord Spalkyn will be arriving later this afternoon. They'll have a company, and half that again from Lords Chaspal and Whethryn."

"And the other two lords?"

"They entrusted their armsmen to Lord Maeldyn as the best commander in the north, saving Lord Gethen."

"My guard will show you to the stables and the barracks. You can either keep the missive until Lady Zeldyan is able to receive it or entrust it to me. I will not open it if you do."

"I'd best keep it, begging your leave, Commander."

"I understand. I will tell Lady Zeldyan as soon as I see her."

Saryn watched as Maeldyn's armsmen headed off, led by the guard, but before she could turn, she saw Hryessa walking toward her, following two wounded men in the green-and-yellow tunics of Lyntara.

"Commander . . . there were several survivors who were hiding in the reeds of the pond over the hill. They were all wounded, and some died there. I thought you might like to hear what these two had to say."

"Thank you. I would."

The two armsmen did not look at Saryn directly.

"Go ahead," prompted Hryessa, "tell the commander what you told me."

"Well . . . ser . . . we was with Lord Deolyn, and we rode half the night before we got here, and we'd no more 'n gotten here when all the rebels attacked. Must have been six companies, and they had a couple of white wizards. That was how they got through the gates. Threw those fire-bolts at anyone who got close to 'em until no one would . . ."

"Lord Deolyn, he had a big iron shield," added the second man. "He finally got a squad back to the gates. He musta beat 'em back five, six times. They just kept coming, especially the ones in red . . ."

Keistyn's forces, of course. Saryn wondered how Henstrenn had managed to get the other lord-holders to take the brunt of the fighting . . . and the casualties.

". . . Lord Gethen, he and his fellows, they had piles of bodies around them. Even the little lord got a couple . . . just too many . . ."

When the two had finished their gory tale, Saryn nodded. "Thank you. You may go."

"This way," Hryessa said to the two.

Before returning to her inspection of the villa, Saryn paused, thinking about the costs of loyalty. Lord Deolyn had proved his faith by answering Gethen's summons quickly, and his reward had been to be killed. Shartyr had been loyal to no one but his own interests and had so far survived. As had Jharyk.

Saryn was about to reenter the villa when Zeldyan appeared, flanked by two Lornian armsmen.

"Did you receive the message from Lord Maeldyn, Lady?" asked Saryn.

"I did. He and a company and a half will arrive later today. Would that they had come sooner." The last words were tinged with bitterness.

"Quaryn is farther than Lornth from The Groves, is it not?" asked Saryn. "Yet you did not receive a messenger."

Zeldyan looked coldly at Saryn.

"That is not what I meant, Lady. I have no doubt that your father sent a messenger. We did not receive such a message. That could only mean that Henstrenn and the other rebel lord-holders were close enough already and in enough force that no messenger was successful in evading them."

Some of Zeldyan's coldness faded. "There was not enough time for Maeldyn and Spalkyn to receive the message and travel here."

"That is how it seems. I just talked to two wounded armsmen from Lord Deolyn's forces who survived by hiding in pond reeds. Lord Deolyn marched his forces through the night to reach The Groves, and they arrived just before the first attack."

"He was always fiercely loyal to Father. He was a good man." Zeldyan shook her head, then looked at the pair of guards. "The commander and I will be inside."

Saryn followed Zeldyan into the front foyer, where the regent stopped and looked at the three still figures laid out on the long table. Then she turned her eyes to Saryn.

"If you would make arrangements for a funeral pyre . . . on the top of the hill beyond the tower . . . at sunset . . ." Zeldyan swallowed, once, twice, then straightened. "The study . . . if you would." She did not look back or sideways.

Saryn followed Zeldyan out of the foyer and down the wide hall and into the study. Someone—most likely Zeldyan, Saryn thought—had picked up the scattered items and put them back in the desk or on it or in the bookcases.

Once they were alone in the study, Zeldyan turned, and asked, "What do you think I should do?"

Saryn didn't want to answer that question. Instead, she said, "Are you and Relyn not the only survivors who could hold The Groves?"

"According to the customs of Lornth, I could not hold anything."

"You could hold it as regent for your brother. He is certainly entitled to succeed his father."

"So you would have me go through the grief of position without power once more? The southern lords will claim I have no authority."

Saryn realized that Zeldyan hadn't fully considered what had happened over the last half season. Only two of the southern lords who had taken up arms were still alive, and the successors to those who had fallen had almost nothing in the way of armsmen. "They would have to bring forces against The Groves once more. Would they wish to do that now?"

Zeldyan looked at Saryn. "You ask much. Why? Why now? You have lost, as have I, for the next Overlord of Lornth will not be friendly to Westwind."

"How will the lord-holders determine which lord becomes the Overlord of Lornth?" asked Saryn.

"There is no rule. It has been generations since the overlord has died without a blood heir." Zeldyan shrugged. "They will bow to the strongest, no doubt."

"That will be Henstrenn. He was smart enough to suggest that Kelthyn and Jaffrayt take the river road, and he managed to maneuver it so that Keistyn's forces took most of the losses in taking The Groves. That leaves Henstrenn with more golds, probably augmented by the Suthyans, and his forces are far greater than those of Keistyn, or of any other remaining lord-holder." Saryn paused, then asked, "Do you want him to be Overlord of Lornth?"

"Part of me no longer cares. Should I? You and the angels came, through no fault of your own, and over the past ten years I have lost all I held dear."

"Six lords in the south, prompted by Kelthyn and Henstrenn, decided that you should not be regent and that Nesslek should die. They demanded you step down, and before you could even respond, they attacked."

"I can do nothing about it. I have less than one company of armsmen left." Zeldyan looked at Saryn. "Do what you will, Angel."

"I would suggest we wait until Lord Maeldyn and Lord Spalkyn arrive. They are levelheaded."

"A few glasses will not matter, one way or another. Perhaps nothing will." She sank into one of the chairs set at an angle to the table. "You must have much to do, Commander."

"Until later, Lady." Saryn inclined her head to Zeldyan and headed out to see how Hryessa and the guards were doing in restoring order to the holding.

By midday, some of the surviving holder staff—those sent away by Gethen—had begun to return. Second squad had completed stacking and arranging the timbers and wood for the pyre on the hill, and the remaining disorder in the villa had been largely removed, although Saryn had cautioned the guards and staff not to disturb Zeldyan.

She and Hryessa also made certain that the kitchens would be able to prepare enough for the additional armsmen. Saryn asked Dealdron to assure that the stables would be ready.

His response was simple. "We will do what is necessary, as will I for you."

Saryn smiled at that, but only replied, "Thank you." She did watch him as he headed toward the stables.

As soon as the outlying patrols reported the approach of Maeldyn and

Spalkyn, Saryn informed Zeldyan, and the two made their way, in time, to the portico of the villa just before the head of the column arrived, and the two lord-holders reined up.

All of the mounts looked tired, as did the armsmen behind the two lord-holders. Saryn could sense the fatigue in both lords.

"Greetings, Lady Regent," offered Maeldyn.

"Lord Nesslek is dead. By definition, I am no longer regent."

"I am most sorry, Lady. We left within glasses of receiving word."

"You have always done your best, both of you."

"As I understand matters, from the scouts I sent out on our way here," Maeldyn said slowly, looking down from his mount, "Commander Saryn and your forces, Lady Zeldyan, encountered the forces of Lord Jaffrayt and Lord Kelthyn on your way to relieve The Groves. You routed both." The dour-looking lord glanced to Saryn. "Might I inquire about the lords in question?"

"They were both killed in the fighting, as were the majority of their forces," replied Saryn. *A bare majority, but a majority.* "When we reached The Groves, it was already too late. Lord Deolyn, Lord Gethen, and Lord Nesslek had been defeated and killed." Saryn nodded toward the archway behind her. "They are there, and we have made arrangements for a funeral pyre for sunset."

"From our approach, I surmised something of the sort," added Spalkyn. "What about the other southern lords."

Zeldyan looked to Saryn.

"Lord Orsynn attempted an ambush last eightday. He did not survive, nor did two of his sons and most of their armsmen. Lord Mortryd begged for aid against an attack by Lord Rherhn, but when we arrived to help, they both turned and attacked us. Both are dead. We have not seen either Lord Keistyn or Lord Henstrenn, but presume that, from their tracks, they took the eastern road to return to their own holdings."

"Or to Duevek," suggested Maeldyn, "which is easier to defend and closer to Lornth." He paused. "The last days have been long. If you would not mind, Lady of The Groves, I would like to settle my men. Perhaps we could talk in greater detail later."

"Later would be best," replied Zeldyan, "even in the morning."

"The barracks kitchen has prepared food," Saryn offered, "and our ostler has adapted the stables to handle your horses."

Maeldyn nodded. "We thank you."

As they led their men past the villa, Zeldyan watched for a moment, then looked at Saryn. "I am not at my best. Thank you."

"I would not be at my best if I'd had to endure what you've had to go through, Lady."

"May you never have to, Angel. No one should." Zeldyan hesitated. "I will be in the study."

"I'll have your supper brought to you, Lady. It will be simple."

"Simple is enough, now. If I can even eat that . . ." Zeldyan turned away and walked resolutely back into the front foyer of the villa.

LXXXIII

As the lower edge of the sun, tinged slightly orange, touched the edge of the roofs of Carpa, the first squad of Lornian armsmen escorted Lord Deolyn's still form, carried shoulder high by six armsmen, from the foyer of the villa out through the portico and along the paved lane toward the east tower. Shortly thereafter, the second squad appeared with Lord Gethen, then third squad with Nesslek's body.

With measured steps, they made their way past the tower and up the path to the top of the hill. All the remaining armsmen and guards were drawn up in formation around the pyre on the hilltop. In a line forward of those bearing arms were Maeldyn, Spalkyn, Saryn, and Zeldyan.

When all three forms were in place, with Nesslek in the center, and the Lornian armsmen back in formation, Lord Maeldyn stepped forward, then turned to face the Lady Regent and the others.

"From chaos, order brings life, and in the end, from that life, chaos leads us all to death," began the stern-faced lord. "Some deaths are timely and come with order. Some are most untimely and disorderly. So it has been with the three men before us. All of them lived honorable lives that were too short; but for one of them, that life was far, far, too short." Maeldyn paused for a moment before resuming.

"Each of these men had characteristics worthy of emulation. Lord

Deolyn was fiercely loyal to honor and to doing what was right, regardless of the cost to himself. Lord Gethen was a good leader, and more than that, a wise man who looked to do good for all of Lornth, and not just for his own holding or personal gain, and who had already lost many of those whom he loved and who loved him because those who embody chaos could not abide such good. Young Lord Nesslek came from a most noble heritage and stood with others far older against those forces of chaos.

"We will miss them, and we will miss what they brought to Lornth and life." Maeldyn stepped back.

Spalkyn stepped forward and, like Maeldyn, turned to face those who waited. "From chaos we came and unto chaos we go. From dull clay is spirit sparked into the flame that is life, and that flame burns our course over the years that we have. In the end is chaos, leaving no sign of where we once stood. All that remains is the memory of what we have been, what we have done, and how well we have loved. May these flames burn those memories into all of us, and may our acts carry on those memories, and so to the end of time."

One of the Lornian squad leaders strode forth and handed a burning pitch torch to Spalkyn, who stood . . . waiting.

Slowly, Zeldyan stepped forward. She took the torch from the heavy-set lord and walked deliberately to the foot of the pyre, where she laid the torch across an oil-soaked plank, then straightened.

After a long moment, she turned and walked gravely back to stand beside Saryn and the two lords.

Saryn stood beside Zeldyan, watching as the flames rose, consuming the wood and the bodies upon them . . . consuming as well the hopes of a woman for her son, the hopes of a regent for a reign of peace and prosperity.

Is this all that Ryba foresaw? The endless battles between chauvinistic lord-holders? A land where respect and restraint occur only at the point of a blade? Where the only way a woman can obtain anything close to respect is by being able to kill greater and greater numbers of men? Isn't something better possible? If it is, is there any other way to accomplish it besides more violence and killing?

Standing before the heat of the raging flames, Saryn couldn't help but ask the last question again.

LXXXIV

Less than a glass after sunrise, Zeldyan, Saryn, Maeldyn, and Spalkyn sat around the table in what had been Gethen's study. From outside on the verandah came the sound of the fountain, muting the sounds of armsmen and guards engaged in various duties around the villa.

"Properly speaking," began Zeldyan, "I have no authority."

"You are the only certain blood survivor of the previous lord-holder," observed Spalkyn. "That makes you equal to any other lord-holder."

"There is also the question of the regency," added Maeldyn, "since the overlord for whom you were regent was attacked and killed by lord-holders rebelling against the will and wishes of a majority of lord-holders. In doing that, Henstrenn gathered together three other lords and brought six companies against Lord Gethen and Lord Nesslek . . . and Lord Deolyn. The question that remains is exactly what we should do." He looked to Saryn. "That is where you, Arms-commander, come in. If I count correctly, you have close to a company and a half of Westwind guards."

"Two squads are Westwind guards. The other four squads are those who have joined us here and have received some training, none more than a season and a few eightdays."

Maeldyn turned to Zeldyan. "You have a company remaining."

Zeldyan nodded.

"And Spalkyn and I have a few less than two companies." Maeldyn smiled, coldly. "Is it also not true that the Westwind and Lornian companies effectively destroyed half of the forces Henstrenn originally mustered against The Groves, and that Lord Keistyn's forces were considerably reduced in the attack on The Groves?"

Zeldyan did not speak.

Finally, Saryn said, "That is so."

"I also understand that you, Commander, have routed and destroyed many of those forces who might have joined Henstrenn in his efforts to usurp the overlordship of Lornth."

"I believe that to be so. Certainly, Lord Orsynn, Lord Mortryd, and Lord Rherhn will not be able to back Henstrenn."

"Nor Lords Jaffrayt and Kelthyn," Maeldyn pointed out. "That leaves Henstrenn with less than three companies . . . at the moment."

"That assumes he doesn't receive forces from elsewhere. Shartyr has avoided being involved, and so has Jharyk," Spalkyn pointed out.

"Jharyk has little in the way of armsmen," Saryn said, "but Shartyr has two companies. So far, neither has seen much point in actually committing troops. Jharyk is, or was, loyal to Lord Gethen. Shartyr is loyal only to himself."

"Shartyr will not weaken himself to support Hennstren." Maeldyn looked to Saryn once more. "Are you willing to use your guards against Henstrenn?"

"I don't see that we have any choice. If he becomes overlord, Westwind and Lornth will be at war in another few years, and Suthya will pick up the pieces of whichever land loses. In the end, both Westwind and Lornth will lose."

"You phrase that in an interesting manner, Commander," observed Spalkyn.

"Interesting or not," Maeldyn interjected with a quick glance at Spalkyn, "even with the commander's forces, we have another problem. The reports I have heard indicate that Henstrenn has several white wizards with his forces."

"They're most likely Suthyan," suggested Saryn. "Lady Zeldyan has pointed out that none were left in Lornth, and the few that remained in Gallos were destroyed when the Gallosian forces were defeated by Westwind."

"How did you manage that?" asked Spalkyn.

"The Marshal dropped a cliff on them," replied Saryn.

"A handy trick if you can manage it."

"It's much easier in the mountains," Saryn replied dryly.

"I don't think we can lure Henstrenn from Duevek into the mountains," Maeldyn said. "Is it worth the risk to attack Henstrenn?"

"We attack him now," replied Spalkyn, "or we will never succeed. We will not have the commander's forces with us in the future, and some of the other southern lord-holders may regroup behind Henstrenn. So might Shartyr, upon reflection and if gifted heavily enough."

Maeldyn looked to Zeldyan. "Do you agree?"

"I would see him destroyed." Zeldyan's voice was like ice. "I will accompany you, so that every possible armsman can be used against him. We should leave as soon as possible."

"At dawn tomorrow, then?" asked Maeldyn, turning to Saryn. "Commander?"

"Dawn, tomorrow," she agreed, even as she wondered why Maeldyn was being so deferential. *It's not just that he wants the Westwind guards . . . there's more there, but it's not the cold and calculating sort of scheming that I sensed with Henstrenn and Kelthyn.*

"Then it is settled." Maeldyn stood and nodded to Spalkyn. "We need to draft a message to Chaspal and Wethryn." He turned to Zeldyan. "If you two would excuse us?"

Zeldyan nodded. "Thank you."

Saryn stood, and said, "We should talk about supplies later. We do have some wagons and teamsters." She felt words were necessary, but also that offering thanks was somehow not appropriate. She also wanted to convey respect and helpfulness.

Spalkyn nodded in return. "Thank you. They will be most useful."

When the two lords had left, Zeldyan looked to Saryn. "When this is over, either you or Henstrenn will be the most powerful force in Lornth, Commander. Will you make Lornth an appendage of Westwind?"

"That I would never do," Saryn replied, almost without thinking. "I wouldn't . . ." She broke off, realizing that she'd been about to say that she wouldn't apply Ryba's views to Lornth.

"You wouldn't do what, if I may ask?" Zeldyan rose, half smiling, if wanly.

"The beliefs left over from Cyador are not suitable for Lornth, as events are proving, but those of Westwind would be equally unsuitable, for different reasons. Besides, why should I be the one deciding Lornth's future?"

"Because, like it or not, Commander, you well may be the only one who can," said Zeldyan gently. "Think upon it carefully."

"First, we need to deal with Henstrenn and Keistyn," replied Saryn, "but I will take your words to heart."

"That would please me. I would like to see some good come from all the blood that has been shed."

Saryn bowed her head. "I will do what I can, Lady."

"I know. If you would not mind . . . I would like to reflect on matters."

"Of course. Until later, then," replied Saryn, slipping toward the verandah door.

Maeldyn was waiting on the far side of the verandah as Saryn left the study. "A word or two, Commander, if you would."

"Of course." Saryn smiled pleasantly, although she remained wary, for all that she believed and sensed that the thin-faced lord was trustworthy.

"What do you want out of all this?" asked Maeldyn. "You, yourself, not Westwind?"

What should I tell him? And how much? "I have asked myself that question, Lord Maeldyn. I don't have an easy or a simple answer. I do know that I don't want women from Lornth fleeing to Westwind because they feel life is intolerable. I'd like to see women in Lornth able to be lord-holders and even overlord . . . lady-holders or overlady . . ." She winced. "I can't say I like the way the last sounds. Lady Zeldyan should be able to hold The Groves without having to find a consort and defer to him. Lord Spalkyn ought to have the right to have one of his daughters succeed him."

"Do you think women would do any better as lady-holders, if you will?"

"Probably not at first, not unless whoever was overlord would back them, but all this fighting between the lord-holders makes no sense, not when Suthya or the Jeranyi would love nothing better than for it to continue to weaken Lornth until they can walk in and take over."

"It may be premature, Commander, but if we defeat Henstrenn, how do you think we should select another overlord—or lady?"

"Gather all the remaining lord-holders who did not revolt and see if they can agree on someone."

"And if they cannot?" pressed Maeldyn.

"I think we would have to see how they cannot agree." Saryn managed to inject a tone of wryness into her voice.

"In the end, it will take great strength to hold Lornth together."

Saryn didn't want to deal with that . . . not yet, even though Zeldyan had already brought up the issue even more directly. "The first problem is to defeat Henstrenn and remove the Suthyan meddling and influence."

"That is true, Commander." Maeldyn smiled. "You are most capable. And you have Lornth's interests more at heart than many lord-holders. I would like to discuss this matter with you after we deal with Lord Henstrenn. You are correct, I believe, that all the surviving lord-holders should be gathered, but we should discuss a strategy with Spalkyn and Lady Zeldyan before we do."

"At that point, we should. I agree."

"If you will excuse me, Commander . . ."

"I won't keep you."

With a pleasant smile, and one that matched a guarded warmth behind the expression, Maeldyn nodded and walked swiftly in the direction of the barracks.

Saryn walked more slowly toward the stables, to check on mounts and to talk to Dealdron about the wagons and what supplies they could and should carry. She couldn't help but think that Maeldyn and Zeldyan were both acting as though their victory were a foregone conclusion. Yet, with chaos-mages supporting Henstrenn, that was anything but a certainty.

Without shields against chaos-fire-bolts, prevailing against Henstrenn and his allies was unlikely and, even if possible, any victory would likely result in huge casualties that would render success only marginally better than defeat because without a strong force to deal with the other lord-holders, indecision and political chaos would result. At the same time, her recent efforts with the chaos-order-knives had made it clear that she did not have either the strength or the ability to hold or maintain large shields for long at all.

Could she do the same thing with her shields as she had with the chaos-order-knives? Make them small and more targeted while sliding the fire-bolts away? *Do I have any choice?*

She smiled wryly. *Why does trying to do the right thing always involve so much more than you ever think it will?* She didn't have an answer for that question, either.

She did know that she needed to practice sliding flow shields that could be used against chaos-fire-bolts. She had a day or two to work on that, and she'd probably need every moment.

LXXXV

The east road was the longer route to Lornth, but shorter to Duevek, given the westward course of the River Yarth south of Carpa. It was also much drier and dustier, and reddish road dust rose and sifted through everything by midafternoon on fiveday. Saryn had been practicing the skill of making small sliding order-chaos-shields on and off for two days. She thought she had a better technique that took less effort, but how long she could keep that up was another question once they got into battle.

"If it's this dusty farther south," Saryn said to Spalkyn, riding to her right, "Henstrenn will see us from kays away."

"Duevek sits on a bend in the river, with hills to the north. It's not as dry there, but the hills would shield us from view until the last five kays or so. By then, it shouldn't matter. One way or another, he'll know. He still has those mages, and some mages can tell from a distance when people are coming. He must suspect we'll attack, anyway, and he will have posted scouts on the roads."

Did Saryn's ability to sense people from a distance make her a mage? Hryessa had as much as said that, but Saryn certainly couldn't throw fire-bolts.

From what she recalled, Duevek sat on a hill overlooking the main southern road from the Westhorns into Lornth, but she'd only seen the keep from the road below and from a distance. "What is the holding like?"

"I only saw it once, as a very young man," returned Spalkyn. "It's on top of a low hill or rise, and it overlooks the town and the River Yarth. The Yarth is narrower there, but still not an easy crossing. The villa is all one story and extensive, but it is set within rather large and solid walls. So are all the outbuildings. The walls must be a good eight cubits high and two or three thick."

Cannon would definitely help here, but with white wizards on the other side, they'd likely use chaos to blow the powder. She frowned. *Is that why they never pursued gunpowder or the like? Or was the reason simply lost in all the centuries since the old Rats colonized Cyador?* "What about the gates?"

"The usual for a fortified keep. Heavy planks, backed with timber, and ironbound. The pivots and hinges are all protected by the walls."

"So they swing inward?"

"Unless you have a moat and a drawbridge, what choice is there?" Spalkyn's question was clearly rhetorical.

Saryn wasn't about to get into portcullises and sliding slot gates and the like. She just nodded, idly wondering if she could use her order-chaos in some way against the gates. *You can't use it for everything. You're not strong enough or talented enough for that.* Again, it would be pick and choose . . . and hope that her choices were the right ones. "What if he just retreats inside the walls?"

"It's not as defensible as Masengyl, but I doubt Henstrenn will want a siege. He wants a victory, and sitting behind walls doesn't make him a leader. That would just erode his support."

Given the brashness seemingly revered by the southern lord-holders, Saryn could see that.

"Also, he can't get his harvest in. So . . . if he stays inside the walls, we just start to burn fields until he comes out. If he doesn't come out, he loses it all, and that will weaken him both in the wallet and in terms of support with both his own people and the other lords."

Saryn hadn't thought of going that far, but she could see the possibilities. Still . . . Henstrenn was the type to sacrifice anything and anyone to his ambitions.

"I'm glad you had those wagons. We can carry more rations," said Spalkyn. "The spare mounts you captured from Jaffrayt and Kelthyn also help."

With Spalkyn's words about the wagons, Saryn couldn't help but think about Hryessa's comments about Dealdron. While she had meant to talk to him on threeday, what with one thing and another, somehow she hadn't gotten around to it. *Was that because you really didn't want to?*

Finally, while Maeldyn and Spalkyn were checking with their armsmen, Saryn rode back to the rear of the column, where, amid the road dust, Dealdron was driving the first of the five supply wagons. There she eased the gelding alongside the wagon.

"How are the drafts holding up?"

"So far, so good, Commander."

"And the wagons?"

"There's one axle on the third wagon that's a trace unsteady, but it's holding so far. We have spares and extra wheels."

"You've thought that out."

"Wouldn't be much help if I hadn't," he replied with a grin, looking to the team.

"You've been a great help wherever you've been," Saryn said with a light laugh. "Even when you could barely walk with that heavy support and splint."

"You made it clear I should be." Dealdron's tone was on the edge of banter, and there was no sense of resentment.

"You don't sound too upset."

The younger man shrugged. "You made me think about things differently."

As he replied, Saryn realized something else. Dealdron's speech was better than it had been when he had first come to Westwind. "You've gone out of your way to arrange matters for me," she said carefully, although she did not sense any of the other teamsters in the wagon, even out of sight. "I appreciate it. I truly do."

Dealdron smiled easily, and she could sense a certain amusement behind the expression before he replied. "You'd like to know why? Is that why you're here?"

"I'm curious," she admitted, wondering why she felt so guarded, but perhaps that was because she'd always had difficulty reading more than his surface feelings.

"You do your best to protect everyone else. You protected me from the Marshal. I didn't see anyone else protecting you when you were ready to drop from the saddle. I don't have very good arms skills, but I can make sure of . . . other things."

She smiled. "Thank you. I appreciate it."

Dealdron looked at her and smiled warmly. "Thank you for telling me."

"You deserve it. I should have said more earlier." After a moment, she said, "I need to head back."

As she rode back to the front of the column, she could feel his eyes on her back, again, and a certain sense of worry and concern emanating from him. She couldn't help but feel touched, but she also worried that, in some way, he was putting her on a pedestal, and that he really didn't understand how much death and destruction she'd created.

Why should that bother you?

That was another question she didn't really want to answer.

Why? Because you might care for him? Because you really don't want to come off that pedestal?

And those were questions she also didn't want to answer.

LXXXVI

Sevenday morning brought Saryn and the forces of the other three lord-holders to a position just beyond the hills north of Duevek. Maeldyn's and Spalkyn's armsmen were in the lead, with Saryn and the others riding behind the scouts and in front of the northern lords' lead squad. The green-blue sky was clear of clouds, but a faint silvery haze cut the light from the white sun just enough that the day was slightly cooler than those that had preceded it. As Spalkyn had predicted, Henstrenn had followed their progress in some fashion because a squad of armsmen was reined up on the section of road a half a kay beyond the last of the hills, waiting under a parley banner.

Saryn could sense no other armsmen nearby, nor did the outriders and scouts see any others. After making a scan with her order-senses, she sent her own first squad forward under Shalya to see what the Duevekan force wanted. Maeldyn, Spalkyn, and Zeldyan waited on their mounts with Saryn while first squad rode out, then returned.

"Sers," said Shalya, reining up before the group, "the squad leader was here to deliver messages to Lord Maeldyn, Lord Spalkyn, and the commander." She eased her mount forward and handed a sealed envelope to Maeldyn, then one to Spalkyn, and the last to Saryn. "He said he was instructed to wait for a response, but no longer than a glass."

"If you would leave us to consider," Saryn said.

"Yes, ser." The squad leader rode a good fifty yards farther up the road to where first squad waited.

"I see that there is no missive for me," observed Zeldyan. "That alone is a message."

"Shall we see what stratagems Henstrenn has in mind?" asked Maeldyn sardonically. "Besides the obvious one of divide and conquer?" He held up the envelope, then slit it open with a belt knife.

Saryn didn't bother with a knife, but broke the seal on hers with her fingers, then extracted the single sheet of parchment, opened it, and began to read.

> Commander—
> You and your beliefs are not welcome in Lornth, and never will be. For all the death and destruction you have caused, none here will ever forget or forgive. Yet, for all that, if you and your forces immediately break off this conflict, none will pursue you or attack Westwind.
>
> Remain here, and all that you are and hold dear will be forfeit, and you will be hounded and harried by all west of the Westhorns, as will Westwind itself, for all the years of all the generations to come.

The signature was that of Henstrenn, and under it was a seal—that of the Overlord of Lornth.

Does he really believe he can do that? Saryn shook her head. Regardless of whether she was successful against Henstrenn, there was no way that Lornth had the resources to hound and harry Westwind, precarious as Westwind's position might be, for year after year. *Is it designed to get me so angry that I'll do something incredibly stupid?*

She finally glanced up and looked to the other two lord-holders. Maeldyn smiled ruefully. They waited for Spalkyn to finish reading his missive.

The heavyset Lord of Palteara lowered the parchment, then fingered his square-cut brown beard, finally shaking his head. "The presumptive Overlord of Lornth has offered me his daughter as a consort for my son and a pardon for my actions against him as lawful Overlord of Lornth. What did he offer you, Maeldyn?"

"Lord Keistyn's younger son as consort for my daughter. Of course, he's but eight, but he didn't mention that. Oh . . . and a pardon that won't mean much because, sooner or later, I'll be poisoned or suffer some sort of accident."

"And you, Commander?" asked Maeldyn.

"The wrath of all Lornth no matter what I do, but neutrality with regard to Westwind if I depart the lands of Lornth immediately."

"Not exactly the most enticing of offers," mused Spalkyn. "None of them."

"They weren't meant to be," replied Maeldyn. "They're meant as justifications after we refuse them and are defeated and slaughtered so that he can say he offered us full redemption of some sort."

"Then we had best make sure that we do not lose." Spalkyn laughed.

"His messenger is waiting," Maeldyn pointed out. "I think we should make him wait longer while we compose particularly irritating replies. Since we have no real choice, it cannot hurt to make him angrier. He doesn't think as well as he believes he does when he is upset."

"That may be," replied Spalkyn, "but I don't happen to carry parchment and pen on long rides to battle."

"I do have a pen and ink," said Maeldyn, "and I believe it will be acceptable to reply on the reverse of what he used."

While Maeldyn was writing his response, Saryn rode forward to where first squad waited and reined up beside Shalya.

"Ser?"

"Send out a few scouts, away from the road. I don't want anyone sneaking up on us while we reply to Lord Henstrenn."

"Yes, ser."

As Saryn rode back toward Maeldyn and the others, she again tried to sense whether anyone was hiding nearby . . . or even approaching. So far as she could tell, no one was nearby, not besides their force and the parley squad.

Once she reined up, she reread Henstrenn's insulting note once more and mentally worked on a response until Maeldyn passed her the pen. Writing in the saddle with what amounted to a quill and an inkwell wasn't exactly easy, but she managed to write out her reply without any terrible errors or ink blots, then read it over one last time.

My dear Lord Henstrenn:

One really should not make threats that one cannot carry out. Such threats have a tendency to make your betters irritated, and such irritation can only redound to your disadvantage. Your attitude toward women is also unacceptable, and the time will come sooner than you believe that you will have to deal with women more powerful than you. Needless to say, your offer is neither practical nor acceptable.

She signed what she had written, then held it for a time to dry. As she folded the sheet and slipped it back into the envelope, she frowned. Something wasn't right. She was sensing a fuzziness somewhere to her left . . . an almost-chaotic swirling, although she could see nothing.

That wasn't right. It was as though her eyes slid away from that patch of bushes that were barely waist high. She thrust the envelope inside her tunic.

"Maeldyn! Spalkyn! Use your armsmen to make the parley squad surrender or cut them down! Using a parley squad to conceal an attack voids any truce!" Saryn turned the gelding and rode back toward Shalya. "First squad! On me! Tight formation!"

Then she rode toward what she thought was the chaos–concealment shield, gathering and weaving order and chaos flows together, even while she drew one of the blades from the knee sheath, rather than from the easier-to-reach battle harness. Behind her, first squad formed a tight wedge. That was a gamble, because a tight formation would suffer greater losses if Saryn's shields failed, but she couldn't protect a wider formation.

She was almost a hundred yards away from the bushes when a fire-bolt arched toward her. Her first attempt at throwing a small sliding shield at the fiery chaos was successful only in that it redirected the chaos just enough that the mass of fire slammed into the sand and dirt less than ten yards in front of her, and she barely avoided riding into it.

Frig!

A second firebolt followed the first, but Saryn managed to deflect it without using much effort, as she did with the third. By then she was close enough to fling the short sword at the chaos-shaded form that she could sense, but still not see. As she released the blade, she added just a touch of order to the point, then smoothed its path and increased its force, using order and chaos.

Less than ten yards from where she sensed the indistinct chaos-mage, flame flared around the blade, and both blade and flame dropped to the ground.

Saryn launched a second blade.

The same thing happened again, but almost at the spot where Saryn felt the white wizard was. When the chaos flared away, so did the concealment shield, revealing a squad of mounted armsmen in brilliant red tunics with gold trim, their sabres ready, and starting to charge toward first squad.

Saryn threw the third blade, at less than thirty yards, directly at the wizard, attired in red as well, and then drew the fourth blade, trying to fashion a narrow and yet thin order-chaos-knife before she released it at the squad of armsmen.

The white wizard flung up a chaos-barrier of some sort, but the black-iron short sword slammed through it and into the wizard, and a pillar of flame exploded in all directions, just as the order-bounded chaos-knife sliced through the center of the red-clad squad of men and mounts.

Saryn guided the gelding right after the chaos-knife because she didn't want to get close to any possible survivors, not without weapons. First squad followed her lead, and the three armsmen in red who had been outside the range of the order-chaos-blade were so stunned that they went down under the short swords of the guards at the outer edge of the wedge.

Saryn could barely see through the dust as she reined up well past the fallen armsmen, but she immediately used her senses to check the area. She could feel no one, and she had only the slightest headache . . . and no lightknives stabbed into her eyes.

So far. She'd have to eat something, though, and drink more than she wanted. That, she was learning from experience, helped greatly.

Were the red-and-gold armsmen Suthyan? She didn't know from where else they could have come.

Shortly, Shalya brought first squad back into formation facing Saryn. "No survivors, ser."

"Recover everything you can quickly." Saryn paused. "There might be one of my blades that's in one piece. There aren't any other armsmen close. Not now. I'm going to tell the other lord-holders what happened. As soon as you're done, if you'd report to me?"

"Yes, ser." Shalya inclined her head.

Saryn took her time riding back, remembering to get out her water bottle and drink, and then eat several of the hard biscuits she'd slipped into a pouch at the top of her saddlebags.

As she neared Zeldyan and the other two lord-holders, she could feel a sense of nausea from the former regent, as well as from Maeldyn.

"Did you capture anyone?" asked Spalkyn.

"No. They were all dead after the first charge. Were the red-coats Suthyan armsmen, or did they belong to some lord-holder I don't know about?"

Spalkyn nodded. "The red and gold are the colors of Suthya. The traders believe in spending others' blood for their gold."

Saryn reined up facing the three. "Since they supplied the mage and armsmen, I don't think there's much doubt that they're behind Henstrenn."

"It didn't do them much good," said Zeldyan.

"Not here," replied Saryn, "but there are likely several more at Duevek, according to what we learned earlier."

"How did you manage all that?" asked Maeldyn.

"We just charged them with cold iron," answered Saryn before asking quickly, "What happened to the parley squad?"

"The moment you started to ride, they galloped off," Maeldyn said. "I decided against chasing them at that speed."

Saryn nodded. "That was probably a good idea. They might have had another trap planned along the way." Henstrenn's ploy just confirmed to Saryn that the lord-holder of Duevek didn't respect either side of a parley flag.

"Another one of Henstrenn's bits of trickery," declared Spalkyn.

"It would have worked if the commander had not acted," Zeldyan pointed out.

"I don't believe you mentioned that you were a mage," Maeldyn said dryly.

"I'm not," Saryn replied. "I can't throw fire-bolts or things like that. I still had to use a blade to kill him. In fact, I ended up using four. The fire that exploded was his chaos against the iron of the blade." That was an oversimplification, but Saryn really didn't want all of Lornth to think she was a mage. Not any sooner than necessary.

"Besides, how could any woman master magery?" added Zeldyan, her words coated with irony. "We certainly can't be trusted to master anything, can we?"

Spalkyn glanced from Zeldyan to Saryn, then to Maeldyn. He looked as though he might speak, then gave the smallest of headshakes and instead smiled ruefully at Maeldyn.

"I think we do have yet another answer as to whether Henstrenn could be trusted as overlord, or even to retain his current holding," said Maeldyn. "I suggest we move forward before the good lord-holder of Duevek can come up with another scheme to delay us."

Spalkyn nodded, as did Zeldyan. Saryn drank some more water and ate two more biscuits.

As soon as Shalya and first squad returned and reported, and the joint force began to ride toward Duevek once more, Saryn eased the gelding back to the wagons.

"Commander," called Dealdron from the seat of the first, "I have your blades here. Four of them, if you need that many."

Saryn eased the mount up beside the wagon with a wry smile. "I'll need all four. How did you know?"

"You use blades. I made sure I had plenty in the wagons for you."

"What about the other guards?"

"They can do with one, if need be. If you are without blades, all will suffer, and they all know that."

"You make me sound like a one-person company," said Saryn as she took the first short sword he proffered, hilt first, and slipped it into the battle harness.

"No, Commander. You are not a one-person company." Dealdron offered the second blade. "A one-person army, perhaps, but not merely a company."

Saryn almost dropped the second blade before putting it into the scabbard in the battle harness. "That's absurd."

"I think not. Why else would the Marshal send you to Lornth?"

"That's obvious enough. She doesn't want an enemy that close to Westwind."

"That is most true, in both senses. Sooner or later, you would cross the

Marshal. The later it happened, the more likely you would win. If it happened soon enough that the Marshal had to defeat you, Westwind would lose as well."

"I'm learning more here about what I can do personally than I ever would have in Westwind," Saryn pointed out, taking the third blade and slipping it into the right knee sheath. "If what you say is true . . ." She stopped. "She couldn't have been lying when she said she wasn't sending me to my death. I would have known. She couldn't lie to me, and she knew that, and she made sure I knew."

"The truth can conceal a greater truth. She wasn't sending you to your death. That wouldn't have served her well," Dealdron said.

"Then . . . why . . ." Saryn shook her head. "You can't be serious. She couldn't . . . could she?" *Ryba is capable of anything. You of all people should know that.*

In response, Dealdron extended the last blade. His smile was sad. "Why do you think I am here? I knew you would not return. So did Hryessa. That is why Daryn and the children are in Lornth."

Saryn took the fourth blade mechanically. It all made sense . . . too much sense . . . and Ryba had seen it all. Saryn had only thought in terms of removing the enemies of Westwind, but not beyond. *I'm a tactician, not a strategist, and Ryba knew that. She knew.*

"And I'm supposed to . . . what?

"Mend Lornth, as best you can." He looked directly at her. "Do you really want to return to Westwind? To do whatever she wants, whenever she wants?"

Saryn swallowed. She knew the answer . . . and so did Dealdron.

LXXXVII

For the next kay or so, Saryn kept going over what Dealdron had said, time after time, all the while wondering why she hadn't seen what was so very obvious. She'd seen Henstrenn's and Kelthyn's machinations from the beginning. She'd been able to read and discern most of the plotting within Lornth, and she'd understood how Zeldyan had been outmaneu-vered. She'd figured out what the Suthyans were doing early on with only a few hints. But she hadn't even considered what Ryba had planned.

Why not? Because what she said was true as far so it went, and you knew she was telling the truth, and it made sense? Because you had no idea you could do what you have? She shook her head. *She said she wasn't sending me to my death . . . but that doesn't mean it couldn't happen. She just might have meant that it wouldn't be her fault, or that she didn't see my death.*

Finally, Saryn pushed those thoughts away. There wasn't anything she could do about Ryba, and not much that she could do about the re-maining lord-holders, not until and unless they defeated Henstrenn and whatever Suthyan and other rebel forces awaited them at Duevek.

Is that it, or is it that you just don't want to think about it? How can you not? She couldn't, not totally, but she also couldn't do anything about any of it, not until they dealt with Henstrenn, one way or another . . . or he dealt with them, in which case none of it made any difference.

She glanced sideways at Spalkyn, who rode silently and with a certain preoccupation, and said, "Do we just show up outside Duevek and expect Henstrenn and his forces will ride out?"

"They'll wait for a time to see what we'll do. We have enough supplies that we don't have to force the walls," replied the square-bearded lord-holder. "We can also take supplies from the town as necessary. If, after a day or so, he doesn't want to face us, we could fire some of the fields and orchards that are his personal lands." He laughed. "We'd want to pick the orchards first, though."

"If we burned the pearapples," countered Maeldyn from where he rode in front of them with Zeldyan, "we could have roasted fruit."

"Pearapples don't roast that well. They just turn mushy. They're bet-ter fried or baked in pies, and burning his grain fields won't give us pas-try."

"I hope he'll bring the fight to us. His people will suffer less that way," Maeldyn pointed out.

"If that is the only reason he has to fight," said Spalkyn, "we'll be in Duevek a long time. He's never been that careful of his tenants and peas-ants."

After several moments of silence, Saryn spoke. "I'm curious. Why aren't there that many archers here in Lornth?"

"Poachers are about the only ones who use bows," replied Spalkyn. "Some hunters do on their own lands."

"I've noticed. Why?"

"For one thing, until you angels arrived, there were more mages around, and a good mage could burn the arrows out of the air. That was especially true when we fought against the Cyadorans, and they were the biggest threat. Arrows haven't ever been that useful against the Jeranyi because they never stayed in one place, and they always attacked in open formations on horseback. Also, they usually attacked just at dawn. Then there was the problem that no one could make bows that could penetrate and still be used from the saddle." Spalkyn shrugged. "So archery wasn't that much use except against other lord-holders, and anyone whose arms-men practiced archery was looked on with suspicion."

Saryn nodded. *Those are answers. Not good ones, but ones that made sense for Lornth.*

"Why do you ask?" inquired Maeldyn.

"I have some very good archers, and I wondered why no one else did."

"They can't stop a charging company, either," Spalkyn pointed out.

Saryn wasn't about to point out that they could. They just couldn't stop a number of companies. "No, but they can reduce the numbers enough that defeating the survivors is easier." Saryn's voice was wry. "I'll be back in a few moments. I need to talk to my captain." She turned the gelding and headed back along the shoulder of the road toward the Westwind contingent.

When she neared Hryessa, she reined up and waited, then eased her mount in beside the captain.

"What is it, Commander?"

"You remember seeing Duevek the first time, on our way from West-wind?"

"We didn't get too close. It's walled all the way around, isn't it?"

"That's what Lord Spalkyn says. He thinks that Henstrenn will wait to react to us," Saryn said. "I have the feeling that he'll try a quick attack before he thinks we're ready. I'd like our guards to be prepared."

"You think we should have the archers in place near the front?"

"Once we get close, have them ready. I'll call for you. Because his keep is walled, they'll have to come out of gates. Gates aren't too wide. Our archers are good."

Hryessa nodded. "I'll go over that with first and fourth squads. They'll be ready."

"We also might need to attack from a distance if they have companies waiting."

"We can handle either."

"Good. That's all for now."

"Yes, ser."

Saryn urged the gelding forward to rejoin the lord-holders.

Despite Maeldyn's concerns about another trap, the only sign that Saryn saw of Henstrenn's forces over the next few kays was the almost-settled dust of the retreating parley squad. Before that long, the joint force was headed eastward from the junction where the old east road had joined the main road to Lornth. That was roughly a kay west of the town of Duevek itself. Before long, they were riding up a lane on the western slope of the hill-like ridge on which Henstrenn's keep was situated.

The vanguard was only a few hundred yards along the lane off the main road before Saryn could sense armsmen waiting just beyond the ridgecrest. She eased her mount forward, up beside Maeldyn. "You might want to call in the scouts or warn them. There are armsmen and a wizard just over the hillcrest."

"You know this?"

Saryn nodded. "About a company's worth."

"What do you suggest?"

"A modified flank attack. We'll hit them from several hundred yards with archers. That's beyond the range of mages with those fire-bolts." *At least the ones I've seen so far.* "If they don't move, they'll lose a lot of arms-men. If they do, we'll either attack or chase them or withdraw, as seems best. Any way it goes, they'll suffer. You know they're there, and if they come down the slope at you, you can be ready. I wouldn't think that they'd charge an entire force with one company, but it might be best to be expect-ing it."

"It might at that," said Spalkyn.

For several moments, even as Maeldyn sent an armsman forward to no-tify the scouts, Saryn concentrated on using her senses to get a feel for the land. Finally, she decided to take the two squads on a more circular route to the left of the road—in a northerly circle—so that when they came into view of the Duevekans or the Suthyans, the road would be between them.

Then she rode back to Hryessa again and pulled inside beside the guard captain. "I'm going to take first and fourth squads and leave you with the other four. There is a company over the hillcrest, waiting. Once we hit them with the archers . . ." Saryn shrugged.

"Do you want us up front, ser?"

"I think not. Let the Lornians take the first charge if there is one. You should be prepared to pull off the lane. The ground to the left is more solid, and there's more room to maneuver."

"I'll keep that in mind, ser." Hryessa paused. "You don't want to take another squad?"

"No. I'm going to try not to engage them. Just inflict casualties."

Hryessa raised her eyebrows.

Saryn laughed. "I'll only engage them if it looks like we won't suffer too badly."

The captain nodded, then turned in the saddle. "First and fourth squads! With the commander. The rest of you, close up!"

Saryn led the two squads away from the lane and the main force, then up the northern edge of the southerly end of the rise, angling their way through the browning knee-high grass and bushes so that they wouldn't come into view of the other company until they were almost on level ground.

As she had suspected, those waiting were clad in red and gold, and the Suthyans did not move as Saryn's squads drew nearer. When she judged that her force was slightly over two hundred yards out, she ordered, "Squads, halt!"

She still could see no movement from the Suthyan armsmen.

"Ready bows!"

"Bows ready."

"Stand by to fire. Target fire!" ordered Saryn.

"Target fire!" repeated Shalya and Klarisa.

The first shafts arched toward the Suthyan company, which still remained in formation. Then the iron-tipped arrows fell, and armsmen began clutching themselves or slumping in their saddles, even as the Westwind archers loosed a second and a third volley.

Four quick fire-bolts flared up, and a good half of the remaining shafts burst into flame, with the arrowheads dropping short of the Suthyans, falling like iron hailstones on the lane and the ground to the south of it.

The entire Suthyan company charged.

"One more shaft! Bows away."

Two more fire-bolts flared, clearing away some, but not all, of the arrows. Saryn sensed that the last chaos-bolts were not so strong as those before.

Do you charge them . . . or withdraw?

Somewhere between a quarter and a third of the Suthyan company had fallen or turned from the charge, wounded, and that left the Westwind force outnumbered, but not by much. But the Suthyans had a white wizard.

"Forward! On me!" Saryn drew a blade from the right knee sheath and urged the gelding forward.

As she rode toward the oncoming Suthyans, gathering and weaving order and chaos together, Saryn realized that she was flanked closely by two guards, so close that they were riding almost stirrup to stirrup with her.

When less than a hundred yards separated the two forces, a fire-bolt arched directly toward Saryn. She used the smallest possible moving order-chaos-shield to angle the fire-bolt into the ground, then raised and hurled the short sword at the center of the oncoming Suthyans.

The blade and the order-chaos-knife linked to it cut through three ranks of the red-clad armsmen before striking the shields of the white wizard. The impact created a sideways flare of destruction that turned even more Suthyans into instant torches, and the hapless armsmen flamed into ashes almost before they could scream.

Saryn drew a second blade and released it, aimed directly at the indistinct shape of the wizard—the only remaining mounted figure in the middle of the Suthyan force.

A smaller chaos-reaction blast followed, and the red-coated Suthyan white wizard appeared amid the shower of flame radiating from him. Saryn drew and cast a third blade, smoothing its way with darkness.

The white mage flung up an attempt at a shield, but the black blade sliced through it and buried itself in his chest. A small flare of reddish white instantly consumed the mage and his mount.

"Do you need another blade, Commander?" called the guard to Saryn's left.

"Not yet." Saryn glanced around, but there were no Suthyans close by, and the two groups of surviving red-coats split by Saryn and the Westwind charge had made no attempt at re-forming and were riding toward the gates of the hold.

As the last handful of Suthyans hurried within the western gates, and the gates closed behind them, the first squads of the northern lord-holders appeared, blades out and ready.

Saryn smiled as she saw that Hryessa had moved the Westwind guards up and to the north of the main body, giving Hryessa more freedom to move, and, incidentally, creating the impression of a far larger force. Then she glanced back at the keep. The white-granite walls looked all too imposing for a force that had no siege equipment and couldn't afford to squander its armsmen and guards. She hoped that Maeldyn and Spalkyn were correct about Henstrenn's not being able to hunker down behind the walls and wait.

Swinging the gelding back westward, she rode slowly toward the combined forces, letting the two squads close on her. From what she could see and sense, she hadn't lost any guards—this time. Saryn couldn't have said why she'd ordered the charge, but she was just happy that it had worked out . . . and that there was one less white wizard to worry about. She also couldn't help wondering how many remained . . . and how powerful they were.

Then she looked back at the keep and the solid granite walls. No matter what the other two lord-holders said, she didn't see Henstrenn and the Suthyans venturing forth anytime soon.

LXXXVIII

For nearly a glass, the joint force remained ready for an attack, before withdrawing to a position almost half a kay back from the gates. During the apparent calm, Hryessa dispatched half a squad to recover what they could from the fallen Suthyans, especially good arrow shafts; but as a result of the efforts of the white wizard, the guards returned with only thirty shafts, along with fifteen usable blades and some coins.

Shortly after the scavengers rejoined the Westwind forces, Maeldyn, Spalkyn, Zeldyan, and Saryn rode some fifty yards north of the main body, where Maeldyn reined up just far enough away from the armsmen that the four could discuss matters without being overheard while still keeping an eye on the gates to the holding.

Although the day was warm, a slightly cooler breeze out of the east kept Saryn from drowning in her own perspiration as she waited for one of the others to speak. Her head ached slightly, and every so often a small lightknife—more like a needle—jabbed at her eyes, but compared to how she had felt after earlier fights, what she was experiencing was relatively mild.

"It doesn't look like they're raging to attack us." Spalkyn's voice was ironic.

"Of course not," said Zeldyan. "He's outnumbered, and he's lost two white wizards. He'll stay behind stone until something makes him come out."

"Or until he can persuade the Suthyans to attack, or he gets reinforcements from somewhere," added Maeldyn. "That won't happen for a while. He hasn't tried to sneak out a messenger yet."

"He will. He'll offer whatever it takes to get someone else to attack us." Zeldyan's words were icy-bitter.

"Even if he does get word out, he won't get any help that soon." Spalkyn laughed harshly. "Maybe not at all."

"That means he'll try to wait us out . . . or until he sees an opportunity," Saryn finally said. "We need to decide what to do about quarters, food, that sort of thing, while we see what he'll do."

"A little less than two kays to the northeast, there are some barns and a dwelling. That's close enough to the walls, but not too close . . ." offered Spalkyn. "If we quartered in the town, it'd be the demons' own time getting out quickly; we'd get caught in the streets."

"Even at two kays, we'll need a company ready at any time," pointed out Maeldyn. "Scouts, too."

"Any farther, and we'll tire out men and mounts getting back in position."

"Henstrenn isn't going to attack unless he can do it without losses or unless all our forces are where he thinks he can defeat us," interjected Zeldyan.

"We need to put some of the armsmen on stand-down now," suggested Saryn. "Leave one company on ready for a glass or so, then have another stand ready."

"The commander's forces have already fought twice today," Maeldyn said, almost blandly.

"Mine can take the first glass." Zeldyan glanced back toward the main body.

"And ours will take the duty after that." Spalkyn then added, "If Henstrenn doesn't attack by a half glass before sunset, I'd suggest we remove to the barns and post scouts to watch the gates and walls."

"And tomorrow?" asked Zeldyan.

"Just have one company at the ready at the barns, and the others there as well. That way, we're all in one place. The rest should be prepared to saddle up quickly, but there's no point in tiring them out and waiting." Maeldyn smiled sadly. "We just need to be far enough away and prepared enough that he can't surprise us, and rested enough that we can attack him if we get the chance."

Saryn nodded. They weren't trying a siege, but a loose holding action until they could come to grips with Henstrenn and the Suthyans. As Zeldyan rode toward the Lornians, Saryn let the chestnut walk toward Hryessa, where she reined up.

"Ser?"

"Have them all back off and stand down. We're going to wait a bit longer to see what happens."

"They've been beaten twice today. Do you think they'll try again?"

"We don't know how many Suthyans and wizards are behind that wall," replied Saryn. "In his position, I wouldn't, but most of the lord-holders here do things I wouldn't think wise." She shrugged. Inside, she had a feeling that Henstrenn wasn't finished for the day, but since she couldn't explain why, she only said, "Just make sure that they're not too far from their horses or their weapons."

Hryessa nodded, then turned her mount. "Squad leaders, forward!"

Saryn rode back to join Zeldyan and Undercaptain Maerkyn, reining up next to the lady-holder, and asking, "What do you feel that Henstrenn will do next?"

"Whatever he thinks will catch us off guard and cost him little. I can't help but notice one thing. He hasn't yet used any of his own armsmen against us, especially against you, Commander."

"Just like he took the east road and sent Kelthyn down the river road."

"Oh, I am most certain that he pointed out to Lord Kelthyn that the river road was the shorter distance to Veryna . . ."

Using the truth . . . like Ryba. Except that Ryba wasn't quite so vicious and self-centered . . . was she?

". . . and he doubtless had some other reason to send Jaffrayt with Kelthyn." Zeldyan's quiet voice was cutting.

After a time, Saryn rode back to rejoin Hryessa and keep watch on the gates to the holding keep with both eyes and senses.

Another glass passed . . . uneventfully.

As the lower edge of the sun touched the rolling hills to the west of the river, Zeldyan ordered her company to withdraw to the barns, and Saryn gave the order to Hryessa for the Westwind forces to follow but to keep their arms at the ready. The Lornians were almost a kay to the northeast of the walls and halfway to the quartering area, with the Westwind contingent some three hundred yards away from the forces of the northern lord-holders, when Saryn heard a trumpet call.

She could sense activity within the gates and immediately ordered, "Westwind! To the rear, ride!" Then she urged the gelding out to the side and galloped up to the new front of the Westwind force. While she would have preferred not to lead with sixth squad, there was no help for it on such short notice. "Forward!"

She and the guards had covered about a hundred yards when the holding gates swung open, and riders in brown and yellow boiled out, heading for the company and a half of the northern lord-holders.

"Ready bows!"

"Ready bows!" echoed Hryessa and the two squad leaders.

"Fire!" snapped Saryn, knowing that any amount of delay would help.

Shafts began to rake the Henstrenn's advancing armsmen, and a number fell, but Saryn could see that, before that long, trying to target the attackers would result in shafts striking Maeldyn's and Spalkyn's forces.

"Cease fire! Bows away. Charge!"

The attackers had barely slammed into the front ranks of the northern forces when a series of trumpet calls echoed from the holding keep, and

Henstrenn's armsmen broke off the attack and galloped back to the holding before Saryn and the Westwind guards could reach them. The gates
closed behind them, and Saryn slowed her guards for the last yards before
she halted a few yards short of Maeldyn.

"Do you always look for a fight, Commander?" asked Spalkyn, grinning broadly as he joined the two.

"I was just going to make sure that they couldn't get away so that you
could fight them," Saryn countered with a smile. Her eyes scanned the
front lines of the armsmen, and came up with several empty saddles, but
there were also a good fifteen or so Duevekan armsmen down and unmoving, although the northern armsmen had gathered up the surviving
horses.

"Lord Henstrenn seems reluctant to fight Westwind." Maeldyn's
words were sardonic.

"I'd hoped to trap them between us," Saryn said.

"He saw that. Much as I hate to admit it, his hasty retreat was the wis-
est course for him."

"He's a slimy, slippery sort," added Spalkyn.

That's something we all knew.

"We might as well all head for the barns," Maeldyn said.

Saryn agreed with that, but she turned to Hryessa, who had joined
her. "Send a half squad to see how many shafts they can recover. If the
gates open, they're to drop everything and ride to join us."

Hryessa nodded and eased her mount away.

"Your archers took down a few of those brown-coats," Maeldyn
noted. "That's something I don't think Henstrenn had expected."

"I'm very glad he didn't." Saryn concealed a frown. Maeldyn's observation raised a question for her. *Why hadn't there been a white wizard with the
attackers?* Was that because they didn't have too many left? Or because
they would only work with Suthyan forces? Or for some other reason?

"He's slippery enough to come up with something else," Spalkyn
said.

"We need to clear the area," Maeldyn said. "Everyone's tired."

"Westwind! To the rear, ride!" Saryn ordered, watching as her force
again reversed the order of riding and as ten guards moved out toward
where the brief skirmish had taken place. She nodded to the two lords. "If
you will excuse me . . ."

As she eased the gelding out to the side of sixth squad and started forward, she thought she heard a few words between Maeldyn and Spalkyn and tried to use the order-chaos flows to catch them.

". . . demon-glad she's on our side . . ." said Spalkyn.

". . . she's not . . . she's against lord-holders like Henstrenn . . ."

Whose "side" are you on? Theirs, Ryba's, your own? Again, she had no solid answer, only the wish that she could find a course that made sense for everyone.

The Westwind force was almost to the first of the large barns when Hryessa slipped her horse into position beside Saryn. "The northerners got the coins and the mounts. They didn't bother with the arrows. Even with the shafts we just recovered, we have less than fivescore remaining for all of the archers."

Saryn nodded. "I knew we were running short, but . . ." What else could she have done? It was best to use a weapon when it was most effective. "Which squad has the better archers, first or fourth?"

"First squad, I would judge, ser."

"Then give all the shafts to the ten best archers in first squad. That will have to do."

"Yes, ser."

"That was your idea, wasn't it? Or do you have a better one?"

Hryessa offered an off-center smile and a shrug. "I had thought about it, but you're the commander."

Saryn could sense that Hryessa agreed with the decision. "You're the captain, and sometimes I don't see everything." She paused. "We need to get to quarters, such as they are. Both the guards and the horses need a rest."

And so do I.

LXXXIX

Eightday dawned gray, with thick low clouds and a brisk wind out of the northeast that Saryn felt was refreshing, especially after sharing with Zeldyan a tiny room in the small house between the barns and eating hard biscuits and harder cheese for breakfast. While Saryn's tunic was warm enough for her, most of the Lornians shivered and fastened up riding jackets.

Although the scouts watching Henstrenn's keep reported no one leaving and no sign of armsmen forming up inside the walls, Saryn wanted to know more. Since she couldn't sense what was happening behind the walls from where the guards and the others were quartered, she decided to saddle the gelding and check for herself.

When she reached the end of the stable, she found that Dealdron had just finished saddling the chestnut. For a moment, she looked at him without speaking.

"I thought you would be riding out," he explained. "I put the extra blades in the knee sheaths, and there are biscuits in the saddlebags. Your water bottle is clean and filled."

"You didn't have to . . ." Saryn broke off the words. Behind his pleasant smile was a deep concern for her . . . and admiration . . . if not more . . . somewhat veiled behind swirling thoughts and feelings. She managed to smile back professionally.

"I did," he replied. "So much rests on you."

"Thank you." She took the reins from him and walked the gelding out of the barn.

Although she had said nothing to Hryessa, when Saryn mounted up outside, a half squad of guards from fifth squad rode to join her. The lead guard inclined her head. "The captain said we were to accompany you, ser."

"Thank you. We'll be riding to check the keep walls." Saryn urged the gelding forward, thinking as she did, *First Dealdron . . . and now this . . .*

Yet she had to admit to herself that going to check on the walls un-escorted would have been dangerous and foolish. As for Dealdron, it was clear that he'd put her on a pedestal and would have liked to have done far more. Yet he had never made even the slightest of improper gestures or comments. *Ostler or not, he is kind and intelligent.*

She shook her head, then smiled ruefully as she considered the male lord-holders—and their sons—that she'd encountered. Maeldyn was the only one she'd found intelligent and perceptive enough for her, not that she was attracted to the outwardly stern lord. Yet . . . a plasterer and ostler she found more attractive than lord-holders?

Saryn almost snorted. Given the lord-holders she'd met, Dealdron was more lordly than any of them, and probably more intelligent to boot, not to mention handsome and kind. He'd also kept learning from the time he had come to Westwind.

As she neared the walls of Henstrenn's keep, she extended her senses, trying to discern any activity beyond the stone barrier. Before long, she reined up a good half kay from the north walls and studied the keep. Even with her senses, she could detect no sign of formations or concentrations of men or horses. She had the feeling that, even if she remained watching all morning, she would neither see nor sense any such activity.

Even so, she did watch as she rode westward to where she could see the lane down to the main road, then back to where she could see the other eastern lane that led down to the main road farther east, then to the town proper. There were no signs of activity or reinforcements.

Finally, after another half glass, she rode back to the barns and the makeshift staging area, where she unsaddled and groomed the gelding before watching as Hryessa directed the newer guards in arms drills.

Midafternoon came, and when the latest report from the scouts con-tinued to indicate that Henstrenn and his forces remained quiet behind the walls, Maeldyn requested that Zeldyan and Saryn join him and Spalkyn outside the stable that was far too small for all the horses.

"Unless we press him," began the dour-looking lord-holder, "Hen-strenn is not going to leave his walls. I'd like to suggest that we burn down the small pearapple orchard closest to the eastern gates. That orchard isn't that close to anything else."

"How many companies should we have standing by in case he does decide to attack?" asked Spalkyn.

"I would suggest ours and those of Lady Zeldyan, with the commander's forces ready to saddle up and ride out quickly, if need be."

"What do you suggest if he does not respond?" asked Zeldyan. "Staying here all harvest, fall, and winter?"

"If need be," replied Maeldyn mildly. "The alternative is far worse."

"We should at least try to provoke him," said Spalkyn.

"He will not respond," Zeldyan replied.

"That may be, but it will be an indication to his people of just how little he thinks of anything but himself."

They already should know that. They just haven't ever been able to do anything about it. Saryn refrained from uttering the thought and merely nodded.

"Then let it be done." Zeldyan's voice was weary. "I will order my armsmen up and join you." She turned and walked away.

Spalkyn nodded and headed away.

Maeldyn looked at Saryn. "You said little, Commander."

"There was little to say."

"Might I ask your views?"

"Torching the orchard will not persuade Henstrenn to do anything that is not in his interest or survival. It may be necessary to show that we gave warning, in order to placate those lord-holders who are not here."

"You do not have a high opinion of lord-holders, I fear."

"I have a much higher opinion of those with whom I ride," Saryn countered.

"Otherwise, you would not be riding with us, I suspect."

Saryn smiled and shrugged.

Maeldyn laughed softly.

"Until later." Saryn turned and headed toward the barn.

Again, Dealdron had the gelding saddled and ready for Saryn, and, once more, a half squad of guards were ready to escort her. This time, the escort was formed of women from first squad, and all bore bows as well.

Saryn rode to the pearapple orchard with Zeldyan. The Westwind guards paralleled the first squad of the Lornian company, taking the shoulder of the dirt lane in single file, then re-forming once Zeldyan and Saryn reined up.

Saryn waited beside Zeldyan at the front of the Lornian company, as armsmen from Maeldyn's squads put torches to the trees.

It took two glasses in the still and hot harvest air before the last tree was nothing but a charred husk. The odor of charcoal, burned wood, and the fainter acrid scent of burned pearapples filled the late afternoon . . . but the gates of Duevek keep remained closed as Maeldyn, Spalkyn, Zeldyan, and Saryn watched.

Once the fire had died away, Maeldyn and Spalkyn rode to join the two women.

"It appears you were right," offered Maeldyn.

"I have the feeling that we could burn the entire countryside to ashes, and Henstrenn still wouldn't leave his walls," Saryn said.

"Would any of you?" asked Zeldyan.

"We'll have to see what tomorrow brings," Spalkyn said. "Henstrenn may reconsider matters after he has thought them over."

"Tomorrow won't change anything," Zeldyan replied tartly. "Henstrenn would sacrifice every man, woman, and child on his lands to save his skin."

"Especially with two women after him," added Saryn.

"Women have often been the downfall of men," said Maeldyn pleasantly, "but you, Commander, have destroyed more than any single woman in the memory of Lornth, or possibly even in the time of Cyador before."

Saryn smiled politely in response to the mostly good-natured banter. "You might recall, Lord Maeldyn, that in every single instance, I was attacked first. In fact, Lord Henstrenn's armsmen offered the very first attack on me when I came to see the regents in the spring. And we were under a parley banner." She paused. "We women may forgive, but we never forget."

"Ever," murmured Zeldyan, a sound so low and under her breath that Saryn suspected she was the only one to hear that single word.

XC

Another two days passed without anyone leaving the gates of Duevek keep, at least without anyone being observed. Saryn had no doubt a messenger or two had left under cover of darkness, and that concerned her, because each day that passed made the possibility of aid coming to Henstrenn more likely. Just before noon on threeday, with a blazing harvest sun beating down on the land, Maeldyn, Spalkyn, Zeldyan, and Saryn once more met, this time in the shade of the eaves of the larger barn.

"He's not going to fight us anytime soon." Spalkyn frowned. "He knows we can't break the walls. He's wagering that we don't have the supplies and patience to wait him out."

"We don't have the armsmen to waste trying to scale the walls," Maeldyn pointed out.

"If we wait too long, the heirs of the other southern lord-holders will gather forces to come to relieve him," predicted Zeldyan. "He has to have slipped out a messenger by now."

"They might rather attack our lands," added Spalkyn dourly.

"The Jeranyi will begin to gather as well," added Zeldyan.

"And the Suthyans in the north," added Maeldyn.

Saryn considered the situation. Sooner or later, she would have to act, because it was becoming clearer and clearer that none of the lord-holders of Lornth had the strength to be an effective overlord. Henstrenn wasn't any stronger than the others, except through the support offered by the Suthyans, and if he became overlord, Lornth would become little more than a vassal state of Suthya. Still . . . she decided to wait just a bit longer before saying anything.

For a time, no one spoke.

Finally, Saryn spoke. "If Henstrenn doesn't engage us by dusk tonight, I'll try something before dawn tomorrow. If it works, the gates will come down at first light, and we can attack immediately . . ." She let her words trail off.

Maeldyn and Spalkyn exchanged glances.

"Might we ask what you have in mind?" Maeldyn looked inquiringly at Saryn.

"A way to break the gates down." Saryn paused. "It will only be good for one set of gates. Which would be better?"

Maeldyn looked to Spalkyn. "You're the only one who's been there."

"That was years ago."

The other three fixed their eyes on the square-bearded lord.

"Ah . . . well . . . back then the eastern gates would have been better. They may well be now. They're stronger, but they open onto a paved area that splits in two ways—to the front of the villa and to the rear courtyard. Coming in that way would trap their armsmen against the western gates."

"The eastern gates, then?" asked Saryn.

"That would seem best," Maeldyn said. "Do you intend to lead the attack, as well?"

"No," replied Saryn. "Someone should be ready to attack as soon as the gates are breached, but I'll be on foot close to the gates when that happens. It will take a little time for us to remount and re-form. It makes more sense for my forces to be in position to keep anyone from being outflanked or to deal with any white wizards." *And I have no idea what sort of shape I'll be in at that point.*

"You want us—" began Spalkyn.

"Lord Spalkyn," interjected Zeldyan firmly. "The commander has so far led each fight since we reached Duevek. She has also led in the battles against five other lords. I may be speaking where I know naught of what is required, but I gather that what she plans to do involves great danger to her." Zeldyan turned to Saryn. "Might that be so?"

"It is dangerous," Saryn admitted. "It might be very dangerous. I had hoped not to have to try it."

"Have you done . . . whatever this is . . . before?" asked Maeldyn.

"Yes. It worked." Saryn looked directly at the stern-faced lord-holder. "Do you want the gates down or not?"

"I will lead my company first," offered Zeldyan in a matter-of-fact tone.

Abruptly, Maeldyn laughed, shaking his head, murmuring about the deadliness of women. When he stopped chuckling, he turned first to Zeldyan. "You have already risked much, Lady." His eyes went to Saryn. "As have you, Commander. We will lead. At what signal should we attack?"

"When the gates fail, you will know it." Saryn's voice was dry. "We will join you as soon as we can."

"You have not been known to tarry, Commander, for which we can all be grateful."

Translated loosely, thought Saryn, *the sooner you join the fray, the happier we'll all be.* But would they be so happy if they knew what had to follow? Saryn thought Maeldyn might suspect, but she doubted that Zeldyan would have considered the matter. "We will not tarry any longer than absolutely necessary. We need most of the blood shed to be that of Henstrenn's men and that of the Suthyans."

Zeldyan nodded.

"How far back should we be . . . and when?" asked Maeldyn.

"About three hundred yards . . . a half glass before first light . . . one Westwind squad will be at five hundred yards, the others slightly farther back . . ."

The four discussed their plans for almost a glass before it became clear that once the basic outline was laid out, there was little else that they could determine with any certainty.

As she walked away from the others after they finished their discussion, Saryn began to worry even more. Could she take down the gates and still have enough ability left to function? To do what else needed to be done? And then to do what was required beyond that?

Did she want to? Saryn shook her head. What real choice did she have if she were to stand behind what she believed?

Dealdron stood at the corner of the barn, as if he had been waiting for her. He smiled warmly. "Good afternoon, Commander and Angel."

"Good afternoon."

"You look worried."

"That's because I am."

"Then you will be attacking the holding tomorrow."

Saryn raised her eyebrows. "You're presuming a great deal."

Dealdron smiled sadly. "I think not. Lord Henstrenn remains behind his walls. You just met with the other lords and the lady. You are worried. You do not show that you are worried unless you are very worried—"

Saryn couldn't help but smile. "That's enough, Dealdron," she said warmly. "You've made your point."

He grinned back at her, clearly amused. "Only because it is in words. In all else . . ." He shrugged.

"I doubt that I know a fraction of what you do in practical skills, things like stonework, plastering, carpentry, horses . . ."

"Skill at arms is most practical in Candar, Commander."

"I would that it were not. I would that . . ." She shook her head. "We do what we must."

"So we do." His eyes fixed on her for a long moment before he offered an embarrassed smile. "When would you like the gelding to be ready?"

"A glass before first light."

"He will be ready."

"Thank you. I need to find Hryessa."

"She's giving the newer ones more training by the smaller barn."

Saryn nodded and turned, walking slowly toward the other barn. The momentary intensity of his glance had unnerved her, more than unnerved her. *Why? Because you might actually feel something for him?*

Tomorrow would come all too soon, she reminded herself. *All too soon.* After that, she could consider what she might feel.

XCI

Not surprisingly, Saryn did not sleep well on threeday night and ended up waking even earlier than she needed to. After dressing without lighting the single lamp, although she suspected that Zeldyan was already awake, she slipped out and made her way through the darkness toward the stable, thinking about what lay ahead.

She wasn't skilled enough with the order-chaos flows to deal with the iron straps and hinges that held the gates in place, but she didn't have to be. All she had to do was link enough nodes in the stone that held the hinges to destroy the support.

All? She smiled wryly. She also had to blow the gates in a way that left her functional afterwards, because taking down the gates was only a prelude to the battle, not the entire battle, as had been the case when she had dealt with the Gallosian army marching on Westwind.

Both Hryessa and Dealdron were waiting for her in the light of the lamp just outside the stable door. Dealdron held the reins to the gelding, already saddled.

"Fourth squad is almost ready," said the captain.

Saryn nodded. They'd decided the night before to save first squad—and the squad's ten archers—for what followed Saryn's efforts with the gates. "And the rest of the company?"

"They'll be ready in less than half a glass. We will leave shortly after you and fourth squad. We will circle to the north so that no one can hear us before we ride toward the gates, and we will stand ready at half a kay."

"Stay well back of the others until the gates are down."

"We can do that, but we will move up to cover you." Hryessa smiled. "The others need to do some of the work."

They do . . . for more than one reason. "We'll let them." *But I don't want very many Suthyan survivors if we can eliminate them without losing too many guards.* "Try to pick off the ones who break and flee. We don't want to have to fight them later. They're the kind who cause trouble time after time."

"Yes, ser."

"I need to be going."

Dealdron handed her the reins, and said quietly, "If you would, Commander . . . take care of yourself."

Not quite impulsively, she put her hand over his for an instant before taking the reins, squeezing it gently, if but for a moment. "Thank you." She could sense his confusion and consternation . . . and found it touching. "I'll do my best."

Then she swung up into the saddle and checked the knee sheaths. Both held blades, giving her four with the two in her battle harness. She hoped that four would be enough. She nodded to Dealdron and Hryessa, then turned the gelding toward fourth squad, formed up some twenty yards away on the flat ground beyond the stable.

She reined up just short of Klarisa. "Squad leader."

"Commander."

"Once we're within a few hundred yards of the walls, I'll need one guard to ride closer with me and take care of my mount. You and the squad will hold for my return."

"Yes, ser. Ishelya will be riding with you. She's one of the best horse-women we have." Klarisa turned. "Guard Ishelya, forward."

Even in the darkness, as Ishelya rode forward, Saryn could see and sense that the guard was small and muscular.

"Sers." Ishelya inclined her head.

"Head out, squad leader," Saryn said. "We want to be five hundred yards northeast of the eastern gates."

"Yes, ser." Klarisa added in louder voice, "Squad, forward. Silent riding."

Close to a quarter glass had passed, Saryn judged, before the squad came to a halt. Only a few lamps glimmering to the southwest marked the darker silhouette of the keep walls and the buildings within the granite barrier.

"Hold here until the gates fall."

"Yes, ser."

Saryn turned to her escort. "Let's go."

While Saryn wanted to hurry, a fast walk was far quieter, and it took a while before she sensed she was perhaps seventy yards from the dark walls. She reined up and dismounted, then handed the gelding's reins up to the guard. "Ishelya," she said, her voice low, "I want you to ride back out another fifty yards and wait. There will be an explosion if I'm successful. When that happens, ride back here with my mount as quickly as you can."

"Yes, ser."

Saryn turned and began to walk quietly toward the walls, using her sight and senses to try to avoid anything that might cause her to trip or stumble. The sound might well alert a sentry. Then, too, a sentry might still see her, but that was less likely in the darkness since she had ridden to a point not opposite the gates, but opposite the walls some fifty yards north-west of the gates. That was so she could walk straight to the wall in an area where there were no lamps close by and hug the wall as she moved closer to the eastern gates.

Dodging around bushes and clumps of grass and piles of other odor-iferous substances made those fifty yards seem much farther . . . and her progress much slower, but she finally stood beneath the walls, trying to ig-nore some of the odors. From what she could sense, there were no sentries posted on the wall above her. The nearest was some twenty yards from the northern edge of the gates.

She glanced eastward. Was there the faintest hint of light along the horizon?

Step by step she edged along the rough outer surfaces of the stone un-til she was within ten yards of the sentry, where she stopped and extended her senses. She was closer than when she had severed the mountain ledge from the mesa . . . but then she'd been in no shape to do much of anything else afterwards. By getting nearer this time, she hoped that it wouldn't be quite so much of a strain on her.

A cough echoed from the sentry, and she froze for a moment, then con-tinued to use her senses to feel for the junctures and nodes in the stone where order or chaos were more concentrated, trying to avoid the iron hinges and fastenings that felt silvery grayish black to her senses. Unlike the rock of the mountain ledge she had exploded, the quarried granite held flecks of order and chaos all along the edges where the stone had been cut, but those flecks were so tiny she could barely sense them. The nodes she did find were more uniform in size and strength, but there did not seem to be quite so many in a given area. That meant she'd have to link more junctures together and tie them to the area around the gate hinges.

Although she knew that she was running out of time, she forced herself to be careful and methodical—linking, joining, smoothing the flows, almost like creating an electrical circuit, except that all the lines were live . . . or would be when enough were connected.

Another cough jolted her, especially the words from the wall above and to the east of where she stood flattened against the stone.

". . . you see anything, Kulyn?"

". . . something out there . . . can't make out . . . maybe a rider . . ."

". . . could be one of their scouts, watching us . . ."

". . . got a real bad feeling, Undercaptain. They got something against us . . . not going away . . ."

The undercaptain laughed. "What can they do so long as we man the walls?"

Saryn forced herself to continue creating the flow of order and chaos targeted at the stone supports of the gates, letting the words drift over her. She had to keep working because the eastern horizon was definitely getting lighter, and it wouldn't be long before she was totally exposed—she might be already if anyone looked down.

"Sargyl says they got a mage, ser . . ."

"Might have a black one . . . you didn't see any fire-bolts coming from them, did you? Besides, the black ones can only defend, and that won't take the walls."

"Begging your pardon, ser, but there weren't many from twentieth company that made it back . . . and they were fighting women."

"Renegades from Westwind, Lord Henstrenn says." The undercaptain laughed again. "If those are the renegades, we're better off leaving the Roof of the World alone."

Saryn almost smiled, but she could feel the energy building, as if everything were flowing toward the stone, and she dropped to the ground, flattening herself as much as she could.

CRUMMPPTT!

Beneath her, the ground shivered and shook for a moment . . . and then something hammered her flat. Waves of light and darkness sloshed back and forth in her skull, then subsided into a dull ache. She lifted her head and glanced around. A pillar of dust rose from where the gates had been, and she could feel the thunder of hoofs as the northern lords' company galloped toward the gap in the walls.

Quickly, she scrambled to her feet and began to run out toward where she sensed Ishelya was riding. No one seemed to notice her. For that, she was grateful. She was also glad she seemed to have some ability to sense and use the order and chaos flows, but the dull ache in her skull reminded her that she needed to be careful . . . very careful.

As Ishelya brought both horses to a stop, Saryn swung up into the saddle, then glanced back toward where the gates had been. Half of Maeldyn's forces were within the walls, and without even trying, Saryn could sense the rising number of deaths. She just hoped most of those were Duevekan or Suthyan.

She turned the gelding toward fourth squad, realizing that the rest of the Westwind forces had almost joined the squad. As she rode toward her force, behind her she began to sense men and mounts milling around, moving slowly westward within the walls.

"Captain! To the western gates! The Suthyans are trying to escape."

"On me!" ordered Hryessa. "To the western gates!"

Saryn let the bulk of the riders pass her before swinging the gelding parallel to the column, noting that Hryessa already had each squad five abreast. Three more guards detached themselves from fourth squad and moved into position, flanking her on both sides. Then, the rest of fourth squad moved in behind them.

On Hryessa's orders, no doubt.

As Saryn neared the western end of the holding walls, she saw that the armsmen riding out through the western gates, even before they were fully open, were clad in red and gold.

"Squads abreast!" came the order from Hryessa, followed by, "Fourth squad hold for the commander! All others, charge!"

Saryn couldn't help but frown, as she began to gather and weave the order and chaos flows once more, hoping she would have the strength to divert at least some chaos-bolts away from the guards.

The first guards reached the Suthyans without a single fire-bolt being cast, and the short swords of the guards ripped into the red-clad arms-men, who fought with a combination of desperation and resignation. That was the way it felt to Saryn.

There aren't any white wizards left?

A few moments later, a squad in red and gold wheeled away from the melee and angled due north from the walls, as if to make a break between the Westwind and the Lornian company that was following the others in though the eastern gates. Saryn could sense chaos amid the withdrawing Suthyan squad.

That's where he is.

The last thing she wanted was any Suthyan mages surviving.

"Fourth squad! On me!" Saryn projected her voice and command, drawing the short sword from the right knee sheath.

"On the commander!" ordered Klarisa.

Fourth squad surged away from the melee and behind Saryn as she rode toward the Suthyan squad. She could sense a concentration of chaos, but no fire-bolts arched toward her.

Then . . . when they were yards from the Suthyans, a single word rang out. "Now!"

A blinding flare of white light flashed before them, so bright that Saryn could see nothing. She could still sense the Suthyans ahead, and the chaos-mage, who had turned his mount to the east and was breaking from the squad.

In the instants she had before she reached the first Suthyans, Saryn focused her order-chaos into an unseen knife wedge barely a yard wide, linked it to the blade, and flung both, directing them toward the fleeing wizard. The order-chaos-knife angled across the few riders to her left, cutting through them, and the black blade slammed through the white wizard's shields.

Another white flare flashed, and Saryn could sense nothing where the white wizard and his mount had been. She still could see nothing.

Just before reaching the first rider in the Suthyan squad, she pulled a second short sword from her battle harness and slashed at the Suthyan, slightly off to her right. His block was weak, but accurate, suggesting that he'd closed his eyes, knowing what was coming . . . the first time.

She ducked, kept moving, and back-cut, before coming up with a direct thrust under the guard of the next Suthyan. She was still operating mostly by sense, although her vision was beginning to return. Another parry and a cut, and she was behind the Suthyan squad.

She wheeled the gelding and attacked from behind.

For a time, the fight continued, but as the guards recovered their vision, more Suthyans dropped . . . and then more. Then, there were but a handful of mounted Suthyans from the small squad.

Saryn was about to move toward them, when she sensed, behind her, a smaller body of armsmen riding from the western gates, immediately beginning to turn south. She turned her head to see that they wore red and black—Keistyn's colors. With that, she wheeled the gelding.

"Fourth squad! To me! Now!"

"On the commander!"

What was left of fourth squad—or those who could respond—formed into a wedge behind Saryn as she rode toward Keistyn's armsmen. As she neared them, she recognized Keistyn himself at the forefront.

"Running away when you can't bully?" Saryn order-flung the words at him. "You don't want to fight when women make it too hard for you, little boy?"

"Do your worst, bitch commander!" Keistyn spurred the big charger directly toward Saryn and fourth squad.

Saryn didn't feel charitable, not in the slightest. She also didn't want to use any more order-chaos than she had to, but her squad was battered and outnumbered. She wove together as much order and chaos as she could and linked it to the short sword she hurled at him, with a wider and thinner chaos–cutting blade.

Keistyn's mouth opened, but no sound emerged as Saryn's blade buried itself in his chest and the chaos-knife continued onward, separating his body—and the bodies of men and mounts beside and behind him—into two sections.

Only a few armsmen on the flanks escaped the deadly wedge, and they turned their mounts almost due south and galloped away.

"Fourth squad! Re-form! On me!" Saryn glanced around, but the only riders outside the western gates were those of Westwind. Then she looked to Klarisa. "How bad was it?"

"We lost four, it looks like, in the first and second ranks . . . because of the bright light. Another four were wounded. They should recover." The squad leader shook her head. "I was lucky. I was behind you."

Saryn wouldn't have called being behind her lucky. Surviving being behind her was.

Hryessa had re-formed the remainder of the company, and Saryn led fourth squad toward the company and the guard captain.

"They're still fighting inside," Hryessa said.

Saryn glanced toward the walls, trying to extend her senses, but that effort brought lightknives and involuntary tears to her eyes. She stopped trying, although she had a sense that the fighting was largely sporadic. "They're just mopping up. We'll stand by and take anyone who tries to escape."

"Yes, ser."

Even without trying, Saryn could sense the agreement behind the captain's words.

Hryessa glanced to the north. Saryn followed the motion and saw one of their wagons rolling toward them, driven by Dealdron.

"I have more blades!" he called as he brought the wagon and the team to a halt some fifty yards away.

He shouldn't have been out here, not that close to the fighting. After a brief moment, she laughed at her thought. How many men had thought the same about women over the years, whenever a woman left "her place"?

Hryessa smiled, then looked to Saryn.

"See if anyone needs any and send a guard to get them."

"Yes, ser."

While Hryessa dealt with the blades, Saryn looked back to the holding walls and the still-open western gates. Someone was riding out . . . but the armsmen wore green and purple, and at the head was Zeldyan.

Saryn waited, even as four guards moved up to flank her.

Zeldyan, accompanied by what looked to be two squads, rode up and halted. The rear squad rode around the first and formed up parallel to it. After a moment, she spoke to Saryn. "I heard your words to Keistyn. It was Keistyn, wasn't it?"

Saryn flushed. "I was angry. He and Henstrenn plotted and plotted, and their plots killed so many who didn't have to die."

"I think everyone heard them . . . everywhere. What did you do?"

"I lost my temper," Saryn equivocated. "Then I killed him. The squad killed most of those with him."

Zeldyan nodded. "Most of those who heard what you said threw down their arms. Some others refused to surrender. It wasn't the words, but the power. For a moment, everything stopped. Even those who fought lost heart. Except Henstrenn."

"What happened to him?"

"Maeldyn went after him. He wounded Henstrenn, but Henstrenn wouldn't surrender. He ran at Maeldyn with a knife dripping something, maybe poison. Maeldyn cut him down. Henstrenn's son was killed." Zeldyan shook her head. "His own father . . ."

"He killed his own son?"

"He was yelling that better his boy die than bow to some bitches."

Saryn couldn't help but wince. With that attitude, she was more than glad Henstrenn was dead . . . but his own son? And what did that mean for Lornth? "We need to ride into the holding."

Zeldyan nodded. "It's over . . . now."

Saryn turned the gelding to head back into the captured holding. She stiffened in the saddle as she heard the faintest of murmurs, somewhere from within the Lornian squads.

". . . demon-damned bitches . . . killed too many good men . . ."

She wanted to turn and demand just where the speaker had been for the past generation with all the infighting and battles that had killed far, far more than what she had accomplished in the last season. *It wouldn't do any good. Men like that already have their minds made up, and facts they won't believe change nothing.*

She kept riding, flanked by her guards, back toward the holding, dreading seeing all the dead and wounded, even as she rode past and around the bodies of mounts and men. Behind her followed the rest of the Lornian and Westwind forces, and behind them Dealdron drove the wagon, doubtless to hold the weapons and goods that would be collected . . . in time.

XCII

For the glass after she rode into the holding of the late Lord Henstrenn, Saryn did very little but observe while the armsmen and guards searched all the buildings and rounded up the few remaining rebel armsmen, most of whom were wounded. Once those tasks had been accomplished, Saryn dismounted in the receiving courtyard and walked toward the white-granite steps leading to the entry foyer of Henstrenn's villa, an elaborate single-story structure set on a knoll within the walls.

She paused when she saw Dealdron's wagon just a few yards west of the entrance and Dealdron standing beside it, loading something into the wagon bed. "What are you doing?"

"Lord Maeldyn and his armsmen fought their way inside. Some of the guards were helping bring out bodies and weapons." He gestured to the cart behind the wagon. "The bodies go there, the weapons and tools here." He paused. "They say they're almost done."

"You're being very diligent." Her voice carried a touch of amusement.

"Too many who have skill with arms forget the costs of those arms, unlike you." He smiled at Saryn. "What is in the wagon will support three companies of yours for over a year. It could be longer."

"What of the other lords?"

Dealdron shrugged. "I just tell them that I am following orders and that they should ask you." He grinned for the briefest of moments. "There are also more than a few silvers you will need. No one else knows how many."

Saryn could not say a word for a moment, not because of what he had said but because of what lay behind the words—a clear devotion to her, at the very least. Finally, she said, "Thank you."

Dealdron just inclined his head.

As she headed up the steps, she couldn't help but wonder why she found his devotion to her so unnerving. He was good-looking and took care with his appearance. He was bright, although his formal education was certainly lacking, but he definitely had worked at learning ... and kept at it. She really didn't care that he'd been a plasterer and an ostler ... *So why does his affection upset you? Because you're actually attracted to him and yet so far above him in position? How many men have found and expressed an interest in younger women not of their "official" stature? Should it be any different for women?* She swallowed as she realized the implications of the question she'd just asked herself. *But why?* Was it because he'd never intruded in the slightest on her, and always tried to please her, not by flattery or deceit, but by doing to the best of his skills what he thought she needed done?

She shook her head. Thoughts about Dealdron would have to wait. *But they can't wait too long,* came a stray thought from somewhere.

She hurried through the villa's front foyer and down the corridor to the right, where a pair of armsmen in Maeldyn's tan and black were stationed outside a door. Stepping between them, she joined Maeldyn, Zeldyan, and Spalkyn in a small chamber, most likely the late lord-holder's private study. That location afforded a view of the town and the river through the study's wide south windows. The four sat around a square table, one Saryn suspected had been used more for gaming than for writing or meeting. She couldn't imagine Henstrenn meeting with even three other people at the same time, not unless he planned to cheat them out of something, either by gaming or politicking.

"What should we do with the prisoners?" asked Spalkyn, whose left forearm was heavily bound.

Saryn refrained from replying immediately, instead using her senses to see if there happened to be any wound chaos in Spalkyn's arm, despite the lightknives that stabbed through her eyes as she did. She found no chaos, but she reminded herself to check later ... when she had recovered more of her strength.

"They can't stay here," said Zeldyan.

"Have them help rebuild The Groves," suggested Maeldyn, "and pardon them if they do. Execute them if they refuse."

"They shouldn't be allowed back on the holding here, either," said Zeldyan. "They served Henstrenn."

"Nor in the town of Duevek," added Saryn. "Other towns in the holding lands, but not Duevek itself."

"That's reasonable," agreed Maeldyn. "Whoever succeeds Henstrenn shouldn't have to deal with that."

"That's another problem," offered Spalkyn. "There are no living heirs to Duevek. No close ones, anyway."

"What happened to his consort?" asked Saryn.

Maeldyn looked directly at her, but did not speak.

"He killed her, too?"

"He was rather possessive."

Rather possessive? How about insanely possessive? Another case where a woman ended up paying for the faults and follies of the man . . . not that Henstrenn hadn't paid as well. But so many others had paid dearly for his ambition and self-centeredness. Saryn shook her head . . . and winced because the throbbing in her skull intensified. *Why did he go to such extremes at the end? Because he wanted power and couldn't stand a woman having it? Or his own consort surviving him? Or was it all about him, proving he was the strongest and that his will would prevail?* Those questions raised another. *Are you any different in that regard? Probably not.* Even so, the lord-holder system of Lornth had proved clearly that, in the absence of the Cyadoran threat, it didn't work. Maybe it never really had, but that failure had been concealed by the infrequent Cyadoran attacks. Whatever the case, matters had to change, for the sake of both Westwind and Lornth.

"So what do we do about it?" pressed Spalkyn.

Maeldyn turned to the bearded lord-holder. "We'd best not jump to a solution. We need to think about that and not act too hastily. There may be other southern holdings facing similar situations. I don't believe Kelthyn could have had any heirs since he had no consort. Whatever we propose should be best for all Lornth. Tomorrow would be best, or even the day after."

Saryn could sense that there was more behind Maeldyn's words, but with her headache and the lightknives that her last attempt to extend her senses had caused, she wasn't about to try to discover what, especially since she had seen, time and time again, how honest the stern-faced lord really was.

"There's no provision for an overlord, either," Spalkyn said.

Maeldyn looked to Saryn. "It would seem appropriate and necessary that we gather all the remaining lord-holders of Lornth to discuss the matter. Do you have any objection to that?"

"So long as none of them brings more than a squad of armsmen," Saryn replied. "There's been enough bloodshed."

"Some of them will claim they need more protection," Spalkyn observed.

"Tell them that we will protect them from each other," Saryn replied. "You might also point out, if they question, that we have attacked no one who did not attack first."

"You might also suggest that they need not come," said Zeldyan, "but that, if they do not, they will have no voice in what happens, and none will entertain their complaints. When would you suggest?"

"Two eightdays from oneday," said Maeldyn. "It may take five days even to get the word to some . . ."

After discussing more mundane arrangements, such as quartering and supplies, the four left the study. They had just started down the hallway toward the entry foyer when a dull *clank* of metal on the stone tiles, followed by a set of lesser *clinks*, jolted Saryn.

"Son of demon!" exclaimed Maeldyn, bending down to recover his belt dagger, still in its scabbard with part of the belt that had held it, along with his coin wallet, and the silvers and golds that had spilled from the wallet.

"It looks like someone cut a lot closer to you than you thought, friend." Spalkyn laughed and began to scoop up some of the stray coins.

Zeldyan glanced back, then kept walking.

Saryn stayed with the Lady of The Groves, sensing Zeldyan had something to say, although she couldn't help but wonder what Maeldyn was discussing with Spalkyn.

"What will you do now?" asked Zeldyan cautiously.

"That will depend on who becomes Overlord of Lornth . . . and how. The whole reason I was sent was to assure that the overlord remained friendly to Westwind."

"You could claim Duevek, you know. There aren't any heirs." Zeldyan glanced back toward where Maeldyn was attempting to find somewhere to put his coin wallet, the dagger and scabbard in his hand, then added in a lower voice. "Maeldyn would certainly prefer you as a lady-holder than any would-be lord-holder from the south."

"I hadn't thought that was an acceptable possibility until a few moments ago." *A possibility, but not one acceptable to many lord-holders.* "I doubt many of the lord-holders would like that." Saryn could also see from where Zeldyan was coming.

"Whatever happens, they will not like it," Zeldyan pointed out. "The more practical the solution, the less they will wish it. Sillek wanted to be practical. He saw war with Westwind as impractical. He was forced to fight, one way or the other, either to fight Westwind or his lord-holders. Since he knew he could not win against the lord-holders, he chose to fight Westwind. He was doomed, no matter what. He did not know it then. That was why I requested your aid."

"And now?" asked Saryn, as they walked though the archway and started down the steps.

"Lornth still needs you, as do I."

What do I say to that? How much should I say? Saryn was silent for several moments before speaking. "What is needed is often not what those who have or seek power would prefer." She glanced to the paved area beyond the steps, where, in the lower portico and receiving area, waited fourth squad—drawn up across from the steps, some twenty yards back— a smaller group of Lornian riders and their squad leader just to the right of the mounting blocks at the base of the stairs, and, to the left, Dealdron, who stood beside the lead horse of the team drawing the wagon, apparently checking or adjusting the harnesses.

"Lornth must accede to what it needs, not what individual lord-holders would have," replied Zeldyan. "You, more than anyone, must know that."

"I know that, but I'm an outsider."

"You have risked more than any lord-holder."

"Except you and your father," Saryn pointed out.

"That may be, but you have power that we did not . . ."

Even with her aching head and the intermittent lightknives stabbing into her eyes, when Saryn stepped down onto the pavement of the courtyard and past the mounting blocks, heading for fourth squad and the waiting gelding, she sensed . . . something and looked up. As she did, the five Lornian armsmen, who had been holding sabres in a salute, charged forward toward Zeldyan and Saryn.

"No more bitch rulers!" yelled the squad leader.

Zeldyan looked up in total surprise.

With one hand, Saryn drew the remaining blade from her harness, and with the other she grabbed Zeldyan's sleeve and threw her up the steps. Then her blade came up into a guard position, because she was almost between two riders.

At that moment, another figure attacked the armsman on Saryn's right, driving a blade up into the man's gut before the armsman's mount ran him down.

Saryn went almost to her knees as she half parried, half blocked the heavy hand-and-a-half blade. Then she dropped her own blade and threw herself into a rolling dive past the second armsman, coming up behind the man's mount, looking for her blade.

She didn't need it. Fourth squad had surrounded the attackers, and in moments, cut all five out of their saddles.

Dealdron lay motionless on the stone beside the mounting block.

Saryn ran toward him.

Even before she knelt beside him, she could see that he was breathing, but that one arm was at an angle that indicated it was broken. She could also sense a mass of chaos within his chest, as if his ribs had been pressed in on his heart.

The arm could wait. She had to relieve the chest pressure . . . somehow.

She forced herself to concentrate, to come up with some strands, some flow of order, straightening . . . forcing . . . coercing . . . the ribs . . . muscles back . . . away. She could sense, despite the brilliant lightknives slashing into her eyes so intensely that she could not see, that the chaos-pressure on his chest had eased . . . mostly.

Slowly, she straightened, her eyes burning. *Ought to be able to do more . . . somehow . . .*

But there was nothing left within her to give, no control of order . . . nothing. She struggled to her feet.

"Commander!" Klarisa reined up beside Saryn and looked down. "Are you all right?"

"Don't put any pressure on his chest . . . Don't. His ribs are broken."

"Are you all right?" demanded the squad leader.

"Don't touch his chest," Saryn said again. "I'm fine," she began to add, when a wall of unseen black and white crashed over her, and she felt nothing.

XCIII

Saryn woke up lying on a wide bed. Her head felt as though unseen hammers were beating on both sides of it, and she could barely see through the lightknives stabbing through her eyes. She thought it was light outside, but was it still fourday? After several moments, she could make out that Hryessa stood on one side of the bed, with Zeldyan on the other.

"Commander?" asked Hryessa.

"I'm here." Saryn moved her fingers, her toes, and turned her head slightly. That made the unseen hammers beat harder. Finally, she sat up, if slowly, swinging her boots over the side of the bed. Her heels barely touched the heavy bedside carpet.

Hryessa extended a goblet. "It's ale."

Probably better than water here at the moment. Saryn took the crystal goblet with both hands and slowly sipped until she finished half the ale. The pounding subsided slightly. The lightknives did not. She handed the goblet back to Hryessa.

"I owe you once more," said Zeldyan quietly.

"No . . . you don't," replied Saryn. "They wouldn't have attacked you if I hadn't come to Lornth."

"If you had not come to Lornth, the same things would have happened, and I also would be dead. Like my son and my father."

"You are kind, Lady." Saryn was too tired to argue. "How long was I out?"

"Out?" asked Hryessa. "Oh . . . it is about a glass before sunset."

"The same day? Fourday?"

"Of course."

"Two, maybe three glasses," Saryn murmured. "How is Dealdron?"

"He is in much pain, but he says nothing. He is in a small guest chamber. We did not touch his chest."

Saryn stood, if slowly and deliberately, waiting to see if she felt dizzy. She did not. "I need to see him."

"Commander . . ."

"He saved my life. I will see him." Saryn walked slowly to the chamber doorway and into the corridor—where two guards stood, hands on the hilts of their blades.

"To the left, ser," instructed Hryessa.

Saryn kept walking until she reached another door with two guards also stationed outside. She looked to Hryessa.

"We did not wish any of the dead Lornians' friends to disturb him." The captain paused. "I will wait here. He should see you both. It will ease his mind."

Saryn opened the door and stepped inside. Zeldyan followed.

Dealdron lay on a bed narrower than the one on which Saryn had awakened but almost twice the width of a guard's bunk. His left arm had been splinted, but his chest had not been bound. Saryn was glad for that, although she knew he would need some sort of brace before he could safely move, but she wanted to be there when he had his chest bound. His forehead was beaded with sweat. His eyes were open, but fixed overhead, almost unseeing.

Saryn stepped forward until she was standing beside the bed. Zeldyan moved up closer as well, to Saryn's right.

"Dealdron," Saryn said softly, "I'm here. Thank you." What else could she say?

He blinked, then winced before speaking, slowly, as if each word were an effort. "I . . . overheard . . . knew they were up to something . . . told Klarisa to be ready . . . didn't know for what . . . should have known . . . done more . . . tried . . ."

Even without trying, Saryn could sense the pain, but she had to *know* if she had done enough. Oh-so-carefully she extended the tiniest order-thread across his chest.

". . . feels better . . ."

The worst of the chaos was gone, and his heart felt normal. As she began to feel dizzy, she released the probe, then laid a hand on his forehead. "You'll be all right. Just try to sleep."

"Are you . . . ?"

"I'm fine, now, thanks to you." She reached down and squeezed his good hand, gently.

"You are . . . my angel . . . Commander . . ." Dealdron closed his eyes, as if the words had taken every last bit of energy.

"Just rest . . . I'll be back to see you later." Saryn lifted her hand, turned, and walked slowly from the chamber.

You are my angel . . . my angel. His words rang in her ears . . . and in her thoughts.

"You care for him, do you not?" murmured Zeldyan.

"He's never asked anything of me, except to please me. And he was willing to give his own life to save mine."

"Would that there were more men like him." Zeldyan paused. "Why is he so devoted to you?"

"I saved his life and challenged him to do his best at what he could." What else could she say? And what was she going to do? For one thing, as soon as she'd recovered, she was going to make sure Dealdron healed—fully.

Then, she froze in place for a moment, recalling what Istril had said seasons before about understanding the price a woman might have to pay for any man who truly worshipped her. *Can I pay that price? Should I?*

She'd just have to see . . . as with everything else . . . But . . . somehow . . . she would.

XCIV

Three days passed before the pounding in Saryn's head fully subsided and another before she could see normally. Part of that was because after two days, she'd used more order to help when the healer had bound and braced Dealdron's chest.

Just before midmorning on oneday, she walked down the wide corridor toward the small study, where she was to meet Maeldyn. The stern-faced lord-holder had quietly requested a private meeting, one that Saryn wasn't sure she was anticipating with any pleasure, much as she trusted Maeldyn.

The Lord of Quaryn stood by the door to the study, waiting for Saryn. "Good morning, Commander." Maeldyn bowed, then gestured toward the open door. "Shall we?"

"Thank you."

Maeldyn followed her inside, then closed the door and seated himself across the square table from Saryn.

"You had some concerns," offered Saryn.

"Two eightdays from now, we are to meet in Lornth to discuss what to do about an overlord and the succession of various other lord-holders," began Maeldyn.

Saryn nodded. "That was what we agreed upon."

"Lord Henstrenn is dead, and so are Mortryd, Orsynn, Rherhn, Keistyn, Kelthyn, and Jaffrayt. And, of course, Lord Deolyn and Lord Gethen. Some of them, such as Henstrenn, Kelthyn, and Orsynn, do not even have male heirs, and there is no lord-holder of Rohrn. In fact, Kelthyn has no possible heirs whatsoever. What exactly, Angel Commander, do you intend?" Maeldyn looked almost guilelessly at Saryn.

"I was thinking of you, as a matter of fact." Saryn was, but only to bring up his name and to determine her course from his reaction.

Maeldyn shook his head, if ruefully. "I am as vain as the next man, but I am not fool enough to think I would ever have the power to rule Lornth. Of equal import is that, while I love my son dearly, he would make a poor overlord. There is also the fact that I do not have the coins expected for such a position. Do not mention Spalkyn, for his son . . ."

"I know," Saryn said quickly. "You are a man of judgment. Whom would you have as overlord?"

"You must realize, Angel, that any lord-holder of Lornth you name will be hated and thought a puppet of Westwind. That would also be true of anyone you found acceptable, even if you did not name such a person. Anyone you would not name or could not support would be an even worse Overlord of Lornth than those who have come before."

"You're saying that I can name no one? Am I supposed to turn Lornth over to the Suthyans or the Jeranyi?"

"I would not wish that on the worst of lord-holders . . . nor did I suggest it. You already act as much as an overlord."

"That would not set well with many." *Almost none, from what I've seen so far.* "Also, I don't even have a consort, much less any children."

"You still are young enough to have children, are you not?"

He's serious, deadly serious. "I could have children, if I so desired, but why me?"

"Because the only one who can heal Lornth is someone powerful enough that no lord would even think of rebelling, and you are the only one in the land who is that strong."

"You're saying that only a tyrant can hold it together."

"Can you think of anyone else? Even the Suthyans would hesitate to strike, knowing that Westwind would aid you. Was it accidental that you just happened to be in a position to halt and destroy the last Suthyan white wizard? Or that you did not even entertain surrender in dealing with most of the lord-holders?"

"I offered terms to a number of the lord-holders." *Not all, but a number.* "They refused to consider them."

"And the Suthyans? Would you have granted them terms had they asked?"

"No," Saryn admitted. "I did not want any of them to return to Suthya."

"Why might that be?"

"So that the Suthyan Council would think twice about sending mages or wizards against either Westwind or Lornth . . . and so that they would have fewer to send if they so decided."

"You see?" Maeldyn smiled. "You already think as an overlord should. In time, if it is not true already, you will be stronger than your Marshal." He paused. "Do not tell me you have not thought about it." His face was serious, but Saryn could detect amusement behind the words.

"I did not . . . not until we reached Duevek. Still . . . just assuming that I agree to your idea, Lord Maeldyn, how will you and all the other lord-holders feel if I insist that every lord-holder name his eldest daughter as his heir, and if he does not have a daughter, his sister's eldest daughter? Or perhaps his eldest son's consort?"

"Do you think that wise?"

"Wise? I don't know, but something has to be done to stop this practice of bloodying the entire land to prove who is mightier."

"How would the daughters prove their ability?"

"I have an idea about that."

"I thought you might." Maeldyn's voice was dry.

Yet Saryn could not sense either anger or dissatisfaction behind the dour-looking lord's words. "I would have them all trained at arms in the Westwind style, and none who could not be guards would be allowed to become lady-holders."

"You seem to have that ability to train women."

Saryn shook her head. "I can, but Captain Hryessa has done all the training in Lornth. I've had little enough time."

"Except to teach my daughters more in an afternoon than I could have in an eightday. Your captain is also most adept at recruiting. In your name."

Saryn smiled wryly. Already, more than a score of local women had appeared outside the holding walls, begging to be trained as guards.

"Before we reach Lornth, you will have more than two companies under arms. That is twice, perhaps four times what any other lord-holder now has available for men at arms. Even your head ostler was able to kill two men."

Two? Saryn hadn't realized that, but she hadn't asked, either.

"Oh, one other matter. Spalkyn, Lady Zeldyan, and I all agree that, should you agree to become overlord, you will also receive Duevek as your holding, as well as Lornth. With two holdings, you will have enough in income, in addition to tariffs, to support the forces required of an overlord."

"And the others? Will they agree?"

"The ones who are no longer with us and have no heirs certainly cannot object. From what Lady Zeldyan has indicated, neither Jharyk nor Barcauyn will object, and that would suggest a majority will support you."

"Or not oppose me openly," said Saryn.

"They will all know that the alternatives are far worse."

"What about Lord Spalkyn?"

"He cannot state so openly, but he would be most relieved if one of his daughters could succeed him."

"They do show promise," Saryn admitted.

Maeldyn glanced toward the study door. "If you would excuse me, Commander, I believe Lady Zeldyan would like a word with you."

"You all have talked this over, haven't you?"

Maeldyn stood, then shrugged. "Like you, we wish the fighting and the bloodshed to end. I especially agree with your point about Lornth needing a tyrant—a benevolent and intelligent tyrant, but one who will not hesitate to destroy a rebellious lord. Times have changed, and if we do not change with them, we will perish. I would preserve what we can, rather than lose all."

Saryn stood. "I would like to talk to Zeldyan before I make a final decision." *As if you already haven't, but there is the business of being political.*

"That is most reasonable and right." Maeldyn smiled knowingly.

Saryn almost shook her head ruefully. She definitely needed Maeldyn as one of her advisors.

The stern-faced lord opened the door, holding it for Zeldyan, who entered quietly. Maeldyn stepped out and closed the door behind himself. Saryn gestured to the table, but only reseated herself as Zeldyan sat down.

"You are going to become overlord, aren't you?" said Zeldyan, although her tone made clear that she was not really asking the question.

"Lord Maeldyn requested that I consider it. I told him that I would not decide until after I talked with you."

"You don't need my approval."

"But your advice and support I do need," said Saryn as warmly as she could. "You will be one of the most influential holders if I so decide."

"You are kind."

"I'm trying to be practical. You deserve to hold your family's lands. You deserve to be the overlord . . ." Saryn hoped Zeldyan would reply.

"The other lord-holders would not agree, and I do not have the power or the ability at arms that you have shown. You have bested everyone who has come against you." Zeldyan smiled. "Besides . . . does either of us have a choice?"

Saryn laughed softly. "You have me, Lady. For everyone's sake, including my own . . . what choice do I have? I cannot return to Westwind. Westwind cannot support another two companies of guards at present." *Nor could I deal with Ryba any longer.* "There is no lord-holder powerful enough to hold Lornth together or to stand against the Suthyans or the Jeranyi." Saryn stopped.

"And what of me, now that I have served your purpose, Saryn?"

"You did not serve my purpose." Saryn smiled sadly. "I came to Lornth with only the goal of preserving your regency. The problem was—"

"That to preserve me, you ended up destroying the Lornth that was, just as the other angels began that destruction in order to save me. Now, what of me?"

"I would still be your friend and your supporter. You hold The Groves, Lady, in your own right, and you may consort as you like, if that is your choice, or not. One way or another, you will determine your family's holdings. I will stand behind you, as I always have. You know, as do Lord Maeldyn and Lord Spalkyn, that the time has come for change." Saryn shook her head. "You may not believe me, but I never left the Roof of the World with this, or anything like it, in mind."

Zeldyan smiled wanly. "That I do know, and that makes it all the sadder, that we could not resolve our differences, and that an angel from beyond the Rational Stars must descend to set things right. You will create a legend, you know, and generations of girls will look to you."

And if that is so, generations of men will curse me. "Only if I am successful, and that will be so only if you and others support me."

"How could I not? You saved my life, and you are the only one who will grant me my due as my father's daughter."

"For your sake," Saryn said gently, "I wish it had not come to this."

"I thank you for those words." Zeldyan offered another sad smile.

Saryn could sense the mixture of sadness, acceptance, and appreciation . . . and the grief beneath, which the former regent might bear all the rest of her days. "I would also be your friend . . . Zeldyan."

"I would be yours . . . also."

"I would like that very much." And that, also, was truth, Saryn knew, for, if matters did work out, Zeldyan might well be the only woman in all Lornth who would understand a fraction of what Saryn felt.

XCV

Immediately after breakfast on fiveday—prepared and served in a cheery breakfast room by a kitchen staff that seemed exceedingly happy to welcome Saryn as the new lady-holder, Saryn made her way down the main corridor to the small guest chamber where Dealdron lay on the wide bed, propped up at a slight angle.

"Good morning," she offered as she stepped into the room.

"Good morning, Commander." His brow furrowed. "I dreamed you were here earlier. So was Lady Zeldyan . . . before my chest was bound."

"We were." *And I have been several times when you didn't recognize me.* "You didn't dream it. She came to thank you for saving her life. She and the other lord-holders have returned to their holdings for the present." Maeldyn and Spalkyn had actually provided an escort for Zeldyan, and half of Maeldyn's armsmen would remain at The Groves, along with what remained of Zeldyan's armsmen, to keep order and control over the prisoners rebuilding and repairing the villa and its outbuildings.

Saryn concentrated on sensing Dealdron's ribs and chest, as she had done two days earlier, when he had been slightly feverish and disoriented. There was still some wound chaos in places, but far less than what she had removed or neutralized before.

The younger man shifted his weight on the pillows supporting him.

"Hold still, if you will."

Dealdron opened, then closed his mouth.

This time, it took only a few moments to remove the chaos, and she could sense that he was beginning to heal. She straightened slightly, then smiled. "You'll be fine, but not all that soon."

"You're a healer, too, aren't you?"

"I can do some healing. I'm not a healer."

"I wouldn't be here otherwise."

"Probably not," she replied with a smile, "but I wouldn't be here if you hadn't attacked those Lornians."

"I only got two of them."

"That was enough. I blocked one other and dived free. Klarisa and fourth squad killed the rest of them. You also saved Lady Zeldyan. She was most grateful."

"The girls who brought me food, they said you were the new lord-holder here."

"For now, perhaps for longer. All the lord-holders will be meeting in Lornth an eightday from next oneday. That will decide who will be the Overlord of Lornth."

"You should be the overlord," Dealdron said. "You have defeated all who came against you, and you are fair and just. Most of them are not."

"I try to be fair," Saryn acknowledged. "Being just is harder."

"You see that. Most do not."

Saryn could sense the warmth and the affection. Had Dealdron not still been so weak and injured, she suspected she might well have sensed a great deal more, and for a moment, and behind a pleasant smile, she had to struggle to maintain her composure. She did bend forward and take his hand for a moment. "You see in me what you would like to see."

"No, Angel, I see what you are and will be."

Saryn swallowed, taken aback by the faith and affection in and behind his words. Could she ever live up to that faith? Yet . . .

She managed another smile as she withdrew her hand. "You need to get well. Then we'll talk about what happens."

"What will happen is what will happen, but whatever happens, you are my angel."

One way or another you will be his angel, but what do you say? She managed a grin. "What kind of angel, we'll have to see."

She did not quite flee his chamber, but she did take several deep breaths once she was back in the corridor alone for a moment. *Whatever might be, living up to his faith might be even harder than what has come before.*

After a time, she headed out of the villa and toward the barracks area to find Hryessa.

The guard captain was watching as Klarisa directed the newer guards and even some recruits, it looked like, through the morning warm-up exercises. When Hryessa saw Saryn, the captain immediately turned and walked toward her commander.

"More new faces, I see," observed Saryn.

"There are a few more every day. Some days, more than a few. You have inspired many."

"Will they stay inspired?" Saryn had her doubts.

"Very few have left. Very few, even after seeing battles and other guards dying."

It was hard for Saryn to accept that life for women in Lornth had been that hard, but it must have been. Otherwise, why would they remain so cheerfully? "We need to think about forming and training a full second company. Who would you suggest as the undercaptains for the two companies? The squad leaders of first and fourth squads?"

"They have been acting as such . . . at times."

"You'll have to watch over them closely." Saryn grinned. "Not that you haven't been."

"I have, but they know what to do. They have watched us both."

Saryn shook her head with a wry expression. *I just hope they've watched you more. They shouldn't be trying some of what I've done.*

"They need to see that a woman can be fearless and successful, Commander."

Saryn didn't want to get into that. "How many should we take to Lornth?"

"I will take a full company with you. If you are to be overlord, we must be prepared. But we must leave some guards here."

"What do you plan?" asked Saryn.

"Second company will be what remains of fourth squad and the newer trainees and the new recruits. Klarisa can be most forceful. We will even have enough for a third company before long. For now, they should certainly be able to hold Duevek."

Saryn winced. Every time she heard the name Duevek, it grated on her. The holding name needed to change as well. "How are those of the holding staff taking matters?"

Hryessa raised her eyebrows, as if to ask why Saryn would even ask.

"Because everyone is so respectful around me. I'd like to know how they feel when I'm not around."

"The women who know how to do things are most happy. Those who try to get others to do their work are not. Most of the men were either armsmen or have left. Those who remain seem pleased. We have had a score of women arrive here who have inquired about work at the holding, and even a few men."

"I take it that you are working on the complainers?"

Hryessa laughed. "I do not have to. The other women are taking care of that. Within a few more days, everything will be close to what it should be."

Saryn nodded. For a time, she was silent, wondering if she should ask the next question.

Hryessa looked at her inquiringly.

Saryn decided to go ahead. "I've just seen Dealdron." *Again.* "What do you think of him?"

"He is a good man. He loves you." Hryessa shrugged. "What else is there to say?"

"What else?" *There are a million other things to say.*

"If you were a poor and powerless woman, other things might matter. You are not poor or powerless. He will never harm you, and he adores you. He is also not dumb. He is good with coins, and has saved much for you and for us."

In short . . . exactly where are you going to do better? The problem was that Hryessa was clearly right, at least from what Saryn had seen of the men in Lornth and elsewhere in Candar. And she couldn't deny that she definitely felt something for him. *More than just something.*

"Oh . . . a messenger just delivered this, Commander," Hryessa said with a smile, extending an envelope. "He wore green and cream."

"Lord Shartyr . . . no doubt a missive of congratulations and support."

"He is not to be trusted."

"No . . . but he's been most careful not to offend or provoke us."

"Those men are the most dangerous."

"Women can be exactly the same if they have power long enough," replied Saryn dryly, thinking about Ryba. "Let's see what he has to say." She broke the seal and opened the envelope, taking out the single sheet and scanning the beautifully written lines.

> My dear Commander,
>
> I have just received word about the treacherous attack by some of the southern lord-holders on The Groves and learned of the tragic deaths of Lord Deolyn, Lord Gethen, and young Lord Nesslek. I have conveyed my sympathy in a separate letter to Lady Zeldyan, but I wanted to express my appreciation for your efforts and success in bringing the malefactors to justice effectively and quickly.
>
> I would also like to assure you that I will support you and Lady Zeldyan and the northern lord-holders in whatever you recommend to the assembled lord-holders when we meet in Lornth, and I commend you for your forbearance and trust that you understand that you have my utmost respect.

The signature and seal were those of Shartyr, Lord-Holder of Masengyl.

Saryn nodded. As she had suspected, Lord Shartyr was extremely as-tute, and not to be trusted in the slightest. *Especially not when your back is turned.* At the same time, the letter did reinforce what Maeldyn had told her.

"He offers you congratulations and support," suggested Hryessa.

"Of course," replied Saryn with a laugh. "You said he was not to be trusted."

The meeting in Lornth was going to be most interesting, especially when she told them what she expected of them. Yet . . . if she wanted to change things, she couldn't leave matters as she had found them. And if she didn't change things, what was the point of all the deaths?

XCVI

Late on threeday afternoon, Saryn sat in the small study, looking at the missives stacked to one side. She picked up the top one, from Lord Whethryn of Tharnya, and scanned the lines.

> . . . have discussed our sad situation with Lord Maeldyn and find, I must say, unhappily, that I agree with his proposal . . .
> would never have hoped for such . . .
> all other alternatives . . . impractical and worse . . .

The next, from the widow of Lord Rherhn, was even less palatable.

> . . . understand that you, as Arms-Commander of Westwind, will play a role in determining my future and that of my sons and daughters . . . as one woman to another . . . can only plead that you will not destroy all that our family has held dear for generations . . .

Saryn wanted to snort at the widow's plea. While the lord-holders had certainly been the prime players, and while the poor women of the towns and hamlets had little say, if even a few of the consorts of the lord-holders had been more forceful, the situation wouldn't have been nearly so bad. *Or would it?* How would she ever know?

Finally, she stood and walked to the bookcase set in the middle of the inside wall, pressing on one of the corner bosses, one that was at the edge of the second shelf and ever so slightly more worn than the others. Then she swung the bookcase away from the wall, revealing a closet—or small room, really, since she'd not yet seen a true closet in any palace or villa anywhere in Lornth. Although she'd sensed the hidden space once she'd started to look for such, it had taken her a while to figure out the trick.

She studied the seven strongboxes on the shelves, then shook her head. She had been required to employ considerable effort with her order-chaos-abilities to open the heavy padlocks without destroying them, since she had yet to find the keys. The number of golds and silvers was considerable, more than enough to pay for the costs of operating the villa and paying the guard companies she would be supporting, possibly for several years. But having that much coin worried her, first because it suggested that the costs were far higher than she thought they were, and second because it re-vealed, again, that Lornth had nothing even approximating a banking sys-tem, another problem that she would need to address—assuming that she could pull off becoming and remaining overlord.

The other thing that she had noticed was the coins themselves. She'd observed earlier that the golds, silvers, and coppers were a mixed lot, some clearly Cyadoran, others Suthyan, or Gallosian, and even a few from Hamor and from someplace called Lydiar. None bore marks of having been coined in Lornth, yet another difficulty ahead. The other thing was that, whatever the source, the golds were all identical in weight and size, as were the silvers, but the size of the coppers varied a great deal, al-though the weights seemed to be the same.

She smiled briefly. In a way, that all made sense.

Her eyes drifted to the smallest of the strongboxes, the one that Deal-dron had used to collect the loot and other items of value from battles and the like. It held close to a hundred golds in coins, and rings and jewels most likely worth several hundred golds, if not more.

He never took a copper himself.

She stepped back and closed the bookcase door, making sure that the catch and hidden lock were both engaged. Then she left the study, walked halfway down the main corridor, and took a side hall out to the north terrace, knowing that Dealdron was seated there.

As she neared, he put his good hand on the arm of his chair.

"Don't get up. Your ribs still aren't healed, and if you slip, you could hurt the arm."

"I am much better, Angel." He grinned.

"I can tell that." Saryn managed not to flush as she took the chair in the afternoon shade beside his. He'd taken to calling her Angel after he'd sensed her reaction to the salutation, although he always spoke respectfully, and the feelings behind the words were a combination of respect and affection.

"Hryessa turned your strongbox over to me the other day. I forgot to tell you that it's safe. I counted over a hundred golds."

"It is all for you."

"I know." While some men would have said so after the fact, Dealdron had told her before the fact as well, and she could also read the truth in what he said.

"What do you think of this place?"

"It is much grander than Westwind. It is not so grand as the Prefect's palace in Fenard, but it is much more pleasant."

"You will have some time to explore it and offer your thoughts on how to change it for our needs."

Dealdron frowned.

"The day after tomorrow, Hryessa and I and first company will ride to Lornth to meet with the remaining lord-holders and perhaps some of the heirs of those who died."

"I will be much better."

Saryn shook her head. "We'll only be taking one wagon, and your injuries are not healed enough for travel, not when such travel is not necessary."

"But . . ."

"You have done enough for now." She smiled. "Besides, I like this place—except for the name—and it's closer to the southern lords and to the roads across the Westhorns. Also, the lords or overlords of Lornth have left a bad impression on everyone. So . . . if matters work out, and they agree, however reluctantly, to my becoming overlord or the like, this is where the center of government will be."

Dealdron gave a quick quizzical frown at the Rationalist word *govern-ment*, a term Saryn realized she'd never heard in Lornth, before saying, "You should call it Sarron."

"That's rather vain, don't you think?"

"No. *Sarron* means *peace* in the old tongue. That is similar to your angel name, but it does not sound quite the same, and it is not spelled the same."

"But the similarity would be helpful, you think?"

"You wanted to bring peace to Lornth, did you not?"

Saryn shook her head.

"Do not let them talk you out of being overlord, Angel." Dealdron's voice was firm. "All you have done and all the lives that have been lost will be wasted."

"Become overlord at the point of a blade, if necessary?"

"As it must be," he corrected her. "I am but a plasterer and an ostler, but I have seen enough to know that a weak ruler is the worst fate for any land."

"What about those who rule by fear?" Saryn wanted to hear what he said.

"Those who rule by fear alone are weak. The proper use of strength is to create respect, not fear. Only those who wish to do evil should be fearful of a ruler."

Saryn wouldn't have phrased it that way, but she certainly agreed with the ideas and the sentiment behind his words.

"And to whom should a ruler listen? Besides you?" she asked with a smile.

"Listen to all," he said, "but make your own judgment."

Saryn sat back in the chair, letting her eyes take in the Westhorns and the dusty road she had ridden down three times, and back only twice . . . and which she now doubted she would ever take again to the Roof of the World.

Her eyes drifted to Dealdron . . . and she smiled.

XCVII

Saryn, Hryessa, and first company had set out from Duevek—the holding and town that *might* become Sarron—early on a fiveday so that they would arrive in Lornth well before oneday. The road was hot and dusty, and those in the fields bringing in the harvest gave the riders a wide berth. Neither Saryn nor the scouts saw any sign of any other armsmen or lords as they neared the town of Lornth a glass or so past midafternoon on sevenday.

As they reached the point where the rutted-and-packed clay of the road was replaced with stone pavement and where the dwellings with their pale pink stucco walls began, a dark-haired woman holding an infant beside a line of laundry just stood and watched. Immediately beyond that first stucco-walled dwelling, Saryn smelled the first whiff of the open sewers, a scent somewhat mitigated, she suspected, by all the recent dry weather.

The first strange thing that struck her was that she saw more people alongside the main avenue. And ahead, toward the square, she could see people coming out onto the street, and even a few windows opening. She could feel eyes turning to her, and the sensation was so powerful that she knew it was not her imagination.

Farther on, two blocks before the square, from those who stood along the avenue and watched, she heard low voices, murmurs that she could barely make out.

"That's her . . . the one with the brown hair that has flame in it . . ."

". . . all wear twin blades . . ."

". . . sad time coming . . ."

". . . see her silver eyes . . ."

". . . every lord . . . didn't bow to her . . . they're all dead . . ."

". . . take an angel from the mountains . . . set things right . . ."

". . . cold as the ice from where she came . . ."

Yet, when she rode through the small square in the center of the town, it was empty, as were the walks flanking the narrower part of the avenue between the square and the green before the palace.

Is that because those with wealth fear what will happen? And those without it hope somehow that life will be better? Saryn didn't know, not for certain, but she suspected her guesses reflected at least some of the truth.

The patchy grass of the green before the palace walls was almost all brown, and dust had drifted against many of the clumps. Saryn's eyes took in the weathered platform where she had held her first and only execution, then moved to the pale pink granite walls of the palace, walls that looked old and tired, now more than ever.

The pair of armsmen guarding the gates straightened as they saw the column of guards approaching, and they remained at attention.

"Commander," offered one, bowing deeply, "the stables and barracks are ready. Only Lady Zeldyan has yet arrived."

"Thank you," returned Saryn.

As she entered the palace courtyard, she saw that some of the grass between the stones had returned, and there was a haze of dust over the pavement.

"It could use cleaning up again," murmured Hryessa.

"I didn't see Undercaptain Maerkyn before Lady Zeldyan left," Saryn said, thinking about the nervous young officer.

"He was killed in the fighting. Some said it was from behind, by the squad leader you killed, Commander," replied Hryessa.

"Oh . . . I should have known."

"I thought you did, ser, or I would have mentioned it."

Saryn almost wondered aloud if anyone had been appointed to take Maerkyn's place, but who could have made such an appointment? The overcaptain and captain had died at The Groves. Zeldyan was no longer regent, and Gethen and Nesslek had both been killed. Her eyes noted that there were two wagons waiting by the front steps to the palace, and two armsmen carried a chest down the steps and placed it in the second wagon.

Once she had unsaddled and groomed the gelding, Saryn headed for the palace. She found Zeldyan in the overlord's third-level bedchamber, packing items into a crate. So absorbed was Zeldyan that she did not even look up as Saryn slipped into the room.

"Zeldyan?"

The blond woman who had been regent straightened and turned.

Saryn could see—and sense—traces of tears.

"Commander . . . I have only taken what I brought here . . ."

"Zeldyan," Saryn said gently, "you should take everything of a personal nature that was either yours or Sillek's, as well as any furniture that has been in your family or his. Also, if there are any golds here, or in strongboxes, they are yours by right . . . and by my wish."

"But if you become overlord . . . ?"

"Henstrenn left quite enough for now, and I have no doubt that you and your father ended up paying out of The Groves strongboxes what others should have paid." *Besides,* **all** *the lord-holders will pay their tariffs, and they'll do so on time.* She'd seen enough to know that they could . . . and she'd see that they would. *Aren't you getting a little ahead of yourself?* "Also, there's the small matter of getting them all to approve of a woman as overlord."

"All you have to do, Commander, is to ask who might be opposed to the idea."

"I suspect all of them except Maeldyn and possibly Spalkyn are opposed."

"That may be," Zeldyan replied, "but all you have to do is ask who is opposed."

"You're suggesting that no one is about to speak up."

"Against you? I would think not. If anyone does, it would be Chaspal. He's not always perceptive. I don't know if there will be any heirs who will try to claim their fathers' holdings, but there might be some stupid enough to show up and try." Zeldyan slipped a small box wrapped in cloth into the crate beside her. "What will you do if that happens?"

"Assuming people look to me, I'd accept any true blood heir . . . and make certain that they are treated exactly like any other lord-holder."

"You can tell that, can't you?"

"I can usually tell when people tell the truth and when they don't."

"Usually . . . or always?"

Saryn offered what she hoped was an enigmatic smile.

"I'll be through here before long," Zeldyan said.

"The quarters here are still yours, and they will be for now, and until you return to The Groves as lady-holder."

"But . . ."

"The guest chamber I had before is perfectly adequate. This has been yours forever."

"Just twelve years. At times, it seems like forever."

"Could we have dinner together, Zeldyan . . . and without you calling me 'Commander'?" asked Saryn warmly. "Please?"

Zeldyan's eyes brightened. Then she swallowed . . . and nodded.

Saryn stepped forward and put her arms around Zeldyan.

XCVIII

Saryn woke early on eightday, half-dreading what the day might bring, knowing that Maeldyn, Spalkyn, and Wethryn had arrived late the evening before, and that most of the other surviving lord-holders would doubtless show up before long. She ate by herself in her chamber, then dressed and checked with Hryessa to make sure that first company was ready for any eventuality, before returning to the palace to see Zeldyan.

The former regent insisted that Saryn use the third-level sitting room for any private meetings. She also suggested that Saryn provide her own guards from first company. Saryn did not protest, and within the glass she was waiting there for Maeldyn, with two guards stationed outside.

"Lord Maeldyn and Lord Lyndel of Lyntara, Commander."

Lord Lyndel? That has to be Deolyn's son. "Have them come in."

Maeldyn stepped into the chamber along with a slightly built young man with tight-curled and short brown hair. "Commander . . ."

Both men bowed, and as she stood from behind the table, Saryn saw immediately the resemblance between the son and his late father. "Lords . . . please join me." She gestured to the table, waiting for them before she re-seated herself.

"I thought Lyndel should meet you before all the lord-holders assembled," began Maeldyn.

"I'm pleased to see you, Lord Lyndel," Saryn said, "although I wish that your accession to being lord-holder had occurred under different circumstances."

"I would have wished that, also, Commander," replied the young man in a voice far deeper than his stature and youthful appearance might have suggested, and not at all like his father's tenor. He smiled politely. "Lord Maeldyn has suggested that it is most likely you will succeed the regents. Although I am young, I must express my concern, especially given that my father sacrificed his life to preserve the regency in the hope of retaining the traditions of Lornth."

Saryn could sense both worry and youthful arrogance behind the smoothly spoken words. She did not reply immediately, letting the silence grow for a time, while she gathered order and chaos flows to her. As she began to speak, she used those flows to project absolute authority over the young lord. "Lord Lyndel . . . I will speak frankly. I did not come to Lornth to seek power. I came here to preserve the regency and the friendly relations between Westwind and Lornth. Ever since I have been here, lord-holders—mostly from the south—have either attacked the Lady Regent or me, all demanding two things—that the regency attack Westwind and that no woman ever hold power in Lornth. Lornth attacked Westwind once, and the result was disaster for Lornth. Westwind is even more established today. I arrived here with a mere two squads of women guards, and we have not only defeated but also destroyed all those who attacked us. I would point out that not once did we attack any lord-holder who had not attacked first." Saryn paused and smiled again, sensing that she had shaken the young lord, despite his massive arrogance.

Sitting on the side of the table between Lyndel and Saryn, Maeldyn nodded.

"Neither the Marshal of Westwind nor I can allow Lornth to destroy itself with internal bickering, and I am most certain that any intelligent lord-holder would prefer to hold his lands under an overlord—or lady— sympathetic to his needs than to have Lornth raided continually by the Jeranyi and racked with dissension until it became a mere province of Suthya. Or would you prefer to find yourself under Suthya?"

"We have always dealt with Suthya."

"The last incursion of Suthyans I dealt with," Saryn pointed out, "because no lord in the north beside your sire had the armsmen to do so. Now . . . not through my doing, but through the doing of your fellow lord-holders, you have barely a handful of the armsmen trained and raised by your father. Exactly how do you propose to stop the next Suthyan attack, not that there is likely to be one . . . unless I leave you to that unhappy fate?"

Lyndel looked to Maeldyn.

"As I pointed out on that part of the journey we shared coming here," Maeldyn said, "even between us, Lord Spalkyn, Lord Wethryn, Lord Chaspal, and I could barely raise a company and a half of armsmen. Commander Saryn's forces have defeated more than ten companies of armsmen. In some cases, not a single armsman of the forces opposing her survived. The Suthyans lost close to three companies, as well as three white wizards."

"You two seem to leave me no choice," protested Lyndel.

Saryn laughed softly. "That is not quite correct, Lord Lyndel. The reason why your choices are so few is because so many lord-holders who are no longer with us chose so poorly. They attacked a land that never attacked Lornth, and they continued to press for such attacks even after it was made clear to them the futility of such. Do you want to hold your lands in peace and prosperity . . . or do you want constant warfare with Suthya and Jerans at best, or total defeat at worst?"

"But . . . under a . . ."

"Woman?" finished Saryn lightly. "Why not? Have all those manly lord-holders you revere supported you and your sire so faithfully? You might recall that Lord Maeldyn and Lord Spalkyn and I were the ones to avenge him."

"No," said Maeldyn quietly. "Commander Saryn avenged him, and you might well mention that to any who press you on the issue, Lyndel."

While Maeldyn's tone was even, Saryn could sense the anger behind the words, an anger directed at the young lord.

For a moment, Lyndel was silent. Then he shook his head. "I must offer my apologies, Commander . . . Lord Maeldyn. Matters . . . are so unlike . . . what I had expected."

"They are so unlike what any of us expected last spring," said Saryn, using the flows of order to press a sense of warmth and friendship on the young lord. "We cannot bring back what of the past has been lost forever. We can only forge a future in which we can all do our best." She could sense that the young lord would not object to her, because, arrogant as he was, he now understood the situation, but that there remained concern . . . and resentment. *There will be more than enough of that for some time to come.* She rose from the table. "I am so glad you came, and I'm certain that you will do well in following your father's example. He was most supportive of Lady Zeldyan and me when we last visited him."

Lyndel quickly stood. "I appreciate your candor, Commander."

"I'm very direct, Lord Lyndel. I find it results in fewer misunderstandings." *More anger, often, but fewer misunderstandings.*

Maeldyn also rose and turned to Lyndel. "I need a word with the commander, but I will be with you shortly."

"Of course." Lyndel inclined his head to Saryn, then to the older lord-holder, before turning and leaving the sitting room.

"I apologize, Commander," Maeldyn offered after the door closed, "but after meeting Lyndel, I thought it best that he meet you before he spoke with others and before everyone met." The stern-faced lord smiled and shook his head. "He's more stubborn than I ever would have been, but I could see him wilt under your authority. You will need that when all the lord-holders meet." He paused. "I noticed that you were most direct with him."

Saryn smiled crookedly. "I've never been that good at indirection and manipulation, and I've never liked people who are."

"I believe you are quite good at discerning it. Am I wrong?"

"No . . . but just because I can detect it doesn't mean I'm particularly good at it . . . or want to be."

"That will make matters harder for you in the days immediately ahead, but far easier with time."

With time and with the understanding that I won't stand for plotting and the like. She wondered how many other lord-holders she would have to replace before the remainder understood. Saryn nodded. "Is there anyone else I should meet? Lord Jharyk has already requested a few moments."

"I don't think there's anyone else you have not already met. None of the holders you . . . dealt with . . . have sons . . . or daughters," he added with a smile, "old enough to act as lord-holders."

"Should we recommend that their consorts serve as lady-holders until their daughters are old enough?"

"It might be best if you were the one to make that determination."

Saryn smiled. "I understand."

For almost a glass after Maeldyn left, Saryn sat and thought about what would be the best and most effective way of dealing with the assorted lord-holders.

It scarcely seemed that long before Lord Jharyk appeared.

Saryn stood.

The older lord looked around the sitting room, then stared straight at Saryn. "I heard words that you're going to replace all the lord-holders with their daughters or some such. Are you going to have my daughter replace me? Don't give me platitudes about whether you will become overlord, either."

Saryn smiled pleasantly. "No. I'm not replacing any existing lord-holders who abide by their duties and pay their tariffs. I'm in no hurry to replace loyal lord-holders. Young Lord Lyndel has already replaced his father, and Lady Zeldyan has taken her father's holding, since she is the only heir. That may also be the case for some of the rebel lord-holders. I do insist that your successor be either your eldest daughter or your son's consort, and that you and I discuss who might be the best steward for the holding."

Jharyk laughed harshly. "That's their problem. My second daughter would be better, but you can meet them both. I'll be an obedient lord-holder. What's most important to me is order in the land and an overlord who will take on the Jeranyi and protect the borders."

"I will, as necessary. I intend to have the other lord-holders follow your example of only having a limited number of armsmen. In return, I'll use the companies I raise and support to deal with problems like the Jeranyi and the Suthyans."

"Will all your armsmen be women?"

"Right now, that's all I have. I plan to have companies of both. I will need more armsmen and guards to deal with those who would threaten Lornth."

"What about Westwind?"

Saryn shrugged. "Westwind has no designs on Lornth and never did. We will trade as necessary. Since our interests do not conflict, I see no problems."

"You don't think women will leave Lornth to go there?"

"There will be far fewer trying to reach Westwind now than would otherwise have been the case. Those who still wish to leave would not have served Lornth well."

"What about tariffs?"

"They will be slightly higher, and they will be paid on time. Most lord-holders will be better off because they won't need so many armsmen. In your case, you'll lose less to the Jeranyi."

Jharyk laughed again, not quite so harshly as the first time. "You take care of them the way you did before, and you'll even have me spouting your praise." He paused. "There will be some who won't take to you."

"I know. They don't have to like me. They just have to be loyal."

"For some that's been a problem. Then, I hear that most of them are dead."

"Those that raised arms against the regency."

"That leaves a few, Commander."

"All we can do is see what they do," she replied.

Jharyk shook his head. "They'd be wise to do nothing. I'm not sure one or two are that smart." He inclined his head. "I can live with what you do. Good day, Commander."

"Good day."

After Jharyk departed, Saryn walked to the window and looked out at the front courtyard of the palace. *How many more will want to see you? How many won't even consider it? How will you handle matters if someone gets unruly?*

XCIX

Saryn and Hryessa walked into the tower council chamber half a glass before the lord-holders were to assemble. Five chairs around a round table filled the center of the dark-paneled room, with the only light from the high windows in the back wall of the chamber, since the wall lamps were unlit.

"Let's put the table against the wall, and line the chairs up along the wall by the door. That will leave the floor space open." Saryn glanced down at the heavy, worn, dark green carpet, which was bordered in purple, with gold intertwined vines and leaves. *Ugly and then some.*

When they had rearranged the room, Hryessa looked to Saryn. "How many guards do you want?"

"Ten. I want the most experienced, and five should be on one side of where I'll stand, and five on the other side. They should be here, waiting. I won't enter until everyone is inside. After I do, and the doors are closed, bring the rest of the squad into the corridor outside."

"The lord-holders . . . they will not like it."

"No. They won't. And they won't like the fact that I'm wearing a battle harness, but they'll each have a single blade at their belt." *And my having two blades at hand will subtly reinforce the impression of power.* "They're going to have to get used to having women with power and weapons around, and now is as good a time as any to start."

Saryn decided to wait on the staircase landing around the corner from the corridor in front of the council chamber, half a flight up. From there, she could sense the lord-holders entering, and Zeldyan had agreed, with a smile, to summon Saryn after Maeldyn had explained the general situation to the others.

When Saryn left the chamber, because she did not want to be anywhere close while the lord-holders arrived and gathered, Zeldyan was outside.

"We rearranged the chamber," Saryn said, nodding for Hryessa to get on with her preparations.

"You could have had the staff do it," Zeldyan pointed out.

"I'd rather not ask anything of them yet, other than what any guest would expect. Have you heard anything I should know?"

"Maeldyn says that most are resigned to your becoming overlord, but he hasn't mentioned anything about succession."

Saryn could understand that. For a historically patrilineal and patriarchal society, what she planned to impose would certainly not sit well, but, for better or worse, she wanted everything out in the open from the beginning. It would make the initial transition less popular, but easier because it was clear who held power, and that would make matters easier as time went by. *That's what you hope.* At the very least, she would know who was so vehemently opposed that she would have to deal with them immediately. "That's something I'll deal with after the issue of being overlord is raised."

"Some may change their minds."

"That's their decision . . . and their consequences."

Zeldyan winced.

"You think I'm cruel? You have lost everyone you loved. I don't want to see the same things happen again and again, and they will, if things aren't changed."

"Saryn . . . women are not any better than men."

"No, we're not, but I can train and educate the women. Right now, I can only kill the men, because they'll fight to the death rather than accept change. I'd prefer not to, but I'll end up having to unless I change matters. And there are a few lords who love and trust their daughters."

"In the end, will the women be any better?"

"I don't know. I hope so, but . . . don't you think we ought to have a chance to see if we can do better?"

Zeldyan only smiled sadly.

Saryn could sense the former regent's feelings—that Saryn was going to pay a very high price for her changes . . . and that, in the end, little would change. *We'll see.*

"You'll enter the chamber with Maeldyn and Spalkyn?" Saryn asked, as much to change the subject as anything.

"Both Lyndel and I will enter with Maeldyn. Spalkyn is going to stick close to Chaspal."

Saryn heard horses outside. "I think it's time for me to disappear for a while."

"And I, also."

Saryn retreated to the staircase landing, and Hryessa ushered the ten guards into position in the council chamber.

Since Saryn could only sense general shapes and some few feelings from where she was, she could not identify most of those who entered the chamber, but she thought she sensed the gruff Barcauyn, and Jharyk, and, of course, Maeldyn, near the end, because he was escorting Zeldyan and Lyndel. She could only sense that the lord-holders talked and moved below, some in apparent agitation.

Almost half a glass passed before Zeldyan appeared at the bottom of the staircase. "You should come."

"How are they taking it?" Saryn came down the stairs and joined Zeldyan.

"Not well . . . but no one has left."

As she entered the council chamber with Zeldyan, Saryn could sense the conflicting emotions—veiled hope, anger, resentment, resignation, worry.

"... wearing blades ..."

"... so are we ..."

"... doesn't seem right ... woman ..."

Once she reached the point midway between the guards, Saryn turned and surveyed the lord-holders present: Spalkyn, and beside him a holder she did not know, presumably Chaspal, Jharyk, Barcauyn, Shartyr, Maeldyn, Zeldyan, Lyndel, and a rotund figure with deep-set eyes, who, by process of elimination, had to be Whethryn. Eight out of what had once been eighteen, if she counted the vacant holding of Rohrn, and who knew how many others might have been present if the holdings taken by Suthya were also included.

Maeldyn cleared his throat, but did not speak.

Saryn gathered the order and chaos flows, a process almost instinctive after all her experiences, and projected both authority and ability even before she began to speak. "I understand that Lord Maeldyn has explained how I came to be in Lornth and all the details of what has occurred since last spring. Although all of you know some, if not all, of those events, not all of you knew what lay behind many of them." Saryn smiled pleasantly. "You are gathered here because Lornth needs an overlord who is strong enough to protect it from other lands, and forceful and able enough to protect you from each other. I did not come to Lornth seeking anything but to support the regency and to keep Suthya from creating conflict between Lornth and Westwind. I was asked to consider becoming overlord. That is why I am here."

"Do we have any choice?" That question came from the lord-holder she thought was Chaspal.

Saryn smiled. "You have had many choices. You could have accepted peace with Westwind. You could have united behind the regency and supported the regents with more than equivocal words and insufficient tariffs, tariffs paid late if at all. You could have rejected the dissension created by the late Lord Kelthyn and others. Most of the lord-holders of Lornth chose not to do any of those, and few indeed protested the acts and words of the rebel lords. That is why your choices now are few. It is also why my choices are few. If I choose to leave you to your devices, within a year or so, if not within seasons, most of you will be dead, and Suthya will rule Lornth. And then I will have to fight another year over these lands and others to stop Suthya. You will pardon me if I tell you that I am less than enthusiastic about that, and I would think you would not find that prospect particularly to your liking."

"Some have said that as soon as you are overlord," offered Jharyk, "that you will turn on each of us in turn and take our holdings and turn them over to daughters or consorts."

"I will not take your holdings from you. I could. That you should know. But upon your death, each of your holdings will go to your eldest daughter. If you have no daughter, you may choose between the consort of your eldest son or the eldest daughter of your oldest sister . . ."

"You will destroy the bloodlines . . ." That was from Chaspal again.

Saryn laughed. "On the contrary, what I do will preserve them. Any child of your daughter has to carry her blood. A man's consort does not always bear that man's offspring . . . as all of you should know. A daughter always bears her own offspring. If you are worried about your blood inheriting, having your daughters inherit is the only absolute way to assure that."

"How can a woman keep a holding?" asked Shartyr. "You might, but women in Lornth are different."

"Do you doubt that women can bear arms?"

"You can bear arms, Commander," offered Spalkyn, "but none of us have trained our daughters in arms . . ."

Saryn smiled. "That is scarcely a problem. Every single one of the guards who defeated those who came against them was born in Candar, and not a one received arms training from their fathers. Every lord-holder's daughter will be trained in arms, and I will supervise that training. They will also be schooled in numbers and other skills needed to run a holding. This should not pose a problem since you will all remain lord-holders and can, if you choose, also add to their knowledge."

Chaspal edged forward until he stood at the front of the group, his hand on the hilt of his sword. "You mock everything Lornth has stood for."

"Not everything," Saryn replied, gathering order and chaos as she sensed the anger and antagonism. "Just the ideas that more fighting among lord-holders will preserve Lornth and that women have no worth at all."

"I will show you worth!" Chaspal's sword was just out of the scabbard, and he had taken but a single step, when Saryn's blade slammed into his chest with such force that chaos-flames erupted, momentarily, before he toppled backward.

Naked blades appeared in the hands of the ten guards flanking Saryn.

In moments, all that remained of Chaspal was a pile of ashes, fragments of leather and metal, and two blades, all resting on a charred patch on the heavy ugly carpet.

None of the remaining lord-holders made a sound, and Saryn again let the silence fill the room before she spoke.

"You can call me a tyrant . . . but that is the way it will be. Any lord-holder who brings arms against another, I will deal with—just as I dealt with Lord Chaspal. In addition, each lord-holder will be limited to two squads worth of personal guards. That should be enough to keep peace on your lands . . . and few enough that neighboring holders will not be tempted into territorial incursions. It will also allow you to keep more of your golds since you will not have to spend them on arms and arms-men . . . although I will increase your annual tariffs slightly to support the guards and armsmen necessary to deal with Suthya and the Jeranyi . . ."

"What of our sons?" inquired Whethryn.

"What of them?" asked Saryn in return. "They can help their sisters run their holdings. They can consort with the daughters of other lords. They can do all manner of things—but they cannot inherit or rule a holding."

"That will bring chaos . . ." muttered someone.

Barcauyn, Saryn thought, but decided against singling him out directly. "Chaos, you say?" Her laugh was mocking and cold, and she added order and chaos flows to the sound that chilled every ear. "Chaos, you say? For a score of years, if not longer, Lornth has been nothing but chaos, with holder against holder, falling prey to the schemes of the Suthyans and the lusts and bloodlust of all too many lord-holders. There will be none of that, not now, nor in the future. I will protect our borders with the same skills that have brought you all to bay, and I will not suffer any outside meddling in the land, not from Jerans, nor from Suthya or Westwind.

"Think about this. I have not raised arms against anyone who did not first raise arms against the regency that was or against me. How many of those lord-holders who perished at my hand could have said that? Not a single one. Also, think about this. I am not taking the lands of any lord-holder except those of Lord Henstrenn and possibly Lord Kelthyn, who brought near ruin on the land. I am allowing the heirs of even the rebel lord-holders to keep their lands, and I am allowing you to remain lord-holders for the rest of your lives, and those of your blood will continue to hold those lands. If you rebel, then you will suffer Lord Chaspal's fate, and your daughters will become lady-holders that much sooner." After a moment, Saryn added. "I will tariff you, as did the regency, and you will pay those tariffs. In return, I will protect you, and I will keep order so that no lord-holder need fear another."

"How will we know you will keep that word?" asked Maeldyn mildly.

"Some of you have seen that I have thus far kept my words about all that I have done. That will not change. Also, think about this. How many of those who rebelled and wished to be overlord could say the same? Lord Orsynn paid the Jeranyi to raid Lord Jharyk's lands because Jharyk was loyal to the regency. Lord Mortryd begged for help from the regency, then joined with Lord Rhehrn to ambush the regency forces. Lord Henstrenn persuaded three other lords to join him in attacking Lord Gethen, then left two of them behind to face me while accepting golds from Suthya to attack the regency. Lord Jaffrayt incited the southern lords to rebel. Lord-holders . . . if you are at all honest, you should see that the record of honesty and loyalty among you leaves something to be desired, especially when the greatest butchery was accomplished by rebel Lornian lord-holders against the most loyal lord-holders—Lord Gethen and Lord De-olyn."

With her words, Saryn did her best to project guilt and shame . . . if only briefly.

"That is past," she went on. "Either the Suthyans or the Jeranyi or both would kill you and take your lands. I will not. Were I so inclined, I certainly could have done so. Could any of you have stopped me? Yet you question me far more than you ever questioned yourselves. My question to you is simple. And before you answer, I will tell you that I can tell if any man or woman lies to me. My question to you is simple: Will you be loyal and not force me to take up arms against you?"

"A moment, Commander." Spalkyn stepped forward and cleared his throat. His hand went briefly to his beard. "I'm not one who speaks much. Some of you know that I near-on lost everything years back. Some of you also know that a company or so of Suthyans attacked my lands this summer. The only help I got was from the commander. She and little more than a squad of her women guards wiped out every last Suthyan and one white mage. I'd not be here without that. She was the one to take on

Henstrenn and three Suthyan companies and three more mages. Not one of the mages and few of the Suthyans survived. Now . . . it seems to me that we've been complaining for years about not having an overlord strong enough to protect us . . . and when we get one, we're going to complain that she happens to be a woman?"

Saryn kept from smiling, knowing that Spalkyn's earlier comments, as well as his remarks, had been Maeldyn's idea.

"Now maybe I'm seeing things different-like," Spalkyn went on, "because I have two daughters who already do well at helping run my holding and a son who won't ever do well at it. It seems to me that the commander is still letting our blood hold our lands. It also seems to me that the Suthyans—or the Jeranyi —don't much care about that. With the commander as overlord or overlady, we might even get Westwind to worry about Suthya, and we sure as the demons won't have to worry about Gallos." He fingered his beard. "I don't know as I can say more."

Surprisingly, Barcauyn stepped forward. "Matters don't always go the way we like. We all know that. I thought I had sons with some sense. They tried . . . I'm embarrassed to say . . . to attack the commander with dirks in a hallway. They're most fortunate that she was kind to them because she could have killed them with her bare hands. They will have scars to remind them. We haven't had much fortune with the last few overlords. It might have been their fault. It might not have been. It might have been the times. But there's a saying about needing fire to fight fire." He nodded to Saryn and stepped back.

Maeldyn moved forward. "The commander asked a fair question. She didn't ask us to like her. She didn't ask us to hand over our lands. She asked us to be good lords and loyal. Is there anyone here who doesn't think that's a fair question in these times?"

"It's a fair question," answered Jharyk. "I can say I will be. But . . . I want the heirs of all the rebel lord-holders to make the same pledge to the commander overlord in person and look into her eyes when they do."

"That's fair," said Barcauyn. "More than fair."

Saryn waited until the chamber quieted. "In return, you have my pledge to support each of you as I already promised, and to support your heirs as well in the years ahead."

After another round of murmurs, a voice came from the group.

"There is one other matter . . ."

It took Saryn a moment to determine the speaker—Whethryn. "Yes, Lord Whethryn."

"Ahem . . . one reason we've had trouble, and you're here, is that there was some question about . . . heirs . . ."

Saryn managed to keep from flushing. "Lord Maeldyn raised that question. The simple answer is that I can and will have children, and that I am young enough to raise them to maturity." She paused. "I haven't exactly had much time to devote to such considerations in the past years, but now that matters are more settled . . . there is someone."

Several chuckles filled the room.

Nothing like backing yourself into a corner . . . with no real way out.

Still . . . she smiled.

C

Saryn stood at the window of the third-level sitting room, looking down at the long shadows cast across the front courtyard by a white sun tinged with the faint orange that came just before sunset. She was Overlord of Lornth . . . or tyrant . . . or whatever. Had that been her fate from the beginning? She had the sense that Ryba had certainly seen that . . . and believed it.

Had she had any choices? She shook her head. *That's a meaningless question.* Each choice followed from the previous choice. In a sense, the day that she had defeated two squads of Henstrenn's armsmen outside of Duevek had led to all that followed.

The same had been true for the other angels—those who survived. Were the "right" choices merely the ones that allowed one to survive and prosper? What of those for whom any choice was wrong—like poor doomed Lord Sillek? Once his father attacked Westwind, Sillek had been left with no good choices. Was that what everyone called fate?

Ryba had dealt with her fate in one way, and she had created and would rule Westwind alone and pass that heritage to her daughter, Dyliess. Nylan and Ayrlyn had left Westwind and Lornth to build whatever they would in what had once been the Accursed Forest of Cyador. And Saryn . . . she had built nothing. Not yet. She had presided over the destruction of a tottering land, using the only means at her disposal, means that she would once have claimed that she never would have employed, only to find herself faced with rebuilding a land that shared few of the values in which she believed . . . and she had agreed, for the sake of all that, to have and bear children, and with a man she would have ignored totally years before.

Can you change Lornth enough that you will make a difference? Not changing Lornth would doom the entire land and possibly Westwind. Would she be successful, or would she find herself in the same position as Sillek?

She smiled faintly. That was what she would find out.

Thrap.

The gentle knock was Zeldyan's. That Saryn could sense. "Come in, Zeldyan."

The former regent and current lady-holder of The Groves slipped into the sitting room that had once been hers, gently closing the door behind her. "You have been here, alone, since all the others left."

"I've been thinking."

Zeldyan offered a sympathetic smile. "You are worried?"

"More like reflective, not that there's not some worry there. I'm trying to do something . . . well, I have the feeling that your lord Sillek was trying to change things, too."

"He tried, but he could not."

"I don't know that I would be here without what he did."

"You are kind."

Saryn shook her head. "I haven't been kind. I've done what I thought had to be done. I think what I did was right. But it wasn't kind. I couldn't even afford to be kind to Chaspal. Any kindness would have been seen as weakness, as an opening for others to test me, and that would have forced me into greater use of force later."

Zeldyan did not speak for a time, standing beside Saryn as they looked down into the courtyard and watched the shadows fade and the twilight slowly fall across the palace.

"I envied you, you know," Zeldyan finally said. "You are always so confident, and so strong."

You don't have to think much when you have few choices, and, so long as you act quickly, that gives the appearance of confidence. "I only did what I had to, in hopes of restoring Lornth and stopping the endless feuding."

"Lornth will be strong again. I know that. But it will not be the Lornth I have known."

"That Lornth could not have lasted," Saryn replied, "even without Westwind. Cyador was fading, and once it faded, so would have Lornth."

"I would not have lived to see my Lornth fade."

"No. It would have taken longer," Saryn admitted, "but we do not choose the times in which we live. We only choose how we live in those times."

"I will be leaving in the morning. I had hoped we could have dinner together again."

Saryn smiled. "I would like that. Very much."

EPILOGUE

Saryn glanced toward the side doorway leading into the main hall of the villa of Duevek. Sarron, she mentally corrected herself, the place where peace begins. She straightened, glancing down at the finery she was unaccustomed to wearing. She'd insisted on trousers and boots for the combined betrothal and consorting ceremony, but she had compromised—slightly—by wearing a brilliant blue and high-collared tunic long enough that the silver-edged hem reached down to midthigh over the black trousers.

Her eyes went to Hryessa, standing by the closed side door, who still wore the uniform of a Westwind guard.

"Not yet, ser," said the Arms-Commander of Sarron, with a smile. "They will wait. Do not hurry, for they will want to remember the day. And you should not be in haste, Angel. This will happen but once in your life."

That was all too true. She had to admit, if reluctantly, that she'd picked Dealdron because he'd been the only man unhesitatingly to put his life on the line for her. *And because he loves you, and because there's some feeling on your part.* Only after the fact had she realized that it had been a wise decision politically, as well, because it avoided any implied favoritism toward any of the other High Holders.

A fleeting smile crossed her face as she recalled Dealdron's words and his feelings when he had been recovering—*What will happen is what will happen, but whatever happens, you are my angel.*

Finally, Hryessa opened the side door and stepped aside to let Saryn enter first.

Saryn walked slowly—she hoped her movements were stately—until she stood almost in the middle of the low dais, empty of all chairs or furnishings. Hryessa followed, but stopped two paces behind Saryn.

Saryn turned to face those assembled before her. Standing arrayed across the hall were the lord-holders of Lornth—and the four lady-holders, all of whom had pledged to Saryn. Four guards stood at each end of the dais. While Saryn had not insisted on anyone attending the ceremony, clearly all had wanted to be there, for whatever reason, even though she had declared that only a half squad of guards would be welcome in accompanying each lord- or lady-holder. At the very front of the holders, on the left, stood Zeldyan, and opposite her, on the right side, were Maeldyn and Anyna. Anyna smiled warmly at Saryn.

"Saryn of the Angels, and Overlord of Lornth!" announced Daryn from beside the main doors to the hall. For the ceremony, he wore the gray of Westwind.

The doors at the back of the hall opened. From outside the hall came a short fanfare on a horn—the same horn that Saryn had used to signal her guards.

"Dealdron of Westwind!" announced Daryn.

Even from that distance, Saryn could see that the smith was smiling broadly as he finished the announcement and as Dealdron walked past him, his polished black boots firm, yet almost soundless, on the marble tiles of the hall floor.

Saryn watched as he moved toward her. His formal tunic was a muted grayish silver, not shimmering, and trimmed in black. His trousers were a gray that was not quite black. All eyes followed him as he reached the dais, then stepped up onto it, his honest eyes taking in Saryn.

She managed to hold a pleasant smile, even though the love and adoration in his expression washed over her, and she swallowed.

Once he stood on the dais, and they both faced those in the hall, she nodded to him, and they turned sideways, so that they faced each other.

A young guard stepped forward with a small green pillow on which rested two matching gold rings, each set with a square emerald.

Saryn turned slightly and took the larger ring, holding it high for a moment before lowering it and facing Dealdron directly once more. "As a token of my faith, with this ring, I ask for your hand, pledging both my hand and my honor."

Dealdron extended his left hand, and Saryn slid the ring in place, adding so quietly that only he could hear, "and my appreciation and affection for all that you have endured and all that you have offered."

She could sense . . . something . . . a feeling that was not only love, but a hope and a belief on his part that she would find love with him. *And he just might be right.*

In turn, Dealdron lifted the smaller ring from the pillow, and Saryn extended her hand. His words were deep and warm as he said, "With this ring, I give you my hand, and all that I have." After he eased the ring onto her finger, his hand tightened around hers but for an instant as he murmured, "For you are and always have been my angel."

Saryn barely managed not to swallow, although her eyes burned for a moment, before she recalled the formal close to the ceremony. "Two hands promised in honor and for the future of Lornth."

"For the future of Lornth!" chorused the assembled guards, holders, and consorts.

She reached out and again took her consort's hand.